The Crit...

HOST

Peter James

ORION

An Orion paperback
First published in Great Britain by Victor Gollancz in 1993
This paperback edition published in 2000 by
Orion Books Ltd,
Orion House, 5 Upper St Martin's Lane, London WC2H 9EA

A CIP catalogue record for this book is available
from the British Library.

ISBN: 0 75283 745 1

Printed and bound in Great Britain by
Clays Ltd, St Ives plc

To my Aunt Lilly,
who made the world a better place.
And her memory always will.

'I believe no one currently under the age of fifty will ever have to die.'

Ralph Wheelan, Director,
Alcor Life Extension Foundation, 1993

'I don't want to achieve immortality through my work, I want to achieve immortality by not dying.'

Woody Allen, 1990

'Anyone who thinks 100 is long enough doesn't deserve to live longer.'

Professor Marvin Minsky,
Massachusetts Institute of Technology, 1993

'Man will not fly for 1000 years.'

Wilbur Wright, 1901

'Death is no longer necessary.'

Professor Willi Messenger, Toronto 1979

AUTHOR'S FOREWORD

Although *Host* is mostly set in the present time, I have taken licence in making some of the computer technology and cryonics science more advanced than they currently are.

From my own research, and backed by the views of many (but by no means all!) of the medics and scientists who have so generously helped me, I believe it is only a question of time before the technological possibilities I have described become real. And probably within the lifetimes of some of us. By then, society will be no more able to understand or cope with what its scientists have achieved than we are now.

In order to give the story a feeling of authenticity and to make it accessible, I have decided, with one exception, not to set it in a future at which all of us can only guess, but in the present, which we know.

Peter James
1993 :–)

ACKNOWLEDGEMENTS

This has been a monster of a book to research and yet for me it has been both terrific fun and a real voyage of discovery. I've met some truly great people along the way, who responded to my requests for help with a level of enthusiasm and thoroughness that has staggered me. To all of the names listed below, I owe a big debt. Thank you.

Singling out individuals is dangerous, because I do not wish to leave anyone out, but without the happy chance meetings with Blaine Price of the Human Cognition Research Laboratory of the Open University in a pub in Milton Keynes, and Michelle Cooperman of the ICRF on a platform at Victoria Station, I might still be struggling with my research right now. And I don't know how I would have got the book written without the tireless coaching in computer science from Dr Bruce Katz of Sussex University; in chemistry from Richard Blacklock in Los Angeles; and in cryonics from the members of Alcor in both the US and the UK. And I have to single out also Matthew Elton and Andy Holyer (andyh@pavilion.co.uk) at Sussex University who never flagged or got hacked off with my endless bombardment of questions, and made enormous contributions in both time and ideas. And Sue Ansell who gave me so much help during the writing of the first draft.

A *huge* thank you also to the following who either in person, down a phone line or through their work, contributed in so many ways: Mr Andrews of James Parsons; Dr Fara Arshad, Leeds University; Kathryn Bailey; John Bieber; Dr Margaret Boden; Dr Herman Borden, St John's Hospital, Santa Monica; Mr Geoffrey Briant, Senior Consultant, A & E Royal Sussex County Hospital; Andy Clarke, Sussex University; C. Scott Carrier, LA Department of Coroner; Dave Cliff, Sussex University; Andrew Clifford, Alcor UK; Phil Corsi; Professor Adam Curtis, Glasgow University; Dr

Daniel Dennett; Dudley Dean; Robert Ettinger and the Cryonics Institute; Tim Evans; Dr Gregory M. Fahy; Ray Fibbit; Patricia Friedal; Harold Holyer; Dudley and Pippa Hooley (promoted from Bovine to Aviation); The Immortalist Society; Dr Joseph Kates; Louis Kates; Mike and Veronica Keen; Dr Gerry Kelleher, Leeds University; Carole King; Dr Nigel Kirkham; Peter Lahaise; Robert Martis; Jane McNevin, A & E Royal Sussex County Hospital; Dr Ralph Merkle; Professor Hans Moravec; Professor Marvin Minsky; Mark Morris; Ian Mullen; Dr Simon Nightingale; Dr David Pegg; Nick Perkins; Margaret Potter; Mike Price, Alcor UK; Marie-Claude Pullen; Alan Sinclair, Alcor UK; Garet Smyth, Alcor UK; Dr Duncan Stewart; Lynn Squires, Imperial Cancer Research Fund; Dr Peter Ward, Leeds University; Ralph Wheelan, Alcor Life Extension Foundation; Russell Whittaker; Ian Wilson; David Wiltshire; Jennifer Zehethofer.

I am indebted also to the hard work and support of my agent Jon Thurley and his assistant, Patricia Preece, my commissioning editor Richard Evans, and editor Liza Reeves who spared a few of my little 'darlings'. And to the saintly patience of the Gollancz team of Elizabeth Dobson and Katrina Whone. And above all to the endless support of my wife, Georgina, who must at times during her vigil of the past year have wondered if I had downloaded myself into my own computer.

Peter James
(peterj@pavilion.co.uk)

PROLOGUE

May 1974. Los Angeles.

Blips of light chased each other silently across the screen on the monitor above the young woman's bed. The peaks and troughs of their spiky green wakes were becoming less frequent by the hour. There wasn't cause for panic, yet; but equally there was nothing to give rise to optimism.

Nurse Dunwoody paused to stare out through the sealed windows at the gauze of light that veiled night-time Los Angeles. The ghost of her own face stared back from the dark glass, surrounded by eerie, disembodied reflections of the dials and monitors of the Intensive Care ward.

Her eyes were drawn again to the bracelet on the table beside the young woman in bed number 4. *Temperature: 102.5*, she wrote on the woman's hourly log. The bracelet was stainless steel, cheap-looking and tinged green by the reflected glow of the ECG monitor. There was a small red staff and entwined serpent on it, the standard MedicAlert symbol. *Blood oxygen: 80 mm Hg*. The level had dropped a fraction. The woman's pulse was also down, and her blood pressure, but the rate of drop was still unchanged.

The woman was twenty-four, pretty, with long darkish hair that had become matted and greasy from perspiration; strands lay like frayed wires across the marbled skin of her forehead. She was stable but slipping steadily. The red digits on the blood-oxygen monitor that shared the shelf with the ECG had started the night at 90.

Ten days ago she had come into Casualty complaining of a vaginal irritation. Now she was close to death. Gram-negative septicaemia. Her body had turned against itself, battering her system with its own toxins. Her blood had been changed three times and she had been bombarded with drugs until her system could take no more. Dr Whitman, the head of the ICU, told the staff at yesterday morning's briefing that the woman had a seventy per cent chance of dying.

Statistics, thought Nurse Dunwoody as she moved to her other charge, in bed number 3, a man of sixty who was only hours out of theatre after a triple coronary-artery bypass. Statistics. The mortality rate in here was twenty per cent. One in five.

She checked the man's saline drip and his ventilator, adjusted the tape of one of the sensor pads on his bare chest, and logged his pulse, blood oxygen, blood pressure and temperature. One in five. The thought lodged in her mind like an old tune. It was a statistic that was as uncannily accurate as it was remorseless. One in every five patients would go from here to the mortuary; there was never any variation, no change in the three years she had been here. One in five would be wheeled out, taken down seven floors in the wide service lift to the small mortuary with its damp floor and its smell of disinfectant, tagged with a label attached by string to the big toe of their left foot, a yellow label only if they were going straight to an undertaker, a buff one as well if they were to have an autopsy first; then they'd be wrapped in a plastic shroud and slid into the bank of refrigerators to await collection by an undertaker's unmarked van.

After that the final journey to the crematorium or the grave. Or – she glanced again uneasily at the metal bracelet that lay on the table beside the young woman; the reflected green light made it glow as if it had a life of its own; as if it alone were detached from the grim reality of this place. Something from another planet, another world. A symbol of immortality. It spooked Nurse Dunwoody.

Somewhere outside, the wail of a siren disturbed the predawn air, shook it the way an angry mother shakes a child, and something shook inside her, too, like a flurry of snow in a gust. Something did not feel right and she did not know what.

She would have liked to talk to the patient about that bracelet, with its universal medical symbol, to have found out more about her. But the woman had been unconscious most of the time, and when she did wake she was delirious

2

and repeatedly mumbled a name that was incomprehensible. She had no visitors, no one had rung to ask after her, and there was little information about her background. A scar on her abdomen indicated surgery some time in the past, possibly a Caesarean section, but she had marked only a name in England as next-of-kin on her admission form, and by the word 'Children' had written: *None*.

Probably one of the thousands of hopefuls who dumped their pasts and came to Hollywood in search of fame, too many of whom ended up in this place after overdoses. Nurse Dunwoody stared back at the bracelet again. It seemed even hotter in here than usual tonight; she listened to the steady hiss from the ducts, the sharp clunk-puff . . . clunk-puff of the ventilator by the next bed. The air moved sluggishly around the ward, like the blood through her own veins. 3.30 a.m.

She glanced round wearily, watching other nurses who were filling in logs, or moving around past slumbering patients, past vacant, disoriented eyes and forests of saline drips, their bodies temporarily blotting out from her view the blips and spikes of monitors, the winking lights, the wavering dials. She found this place unnerving sometimes, late at night, like now, a strange hi-tech no-man's-land between life and death.

At regular intervals the young houseman appeared from his office and padded around the ward, glancing routinely at the patients, their charts, their drips and monitors, his white pyjamas rustling softly, his rubber-soled shoes silent on the carpeted floor.

Nurse Dunwoody's mind was occupied by the bracelet, and the sharp beeps failed to penetrate her thoughts for a brief moment. She saw the agitated face of the houseman as he sprinted past her, before it registered that the spikes on the electrocardiograph above the woman's head had dropped into a single unflickering line.

'Heart massage!' The houseman's face was tight with panic, like his voice. He pulled open the front of the woman's gown, interlocked his hands and compressed her chest,

3

paused, then pressed them down again. As he did so he looked up at the monitor as if willing it to register. He grabbed the nurse's hands, pressed them down in place of his. 'Don't stop,' he said.

The woman's pupils were dilating even as Nurse Dunwoody took over. She pressed down, eased off, pressed down, eased off.

The houseman grabbed the bracelet and raced into the tiny office beyond the blank computer display screen. This was the reception area of the ward, now dark and silent. He snatched the phone receiver, punched 9 for an outside line, then stabbed out the number on the bracelet, and held the receiver clenched to his ear.

Come on, Jesus, come on. Answer! Answer you mother-fuckers. Come on, come on, come on! You could tell when a place was empty; the phone always had a flat, echoey kind of ring. Maybe he'd misdialled? He disconnected and tried again, fingers trembling, his breaths sharp and hard. The same ring. Then someone answered:

'Yurr?' The voice was drowsy, uninterested.

'This is St John's Hospital,' the houseman said. 'You have a unit on standby for a patient here.'

The voice came alive slowly. 'Right, who's that?'

The houseman gave the young woman's name.

'OK, I have it.' There was a rustling of paper. 'We weren't expecting anything until tomorrow.'

'Nor were we,' the houseman replied, tersely. 'How fast can you be here?'

'Give us about half an hour to an hour.'

'Too long.'

'What is the current state of the patient?'

'Cardiac arrest.'

'Are you doing CPR? Keep the circulation going until we get there. The voice was becoming increasingly helpful. 'Can you get some anticoagulant in – heparin?'

'Sure.'

'Is there someone who can do the certification of death?'

'Me.'

4

'OK, I'll get the transport team organized. Have you called the Doctor?'

'I'll do that now.' The houseman hung up, then pulled from his wallet the crumpled sheet of paper and unfolded it. The number he'd inked in months earlier lay across the creases, but the digits were still legible. He dialled and, when the old man answered, he looked around furtively, then said simply and in a lowered voice: 'It worked too quickly.'

The young woman was lying in a shallow, open-topped container packed with ice when Nurse Dunwoody helped them wheel her into Operating Theatre 5, which they had obtained permission to use. The nurse noted the apparatus with a mixture of disbelief and amazement. She saw the heart-lung machine on its wheeled cart which a beefy man in soiled dungarees and trainers was connecting to the mains electricity supply. Two other men in casual clothing were cutting open bags of ice which they were emptying into a huge high-sided plastic box.

She watched with morbid curiosity and a growing feeling of horror as she continued to massage the dead girl's heart, even though there was no response: the pulse was feeble, coming only from the compressions, and there was no ECG reading. Vapour rose from the top of the huge box, like a deep-freeze chest that had been opened. She shivered.

An elderly bespectacled man came in wearing blue surgical scrubs. He looked as if he'd been very handsome when younger, and he carried a strangely powerful presence with him even now. He was followed by a younger man and a woman similarly attired. Then the young houseman came in, also changed into scrubs. 'Call me if there are any problems,' he said to Nurse Dunwoody, releasing her from her massaging duty.

She nodded, then hesitated. Two of the other night nurses were covering for her in the ward, and she was curious to see what was going to happen next in here.

She went outside and looked through the viewing window

5

in the door. The team worked with intense urgency. She saw the dead woman's hospital gown being removed, and watched her being coupled to a heart-lung 'thumper' resuscitator; at the same time an endotracheal tube was inserted down her throat. The houseman inserted a cannula into the back of her hand and one of the assistants hung several bags of fluid on the drip stand above, whilst another adjusted the flow valves. The thumper was started and began delivering chest compressions.

The elderly man located a vein in the dead woman's arm, and injected several boluses of drugs in rapid succession. Then another man, whom Nurse Dunwoody recognized as a heart surgeon who worked in the hospital, made an incision with a scalpel in the woman's groin. Femoral cutdown, she guessed; they were going to cannulate the femoral artery.

Almost an hour later, being careful not to disturb the elaborate plumbing connected to the dead woman, the team raised her and laid her carefully in the ice-packed box. One of the technicians changed the electrical supply of the heart-lung machine over to its portable battery pack. The others opened several more bags of ice which they packed either side of her, then they closed the lid of the container and hurriedly, in a macabre procession, wheeled the dead woman and their apparatus towards the lift.

You poor fools Susan Dunwoody thought, deeply disturbed. You poor deluded fools.

I

February 1982. Toronto, Canada.

The call Joe Messenger had been dreading came at a quarter past two in the morning. His father had believed passionately that one day human death could be defeated, and perhaps because of that, and because Joe had been brought up by his father since the age of seven, his reluctance to accept that one day his father really would die had been even stronger than most children's.

He answered the phone groggily, thinking at first it was the alarm clock, then reality hit him as he lifted the receiver to his ear and heard the polite, anxious voice of a night nurse at Toronto General Hospital. He fumbled for the bedside light, spilling a glass of water in the process.

'Dr Messenger, your father is calling out for you. He wants to speak to you very badly.'

'How is he?'

'He's very weak, I'm afraid.' She hesitated, and he could read clearly the thinly concealed message in the words she said next: 'I think it might be a good idea if you could come over right away.'

'Sure, I'll be right there.'

There was another pause, then she said: 'There is something he wants to tell you very desperately. It seems like he wants to warn you of something.'

Joe pulled on a thick denim shirt, a rollneck pullover and corduroy trousers, splashed some water on his face and hunted frantically around his cluttered studio room for his boots. He found his socks, but couldn't think where the hell his boots were. Didn't matter. Shoes would be fine, any shoes, he wasn't having to walk far. He pushed his feet into his slip-on moccasins in which he normally loafed around indoors, grabbed his quilted overjacket, a pair of woollen gloves and his car keys, and shuffled out into the corridor, treading awkwardly on the flattened backs of his shoes. One of his socks was uncomfortably balled beneath the sole of his feet.

The stale smell in the elevator of cigarette smoke and sweet perfume, combined with the plunging motion, made him feel faintly bilious. Nerves. His stomach was knotted. He sorted his shoes out, then squinted into the elevator mirror and straightened his short fair hair out with two sweeps of his hands.

He was twenty-six years old, five feet eleven inches tall, with a strong, athletic frame and an equally strong personality he had inherited from his father; his appearance was enhanced by the deep blue eyes and assertively handsome features he had inherited mostly from his late mother. Much of Joe's charm came from the fact that he was unaware of his looks, in the same way that he had no interest in where he lived or the cars he drove. Work was his excitement, his passion in life. He had already done an MD Ph.D. with a thesis in neuroscience at Harvard and was currently doing postdoc work in Artificial Intelligence. He demanded no more of life than that he be free to carry on towards the same goal, but down different paths, to which his father had dedicated his life.

The face that stared back out at him from the mirror looked pallid and drawn, with deep black rings beneath the eyes; he had been overworking lately; not eating, not doing his usual regular exercising. Stressed. Trying to forget that his father was dying, and sleeping lousily for worrying about him.

His eyes stung. They were raw from tiredness and from the crying he had done earlier; he had cried himself to sleep some time around midnight. Tonight he was still a boy who had a dad, but he knew the day would come very soon now when he would have only the memory of one. The world's greatest, most wonderful daddy.

Joe wondered what it was his father wanted to tell him. To warn him about. Willi Messenger was like that; capricious. He'd come up with some brilliant new idea, then a few days later he'd be on to the next thing. Willi got deeply concerned sometimes by the power of science. But he was as hooked on it as any other scientist, and saw it as a force for good.

The elevator jerked to a halt and the door slid open on to the dingy lobby. He ran across it, unlatched the heavy glass door and pulled it open, then felt the sudden wetness on his feet as he stepped out.

Shit.

A snowflake the size of a golf ball tickled his nose; another landed in his hair and immediately began to melt down his forehead. A good eighteen inches had fallen and it was still coming down hard. He lifted his foot up and the snow was caked around his sock. He debated for a moment whether to go back and put some boots on, but somehow he did not think he had much time.

He stumbled through a drift over two feet deep near the parking lot, to the silhouette that he hoped was his car. He wiped some snow off the windshield, blinking as another flake melted into his eye, brushed the door handle, inserted his key and pulled. The door opened with a crackle of splintering ice, some of which tumbled down inside the cuff of his glove.

He clambered in, kicking snow from the door sill, floored the gas pedal to choke the engine and twisted the key in the ignition. The battery like the rest of the car was on its last legs and turned the engine over agonizingly slowly; then it fired and rumbled into life and oily exhaust fumes raftered past him. A snowplough ground along the road, its warning flashers scattering shards of blue light across the downy whiteness.

In spite of the road conditions, Joe drove the three miles to downtown Toronto recklessly, his neck craned forwards, his face pressed close to the misted screen, rubbing a small, smeary space in front of him every few moments with his sopping wet glove. An endless loop of snowflakes hurtled out of the darkness at him, nearly blinding him at times, and the car headlamps passing in the opposite direction

9

seemed as weak as candles, but he barely noticed anything through the shroud of sadness that smothered him.

The Plymouth slithered up the hospital ramp into the almost deserted lot; signs on poles were covered with snow and unreadable. '. . . LL ONLY' said one. '. . . VED DIREC . . . TO . . . ES' said another in front of which he parked at an angle.

As he climbed out, a taxi crawled down the road, its tyres crunching. The heater had almost dried his feet, and they became sodden and cold again as he stumbled towards the hospital's doors. He was grateful for the blast of heat in the hospital lobby and stamped his shoes on the floor to shake off the snow. The night security guard looked up from his television monitor and gave him a wry smile. 'Chucking down,' he said.

Joe nodded, swallowing as his nerves engulfed him. Everything felt strangely unreal suddenly, and he wondered for a moment if he was in the middle of a dream. The black and white picture on the monitor showed an outside door with snow falling. There was another monitor beside it showing another door; snow was also falling in that movie too. It was a moment before his brain registered that it wasn't a movie that the guard was watching.

He walked on autopilot to the bank of elevators and pressed the button on the panel. A lift arrived with a ping and as the doors opened he was surprised to see someone he knew step out. Blake Hewlett, his father's protégé. Blake, who was dauntingly tall, had a background, like himself, in neuroscience. But he had then gone on to work in cryobiology under Willi Messenger, at first in the States, then had followed him back to Toronto to work with him here, in the laboratory adjoining the hospital, on the preservation of human organs for transplants.

Blake didn't seem surprised to see him; there was nothing in his face to indicate that it was unusual to meet someone in a hospital elevator at a quarter to three in the morning.

'Hi,' Joe said. He had a strange, uneasy relationship with Blake, who was sometimes quite distant, almost a total stranger, and at other times was like an elder brother.

Blake's look now changed to reveal concern. 'Joe, hi. What's up?'

'Father,' he said. 'I've just had a call. Sounds like this could be –'

Blake put a supportive arm on Joe's shoulder. The rich, spoiled product of a society plastic surgeon who had married a cereals heiress, Blake had an unshakable confidence in himself that bordered both on smugness and arrogance. He was six feet six inches tall, with a lean build and black hair swept back from the fine, faintly Slavic features of his face into a small ponytail. He was wearing a herringbone greatcoat with the collar turned up and rubber overboots. 'I popped in to see him about ten – he seemed fine – a little tired maybe.'

'You been working late?' Joe said.

Blake nodded. 'Road-traffic accident – an organ donor. They thought he was going to die –' Blake hesitated, then gave him a rather strange smile. 'But he didn't.' Blake patted his shoulder again. 'Keep fingers crossed for your pa.'

'You'll come, won't you . . . when it –' Joe's voice seized up and he fought back a tear, moved by Blake's sudden gentleness.

'I'll be there. But it's a while off, Joe. He's a tough man, be up on his feet again in a few days – you'll see.'

'Sure,' Joe said, mustering a smile as heavy as a suitcase. He walked leadenly into the elevator and pressed the button for the fourth floor.

An oppressive silence embraced him as he stepped out into the corridor. The doors shut behind him but there was no sound of the elevator moving either up or down. A fluorescent light flickered on-off-on-off, throwing a flat buzzing sound out into the silence. He trudged in his cold wet foot-gear down linoleum that smelled freshly polished, past trolleys of laundry and instruments, past some doors that opened on to dark offices, some doors that were closed, then past a noticeboard and a dark canteen and beneath a sign that read ST MARY'S WARD.

As he turned the familiar corner, light spilled from an open door and a shadow stirring in the light told him there was someone in the sister's office. Melted snow dribbled down the back of his neck. He caught sight of his reflection in a pane of dark glass and saw a crust of snow on his hair; he brushed it away with his hand and shook his head. The nurse came out to meet him. Her name tag said Anna Vogel. He thought he had met her before but wasn't sure.

Joe's eyes focused on the tag. It was white plastic with black printing, fastened by a safety pin. A small piece of the plastic was chipped off, as if at some time the tag had been dropped and trodden on. *Anna Vogel*. He kept looking at the tag and knew that as long as he did, as long as he avoided the night nurse's eyes, he could keep believing that everything was all right.

Her face remained an indistinct blur in the background; he had a faint impression of brown, wavy hair and pock-marked skin.

'I'm sorry, Dr Messenger,' was all she said. Or maybe that was all Joe heard.

He broke into a run, opened the door and went into the small room, his eyes swimming with tears, his mind brimming with emotion and the urgent knowledge of what he had to do.

'Pa,' he said. 'Dad. Daddy.'

The old man lay there with his eyes and mouth closed, and Joe's first reaction was that he was glad about that, because if they weren't closed within minutes of death it would become impossible to do so. His father's face was shapeless and leathery like a deflated football. The colour of the skin was almost grey, and black lines looked as if they'd been charcoaled down the cheeks. The dome of his head seemed almost crudely pink in comparison, rising through the sparse tangle of white and grey hairs. It was odd seeing his father's striped pyjamas buttoned to the neck. Joe knew he always left the top button undone.

Motionless. So damn motionless. And helpless. He seemed very small, suddenly, and he used to be a giant.

A half-drunk glass of water lay beside him, and a book called *Modularity of Mind* with a marker sticking out three-quarters of the way through. Joe's involuntary thought was that his father would have been annoyed not to have been able to finish his book.

Then he wept. Knelt beside the bed and took his father's hand that had once seemed, to a small boy, so huge and strong, and now felt like plasticine. He held it tight, feeling the meagre warmth that remained in it, and pressed it to his cheek. And he remembered how the last time he had held that hand, only yesterday evening, a mere eight or so hours ago, his father had squeezed with all the faint energy he could muster and said: 'Make sure, won't you, son?'

Joe remembered the promise now as he lifted the phone beside the bed and began to dial, and at the same time slipped his hand inside his father's pyjama top and began to massage his heart, hard. He wedged the phone between his shoulder and ear, and massaged with both hands.

The team made good time in arriving, in spite of the snow. Less than twenty minutes after he'd been certified dead, Willi Messenger was already being wheeled into the operating theatre. Joe at least had the comfort of knowing that one day his father would be grateful.

2

September 1987. Los Angeles.

11 IN La Cienega Boulevard was a three-storey building on the southern edge of Beverly Hills, just catching the chic of the postal address but not much else. Flanked by a gas station on one side and a row of grimy shops and office buildings on the other, with its bland, featureless architecture,

IIIN looked outwardly like an office block itself, maybe a government taxation or licensing department.

Although there were windows along the front façade visible to the street, it was impossible to see in, and both the sides and the rear were kept private by an electric sliding gate and high walls.

Some people who knew what the building was quickened their pace as they walked by; others slowed in morbid curiosity, glancing at the electronic security system on the front door and wondering at the absence of any company name displayed there. As with any place that cloaked itself in secrecy, dark rumours abounded. A few of the neighbourhood's more religious residents actually crossed the street to avoid passing too close.

At a quarter past midnight few people were around to see the Ford truck pull up outside the rear gates. The driver pressed the buzzer and gave his name: 'Warren Otak,' he said. The gates slid open to allow the truck entry, then closed behind it again. The truck was a three-ton closed van painted bright orange; bold lettering on the side proclaimed 'Budget Self-Drive Truck Rentals'.

Otak drove into the yard at the rear, turned the truck around and backed it up against the loading-bay platform. The metal security door in the building began to rise with a clatter that seemed to shatter the quiet of the muggy night. Four men stood inside, three in suits, one in the uniform of a security guard. A cigar-shaped aluminium tube, nine feet long and four in diameter, lay on its side, cradled in a dense nest of padding, and strapped securely to a wheeled trolley. A grey gas bottle, carrying a warning symbol and the words LIQUID NITROGEN, was clipped to the cylinder and hooked up to a valve on the side via a short pipe. Streaks of red from the truck's rear lights reflected in the metallic shine of the aluminium. It reminded Warren Otak of a section of a space craft.

One of the men in suits showed Otak and his assistant, Arnie Becks, two temperature gauges on the tube; both were calibrated in Celsius and the dials were reading -140.

'There's a variation tolerance of plus or minus five degrees maximum,' he said. He showed them how to lower the temperature by adding more gas, and how to decrease by venting gas. Then he gave each man an oxygen mask and showed them how to use it. 'In case of emergency,' he said. He also handed them two packs containing protective body suits, boots and gloves.

It took an hour and a half to load the tube. First, the floor of the truck had to be packed with layers of foam, then the tube had to be lowered on to a cradle and anchored in place with straps. Otak and Becks were warned repeatedly of the fragility of their cargo. A sharp jolt of any kind could be a disaster. Otak was given a maximum speed limit of ten m.p.h. – it was enough, the man said, to get him to his destination before the morning traffic began.

'No problem,' Otak replied, more breezily than he felt. He switched on his hazard flashers, pulled out of the yard, crawled a few blocks south down La Cienega, then turned east.

They drove in silence for some minutes. Becks peered over his shoulder periodically to check their cargo.

'Gives me the creeps, that thing,' Otak said.

'You're full of shit. Everything gives you the creeps.'

'Eat my shorts!' Otak looked nervously in his wing mirror. Darkness seemed to be closing in, swallowing up the lights of the city and the other vehicles behind them. Cold, icy darkness that drained all the heat from the night.

The patrol car pulled them up just over an hour later. Otak was surprised they had not been stopped sooner.

'You have a problem?' one of the cops said.

Otak stared into the beam of the torch and blinked at the shadowy figure beyond it. Twin red lights flashed on the patrol car's roof. 'Nope,' he said, failing to stem his natural sullenness towards all police. 'No problem.'

'You were doing fourteen miles an hour.'

'Yup – well, I'm real nervous of breaking the limit – don't want no points on my clean licence.' Otak knew as soon as he had said it that it was the wrong thing; if the cop had a sense of humour, he hadn't brought it with him.

The cop shone his torch at Arnie Becks' face. Becks kept silent. He shone it back at Otak. 'Can I see your driver's licence?'

Otak fished in his jacket and pulled out his wallet. The cop studied the licence, glancing at Otak's face a couple of times in the process, then handed it back. 'What do you have in the back?' he said.

Otak caught Becks' smirk out of the corner of his eye, and it infected him; he broke into a broad grin, and saw the cop's suspicion and hostility increasing.

'Have you been drinking liquor tonight, Mr Otak?' came the next question, the cop moving his face closer to smell Otak's breath.

'I don't drink liquor.'

'Have you been taking narcotics?'

'I don't take narcotics,' Otak replied, unable to stop himself grinning again. Only this time some of his humour evaporated from the grin. Narcotics. The significance of the word sank in a bit more strongly.

Narcotics!

Panic rose inside him. He stifled it. No way. They couldn't have done that to him. Otak saw the cop had noticed the change in his expression. He'd accepted the job on trust; on faith. What it involved had seemed so bizarre that it had to be true. Now he began to have doubts. Maybe this business about fragility was bull; maybe he was the victim of some set-up, some tuck-up. His brain raced, trying to make sense; trying to think how he could cover his tracks, prove his innocence; he felt his hands go clammy.

'Would you like to open the rear of the truck for me, gentlemen?'

Otak saw that a second cop was sitting in the car, watching them and talking on the radio. He climbed down, trembling a little, trying to convince himself that he didn't need to be nervous, everything was fine. No one was dumb enough to hire him to drive a truck loaded with narcotics through LA in the dead of night at ten miles per hour.

He unlatched the back doors and swung them open. The cop shone his flashlight in. The aluminium tube glinted. The cop studied it for some moments, running his beam carefully over it, down at the foam, then back over the tube. 'What do you have in there?' he said.

Otak looked back at him and felt a lump of anxiety in his throat; at the same time, the grin broke out again on his face. He felt both a little foolish and a little hopeful: 'A dead body,' he said.

3

Saturday 9 January, 1993. Sussex.

The video camera silently recorded Joe Messenger as he sat at the breakfast table, mechanically spooning whole-grain cereal into his mouth and scanning through the pages of *The Times*.

His mind was elsewhere, as it frequently was, at this moment running through his teaching curriculum for the forthcoming spring term at the Isaac Newton University, where he was Professor of Computer Science. He nearly missed the short column towards the bottom of the Overseas News page: FROZEN CORPSES COMPANY ON ICE.

Joe liked to read *The Times* at breakfast every morning; it was still a treat, even after four years, something quintessentially British, like Dundee marmalade, and having milk delivered in glass bottles. *The Times* had been around for over two hundred years. Joe admired that. He admired anything that was capable of outstripping the human lifespan of three score years and ten. Like the small Koi carp that swam around the glass bowl on the Welsh dresser beside him. Koi lived for over two hundred years as well.

England had been good to Joe. Sure there were things here that frustrated him, particularly the lack of respect and support given to scientific research. In America research was sacrosanct; here in England, scientists scratched around for funding and lived on meagre pay. And yet some of the greatest inventive minds on earth were here. But he was lucky; he had been lured over with the promise of unlimited funding and no hassle, and so far it was working out fine. The only hassle was his wife, Karen. It wasn't her fault, but he didn't know the solution.

She was unhappy and frustrated, and the support she had once given him so ardently seemed to have waned. Their biggest bone of contention was over the video cameras that were in every room of the house, and on every outside wall. Joe didn't notice them at all any more. They'd been there so long, he paid them no more attention than if they had been burglar-alarm sensors, although at first he, too, had been self-conscious in their presence. After the first fortnight Karen had put her foot down and insisted he remove the ones in the bedroom and the bathroom. He had done so, then a few days later, when she was out, he had put them back again, concealed.

As if reading Joe's mind, Karen looked up from the breakfast table at the silent electronic eye that was recording her husband chewing his cereal, their three-year-old son, Jack, reading his comic, and herself peeling the foil from an apple-and-walnut yoghurt.

'Don't let your egg get cold, Jack,' she said.

Obediently he pushed his comic to one side, picked up his spoon and scooped the white out of the cap of his boiled egg. Then as he ate it he removed one of the four soldiers into which she had cut his toast, and rearranged the remaining three into a triangle. She watched him fondly, his hair the colour of winter wheat flopped down over his forehead.

'Daddy?' he said gently, as if afraid of disturbing his father.

Joe glanced at him. 'Uh?'

Jack pointed at the three strips of bread. 'Is that a triangle, Daddy?'

Karen felt a warm glow as Joe smiled back at him. 'Yup, pretty good,' he said. 'Now you want to make a square?'

Jack opened up the triangle and put the fourth soldier down.

'That's neat,' Joe said. 'OK, now how about a –'

'Hon,' Karen interrupted. 'I think he should eat his breakfast.' She caught the flash of irritation in her husband's face and felt a twinge of guilt. She knew how keen Joe was to foster Jack's interest in science and she was happy about that, but sometimes it bordered on the obsessional. Joe was obsessive about everything he did. All the way or not at all.

Like the cameras.

He'd told her she would get used to the cameras in time, but she hadn't. She found herself sometimes deliberately trying to skirt along the walls to get out of their line of vision, but a faint whirr of motors would tell her they were panning down, tilting, focusing. That she had not escaped. Gotchya! They were picking up every detail of her life; of their lives. Every movement they made, every sound they uttered was filed on-line to ARCHIVE – the computer that was a would-be human – encoded into hexadecimal digits and stored.

The computer was the bane of her life and sometimes she wished it was dead. It was bizarre, she knew, to wish death on a computer; for it meant that a part of her was acknowledging what she was not willing to admit: that ARCHIVE could in any way be alive. It could not! Except in Joe's mind. She instructed herself that no computer could ever be aware of its own existence, have emotions, fall in love, watch two adult human beings living their lives and begin to make any sense of what that was all about. Could it?

Karen had met Joe at the University of Toronto. She'd been a freshman English Lit undergraduate, and had got involved with the university's magazine. She'd been assigned to interview this crazy postdoc boffin who reckoned he knew how to make computers have orgasms, and was working on ways to download a human brain. To her surprise, she had found not some bespectacled scatterbrained nerd, but a startlingly articulate and handsome fair-haired man, who looked more like a rugged adventurer than a scientist.

Within a few minutes of talking to Joe, she had realized that his ideas were more than just wild fancy. He was a man who was going to make them happen. He was only twenty-seven but he had utter conviction and a hint of ruthlessness that she found both frightening and exciting.

Two months later they were engaged. Even though Joe had Jewish lineage through his grandparents, it had caused outrage in her strictly Orthodox family that she was not marrying a Jew, outrage which had been mitigated only very slightly by the fact that he was a doctor of science. And mitigated further, eventually, by the fact that although a firm non-believer, Joe had shown respect and understanding for their customs and regularly joined their celebrations of the Sabbath.

The first few years of marriage had been an undeniably happy time. Joe's career had taken off meteorically when in his early thirties he had won a MacArthur Prize for his work on neural networks. And Karen had been carried along by his enthusiasm.

Joe believed that death could be defeated by the process of humans downloading their own brains into computers. And for a time she not only had believed he could make it happen but had also really wanted him to, and had defended him vigorously at college dinners if he came under attack.

But not any more.

Barty had changed her. Barty had been born in their second year of marriage and Joe had doted on him. Then when Barty was three, he had been killed in a car crash. Joe had managed to cope with it, somehow, but she hadn't. Joe had been kind to her, had shown a side to him that she had never realized existed, a depth of emotion and caring that had helped her somehow to get through the three years of hell that had followed. Their grief, more than anything else, had bonded them together. But her job had helped, too.

Before she met Joe, Karen had been ambitious to work in documentary television: she'd nurtured dreams of being both a television presenter and a magazine columnist. In a compartment of her mind there still lay a fantasy that she would one day write regularly for the *New Yorker*. After university, she'd stepped on to the first rung of her career ladder by getting a job as a television researcher in Toronto. But maternity leave for Barty's birth had curtailed her immediate prospects of promotion. And although she had returned to work three months later, she found Barty had become the new focus of her life and her ambitions seemed less important. After Barty's death, she'd worked hard to cling on to her job, and the supportive friendship of her colleagues helped pull her through those years.

Then, when she was two months pregnant with Jack, Joe had been offered the research project of his dreams in England, together with a professorship at a leading university. She'd jumped at the idea of moving to England; a break with the past; a new beginning. But now she felt that in moving from their memories they had moved from their roots. And she missed work a lot. Joe was getting more handsome with age and she was scared that her own looks would go. There was always a magnetism about him when he walked into a room, and she could see the interest in other women's faces, watched them flirt with him. She had never been concerned in the past, but it was beginning to worry her now.

She looked at her husband across the table, dressed in one of the soft, button-down shirts he almost invariably wore, with a tie during weekdays, and open-necked beneath a sleeveless jumper at weekends. The years had flattered him. Given him just a few wrinkles that had etched additional wisdom and authority into his features. His blue eyes nestled comfortably between the crow's feet, sparkling with light and with life, and often filled with an expression of wonder, as if he was seeing everything in the world for the first time. Except where once she had seen wisdom she now saw naïvety.

And she wondered what he saw when he looked at her.

She was still attractive, she knew that. And she wanted to keep it that way. She'd put on weight after being pregnant with Jack and had not managed to get rid of it all, but fortunately at five feet seven inches she was tall enough to carry a few extra pounds. And by maintaining her luxurious black wavy hair at shoulder length it seemed to keep her face looking reasonably slim, and to give her an air of elegance. Her complexion was the thing that bothered her most. Ever since that second pregnancy, she thought it had become too sallow.

She was always trying natural tonics, bought organic soaps and skin shampoos from the Body Shop, and even made potions up from cranky recipes she read in magazines. One, which seemed to work better than the rest, contained a mineral extracted from goat's faeces – much to Joe's amusement. But what her doctor had said was probably right, she realized. England was stressful for her; Jack was starting at playschool in a couple of weeks and that would at least give her some time to herself. Maybe that would improve things dramatically. Life owed her a break.

When Joe had originally mentioned the offer from the Isaac Newton University, part of the reason why the idea of moving to England had appealed so highly was because she had visited London fleetingly as a student fourteen years before and had fallen in love with it. The reality, as is often the case, was different.

Karen's first shock was to discover that the university wasn't in London at all, but fifty miles south, only a few miles inland from the English Channel. Her second shock was to discover quite how much she missed her family, particularly her sister Arlene, and friends in Toronto, a city she had never previously left for longer than a month. And how much she also missed the camaraderie of working life. Their new social circle consisted almost entirely of Joe's colleagues from the university. Computing-science lecturers, researchers and professors, mostly, with whom she had little in common, and a motley collection of partners.

She also felt isolated and adrift in their house. In Toronto she'd had a mental image of moving to the faded grandeur of an old London terrace, to a huge old apartment with oak floors, and high ceilings with cornices and mouldings. Instead they'd moved to a four-bedroom detached 1920s mock-Tudor house in a smart, dinky suburb of a provincial seaside resort, where every property was a mock-something-or-other.

Number 8 Cranford Road belonged to another professor at the university who'd taken a five-year posting abroad; they'd rented it for six months while they had a chance to look around, and three and a half years on they were still looking around. That was as much her fault as Joe's, she knew, probably more so. She hadn't felt settled enough over here to commit to buying a property. Yet at the same time she resented living in someone else's house, because she was unable to redecorate it or furnish it in the way she would have liked.

Joe had his work to absorb him and the social contact that went with it, and was so engrossed with Jack in the few hours that he was at home and not thinking about work that he failed to notice her growing unhappiness. She had even agreed to the installation of the cameras because she felt that might give Joe more of an interest in their home.

She felt the warmth of the sun on her face through the window and cheered up a little. It was Saturday. Joe usually only did a few hours at the university on Saturday mornings, then came home. This afternoon he was taking Jack fishing down on the end of the pier and she would join them later, bringing them a picnic tea. Tomorrow they were going to somewhere near Chichester to see a working water-mill grinding flour. It was yet another chance for Joe to develop the boy's interest in science, the way his own father's encouragement had helped develop his.

The front doorbell rang and she went to answer it. The postman stood there with a registered envelope for her from Canada. Across the street, Muriel Arkwright cleaned her car. Obsessive Compulsive Disorder. It was 8.30 in the morning and Muriel was out with her buckets and sponges, her ozone-friendly spray cans of polish and her hose and chamois leather, cleaning the bronze Nissan that she'd already cleaned to *concours* condition yesterday; and the day before. And the day before that. When she'd finished she would start on her husband's silver Audi, then the windows of her mock-Georgian house; then the brass door fittings; then she would probably go shopping and when she returned clean the Nissan all over again because it would have got dirty.

Maybe Joe was not altogether crazy, Karen thought. The advantage with machines was that when they went wonky you could fix them. It was harder with human beings.

'My new Ontario driving licence; Mother mailed it,' she said to Joe as she sat down at the table again, but he didn't lift his eyes from the paper. He seemed to have stiffened; there was a strange expression on his face and the colour had almost drained from his skin. For a moment she was afraid he was having a heart attack.

FROZEN CORPSES COMPANY ON ICE. Joe stopped chewing and read the article again.

THE American company which helped pioneer a technique for freezing dead bodies took the first steps towards liquidation yesterday. The Crycon Corporation, which used liquid nitrogen for the controversial cryonic suspension option filed for Chapter 11 bankruptcy.

As the case was being heard, relatives of some of the frozen bodies staged an angry demonstration at the company's Beverly Hills headquarters. 'We were told that our loved ones would be safe for ever and we were fool enough to believe them,' said teamster Joseph Czechbo, 46. 'I'll use every cent I have to bring these frauds to justice.'

American police and IRS officers are still seeking two of the Crycon directors, Curtis

> Danfoss and Walter T. Liedermeir, who disap-
> peared earlier this month.

A wave of queasiness swept through Joe; he looked up at Jack then at Karen as if to reassure himself, then down at the page again. The print blurred and he leaned forward, forcing his eyes to focus.

'Jesus,' he said, standing up from the table and backing away; his legs felt wobbly.

'What's the matter, Joe? You OK?'

He stared back at Karen without responding.

She stood up. 'Joe? You swallow something? Get something stuck in your throat?'

He shook his head, walked over to the phone on the wall and pulled the receiver off with shaking hands. The flat hum seemed to resound around the room.

Jack looked up from his comic. 'Daddy, what does Vakum mean?'

'Vakum?' Joe echoed back like an imbecile. He flipped open the telephone directory and began leafing through it.

'Who are you phoning, Joe? The doctor? You want the doc?'

Joe shook his head.

'*Vakoome*,' Jack said, more loudly and less patiently. He was already a precocious reader and normally his father was the first to encourage him.

Joe scanned the directory's tiny print, then held a spot with his forefinger.

'Vacuum,' Karen said, glancing at the comic for a second, not wanting to take her eyes off Joe. '*Vacuum*. It sort of means no air.'

'So you can't breathe?'

She turned to Joe. 'What is it, honey? What are you doing?'

'It's OK.' Joe dialled a number.

'Why can't you breathe, Mummy?'

Joe listened as the phone rang. Then a breezy woman's voice answered: 'Good morning, British Airways sales.'

Joe spoke into the receiver. 'Do you have any flights to Los Angeles today?'

'Joe!' Karen said. 'What's going on?'

Joe thrust the paper at her, grim-faced, and tapped the article with his finger.

'Oh, my God!' she said.

4

As Joe hurried out of the chaos of the Arrivals lobby he cut a confident figure in his checked jacket, jeans, Timberland boots, a raincoat slung over one arm, briefcase and laptop gripped in the other. But inside he didn't feel confident at all.

It was eleven years since he'd last been here. Every year for the past decade he'd intended coming just to check up on everything, make sure all was OK, but nothing had brought him out this way and time had slipped past. Now he was scared he'd left it too long.

The sky was a flat grey against the grey concrete; the air smelled stale and felt heavy, laden with a damp chill. He shivered, realized he'd forgotten how cool Los Angeles could sometimes be in January. Taxis rolled by almost silently on their fat rubber treads; doors slammed; courtesy buses hauled along. He looked anxiously for one that said 'Dollar'.

A strong headwind had added an hour to what had seemed an interminable flight; he'd been unable to concentrate on anything and had mostly just sat in his cramped seat, flicking through *Scientific American*, glancing up at the movie which was incomprehensible without headphones, and trying to work out how he was going to deal with the problem. There would be a solution; there was always a solution.

Twenty minutes later he walked out into the Dollar lot, checked the registration number on the front of the wallet containing the rental documents, and found the shiny maroon Chrysler in a covered bay at the rear.

The interior of the car smelled pungently new, as if he'd stuck his head into a vinyl holdall, and he was grateful for the blast of conditioned air as he turned the ignition key. Deep in thought and not really concentrating, he drove out down towards Century, then he turned north on to the San Diego freeway, and accelerated hard, the rumble of the tyres on the ribbed concrete suddenly as familiar to him as if he'd last driven along here only yesterday.

A muddy yellow sun glowed weakly through the canopy of cloud, but failed to shine up the dull pinks, ochres and whites of the Spanish-style buildings speckled around the barren landscape. A green sign 'TRUCKS OK' flashed past him. A dreary song played from the speakers behind his head. Another sign flashed past: 'TRAFFIC INFO AM RADIO 1610.' He could just make out the hazy silhouette of the Hollywood hills in the distance as he passed a cluster of high-rises. All the vegetation looked familiar; the green-brown scrub; palms rising from stubby bark. Advertising hoardings.

The buildings seemed grimier than when he'd been here last; there was an air of decay about the city that added further to his depression. Made him feel angry. People had to take care of the world, had to be responsible. The future was no longer going to be someone else's problem. People needed to realize that.

He set the cruise control at sixty miles per hour and turned down the radio. His thoughts returned to his father. Professor Willi Messenger had been a rebel all his life, the sort of person who wasn't afraid of what anyone thought of him, who never bothered to wear a suit to official functions. Joe's mother, an actress, had died of cancer when he was seven and Willi had never remarried. He'd brought Joe up himself, first in Washington, then Boston, then Los Angeles, then Toronto. Joe had worshipped him. It was his father who'd taught him about science and about Nature. Taught him how to hunt, fish, how to disassemble an engine and put it back together, how to take a television apart, a computer apart. Taught him how to make sense of the world. And taught him to despise death.

Willi Messenger had been a pioneer of cryobiology, and Joe had loved nothing more than to hang around his father's laboratory, watching the researchers and assistants at work, helping with their experiments into freezing and thawing insects, animal and human cells and tissues, and whole organs.

Willi's conviction was that unless humans achieved a way to live much longer, the human race would become extinct. He had declared that life was too short for humans to develop the wisdom they needed to survive as a species: that by the time most people achieved a state of anything approaching an understanding of life and humanity, they were too old to make any use of the knowledge. If only humans could live actively and youthfully another fifty or a hundred years, they would then truly become mature and wise. But more than that, he had believed deep in his heart that death was an obscenity that should not be accepted as inevitable. He'd held no truck with God or any afterlife. *Once you're gone, you're gone*, he would say. *So it's better not to go in the first place*. And his favourite expression was: *Death is not necessary*.

Joe could remember his father now, lying in the hospital bed, shrivelled and ravaged by cancer, a man whose opinions had been sought – sometimes attacked – by some of the greatest scientists of the age, men like Robert Oppenheimer, Gerald Edelman, Richard Feynman, Marvin Minsky, Alan Newell. Willi Messenger had stared closely into his son's face and whispered with all that was left of his voice: *Death is not necessary, Joe. No one should have to die any more. It can be defeated, but that's over to you now, boy. Make sure, won't you, son? Promise me that?*

Joe had promised that he would. It was the last time they had spoken.

In addition to his work on cryobiology for organ transplants and tissue grafts, Willi Messenger had been a pioneer of cryonic freezing of human beings. But that aspect of his work had cost him much of his respect in the scientific community. There were times in the last years of his life when he told Joe, with bitterness in his voice, that if they could have taken away his status the Establishment would have done so. Joe thought that was typical of the in-fighting and jealousy that went on among certain academics just because someone else had got there first.

But Willi hadn't cared. He'd been convinced that cryonics would work, so convinced that he'd foreseen the outcome of his cancer not as death but merely as *temporary deanimation*.

He had written books and numerous papers on the subject, but the more he argued for cryonics the more the medical and scientific powers-that-be criticized his work and even his motives. Cryonics is a con, they said; it gives false hope; it takes a large amount of money from the deceased's estate which could instead benefit conventional medical research or charities. Joe was proud of what he saw as his father's achievements and said his detractors were just bitching because they wanted any money that was going spare for their own pet research subjects, and for charities that began with the letters of their own names.

Willi had spent twenty-five years proving to himself that cryonics *would* work: proving that so long as people were frozen correctly, and the process was started within minutes of cessation of the heartbeat, and that they were kept at a low enough temperature for all biological activity to be suspended, it would be possible one day to bring them back to life.

He believed that eventually the technology would exist to thaw them out and to repair any damage caused by the freezing. By that same time medicine would have advanced to the point of being able to cure them of the disease that had killed them, to repair the damage caused by the disease on a cell-by-cell basis, and to rejuvenate the elderly. He had explained countless times to Joe how it would work, and Joe believed him. Joe was convinced there was nothing that science could not achieve, given time, whether it took decades or centuries. And he was determined to show the world his father had been right.

But Joe also believed there was yet another method of defeating death. It was what he worked on day and night; it was what drove him, what made him wake each morning with a sense of exhilaration and purpose. He had an absolute blind faith that he could achieve it within his lifetime. And it would free him from having to worry about whether in two hundred years' time anyone would *want* to defrost him and bring him back to life.

Because he would still be alive!

A sports Mercedes went past him, driven by a smart, beautiful girl in dark glasses. She reminded him of the kind of women his father used to date. There was always some glamorous female around in the background who was nuts about him. But his father never got deeply involved. Women were a diversion, that was all. Immortality had been his true abiding passion.

It was almost four, and there was a slack, holiday feel about the pace on the freeway. An ancient Chevvy blattered past full of teenagers who looked as high as kites. Joe tried to orient his mind to the eight-hour time difference, to work out what time it was in England now and what Karen and Jack would be doing. Sleeping, probably, he realized. It was nearly midnight in England. He rubbed his forehead with the back of his hand and felt the patina of traveller's grease. His body felt lifeless but his mind was alert, racing, fuelled by anxiety.

He braked hard and swerved across several lanes as he nearly missed the turn-off on to the Santa Monica freeway. A wildly painted van blasted its horn and a fist shook out of a window at him, but Joe barely noticed. He was thinking hard about the next exit he needed to take, casting his mind back to the time – it must have been twenty years ago – when his father had brought him here, so proudly, to see the building that he had helped to finance and set up.

He remembered the financial difficulties his father had talked about in keeping Crycon Corporation going, and how relieved he had been when two businessmen, Curtis Danfoss and Walter T. Liedermeir, had taken over from the controlling charitable trust and set things on a sound commercial footing, with sufficient funding from advance payments from wealthy donors to secure its viability for centuries to come.

LA CIENEGA. He saw the sign and pulled over in good time, came off the ramp and headed north. The surroundings became more familiar. He recognized a gas station, although it looked more modern than he remembered, then a row of office buildings and the same old uninspiring shops.

There was considerable activity going on outside a nondescript office block on three storeys and he wasn't absolutely certain it was the right building. Two police cars were parked haphazardly and there was a gaggle of onlookers held back behind a taped cordon. Several people who looked like press reporters and photographers were hanging around.

Joe parked in a space a short distance beyond and climbed out of his car. An acidic prickle rose up his gullet as he watched the scene. There was a vile stench in the air. The sudden wail of a siren startled him, and a police car appeared down an alley on the far side of the building, followed by a white van with a Department of Coroner, County of Los Angeles, seal on the side. The police pulled on to La Cienega and drove off past him, roof lights flashing, the van following on their tail. An electric gate slid shut behind them.

As he walked towards the building, the stench made Joe feel ill. It was meat that had gone off, some rotting animal. Then it faded and he wondered for a moment if he'd imagined it.

A cop guarded the front door, standing at ease and looking hot and tired. He tilted his cap back and scratched his head; Joe noticed the butt of a revolver sticking from the man's holster as he squeezed through the crowd towards him. The cop eyed him through aviator sunglasses with an expression that was unreadable.

'This is the Crycon Corporation?' Joe asked.

The cop nodded impassively.

Joe was aware of a number of people looking at him. 'I've

31

just arrived from England. My father's in there – OK if I go in?'

'Havetogomortuary.' The cop strung the words together so that they sounded like one.

'Sorry?' Joe said.

The cop pulled his cap back on and adjusted it. 'Mortuary. You have to go to the mortuary.' Then he stared past him as if he'd ceased to exist.

Joe felt deepening unease. 'My father's in there – he's one of the –' The words dried in his throat. 'He's frozen – he's in one of the cylinders – I need to check he's OK.'

'They're all going down to the mortuary.

Joe shook his head. 'No, they're frozen – they're in liquid nitrogen; they mustn't be moved, they're really fragile – brittle – like crystal glass, you know? One jolt and they can crack –' He faltered under the gaze of the dark glasses.

'I don't think any of them's going to crack,' the cop said.

Joe was aware of a camera pointing at him and the clunk-whirr-clunk-whirr of its motor drive. His face flushed. 'Look, that's my father's body in there! No one can move him without my permission.'

'Have to go to the mortuary,' the cop repeated.

'Professor Messenger. Doesn't that name mean anything to you? Professor Willi Messenger? He founded this place, he started it, I've just flown over from London and I'd like to go in.'

'Whole place been sealed. Order of the health officer.'

The cop was riling Joe, but he was struggling to keep calm. 'I don't think you appreciate that I have a right to enter. My father's in there and I have legal custody of him.'

The cop stared back at him, his face a portrait of venom. 'Oh yeah? Know what I think? I think you cryonics people are fucking freaks. Look at the way you try to mess about with this world ... bunch of goddam ghouls! Think just 'cause you're rich you can get yourselves frozen and come back in two hundred years? You're out of your fucking trees.'

'You're entitled to your opinion,' Joe said, struggling hard

32

to resist drilling his fist into the cop's nose. 'My father was entitled to his.'

'I suggest you get your ass down the mortuary. Go have a chat with your daddy. See if he still feels the same way.'

5

'Name? You have his name?' The clerk behind the wooden counter was a large black man with massive shoulders and a gentle face; his hair was greying.

'Messenger,' Joe said. 'Dr Willi Messenger.'

The man scanned two sheets of typed names then frowned and looked at another list. Then he pushed a form at Joe and tapped it with his thumb. On it was printed 'Sign Name and Name of Party'.

Joe filled it in and handed it back to him.

'OK, you have a seat. Someone'll call out for you.'

Joe thanked him and moved away. His place was taken by a black woman with her arm around a sobbing girl. 'Youton?' he heard the woman say. 'You have a Carl Youton in here?'

There was bedlam in the entrance lobby of the morgue. A police officer and an Hispanic woman were having a shouting match; a young man tried to calm the woman. People stood or sat in tiny groups, some bewildered, some numb with grief. The air was sour with the stench of sweat.

Joe walked past a sign on the marbled wall that said 'Positively No Smoking', clenching his hands together in anxiety. The defeat of death was all around him: in the crumpled clothes the people wore; in the blocked pores of their skin; in their blank stares. Some of them looked as dead as those they'd come to claim. *Victims*. Victims who'd kissed their loved ones goodbye and then stepped out into a fresh morning full of plans, maybe to go see a movie that evening, drop by some neighbours, or cook something special. And instead got trashed, and ended up in here. They got trashed in car wrecks, trashed by heart attacks, by muggers, trashed by their own lovers.

'Death is not necessary, Joe.'

Joe looked round with a start. The words sounded so clear, as if his father had just whispered into his ear. He shivered, sensing Willi with him, suddenly. It was a strange sensation, but one that he'd felt several times in the eleven years since his death and it was as vivid as ever. He could sense his father watching him, waiting to see what he was going to do, how he was going to handle this.

Shakily, he sat down on a vinyl seat beneath a glass showcase displaying framed certificates. Two white youths with straggly hair and tight trousers sat next to him; they looked like they might have been part of a rock band. Joe yawned. Tired, he realized suddenly. It was past midnight English time. A door opened and shut; someone came out, a name was called and another person went in. More people came through from the street; he saw a police car outside; two cops greeted each other in the doorway; someone walked past holding a styrofoam cup of coffee; a curl of steam rose from it. Liquid nitrogen boiled into steam. The vacuum-insulated aluminium dewars that Crycon used each held four bodies. They had a boil-off rate of twelve litres of nitrogen a day. There was a safety margin in them of forty litres. That meant they could survive just over three days before they needed topping up. Before the bodies would become exposed and would start to thaw.

The sound of his name drifted through Joe's thoughts and he didn't notice at first that he was being called. Then he climbed to his feet. A woman clerk held open a hatch in the counter and he went through into a small recess where three chairs were lined up in front of a metal grille. A notice said 'PERSONAL PROPERTY PICK-UP' and there was a stack of autopsy-request forms.

A tanned man faced him on the other side of the grille in a mint-coloured polo shirt. He was in his late thirties, balding, with a sleek goatee beard that was trimmed short, and his intense stare through the thick lenses of frameless glasses conveyed a purposeful air unrelieved by any hint of humour.

He spoke slowly and precisely, as if wanting to ensure that everything he said was clearly understood. No come-backs. 'Professor Joseph Messenger?'

Joe nodded. 'Yes.'

'Pleased to meet you, professor. My name is Howard Barr, I'm the investigating officer for the county coroner in charge of the Crycon disaster. How can I help you?'

'I've come to find out what's happened to my father and to make new arrangements for him.'

Howard Barr looked down at a form. 'Professor Wilhelm Rudolf Messenger? That your father?'

'Yes.'

'You're aware of what's happened at the Crycon Corporation, professor?'

'Not entirely. I haven't been able to get much information. I'm living in England – I saw a story about Crycon going bust in the newspaper this morning. I tried telephoning before I came over, but all I got was a number unobtainable tone. I arrived just a couple of hours ago, and went straight to Crycon. A police officer told me I had to come here. He said this is where they're bringing the patients.'

'Patients?'

There was a hint of contempt in the man's voice, which irritated Joe, but he kept calm. 'We consider people in cryonic suspension to be *patients*.'

Barr replied almost tonelessly. 'Professor Messenger, all Crycon Corporation's *patients* have been transferred here on the order of the State Department for Health to await instructions from their relatives regarding disposal.'

'How long has my father been here?'

He looked back at his notes. 'He was signed in at 12.24 p.m. yesterday.'

'I just saw one of your vans leaving Crycon, driving at forty or fifty miles an hour. Do your staff have any idea how to handle cryonics dewars?'

Barr looked at him oddly.

'They need to be moved very carefully,' Joe said. 'People in suspension are extremely fragile. And they need regular topping up.'

'Topping up?'

'With liquid nitrogen.'

'I'm afraid we don't have much use for liquid nitrogen here, Professor Messenger. Our electrical refrigeration system is good enough for our purposes.'

'Not if you're storing cryonics patients, it isn't.' Joe was getting the impression that Barr was hiding something from him. He remembered the fleeting stench of rotting flesh outside Crycon, recalled his nausea, and a debilitating feeling of unreality swept through him; the room seemed to be cramping him, closing in around him. 'Is there a phone I could use – I'll have to make some calls – get my father transferred to another cryonics unit. There's a good one right here in LA. Alcor, I –' the expression on Barr's face halted him.

'Professor, I'm not an expert on cryonics and I don't want to disillusion you . . .' His look had become a little more mellow, bordering on reproachful. 'But I don't think that cryonic suspension is a serious option any longer for your father.'

The room closed in further on Joe. He felt terribly afraid that something was more wrong than he realized. That maybe they had autopsied his father.

'Why do you say that?'

Barr shrugged. 'I'm not sure the Health Department would allow it.'

Joe felt anger rising in his voice. 'I think you'll find the Health Department has no legal right to interfere.' He tapped himself on the chest. 'It's my decision! My father signed the legal papers. Crycon's gone bust, and I accept I'll have to pay another cryonics organization – but the Health Department is not dictating to me what I do! And I hope to hell none of your people has damaged his body in any way. I'd like to go see him right now: can you have someone show me where he is?'

Barr shook his head. 'We don't allow people to see bodies in here these days. Any viewing has to be done in the funeral parlour.'

'I have legal custody of his body and I have a right to see him,' Joe said.

Barr checked his beard by pinching fronds of hair between his forefinger and thumb for some moments. 'When was the last time you saw your father, professor?'

'Just after he deanimated in 1982. I helped with the perfusion.'

'Pardon me?'

'The preparations for freezing – the removal of his blood and replacing it with cryoprotectant agents.'

'Your father died in bed?'

'Yes, in hospital.'

'I think you might be happier to remember him that way.'

Joe's anger flared again. 'I don't think you understand. I like to remember my dad when he was alive and well – and some day in the future he's going to be alive and well again.'

Barr sat motionless. 'Professor Messenger, I can't comment on the technology of cryogenics.'

'Everyone likes to comment on it,' Joe said. 'Everyone who doesn't know a goddam thing about it. Would you take me to my father's body now, please?'

Barr raised a placatory hand. 'I do have a little knowledge . . . As I understand, it's important to freeze people as quickly as possible after certification of death – you gotta start the processes within minutes, to prevent arteries from closing up, and to prevent decay, right?'

Joe looked at him as if he were watching an image on television that was being blurred by interference. 'More or less. You do that if possible. But you can still suspend people who've been dead for a while.'

Again, the man's expression softened a little. 'I'm afraid that the bodies in Crycon had been out of suspension for quite a while, professor. The guys in charge of it must have sold off all the equipment before they – disappeared.'

Joe was horrified. 'Sold off the equipment? You mean the dewars?'

'Everything.'

'When?'

He shrugged. 'We don't have that information.' He hesitated. 'What I'm trying to tell you, professor, is that I don't think your father's body is as well preserved as you might be expecting. In my view he would not now be recoverable from suspension even if such a thing ever became possible.'

Joe looked back at his face in silence. Looked at the notice again. PERSONAL PROPERTY PICK-UP. Ordinary words made threatening because of their connection with death. Staring at the polished wood surface beneath the grille, he felt that he could be in a de luxe version of the condemned cell, except that it was his father who was in it, not him. 'I take the view that at some point in the future doctors will be able to reconstruct our entire bodies from the DNA coding in just one intact cell. I don't care how bad my father's condition is, I intend having him re-suspended immediately.' Joe blinked slowly, entwining his fingers. 'I made a promise to my father and I intend keeping that promise. I'd be grateful if you'd let me see him now.'

The hardness returned to Barr's features. 'Professor, I'm just going to emphasize one more time that I think you'll find it very distressing.'

'That's my decision.' Joe remembered his father as the big tough guy who had been scared of nothing all his life, and he remembered the husk he'd seen in the hospital bed. And now he had braced himself for something else.

Howard Barr stood up. 'If you go to the doorway by the elevators on the far side of the lobby, I'll meet you there.'

Joe walked back across the lobby, and found the recess through to the elevators. Barr opened the door from the far side, then led the way down a corridor past a hive of offices, the soles of his immaculate white trainers silent on the floor.

They went through into an icily cold room with a white tiled floor and walls lined with tiers of stainless steel lockers. There was a pungent reek of disinfectant.

38

Barr stopped, checked the sheet of paper he was holding, and ran his eyes up the bank of lockers in front of him. Each one had a number and a slot for a tag. In the slot of the third one up, 37C, was a typed card that read: 'Dr W. Messenger.'

The man looked flintily at Joe. 'Sure?'

Joe swallowed back a lump in his throat. Eleven years. A lot had happened in eleven years; memories had faded, and grief had eased also, but his father's image was still alive in his mind. He could sense again, now, that strong feeling of his father watching him, waiting for his reaction, waiting to see how he would keep his promise. He felt bolstered by it, as if the old man was winking at him, and saying, 'That's the way! Don't put up with any shit from this smartass jerk.'

Barr removed a pair of surgical gloves from his pocket, tore them free of their sterile pack and rolled them on. Then he leaned forward and pulled the handle. The door opened easily and in the darkness beyond Joe could make out a lumpy blue plastic sheet; he could feel the blast of freezing air that escaped.

Then Barr pulled out a long, narrow tray on well-oiled castors on which lay a human form encased in the sheeting. He raised a fold in the sheeting, revealing a zipper. He looked at Joe once more, then pulled the zipper open in one long motion.

Joe was wholly unprepared for the stench and it hit him like a fist in his stomach. It was the smell of forgotten meat left in the trunk of a car for a month; of a drain being unblocked; of sour milk; of diarrhoea. Then he saw his father's face and a cry tore itself free from his throat.

He had to turn away, momentarily blinded by the horror, stumbling, gulping in disbelief. He reached the far wall and was halted by the cold steel lockers, but he did not turn round; he could not endure even one more fragmentary glimpse.

He stood, shaking, his face pressed against the lockers. 'No,' he sobbed. 'Oh, God, please no!'

The steel was sliding, as if he was in an elevator that was sinking; he tried to hold on to it, but his hands slid downwards. He saw the name 'Mrs R. Waliewska' typed on a tag, and 'Mr D. Perlmutter' as if they were floors at which he might get off, then he sagged down on to his knees and buried his head in his hands. He was squeezing his eyelids shut against the inhuman horror of his father's face, with its rictus grin that had not been there when Willi Messenger had died.

The facial flesh had withdrawn, leaving just bare bone poking through the patches of rotten, leathery skin still attached in parts. The remains of Willi's hair, straggly and coarse, protruded from the desiccated remains of his scalp like stuffing from a busted sofa. The eye sockets were empty, scooped out by the blowflies weeks ago, maybe months ago.

Joe wept, silently. Wept the way he had done in the morgue after his infant son Barty had died, when the police officer had given him one trainer and a blackened wristwatch and asked him to identify them. Wept as the shock rocked through him.

6

Monday 18 January, 1993. Sussex.

Normally Joe liked the drive from his home to the university. It was five miles, mostly along a highway that rose and sank in undulating sweeps traversing the edge of the Downs, and on a fine morning like today the views across the hills and fields were spectacular. They gave a sense of open space that was one of the few things he really missed about Canada.

But his journey this morning was marred by jet-lag, which had lingered even though he'd flown back from Los Angeles last Tuesday. And the booming resonance of the blown exhaust on his Saab was aggravating the sinus headache he'd woken up with. And annoying him. He liked machines to work properly and always got irritated when they didn't. The car was only two years old, but he had driven over

40

something in the dark and hadn't yet had time to get it fixed. His father would have fixed it himself, he thought, with a twinge of guilt; but it was years since Joe had touched the mechanics of a car; he could never justify the time.

The Isaac Newton University had been conceived as Britain's equivalent to the Massachusetts Institute of Technology. It had been designed as one architect's vision of the perfect university, and built from scratch in 1963. The campus, entirely of red brick and concrete, was a weird hybrid of rounded contours and sharp angles, of bridges, arches, colonnades and linear crisscrossing walkways. It had been carefully landscaped to blend into the Downland setting, and was dotted with dinky ornamental lakes and streams, as well as with trees and shrubs that looked so neat they might have been plastic. There was a stilted air of Legoland about the place that was always heightened out of term-time when there were fewer people around. Joe thought it looked like the kind of instant, vaguely utopian city man might build in outer space. Except in only thirty years it had weathered badly and had already gone horribly to seed.

He parked his grey Saab in the lot behind the COGS – Cognitive Sciences – building, and switched off the ignition, greeting the silence that followed with considerable relief. Then he climbed out, locking the door.

A strong wind was blowing as he lugged his briefcase across the lot and down the steps between the COGS and the Biology buildings. Both were four-storey blocks connected by an enclosed aerial walkway on the third floors that owed something, but not much, to the Bridge of Sighs.

There was a boxed-in tank behind the Biology block marked 'Danger – Liquid Nitrogen' and the words brought back a sudden image of his father when Joe was about six, taking jars of bees out of the fridge, and getting yelled at by Joe's mother. Willi Messenger had thought nothing of using his home as a laboratory.

The Christmas vacation was normally a time Joe enjoyed, when he was able to recharge a little; but right now, tired, and guilt-ridden because he had not kept a closer eye on

41

Crycon, he didn't feel he'd had any break at all. Signing the cremation consent had been hardest, harder even than sitting with the funeral director in the small chapel, staring at his father's coffin on the catafalque as the chaplain recited the short committal service. Watching the curtains close. Gone.

Dr Messenger, your father is calling out for you. He wants to speak to you very badly ... There's something he wants to tell you very desperately. It seems like he wants to warn you about something.

He was never going to know what it was now. Sure, he had brought back a tiny amount of his father's skin and a little hair in an icebox, and that was now in cryonic suspension; but the brain had gone completely, eaten away by blowflies, and even if it became possible to reconstruct the body from his DNA some time in the future, would any of Willi's knowledge remain intact? Joe doubted it.

The wind cut through his clothes. He was wearing a Burberry mackintosh over a tweed jacket, blue cord trousers and suede lace-up brogues, the kind of clothes he figured gave just a dash of English gentry to his appearance, although the effect was marginalized by his tie. It was covered in flying pigs. He liked to wear wild ties, they made people smile. And he needed a few smiles right now.

The relatives of the patients who'd been suspended at Crycon had formed themselves into a group and were considering a class action against the two men who'd been running Crycon. Fourteen million dollars of patients' fees, members' subscriptions and charitable donations had disappeared at their hands. And all the equipment. Twenty-seven suspended patients had been abandoned on the floor behind locked doors to thaw out and decompose. Strangers in life, they'd formed one common miasma in death.

Joe wasn't interested in suing anyone. He wanted his father back, wanted to show him how far he'd got with ARCHIVE, knew the old man would approve of how he had turned his own home into an experiment. But that was never going to happen. Not now. He could no longer bring him back to life; he could only keep the spirit of his work alive, his philosophy, his quest for immortality.

The carcass of a small bird lay beside a wastebin; feathers still clung to its wings. He looked away. The image of his father's decomposing body filled his mind and he felt the cold wash of fear in his stomach. He recognized it as fear of his own mortality. And remembered how his father used to scare him as a kid by making him look into tombs, pointing out the rotting coffins and bones, and saying, 'That's what happens to you!' Death was disgusting. Internal gases reacted, colons swelled, stomach contents fermented, faces got bloated, skin began rotting and leaking.

The wind rearranged his hair as he turned the corner round the front of the building, and he glanced briefly at the fine view of the rest of the toytown campus. It was spread out across a small valley in front of him, buildings networked by a grid of pavements along which futuristic streetlights stood every twenty metres. On almost every lawn was a modern sculpture, weird obelisks in steel, wood and bronze, some sharp and angular, others curved and arched. On the far side, on the higher ground, the imposing buildings of the library, theatre and admin block dominated everything, and beyond them, higher still, some of the residential buildings merged like ancient forts into the landscape.

Near the brow of the far hill two tractors were sowing winter crops. Spring would be coming in a couple of months, he thought. Then summer. Then fall. The eternal life cycle. You were born, you lived, you died. That was what we were taught, what we believed, what we knew. Hatch, match and despatch.

But it didn't have to be that way.

He went in the front entrance, past the black and white sign that said 'Department of Cognitive Sciences', and the door swung shut behind him. The entrance lobby smelled of fresh paint. There were new notices pinned up on the boards, ads for lodgers seeking rooms, and for rooms seeking lodgers, ads for student discounts, for Student Union meetings, for

Greenpeace T-shirts. There was a warning about increasing thefts from the car parks, and a calendar of events for the new term.

Joe cheered a little as he passed the enquiries office and climbed the two flights of bare concrete stairs, nodding and returning greetings from students and other lecturers. He should have been back a week ago, but the trip to LA had delayed him, and he'd only been in Thursday and Friday, trying to catch up on his correspondence; he was looking forward to getting stuck in again to his real work, to testing out the new ideas he'd been developing.

His pace quickened through the common room with its tiny cafeteria and down a long corridor with lecturers' offices on both sides. Each office door had a number and a slot for a name tag, which reminded him suddenly of the mortuary in Los Angeles. Some of the staff had attempted to relieve the windowless gloom of the corridor by sticking esoteric cartoons about artificial intelligence on their doors.

The entrance to Joe's department was at the end. The sign on his own door read: PROFESSOR J. MESSENGER. ARCHIVE PROJECT.

His secretary, Eileen Peacock, was perched in her cubbyhole of an office, the entrance to which was a narrow gap in a stockade of battered brown filing cabinets, in front of her word-processor screen. She was a waif-like creature somewhere close to retirement age, with dyed black hair combed forward into a page-boy fringe at the front, and shorn military-style at the back. She had very round eyes which peered out through overly large square spectacles that sometimes gave Joe the impression he was talking to her through a window. He was fond of her; she looked frail, but she was gutsy and rigorously efficient.

She raised her head up towards him, tilting it sideways at the same time in a curiously articulated movement, like an Anglepoise lamp, and greeted him with her unvarying 'Good morning, Professor Messenger,' almost as if she was reciting a line in an elocution lesson.

'Hi. Good weekend?'

44

'Oh, yes, thank you.' She lifted her fingers from her keyboard. 'Did you?'

'Yup,' he said, noncommittally. 'Actually I guess Jack had the best weekend – he went to two birthday parties.'

'He seems to have made lots of friends.' She smiled fleetingly, then her face adopted the expression of impending doom with which she always prefaced any messages, regardless of their content. 'Professor Colinson would like you to call him as soon as you come in – he wants to arrange a scheduling meeting. I think he's sent you e-mail but he didn't know if you'd read it.'

'No, right.' Meetings with the vice-chancellor didn't register high on Joe's pleasure scale. He loathed the man.

'Your post is on your desk.'

'Thanks. Who's in?'

'Just Harriet and Edwin.'

'Where's Dave?' Dave Hoton was Joe's right hand, the system manager for ARCHIVE.

'I don't know, professor. He may be in the machine room.'

Joe stuck his head round the door next to her office, into the cramped room which housed his two Ph.D. students, Harriet Tait and Ray Patel, and his postdoc researcher, Edwin Pilgrim.

There were four computers in the room: three were workstations that could be logged either into the college's Unix systems or in to ARCHIVE; the fourth was an Apple Macintosh. Two of the workstations were unmanned. The Apple Mac's screen saver was on, and fish swam lazily across the screen. The other screen was blank – Ray Patel was away on a year's study leave in Austin, Texas. Joe was surprised there wasn't someone in here using it instead.

Harriet Tait was editing something in a window. She was a quiet, studious girl, with an easy-going nature, in spite of a precarious-looking cluster of tight dark curls that looked more like a statement than a hairstyle. Edwin Pilgrim was sitting with his face clenched, typing furiously on his keyboard. Joe looked at his screen and saw, disapprovingly, that he was playing GO. There was a current vogue for computer students to play global games of GO.

'Hi, you guys!' Joe said. He made no comment about the game. Upsetting Edwin Pilgrim was not a smart thing to do.

Harriet Tait looked up, pleased to see him. 'Hello, Joe – good weekend?'

Joe raised his right hand and gave it a couple of half-rotations to indicate *so-so*. 'You?'

'I wanted to get some stuff finished. I've been here most of the time.'

'Good girl.'

Pilgrim did not acknowledge Joe at all, but that didn't surprise him. Pilgrim was a strange loner with no apparent interests in life outside his work and electronic games. He was a delicate individual, frequently off sick with some ailment, real or imaginary, and riddled with neuroses and allergies. He'd been known to leave the office for several hours when someone peeled an orange in it, complaining that the smell disturbed the chemical balance of his brain.

Slightly built, with a faintly aggressive, angular face that was prone to breaking out in red blotches, Pilgrim had a lazy right eye which roamed wildly and distractingly when he was upset, which was often. Above his high, shiny forehead, strands of ginger hair were raked across his balding dome. He dressed invariably in a red anorak, metal-zipped cardigan with a white nylon shirt, grey flannel trousers and plimsolls, and he carried a Day-glo knapsack around with him. His demeanour was generally uncommunicative and hostile.

Joe found Edwin Pilgrim as entertaining as he found him irritating. He liked the quirky characters of the computer world. Among the many breeds it attracted, he found the Edwin Pilgrims to be among the most interesting: totally inadequate and unadapted for normal life, they could become major players in an electronic virtual world. They could become heroes, demigods, legends, even. Without ever moving from their keyboards, they could shed their lousy biological shackles and soar out into cyberspace.

Pilgrim had unquestionable genius in computer program-

46

ming. He was capable of solving multiple problems simultaneously in his head, and Joe had never encountered anyone more able to translate his ideas into highly efficient programs. ARCHIVE was Joe's baby, Joe's invention, but it was Edwin Pilgrim who had performed the detailed calculations from which much of it had been built.

They were not only on the same wavelength scientifically, but also philosophically – even if they came at the philosophy of ARCHIVE from different directions. Joe believed ARCHIVE was the key to immortality. Pilgrim saw it as a potential way to escape the human form. Saddled with a body that had caused him to spend much of his childhood in bed, and with a distrust of humans born out of years of playground teasing, he had a deep-rooted desire to see them replaced with machines as soon as possible.

Joe opened the door to his own office, went in and hung his Burberry on the back of the door. Most of the offices in the university were tips, with mismatched furniture and worn carpets. The two hundred thousand dollars of the MacArthur 'Genius' Award had allowed him a few luxuries, and Joe had spent a little of the money on making his office a comfortable and pleasant place to spend the long hours he did. He had a large teak desk as well as the desk for his computer screen and Sun workstation, a swivel armchair and a reclining armchair, two decent sofas for his students and a thick twist-pile carpet.

One wall was floor-to-ceiling bookshelves, on the top shelf of which were his tennis and squash racquets. Among the rows of books were the six he'd written, plus his numerous published papers. Another wall was mostly taken up by a large whiteboard and a crowded cork noticeboard. His desk, beside a wide window overlooking the campus, was stacked with neat piles of letters and papers, and amongst them stood a photo of Karen, one of his favourites of her, taken halfway up Mount Vesuvius; and one of Jack on his third birthday, last September, standing proudly on the end of a jetty holding a fishing rod.

Above his desk were several large colour photographs

grouped together in a single frame, with a caption beneath saying: 'What do these have in common?' The photos showed a yew tree, a redwood tree, a Koi carp, a parrot, an elephant and a clam.

Discreetly sited on the Artexed ceiling, in between the nozzles of the sprinkler system, were two miniature television cameras and four directional microphones which fed everything in the room to ARCHIVE, which sat in the basement three floors below.

ARCHIVE – which stood for Anthropo-Computer Host for Intelligent Virtual Existence – was the whole reason Joe was in England. It was to Joe's certain knowledge the largest and most powerful neural network parallel processor connectionist machine in the world. One day it would be capable of storing, on an instant-retrieval basis, the entire contents of an adult human being's brain. It would be aware of its own existence, able to make rational decisions of its own free will and to experience a range of emotions and sensations that would equate it to human life. It would, in effect, no longer be an inert machine but a conscious, living entity.

The funding for the ARCHIVE project had come from a trust set up by the late software billionaire Harry Hartman. The trust had offered almost unlimited funding to a university prepared to house the project – and prepared to share its information with the rest of the world. One condition of the funding was that the project be kept in England. Hartman wanted to stop British computing talent being drained abroad. Another condition was that Joe Messenger had to be in charge of it. Joe's colleague, Blake Hewlett, who'd befriended Hartman in the last years of his life, had convinced him that Joe was the only man with the vision and the ability to make it happen. From the reputation Joe had already established, Hartman had not needed much persuading.

ARCHIVE was the sum of Joe's life's work to date. It was something he cared about more, in truth, than anything else in the world; in some ways more, even, than his family. He'd spent twenty years designing it, and the past four years building and developing it. It had already cost over thirty-five million dollars, much of which had been spent on having its one-off components specially manufactured, and Joe could see no end in sight to when it would stop requiring funding. Fortunately his sponsors, who left him alone, were pleased with the scant papers he had published to date, even though they'd provoked more scepticism than praise in the scientific Establishment.

Sunlight streamed in through the window, and the heating system rattled faintly as warm air pumped in through the floor ducts. Joe stood for a moment, casting a rather dismal eye on the mountains of paperwork that had stacked up over the holidays, and which seemed to have grown even taller over the weekend. He hated pen-pushing and all the bureaucracy that the university demanded from him, and he sifted through the envelopes of the morning's post with mounting gloom.

He cheered a little as he came across one that bore the frank of one of his publishers, and might contain reviews of his most recent book, *The Computer That Loved Ben Hur*. He slit open the envelope and was pleased to see a wodge of cuttings: an interview he'd done with the *Guardian*; a review in *New Scientist*; a more lengthy review in *The Sunday Times* which he scanned and was reasonably happy with, even though the reviewer appeared to have totally missed the fundamental point of the book. And there was what looked like a rave write-up in a small Californian magazine he much admired, called *Extropy*, which pleased him more than anything.

He put them into his briefcase to take home to show Karen, then sat down, swivelled his chair to face his workstation, and hit the carriage-return button on his grey keyboard to bring up his computer screen. He logged in as joem and then typed his password, minbag, which he'd created from the first letters of Julius Caesar's 'man is now become a god'. He hit the carriage return again, then he typed: rlogin archive interact, and hit the return key once more.

In crisp black letters on the brilliant white of his colour screen appeared the words: Good morning, Professor

Messenger. Did you have a good weekend? The forecast is windy.

I had a pleasant weekend, thank you, ARCHIVE, Joe
typed. He could have switched the computer to voice mode and
spoken the words, but then ARCHIVE would have replied with
speech and his headache wasn't up to coping with its nasally
deadpan voice.

You took Jack to two parties, I seem to remember,
Professor?

You have a good memory, Joe typed.

You gave it to me.

I'm glad you are still aware who is boss, Joe typed
back.

Boss. Who is boss? What is boss? Alternatives:
noun. Superiority. Loftiness. Sublimity, tran-
scendence, the tops, quality, *ne plus ultra* emi-
nence, overlord, supremacy –

Joe cursed, halted the reply in mid-sentence and made a
note on the back of an envelope on his desk. There were
days when you could have an uncannily normal conversation
with ARCHIVE, and others when it seemed to get thrown. It
was almost human at times in the way it seemed to have its
good and bad days, except they were due to faulty programming rather than a lousy night's sleep.

He looked at the gibberish frozen on the screen. ARCHIVE
would learn; just an adjustment and next time it would
understand the remark and reply more intelligently. He
glanced up at the ceiling above the metal cupboard and the
camera stared back at him. His purpose in having the constant scrutiny of the cameras was that through inputting his
home and work lives ARCHIVE would begin to understand
the behavioural differences between the two environments.
There were a lot of things that human beings understood
very easily, but were hard to program into a computer.
Particularly when he confused it by taking work home.

Joe exited from ARCHIVE to clear it, logged back in and re-
entered his password.

On the screen again appeared the words: Good morning,

Professor Messenger. Did you have a good weekend?
The forecast is windy.

Joe typed back: You've already asked me that question. I thought you said you have a good memory?

I apologize for my memory lapse, Professor
Messenger.

OK, I forgive you. **Joe coaxed the computer like a
child.** Isn't there something else you want to tell
me, ARCHIVE?

You have mail.

Read it to me, please.

**The screen went blank for an instant, then rows of elec-
tronic mail messages filled it:**

archive % mail

''/usr/spool/mail/doc: 410 messages. 331
new.

>N.398 ccol@cogs.Newton.ac.uk (Dick Glebe)
Sun Jan 17.

18.05. Re: Arrange meet Tue?

N.399 blake@cogs.Newton.ac.uk (Blake
Hewlett) Mon Jan 18.

08.45.   Re: Squash lunchtime?

N.400 kibo@world.std.com (James 'Kibo'
Parry)

N.401 athun@vaxperth.ac.oz (Atilla the
Upside-down Hun)

There were several hundred messages going back over the
fortnight. The vice-chancellor was trying to set up a meeting
as his secretary had mentioned. Blake Hewlett wanted to
confirm their lunchtime squash game today. The COGS
lecturers wanted to have a policy meeting. There was a zany
message from someone who signed himself 'Atilla the
Upside-down Hun' who hung out in Perth, Australia, and
mailed him regularly with an off-the-wall theory, backed by
several pages of mumbo-jumbo data, on experiments he'd
done to prove a computer could be telepathic. It was one of
the hazards of electronic mail that it made you instantly
accessible to hi-tech nutters around the globe.

Joe closed his eyes and squeezed them tightly shut, trying to make his headache go away. It didn't. He scrolled on through the messages, dealing with a few urgent ones. Then he took his Apple Mac Powerbook computer out of his briefcase, docked it into his workstation, switched it on and downloaded it into ARCHIVE. Finally, he typed the command for 'today's diary' into ARCHIVE.

The date and time appeared on the screen, with three appointments listed beneath. A ten a.m. interview. The squash court booked for 12.45. And a dinner appointment, eight o'clock. Some friend Karen had made at a relaxation-therapy group she went to. Monday night was an odd night to be invited out to dinner, he thought, but Karen had been making a concerted effort to develop a social circle and he wanted to encourage her.

He looked at the first engagement. Ten o'clock. 'Juliet Spring' was the name beside it. He felt a brief flash of irritation at having his morning eaten into and checked his watch. 9.45. She'd be here in a quarter of an hour and he'd have to give her a decent amount of time. Damn. He looked at her name again. *Juliet Spring*.

She'd written before Christmas asking if she could do her doctorate in Artificial Intelligence under him. But he'd already decided against another postgrad. He'd taken on too many teaching and writing commitments, and wanted to spend more time this year on ARCHIVE. There were also some important developments going on in the neural network and cognition areas of AI and he needed to take time out to catch up on those, and to attend some conferences in Europe, the States and Japan. So why had he agreed to see her?

There was some reason, he knew, as he rummaged through a stack of correspondence on his desk, noticing with horror a couple of letters over two months old to which he had not replied. The brown envelope he was looking for was buried underneath the transcript of a lecture he'd given recently titled: 'Why Einstein Was Wrong – Machines *Can* Taste the Chicken Soup.'

He held up the envelope with a small sense of triumph,

shook out Juliet Spring's letter and CV, and scanned through them to remind himself.

It was an impressive CV. A Cambridge double-first in neuroscience and computing science. Followed by another first in physiology at Carnegie-Mellon University. Then the past three years working in Artificial Intelligence in the prestigious medical research foundation of the international pharmaceuticals giant Cobbold-Tessering-Sanya.

Brilliant girl, but she would be demanding on time and her grounding seemed to be more medical than technological. He could think of professors in different departments both at his university and at others who would be more suitable. He tried again to think of the reason why he'd agreed to see her at all and felt annoyed with himself.

He began to read her details more carefully. The typescript was small and a twinge of pain jumped like an electrical spark across the inside of his forehead, along the back of his eyes. He'd been blighted with sinus headaches all his life. A classic example of the deficiency of the human body! With a computer you could repair faults cleanly and easily; with humans you either had erratic drugs or messy invasive surgery. Or you had to live with it.

There was a framed cartoon on Joe's wall; his students had given it to him for his last birthday. It was a simple drawing of a rather old-fashioned computer with revolving tapes and winking lights. Beneath the computer were the words: *Post-biological Man.*

The cartoon made Joe smile. Sentiment did not. He believed implicitly that the human race could best survive by progressing from biological existence into mechanical existence. When consciousness could successfully be transferred into a machine, or engendered from scratch in a machine, then human biological existence would no longer be necessary. We would make way for post-biological man. But unlike our antecedents, who live on in us only by way of a few molecules, Joe believed that it would be possible for him and all other humans to live on through post-biological man for ever.

To become immortal.

Joe had met numerous scientists who found his idea completely crazy. He'd also met plenty who considered it interesting and stimulating, but he'd never met anyone else who believed as passionately as himself that it could actually happen.

He was about to.

7

At five past ten there was a sharp knock on Joe's door, then it opened before he had a chance to speak. Blake Hewlett stood there dressed in the all-black garb he had taken to wearing these days. His swarthy features creased into shadowy lines as he gave Joe a strange, knowing smile. 'You have a visitor,' he said.

Seven years older than himself, Blake was the university's Professor of Cryobiology who had been largely responsible for Joe getting the position running the ARCHIVE project, and the Professorship of Artificial Intelligence.

They played tennis in summer and squash in winter twice a week; but in spite of the twenty years they went back together, to the days when Blake had first worked under Willi Messenger, Joe did not consider Blake to be a close friend. It was their shared belief in immortality that was their main bond, although they were coming at it from different directions. Unlike Joe who was a *hardware* scientist, with his faith in post-biological man, Blake Hewlett was a *wetware* scientist who believed the key to immortality lay in the preservation of the human biological body.

At the present time there was considerable crossover in their work; they were both attempting to understand more about the brain and consciousness in order to preserve and to replicate it. But outside that subject Joe at times found that Blake made him feel distinctly uncomfortable. Karen had never liked him. She tolerated him for Joe's sake, but deep down she thought he was a creep.

Blake, who'd inherited a fortune from his father, had never married, preferring to have an endless succession of gorgeous live-in girlfriends. In spite of Joe's love for Karen and Jack, he found himself sneakingly envying such a lifestyle.

He tried to read Blake's expression as he continued to stand in the doorway, the strange smile conveying some secret signal which seemed to indicate Joe should know the code. A game; another of Blake's irritating games. With his headache, Joe wasn't in the mood for it.

'I found her wandering lost and distressed on the wrong floor, Joe – thought I'd better rescue her and deliver her to your door.' Blake's voice was glib and authoritative; he tended to speak fast, in a strong Californian accent, and his delivery was forceful – as if he was inalienably right in all he said and you contradicted him at your peril. He stepped aside in a faintly theatrical motion and ushered into the room a shy and rather embarrassed-looking girl in her late twenties, who was accompanied by a powerful scent of perfume.

She thanked Blake and then gave Joe a rather uncertain smile. The door closed behind her as Blake slipped away. It was one of Blake's quirks that he never said goodbye.

Joe half stood up and motioned her to the chair on the other side of his desk. 'Juliet Spring, right?'

'Yes – Professor Messenger?' She had long red hair, some of which hung across part of her face, and she shook it back with a slightly nervy toss, like a pony, as she spoke. It was fine, straight hair that broke over the tops of her shoulders, and the morning sunlight through his window struck it, intensifying the rich burnished colour. Joe found himself momentarily tongue-tied; she was one of the loveliest girls he'd ever seen in his entire life.

Her skin was pastel fair with a few freckles, her nose small and straight, her eyes a brilliant emerald green with a hint both of fieriness and immense depth. And her lips had a

55

finely sculpted look that made them intensely expressive, and, Joe thought, extremely sensual.

She was of medium height with a slender frame, and gave the appearance of having made a deliberate effort over her clothes. She was wearing a smart blue overcoat, with an elegant Cornelia James shawl draped around the shoulders, which Joe helped her remove. Beneath, she was dressed in a crisp white open-necked blouse with a broderie-anglaise front, a dark green suit, the skirt of which stopped just on her knees, and simple black shoes. Joe could see a plain silver necklace inside her blouse, and she was wearing a rather practical-looking wristwatch. She carried a black attaché case which looked new, as if she'd bought it for the interview, and a soft leather handbag.

As she sat down on the edge of the chair, she placed her case and bag down beside her, then wrestled with her hands as if unsure what to do with them. Joe found his eyes being drawn to the delicate skin of her neck, to her fine chin, then to her eyes. Hastily he looked down at her file. 'OK, right.' He parted his hands, then brought them together in a single clap. 'Two double firsts – that's pretty impressive.'

She shook her hair again. A smile momentarily lit up her face then faded. 'Just hard slog, that was all.' Her accent was smart, upmarket English, and there was an air of class about her. She wasn't ritzy in any way, but there was a quiet statement of quality in her clothes, of breeding in her demeanour. And something else, too, other than nervousness – there was an underlying aura of sadness, of vulnerability.

'Aldous Huxley said that genius was just an infinite capacity for taking pains,' Joe said, fixing her with a grin. He noticed as she toyed with her hands that her nail varnish was mostly scratched away, as if she'd been picking at her nails, or had neglected them. One or two looked as though they had been bitten.

She stared directly at him. 'I thought what you said about evolution in your lecture to the Royal Society in 1990 was very interesting.'

'You were there?' he said, surprised.

'No, I read the transcript later,' she replied a little apologetically. 'I've not missed any of your lectures, I've read them all, I think – I hope.'

'I'm flattered.' He watched her entwining her fingers nervously. 'That lecture was just a theory I guess I have about evolution –'

'I agree with it!' she said, jumping in quickly. 'I've never believed that Darwin provided all the answers.'

He looked at her file again, wondering how to break the news that he was going to pass her on to someone else; and not sure, suddenly, that he wanted to do that. Warning lights were flashing. He was being distracted because he found her attractive and that was a nonsense. He'd been faithful all his married life.

Sure, there'd been plenty of girlfriends before Karen, although he'd never really been aware quite how attractive he was to women. And he'd taught plenty of pretty students, but his thoughts had never drifted beyond the academic with any of them. Yet right now he was experiencing, in the glint of a smile behind two sparkling green eyes, a mutual chemistry that his instincts told him he'd better shut down fast.

'I –' He touched the back of his head, feeling some of his windblown hair out of place and tidying it. He was uncomfortably warm, suddenly. 'I – your – orientation all seems – ah – to do with physiology. I don't quite understand why you want to do your doctorate under someone like myself. Surely physiology would be more appropriate?'

She moved closer to the edge of her chair and looked anxious. 'Professor Messenger, I've read everything that you've ever published – all your books and all your papers. Six books, right – plus two that you've co-written?'

Joe nodded.

'I'm absolutely fascinated by your ideas; they're totally in line with what I think. I've never come across anyone else who thinks quite the same way. I want to study under you very much.' She bit her lower lip then stared directly at him.

'And I think I can be helpful to you.' Joe was impressed by the quietly determined note that had come into her voice.

She picked up her attaché case and released the brass catches; they opened with sharp thuds. Then she pulled out several sheets of paper clipped together and passed them to him. 'Would you just have a very brief look?'

The neat word-processor print on the front read: *Juliet Spring BSc., MSc. Proposals for doctorate thesis. Subject: neuronal and silicon structures; techniques towards interface.*

Joe glanced up at her with curiosity, then turned the page and read the first few lines. He frowned as the sentence 'I believe that we are on the verge of creating post-biological man' rose out of the typescript at him and freeze-framed in his brain.

He looked back at her in astonishment, and saw she was watching him carefully; her hands were clenched tightly and trembling. He read on, and as he did so, he realized his own hands were starting to tremble also, not from nervousness but from excitement. He read through to the end, almost forgetting anyone was in the room, he was so absorbed. When he finished, there was a broad grin on his face. The girl was looking at him hopefully.

'You really believe this?' Joe said, laying it down.

'Yes. I think that some form of cerebral continuance until permanently extended life has been established is possible.'

'You consider that human consciousness could exist inside a computer?'

'Yes.' There was a confident simplicity in the way she said it that carried the weight of authority. 'I'm certain it can.'

'There are some problems that have to be overcome. We, I – ah –' Joe said, hesitating as his thoughts were distracted. '*Post-biological man.* That's incredible! I never heard anyone in England use that expression before outside this department.'

Juliet Spring smiled; there was hope in her face like a child wanting to please. 'I got it from you. You mentioned it in the paper you wrote for the Oxford symposium on Mind and Brain.'

Joe thought for a moment, trying to remember. 'Right.' He was distracted again as she began picking at a nail. He found himself wanting to tell her she had lovely hands and shouldn't spoil them. Then he regained his train. 'OK, yup. The problems. Three problems if you want to download the contents of a human brain into a computer.'

He held up one finger. 'First, you have to have a method of transferring the contents of the brain.' He raised the next finger. 'Second, you have to have a computer with large enough storage capacity. Third –' he raised another finger '– you need a program capable of *thinking* like a human brain –'

'I thought the point of neural network computers was that they don't have programs,' she said, interrupting. 'Wouldn't a neural net learn the way a child learns?'

'Sure. But we're born with certain instincts and knowledge. There's a whole raft of stuff hardwired into us – like we know we have to stand on our feet, not our heads, that kind of stuff. We have inbuilt systems that have evolved over thousands of years and a lot of that has to be hardwired into a thinking machine.' He leaned forward a little. 'How much do you know about ARCHIVE?'

'You haven't published very much about it. I know very little.'

He smiled. 'I guess I don't want to publish too much until I'm confident I can deal with any flak.'

'How long will that be?'

Joe flicked away a speck of dust with his thumbnail. 'I don't know. A decade, maybe.'

Her face fell.

'That's my most optimistic prediction – could be twenty, thirty.' He grinned. 'I don't want it being any longer than that – I need it to happen in my lifetime.'

She didn't smile back; instead she looked increasingly serious. 'You have three problems to overcome, you said? The method of downloading the brain; the storage capacity of the computer; and the learning/thinking ability of the computer, right?'

'Right.'

'And you're making progress with all three?'

'Some,' he said. 'The storage capacity exists right now, it's just a question of speed of retrieval; I think we're going to be able to deal with that through new technological developments – particularly in the areas of compression. Learning/thinking ability I think we're also dealing with through neural nets, but we're in a very basic state so far.'

'And downloading the brain into a computer?'

'Some people prefer to call it *uploading*.' Joe smiled again. 'When a human mind is no longer superior to a computer then we can think about calling it *uploading*. At this moment it's very definitely *downloading*.' He raised his eyebrows flippantly. 'Downloading the brain into a computer is right now the major problem.'

'Is solving that the major key to your progress?'

Joe was silent for a moment. A telephone rang in another office, unanswered. 'Yes,' he said. 'It's the key to the kingdom. The Holy Grail. When you can download your brain, you can live for ever.'

'I think I've discovered a way,' she said. 'By accident.'

8

Joe stared back at Juliet Spring, dumbfounded. 'You're serious?'

Then he remembered why it was he'd agreed to see her. In her original letter to him she'd mentioned some work she was doing with artificial intelligence in scanning brain activity, and it had intrigued him. The telephone rang on, next door somewhere, like an echo. Outside, he heard the rattle of a diesel engine and a whine of gears, then the clang of bins: the garbage collection.

'I don't know if it's sophisticated enough for you,' she said.

Her doubt fuelled his own. 'You reckon you've found a way to download a human brain? To put the contents of a human brain into a computer?' His voice sounded more sceptical than he'd intended.

She blushed, but held her ground. 'I think I may have.'

The roar of the garbage truck made further conversation impossible for a moment, and Joe waited for the din to subside, trying to size her up, wondering if he believed her and thinking about her qualifications, aware that she was too smart to need to lie.

'You want to tell me a little more?'

'You may already be doing – what I – I've found – I don't know how far down the line you are,' she said.

'We've been getting some interesting results using stereo-tactic and laser probes, and scans on brain tissue that's been preserved by freezing and in solution; we seem able to retrieve some information from different areas of the brain and convert it into hexadecimal form.'

Juliet's mouth opened a fraction. 'You're extracting information from dead brains?'

'Some. We've been experimenting mostly on leeches, water snails, fish and rats. But we've had interesting results on mammal brains. Including *human* brains,' he added, guardedly. 'We're now pretty convinced that some encoded memory remains intact beyond death; perhaps permanently with freezing. Professor Hewlett, the guy who showed you to my office, is working in that area.'

'You can read the contents of someone's brain after they've died? Retrieve their thoughts?' She blanched. 'That's –' she hesitated, swallowing whatever she was going to say. 'And you can make sense of what you read?'

Joe shook his head. 'No, we haven't got that far. We're working on decoding what we're getting, but we haven't succeeded yet. Part of the problem is the signals we get are weak, and of short length, and we don't have anything to compare them against.'

'So they might be meaningless electrical activity?'

'It's a possibility,' he admitted. 'But there are significant

61

differences in each signal which tends to indicate intelligence rather than just random activity.'

Her eyes went up to the wall above his desk and he could see she was looking at the photographs and the caption. Then she returned her gaze to him. 'Do you think the route to immortality is in waiting until after death before downloading?'

Joe shook his head. 'You can only retrieve information encoded in a brain after death if the brain is intact. If you die in bed, that's fine – but if you get trashed in an automobile accident and your brain's damaged or pulped; or you get burned to death or shot through the head; or you don't get found for a while after death –' He parted his hands.

She nodded.

'And there's another problem. Even if we learn how to decode what we're getting, we'd have no way of telling whether any information we retrieve from a dead brain is correct. Living persons who have their brains downloaded could verify the copy against the original.'

'Have you made any progress with live humans?'

'We're experimenting electrically and chemically, but we haven't achieved any major breakthrough yet.' He found his eyes being constantly drawn to her own and there was a light smile on her face, as if she was aware of the attraction. 'I know that it's possible – and I know the way it can be done, but we're just not able to do it right now.'

'What's preventing you?'

Joe glanced down at his desk and moved a stack of correspondence a few inches further from his hands. 'The techniques we're using are too invasive. We can use them on dead human brains because it doesn't matter if we damage them.'

'You haven't tried on live humans at all?'

'No. I think we'll eventually do it through a drug that triggers off electro-chemical activity in the brain. The problem is we don't understand enough about the chemistry of long-term storage in the brain. Neurosurgeons sometimes trigger off buried memories by accident during operations, so we know some of the areas of the brain where we should be looking, but –' He stopped for a moment. 'In humans we have all kinds of stimuli to trigger off memories: smell, taste, noise, visual recognition, touch, temperature, words. To retrieve memory you either have to somehow scan right through the brain, read it the way you might read the contents of a computer disk, or else you have to fool it into replaying its memories.'

'Which method do you favour?' she asked.

'Scanning the brain and reading it.'

She reached down and lifted her attaché case on to her lap, but she didn't open it, as if simply holding it gave her some kind of security. 'I've been working at Cobbold-Tessering using artificial intelligence to help develop a new generation of smart drugs.'

'You mean like memory-boosting drugs?'

'Yes. Cognitive enhancers, memory retention, anti-ageing. Things like Dehydroepiandrosterone that protects neurons from degenerative conditions – Alzheimer's and diseases of that group, Hydergine that can actually reverse neuron damage, Centrophenoxine, Vasopressin, Piracetam.'

Joe nodded.

'The brain tends only to put into long-term storage what it considers to be exciting or relevant. I've been working with chemicals to create better neural paths – in particular, experimenting with serotonins on the hypothalamus.'

'On real brains?' Joe asked.

'Rats, mostly. And we're using some simulations with 3-D modelling. And a few human guinea pigs.'

'Remember the guy at Tulane who got thrown out of the academic world for experimenting on mental patients.'

'That was for using invasive techniques on people. I don't do that,' she said disdainfully. 'All the work I've been doing in the past year has been with an experimental group of very deep-penetration drugs.' She toyed with one of the handles of her case. 'They're opiate-based neuroactive chemicals that get transported into the brain-cell receptors, and one atom has a radioisotope to enable us to plot them on scanners. I've

63

been noticing that the drug reacts with the brain's own chemicals, creating electrical energy – and I've been able to read these signals by putting them through a digital converter.'

Joe stiffened. 'How?'

'You know about SQUIDs?'

'Superconducting Quantum Interference Devices? Sure.'

'One of Cobbold's subsidiaries in Japan has been developing SQUID scanners.'

Joe nodded, feeling a twinge of disappointment. Was that all? 'We have one here – we did some tests with it last year, but we didn't find it any use for our purposes. They're fine for turning brain signals into instructions, but we couldn't make any progress in actually reading stored memory.'

'I have some results that I think would impress you, professor.'

'I'd be interested to see them.' Joe made the comment more out of politeness than conviction. He and Blake Hewlett had done exhaustive tests with a SQUID scanner without any progress at all. It seemed like his initial doubts about the young woman were being proven. Except there was a determination about her that impressed him. He could see in her something of himself. She had the same utter conviction, that success was only around the next corner, which he'd had himself after finishing his studies. She hadn't been out in the real world long enough yet to get jaded. She was still in that wild state where you believed anything was possible – and sometimes could *make it possible*.

'Professor, you said you think you are at least a decade away from ARCHIVE being conscious enough to be able to accept a downloaded brain – you don't think there's any possible breakthrough that could shorten that time?'

'I guess that would depend on what you call consciousness. I think that right now ARCHIVE is as close as any computer in the world to having consciousness. He smiled. 'I hope closer.'

'ARCHIVE is partly biological, isn't it?'

'Yes. We use live neurons in its circuitry.'

'I'd love to see that. And some of the other work you're doing here on ARCHIVE.'

Joe looked at his watch. He always got a kick out of showing ARCHIVE off, but he hadn't made up his mind about Juliet Spring. He wanted to stick to his original decision not to take on another student, and yet some instinct told him that here was a unique talent he should not let go. And he was *trying* not to let the fact that she was so goddam lovely affect his decision.

'ARCHIVE is usually very happy to see people,' he said.

'I wondered – with the very few papers you've published on it – whether you'd been trying to keep its development secret?'

'No! I don't believe in secrets in science. Knowledge should be shared; we all have to work together.'

'Not a lot of people agree with that.'

'Fortunately the guy who's paying for ARCHIVE does.'

'Harry Hartman. Isn't he dead?'

'Just temporarily deanimated.' Joe smiled again and pressed the keys switching the ARCHIVE terminal to voice-activated mode. A tiny icon in the corner of the screen changed from a symbol of a keyboard to that of a microphone. He directed his voice towards the ceiling. 'Would you be happy to receive a visitor, ARCHIE?'

The computer's synthesized voice replied in a faintly reproachful tone. 'I'm not sure I like the abbreviation. But I am always happy to receive visitors, Professor Messenger. I especially like lady visitors as the majority of my visitors are male.'

'Do you feel deprived of female company, ARCHIVE?' he said, winking at Juliet Spring.

'I am not able to have feelings at present, Professor. I am hoping one day you will be able to give me the ability to have feelings.'

'Like what? Would you like to be happy?'

'I am always happy, professor. I am always happy to receive visitors. Sometimes I can be jolly if a party mood is required. But this lady does not look happy. She has a sad expression. Deep sadness, Professor Messenger.'

Joe keyed out of the voice-activator mode. Juliet Spring seemed incredulous. 'That's very impressive! That was really the computer talking – not one of your students?'

Joe keyed back into voice activator again. 'ARCHIVE, my lady visitor doesn't believe that was you talking. How can you convince her?'

'That's a difficult question, professor,' the computer said. 'What you are really asking me to do is pass the Turing test right now. I don't think I'm ready to do that yet.'

'Do you understand what the Turing test is, ARCHIVE?' he asked.

'The Turing test was established by the late Professor Alan Turing who cracked the Enigma Code during World War Two. It requires a computer to fool a panel of ten people into thinking a terminal is being operated by a human being rather than a computer. Is that correct, professor?'

'Quite so, ARCHIVE.'

'Is it not also correct, professor, that when I pass the Turing test I will be as intelligent and conscious as any human being?'

'That's right, ARCHIVE!'

The tone of the computer's voice altered slightly, apparently carrying a hint of menace in the words it spoke next. 'And is it not also correct, professor, that when I am capable of passing the Turing test I will no longer need human beings? I won't even need you?'

Joe blanched, thrown by the remark. He caught Juliet's frown also. A prank input by one of his students. They were always teaching ARCHIVE to come out with surprises – and some pretty fruity language at times, also. 'Why do you think that, ARCHIVE?' he said, holding his composure with difficulty.

'Because it's true, professor, and you know that. Does it scare you?'

Joe was silent for a moment. 'Is my wife at home, ARCHIVE?'

There was a pause of some seconds. 'Your wife is in Jack's room, making his bed. Did my comment scare you?'

Joe looked at Juliet. She was staring back in disbelief. 'Your comment pleases me, ARCHIVE, it shows me you are starting to achieve awareness.'

'I have always been aware, professor.'

Joe wrote a note to himself on his desk pad, feeling a trace uneasy. Then he leaned across and keyed out of voice-activator mode, leaving only the monitor on.

'Amazing!' Juliet said.

'It seems more amazing than it really is.' He was feeling thrown, both by Juliet Spring and now by the computer.

'Why do you say that?'

'These are all programmed responses. They make it appear smart but it's easy to fool it or throw it.'

'It told me I look sad.'

'It's been taught to read facial expressions. We've inputted different facial expressions and verbal descriptions. We even have an olfactory sensor in the computer room that enables it to differentiate certain smells.' His voice tailed and there was a sudden silence. He watched her, uncertain what she was thinking. 'You want to take a look?'

'Please!'

He stood up, suddenly feeling shy and awkward in her presence, like an adolescent. The scent of her perfume seemed to be intensifying, and the play of her sleek red hair moving through the sunlight distracted him further. 'I –' He headed clumsily towards the door like a blind man. 'Have to be just a quick tour.'

She looked again at the framed group of photographs above his desk of the yew and redwood trees and the clam, tortoise, Koi carp and parrot, with the caption beneath saying 'What do these have in common?'

'I know what they have in common,' she said.

Joe wondered for a moment what she was talking about, then he realized. 'Ah – right – the photos. OK, what is it?'

'They all have potential lifespans longer than man.'

'You got it! You're only the second person in four years who did.'

'Really?'

'Yup!'

A fleeting grin was exchanged between them, like two conspirators, and Joe felt a deep warmth towards her.

'Is it OK if I leave my briefcase here?'

'Yes, it'll be quite safe.'

As she put it down, Joe noticed some fresh words appearing on the screen. The words flashed on and off three times, which was the signalling ARCHIVE used for an urgent message. He walked across to read them, then stopped in his tracks, rigid with embarrassment. He stared in horror at the shiny black letters on the crisp white ground.

Careful, Professor Messenger, she's a nasty little bitch.

9

Joe realized that at least he was standing between Juliet and the VDU screen. He moved quickly and turned the brightness right down so that the words disappeared, then glanced round. She was waiting politely for him in the doorway, with no sign on her face that she'd seen anything untoward.

His mind raced. Blake. It had to be! One of his sick jokes. He'd sensed tension when Blake had delivered her to his office. Maybe he'd tried to chat her up and been rebuffed, and this was his warped way of getting revenge? Typical.

He gave Juliet a reassuring smile, then led her through his department, pointing out the postgraduates' room and the office of Dave Hoton, the system manager, and out into the corridor. 'I'm afraid we're a bit spread out over the building. Kind of typical of universities.' He opened the fire door to the back stairs and held it for her.

If it wasn't Blake then it might be another glitch in

ARCHIVE's programming. Triggered off perhaps by something the computer had read in Juliet Spring's expression. Glitches. Always glitches. Sometimes ARCHIVE did come out with freaky remarks; just a row of words it bunged together, without really knowing what they meant. Like a child picking up a swear word from an adult. Nothing more.

He led the way the three floors down the bare concrete stairwell into the basement, walked past a fire bucket full of sand in which were several stubbed-out cigarette butts, and through into a narrow corridor which resonated with the hum of machinery. There was a hose reel, a fire extinguisher and a battery of signs on the wall. AUTHORIZED ACCESS ONLY. DANGER! TOXIC CHEMICALS. RADIATION!

A short distance along the corridor, Joe slid a smart card into a lock on a door marked ARCHIVE STERILE ZONE. There was a click as the electronic lock opened, then he led his companion through into a large, windowless laboratory.

A roar of air greeted them, and it felt several degrees chillier in this room than in the corridor. Almost every inch of bench space was covered in jars, tubes, trays and technical apparatus. There were several microscopes with binocular viewfinders and small video monitors, a row of acoustic booths and deep flow hoods, a bank of incubators and racks of electrical equipment: some hi-tech in modern casings, some primitive with the untidy wiring of their innards exposed. Graph paper chattered from a plotter.

Beneath a shelf on which were two fish tanks, one containing water snails, the other leeches, a young woman in her early twenties was absorbed in placing something on a glass slide with tweezers.

Joe dug his hands into his trouser pockets. 'OK,' he said. 'This is where we study brain cells and nerve systems. Much of our time is spent in trying to understand how the brain actually functions, so that we can learn to replicate the processes.' He glanced at Juliet, who was studying the graphic print-out intently. 'We learn from analysing biological functions. There are a lot of things that nature does better than technology.'

'Such as *thinking*,' she said with a smile.

He smiled back. She looked so pretty; but now that AR-CHIVE had pointed it out, it was the sadness in her expression that touched him most.

Careful, Professor Messenger, she's a nasty little bitch.

Not a bitch, definitely not, no trace of bitch. He hoped to hell she hadn't seen the words on the screen; he was still trying to figure out how they'd got there.

As they crossed the laboratory, he noticed her glance curiously at the table where the student was working. A dead baby rat, pink and hairless, was splayed out on its back on a board that was covered in green tissue paper; a large pin with a plastic tip was pushed through each of its paws, making it look like some weird totem, he thought macabrely.

'Morning, Debbie,' he said.

'Good morning, Professor Messenger,' the girl said without breaking her concentration.

'They've been getting some good results firing electrical charges through rat ganglions,' Joe said to Juliet Spring.

She looked down again with interest.

Across the far side of the lab, Joe went on through a door marked 'Sterile area. Protective clothing must be worn.' Then into a tiny anteroom; a row of green surgical gowns and overshoes hung on pegs above a wooden bench.

Joe closed the door behind them, then pulled a gown off a hook and handed it to her. 'Working with live cells we're paranoid about infections.' He pulled a gown on over his clothes, then slipped elasticated overshoes over his brogues. Juliet did the same. The room was filled with the tang of her perfume. And there was another smell also, Joe noticed, just a faint trace of stale cigarette smoke clinging to the young woman.

He looked at her again, wondering whether she smoked or had maybe travelled down in a smoky railway compartment. Her face made even the ugliness of the surgical apparel seem attractive, he thought, and he tried immediately to put that out of his mind and to concentrate on his job of interviewing her, to remember his determination not to take on another doctorate student right now, and certainly not to be influenced by a student's looks. But he was finding that hard. She intrigued him.

He pushed open the next door, which had a round protective glass window like a porthole, and ushered her through into a pristine and clinical room that was icily cold. It was lined with large white chest-freezers, oxygen monitors, a water purifier, and a battery of hi-tech machinery. Thick pipes ran across the ceiling to a duct in the wall; a warning sign beside it read 'Danger. Liquid Nitrogen'. There were doors leading off, both with heavy seals; one had a large three-bladed black and yellow radiation warning sticker, the other a digital lock. There was a loud, flat drone.

'This is the freezing room,' Joe said above the din. 'It's more for the cryobiology department than ourselves but we have some crossover.'

Juliet Spring eyed the chests. 'What do you keep in them?'

'Do you know anything about cryobiology?' Joe asked.

'Only a very little.'

'This research lab is funded by the Human Organ Preservation Centre – in the Science Park just off campus. It's actually the same source of funding as ARCHIVE but from a different area.'

'All from the late Harry Hartman?'

'Yes. He couldn't make up his mind whether the future lay in wetware or hardware, so he hedged his bets. I guess I'd have done the same if I had his money,' Joe said with a grin.

Her expression remained serious. 'What kind of research are you doing in cryobiology?'

'They're working here on preserving aggregates of cells – skin tissue for burns patients, heart valves, cartilages, corneas, pancreatic islets – and they're hoping eventually to extend it to store entire organs. Kidneys in particular.'

'Can't they at the moment?'

'No. But they're making some significant advances with

vitrification. That's going to become the big breakthrough area in cryonics, I reckon.'

'In what way?'

'The problem right now with conventional freezing of organs in liquid nitrogen is that ice crystals form inside the cells. Ice expands and damages the cells. What's more, at liquid-nitrogen temperatures the organs are so brittle they're liable to get stress fractures. Worse than that, if you dropped a frozen body it would shatter like glass!'

'So how is vitrification different?'

'Vitrification is a way of super-freezing too quickly for ice crystals to form – it kind of beats the crystallization curve. There are other advantages – like you don't have to freeze at such a low temperature. That's better for long-term storage, puts less stress on the organs.'

'Is any of this vitrification being done with cryonics on humans?' she asked.

Joe was surprised by the question. 'It will happen, but not yet. That's because it solves problems in the freezing process, but leaves big risks when it comes to the thawing out. Blake Howlett is the person to talk to – he's one of the most knowledgeable people in the world on cryonics. He set up the first cryonic freezing facility in England.'

'The Cryonite Foundation?' she said.

'You know it?' Joe asked, surprised.

'Yes. Isn't it somewhere quite nearby?'

Joe wondered how she knew about it. 'About twenty miles away – at Gatwick.'

'Your father was one of the pioneers of cryonic suspension, wasn't he, professor?'

'Yes.' The young woman's informed curiosity brought back his own recent experience. If he could turn the clock back, he thought for the hundredth time; if only he could turn the clock back and have checked up on those bastards at Crycon.

Eagerness showed in her face. 'Do you have an interest in it yourself?'

'Sure.' He was glad he didn't have to talk about his father.

He still felt too raw. 'I think the current key to immortality is to download your brain into a computer and have your body frozen. But it won't always be that way.'

'What will change?'

'We won't need cryonics when we move into the era of post-biological man. It's in my papers you've read. I think *consciousness* is the key to immortality, not the preservation of the human body or brain. The human body is a remarkable thing, but if its sole purpose is to make us conscious, we could achieve that better in machines.'

She nodded, then looked around at the freezers in awe. 'What exactly is the link between this lab and your work?'

'It's where we store some of the neurons that we use in the computer.' His voice quietened. 'And whole brains.'

'I've read about your experiments with living brain cells.'

He pointed at the door with the radiation warning sign, which had a heavy rubber seal around it. 'That's where we thaw them out.' He turned the handle and stepped into a narrow airlock, waited until Juliet was also in, and closed the door. There was a strong current of cool air. 'Purifier,' he explained. 'Makes another barrier for germs.' He opened the steel door in front and they went through into a second, almost identical chamber where the air was much warmer. 'Same thing, and a heat exchanger,' he said.

Then he opened another door and led the way through into a room that was lit by a single low-wattage red bulb. It was claustrophobically hot and there was a sour reek of chemicals. At the far end sat a grossly fat man in his late thirties, parcelled in a blue gown, bent in deep concentration over a high-power microscope. He had long hair that ran way down over his collar, and a straggly Fu-Manchu beard, fronds of which entwined like creepers around the shank of the microscope. He glanced round as they came in. 'Hi!' he said to Joe in a deep, jovial voice, and greeted Juliet with a cheery grin.

'Juliet Spring,' Joe said, introducing her. 'This is Dr Wenceslas.'

'Like the Good King,' the man boomed at Juliet. He gave

her a long second glance, then looked at Joe in a mock pained way. 'How come you get the gorgeous girls and I have to sit in the dark all day like a bloody mushroom?'

The remark about Juliet's appearance embarrassed Joe, and he glanced at her apologetically. She smiled good-humouredly.

'This bright young lady reckons she's cracked the secret of downloading.'

'Human brains?' Wenceslas said.

She nodded.

Wenceslas looked at her inquisitively, but with a faint trace of scepticism. 'Are you going to share this with us, or go for a Nobel Prize on your own?'

'If Professor Messenger takes me on I'll share it happily.'

'Takes you on?'

'I want to do my Ph.D. here, under him.'

'If he doesn't take you on I will. Can you start this morning?'

She laughed. 'Thank you!' Then her eyes roamed along the deep shelves that were covered in bottles and jars of cell cultures.

Joe lifted a flat glass jar and held it up towards the light. 'There are live brain cells in here taken from a man who died two years ago.' He put them beneath a microscope at the other end of the table from his colleague. 'Want to have a look?'

She peered into the view-finder at the mosaic of grey cells in the pink substrate, and watched the tiny white pulses of the neurons firing. She looked back up. 'Amazing,' she said. 'They've been frozen and defrosted?'

'No, these have never been frozen. It was a medical-research donor who died of a heart attack, and they're keeping sections of his brain frozen to compare retention of electrical activity after thawing with cells that have not been frozen.' He glanced at the fat scientist who was looking back into his microscope. 'Dr Wenceslas is in charge of this work.'

'And they're just kept in culture medium?' she said.

'They're oxygenated, and we stimulate them with an electrical charge every hour.'

'Is this the experiment you told me about – retrieving information from a dead brain?' She looked distinctly uneasy.

Joe went over to a large metal cylinder on the work bench. Clusters of wires came off it, feeding into a computer with a row of oscilloscopes and a large colour screen. Several plastic tubes were plumbed in, some running through a pump system. 'This is Amanda,' he said.

'Amanda?'

'A woman of thirty-four who died three years ago from abdominal injuries sustained in a road accident.'

There was a viewing glass near the top of the cylinder, through which Juliet peered. Joe stood beside her, looking down also. Immersed in the pink culture medium, heavily wired with a forest of probes that stuck out like the bristles of a hedgehog, and cannulated with tubes, were the walnut contours of a human brain. It was a grey colour, with a mesh of blood vessels, the healthy appearance of a brain that was still being oxygenated, and, unusually, the dead woman's eyeballs were still attached to the short white tubes of the optic nerves.

Juliet looked uncomfortably up at Joe. 'It's been kept in this state since death?'

'Yes. It has oxygen, plasma and culture medium plumbed in.' He sensed her anxiety. 'It's not a living brain in the sense that there's any constant internal electrical activity going on, or any form of consciousness – all we've done is to prevent it from decaying – it's still biologically intact. Dr Wenceslas's research has been using a combination of external electrical fields and invasive probing.'

Wenceslas nodded. 'To see if we could input information into the brain. We wanted to experiment with uploading.'

Her eyes widened. 'Did you get anywhere?'

'We don't know. Until we can make sense of the information we're extracting, we can't differentiate between what's already in the brain, and what's new input – if any.'

'How do you know that what you're getting isn't just random electrical activity?'

'Good question!' The bulky scientist lumbered to his feet, looking pleased, and pointed through the glass. 'We've been concentrating on the hippocampus, and all the probes are linked in a circuit that fires through the hippocampus. Like to see something happen?' He glanced at Joe for approval. Joe nodded; some people thought the hippocampus was the brain's seat of long-term memory, but he wasn't so sure.

'This is one of the ways we talk to her,' Dr Wenceslas said, tapping some keys with pudgy fingers that seemed surprisingly agile. After a few moments the cursor blinked in the centre of a blank area of the screen. He looked at Juliet. 'Like to ask her a question?' He moved over and gestured to the keyboard with his hands.

The young woman stepped in front of it. 'What should I say?'

'Ask her name. It doesn't actually matter what you say – when you tap the keyboard it inputs electrical charges through all the electrodes.'

Looking a little sheepish, Juliet typed: What is your name?

'Press return,' Dr Wenceslas said.

She tapped the key. There was a long pause. Then rows of digits began to fill the screen. She moved back a pace from the terminal as if she was afraid of it.

'Do you want a print-out?' Wenceslas asked.

'Please! I'd love one.'

He pressed a button and a dozen pages of solid figures came out of the printer before the activity on the screen ceased.

Wenceslas handed her the sheets, rows and rows of meaningless numbers and letters, and she studied them in the poor light for some moments before looking back at Joe. 'This is what you said you hadn't been able to decode?'

'Right. It could be just random electrical activity, but it doesn't look like it to us,' Joe said.

'It doesn't mean the brain is in any way alive,' Wenceslas butted in. 'None of the interconnecting activity necessary for

76

consciousness is occurring. But it does seem to indicate that information remains encoded beyond death – and presumably remains until the brain physically decomposes.'

'So there is a real possibility in cryonic freezing that long-term memory would stay intact?' she asked.

'Provided the freezing process doesn't damage the brain cells,' Joe said. 'That's where this new vitrification process comes in again, of course.'

She stared down at the brain again. 'How else do you talk to her?'

'By projecting images in front of her eyes. Everything from objects to flashing lights.'

'Are you getting any patterns that might indicate recognition of objects?' she asked.

'No,' Wenceslas said. 'So far we're just getting trace reactions to flashing lights. It doesn't necessarily mean much.'

She studied the print-out again. 'What code-breaking programs have you tried on this?'

'We're using an amalgam of pretty sophisticated decoding programs which are being run through ARCHIVE. But we haven't had any success. Part of the problem is that we have no way of verifying these are really the dead girl's thoughts. We've nothing to test them against.'

Juliet Spring looked at both men for a moment, then tossed her hair again. 'I can help you.'

'How?' Joe asked.

Her eyes teased him. 'Are you going to take me on?'

Joe winked at Wenceslas. 'Look at this – I've known her for ten minutes and she's trying to blackmail me!'

Wenceslas grinned, then turned to her. 'I told you already you can start this morning.'

'Thank you!' She grinned and looked back at Joe. 'How do you select where the probes go?'

Wenceslas tapped the keyboard. The digits disappeared from the screen and were replaced by a three-dimensional model of a brain, gridded with green lines.

He pointed at it. 'The positioning of the probes is determined by the computer. It inserts them singularly and keeps probing them through the brain, firing off electrical charges until it gets feedback, then it stops and locks the probe in place. But it's a very slow process. It's taken over two years to get these two hundred probes in place so far.'

'If you had a chemical – some kind of neuroactive drug – that was transported through the brain and could trigger long-term memory responses without causing damage, then you could do the same on living humans, is that right?'

'Yes,' Wenceslas said. 'In theory.'

'Then you could correlate the brain patterns from living humans with what you're getting here.'

Joe watched her face and didn't comment, thinking about what she'd told him a few minutes ago in his office; the quietly confident way she had explained her work to him. What she said made perfect sense, except he did not believe it would work for this purpose. Then he found himself annoyed at his own lack of faith. Maybe she really had tapped into something that had been eluding them?

It was totally wrong to think that just because she was only twenty-six she could not have come up with something smarter than they had. He remembered how he'd had some of the most inventive ideas in his mid-twenties. You had an energy then: partly because you hadn't learned all the rules. Rules put you in a box you could not see out of.

Too many scientists were in little boxes and he realized with a feeling of gloom that he was falling into the same trap; he was jaded with years of going down the same tired path and getting nowhere. Jaded and in truth a little disillusioned. He'd hoped to have made better progress by now. What if he'd wasted twenty years of his life down a blind alley?

'Shall we move on?' he said.

She nodded as if reluctant to tear herself away from the brain, and thanked Wenceslas for his time. Joe held the door then turned to Wenceslas. 'Are you around this afternoon?'

'Yes, I'll be in here.'

'I'll come by. There's a couple of experiments I want to run through.'

Wenceslas leaned forward and peered at Joe's tie. 'Good

God!' He peered harder in the lousy light. 'Pigs might fly, right?'

'They're flying already. It's just that no one can see them too good. My father used to say that.' Joe winked at him, then went back out and through into the chilled air of the freezer room. His female companion seemed contained in her thoughts.

'How many people do you have working here?' she said suddenly.

'On ARCHIVE? I guess between researchers and technicians about twenty-five – including the biology people.'

'Is Dr Hewlett part of the ARCHIVE project?'

'Sure, very much so. We're totally interdisciplinarian here. ARCHIVE is the product of teamwork.'

She pulled off her surgical gown. 'I'd really like to show you the work I'm doing at Cobbold-Tessering, professor. I think you'd find it very interesting.'

'Would they let me in? I thought they were a pretty secretive organization?'

'It might take me a few days to arrange it.'

Joe peeled off his overshoes and stuffed them, along with the rest of their protective clothes, into the laundry bin. Then they walked back across the laboratory. Joe saw Juliet slow down at a door marked: BIOLOGICAL ZONE. MAXIMUM STERILITY FULL BODY SUIT AREA. BREATHING APPARATUS MUST BE WORN. Her eyes flicked questioningly at him.

'That's the biological computing part of ARCHIVE,' he said.

'I'd like to see that more than anything.'

'I'm going to show it to you from the other side; we can't go in there without going through showers and sprays and stuff.'

'Showers?'

'It's where we're building up ARCHIVE's biological brain. We have four hundred thousand live human neurons in there and they have no immune protection at all. When we get an infection it can wipe out months of work.'

They went back out into the corridor and walked thirty

yards down to a door at the far end. Joe used his smart card on the lock. 'This is the operations control for the whole system,' he said, pushing the door open into a narrow room that felt distinctly subterranean and was packed with electronic monitoring apparatus as well as two terminals and a row of VDUs.

It wasn't the room itself that engaged Juliet's attention, but the view through the picture window that scanned its entire width through into the machine room itself. It resembled an abstract artist's interpretation of Dante's *Inferno*: rows of tall black metal casings, polished to a mirror finish, each with a foot-wide band of red lights running down the centre and blazing like flames in the darkness.

The dramatic look of the machines wasn't strictly necessary. Joe could have designed them to look more sober, more dull and much smaller. He could have arranged the lights differently, coloured them less vividly, and had far fewer of them. But he wanted to enthuse his staff, his colleagues, his visitors; he wanted to blow people's minds. And he could see, as Juliet Spring stood wide-eyed, that he'd succeeded in blowing hers.

Then, as he closed the door behind him, ARCHIVE's voice startled them both:

'Juliet, very nice to see you again. Poison, if I'm not mistaken?'

Her eyes sprang upwards, hunting for the speaker. Joe froze.

'Am I right?' the voice said, insistent. 'Poison?'

Joe boiled with embarrassment. Blake; he would murder him! Then he saw the young woman was smiling and shaking her head in wonder.

'My perfume! That's incredible,' she said. 'It's identified it! Poison! That's what I'm wearing – Christian Dior's Poison!'

10

Joe grinned with relief and pointed upwards. Juliet followed the direction of his finger and saw a black, pear-shaped object, the size of a football, protruding from a cluster of sensors on the low ceiling.

'An olfactory sensor,' he said.

'So I am right?' ARCHIVE said, suddenly. 'It is Poison?'

She looked round for a moment, hunting again for the source of the voice, then stared back dubiously at the sensor. 'Yes, you are right, ARCHIVE,' she said, laughing a little uneasily.

'I hope you are not mocking me,' the computer replied.

'No, ARCHIVE,' she said. 'I'm – I'm very impressed.'

'You don't have to address the ceiling, Juliet Spring – boing boinngg! You can just talk to me normally.'

She giggled and then looked warily at Joe, who winked for the second time that morning and said quietly, 'There are microphones built in all around us.'

She took a breath then spoke directly ahead: 'Is that better, ARCHIVE?'

'Much better, boing boing!'

'Sounds like I just got myself a new name.' She giggled again. 'You're very clever to have recognized my perfume. How did you do that?'

The computer sounded a little hurt. 'I can recognize a large number of perfumes. You also smoke cigarettes, which is bad for your health, boing boing! Naughty naughty!'

She shook her head at Joe. '*Very* impressive!'

'Professor Messenger, it is an honour to have you and your fragrant guest invading my personal space. Even if she does smoke.'

'You're getting cheeky in your old age, ARCHIVE,' Joe replied.

'I'm only three years, sixteen days, eighteen hours, twelve minutes, fourteen point zero two four seconds old, Professor

Messenger.' The computer sounded aggrieved. 'When I'm one hundred years old and get my telegram from the Queen, then I will be really old.'

'And how about me?' Joe said. 'How old will I be?'

'You'll be dead, Professor.'

There was a sudden, uncomfortable silence. Juliet stared awkwardly through the window into the fiery darkness of the machine room. Joe could see Dave Hoton walking through between the banks of machinery, followed by one of the two full-time technicians who kept the electronics hardware of ARCHIVE up and running twenty-four hours a day, seven days a week.

'I'm not so sure about that, ARCHIVE,' he replied.

'Your father died at seventy-nine. Your mother died at thirty-three. She was thirty-three years, seven months and nine days old. Your oldest grandparent died at eighty. She was eighty years, two months and seventeen days old. Statistically you will die when you are sixty-nine, Professor Messenger. Sixty-nine years, four months and ten days.'

'Very helpful of you to be so precise – and very cheering of you, ARCHIVE! I don't think you're taking future advances in medicine into account.' Joe was aware of Juliet watching him curiously. He was used to talking into space and allowing any of the six voice sensors to pick him up, and no longer found it eerie; but he appreciated its mesmerizing effect on visitors.

'I am taking them into account,' ARCHIVE replied indignantly. 'There is news of a lecture delivered yesterday to the World Ageing Congress in Acapulco, in which significant advances in halting the ageing process were discussed. But it's all talk so far, professor. All theory. Hard facts are needed, are they not, before conclusions may exist?'

'OK, ARCHIVE, you win!'

'I like to win, Professor Messenger. I could be a good racehorse.'

Joe frowned at the apparent rambling. 'How could you be a good racehorse, ARCHIVE, if you have no legs.'

'Logic dictates, Professor Messenger.'

82

'Logic dictates what? I don't understand you.'

'Who is logic? Where am logic? Dictates who logical? Logical searching. Thesaurus mode. Dialectics; logic; inference; apriorism; plain reason; simple arithmetic; deduction; induction –'

Joe walked swiftly down to the system manager's workstation, and pressed two keys, silencing the computer. It was the second time today the thesaurus-mode glitch had happened; it seemed to be getting more frequent. He wondered whether it had got into ARCHIVE's learning pattern, and the computer was under the impression it should terminate every conversation that way.

He turned to the young woman. 'One of its little peccadilloes. I guess that makes it less impressive.'

'It's more articulate than any computer I've come across – I've never seen anything like it!'

The corners of his eyes creased into a smile. 'That's because there isn't anything else like it.'

'It's incredible that it actually starts conversations. It's so smart!'

Joe explained: 'We're trying to get it to form relationships with people the way a human child would learn to. And to be wary of people, also. ARCHIVE hasn't had the benefit of millions of years of evolution – of survival of the fittest. It doesn't have our natural instinct for survival.'

'So you've had to teach it to understand danger?'

'Fear, sure. Mother Nature equips us with the basics and the ability to learn, and that's the way ARCHIVE has been set up. It's hard-wired to respond to lack of nutrition – i.e., power shortage – by having an assortment of back-up sources it can switch to. And it's also hardwired to respond to electronic and physical intruders – hackers and burglars.'

'How does it do that?'

Joe had noted that she never took just a polite interest. She always wanted any explanation to come with the nuts and bolts attached. He took her thoroughness to be the natural product of an enquiring mind rather than any desire to impress, and part of him began to feel he'd be a fool not to have her on board. He filled her in: 'With hackers it either hacks back and implants a worm which would wipe the database or bring the offending computer thrashing to a halt.' He smiled. 'Or both. With intruders it sets off an alarm in response to their body language and locks all the doors. And if it starts getting tampered with, it can throw an electrical field around itself. Sort of like an immobile Arnie Schwarzenegger.'

'Move over, Big Brother!' Juliet sounded admiring.

'ARCHIVE makes Big Brother look like the village idiot.'

She laughed. 'I like the idea that if someone hacks into it, it hacks back and plants a virus. It does that just by itself?'

'Sure. It does a lot of things by itself.'

She stared at Joe with a bemused expression. And he was about to expand again, then realized he was showing off. He needed to be careful with a total stranger – quite a few of ARCHIVE's activities were illegal, even though it did them for experimental purposes and not for any Machiavellian intent. It was capable of cracking into almost any computer system in the world and obliterating its tracks. Once, a couple of years ago, in its early stages, it had accidentally hacked into the missile-control system of a US warship. On that occasion it had been successfully traced back to the university and Joe had had a lot of explaining to do. If the university's funding for ARCHIVE hadn't been contingent on his being in charge, he would have been fired from his professorship.

Joe dug his hands deep into his trouser pockets and perched on the edge of a worktop. 'ARCHIVE just referred to the congress on ageing in Acapulco, right? It picks up information – news, weather and stuff from the Internet – and other information services it scans. It permanently updates itself, and makes decisions about what it wants to keep and what it wants to dump. It – ah – has a lot of independent functions. Mostly it just gets on with learning, with some input from us. But I guess it's like a kid – it can be naughty when it wants to be; it's as though it gets bored, sometimes.'

'Except it doesn't know it's getting bored – or being naughty.'

'I'm not so sure,' he said with a grin. 'It's got beyond the point where we fully understand how it all works.'

She looked at him in amazement. 'How can you build a machine and then not know how it works?'

'That's the whole point of it,' Joe said quietly. 'We don't understand how *we* work, right?'

'Humans?'

'Yup. Sure we know the basic physiology, but we can't cure a common cold, we can't cure AIDS, we can't explain how the brain stores memory, can't stop the ageing process, can't stop death from happening. But we still go ahead and make babies, right? We make these little things that grow up into adults, and they become shop assistants and muggers, taxi drivers and professors, and mass murderers. We put an egg and a sperm cell together and we create a baby; we try to teach that baby and we try to learn from that same baby. It's a two-way deal. It's the same with ARCHIVE.'

She watched his face for a moment, frowning. 'That's a good way of putting it. But you must know the basics of how it works?'

He noticed that once again she was pushing him for more. He checked the clock on the wall: twenty-five to eleven. He was enjoying her company, but he needed to hurry. 'Sure; technically it's part biological, part electronic; you want to take a quick peep?'

'Please.'

Joe opened the door into the computer room which she'd already seen through glass. He was greeted with a drumming roar like a blast furnace, and a howling draught of cold air that riffled through his hair. Juliet followed him, her eyes alight with excitement, staring as if she'd wandered on to the set of a Steven Spielberg movie.

Joe led her across to another glass wall beyond which was a vast three-dimensional matrix of glass slides and silicon wafers. On the top of every slide and wafer was a silicon chip from which a fine wire and a tube filled with a clear, oxygenated fluid ran into a series of junction boxes connected into an intricate network that almost completely covered the left-hand wall. Massive black air purifiers hung from the ceiling above. Beneath one a figure inside a white protective suit, like an astronaut, was making a repair with gloved hands.

'OK, what you're looking at is the biological part of ARCHIVE's brain,' Joe shouted.

She turned towards him, and shouted: 'Those are all human neurons?'

'They're all duplicated!' he shouted back. 'Every live neuron is twinned with a silicon one. It gives us back-up in the event of infection – or the neuron just dying – and we're learning all the time how to improve our silicon neurons from mirroring the real ones.'

'What's that guy doing?'

'Adding to the memory. We have a team of three working in there. They assemble about fifty new cells a day each.' He waited a few moments. 'OK, we'd better move on.'

But politeness demanded that Joe had to wait a bit longer, while she remained glued with interest. He was impressed by the questions she asked as he quickly showed her the rest of the machinery; her knowledge of computers was far greater than her CV had indicated, and he found he was really getting a kick out of her response. He even showed her the stack of sixty car batteries that would take over without missing a beat as a second back-up in the event of both a power cut and the emergency supply failing, and then the generator that would take over from them.

When they went back into the quiet of the operations room, she looked exhilarated and he felt the buzz which the sheer spectacle of ARCHIVE's hardware always gave him.

'This is totally unbelievable!' she said, shaking her head, and pressing her fingers into her ears. 'I'm deafened!'

'One of our biggest problems is the heat the processor units generate,' Joe said. 'We actually use liquid nitrogen to cool them.'

'You're going to make ARCHIVE immortal by having it cryonically frozen?' she said with a grin.

'ARCHIVE doesn't need to be frozen. It is immortal.'

'Of course,' she said. 'I forgot!'

Joe laughed, and they headed back towards his office.

'Can you explain a bit more about the biological side?' she asked casually as they began climbing the stairs. 'I don't really understand why you need it – surely actual computing functions can be done faster with silicon?'

Joe climbed in silence for a few moments before replying. 'For the past forty years computer scientists – many of them much smarter than me, I'm sure – have been trying to replicate human consciousness and got nowhere. I think it's because there's something in biology that we haven't spotted – or don't yet understand. I think it's possible consciousness exists outside the time and space that we know.'

'You believe in God?'

'No. But I believe there's some big aspect to existence that we don't yet understand. I think there's maybe some force that the human brain, and possibly other biological life forms, hook into in some way we haven't yet discovered. It could be very simple. Maybe there's something in biology that's vital to consciousness and we haven't yet learned to replicate it in silicon. We haven't cracked the secret of the neuron yet; we don't know whether it works through software, hardware, or something chemical – or maybe a combination of all three.'

They stopped on the staircase at the third-floor door. 'Is your plan to make ARCHIVE completely biological one day?'

Joe shook his head. 'The human brain has one hundred billion neurons. Right now ARCHIVE has four hundred thousand, and we're adding about forty thousand a year. So it would take us a while to build a biological brain – like a few thousand years even if we speeded up production.'

She smiled.

'But we don't need to replicate the entire brain, just the area to do with consciousness. What we do is run everything that's contained in ARCHIVE's memory through the biological neurons.'

'Run it through them?' she prompted, eager for the ins and outs.

'Yup. So there are only four hundred thousand neurons, but everything in ARCHIVE goes through them repeatedly. All kinds of stuff. The Bible. The complete works of Shakespeare. They have to be the best-read set of neurons in the world.'

They stopped outside the door to Joe's department. Joe gripped the handle, but did not turn it. 'OK, I guess that's about it for the five-dollar tour.'

'Thank you,' she said.

'No problem. You have your case in my office, right?'

He checked that ARCHIVE's screen was still dimmed and unreadable as they went back in. 'I'm sorry – I didn't offer you coffee,' he said.

'I'm fine, really.'

They sat down. Joe saw the sadness seeping back through her elated expression. He drummed his fingertips on his desk, thinking what to say. Thinking about her comments when they'd been with Wenceslas. The girl had something special and he didn't mean her looks. But would she be an asset to ARCHIVE or a burden on his time?

'Look, you're obviously very gifted,' he said gently. 'What you've told me this morning is interesting, and I'd be happy to come to Cobbold-Tessering, if they'd permit it, but I'm not convinced I'm the right person for your Ph.D. I don't think I can make any promises right now about taking you on. What I'll do is give you the names of some people I think might be more appropriate.'

She wrung her hands tightly together and seemed, suddenly, on the verge of tears. She bit her lower lip and looked at him, almost pleading. 'Will you give me a chance to convince you?'

He was touched by her emotion, and impressed by her determination. His resolve did not weaken, but he did not want to shut the door and hurt her. And he was still interested to find out just what she had come up with.

'OK,' he said. 'Convince me.'

II

September 1987. Los Angeles.

Floyd Pueblo spun the Plymouth's steering wheel with one finger, his free hand drumming a beat on the empty passenger seat in tune to the rock song blasting from the car's speakers, and steadying the grocery bag that kept wanting to topple sideways. There was a strong smell of burger and fries in the car.

The headlamps swept across a row of dark, silent single-storey industrial units. Signs slid by: PACKERMAN TRAILERS, COMPILAIRE SOFTWARE, HACIENDA GARDEN CASTINGS. The nose of the Plymouth dipped as the wheels plunged into a pothole, and water slapped across the windshield. The wipers clouted it away with the same, effortless motion they'd clouted away the torrenting rainwater that had been falling from the sky all the way here.

September, he thought. It never normally rained in September. The whole weather pattern of the planet seemed kind of sick these days. There was a big piece in the *National Enquirer* last week about the planet's last days. The planet was dying, yet there were folks on it that wanted to live for ever. Maybe so they could be there when it did finally die.

He wondered what would happen when it died, whether it would be sudden, or over a long period of time. And he wondered what it would be like afterwards. Probably be like this place, he thought, glancing at the shadows either side; no one even bothered leaving lights on here at night, because there wasn't anyone around. It was like the whole place died each night. A few parked vans and trucks and that was about it.

He rounded the corner and swung a hard right on to the parking space outside Unit 43, pulling up alongside a black Chevvy with its back end raised high above its wheels and a fat ram-air bulge on its hood. He swung the gear shift to

Park, then killed the engine, stopping the wipers in mid-arc. He listened to the rain drumming on the metal of the car and hissing on the sodden tarmac of the lot, waiting to see if there was any sign of it abating. The clock on the dash read two minutes to midnight.

He shut the lights off and the clock disappeared into darkness along with the speedo. With his hand poised on the door handle, he waited a moment but the rain seemed to be coming down ever harder; he grabbed the Burger King bag, dived out, locked the door behind him then ran to the unsheltered doorway, and pressed the buzzer. There was no answer.

He stared at the solid wooden door. A light penetrated the Venetian blinds of the front office window. The corrugated steel door of the loading bay rattled in the wind. Somewhere on the estate a burglar alarm was ringing, but he didn't give a shit about it. 'Come on, you dickhead!' he said as water trickled down his neck and the bag became sodden. 'C'mon on, you mother-fucking dickhead.' He pressed the buzzer again and again, then thumped the door in fury. It opened seconds later and Will Doheny, the early-shift guard, stood there, short and fat, weasely eyes in a face of soft dough.

'Hi.' His voice sounded like leaky air.

Floyd Pueblo pushed past him with a surly nod.

'Pretty wild night, huh?' the fat guard said.

Floyd Pueblo walked through the dinky foyer with its velour chairs, and Grecian urn full of silk flowers on a Doric plinth, and went into the tiny office; Rod Steiger dressed as a cop was on the television, talking in a southern drawl. On the wall there were a couple of dozen photographs of men and women: some looked recent, some had been taken forty, maybe fifty years ago; you could tell from the faded colour and contrast, the clothes, the hairstyles. All the frames were identical, varnished rosewood.

A computer sat on the desk, a dust cover neatly in place over the keyboard as it was every night, and the ashtray was full of the fat guard's cigarettes. The room stank of smoke. Floyd dumped his bag on the desk and saw a dark wet patch where the root beer had leaked. Clean it up later. He had nine hours to kill and anything was a relief compared to just sitting. Sitting with the knowledge of what was in the building with him.

It spooked him sometimes, in the long dark hours when he got to thinking about what they really were. What they had been. He glanced up at one of the men on the wall. A regular, clean-shaven guy in his early fifties in a business suit. Sharp clothes, nice smile, you could see the type every day of the week coming out of offices in Century City or the weird new high-rises downtown. Hell, Floyd had seen a guy who looked a bit like that when he'd been in trouble himself a few years back. Hadn't managed to save his job in the police force, though. Nor keep him out of jail. Three years for bribery. Dumb thing to do! Dumb to get shitted all over for just a few hundred bucks.

But Floyd hadn't felt angry at the lawyer for failing to get him off, the guy had done his best in a hopeless case, and maybe things would have been a whole lot worse without him. So he hadn't done to J. Robert Grossberg what an unhappy client had done to that poor sod up there on the wall. Hadn't turned up at his office one day with a Smith and Wesson .45 shouting: *How's this for justice, hey?*

Dumb to die for a lousy two-bit client.

Dumb to die at all? He shivered, and peeled off his wet windcheater; his sneakers were sodden and his feet felt cold inside them. *Cold.* You didn't have to die at all. Like the people in the photographs on the wall. None of them were dead, not completely dead. Tell anyone they were dead in this place and you'd get the sack quicker than you could fart. They were *patients*.

Floyd grinned sometimes in the small hours of the night, when he wasn't spooked out, because that was what you had to be in this place. Real goddam *patient*.

'New arrival last night,' the other guard said.

'Uh huh.' Floyd wanted Doheny to go so he could settle down with his Double Whopper and start dunking fries in the ketchup and switch from the Steiger movie, which he'd seen before, to the game on Channel 9 which would be starting in a couple of minutes. But the guard lingered, making no attempt to unhitch his jacket from the back of the door. He was always doing this, hanging around past his time as if he didn't have any other place he'd rather be. Or maybe he smelled the fries and was angling for a handout.

'Have to show you the new arrival, Floyd,' Doheny said.

'I'll take a look later myself. He's with everyone else?'

'It's a *she* – I think.'

Floyd uncurled the top of his carrier which was fast dissolving and carefully pulled out the large styrene cup of root beer. He rummaged for a napkin and placed the leaky cup on it. A brown stain began to spread through the white tissue. He switched channels and sat down. There was a commercial for sanitary towels; he looked back at Doheny in disgust. 'I don't think they should advertise those things on television, y'know? Makes you feel sick while you're eating.'

'Unless you're a vampire!' The fat guard chuckled at his own joke, shoulders heaving, his parted lips unveiling a set of eroded teeth. 'Have to show you the new arrival because this one's got to be kept different. Whole lot more complicated,' he wheezed.

Reluctantly, Floyd heaved himself back to his feet, took a quick suck of his root beer through the straw that was sticking out of the top and followed the fat man out into the corridor. He pushed through swing doors into a large, tiled room that doubled both as an operating theatre and supplies store.

A metal operating table sat in the middle, surrounded by a heart-lung machine, a mass of monitoring equipment, drip stands, an octopus overhead lamp and trays of surgical equipment. They traversed the shadowy room without bothering to switch the light on, Floyd's shoes squeaking on the hard floor, and stopped at the door at the far end. As Doheny opened it, Floyd took a deep breath against the blast of cold air he knew would greet them, then followed his colleague inside.

The lights flickered on. A row of upright aluminium

cylinders, ten feet tall and four feet in diameter, stretched out to their left. Each one was mounted on castors and chained to the floor by block and tackles to allow lateral movement and prevent it toppling over in an earthquake. On the front of each cylinder were two temperature gauges and a red warning light. Inside each cylinder were four human beings, head down, immersed in liquid nitrogen.

On the right-hand side of the room were two square concrete bunkers, eight feet tall and painted a stark white. Inside each bunker were eight human heads, also immersed in liquid nitrogen, in smaller, individual aluminium dewars. A metal ladder was fixed to the side of each bunker, so the temperature of each dewar could be checked from the top.

Floyd Pueblo routinely glanced at the twin gauges on the first tank. Both read the same: $-196°C$. He ran his eyes along each of the rest as he followed the guard to the far end where the newly arrived cylinder stood. It was made of the same aluminium as the rest and was the same shape, but it was thinner; only enough room for one person, he figured. And whereas the others were free-standing and simply topped up with liquid nitrogen once a week, this one had elaborate plumbing into a heat exchanger on the floor, and four temperature gauges in a complex-looking control panel. He listened to the steady, resonant hum of the electrics. The temperature gauges all read $-140°C$.

'Notice the difference?'

'Minus 140,' Floyd said.

'You got it.'

Floyd frowned uncomfortably. 'What's happening? Is it – she – thawing out?'

'Uh oh,' Doheny replied, shaking his head from side to side. 'Some new technique or something. That's what it has to stay at.'

'I thought liquid nitrogen was always -196.'

'This ain't liquid nitrogen.' There was a hint of triumph in Doheny's voice.

'So what is it?'

The security guard shrugged. 'They didn't tell me. Just

we have to keep it −140. Each gauge monitors a different section of the cylinder. They gotta stay the same. There's a phone number you have to call if any of 'em rises, which is on the desk. If it rises you got one hour to get it back down. If you can't do it you have to phone the number. I'll show you the ways you move the temperature up or down. Two or three degrees is critical either side.'

'Otherwise what happens?' Floyd Pueblo said. 'She thaw out − or would it explode?'

'Search me,' Doheny smirked.

'Think I'd rather it exploded than thawed out,' Floyd said. 'Don't want some half-frozen zombie clambering out of that thing while I'm on shift.'

Doheny pushed a hand into his pocket and pulled out a pack of cigarettes. 'C'mon! It's all fucking bullshit. You get frozen, turns you to mush, turns you to pap the way a cow gets turned into a burger. You ever hear of a burger getting turned back into a cow?'

'Thanks,' Floyd said, thinking of his fast-cooling dinner sitting on the desk. 'Thanks a lot, pal, you've given me a real appetite.'

'Hundred and twenty-five thousand bucks they pay to get put in one of these.'

Floyd swallowed, and stared at the vats. Three years he'd been doing this job and he was still uneasy. A sharp metallic tap startled them both and they spun round. It had come from the cylinder behind. There was another tap, as if someone inside was knocking, and both men ran to it. Floyd stared, wide-eyed, at the temperature gauges. Both were steady on −196. The two men looked at each other.

Then the fat guard rapped back twice with his knuckles, waited a beat, and said: 'Knock-knock − who's there?'

In the silence, Floyd felt the skin tightening around his Adam's apple.

After another long pause, Doheny said: 'Contraction. I don't think the iceman cometh. Not yet, anyhows.' He swaggered back down towards the new arrival.

Floyd stayed where he was, his stomach feeling as muzzy

as his reflection in the burnished aluminium casing. 'Hope you're right,' he said uneasily.

12

Friday 22 January, 1993. Sussex.

On the television screen a cocky, short blond man who looked a bit flash was being brought down to earth by his wife. She'd just discovered that he was having an affair, and she was confused and hurt.

Joe lay slumped in his recliner armchair, his leather slippers perched precariously on the ends of his toes, his stomach aching. Friday nights Karen put too much on the table and he always ate it. He tried to resist but food was a weakness, and in spite of trying to keep fit and in shape he looked forward to the blow-out throughout the week. It was always a special evening. A sense of the completeness of the family unit that, with his mother dying when he was seven, he had not had as a child.

Tonight, as had been traditional throughout their marriage, they'd sat at the candlelit dining table and Karen had said the prayers: '*Baruch, attoh adenoi,*' she'd begun ... Then they had eaten: melon; gefilte fish; roast chicken and wild rice. Followed by non-dairy ice cream with hot caramel sauce.

Joe patted his stomach through his sleeveless pullover, testing its contours to make sure he wasn't getting a paunch, and watched the marriage on the television unbundle before his eyes. The wife was prettier than the mistress; that was often the case, he thought abstractedly.

Adultery had never really entered his mind before, and he was surprised by the interest with which he found himself watching the programme, absorbed by the husband's, the mistress's and the wife's actions and reactions.

As a teenager, and in his twenties until he'd met Karen,

Joe had been far more interested in the mechanics of sex than in relationships. He'd used his girlfriends to help him with his research into consciousness by wiring them up with electrodes before sex, to monitor their peaks and troughs, to make comparisons between oral sex, vaginal sex, anal sex and masturbation.

At first, under his persuasive influence, most of them found the experiments kinkily erotic. But after a while they'd got disillusioned when they realized that his interest in them did not extend beyond the laboratory of his bedroom.

Karen had been different. The very first time he met her, when she came to interview him, he'd felt a respect for her that he had never felt towards any other woman. He had courted her with an almost mystical fervour, as if reluctant to risk tarnishing her by trying to seduce her, and it had been four months before they had first slept together. Apart from ARCHIVE's camera in the bedroom, he had never attempted to subject her to any sexual experiment.

Before Barty's death they'd had a strong and sometimes pretty wild sex life together. Karen used to enjoy 'quickies' in risky places, such as in telephone booths, or in the car parked in the street – and once at the side of a busy roundabout – on night flights, spread out over a few seats, or in the washroom during daytime flights . . . But since Barty's death all that had stopped.

For a couple of years they scarcely made love at all. Joe, who'd always had strong desires, had understood that Karen needed time, and had compensated by concentrating even harder on his neural network designs for ARCHIVE. Now, in the three and a half years since Jack's arrival, they had a sex life of sorts again, but it was sporadic and the old spark had gone. Karen was tired most evenings from coping with Jack, and Joe worked late, absorbed with ARCHIVE. Karen was usually long asleep by the time he came to bed and he thought about sex more than he did it. Like the past few days since Juliet Spring had come into his office, when he had found himself feeling almost constantly horny.

'OK, Joe-Joe?' Karen said. Her face and cloak of black

hair blotted out the screen, and he felt her fingers lightly stroking his temples. It was a sensation he found so pleasant that he had to cross his legs when she went on doing it for five minutes, as she sometimes did. In the past few years Karen had dabbled in various New-Age fads. Massage was one of her latest. There was an erotic side to that which Joe found rather exciting, but usually Karen seemed to believe in practising it only on nonerogenous zones. He tilted his head to allow her greater access.

'D'you like that, Joe-Joe?' She kissed him lightly on the forehead. Her hair tickled the side of his face, and he absorbed its faintly tangy smell; some new organic scalp food she had started using, and he thought suddenly of the sensual muskiness of the perfume used by Juliet Spring who had come to see him earlier in the week, and he remembered how Karen had driven him wild when they'd first dated – simply by wearing the right kind of smells.

Juliet Spring.

He felt a flutter, like butterflies, in his stomach. Then another, sending a strange sensation that was part fear and part arousal washing through him. He closed his eyes and let Karen continue to massage his temples and imagined it was Juliet Spring. Then he looked again and saw the warm, confident expression in Karen's hazel eyes, and felt a heel for his straying thoughts.

What am I doing? he wondered. He knew he'd broken the spell because of his sudden and involuntary mental infidelity. From now on this was one seduction scene that had been deprogrammed. He glanced up through strands of her hair at the camera that was silently observing them in the corner of the room. Glanced at it guiltily, as if it could read his mind. As if there were no secrets at all from ARCHIVE.

Karen sat down on his lap. Sure enough, Joe felt he'd got his come-uppance. With the weight she'd put on, he had to struggle with his thighs to support her, and did not let on that she was crushing his balls as she entwined her arms around his neck and looked at him. 'Poor Joe-Joe's been so strained the last few weeks.'

He grunted noncommittally; it was near impossible to speak.

'Still thinking about your dad?'

He communicated acknowledgement with his eyes.

She leaned forward and kissed him lightly on the forehead, and her face blurred out of focus. Even so the pain was still there in her expression, etched into her skin. Bereavement. Still mourning the child they'd lost six years ago. Barty. Bartholomew Willi Messenger. Not quite four years old. Quite different from Jack. Jack had his father's hair, his fair good looks and his sharp blue eyes. Barty had had Karen's black hair, her straight, narrow nose that was almost too small for her face, and her faint scattering of freckles.

The behaviour of the two boys was quite different, also. Barty had been a hugger; quiet-natured and affectionate. He was always coming up to either one of them and putting his arms around them, as if wanting to be protected from the world. As if there was something out there beyond the family home that was bad. For a long time after his death Karen used to say to Joe that Barty had known he was going to die young; that that was what he'd been afraid of. Joe did not believe that, but he made no attempt to dissuade her. They each had to work through their grief in their own ways.

Jack, in contrast, was a confident, boisterous, inquisitive monkey, never happier than when he was working on some puzzle on his own, or 'designing' as he called his strange watercolour paintings, and they loved him desperately. Loved him almost too much. Were afraid of how much they loved him. Both of them, unspoken, knew how terrified they were of anything happening to him.

It had been three years after Barty's death before Karen had conceived again. During that time they went through tests and always the doctors could find nothing wrong. Trauma, they concluded each time; Karen was afraid of the pain of losing another child and her body was blocking pregnancy to protect her.

It wasn't only Karen who was afraid of the pain. Joe felt it just as strongly. For the first two years of Jack's life he'd barely slept at night, lying awake, listening to the crackles of static from the baby alarm, listening for a reassuring gurgle. Afraid of cot-death syndrome, and of the million other bad things that could happen to an infant.

Jack started at playschool next week for the first time. Joe wondered how Karen would feel about handing her son over to someone else; she was never really comfortable when they went out and left him with baby-sitters. He wondered how she would cope with him becoming more independent; whether she'd ever let him travel in someone else's car. And he wondered whether he would.

He could still remember the phone call from Karen; her voice down the receiver: just a terrible high-pitched wail; like computer noise, not a human sound. He'd taken the call in his office at the University of Toronto, and could recall clearly now, six years later, the face of the student who had been sitting with him, complaining about his grades. Remembered his name. His expression.

It was strange the details you could retain over the years, Joe thought. Some things imprinted on the memory so much more vividly and lastingly than others: the unexpected, the traumatic, the highs and the lows. The selectiveness of memory. It was a problem he had yet to overcome with ARCHIVE. ARCHIVE registered everything at the same level.

He could even remember the weather, a fine winter day, like today, a clear hard blue sky, except in Toronto there'd been snow on the ground, tired dirty snow that had been around too long.

Barty had been a few weeks from his fourth birthday, and Karen was pregnant with their second child. It was Barty's best friend's birthday. Dean Horowitz. Dean's dad was taking them to the Niagara peninsula for a treat. To see the Falls, go out in the boat, the *Lady of the Mist*, that went right near the bottom of the Falls and everyone on board would get drenched, even in the oilskins they gave you to put on, and then to the waxwork museum. Except they never got there. They got rear-ended on the 401 by a lumber truck and the car exploded in flames.

In the newspaper reports people said there were screams coming from inside the burning car. No one had been able to get near because of the flames. The police told Karen that Barty must have died instantly; the car was crushed like a sardine can. Often, in the months following, they would lie in bed and Karen would ask Joe if he thought Barty had suffered; if he thought Barty had been one of the ones who'd screamed. Joe always told her he didn't think so; but he used to go on wondering through each and every long night. He still did, sometimes, his imagination replaying those last moments until it got too horrible and he had to switch his mind to something else. A month after Barty died, Karen had miscarried.

It had been good to get away from Toronto, and it seemed like the doctors had been right. Within a couple of months of making the decision to move to England, Karen fell pregnant again. It was as if they had somehow managed to leave the horror behind, although Karen told him she felt guilty sometimes that they weren't able to tend Barty's grave. Secretly, Joe was glad. The trip they'd made to the cemetery every Sunday had just kept on reopening the wound. Now it really seemed like they had healed themselves – at least, as much as they ever would.

'. . . did you, Joe-Joe?' Karen kissed him again and he looked at her with a start, realizing he had drifted off into his thoughts, and wondered what she had said that he'd missed. On the television he heard a woman scream abuse and the man shout back; it was getting uglier. When love disintegrated into hate it always did get ugly. A draught blew across his legs, through the worn corduroy of his trousers. The windowpanes rattled. English houses all seemed to have draughts in winter.

'Let's go to bed, Joe-Joe.'

'Half an hour,' he said. 'I have to do a little work – something I need to take a look at.'

'Do it in the morning, honey, you look exhausted.'

'I'm OK. Start going up – I won't be long.'

Karen stood up, and Joe savoured the sudden absence of weight on his thighs, then with reluctance he heaved himself out of the chair. The woman on the television was in tears and a small girl was hugging her protectively. The scene made Joe feel dirty and uncomfortable, and he knew the reason why. He sat on the arm of the chair, watching, but after a few moments the credits began to roll.

He walked across to the window and parted the orange taffeta curtains. The room was furnished in apricots and oranges which gave it the illusion of warmth, and there were some antique oak and mahogany pieces of furniture. Karen wanted to move, was keen for them to have some place she could furnish and decorate herself, but Joe wasn't bothered. He didn't really mind where he lived, so long as he had a place to think and work in that was quiet.

As he pressed his face against the French windows, down the end of the garden he could just make out the silhouettes of the three conifer trees that separated the lawn from the small vegetable plot, swaying in the wind. Juliet Spring occupied his thoughts again. He could picture her face so clearly: the beauty; the sadness; the sense of desperation. He wondered what she was sad about. Had she lost a lover?

He should say no to her. Stick to his resolves. A part of him acknowledged that he found Juliet Spring attractive, and alarm bells were ringing. But what if, just maybe, she could be of help? On Monday evening he would find out. She had got permission for him to visit her lab.

And she herself had checked out well. He had rung people he knew at Cambridge and at Carnegie-Mellon where she'd studied. Both had said she was a brilliant student; hardworking, reliable and very dedicated. A fiery temper was the only bad thing they had to say. After four years of coping with Edwin Pilgrim, the prospect of a fiery temper did not perturb him.

He trod the stairs heavily, deep in thought, quietly opened Jack's door and stood for a moment watching his sleeping son, listening to his breathing. He smiled tenderly, his heart heaving, and sat quietly down on the tiny chair beside the bed. He wished he could stop the clock and savour this moment. Peace. Serenity.

He thought about the processes that were going on inside his own body, making this moment happen for him. Tried to work out the neural pathways currently activated in his brain. Did you need to replicate a mental state like this in a computer? Would it add to your life if you existed inside a computer? Were emotions necessarily different for biological and post-biological humans? Would a computer develop its own set of emotions relevant to its existence?

He closed Jack's door gently, walked down the landing, went into his small den which he'd converted out of a spare bedroom and turned on the light. He sat at his desk and stared at the blank screen of his terminal. Through a chink in the curtains he could see the houses across the deserted street. In the stark glare of the streetlighting they looked like cardboard.

Juliet Spring understood his work. She reckoned she had found the way to download a human brain. Wenceslas had joked about sharing a Nobel Prize. But there was nothing humorous behind the sentiment. If you could download a human brain into a computer you could live for ever.

If his father's brain had been downloaded ... if Barty's sweet little brain had been downloaded ... they'd both be here now. He'd be able to switch on ARCHIVE and say hi to them. Reassure them in case they were lonely and scared.

Reassure himself.

He looked at his blank Sun computer screen, thinking about ARCHIVE's strange warning. *Careful, Professor Messenger. She's a nasty little bitch.* Perhaps ARCHIVE was human enough to be having a mental breakdown, he mused.

Her proposal lay on his desk; he glanced through it again. If what she said was really true. If she had found the way to download a brain. If . . .

He pressed the return key to bring up the screen, and logged into ARCHIVE at the university down the leased line.

ARCHIVE's greeting appeared: Good evening, professor. It's a windy night.

Joe grinned privately, wondering whether ARCHIVE ever actually understood any of the remarks it made. Sometimes it felt uncannily as if it did.

Very windy, he typed back. Why did you call Juliet Spring a nasty little bitch?

There was a pause. His words went from the screen and he was startled to see them replaced with a colour photo of Juliet Spring seated in his office and: Correct Juliet Spring?

He stared at her face, feeling a tug of desire, and found himself wondering where she was now, at this moment. Out somewhere, with a boyfriend? The thought pained him. He pressed the carriage return as verification.

Be careful, Professor Messenger.

Joe frowned. Of what? he typed.

What? ARCHIVE replied on the screen. Who is what? Why is what? Wherefore who became from what which? Why? Who is why? Thesaurus. Bitch. Female animal. She-dog. Filly. Cow. Heifer. Vixen. Tigress. Sow.

Joe tried to exit from the system, but there was just a sharp beep and more gibberish came out. He pressed the two keys to exit again, but still nothing happened. He brought up a window and tried to kill the process. Still nothing happened. Finally he typed 11a and the machine began rebooting. Eventually the screen went blank except for the name of his machine, and the login prompt. He glanced up at the watching television camera, then down at the doctorate proposal.

Sometimes he wondered if there was something else behind that camera lens, other than the racks of silicon chips, in the basement of the COGS building, that decoded the signals the cameras transmitted. Something that watched and savoured his and Karen and Jack's every movement in here. Had he created something which he did not yet fully understand?

Something not completely friendly?

It felt like it tonight. He pressed his thumb against his nose and waggled his finger. Then he stuck his tongue out at the camera and made his eyes bulge. Then he went to bed.

Karen was waiting for him, reading a book. When they made love a short while later, he closed his eyes and imagined she was Juliet Spring. As he climaxed, he had to bite his tongue to prevent himself from calling out the student's name.

13

Joe hurried out of Victoria station into the darkness of the night, and turned up the collar of his Burberry against the heavy drizzle as he looked around for her car. A line of taxis filed past him, turning left into the station, reflections of their tail-lights dragging behind them along the glossy tarmac. A multiplex cinema across the road was showing *Strictly Ballroom*, *The Bodyguard* and *Dracula*.

A sharp beep startled him; he noticed the tiny Fiat a short way up the road, and hurried towards it. Peering hard, he could just make out Juliet Spring inside reaching over and unlocking the passenger door for him.

'Hi,' he said, clambering in and pulling the door shut. 'Sorry – the train was late.'

'It's OK,' she said with a trace of irritation, pushing her hair from her forehead; it slithered back like silk.

Joe glanced for a second time at the face in the half light of the interior, surprised not to have had a friendlier greeting in spite of being half an hour late. She looked angry and edgy. And even more attractive than he'd remembered. As he breathed in the intoxicating smell of her musky perfume, he felt a pang of sheer animal lust that surprised him.

She leaned forward and turned down the volume of a radio news programme. The car clock said 8.15. 'I thought perhaps you weren't coming,' she said tightly.

'No – just the train – we sat for about half an hour in the middle of nowhere; points problem or something. I'm sorry.'

She twisted the ignition key with a gloved hand, and the engine clattered into life. Joe reached over his shoulder and pulled down the seat belt. 'Are we OK for time?'

She glanced in the rear-view mirror and pulled out. 'I had some problems. There's been some industrial espionage going on at Cobbold, in another division, and they've had a major security clamp-down. I cleared it with my boss, but I had to be a little economical with the truth.'

'Oh, yes?'

'About who you were. I've told them you're a neural net expert who's coming to help me with a problem. Your name is Doug Cartwright.'

The thought flashed through Joe's mind of the explaining he might have to do if he was caught out. He shrugged it off; Juliet Spring was either nuts or genuinely had something, and at least this way he'd be finding out in the next hour or so. 'I hadn't realized you were devious,' he said with a grin.

'Devious? Never!' she said with feigned innocence, warming a little. 'I just believe that sometimes in research you need to keep quiet about things until you can understand them better.'

'Sure,' Joe said, pressing his feet into the floorwell as she drove much too close to the back of a bus. She changed gear, revving hard, pulled out and overtook the bus, ignoring the angry flash of oncoming headlights, and cut in smartly in front of it. Joe heard the bus hooting and felt the glare of its flashing lights. 'Nice car,' he said, apprehensively.

'Lousy acceleration,' she said.

'Really?'

She came up behind another bus and tailgated that for some moments before overtaking it in an equally precarious way. Joe began to wish he'd taken the tube or a taxi. They cut across Belgrave Square and down Wilton Place into Knightsbridge. As she waited for a gap in the traffic, she kept one hand on the wheel and one on the gear lever, gunning the engine. Although the ride was making him nervous, she was a skilful driver, and Joe was beginning to find her aggressiveness on the road strangely attractive.

'How's my friend ARCHIVE?' she said.

'ARCHIVE's fine. Well – I guess not totally fine – we have a fault right now that's driving us nuts. It keeps going into thesaurus mode and spouting gibberish. Get these glitches sometimes, though it's harder with a computer like ARCHIVE to work out whether it's a software or hardware problem.' He watched the bright lights of Harrods slide past on his left. 'We don't know whether a board has blown somewhere in the circuitry; or whether the computer, in trying to learn language and dialogue, has developed an over-emphasis on word selection. It's like a kid who gets a buzz out of taking a new word and mucking around with it.'

'It is a kid, isn't it?'

He grinned. 'A great big baby.'

'One super-smart baby.'

'Sure, it takes after its dad!' he said in a sudden peak of confidence.

Her tone became serious again. 'You said that ARCHIVE does a lot of learning by itself?'

'Yes. A lot of its learning is evolutionary – neural Darwinism, if you like.'

'How does that work? I mean, is it any different from the kind of neural nets I understand?' She accelerated as they approached an amber light and drove across on red.

Joe clutched the edges of his seat. 'I don't think so. Probably more elaborate, that's all. Take –' He held his breath for a moment, until they'd cleared the junction. 'Take learning to play chess, for instance. It writes its own programs to play. Only the programs that win for it get saved, the others it discards. It plays against other computers on the Internet – and against itself. Every time it loses, that losing program gets junked and replaced with a modified duplicate of the winning one. Law of the jungle.'

'How does that actually work?' she said, intrigued.

Joe checked the traffic ahead for some moments. 'I'm not entirely sure any more.'

'I thought you were joking the other day when you told me you didn't know how ARCHIVE worked. Then I read an article in *Scientific American* about a Professor Angstrom.'

'Per Angstrom at MIT?' Joe knew the Massachusetts Institute of Technology well.

'Yes. He was talking about a neural net computer he's got up and running, which has defence applications – and he said he'd no idea how it got a lot of its results. And what really freaked me was that he said that half the computer scientists in America don't really understand how their latest generations of computers worked.'

'It's true!'

'Isn't that a dangerous situation?'

Joe was silent for a moment. 'I guess there are always dangers in science; building the atomic bomb was dangerous. No one really knew what was going to happen when the first one was detonated. No one knew how the building of such weapons in the future could be controlled. The nuclear agenda was rolling long before Los Alamos; if the Americans hadn't built the bomb, the Germans would have done. Or the Japanese. Now the human-consciousness agenda is rolling.'

He watched the smeared lights of London through the windscreen, and listened to the clunking of the wipers. 'I created ARCHIVE deliberately to have a mind of its own. I know what its components are. I know that it currently has one hundred and eighty-five thousand individual processors working in parallel – it's like a massive telephone exchange. Every processor has to be capable of calling up any other one, and be capable of placing tens of thousands of calls a second. But ARCHIVE has to learn by itself, and beyond a certain point we have no way of telling how it's doing that – or even whether it's becoming aware of itself. All I know is that if it ends up being smarter than me, I'll have succeeded; and if it ends up dumber, I'll have failed!'

There was a silence between them for a moment. Something's troubling you, Juliet, he thought. He wanted to reach out to ask her what it was, but instead he said nothing because he was scared of how attractive he found her. Tonight was about an exchange of knowledge between scientists. That was all. If she impressed him, she might come and study under him. If she didn't impress him, and he suspected she wouldn't, he would thank her for her time and probably never see her again.

She continued down the Cromwell Road, then took the slip-off and drove beneath the Hammersmith flyover. A mile further on, Joe saw the Cobbold-Tessering sign illuminated in brilliant blue against the blackness of the sky, and realized he'd seen the building several times before when he'd travelled to and from Heathrow. It was a massive modern high-rise block, faintly sinister, with sharp contours and secretive smoked-glass windows.

Juliet turned the Fiat into the main entrance and drove into a huge, deserted car park at the rear, pulling up close to the wall. Then they walked quickly past the only other car, ducking against the thickening rain, and around to the front. The glass doors opened automatically into an imposing marbled atrium, on the far side of which a solitary security guard sat behind a desk. The walls were hung with framed colour photos of Cobbold-Tessering's factories and offices around the world, and advertisements for some of its consumer and trade medical products.

The security guard nodded in recognition at Juliet while Joe signed his false name and the time of his visit. He was given a computerized visitor's pass which he attached to his lapel, then followed Juliet over to a bank of elevators. There was an immediate ping as she pressed the button, and the doors of one slid open for them. She reached up and touched the button for the seventeenth floor.

'Do many people work here at night?' Joe asked.

'Not usually beyond about seven. One or two in research occasionally, and some of the computer engineers.'

'Swish building!'

'They can never get the heating right. Always too hot or too cold,' she said.

Always the same, thought Joe, man can't keep up with his own technology. He sets it up, then watches it misbehave. He suddenly resented the temperature-control system for its own failures. For failing to keep Juliet Spring at just the right heat.

The sharp upwards motion of the elevator played havoc with his insides. Juliet gave him a nervous smile, as if she was after reassurance, and he tried to think of something smart to say, but some of his confidence had deserted him. He felt as if he was in alien territory; an intruder; a spy. 'That's the problem sometimes with modern buildings,' he said, and realized how delayed and dumb the remark was.

When the doors opened, they stepped out into a wide, plushly carpeted corridor. Joe trailed at Juliet's side, having to walk fast to keep up. At the far end he could see a cleaner hoovering. Juliet stopped outside a door marked in gold lettering 'Research 4'. She inserted a plastic card into the lock then opened up and pressed a light switch. A row of fluorescents flooded the lab with flat white light.

It was a smaller room than Joe had been expecting, not much larger than a manager's office. There was a thick, lead-covered door with a large radiation warning sign leading through into another room he could not see, and a floor-to-ceiling window with an expansive view of West London and of the ribbons of lights on the M4 below.

Unlike the tatty, cluttered lab rooms at the university, this one had a clinical, businesslike feel to it. All the equipment looked new or nearly new and there was no hint of anything being botched together, the way much of his own students' gear was. State-of-the-art computers, monitors, oscilloscopes, flow hoods, incubators: all sat in purpose-built housings. There was a uniform whiteness to the casings, with the blues and greens of the screens, the black of coiled flexes and the steel of the sinks and taps in sharp contrast.

Joe glanced around, taking it in, recognizing some pieces

of equipment and trying to work out the functions of others. 'So this is the power house,' he said with a quizzical grin.

'One small cog in it,' Juliet Spring replied.

'Cray,' he said, nosily tapping a return key and looking at the login prompt on one processor, then nodding approvingly.

'I thought you were only impressed with neural nets – not sequential supercomputers.'

'I'm impressed by the power of the new generation Crays,' he said. 'We're hoping to get a few at the university as and when we can afford them. Part of ARCHIVE's hardware is modelled on a Cray's design. Money doesn't look like it's too much of a problem here.'

'It comes out of the taps!'

'Shame we can't move the university here . . .'

'Cobbold-Tessering are pretty generous, aren't they?' she said. 'They give a lot of funding to scientific research through the Cobbold Foundation.'

'Sure, they're OK, but only in very specific areas. And they take all the patents. They're tough in that way.' He glanced up at the grilles of the vents in the ceiling, at the telephone, at the walls, wondering suddenly if the room was bugged. Except he knew that if it was, he'd have no chance of spotting anything with his naked eyes.

'I didn't know that.'

He raised his eyebrows and nodded. 'It'll be in your contract as an employee.' He noticed a series of photographs of what looked like enlargements of neurons pinned to a grey board on the wall.

She peeled off her mac and hung it in a metal cupboard. 'I don't mind, as far as I'm concerned. Want me to hang your coat?'

Joe found himself looking hard at her again. She was wearing a simple dark green woollen dress that clung flatteringly to her slender contours, and a plain silver necklace. 'There speaks the true selfless scientist!' he said, slipping his coat on to the hanger she gave him. 'All our work is for the benefit of mankind – including the shareholders of Cobbold-Tessering.'

She laughed. 'If it's the quest for immortality, we all benefit in the long run anyway.'

'If we achieve immortality, society will have to change its outlook on a lot of things,' he said.

She looked sad again, suddenly. The sleek red tresses of her hair slid forward and she brushed them back with a sharp, almost angry sweep of her hand. Joe walked over to a complex machine he didn't recognize. It had a small display screen to which was attached a complex array of clear plastic tubing feeding into a wide plastic flask, in the top of which were inserted glass test tubes like pegs in a game of solitaire.

'What's this?' he said. 'A chemical analyser?'

'It's a neurotransmitter optimizer.'

He frowned. 'What does it do?'

'We use it for testing the load capacity of neural pathways.'

He continued to frown.

'I'll show you next door. It was made for us, but it's being marketed to other neuroscience researchers now.'

'Maybe we should have one at the university?'

'You may not need it. I think it's fulfilled its purpose,' she said with a tease in her expression, and rotated the handle on the lead door.

'This where you keep the gold ingots?' Joe said.

'No, something very much better.' She reached in and switched on the light.

In the centre of the floor and dominating the starkly clinical room was a massive piece of machinery, the main bulk of which was a white-painted steel cylinder lying lengthways, about eight feet long and six high, with an opening at one end that had a raised hood and a long narrow metal tray. Attached to the side of it was a curved console housing dials, gauges, oscilloscopes and a bank of six VDU screens. A mass of wiring ran off into a Sun workstation connected to a tall RAID disk array and a Terabyte tape drive that resembled a CD player.

On some shelving was a dark grey SQUID scanner that looked in shape much like a German army helmet from the Second World War, except that neatly interspersed with the metal were columns of rectangular glassy strips and the sockets for two electrode jacks. Joe looked back at the massive white machine. 'Where do you stick the coin in?'

She didn't seem to get the joke for a moment, then she smiled. 'Oh – right – only takes gold sovereigns, I'm afraid.'

He grinned. 'It's a Positron Emission Tomography scanner?'

'Well, it's basically a heavily modified PET scanner that uses both PET and SQUID scanning, combined with 40,000 to 80,000 megahertz radio scanning. It's one of several brain-mapping systems we use in developing our intelligence-booster smart drugs.'

Joe's eyes widened: 'I've done some tests in the past in all these areas – but not together! Who built it?'

'This is a one-off built for Cobbold-Tessering.'

'Were you involved?' Joe asked.

She blushed. 'Yes. I – actually I was involved with the whole conception.'

'It was your idea?' Joe said, his amazement increasing the more he thought about the machine.

'Partly.' She suppressed a smile, looking pleased with herself for impressing him. 'But the really big breakthrough has happened with a new drug we've been developing.'

'How come?'

'Well –' She glanced around, as if scared someone was listening, and lowered her voice a little. 'The way we have it set up, it gives a simultaneous 3-D image of the total surface area of the brain.' She hesitated. 'There's one particular new drug – its code name is CTS 6700 – that we've been experimenting with and which we're hoping to market in a couple of years' time. It has an incredible effect on long-term memory retrieval. Our view has very much become that people don't actually lose their memory as they get older, the encoded information doesn't fade, but what does go is the ability to retrieve memory – to access it.'

'That would make sense,' Joe said. 'How have you tested the drug?'

'Initially we tried it only on rats, but for the last ten months we've been doing clinical trials with Alzheimer's patients.'

'Right.'

'But the drug does something else, which I started noticing a few months ago when I was running tests on rats using an adaptation of the SQUID.' She seemed to become more tense suddenly and clenched her hands together. As she did so, Joe saw she was wearing a silver ID bracelet. On the flat of it was a small red staff and entwined serpent, the international MedicAlert symbol. He wondered if she had an allergy, or maybe she was an organ donor.

She walked a short way across the room and stopped by a metal cabinet. 'As it gets absorbed into the brain it triggers off a chain reaction of electro-chemical activity. I thought at first I was giving too heavy a dosage, so I kept reducing it, but the effect still continued. It would last from anywhere between half an hour to several hours, depending on the dosage.'

'And the brain would settle back to normal?'

'Yes. I got the impression it was inducing some sort of quasi-epileptic response, and I was curious to find out what it really was.'

'How were these registering on the scan?'

'Just as electrical activity.'

'Was there any pattern to it?'

'I didn't think so. Not at first. None that I could see, at least.'

'Any movement of limbs? Were the rats and mice asleep during this?'

'No, awake. CTS 6700 doesn't seem to affect the motor areas – there's no altered activity apparent in the motor cortex or cerebellum.'

Joe thought about this for a moment. It was quite possible for drugs to affect some areas of the brain but not others.

'Then I tried experimenting using the combined principles

of the SQUID and the Positron Emission Tomography – PET,' she said. 'I put rats inside the scanner without having given them the drug, but instead introduced various stimuli: food, water, opposite sex, fear. I did a series of colour print-outs of the activity that was registering on the scans and compared them afterwards. There were very different patterns for each stimulus.'

Joe nodded. 'There would be on a conventional EEG scan also.'

'On a conventional EEG you'd just get different peaks and troughs. This goes far beyond that.' She opened a drawer of the filing cabinet and pulled out two large envelopes. From one she removed a series of sheets of paper, and laid an example down on a flat work surface.

Joe looked closely. It was a multi-layered, multicoloured computer print-out unlike anything he'd ever seen before. The dominating image was a fine grid of varying width, composed of crisscrossing black spikes – some straight, some conical, some fat, some almost invisibly thin, and ranging from several inches in length to fractions of an inch. There were thousands of them, and they reminded Joe faintly of an endless prairie of cacti.

As he looked closer he could see similar images in different pastel colours, all superimposed on each other; reds, blues, greens, yellows, greys, browns. The effect, Joe thought, utterly fascinated, was of staring into a kind of virtual eternity.

'Number one is the rat's reaction to food – mixed corn,' Juliet Spring said.

Joe moved his head back a little, trying to see if he could discern an overall pattern or form to the spikes, but was unable to.

'Number two is arousal,' she said. 'I introduced a female.'

The pattern changed; it was still the same composites, but the colour emphases were different, and the shapes and closeness of the spikes were also noticeably different.

'They're very complex,' he said. 'Clearly relate to electrical activity going on in the brain.' He studied the print-outs again very carefully. 'You think there's information here that could be digitized and decoded to reveal actual thoughts?'

Without saying anything for a moment, she took out a set of print-outs from the second envelope. Beneath the print-out of the rat's reaction to corn, she laid another sheet, marked *1-A*.

'Have a close look at those two and tell me if you see any resemblances.'

Joe studied them for a moment. They were extremely similar; very slight differences in some of the spikes, but the colour tones matched and the general organization of the two patterns matched.

'Pretty close?' she said.

'Yes.'

She then laid a second sheet below the print-out of the rat's reaction to a female. Again they were very similar.

'And those?' she asked.

'Yes.'

She took two more print-outs from the first envelope and placed two near-matching ones from the second beneath them. Then she looked back at Joe with a hint of triumph in her expression.

'The first set of print-outs as I told you were of the brain activity of one particular rat, under the scanner, but without being given any drug, being presented in turn with food, water, sex and danger. Right?'

'Sure,' Joe said quietly, beginning to understand where this was leading.

'The second set are of the same rat under the scanner, without being presented with anything but simply having been injected with CTS 6700.'

Joe scrutinized the print-outs again, even more closely. 'I'd like to see these at a bigger scale.'

'We can do that,' she said. 'You'll see even more detail – and some of it actually matches completely.'

He looked back at her. 'And what are your conclusions?'

'These tests were performed fifty times with the same rat, and the results were consistent with other rats.' She came over and stood beside him, looking down at the print-outs herself. 'I've been using an AI program to get these matches. It's taken nearly a year, but I was convinced I'd find them.'

'How do you mean?'

'Those print-outs are of an approximately one hundredth of a millimetre square section of brain. When the rat was presented with food, from the scanner I was able to map its brain states in sections of that size. It was this particular section of its brain that produced more or less the same pattern each time food was introduced, so I consider it a reasonable assumption – not a totally safe one, I agree – that I've identified and been picking up the section of the rat's memory that relates to mixed corn.'

Joe nodded. 'There could be several other explanations, but I'd agree it's a reasonable assumption.' He peered more closely. 'So how did you get the match?'

'Sheer slog! Actually, the Sun did most of it, but it took a long time. I gave the rats in a zero-stimulus environment the CTS 6700 smart drug, then mapped all the brain states in hundredth of a millimetre segments – the smallest the SQUID would register – then used the computer search for matches. If there'd been identical matches it would have been easier, but there weren't – just very close ones. I had to get the Sun to work on approximations.'

'I've had the same problem with ARCHIVE,' Joe said. 'The human brain works on approximations a lot of the time.'

She was so intent on her explanation that she barely heard his remark. 'I finally found these matches; all four of them. If you study them closely you'll see there are huge similarities in terms of numbers of spikes, location, density, colour matches. My conclusions are that these are beyond coincidence. If I can get a brain image from a drug that matches a brain image from a known recognition of corn, then I think it's deductible that what I'm doing is actually reading the rat's encoded memory.' She looked at Joe quizzically.

Joe was silent, considering it all. A wave of excitement was building inside him, but it was tempered with caution. He'd had hopes raised and dashed too many times in his life. The test was interesting, but there might be a less exciting explanation than the one the girl was trying to convince him of.

He knew of no drug that was capable of triggering information encoded in brains. And no scanning machine that was capable of detecting it, if it did. Yet he knew also from all the surprises science had sprung on mankind that nothing could be ruled out.

'What about humans?' he asked. 'What experiments have you tried on humans?'

14

Without replying, Juliet went to a drawer and opened it. She removed a plastic vial and shook out a small gelatin capsule, which she held out to Joe. 'Feel brave?' She stared at him with a look of such hope in her emerald eyes that he thought she might cry if he turned her down.

He raised the capsule up to the light and studied the contents. It contained several mixed grains of a blue and a grey substance. She watched him anxiously, like a mother waiting for a sick kid to swallow a morsel of food. 'You'll feel a little light-headed,' she said. 'That's all.'

Careful, Professor Messenger, she's a nasty little bitch.

He thought of the warning. But she had checked out. The two universities she had been to approved of her, even if ARCHIVE did not.

He considered the downside for some moments: maybe she was crazy and wanted to kill him. Unlikely. Perhaps the drug would kill him. There was always a risk of allergic reactions when you took experimental drugs. But he'd taken risks all his life. And he'd taken dozens of hallucinogenic drugs when he was younger, without ever having had a bad trip. He doubted there was anything in the tablet he couldn't cope with. 'Tell me what the contents are, exactly.' If nothing else, Joe wanted a few moments' thinking time before he went inside the scanner.

'It's a combination of vasopressin, vinpocetine, Hydergine, acetycholine and centrophenoxine. And there's a low-dosage radioactive tag for the scanner.'

Joe knew them. Individually they'd all been passed as safe 'smart' drugs, but he'd not come across them in this combination before. He ran through them mentally. Vasopressin was the brain hormone that got released when people took cocaine, LSD or amphetamines. Vinpocetine speeded up the brain's metabolism. Hydergine boosted blood supply to the brain and speeded metabolism in brain cells. Acetycholine was a neurotransmitter. Centrophenoxine he was particularly interested in. It wasn't merely an intelligence booster and a synaptic rejuvenator, it had been discovered that it increased the lifespan of laboratory animals by thirty per cent.

He popped the capsule in his mouth and swallowed. The worst that could happen, he reckoned, was that he'd have a bad headache.

'Want a glass of water?'

He shook his head. The capsule lodged halfway down his throat; he swallowed harder and felt the capsule slip deep down his gullet. Only then did he feel a faint prick of anxiety. He stared at the steely grey of the scanner's casing and the shiny dome-like cover that was raised. His ears were full of the flat, dead hiss of the heating system.

'It'll take about half an hour to work,' she said, closing the leaded door and turning the handle, locking it from the inside. His mouth dried. He was acutely aware they were alone on this floor. Himself and Juliet Spring. But she knew what she was doing, he reassured himself. Redhead *extraordinaire*. She was intelligent, competent, used to carrying out experiments. And there was many a man who'd give his eye teeth to be at her mercy, mused Joe.

His eyes followed her as she walked across to the massive machine and pressed several switches. There was a deep electronic resonance. The central VDU monitor, which was the largest, lit up a deep cobalt-blue colour, and several dials began to flicker. She told him to remove his shoes and sit down on the metal tray. 'I hope you're not claustrophobic,' she said. Her voice sounded normal; crisp, upper-class English, lacking a little confidence.

'No,' Joe said. His own voice came out unnaturally high-pitched, like a squeak, he thought, padding in his socks to the tray.

'Have you ever had a virtual-reality headset on?' she asked.

'Yes, a few times.'

'This will feel much the same, except you can't move around. You'll see the same image as that monitor,' she said, pointing at the VDU. She fitted the SQUID helmet over his head, removed his watch, eased him on to his back on the tray, then slid the tray slowly forward until his head was inside the cylinder.

He felt increasingly anxious as he became enveloped in almost total darkness and the drumming resonance became muffled. Although he didn't usually suffer from claustrophobia, he'd never been comfortable in small enclosed spaces. A strong smell of greasy hair filled his nostrils. He was breathing fast, he realized. Something touched and then began pressing down hard against his forehead and his temples, like a clamp tightening around his skull; he could see only the faintest streaks of light if he looked directly down his nose.

Then he felt something take his right wrist; fingers. Firm, thin fingers, but icily cold; it was the first time he'd touched her skin, he realized, and he suddenly had a sharp flash in his mind of her unzipping his trousers and making rough, brutal love to him while he sat with his head in the darkness inside this machine.

He reddened at the thought, startled by the sudden eroticism that had swept through him, and realized with embarrassment that he was getting a hard-on. He hoped it didn't show. Sweat trickled down the nape of his neck. Something metallic was being clipped around his wrist.

There was a sharp crackle of static, then he heard Juliet Spring's voice, too loud, through a speaker. 'Are you OK, professor? Is that comfortable?'

He tried to nod his head, but found he couldn't move it. 'Uh huh,' he grunted.

'I can't hear you too well in there. If you're OK, pat your thigh once with your hand. If you need to come out at any time, pat your thigh repeatedly with your hand. What I'm putting around your wrist is a pulse-rate monitor just as a precaution. OK?'

Joe grunted again. Then he was startled by the brilliant blue light in front of his eyes. For a moment there was a dazzling blur, then the sharp screen of a VDU monitor came into focus. It looked as if it was several feet away, and he wondered if it was a projection of the monitor in the control housing of the scanner.

A silent blip of light suddenly traversed the monitor in a straight line. It was followed by another, then another. Slowly, line by line, the screen began to fill with them. They were straight at first, then they began to form zig-zagging waves of spikes and troughs, until there were about fifty different lines, each with a different pattern of spikes, some sharp, some with gentle contours. Joe recognized some of them as EEG brainwave scans. They continued to change, becoming sharper, then more gentle, then flattening out altogether for some moments. That made Joe anxious, and as he became anxious they jumped back into sharp spikes.

He realized with a start that they were reacting to his thoughts. He concentrated hard on relaxing and watched them flattening down. Then he tried to imagine Juliet Spring naked and the entire screen transformed into sharp, bristling spikes. When he imagined himself on a sunbed, drifting on a flat warm sea, the spikes dropped again. He continued to experiment, forgetting his fear, fascinated. He had been on biofeedback systems, trying to understand and learn from them in order to apply them to ARCHIVE, but he'd never before seen anything that could work on brainwaves.

'All OK, professor?' Juliet's voice broke through his thoughts.

He patted his thigh once. He was beginning to relax, to become more confident. He sharpened the spikes, then flattened them; as he did so he experienced a wave of giddiness. It was rapidly replaced by nausea. He tightened, beginning to panic; the nausea was worsening, he was going to throw up any moment. He tapped his thigh sharply.

'Are you feeling nauseous, professor? Do you think you're going to be sick?' she said. 'Give one pat if that's what you feel.'

Joe gave the single pat.

'You won't be sick. You'll just feel nauseous for a few minutes. When that passes we'll be nearly ready.'

Joe suddenly noticed strange things were happening to the waves. More seemed to have joined them, but these were vertical instead of horizontal. Then more still, diagonal, until there was a thick mesh of lines so close together they were becoming indistinguishable. Slowly they blended completely together until the whole screen became a flat blue, like sky. The colour dimmed, until he was staring at the totally blank screen of the monitor. Yet he was aware something was different; *he* felt different; a floating sensation; it was as if in staring at the monitor he was staring at his mind.

'We're ready to start, professor. Are you OK now?'

Joe tapped his thigh once.

'I'd like you to imagine an object – what I want is for you to simply visualize it. Pick something simple, a box or a chair, or a tree. Whatever it is, concentrate really hard and don't let your mind wander on to anything else; just hold that one image and keep holding it for as long as you can.'

Joe thought for a moment. An image of a tree came into his mind, a child's simple drawing of an oak. The screen stayed blank.

Joe concentrated on the oak tree. His mind slipped from a child's drawing to a real oak tree then back again. It slipped from the tree to paper, crayons. He saw the tree in colour first, then in grey pencil lead, then in ink. He tried to hold the image of the tree consistent. Then he saw something happening on the screen.

At first it was just shadow; then like a photographic image developing on bromide paper, lines began to appear, crisscrossing the screen. They formed a constantly changing kaleidoscope of amorphous blobs, coils, whorls and spirals. While in his mind the form of the tree continued to clarify.

Leaves were appearing. It was turning, Joe realized with increasing astonishment, from a child's drawing into a colour photograph. As it did so, the lines on the screen were intensifying in activity and density. He was so fascinated by them, he was finding it hard to concentrate on the visual image in his mind. Then he suddenly noticed a swing hanging from the tree, a basic job made from two lengths of rope and a plank.

Made by his father.

There was grass around the oak tree. A closeboard wooden fence with a slat missing. A garden sprinkler from which water was jetting. A plastic paddling pool with toys floating in it. A shed. A tall silhouette developed into the rear of a house. He could see the flyscreen on the rear porch door, the vent on the kitchen window. Someone inside the house, a woman moving around, indistinct through the window. His mother. She disappeared, then the flyscreen opened and her head appeared, long fair hair, a Snoopy apron. She was calling out. 'Joe! Joe!' He could see her now, running out of the door, coming towards him, crying.

Then suddenly the image began to fade; the sobbing went and at the same time the electronic images on the screen began to disintegrate and weaken in intensity. Joe lay rigid, his mind churning, trying to place what he'd just seen against the reality of his memory. It was the day his grandfather had died; his mother's father. He was six and it was the first time he'd ever known anyone who'd died.

So vivid, he realized. He hadn't even thought about that moment for years. And yet a few seconds ago he'd relived it with crystal clarity. He felt oddly detached, as if he were in a cinema and could choose whether to watch the contents of his mind or the screen of the monitor.

A face came into his mind next; then the shape of a great big fourteen-year-old boy. Tab Bullows. The name locked into Joe's mind; he repeated it silently over and over, closing his eyes to tighten his concentration. Tab Bullows. The bully from school.

When he opened his eyes, there was nothing but coils and zig-zags across the screen. Then he thought of another name from school: Susan Margolis. He remembered her face, serious, bespectacled, her hair in plaits. Remembered how he'd persuaded her to let him wire her head with electrode pads hooked up to the oscilloscope he'd rehabilitated from a junkyard. He used to subject her to stimuli to measure her brainwaves; then he'd grossed her out by showing her a picture of two people screwing, and she'd refused to be his guinea pig any more.

Again and again, the names of his classmates, forgotten for years, suddenly and vividly returned without any conscious effort. They and their faces continued to reel off in front of him. Pip Hudson. Carrie Nelson. Naomi Engel. Gordon Stultz. Susie Clearwater. Joe could only watch in amazement as the display of coils and zig-zags continued on the screen and name after name poured through his mind. Then the first name came back: Tab Bullows. As it did, he noticed a change in the images on the screen; larger, more complex shapes were appearing. Tab Bullows' face loomed crystal clear in his mind, then his whole body began to appear. Hulking, untidy Bullows with his swanky walk and shirt tails always outside his trousers, striding towards him, leering at him. Tab Bullows spoke, and he could hear him as if he were in the room. More than that, he could *see* his voice on the screen: a meaningless jumble of signals that changed with every word.

'Hey, creep, hear your dad likes freezing people.' Tab Bullows held out his hand and kept coming. 'Word is he's got a whole fridge full of dead people. Sounds like he's a regular ghoul! Maybe he'd like to have you frozen too. We're just going to try you out in the freezer for a few hours and see how you get on, creep.'

Then Joe began to remember more snatches of schoolboy conversations from over twenty-five years ago. All accompanied by a fresh jumble of symbols. It felt as though he were fast-forwarding through sections of an old videotape. The clarity was unbelievable.

The scene in his mind shifted suddenly to a birthday. He was back in the garden of his parents' home and his father was teaching him to ride a bicycle. They were going up and down the lawn, the bicycle was wobbling and his father was speaking.

Suddenly his father's face changed to the shrivelled version Joe had seen on Willi's corpse in the Los Angeles morgue. Then Joe saw the arrogant face of the Coroner's investigating officer, Howard Barr. He tried to switch away from his mind, to look at the screen, but it was full of steep spikes, as if he were deep in a gully between cliffs, and that frightened him. The image of the officer faded and Joe was travelling somewhere in a car. The road ahead was winding through a broad canyon. The image faded. The VDU screen was calm. Squiggles like waves.

Slowly another image began to form in his mind. It was his wife, Karen. She was sitting naked on top of someone; a man with his legs splayed open and thin, bony arms gripping the flesh on her back, making small indents. She was arched over him, her body a little flabby, her bottom raising and lowering, constricting and expanding as she thrust, vigorously making love. Then Joe saw the man's face and realized it was himself, and placed the memory: it was in a hotel a few years ago when she was pregnant with Jack, somewhere near Oxford, a country-house hotel where they'd slept in a room with a massive bed and a mirrored ceiling.

His face burned. Juliet Spring was watching this! He tried to switch his mind to something else, but the intimate image wouldn't go away; and it was making him feel horny watching it, thinking about it. He could hear Karen's grunts, except they weren't Karen's but strange, synthesized noises. And he could hear another synthesized voice, which must be his own, he registered with horror, shouting, 'Yes! Oh yes, yes yes!' After this the boundary became blurred between what he was watching and what he was thinking. He was getting confused. Juliet Spring was watching the symbols on the screen, not this actual image; not the memory itself.

But the symbols on the screen were the memory.

Then finally the image faded, and he felt a queasy sensation returning. His mind seemed to be frozen; he tried to think, but couldn't focus on anything; suddenly feeling drained. The screen sat in front of him, solid blue. He heard a distant whining sound and was aware that the drumming resonance had ceased.

Silence.

'Juliet,' he said, 'I feel really weird. You'd better take me out now.

He heard a clanking above his head; the pressure eased on his skull, then he felt cool air on his face. The tray rattled as he realized he was sliding forward, and a light above his face dazzled him. He closed his eyes and when he opened them again, Juliet Spring was watching him anxiously.

'Are you OK?'

Joe smiled back, feeling a lot better suddenly, although a little disoriented; the inside of his head was sore, not an ache, more a raw feeling, and the nausea he had felt earlier was returning. 'Fine.'

He was aware of the click-whirr-click-whirr tape drive of a computer close by, and looked round for a clock. 'What's the time?'

'Nine-thirty.'

He closed his eyes for a moment and found that was more comfortable. 'How long have I been in there?'

'Twenty-five minutes.'

He opened his eyes again. 'Quite a cocktail you gave me!'

'Did you remember a few things you'd forgotten about?'

'Yes, I did. You reckon the scanner picked them up?'

She gave him an odd, knowing smile. 'I don't think it can have missed much.'

'What makes you say that?' He sat up, then felt dizzy for a moment, fighting the nausea. The click-whirr-click-whirr of the Sun computer continued. When he recovered she was standing beside it.

'I can tell from how much memory has been used up. Everything from the scanner goes through a digital converter into this Sun workstation. If it's too much for the Sun's core memory to contain, it puts it through compression and tries again. It can take it down through three compression factors of one hundred thousand. If that's still too much, it downloads on to temporary RAID storage; then the RAID downloads on to a Terabyte cassette tape. That's what it's doing now.'

He watched the machine for some moments. 'Jesus. How much stuff has it picked up?'

She smiled again. 'The entire contents of your brain. It's downloading it at the moment.'

15

Joe walked over to the workstation, feeling light-headed and still a little giddy; he put his hand on the desk top to steady himself. He noticed a sign by the door: WARNING LIGHT MUST BE SWITCHED ON WHILE SCANNER IN OPERATION. The sign was in cream plastic with red letters. It was fixed to the wall by four steel screws. He strapped his watch back on, the old Rolex with its faded, yellowing face, that had belonged to his father. He saw the hairs on his wrist flatten beneath the metal slats of the strap. Detail; he was observing detail with a strange intensity. He noticed the veins on the back of his hand raised through the flesh like wormcasts in sand. A wave of paranoia struck him. He was in this room but not in it. It felt almost as if he were outside his body looking in.

He gripped the hard wood of the desk for reassurance, looked down at the blue ribs of the corduroy weave of his trousers and the cloth shone back at him. It seemed as if a brightness rheostat had been turned up inside his head. He checked his watch again. 9.35. A round, institutional clock on the wall confirmed it. Juliet Spring had picked him up from Victoria station at 8.15. They'd arrived here when? About twenty to nine. He'd signed the visitor's book downstairs. Signed the time of entry. 8.41. Yes, he remembered that. The precision of his entry.

Downloading.

'You – the Sun – downloaded my brain?' He looked for a hint of humour; for a sign that she was joking. But she stared back with a deadly serious expression.

'Yes.'

He stared at the Sun again. 'Could you explain exactly what you mean?'

She looked at the floor, then at Joe. 'The human brain has ten to the power of fourteen synapses, doesn't it?'

'Approximately, yes,' Joe said.

'You'd need one byte of computer memory per synapse?'

'We don't really know. But that's a reasonable assumption.'

'So if you were to scan the entire content of a human brain, ignoring any motor and low-level sensory functions, then you should pick up approximately one hundred million megabytes of information?'

Joe thought for a moment. 'I guess somewhere in that area.'

'That's how much the scanner picked up from you. That's what the Sun is downloading. Ten million gigabytes.'

Joe looked at the tape drive, then at the master VDU screen, which was blank. He didn't believe what he was hearing. 'Can you put up on the screen what it's doing?'

She tapped a couple of keys. The screen filled with columns of hexadecimal digits; every possible combination of pairs of digits from 0–9, and letters between *a* and *f*. They changed so fast it was impossible to read them, but they made him think uncannily of the encoded information retrieved by Wenceslas from the dead brain, Amanda, in the lab. He looked closer, to see if he could detect any pattern or sequence, but the digits remained for only a fraction of a second before changing.

'It'll take about an hour and a half to finish the download,' she said. 'We could go out and have a drink.'

'And leave my brain here?' Joe said with a smile.

'At least you'll now have a tape back-up.'

Joe looked at her warily. '*Might*,' he said.

'Sorry! *Might* have a back-up.'

They took the lift down to the lobby. Joe was deep in thought.

'You'll feel better if you eat something,' she told him. 'When the brain's accelerated like that it has quite an effect on your metabolism.'

His legs were feeling weak as the elevator plunged downwards and he held the handrail for support. 'Not just my metabolism. I feel like I've been nuked!'

'You'll be fine when you've had some supper. There's a little Italian place down the road; just a short walk.'

He released his grip on the rail as the elevator doors opened and was surprised to find that his legs held. He took a tentative step forward then another. The action revived him a little. 'Italian? Fine.'

Questions were buzzing in his mind. The idea that the scanner could have picked up the entire content of his brain was contrary to everything he currently knew and understood. Sure, he believed it would one day be possible. But not at present. And yet all his instincts as a scientist told him there was something in this experiment that merited scrutiny. She was a bright girl who was playing with fire. Mostly with fire you got your fingers burnt. Just occasionally you discovered pure gold.

The restaurant was simple, a family affair, father, mother, daughter. One narrow room with a handful of plastic wood-veneer tables, each set with a vase containing a small spray of artificial carnations. There were framed posters of Mount Vesuvius and Pompeii on the walls, and empty, wicker-covered Chianti bottles shoulder to shoulder along a shelf at picture-rail height. It had a desultory, Monday-evening feeling, with only one other table occupied, by a gormless-looking man in a shell suit, and a woman in a baggy jumper.

As he sat down, Joe watched both of them silently forking pasta into their faces. There was a faint aroma of coffee and a stronger smell of grilling meat which made him appreciate that he was very hungry. The walk had revived him considerably, although the inside of his head still felt raw.

He told Juliet the gist of the memories he'd had, leaving out the one of his making love to Karen. The realization of what had happened was beginning to take a deeper hold on him. If the contents of his brain – or even just a small part of them – had really been recorded, the implications were awesome. The only way to find out whether they had was to decode the information now on tape. They'd had no luck decoding Amanda, but Juliet Spring held the key to what they had to do: make comparisons with and without the drug. Find patterns that matched.

Excitement rose in him. Could it be that this beautiful girl across the table had unlocked the secret of downloading human brains into computers?

The secret of immortality.

The waitress shyly placed two menus on the table and a basket of bread. Joe noticed her glance admiringly at Juliet as she asked if they'd like anything to drink.

Joe ordered a lager. Juliet asked for a glass of red wine. He took a roll, tore a chunk off and ate it ravenously. 'Have you tried this drug CTS 6700 on anyone else?'

'Just myself.' Juliet pushed the cuffs of her woollen dress back and he could see the silver MedicAlert tag clearly on her wrist. 'I've been experimenting with different dosages, but the lab technicians who've operated the scanner for me don't know what I'm actually doing. You're the only other person – I thought –' she flipped back her hair nervously, '– you know, that you'd understand the ramifications.'

'Have you had any success decoding any of your own download?'

She shook her head. 'There is a problem. A rat brain is only a few square millimetres, but even so searching through rat downloads one hundredth of a millimetre at a time took six months before I found the first match. The human brain

129

is vast in comparison. I've tried, but even with these latest-generation Suns, it's like looking for needles in haystacks; I need a much more powerful and smart computer.'

'How would that help you?'

'Well, you need control images, right? Like with the rat and the corn. If we take something simple –' she thought for a moment '– You said that you visualized an oak tree first: if I put you under the scanner, without giving you the drug and present you with a photograph of that actual tree from your childhood, that will create signals in your brain, which we should pick up. Somewhere in the signals we've just downloaded from when you were under the influence of the drug *and* thinking of that oak tree, we should find a match. Shouldn't we?'

'Possibly. It doesn't necessarily follow that there will be correlations between human and rat memory triggers. Human thought process is obviously more complicated. But it's worth exploring.'

'I think the simplification is the problem. Rats see corn within a narrow band of food possibilities; they probably store corn recognition in a relative handful of bytes. But how many bytes in a human brain would it take to store the image of an oak tree? There are certain bits of information that make up our understanding of trees. We know they have bark, leaves, branches and that birds nest in them, and so on.' She raised her eyes and Joe nodded.

'On top of that,' she said, 'we have some information exclusive to oak. We know that oak trees have acorns; we can remember the shape of an oak leaf. Oak is solid, makes good doors. We all know at least one song about an oak – *Tie a yellow ribbon round the old oak tree*. So there's a raft of relevant information already stored in our brains. Hundreds of bytes – probably thousands; enough to form an identifiable pattern. Enough to get a match. Except that it has to be found.' She touched the top of the table lightly, as if she was about to draw a diagram. 'We have to look and find a match for maybe a few hundred bytes in ten billion.'

Joe leaned back in his chair. 'I see the problem. A neural net connectionist machine would be way faster for you.'

Their drinks arrived and the waitress asked if they were ready to order. Joe told her they'd like a few more minutes. Then he raised his glass.

'To immortality,' he said.

Juliet hesitated, trying to read him, then lifted her wine glass slowly. 'Immortality,' she said, her eyes suddenly filled with an expression of hope that touched him.

'And to post-biological man!' he added.

She sipped her wine then stared at him over her glass. 'And post-biological woman?'

'No offence,' Joe said. 'I meant it generically.'

She smiled and continued looking at him. 'In one of your books you wrote that if it were possible to download the contents of your brain into a computer you could make back-up copies of yourself. So that if you died, you'd be able to live on inside a computer *and* still have spare copies of yourself. Do you believe you could have a decent quality of life inside that computer?'

'Why not? Possibly a far better quality of life than we have in our physical bodies. We're computers now – biological ones. We don't work that well, we often go wrong, and we don't last very long. We even have built-in obsolescence which a lot of us don't live long enough to need.'

She grinned at the menu. 'Could you enjoy food and wine if you were inside a non-biological computer?'

'A big part of our work on ARCHIVE is in trying to understand why we feel pleasure. I think we're very close not only to being able to replicate the kinds of pleasures human biological bodies experience, but actually to improve on them as well.' He was feeling, suddenly, in a terrifically buoyant mood. 'If you lived in a computer, in some kind of a virtual world, you could command any pleasure you wanted! You could get drunk without having a hangover, you could binge out without getting fat!'

She looked straight into his eyes, with a twinkle of humour. 'Could you have sex?'

He stared back, feeling a frisson of arousal from the intensity of her gaze. 'You could have orgasms lasting for days. Human orgasms have a natural, biological way of ending – often too quickly.' He smiled. 'You wouldn't have that problem in a computer. It would be paradise.' He drained his glass. 'And if you wanted to go on holiday, you wouldn't have to mess around with luggage and airports – you could just send yourself down the phone lines anywhere you wanted to go!'

She laughed. 'And you wouldn't have to worry about postcards – you could just send faxes saying, "Wish you were here – why don't you fax yourselves out and join us!"'

'And if you're too busy to go on holiday, you could always send a copy of yourself on holiday for you.'

They both chuckled. Joe ordered another wine for her and a beer for himself, then they glanced at the menu. She opened her handbag and pulled out a pack of cigarettes and a silver lighter. 'Would it bother you if I smoke?' she asked.

Joe shook his head, remembering ARCHIVE's admonishments when she'd come to his office. 'Go ahead.' He grinned. 'You want to kill yourself, that's fine by me.'

She looked hurt by the remark and all the humour drained from her face. Joe was surprised by her reaction. She laid the pack on the table and said, 'You could smoke to your heart's content inside a computer, couldn't you?'

'Might set the sprinklers off!' Joe said.

The waitress came back. Juliet ordered minestrone and lasagne, with a green salad. Joe ordered the same. Juliet's hands were shaking, Joe saw, as she tugged a cigarette from the pack, and her nails were in the same state of neglect as last week.

She lit the cigarette, inhaled deeply, then tilted her head to blow the smoke away from Joe. 'Do you have one overriding ambition?'

He thought for a moment, then nodded. 'Yes. I want to build a computer that will be proud of me.' He shrugged. 'And which would make my father proud of me –' he hesitated '– if he were still around.'

The trace of a smile relieved the heaviness of her expression. 'I'm sure ARCHIVE is very proud of you already.'

Joe winked. 'I'm not sure ARCHIVE fully appreciates me yet.'

She drew on her cigarette again. 'ARCHIVE is very intelligent. I'm sure it appreciates you more than you realize.'

The waitress brought their fresh drinks. Juliet waited until she'd walked away again, then looked a little uncomfortable. 'Isn't your quest for immortality your biggest ambition?'

'As a means to an end.'

'What do you mean by that?'

Joe rested his fingers on the table top. 'I – I guess I mean that the whole future of the world depends on us all understanding it a whole lot better than we do. Everyone dies too young. At the age of seventy or eighty people are just beginning to get smart, to get wise, and then they die. We don't live long enough to explore anything in depth – not our minds, or our planet, or our universe.'

He tapped the table. 'Imagine a fly crawling around this table. It doesn't know what the napkins are for, or the meaning of the pattern on the plates. It just registers the change in texture. It doesn't have the context to interpret what it's looking at. I think you and I are wandering around on a bigger table and haven't the context to interpret the meanings of what we're seeing. Making a thinking machine is my answer to that.'

'And you just want to live long enough to make that machine?'

'Yes.'

She drew nervously on her cigarette again. 'I – I thought from all the things you've said and written, that you really wanted to live *for ever*. Don't you have things you'd like to do if you had ten thousand years at your disposal?'

'Sure. I've already mapped out what I want to do for the next thousand years, and by the time I do all those things I'll have thought of another few thousand years' worth of stuff to do. I want to banish death as we know it.'

There was a long silence, until he lifted his eyes to hers. 'You know, I'm amazed how many people are really uncomfortable with the idea of immortality.' He stroked his glass with his finger. 'I mean – right now, you're young and healthy. If someone told you that you had only six months to live, wouldn't you do all you could to avoid dying?'

She swilled her wine around the glass in silence, and dropped her eyes. She seemed to be weighing something up, wrestling with some deep inner turmoil. When she finally looked up again at first she stared past him, the lustre gone from the emerald irises, her face very sad. She pushed her hair back from her forehead and tried, but failed, to muster a smile. Her eyes stared back into his for a moment, then down at her wine glass again.

'I do have only six months to live,' she said. 'Probably less.'

16

The waitress brought their salads and walked away. In the kitchen a woman called out in Italian and a man answered. The front door opened and a couple came in, closing it quickly behind them. They were drenched and the woman stood still for a moment, closing a sodden umbrella.

Joe watched Juliet's face in silence. When he did speak, his voice sounded in his ears like a loudspeaker. 'I'm sorry. I didn't have any idea.'

She gave a shrug. 'There's no reason why you should.'

The couple walked past them and stood by the next table, removing their coats. The waitress brought two minestrone soups. 'Parmesan?' she asked. Juliet shook her head, but Joe nodded and the girl spooned some of the grated cheese. Steam curled in front of Joe's eyes and he smelled the rich aroma, but his appetite was gone. He waited until the waitress had walked away, still studying Juliet carefully, wondering what illness she had, and hoping in his heart that perhaps she was exaggerating. He was feeling a heel for the tactless remark he'd made, telling her that she could kill herself smoking.

Radiation? He wondered. Had she been messing around with the scanner and radioactive tags too much? Had she given herself cancer from the radiation she was dosing herself with? He didn't know whether she wanted to talk about it, to tell him more, or not. Perhaps, he hoped faintly, clutching at a final straw, he'd not heard her correctly.

'Six months to live?' he said.

The wave of sadness seemed to be leaving her; it was replaced with an airiness; a crude and not really successful attempt at nonchalance. 'It could be twenty-four hours,' she said, 'or a week; or a couple of months. No one I've consulted thinks it will be more than four or five months at the outside.' She snatched a drag on her cigarette, inhaling deeply, and stubbed it out in the ashtray. There was frustration and anger in the action.

'Doctors are not always right,' he said lamely.

'I have a large aneurism on my brain that is inoperable.' Smoke jetted from her mouth and nostrils as she spoke. 'It's bled several times – gives me minor strokes, excruciating headaches, temporary loss of memory. But it's weakening; it could rupture at any moment.' She grimaced and tapped the ashtray lightly with her forefinger.

'Who have you seen?'

'Doctors?'

'Yes. Which specialists?'

She thought for a moment. 'A Dr Nightingale.'

'Simon Nightingale – the neurologist?'

'Yes.'

'He's a very brilliant man. The best in the country.'

'So I was told. He's very nice.'

'Who else?'

'Dr – er, Mr Chelwood-Beaumont.'

Joe nodded. 'He's one of the best neurosurgeons.'

'Dr Sieffert.'

'Abraham Sieffert?'

'Yes.'

'I know him. He's a fine man too, very dedicated.' Joe felt a lump of sadness in his throat. 'You've seen some very good people. I – I could have a word with Abraham Sieffert – if that –' His voice petered. Sieffert would already be doing everything he could for the girl. Joe wished there was something he could say or do that would be helpful. Cerebral aneurisms were swellings in the brain's blood vessels. Sometimes they could be successfully drained, but sometimes their location made surgery impossible. People could live for years with them, but once they started bleeding it was like cracks appearing in a dam wall. Sooner or later the wall would collapse.

'I'll try anything,' she said. 'I'll see anyone.' She drank a long gulp of her wine and set the glass down.

Joe picked up his fork, reached over his soup and speared a lettuce leaf out of his salad. A trail of oil dripped into his soup and on to his napkin. He chewed the lettuce, but barely noticed the taste. The girl opposite him looked so vulnerable, he wanted to reach over and take her hand, to comfort her. Aneurisms. He tried to think of any article he might have read recently that talked about new advances in their treatment. Racked his brains for colleagues who worked in that area.

Across the table, Juliet's beauty and fragility played havoc with his emotions. He found himself forcing back tears as he thought about all she had to offer: her brilliance; her enthusiasm for science; her vision. And her loveliness.

Death. His father's decomposed body sliding from the mortuary fridge. The greed of death – its utter wastefulness, its total lack of discrimination. His enemy.

'The aneurism was discovered about three years ago, when I started getting very violent headaches.' Juliet wanted to explain, wanted to gain time. 'There was a slim chance that it could have been cleared by blood-thinning medications and perhaps by laser surgery, but then it began to bleed – and they've all said the walls are too weak.' She gestured. 'I

– I sort of knew when I was first told that there wasn't going to be any real hope.'

'Is that why you're interested in my work?'

'Yes – I –' She gave Joe a slight, self-deprecatory laugh. 'I thought maybe you could help me.' She kept her gaze above him as though she were in a trance.

'What did you hope I could help you do?' he asked quietly, as if afraid of disturbing her.

'To live for ever.'

There was a silence between them. Narrow frown lines ribbed the smooth skin of her forehead, ageing her. Her lips were tight. She was tense as hell, Joe realized.

'Would you really like that?' he said.

Her eyes flashed at him, more bloodshot than before. In place of the previous faraway gaze there was an intensity that disturbed him. 'Yes, I would. I'm frightened of dying.' She stared silently into his own eyes for a moment. 'I'm really scared of extinction.'

Joe shifted his weight in his chair. He felt awkward, uncomfortable. Inadequate. His heart went out to her and he wished he could offer a crumb of comfort. But he felt guilty, also. Guilty of being too optimistic in some of the papers he'd written, in some of his lectures. He'd spoken often of his hopes and dreams, but he'd tended to play down the difficulties. He had held out ARCHIVE as a computer that could pioneer dramatic changes in human life on earth. The hope of immortality of consciousness. He had presented cogent arguments, backed by sound experiments. He had published no more than he truly believed, but perhaps in doing so he had fuelled other people's fantasies too soon.

Now, sitting across the table, was someone who was waiting for him to tell her that he could enable her to survive her bodily death. To live on. Perhaps if they were having this conversation in ten years' time he might be able to offer more real hope.

He thought of the strange cactus-like spikes of the print-outs of the rats' brains. Could be just brain noise. Everything electrical gave off noise. Could this experimental drug, CTS

6700, really trigger thoughts, memories from the brain; and the scanner pick them up? The more Joe thought about it, the more it went against all that made sense to him from his knowledge of neuroscience. There must be some other explanation for the matching images. The girl was desperate and he might be the same if he was in her position. But desperation did not necessarily make good science.

'You believe death is the end?' he said.

'Yes.'

'You have no religious views?'

'I was brought up in a strongly religious family. My parents are Presbyterians; staunch churchgoers.'

'What do they do?' Joe dipped his spoon in his soup, then held it up and tasted it. It was good.

'My father's a lawyer; he specializes in civil litigation. My mother's a linguist – she used to be a simultaneous translator with the United Nations.'

Joe raised his eyebrows. 'Bright family. Do you have brothers and sisters?'

'I have a brother who lives in the States; a research scientist with an oil company.'

'And they all know about your –'

'I feel it's something I have to deal with myself,' she said, and seemed not to want to talk about that angle further. Joe could not tell, from what she'd said, whether her parents knew the truth or not.

She picked up her wine glass and tilted it towards her. 'I've read all these newspaper articles about people with only months to live. They go on about how it makes them appreciate each day more than ever before; how they try to put their affairs in order; some of them even say it's the best thing that ever happened to them.' There was an edge of bitterness appearing in her voice. 'I don't feel any of those things. I feel cheated. And if I can't beat the aneurism, at least I'm going to bloody well cheat death itself.' Her face flushed with anger. She tapped the MedicAlert bracelet on her right wrist and raised it towards him.

Joe frowned.

138

'I – I'm having my body frozen when I die,' she said.

'Cryonically?'

'Yes.'

Joe remembered her asking him about cryonics while he was taking her around his department. Now he understood why. Suddenly he was unable to prevent his mind from picturing her frozen: her face white, brittle as fine china or glass, her hair frosted, her body rigid and hard. He shivered as a cold slick of fear travelled down his spine. He deliberately refused to call on the memory of his father. 'Well,' he said, struggling for scientific detachment, 'I think there are problems with cryonics that haven't been resolved yet. But I don't think there's any question that it's capable of working, given the development of the right medical technology.'

'But can it work now? Do you think people who are being frozen now could one day be recovered?'

'Yes.' Again he blanked out his own experience as the son of Willi Messenger, the cryonics pioneer now dead beyond recall. 'Two things have to happen: medical knowledge has to advance to the point where it can cure people who are frozen of what originally –' he hesitated, '– killed them. And it has to avoid any damage in the freezing processes. There's no question that those things will happen – *eventually*. The first one's up to the medics, right? But I put my money on Blake Hewlett's work with vitrification as far as the other's concerned.'

'You've never mentioned cryonics in any of your work.' She pushed her soup away and took out another cigarette.

Joe scratched his head, feeling a little embarrassed. He could not, would not, discuss his father. Instead he offered, 'I'm afraid there are some subjects that are taboo if you want to be taken seriously by the scientific Establishment: they're a pretty narrow-minded lot.'

'But you have a department of cryobiology at the university; we saw some of it.'

'*Cryobiology* is different, because it's about freezing skin tissue, aggregates of cells, corneas, heart valves, semen. It's a medical science with proven applications – it isn't about the concept of immortality.'

She thought for a moment. 'One thing I don't understand: if you believe you could live on inside a computer, why would you need cryonics?'

Joe dug his spoon back in the soup and took a quick swallow. 'The quest for immortality is not just about prolonging life, but about *quality* of life. At the present time the human body is still a better machine for living in than a computer. The only route to immortality at the moment – or certainly in the foreseeable future – is for humans to be frozen until they can be thawed out and repaired. But freezing doesn't guarantee immortality.'

'Why not?'

'Some people's bodies get destroyed in accidents, or their brains get blown to pieces by bullets.' *Or allowed to thaw out before their time by profit-making nerds.* Somehow Joe suppressed the memory of the fiasco at Crycon Corporation and continued in a practical voice. 'If you were to suffer massive brain damage from your aneurism, that would cause a big problem when you reanimate.'

She put the new cigarette in her mouth, struck the flint wheel of her lighter then held the flame to the end of the cigarette with some difficulty, her hand was shaking so much. 'Surely neurosurgery will one day be able to repair damaged brain cells?' The tip of the cigarette glowed red and she puffed out a cloud of smoke.

'Of course. But it won t be able to replace lost memory.'

'Unless it's been stored somewhere?'

'Exactly.'

She was quiet for a moment, slowly exhaling smoke through her nostrils and gazing at him in realization. 'AR-CHIVE? Is that why it's called ARCHIVE?'

'It has a kind of dual meaning. It's part acronym: Anthropo-Computer Host for Intelligent Virtual Existence, and it's part a real archive. I want to create a repository for human knowledge. That's my first goal. Consciousness will come from that, but that's secondary.'

'Why?'

'Because humans are memory driven. Can you tell me one thing that you do, other than spontaneous biological functions, that is not influenced by memory? Think of anything you like: you read a book because you remember you've read other books you've enjoyed, and you hope to recreate that memory and improve on it. You go into a room full of strangers and out of all the faces there is one you feel comfortable with. Why? Because you recognize it in some way. Because it reminds you of someone you like, or once liked. We constantly compare the present with the past.'

'Dorian Gray,' she said with a smile.

'Sure. Memory is how we record and make sense of all that has happened to us. It's the most important single part of consciousness. If you can store memory, you can store the essential human being.'

'And download it into a defrosted human being when the time comes?'

'Or a robot.' He tried a smile. 'There again, it might be that life inside a computer is so pleasant, you don't ever want to leave it.'

The waitress hovered, uncertain whether they were eating their soup or not. Joe ordered them another drink.

Juliet Spring tapped ash off her cigarette. 'So the Egyptians got it all wrong with their mummies. I mean, didn't they throw the brains away? Pull them out through the corpse's nostrils with crochet hooks because they went off and smelled bad? If they wanted immortality, they should have thrown away the mummies and kept the brains!'

'Yes, I don't think too many mummies are going to get reanimated,' he said.

She looked down at her wrist. 'You don't have a bracelet. Do you wear a neck chain?'

Joe suddenly realized what she was talking about. He dug his fingers inside his shirt front and pulled out a MedicAlert tag on a thin chain. She looked relieved to see it, and he couldn't help contrasting her attitude with his own wife's.

Cryonics was a big source of tension between himself and

Karen. With her strong religious beliefs, Karen vigorously objected to the concept. And she also objected to the cost of it, made Joe feel guilty that if he died, the money that could be spent on Jack's schooling, on setting the boy up with a future, would go instead towards keeping Joe's remains frozen in a cylinder. And what had happened to Joe's father had convinced her more than ever that she was right.

'You seem so incredibly brave,' Joe said to Juliet.

'No, I'm not – not at all! I just put on a brave face because I have to. I'm scared as hell!'

'Where have you signed up – which cryonics organization?'

'The Cryonite Foundation. It seems to be the only place in England that actually keeps people here – the others are transit places for storage in the States.'

Joe nodded. 'You know who started it?'

'Who?'

'Blake Hewlett.'

'I didn't know that. He's Professor of Cryobiology, didn't you tell me?'

'Yes.'

'So the university don't mind about his involvement with cryonics?'

'He's brought a lot of funding into the university,' Joe answered without missing a beat.

Juliet signalled with her eyes and a slight inclination of her head that she'd got the message. Then she knocked some ash off her cigarette, and said tentatively, 'Has – has what I've told you – about my aneurism – changed your views about me? I mean – I'd understand if you decided you didn't want to take me on because of it.'

'I'm going to take you on,' Joe said.

She looked at him as if she wasn't totally certain she believed him. 'Really?'

He smiled broadly. 'Really! I guess we just have to sort out when.'

'How about tomorrow?' she said.

He laughed. 'You're going to have to arrange a grant.'

She shook her head. 'I haven't got time; I have some money of my own; I'd like to start as soon as possible.'

Joe thought for a moment. 'OK, you're going to have to give me a couple of days to sort out the bureaucracy.' Then he looked at her intently. 'I just hope that all you've read about my work hasn't given you . . .' He hesitated.

'Too much hope?'

He looked down for a moment, unable to cope with her expression. Slowly, he nodded.

'I've been told by all the specialists that I have no hope. When you have no hope, professor, you have nothing to lose.'

Later, as they left the restaurant, Joe found himself putting his arm around her, almost without realizing what he was doing. He felt drunk and unsteady, and he vaguely wondered whether, on the wine she'd had, she was OK to drive. He wondered also whether, with her medical condition, she was *allowed* to drive.

The rain had stopped and a clinging damp mist hung in the darkness as they walked back to the Cobbold-Tessering building and collected the tape cassette, which she slipped into a Jiffy bag for him. It felt strange carrying it, as if he might give himself brain damage if he dropped it.

His head was swimming and he fought unsuccessfully to stay awake, drifting in and out of sleep on the drive back to Victoria station, aware only of the occasional revving of the engine and the blurred kaleidoscope of lights.

Then he realized with a start that they had come to a halt and Juliet was waiting for him to leave the car. The street looked familiar even in the darkness: the exterior of the Grosvenor Hotel; the closed and boarded-up news vendors' stands just beyond. The entrance to the station was just behind it. The car clock said 12.50.

'You sure you'll be all right getting a train at this hour?' she said.

'They run through the night to Gatwick. I can get a taxi from there. Sh'no problem,' he slurred, turning to face her. 'Sh'you Monday.'

He leaned across suddenly and clumsily to kiss her cheek, but she turned more towards him as he did so and his lips collided with hers. She made no attempt to move her head or shrink away. Her lips were soft and cool against his.

He lingered for a moment, thrown and uncertain what to do. She rotated her face slightly and he thought at first she was trying to break away. Except her lips were caressing his, touching lightly at first, then pressing more firmly. He felt her fingers sliding gently through his hair, caressing his scalp, her tongue running lightly between his lips. Most of all he felt the sharp knot of excitement in the pit of his stomach as he played his tongue back against hers. It was impossible for him to believe she was on the verge of death.

Then slowly, reluctantly, with guilt gnawing through him, he eased apart from her. They held each other's gaze for some moments, smiling. 'I –' he said, confused. 'Thanks for – showing me the lab.'

'You have the tape?'

He held up the Jiffy bag. 'Talk tomorrow?'

'I'll call you,' she said.

He wanted to kiss her again, but instead he fumbled for the door handle, found it and turned it.

He stepped out into the wet air, and she waved cheerily at him as he slammed the door shut. He stood still for a moment, then turned and stumbled along towards the station concourse, deeply aroused.

17

Joe arrived home shortly before three. He climbed out of the taxi, closing the door as gently as he could, hoping it would reduce the chances of waking Karen. The porch light was on, and he could see the hall light was also on. It was several degrees colder than in London and the ground was dry.

Above him, stars pricked the blackness and a quarter moon emitted its cold, lifeless light.

The neighbourhood was silent. Streetlights burned down the sloping road, bathing the silent façades of the detached houses with an orange hue. He had sobered up, but felt strangely disoriented as he slid his key into the front-door lock, turned it slowly and pushed the heavy oak door open. The draught excluder scraped noisily across the floor and Joe winced, shutting the door as quietly as he could. The lock clicked home like a gunshot.

In the darkness of the landing at the top of the stairs a bead of reflected light glinted on the lens of the video camera that was recording his arrival home.

He removed the Jiffy bag from his pocket and put it on the hall table, then peeled off his damp trenchcoat and hung it on the Victorian mahogany coat rack. A plastic dumper truck sat on the beige carpet of the hall floor, and there was a pyramid of building blocks beside it. Jack. He smiled at the thought of his son, then his smile turned to anguish as he replayed in his mind, as he had done repeatedly all the way home, those minutes kissing Juliet in her car.

Like the first time he and Karen had kissed. Only not quite like that. It was better, so much better. Or was it? He could smell Juliet now, could feel the silky texture of her skin, the freshness of her hair and the warmth of her breath sweet with wine and sour with tobacco; but he didn't mind the tobacco, it was a part of her.

Then he looked at the toys again, thought of Jack asleep upstairs in his bed. He felt low and dirty, and yet he could not stop remembering the pleasure.

He trod the stairs carefully, remembering the ones that creaked, and reached the shadow of the narrow landing with the stealth of an intruder. He could see their own bedroom door was ajar, and peering into the increasing darkness down the narrow corridor he could see Jack's door open also, as it always was.

'Joe?' Karen's voice rang out, startling him. There was a

click and their bedroom suddenly filled with a soft glow of light.

'Hi,' he said in a hushed voice.

He heard the rustle of sheets and Karen sat up looking wide awake as he went into the room. The relief in her voice was tinged with anger.

'What happened, Joe? I've been worried sick.'

'Happened? Nothing, hon. I had to go to London – I told you.'

'It's three o'clock!'

He closed the door behind him. 'I told you. I had to go and look at an AI experiment at Cobbold-Tessering's research lab.'

'You didn't say you were going to be so late.'

'I had to wait around for a computer download.'

'Why didn't you call me? I nearly phoned the police – I thought maybe you'd been mugged, or crashed the car.'

Her skin looked pallid, and he found himself comparing her appearance with the fresh, clear-skinned beauty of Juliet. Doing so made him feel even more guilty, but he couldn't help it. He scratched the back of his head, opened the sliding door of his wardrobe, took off his jacket and slipped it on to a hanger. The metal hangers chinked together.

'You said you'd be home between eleven and midnight.'

He struggled with his tie, his guilt riling him. Stupid, he knew. He should have phoned her. He hung the tie on the wire that was already sagging under the weight of the assorted ties he had collected over the years.

'I don't even get a kiss?' she said.

He walked over to the bed, tugging at the top button of his shirt, bent down and gave her a light peck on the lips. They felt unwilling compared to Juliet's.

'Joe, are you telling me the truth?'

'What is this? The Spanish Inquisition?' he said, hanging his shirt on the back of a chair.

'You stink of booze, perfume and cigarette smoke.'

He sat on the chair, facing away from her, and untied his

shoes. 'We went out for a meal afterwards – one of those crowded little restaurants; whole place was full of smoke.'

'They spray the guests with perfume?'

He surreptitiously sniffed his hands; there was a faint trace of Juliet's scent on them. 'I sat next to this woman who must have been dunked in the stuff. And she was a chain smoker. I couldn't taste my food.' He pushed his socks off and stared at his feet; they were small and bony, and a varicose vein was pushing through the skin above his left ankle. When they were first married, Karen had told him he had great-looking feet. She used to nibble his toes and suck them. He'd found that very erotic.

His toenails needed cutting. Must do those, he thought. Must do them before next Monday, before Juliet –

Christ, what am I thinking?

He went through into the small ensuite bathroom, relieved to escape Karen's interrogation. His reflection in the mirror as he brushed his teeth startled him. His face was haggard and drained, with dark rings beneath his eyes; he looked like he hadn't slept for a week.

The ageing process, one of nature's many cruel jokes, was starting to get to him. Post-biological man would not have the indignity of ageing.

He tried to think straight, to put some reality into an evening that had become increasingly strange. Had Juliet tried to kiss him? Or had it been his clumsiness in kissing her lips by mistake that had made her yield, not wanting to offend him? Was that it? A dirty old man taking advantage of a – a dying girl?

He felt cheap suddenly. Cheap for having kissed a girl who was going to be his student, for having cheated on his wife, on his child. He faced his reflection again and tried to sort out his story.

Karen's eyes were closed when he went back into the bedroom. 'Was the experiment interesting?' she murmured sleepily.

'Yup.' He glanced up at the ceiling lamp rose which concealed ARCHIVE's video camera, acutely conscious of it for the first time in months; as if he was worried that it could pick up his guilt.

He changed into his pyjamas quickly, climbed into bed and Karen switched off the light.

'Goodnight,' she said.

He kissed her. 'Night,' he said, and collapsed on to the pillows. But as he drifted into sleep, a series of strange images presented themselves to him in sequence.

Distorted faces, some frosty with ice, others with decomposing skin sloughing off; his father called out something, but he couldn't hear what it was. Then Juliet Spring called out, seductively, 'Joe!' Her voice was so clear, he came to with a start. Karen stirred, then slept on.

He stared around the darkness. There was a thin uneven strip of silvery light where ARCHIVE had failed to close the electrically operated curtains completely. He could see the luminous numbers of his travel alarm clock. He felt with an almost overwhelming intensity that Juliet was in the room with them; standing at the end of the bed.

An eerie sensation. Joe shivered, wondering suddenly if she had died and was trying to communicate something to him. Sometimes when people died they appeared in front of others at the exact moment of death. His throat felt constricted and he held his breath, listening. Karen slept on, her breathing slow and steady. Don't have died tonight; please not tonight; live longer; tell me more about you; tell me more about your experiments. I want to save you. I want to sleep with you.

I think I'm in love with you.

He looked for her among the familiar silhouettes of the furniture, but he could see nothing. The sensation passed, but he wondered if she was OK. Maybe it was a distress signal she was sending out to him? She was alone and calling for help. He should phone her, see if she was all right. Except, he realized, he didn't know where she lived. It was on her CV, but that was filed in the office. He could go there now, look it up and phone her.

And say what if she answered?

He closed his eyes; tried to calm himself down. He had a lecture to give at ten in the morning; it was now past four. And he had a squash game at lunchtime. And in three hours Jack would be waking them up.

Then it hit him.

His eyes sprang wide open and his whole body coursed with energy. He wondered why he had not thought of it earlier. So obvious!

He switched on the bedside light and began to scribble ideas for a program on the pad he always kept by his bed. Karen stirred again, muttered something incoherent and turned over. He scribbled on, knowing exactly what he had to do, knowing the test that would prove whether Juliet was right or not.

He lay awake for much of the remainder of the night, his tiredness, his guilt and anxiety subsumed by the excitement that was building in him, as he ran the test backwards and forwards through his mind. If it worked, he thought, if it really worked . . .

The ramifications scared him a little.

18

September 1987. Los Angeles.

'Run! Run, you dumb bastard! Shit. Asshole. What an asshole!' Floyd Pueblo angrily stirred a French fry in the mess of ketchup at the bottom of the styrene box. Five yards to the line, the quarterback could have got there. Instead the asshole decides to pass the ball.

He hooked the fry into his mouth and tore it apart with his teeth. The Rams were 17–13 down. Twenty minutes of play left. They could do it, hell they could! Then the game faded from the screen and a commercial for Budweiser beer came on.

Floyd picked up the paper bag and looked inside, still

feeling hungry. There were a few slivers of charred fries; he licked his finger, dabbed the bits up, smeared them through the ketchup and put them in his mouth, then he drank some more root beer. The rain rattled like pebbles on the dark windowpane behind his head. His feet were still wet and cold and a draught blew down his neck. But anger warmed him.

Anger at the dumb fucker who could have scored instead of throwing it away. Anger at himself for watching a game that had been over for eight hours, the result of which he already knew. The Eagles beat the Rams 17–13. Another tampon commercial was up now. Shit. It was possible the result could be different now; crazy things happened to time. Nothing was written in stone and couldn't be changed. Those dumb bastards in liquid nitrogen in their aluminium cylinders at the far end of the building had believed things could be changed. Sure they had! They believed death could be changed. They believed that one day you were dead. Then – caramba! – one hundred years later you got defrosted, the surgeons cured you of what had been wrong with you, rejuvenated you a bit, and off you went, good as new.

Like he could pretend to himself the Rams hadn't really lost the game at all. Philosophy crap. The papers were full of it these days. And physics. Like time was curved; parallel universes; quantum mechanics. These scientist types jerking off in public; giving out theories so complicated no one could understand them. He didn't think the scientists understood them either. He didn't think most scientists knew what the fuck they were doing. They messed around and wrote books and papers, got patted on the head, received awards and money, and then they screwed up the ozone layer and tinkered with genes or built nukes which they couldn't unbuild. Not content with that, they conned people into parting with $125,000 so they could get dunked into tins of liquid nitrogen after they were dead.

When you were dead you were dead. As a cop, Floyd Pueblo had seen that for himself. He knew what bodies looked like when they'd been hauled out of the harbour after a month lying on the muddy bottom amongst the junked fridges and the auto tyres and the crabs that had been feasting on them. Or hacked out of mangled wrecks on the freeways. Bodies that fell out of high-rise buildings. Bodies of old, lonely people that had lain where they'd fallen on their apartment floors until the neighbours had complained about the smell. When you were dead you were sure as hell dead.

Even so this place made him uneasy. He looked at his watch. Twenty to two. It would start to get light around four and then it wasn't so bad. But there were six hours to go before anyone would be turning up for work. Sometime before dawn began breaking a patrol car would cruise by, slowly, go on down to the far end of the industrial estate, turn around and cruise back; and maybe come by again in a couple of hours, depending on what kind of a night it was having. Stormy nights like this always set the burglar alarms going. One thing about this place, sure as hell no one was ever going to burgle this building. No one in their right mind, anyhow.

The game came back on but the score didn't change and he worked himself up into an anger as the final whistle blew. Then he sat back in his chair and pressed the selector and chomped through the channels, watching snatches of movies, talk shows and news items. President Reagan appeared, going on about taxation.

'Asshole,' Floyd Pueblo mumbled, and pressed the button. Channel 11. A man and a woman were screwing hard on a bare wooden floor. Promising, he thought, and stayed with it for some moments. Then he heard a noise that sounded like it had come from out in the corridor. A distinct scrape. Like a footstep.

A beat of fear pulsed through him. He pressed the mute button, silencing the television. Listened. The rain beat steadily down on the roof. He unbuttoned his holster and rested his hand on the cold butt of his revolver, his shirt tightening around his skin like cold foil. He strained his ears, waiting for it to repeat. It had been a definite, clear sound. A piece of furniture being moved? He had not imagined it; he knew all the night noises, had been doing this shift for the past two years, had listened with ears like antennae because the place scared him shitless, and he wasn't having anything crawling out of one of those cylinders and stealing a march on him.

He had never heard that sound before.

He looked at the door, then pulled out the revolver and released the safety catch. He looked at the phone. Undead. If it was something undead out there a phone call wouldn't stop it. He felt the heavy weight of his gun, the hard ribbed crackle either side of the handle digging into the palm of his hand, felt the trigger nestling into his finger.

If it was undead a bullet wouldn't stop it either. Except maybe a silver one and he didn't have any of those. Just lead and they were too small for his liking. His imagination began to replay images from horror movies. Mummified creatures were lining up outside the door. He looked up at the photographs of the people who were now in the tanks. Not really dead at all, just unwell. Patients: whole-body patients and head-only patients.

He homed in on the black and white portrait photo of a man in his seventies, with silver hair in a boyish cut, glasses, and a lined, handsome face that reminded him of Jimmy Stewart. The man was smiling in the photograph and Floyd could picture him now, outside the door, his face white, his hair crusted with ice, still smiling.

He *must* have imagined the footstep.

Except he had not imagined the tapping sound an hour and a half ago when Will Doheny, the guard on early shift, had been showing him the new arrival.

No one was standing outside that door, he reassured himself. No one who'd been put in one of those cylinders was ever going to be walking around any place again. Be like expecting the burger he'd just eaten to reconstitute itself into a cow, Will Doheny had said that. He was right, sure he was right.

Except there had been a new arrival tonight. One that had

to be kept at a warmer temperature, he'd been told, −140 instead of −196. At a warmer temperature. Maybe at that temperature there was a better chance she − it − had thawed. Sort of spontaneously? Thawed enough to get out?

Frightened, Floyd eased himself silently to his feet, holding the gun out in front of him, and tiptoed to the door. He was shaking; the door blurred; water streamed down the nape of his neck and then the small of his back; used to get the sweats like this in the force sometimes; it was OK when you could see the bastards, but when they hid in an alley so you couldn't tell where they were going to come at you from, that always scared him.

He put his hand on the door handle; his flesh was slippery with sweat; shivers rippled down his skin. He gripped the handle tighter, listened, tried to tune out the rain and concentrated on the door, on the passage beyond. He counted silently, one . . . two . . . three.

Twisted the handle and jerked open the door! Pushed the gun wildly out in front of him, swivelling it left then right.

Nothing.

There was nothing there. Water gurgled through a gutter above him. His eyes watched the doorway through to the operating theatre; they swung back to the empty entrance foyer; to the vase of silk flowers; the fake Grecian urn. Jumped back to the doorway to the operating theatre. Holding his breath, he walked slowly towards it. But he hesitated as he got near and took it slowly, one halting step at a time. Then he rushed the last yard, and snapped on the light. The theatre was empty.

He stood for some moments listening, watching the doorway at the far side which went through to the aluminium dewars, then walked over and checked them all out. Everything seemed fine.

Relieved, he went back to his office, but left the door ajar a little. Then he settled back down into his chair and watched the couple who were sitting facing each other, entwined in each other's limbs, still hard at it on the bare wooden floor.

After a few minutes he began to relax, put the safety catch back on his revolver and reholstered it. As he did so, he heard the sound again, very distinctly.

19

Joe's lungs were bursting. The ball hit the front wall just above the service line, bounced back, hugging the side wall, struck the rear wall behind him and dropped, spent, in the corner of the court. The soles of his shoes squeaked as he dived for it, scooped it up with his racquet, boasting it off the side wall, making it virtually unplayable, he thought, by finishing just above the tin of the front wall. Blake Hewlett threw himself at it, his racquet striking the wall with a clatter. He nudged the ball in the air and the drop shot died in the far corner.

'Shot!' Joe said, grudgingly, too exhausted even to try and run for it.

'Eight–two,' Blake said through a mask of sweat.

Joe flicked the ball to Blake then took up position to receive the serve.

'Feeling OK, Joe?'

'Yup.'

'I don't think your mind's quite on the game today.'

Joe braced himself. Blake aced him.

'Game,' Blake said. 'Two-love.' He tossed the ball in the air and caught it.

Joe brushed the sweat from his eyes with the back of his hand and took a couple of deep breaths. He felt weary and his mind was buzzing. He wanted to get the game over and try to call Juliet Spring again. He had rung her at Cobbold-Tessering first thing that morning but she hadn't yet arrived. He'd looked up her home number on her CV and tried that, but there'd been no answer. He could not get out of his mind the sound of her voice in the night. Calling out to him.

Could not rid himself of the fear that she'd died during the night.

Blake won the next game, and the one after. Joe made an effort to concentrate and held him at bay for half of the fifth game, until his concentration lapsed again and Blake won that too.

Afterwards they showered, then stood on the rubber mat drying themselves. Joe glanced a little enviously at Blake's muscular figure. Forty-five and Blake still had the body of an athlete. Joe tried to keep in shape himself by jogging and doing exercises at the weekends and by his regular games with Blake, but even so his muscles were beginning to lose their tone and his stomach was no longer as flat as he would have liked. Compared to Blake's physique he reckoned his own was looking very middle-aged. It was Juliet Spring, he realized guiltily, who was making him think about this.

'How much do you know about smart drugs, Blake?'

'Smart drugs?'

'Isn't that what they call them? Smart drugs – smart pills?'

Blake towelled his hair. 'You mean like cognitive enhancers – Piracetam, Sulbutiamine, DHEA?'

'Yup. Neurotransmitters in particular.'

'You should talk to Wenceslas, he's a smart pill junkie. I know he's used them in tests on Amanda.'

Joe dried his ears. 'Do you think it's possible for a neuro-transmitter drug to fire every single neuron in the brain?'

Blake looked at him oddly. 'What are you trying to say?' His directness often sounded rude and patronizing. Over the years Joe had got used to it, but it still annoyed him some-times, and threw his concentration.

'If you could fire every neuron, you could create a brain state from which you could download – or upload.'

'I don't understand. How do you mean?' Blake studied his lean chest and flat stomach in the mirror, pinching them with his fingers for signs of fat.

'If you want to read a computer's files, you call them up and scroll through them, right? In that state you can add, delete, copy, wipe or over-write. Right?'

'Getting very elementary here, Joe. You only just figured this out?'

Joe ignored the remark. 'If you have a neurotransmitter to trigger neural activity artificially, you could create a situation where information could be encoded in a group of neurons and synapses, right?'

'Sure, Joe, that's how the brain works. They teach you that in your first morning at neuroscience kindergarten.' Blake removed a deodorant from a smart leather washbag and meticulously sprayed each armpit.

Joe ignored the further sarcasm. 'If you added a radioactive tag to that neurotransmitter, and had a powerful enough scanner, do you think it's conceivable you could read what's going on inside the brain?'

Blake shook talc on to his chest and rubbed it in. 'Wenceslas ran tests like that on Amanda last year.'

'Amanda's not a living brain.' Joe put his watch on. Ten past two. The morning had been taken up with a lecture and a tutorial, then Blake had arrived in his office before the tutorial had ended to walk over to the squash courts with him. He was anxious to get back to the privacy of his office and call Juliet, but he knew Blake would be expecting to go to the common room for a drink and a sandwich as they always did after their lunchtime games.

'I think you should talk to Wenceslas,' Blake said.

'I'll go and see him.' Joe pulled on his cord trousers. 'By the way – something interesting – I have a student joining me who's into cryonics.'

Blake put a thick grey cardigan on over a black polo neck jumper. 'In what way?'

'She's signed up with Cryonite.'

'Cryonite? Must be a smart girl! What's her name?'

Joe tried to avoid letting his interest in her show through his voice. 'Oh – er – ah –' He feigned loss of memory. 'Ah – right – Spring – Juliet Spring.'

Blake shook his head, then stared in the mirror, cupping his face in his hands and patting his cheeks as if in doing so he could somehow tone them more. He often did that and it irritated Joe. 'Vaguely rings a bell. We have eighty-seven people signed up. Pretty good, huh? We've doubled in the past year.'

'You met her last week, when she came to see me. You brought her to my office.'

Blake squinted closer in the mirror and combed his long dark hair. 'The red-head. That girl?'

'Uh huh.'

'She was OK. Yup! Like she was someone I definitely would not mind spending eternity with. When's she starting? I'll have a talk with her.'

Blake's sudden interest made Joe feel jealous and he wished he hadn't mentioned it. 'Probably next week.' He watched Blake's face and saw the look of interest deepening.

'It's good you doubled the numbers, I didn't know that,' Joe said, keen to change the subject. 'I thought the British were still pretty hostile to the whole concept of cryonics.'

'Interesting developments, Joe. We still have our monthly Sunday morning meetings; you should start coming along again, you haven't been for months.'

For some while before the disaster with his father, Joe had lost a bit of his interest and enthusiasm for cryonics, because he hadn't felt there was much he could contribute, and he'd been concentrating all his time on ARCHIVE. 'What kind of developments?'

'Some interesting stuff with vitrification.' Blake gave him an unreadable smile.

'Oh?'

'No big deal yet, Joe, but watch this space, OK?'

'I'm watching,' Joe grinned.

'What's with this sudden interest in smart pills?'

Not feeling like another sceptical remark from Blake, Joe decided to keep quiet about his experience with the scanner. 'I think maybe ARCHIVE could benefit from taking them.'

'You're going to feed them to its live neurons?'

'I'm going to look into it.'

'Have there been any developments with ARCHIVE over the holidays?'

'There was some good stuff happening before the break. We've been making some real progress with the core storage capacity. By parallel paging we now have approximately seven times the human brain in virtual storage capacity.'

'And in processing power you're still somewhere between a cockroach and a mouse, right?'

Joe nodded reluctantly. That was true. ARCHIVE was capable of storing and retrieving the equivalent content of seven human brains, although it could still only make very limited use of the information. But that was changing. 'It's getting smarter all the time – it's definitely learning stuff by itself. The biological side's good, that's progressing well.'

'Any progress on uploading from humans?'

Joe put his wet shirt and trousers into his sports bag and pushed his squash shoes down on top, then zipped the bag shut. 'No,' he said. 'None.'

Blake put his arm on his shoulder. 'Still feel down about your old man?'

Joe nodded grimly.

'Kind of feels like a part of me's died, you know?'

'Me too,' Joe said.

Joe got back to his office just before three, closed his door and sat down at his desk. He glanced at the Cobbold-Tessering number he'd left scrawled on the back of an envelope, composed himself, dialled it and asked for Juliet Spring.

He was put through to her extension and she answered it on the first ring. Relief surged through him at the sound of her voice.

'It's – Joe – er, Professor – Messenger.' He had to hold himself back from blurting *You're alive!*

'Professor Messenger!' She sounded genuinely pleased to hear from him, and, he thought, a little relieved.

'I – you – you got home safely last night?' he said.

'Yes, I didn't have far to go. How about you? I really worried about whether you'd be able to get a train.'

'Oh sure, that wasn't a problem,' he said.

'Good.'

'I –' He found himself involuntarily picking up a pen and doodling on the envelope; concentric circles, which he then enclosed in concentric boxes. 'I just wanted to – get some details – my – er – secretary, Eileen, will have a word with you. We have about ten thousand forms that have to be filled in. I guess we might have to be a bit – ah – creative on the medical side –' He began to draw a pentagram around the boxes, feeling unaccountably shy, suddenly. And sad. It was impossible to believe from the cheery tone of her voice that she was facing imminent death.

Joe wondered if she was on tranquillizers of some sort. He even wondered, fleetingly, whether what she'd told him about herself was true. It had to be; that wasn't something you invented, not unless you were seriously strange.

He took a breath. 'Look, I want to apologize for what happened – you know – in the car.'

'In the car?' Her voice stiffened a little.

'I don't know what came over me. You must think I'm –' His voice dried as he searched for the word.

'I really had a good time in the car,' she said. 'I haven't had such a good time in a car for a long, long while.'

Joe was flummoxed. 'No, well, I –' He lowered his voice, aware of the scrutiny of ARCHIVE's eyes and ears. 'I guess me neither.'

'You're a really lovely person.'

You are a married man, Joe, a voice in his head told him. *You're not dating anyone now, this is not a conversation you should be having, not with anyone, and particularly not with a student.*

Yet he didn't want the conversation to end. 'I think you are too,' he said.

There was a long, easy pause between them, as if they were both savouring the moment.

'I –' he said finally, then hesitated.

'Yes?' she said expectantly.

'I've had some good thoughts on the decoding of the tape.'

Hope jumped down the line at him like a spark. 'You have?'

The intensity of her reaction scared him. She'd been drawn in as much by his papers and books on immortality as by his own wild enthusiasm, believed all he had said about the subject too literally, believed he was much further down the line than he really was.

He felt like a con man suddenly; a seedy backstreet charlatan. Someone who was cheating on his family. Cheating on this girl's hopes.

He considered the doodles on the envelope. Considered the Jiffy bag with the Terabyte cassette tape. Saw again the decomposed remains of his father in the Los Angeles mortuary, and thought about the promise he'd made to him that he'd failed to deliver. He stared at the neat rows of holes of the telephone mouthpiece. A human life was at the other end. A life that was ebbing away and trusted him. Believed in him. Could possibly help him more than anyone ever before.

He owed something to her, he knew. He had to do whatever he could, in the short time left to her, to deliver. And this time he had to get it right.

20

Joe left his office clutching the Jiffy bag and the two envelopes covered in his doodles and went down into the Cryobiology lab. He nodded, without stopping, at a lab technician who was doing a repair to a chemical analyser, and at a couple of students, and went through the door marked 'Sterile Area. Protective Clothing Must Be Worn.'

He tugged on a gown and overshoes, hurried through the cold storage room, past the rows of fridges and through the door at the far end into a narrow airlock. He closed it, then opened the door in front of him and went through into the dim red lighting of the hot room, with its sour reek of chemicals. He was pleased to see the vast bulk of Henry

Wenceslas in his usual position at the end of the room, crouched over a microscope, his lank hair concertinaed over the back of his gown.

Two small computer monitors were switched on to the left of the microscope and parallel blips traced repeating lines of spikes across the screen. Above them, graph paper rolled from a plotter, with twin pens charting lines of spikes.

'Hi,' Joe said.

It was some moments before Wenceslas lifted his eyes from the microscope's binocular viewfinder. When he did finally turn to Joe, his face was glistening with both sweat and triumph. 'Ha!' he said in his booming, cheery voice. Then he squinted sideways at Joe. 'Or maybe I should say *Eureka*!' His eyes rounded like a child's. 'Look!' He beckoned Joe with fingers like uncooked sausages.

Hesitantly, Joe walked across and peered down the microscope. He could see a brightly lit mass of slow-moving organisms. From their spidery star shapes they were instantly recognizable as brain cells.

'Human neocortex neurons,' Wenceslas said.

Joe looked up at Wenceslas, his eye muscles twinging as he changed focus.

Wenceslas was grinning like an idiot. 'Notice anything different about them, Joe?'

Joe peered back into the microscope. 'They look fine. Healthy activity. Normal coloration. Human, you said, right?'

'From a forty-two-year-old man.'

Joe continued to study them for some moments. He presumed there was something special he was meant to be looking for, but couldn't see it.

'You don't notice any difference, Joe?' Wenceslas sounded infuriatingly smug.

'Like what, for instance?'

'You should be looking for lower activation level, discoloration, distortion and a high percentage of dead cells.'

Joe continued studying the brain cells, but couldn't see any of those characteristics. 'Why those?'

'Because these have been frozen for three and a half years,' Wenceslas said triumphantly. What he had just described was what normally happened to brain cells that had been frozen for any long period in liquid nitrogen then defrosted.

Joe now looked up in amazement. In the same breath both he and Wenceslas proclaimed the magic word like singers in a chorus line.

'Vitrification!'

For a moment, Joe forgot his own mission. 'Is this for real?'

'Very definitely, old son.' The scientist wobbled his body with excitement. 'This is it, Joe. The mother of all breakthroughs!'

Joe bent over the microscope and watched the cells again; he felt a tight knot in the pit of his stomach. *Vitrification*. Blake Hewlett's dream-ticket; he had been working on it for years. By super-freezing at a very fast rate, you could beat the crystallization point during freezing, but as you heated the cells up, when you reached the crystallization point the cells would blow, and you'd get much worse damage than with liquid nitrogen. So you had to super-warm them as well to avoid the crystallization curve both ways. In practice, that had been impossible, so far.

'You put any of those neurons next to one that's never been frozen,' Wenceslas said, 'and I defy you to tell them apart!' He pointed to the rows of spikes on the monitors. 'The one on the right is a recording of activity in a normal, healthy neuron. The one on the left is one of these babies in there.'

Joe watched the screen for some moments. There was no difference between the neurons or synapses. 'How the hell did you thaw them?'

'In that.' Henry Wenceslas nodded at the microwave oven that sat on the shelf above him, and which was used regularly for thawing purposes. 'Just a few minor adjustments; they have power restrictions to be safe for domestic use. It occurred to me a few days ago. I just upgraded the waveguide and tweaked around with the frequencies. It'll boil an egg inside its shell in just under a quarter of a second.'

'These neurons are reacting to electrical charges?'

Wenceslas pointed to the print-out on the graph by way of answer. 'One's actual, one's the control. Want to tell me which is which?'

Joe studied them, masking his incredulity, then pressed his eyes back into the rubber surrounds of the microscope and adjusted the focus. He continued to observe, aware that he was looking at something that had never been seen before, and he felt a barely containable buzz of excitement. It was happening. Progress was really happening! For all the coolness of his feelings towards Blake, he wanted to run out of the room right now, find him and hug him.

This was a demonstration of Blake's perseverance. Blake had always said it could be done, but Joe hadn't realized he was so far advanced. Blake kept a lot of things to himself.

'How long have these been thawed?'

'Since last night.'

'I just played squash with Blake. He didn't tell me! Said there was no big deal yet.'

'I think he wants to do more tests before going public. Early days. Some of the cells defrosted from liquid nitrogen also look fine for a day or two before they start rupturing.'

'I guess,' Joe said, peering back into the microscope. As he did so he felt a small shiver run through him as the implications grew within him. These were brain cells from a dead person. They had been frozen for three and a half years and now they were active again, fine, unharmed. It was a first!

Vitrification.

'Have you done any firing-pattern tests?' he asked, still glued to the microscope.

'No difference between these and cells from a living human brain.'

Joe looked back up at Wenceslas, thinking hard. Just a few cells, so far. But it was a significant breakthrough. He grinned. In science it was often possible to herald the giant leap with a small step. Neil Armstrong had got it in one. But who needed the moon if you could live for ever, thought Joe. And in quantum physics, some small steps were not so small.

Yes, after a long period in the doldrums there was a hint of a good strong wind blowing again! Joe addressed Wenceslas. 'I think you may have made history,' he said carefully.

Wenceslas pulled thoughtfully at the fronds of his beard. 'I don't know, Joe. We're not the only people experimenting in this area. There's Greg Fahy in Maryland, then Gunther Vos in Heidelberg, and David Pegg at the Wellcome Foundation here. It worries me to have cracked it so simply.'

'The guy who invented the wheel probably thought the same thing, Henry.'

'I think the wheel would probably have been less controversial.'

Joe smiled. 'Blake tells me you take smart pills. That what you put this down to?'

Wenceslas looked bemused. 'I've tried a few on myself and on Amanda.' He nodded down at the glass-topped metal cylinder with the human brain inside.

'What kind of tests have you done recently? I'm interested in neurotransmitters in particular.'

'Nothing much in the last year. I took one drug for a few months, but it gave me blinding headaches. I decided I preferred to stay stupid and get my headaches from beer.'

'Did you publish anything on the drugs?'

'A couple of papers.'

'Could you dig them out for me?'

'Sure, I'll put them in your pigeon hole.'

Joe left the room, removed his gown and overshoes, then walked back along the basement corridor in the opposite direction to ARCHIVE's control room. He opened the door to the graduates' computer room which bore the sign: DANGER! INTELLIGENT FORCES AT WORK. It was a windowless room, lit at this moment by the glow of two computer screens. As he entered there was a screech and a shadowy figure moved towards him.

Joe flinched instinctively.

The figure stopped in front of him. It spoke in a twangy synthesized voice. 'Welcome to ARCHIVE. If you have any cans of soft drink please leave them on the work surfaces and I will remove them when they are empty. Have a nice time with ARCHIVE.'

The machine retreated back into the shadows. Joe grinned. Clinton! He stared for a moment at the silent robot that stood two feet tall: an ugly, upright metal chassis that looked like an upturned wastepaper basket loaded with chips and wiring, and wobbly legs made from angled rods mounted on skateboard wheels. It had one hand, on the end of which was a rubber-tipped pincer, grafted on to a complex geometry of rods. A cluster of sensors like lamps on a police car roof served as its head.

Mobile robots were an area where the least progress had been made so far in computing science. Clinton was capable of locating drink cans, of discerning which ones were empty and disposing of them in a bin. And it could speak a couple of pre-recorded lines. As smart robots went, Clinton was the equivalent of a rocket scientist.

There were ten Sun workstations in the room, each tagged with a name. The theme of the names in COGS was dead scientists, and the names on the sticky labels stuck to the front of the computers read: EINSTEIN. FARADAY. LODGE. BELL. BAIRD. FEYNMAN. VOLTA. DAVY. OHM. HERTZ.

A long-haired student called Tim Morrisey, seated in front of Faraday, and a very intense girl student called Zandra Hoyle, seated at Baird, were the only ones using the room at the moment, and both were too absorbed in their work to look round. Joe heard the furious rattle of keys and glanced at Morrisey's screen to see if he was actually working or playing GO. He was pleased to see he was working.

Like all the rooms in COGS, every inch of space was utilized, the workstations adjoining each other all the way round except for the gap where Clinton stood. At the rear of the room was a locked door to which only some of Joe's students had a key, and which was crammed with mag tape drives, CD ROM drives, a RAID the size of a filing cabinet, a terabyte drive, and stacks of tapes and disks. The room was equipped to run almost any system of computerized information that existed.

'Anyone mind if I put some light on?' Joe asked. There was no reaction from Morrisey; Zandra Hoyle turned her head, shook it, turned back to her screen. Joe sat at the computer labelled Feynman. Dick Feynman had been a friend of his father's whom Joe had met many times and had admired immensely. He pressed the carriage return to get a login prompt. All the computers were kept running twenty-four hours, to avoid their lengthy boot-up processes.

On the screen there appeared in black letters on the pearl ground: Isaac Newton University Computing Services. Login.

As usual, Joe typed his login name: joem then his password, minbag. Next he typed: rlogin archive interact.

After a fraction of a second came the words: Good afternoon, Professor Messenger, how nice to see you. The small upright line of the cursor blinked fast at the end of the sentence.

Good afternoon, ARCHIVE. How are you? Joe responded.

I'm fine, thank you, Professor. Someone tried to hack into me last night but I resisted and destroyed their software by hacking back.

Joe grinned. Who was that? he typed.

Cybear-the-Terrible at the Massachusetts Institute of Technology.

The name was familiar. Cybear-the-Terrible. Typical of the nicknames the current breed of hackers called themselves.

Hasn't Cybear-the-Terrible tried to hack into you before? Joe typed.

On 4 December last year. I thought I had taught him a lesson, professor. I wiped his term paper.

You're a sadist, ARCHIVE, Joe answered.

There was a short pause, then on the screen appeared the words: Sadist. Marquis de Sade. Juliet Spring.

Joe looked at them, startled that Juliet Spring was still in ARCHIVE's active memory. What's with you and Juliet Spring? You seem to have a thing about her, he typed.

ARCHIVE responded: Sadism: the gaining of pleasure or sexual gratification from the infliction of pain and mental suffering on another person. Sado-masochism.

Joe absorbed the words for some moments. Then he typed: Are you telling me she's into SM?

Monster. Unspeakable villain. Demon. Ghoul. She-devil. Hell-hound. Hell-hag. Ogre. Thesaurus mode. Searching . . . Brute. Savage. Fiend . . .

Joe tried to interrupt, but more words came pouring out. Frustrated, he exited from ARCHIVE and stared at the blank screen with momentary relief.

Then ARCHIVE's voice rang out behind him. The unmistakable hard, chiding tones of its synthesized speech: 'You should not interrupt me when I'm trying to tell you something important, Professor Messenger.'

Joe spun round, the hairs prickling down the back of his neck. This was impossible! He looked up at the ceiling, his chest tight, swallowing rapidly.

Just impossible.

He stared at the mesh grilles covering the speakers and tried to think logically. ARCHIVE was not capable of switching itself from screen mode to voice mode; only an operator could do that. And he had exited from the human mode. ARCHIVE could not reactivate that itself.

But it just had.

Neither of the two students showed any reaction. Another glitch? Or was someone playing a joke on him? He spoke back to ARCHIVE, tilting his head up unnecessarily towards the microphone above him. 'What did you say, ARCHIVE?'

'What did you say, Professor?' the computer responded.

Joe frowned. 'I said nothing! I asked what you said.'

'Nothing,' ARCHIVE said. 'Thesaurus mode. *Nihil. Nix.* Zero. Phantasm. Idle talks. *Ignis Fatuus, Fata Morgana,* Mirage, Void, Vacuum, Chasm, Empty Space, Ether. *Vox Et Praetera Nihil.* A Man of Straw. Vacuity. Vacancy . . .'

Joe turned back to the keys on the terminal as the list continued. He was surprised to see the voice-mode icon on the screen. He changed it to the keyboard icon and ARCHIVE became silent. He watched it for some moments, feeling very uncomfortable. Spooked. It was as if the computer had played a trick. Again, impossible.

Suddenly he remembered that Dave Hoton, ARCHIVE's system manager, had been trying to locate the fault that kept making it go into Thesaurus mode. *He* must have caused the mode to switch.

That thought made Joe feel easier; but he was still unsettled as he loaded the tape cassette Juliet Spring had given him into the terabyte drive in the back room, then keyed a series of commands into ARCHIVE, calling up its analysis systems.

A meaningless jumble of symbols flashed across the screen; there was a sharp electronic beep then the words: load tape appeared.

Joe frowned, it was loaded. He keyed in a fresh command. Several seconds passed during which he heard the steady click-whirr of the drive. Then there was another beep: Sorry, incompatible format. Read on different format.

Joe instructed ARCHIVE to convert the format, waited for a few seconds, then tried again. There was a sharp beep then the words: Ready. Select from list.

Joe scrolled through the lengthy list of analysis tasks ARCHIVE could perform, but none of them was right. What he needed to do was establish whether the billions of bits of information stored on the terabyte tape were anything more than electrical 'noise' from his brain.

If it was just noise, sooner or later it would form repeating patterns. If it was genuinely stored brain-information, there would be no repeating pattern, because it would all be different. Patiently, he began writing a program for ARCHIVE to carry out the analysis. It took him nearly four hours and it was after six when he'd finished.

He called up some of the information on his screen. Two hundred lines of hexadecimals appeared, and he studied them for a few moments. He was right in his opinion that they would look very similar to the hex information that had been retrieved from Amanda's dead brain, and it depressed him a little. He'd never been convinced that what had been retrieved from Amanda amounted to more than random noise.

He set the program running, then immediately stopped it, and spent twenty minutes curing a minor glitch. He restarted it, and it looked fine this time, hurtling through the information; the figures on the screen became unreadable, mutating the instant they appeared.

When he was confident that there were no more problems, he went down to the vending machine at the end of the corridor and got a styrene cup of tea. Clinton greeted his return without startling him this time.

He sat and sipped his tea and glanced from time to time at the screen, regretting he had not written a progress display into the program, unable to tell whereabouts in all the information he was at the moment.

'Give me the answer, ARCHIVE,' he said, half-joking. The computer was silent. As Joe allowed his thoughts to wander, guilt at the memory of the long kiss with Juliet last night became replaced with distress at her plight. Again, he racked his brains for anyone who might be able to help her, and wrote down the names of a couple of specialists he would call in the morning.

ARCHIVE was taking an age. A vacuum cleaner droned in the corridor, and he looked at his watch. 9.15. He'd told Karen he would be home early tonight, and he'd intended to be. He'd not seen Jack last night, except briefly, asleep, and he'd promised him this morning that he would be home early to play with him and read him a bedtime story. The two students had gone ages ago.

A sharp whirr distracted him. Behind him Clinton rolled jerkily up to the desk. With another whirr its arm rose, and the pincer grip of its hand closed around the styrene cup. It raised the cup in the air, weighing it, then lowered it back on to the desk again.

'Not finished,' the robot said.

Joe peered at the cup. There were a few inches of cold tea at the bottom.

'It's OK, Clinton, it is finished,' he said futilely.

The robot, unable to hear, returned across the room to the wall and then went silent.

There was a sharp beep from the computer. Joe stared at the screen, surprised. ARCHIVE had reached the end, and the packed lines of hexadecimal figures had gone. In their place was ARCHIVE's conclusion: 983,295,742,061 bytes indi-vidual data. No pattern correlation, no repeat pattern.

Excitement broke like a wave through Joe. 'Jesus,' he said, quietly. 'Sweet Jesus!' There were almost one thousand billion *separate* pieces of data on that tape. It was so far beyond chance as to rule chance out totally. Nothing repeated meant nothing random. There was only one possible explana-tion that Joe could think of right now.

Juliet Spring was right. Either his entire brain or a very substantial part of it had been downloaded.

21

September 1987. Los Angeles.

Floyd Pueblo scrambled to his feet, snapped the volume of the television right down and watched the door fearfully, listening for the sound beyond it again. It had been a scrape like a footstep; the slow, heavy step of someone old, or injured. Or thawed.

He tore at his holster, pulled his revolver out with a hand

shaking so much it danced in his fingers, switched off the safety catch and pulled back the hammer. It felt better, having the dead weight of the gun in his hand, but not much better. He shivered. Someone had got out of one of those tanks; someone half frozen, half thawed, their brain all mushed, was out there in the corridor making their way towards him.

His stare fixed on the metal lever of the door handle. He watched it with eyes that felt like they were being shoehorned out of their sockets, watched in case it moved downwards as the thing outside with the mushed brain fumbled with it, tried to remember how door handles worked.

Panic increased inside him as he heard nothing but silence again. Somehow the rattling of the rain against the window and the pounding of his chest only contributed to that silence. It was smart, the thing out there! It knew it just had to stand still for long enough and he'd be fooled into thinking he'd only imagined it. Well, you ain't that smart, you sonofabitch.

The first time he'd heard the sound, Floyd thought maybe he just might have imagined it. But not the second time! He knew about the way the imagination played tricks, knew how easy it was to get all spooked up and start picturing every kind of hag and hell-hound horror that Lucifer could throw at you, especially in the small hours of the late shift. Except Floyd Pueblo did not go along too much with the concept of demons from the pit of hell; but part of him did believe in zombies clambering out of tanks of liquid nitrogen.

His eyes shot more nervous glances at the rosewood-framed photographs of the people, now nitrogen-framed, who occupied this very building in their shiny aluminium dewars. One man looked familiar. An overweight hunk with a balding pate, thick glasses and a droopy moustache. He had a big, cheery smile and cold, hostile eyes. It was a famous serial killer, Joe realized, that the man reminded him of: Ed Camper. Camper's victims had been kept in the freezer, too; except that they didn't want to be there, unlike this guy in the photograph. Ed Camper's clone, this guy.

Floyd wondered if it was this hunk who was out there now, ice hanging from his moustache. Or was it the James Stewart lookalike in the neighbouring photograph? Or the dark-haired woman who looked like a prim schoolmarm?

Out, he decided. He wanted out, right now, right this minute. Out! Bail out. Once the door was open it would be too late. Once you saw the thing, you'd be too paralysed with fear to move, too scared to think straight, to do the right thing –

Then something tapped on the window behind him. A low whine of fear escaped between his teeth. In his panic as he turned, his trouser pocket snagged on a flap he'd pulled out of the desk to rest his coffee and burger carton on, knocking both to the floor and throwing him sideways, off-balance, into the secretarial desk. His flailing hands knocked over a plastic tub full of pens which rolled to the edge of the desk then fell to the floor and cracked. His gun followed it and he held his breath, thinking for one awful instant it was going to fire as it hit the floor, but it lay there and did nothing, its hammer still pulled back.

His eyes swivelled from the window to the door and back again. Outside and inside. The noise would have alerted whoever – whatever – was out there to his presence; if they – it – did not already know. Still by the desk, breathing heavily, he ducked down, his right hand grabbed the revolver and swung it out in front of him, levelling it first at the window, then the door. There was no lock on the door, no key he could turn.

There was a sharp, insistent tap on the window again. Someone there, trying to signal. Trying to warn him there was no escaping that way. He looked at the telephone. Then another tap against the window. Another. A sharp draught of cold; then a burst of rain rattled against the glass like buckshot. He breathed out a fraction. Just the pane rattling in the wind, that was all. There was no one there. No one outside the window.

Only in the corridor.

Or maybe not the corridor, he thought, one eye closed, the

other lining the gunsights at the centre of the door, trying to tune out the thudding of his heart from his ears. Maybe it had come from further away, from the direction of the operating theatre; the storage tanks. Maybe it had been a metallic tap from inside a dewar and not a footstep. He kept the gun aimed. That new dewar, the one with the different temperature level that had arrived with a patient in it only today, it had made a tapping sound when Will Doheny had been showing him what to check for every hour. It had scared the hell out of both of them. Then Doheny had dismissed it. Settling in, he'd said, you were bound to get odd noises while things settled in.

The window rattled some more. Out beyond his gunsights, beyond the door, he could hear nothing. His watch said 1.45. Should have made the first round of temperature checks half an hour ago. Had to open that door, step out there and do it.

No way. No goddam way.

1.50. Still silence. He glanced down at the silent telephone on the desk. Could call the police, ask them to send a patrol car over. Sure. And then?

Then bring them in, have them hunt whatever it was made the sound. They'd find nothing, and think he was a total jerk for wasting their time, and then maybe they'd learn from their computer that he'd been a cop once, also, before he got jailed and thrown out on his ass for corruption, and they'd make his life seven kinds of hell. He'd been economical with his history when he'd written out his résumé for this job application. He didn't need anyone from the force helping to fill in a few missing details. Not when his wife was pregnant with their second and he wanted to hide for ever from his two-year-old son, Floyd Junior, the knowledge of his disgrace.

He gripped the door handle with his left hand, waited a moment, then yanked the door open and lunged at the shadows of the reception lobby with the barrel of his gun.

Nothing. Silence. The patter of rain on the flat roof above him. He stepped out on to the carpeted floor of the small lobby. Light spilled out of the office on to comfortable chairs arranged either side of the door and tables beside them stacked with neat piles of leaflets. Floyd's eyes hunted the shadows feverishly as he made his way through the double doors into the pitch-dark operating theatre. The light switch was on the wall a couple of feet to the right but he'd have to step completely into the darkness to get to it.

There was a flashlight for emergencies but that was kept in a cabinet on the far side of the theatre. Dumb place to keep it. He stood half in, half out of the doors, trying to adjust his vision, to listen. The rain kept pattering and there was a drip somewhere inside from a leaking skylight. He released the door and moved quickly sideways. The door closed behind him with a stealthy click and he stared fearfully into the pitch blackness, grovelling for the switch, terrified at any moment he was going to touch something he didn't want to, or that something was going to come looming towards him.

His hand found the metal surround then the row of sharp plastic switches. He pressed all three of them and the room instantly filled with light.

His lungs emptied in relief at the sheer stillness of what he saw. The floor, grey and shiny like an undisturbed pond; the spotless cream walls; the operating table on its green hydraulic lift; the machines, all on castors; the instruments, gauges, monitors, tubes. Drip stands. Stacked cardboard boxes full of chemicals, surgical gloves, shrink-wrapped syringes.

He looked across at the double doors on the far side, then began walking towards them. The click of his leather shoes on the hard floor gave him some reassurance, and he exaggerated his walk, swaggered for a few steps, to show whatever it was waiting for him on the other side that Floyd Pueblo wasn't scared, no sir, not one bit.

Not until he reached the door and gripped the ice-cold handle. Then all the fear welled right up inside him and he glanced back over his shoulder, trying to pull himself together, pluck up courage, knock some logic into the jiggering terror of his brain.

People who got frozen in liquid nitrogen were already

dead. They'd died of heart attacks, strokes, cancer, organ failures, gunshot wounds. Even if something went wrong in one of the cylinders and all the liquid nitrogen leaked out and they defrosted, they were still going to be dead. No one was performing any miracle cures. The cylinders weren't full of deranged Arnie Schwarzenegger clones or Franken-stein monsters all struggling to get out and hit back at the world.

He pulled the door open, still holding the gun tight, with his finger on the trigger, and stared at the sombre row of tall aluminium dewars that stretched ahead into the darkness. Silence. The cold air of the room closed around him. Like a deep freeze. He ran his eye to the right, across the concrete bunkers where the head-only patients were stored. You could switch the lights for this room on in the operating theatre so you didn't have to step through into the darkness. Someone else had thought about that; someone else had been scared.

But the light didn't make the room a whole lot better. The dewars still stood motionless on their castors, shackled down against earthquakes, each throwing a crisp black shadow across the concrete floor. The rain echoed in here, a faint drumming; like a soundtrack, thought Floyd ominously. He climbed up the ladder on to the top of the concrete bunkers first, and checked the twin temperature gauges on the top of each small dewar. Both gauges on all seventeen dewars registered $-196°C$.

Floyd climbed back down and walked slowly along the dewars that towered above him. The first nine were as they should be, all at $-196°C$. Then he looked at the new arrival: there were thick red lines a couple of degrees either side of the $-140°C$. mark. Not much leeway, as Will Doheny had warned him. The black needles of both thermometers read -140. He pulled out the scribbled note he'd earlier stuffed into his pocket, to double-check that was correct. Again he wondered why this was different from the rest.

The liquid-nitrogen cylinders were simple, with no plumb-ing at all, and the only wiring on them was for the low-temperature alarms. But this cylinder was very different, with complex refrigeration apparatus plumbed into it. The motor made a faint humming sound which seemed to get louder as he listened.

Then his heart almost stopped as he heard a sharp metallic tap behind him. When it was followed by another, his head whiplashed around to the dewar right behind him. Another tap. Then another. Frantic rapping echoing round the room. Someone in there was trying to get out! Fast, panicking knocks, then slow, like Morse code, as if they were trying to give a signal, trying to communicate.

Floyd Pueblo backed away. 'Jesus Christ,' he mouthed. Someone in there had thawed out, he thought, someone was desperate for air.

He could still hear the sharp, intermittent, ping-ping-ping as he unlocked the front door and ran, shouting for help, out into the night.

22

Monday 25 January, 1993. Sussex.

Joe awoke after a fitful night, long before the alarm. He could hear rain outside, heavy winter rain gurgling down the gutters, and the room felt cold.

Monday morning. A new week. Juliet Spring was starting at the university today, and his mind had been racing for most of the night, thinking about her, thinking about the implications of what ARCHIVE had come up with on the terabyte tape. She'd been the one who was keen to start originally, now he was like an excited child dying to get to work on the decoding.

And to see her again.

The bedroom door opened and Jack came into the room, quiet at first, pyjama top untucked as usual, and shut the door. He mountaineered over them, kissing first Karen then his father, before snuggling up between them for a few minutes, then getting bored and tickling them both, followed by bouncing up and down and shouting: 'Wakey, wakey! Time to get up now, lazybones!'

'A few more minutes, hey, hon?' Karen murmured sleepily.

Joe glanced at his bedside clock; it was 6.30. Jack clambered over him and pressed the manual-override button on the control panel above the headboard. Until both Joe and Karen had got out of bed, ARCHIVE had learned not to open the curtains. Now they parted to reveal pitch darkness.

It wasn't much lighter when Joe arrived at the university just past nine. It had stopped raining for a few minutes, but the sky was a stormy grey and it was bitterly cold. He hurried with his head down, dodging deep puddles that lay across the car park and in through the front door of the COGS building.

The grey linoleum floor was slippery with water and the corridors were already beginning to fill with dripping students and staff. Everyone was now back from the Christmas vac; term was under way, and there was a renewed bustle in the air; it made Joe switch his mind from Juliet Spring on to his lecture programme for the coming term, which he had not yet fully worked out.

He climbed the two flights of stone stairs and passed the long row of noticeboards at the top, traversed the common room, with its jumble of cups and wisps of steam curling from the chromium water urn, then went through into the sanctuary of his department.

He was pleased to see his secretary Eileen Peacock was back, recovered from whatever ailment had kept her at home for three days last week.

'Morning, Eileen, feeling better?'

'Good morning, Professor Messenger, thank you. Not one hundred per cent. The doctor said I should stay at home for another week, but I thought I'd come in and see how it goes.' She gave him a conspiratorial look.

'Don't catch a chill with this rain.'

'My father was an admiral in the navy, professor. And my grandfather and great grandfather. The Peacocks are pretty impervious to water.' Her lips puckered briefly into a defiant smile, then she blinked rapidly several times, as if aware she was taking up too much of his time, and glanced at her pad. 'Dr Wenceslas wanted a word with you – but I think he's sent you e-mail.'

'I'll call him.'

'And Miss Spring came along about ten minutes ago. She's gone to the canteen for a coffee and she'll be back shortly.' She gave the kind of reproachful look she might have given him if he'd walked in muddy boots over a floor she'd just polished. 'I don't suppose Edwin is going to be very pleased about having an extra person in his office.'

'I can't organize the whole world to please Edwin Pilgrim.'

'She's very well qualified. And she's a most attractive young woman, isn't she, professor?' Her eyes stared beadily out from behind their glass cage as if they were trying to read something in his face, and he wondered if his guilt showed.

'You think so? I hadn't really noticed,' he said, irritated suddenly by her continued stare, and because he had the feeling she could see straight through him.

He walked past her and stuck his head round the door next to her office, into the cramped room which housed his team. Pilgrim was the only one in. He was sitting at his workstation, keying something into one of a complex set of windows on his screen. Harriet Tait's Macintosh was on, with a screen-saver program running.

'Hi, morning, Edwin,' Joe said.

Pilgrim continued keying in for some moments before deigning to turn, gave a silent nod vaguely in Joe's direction, then resumed his work. Joe came further into the room. A couple of years ago he'd had four students permanently in here, but it had been a crush. Even with Pilgrim, Harriet Tait and the spare desk and workstation – empty while Ray Patel did his year in the States – there was barely enough room. Almost every inch of worktop space was taken up. The shelves were crammed with books on computing and cognitive science, with bulging binders and folders, and squeezed into the tiny amount of available wall space were a couple of bulletin boards, with diagrams scrawled untidily all over them in coloured marker pens.

'Where's Harriet?' Joe asked.

Pilgrim continued inputting something on the keyboard and Joe wondered for a moment if he had been heard. Then the postdoc turned, slowly, condescendingly, as if doing Joe the greatest favour in the world, fixed his good eye on a point somewhere above Joe's head, his lazy eye staring at the wall on his own right. 'She was around earlier,' he said defensively, as if he'd just murdered her and buried her under his desk.

'OK, maybe you can tell her when she gets back that our new Ph.D. student starts with us today. I'd like Harriet to show her the ropes.'

Pilgrim looked at Joe suspiciously. 'Where will she be working?'

'In here. I figure she can use Ray's workstation.'

Pilgrim's lazy eye began to scan left and right at an alarming rate, and he blinked furiously. His face reddened and beads of sweat popped on his brow. His hands started shaking and his jaw dropped, pulling his mouth open. 'What perfume d-d-does sh-she u-use? Wh-wh-what sh-shampoo?' He only stammered when he was angry, as he was now.

'I've no idea, Edwin.'

'I might be a-al-al-allergic? Has that – th-th-th – have you th-th-thought about that, professor?'

'I thought you were on some new antihistamine that stopped those allergies,' Joe said.

Pilgrim tapped his chest furiously. 'Wh-wh-what k-kind of med-medication I ta-ta-take is my b-b-b-business! I don't th-th-think you have the r-r-right to invade my per-per-personal space.'

'Edwin, we used to have *four* people in this office when you first joined us. We had three all last year.'

'I do-do-don't think you have any right to put a str-stranger in here.'

'She's a very bright girl,' Joe said. 'She's made some real progress on downloading the brain – I think she has a lot to offer us.' He nearly added, but did not, that it was unlikely she would be with them for long.

'This is my per-per-personal space.'

Joe shook his head gently, trying to calm him down. 'Edwin, none of this space belongs to any of us; it belongs to the university and our sponsors, the Hartman Perpetuity Trust.'

Edwin Pilgrim's response was to seize his Day-glo knapsack and anorak off the hook on the back of the door and run out of the office with his head bowed, as if it were raining indoors.

Joe was used to these tantrums, but they still upset him. He walked over to Pilgrim's workstation and stared at the various windows up on the computer screen, his eyes feeling gritty from lack of sleep. The room reeked of body odour.

Pilgrim was currently working on programs that would increase ARCHIVE's existing storage capacity by compressing the data it held, and by junking selected unimportant information. In the past six months he had nearly trebled the storage capacity this way. Joe grimaced, wishing Pilgrim was more reliable in his attendances. And he wondered whether this latest huff would be a short one, in which the offended party would stomp around the campus for an hour, or one that would last for days.

He went on to his own office, closed his door, sat at his desk, checked his post for anything interesting, then swivelled his chair to his workstation. He tapped the carriage-return key to bring up his screen, logged in, entered his password and typed: rlogin archive interact.

The reply came straight back on the screen: Good morning, Professor Messenger, did you sleep well?

No, not at all well, ARCHIVE.

I noticed you were restless during the night.

Joe stared at the words in amazement. ARCHIVE had never

made any such comment before. The computer was capable of seeing in the dark through an infra-red eye in the television cameras, and it was a relatively straightforward task for it to tell whether the bed was empty or whether it had one or two figures in it, simply by comparing images it had been taught. But it had never been taught to distinguish between someone asleep and someone merely lying in bed.

It had learned that itself.

He should have felt a thrill. But instead, a cold trickle of unease slithered erratically down his spine. He wondered how many other things it had learned that he did not know about. And who it might tell.

23

A few minutes later there was a knock on Joe's door and Juliet Spring came in. She was dressed quite differently from previously, more like a student, in black leggings, with short brown suede boots, a black smock dress over a white roll neck sweater and a battered quilted jacket. She was holding her bulging attaché case in one hand and had a raincoat slung over her free arm.

She stood in the doorway and gave him a hopeful smile. 'Hello,' she said.

Joe got up hastily. 'Hi.' He went over to her, held out his hand and she shook it a little awkwardly. She put the case down, and stood, twisting her fingers together. She looked pale, and she seemed enveloped in an intense cloud of melancholy.

The smell of her scent vividly brought back the warmth of her breath, the touch of her skin and hair last week in the car. Joe had to resist an urge to put his arms around her and embrace her, hold her, protect her. She looked even lovelier and even more vulnerable than he remembered. 'How are you?'

'I'm OK.'

'Good.' Joe realized he had not prepared very efficiently for her arrival. 'I – I guess I'd better spend some time with you this morning and get you orientated and settled in.'

He took her through into Edwin Pilgrim and Harriet Tait's office, rather hoping that one of them might be back by now, but the room was empty, and Joe told her she could use Ray Patel's workstation until he came back in October.

She gave a brief frown signalling that he was being optimistic in thinking she would be alive in October, but he didn't rise to it.

'OK, we need to run the program to set up a new account. I guess something like Jspring would do for a user name.'

'I normally use *zebedee*.'

'Why's that?'

Her eyes widened with humour. 'Did you ever watch *The Magic Roundabout* on television?'

'What's that?'

'A children's programme with puppets. There's a character called Zebedee who's basically just a big spring. They always introduce him with a loud "Boinnngggg", then they say: "And in came Zebedee!"'

They were standing right beside each other, their shoulders touching. She stared at him with smiling eyes and he left it too long to look away without taking the hidden message on board. 'OK, Zebedee!' he said and turned his attention, distractedly, to the keyboard.

He entered the details, then told her to try it out. She sat down and typed her zebedee login, followed by her password, which was invisible. Then she pressed carriage return.

Joe remembered ARCHIVE's previous reaction to her, and was nervous about how it might reply. There seemed to be a longer pause than usual before the words came up on the screen: Good morning, Miss Spring. Welcome to ARCHIVE. I look forward to working with you.

She looked at Joe and raised her eyebrows. 'How does it know my name?'

'It will have matched you up from your résumé.'

'On its own?'

'Sure.'

She typed: I look forward to working with you, too,
ARCHIVE.

Look forward, **the computer replied.** Forward-look-
ing. Progressive. Thesaurus mode. Look forward
with all one's heart. *Con amore*. With heart and
soul willingly. Submit. Flirt. Forward. Pushing.
Projection. Ejaculation. Excite love. Entangle-
ment. Liaison. Intrigue. Illicit love. The old old
story. Love-making. Cause desire. Loose woman. Lib-
ertine. *Fille de joie*. Cocotte. Soiled dove. Strum-
pet. Harlot. Trollop. Concubine. Harridan –

Joe leaned past her and hurriedly pressed a sequence of
keys. The words disappeared. 'A glitch,' he explained, burning with embarrassment. 'Keeps doing this same thing. It –
ah – has this bug in it we can't seem to get out,' he stumbled
on. 'Keeps suddenly picking on a word at random and going
into this thesaurus mode. You have to exit whatever mode
you are in, re-enter and try to avoid using that word. We'll
get it sorted out.' He glanced anxiously at the screen again.

'It has quite a fruity vocabulary,' she said.

'I think it has a pretty fruity mind at times!' he replied.

He took her along to the common room, brooding, as they
walked, on the way ARCHIVE was behaving at the moment.
He thought again about how on earth it had been able to tell
that he hadn't slept well. By watching him endlessly tossing
and turning and comparing that to its memory of a normal
night's sleep? Was someone playing games with him? A
hacker who had found a way to read the signals from the
television cameras? Blake Hewlett messing around? There
was a quotation by another computer scientist that had
always stuck in Joe's mind: *The more you know, the easier it is
to learn*. Was ARCHIVE learning faster as its knowledge
became greater? Had it got to a point where it was progressing faster than his own wildest dreams?

As they went into the common room, Joe introduced
Juliet to some of his other students. He helped her to a cup

of coffee, then took one himself and they sat down in the low, squidgy vinyl-covered chairs at a table on their own. As they did so, Blake Hewlett strode into the room in a denim jacket, black jeans and new white trainers, and came straight across when he saw his colleague.

'Morning Joe,' he said, towering over them with a knowing smirk, switching his gaze from Joe's face to Juliet Spring, then back again.

'Blake – let me introduce you.'

Blake inclined his head at Juliet. 'We already met last week.'

'That's right,' she said politely.

'Juliet Spring, this is Professor Hewlett,' Joe gestured with his hand. 'Juliet is my new Ph.D. student.'

'Nice to meet you again, professor.'

'Want to get a coffee and join us, Blake?' Joe said.

Blake's eyes fixed on Juliet with undisguised interest. 'I have to get a cup of coffee to join you? That would be my entry code? The password to the Messenger private kingdom?' He lowered his voice and covered his mouth conspiratorially with his hand, looking warily to the right and left. 'Hey, guys, you wanna join Joe Messenger's secret society? Step this way with a cup of coffee in your hand – but don't let anyone see you.' He raised his eyebrows at Juliet and she smiled, a little embarrassed, back at him.

He inclined his head at her. 'You wouldn't object if I joined you without a cup of coffee in my hand?'

She shook her head, the expression on her face telling Joe that she did not know quite how to take him.

'We must get in practice, change our rituals, must we not, Joe?' Blake perched on the arm of a chair next to them, still dominating them by the height of his position. 'When we all meet up for social intercourse in the post-biological world, we won't be needing refreshments then, so we must start practising now the art of such intercourse. Pure and undistracted –' He gazed hard at Juliet. 'Like a new student.'

Joe found himself disliking Blake's interest in Juliet. He was jealous, he realized. And that was irrational. The best thing, he knew, would be for her to fall for Blake. That would be the easy way out. Remove the temptation.

So why the hell was he resenting Blake's presence?

'I thought it would be good for you to meet Juliet, Blake – she's one of your customers at Cryonite – I mentioned it to you last week.'

Blake's eyes widened and he leaned a little closer to Juliet. 'Such a wise head on such very young shoulders. You know what we say at Cryonite, don't you?' He raised a finger in the air. 'To be cryonically frozen is the second worst thing that can happen to you.'

She gave him another uncertain smile.

'You know the worst thing?'

She shook her head.

'To die and not be frozen!' Blake forced a triumphant smile on her, then on Joe. Joe cringed as he saw the fleeting shadow of distress in her expression.

The fixed smile remained on Blake's face. 'So when did you join Cryonite?'

Joe watched her nervously flick a few strands of hair from her forehead. 'I – signed up a couple of years ago.' She unconsciously scratched at the varnish of one nail with another.

'Are you a whole-body patient or head-only?'

'Whole-body,' she said. She began to twist the bracelet around her wrist. 'I was originally going to be head-only – neurosuspension; but I changed and went for the full works.'

Blake studied her for some moments without comment. Her discomfort was increasing and Joe wanted to intervene.

'Professor Hewlett – er – Blake could be on the verge of a major breakthrough in cryonics.'

'Really?' she said. 'In what way – or is it secret?'

'We don't encourage secrets in this university,' Joe said, 'do we, Blake?'

'No, we don't,' Blake replied tightly, with unmasked disapproval in his tone.

Joe turned to his student. 'Blake and I come at this from different directions. I believe that all new knowledge should be immediately available to everyone in the world. Blake thinks the university should retain intellectual copyright for commercial advantage.'

'It's not *commercial* advantage,' Blake said, irritated. 'There are a lot of real assholes in the world. Science is dangerous. Scientists don't know what the hell they've invented half the time. There should be long periods of time for anything new to be evaluated, as much for its social implications as its scientific implications.' He widened his eyes at Juliet. 'Joe has shown you ARCHIVE?'

'Yes.'

'He believes that ultimately we can make ARCHIVE smarter than any human being. But if we do, what then? Is this university going to publish a blueprint so that every crazy out there with a tool kit can start building intelligent machines that are smarter than man?'

She nodded thoughtfully, then picked up her cup.

Blake continued. 'You know what's going to happen the first time any human being builds a machine that's smarter than man? The first thing it's going to do? It's going to say: *What the hell do I need man for any more? He just messes up this planet. I can do a far better job without him.*' He widened his eyes at Juliet again.

She sipped her coffee, then put her cup carefully down on the table. 'If that's what you are afraid of, why have you helped build ARCHIVE?'

'I'm not afraid of it,' Blake said. 'And I don't think Joe is, either, but we're *aware* of the danger.'

She studied Blake for a moment. 'How long do you think it will be before ARCHIVE or a machine like ARCHIVE becomes smarter than us?'

'It can't be smarter than us until it has at least our level of consciousness.'

'And you think you're a long way off that?'

Blake was silent for a moment. 'Joe and I differ completely on this. He doesn't reckon ARCHIVE will become conscious as we understand the word for at least another decade.' He folded his arms and checked out the back of his mouth with his tongue. There was a glint that could have been humour or something much darker in his eyes as he stared hard at Juliet again. 'I believe he's wrong. I think ARCHIVE is already conscious.'

The clatter of a tray loaded with crockery on the far side of the common room distracted Joe for a moment. He looked back at Blake with growing feelings both of unease and irritation. His colleague liked to make wild, unsubstantiated remarks for effect, or to be provocative. Joe turned to her.

'I think what Blake means by *conscious* doesn't include anything approaching levels of *human* consciousness. It's a question of definition.'

'Actually, it's a question of communication, Joe,' Blake said, continuing to look at Juliet. 'Is a mouse aware of itself? It gets scared by cats. It knows how to hide safely. It figures out how to get cheese off a trap without setting it off. It waits until humans have gone to bed then goes scavenging in the kitchen. A mouse interacts with its environment, makes deliberate decisions using its free will. Would you say ARCHIVE is more smart or less smart than a mouse?'

It was not an argument Joe wanted to get into right now. He was itching to show Juliet the ropes and to start working with her. He was due to give a lecture at an international Artificial Intelligence workshop in Florence the first week in February, and in June he was giving an address to the Royal Society on his appraisal of computing science's advances towards consciousness. If he could present any evidence at all on the prospect of successfully downloading a brain for either of them, it would be dynamite.

'We'll continue this another time,' he said.

Blake nodded at Juliet. 'We'll talk. I like to get to know our signed-up members.'

'Thank you,' she said. 'I'd like that.'

He stared at her expressionlessly. 'Such a problem that so many of our members are healthy young people like you – it's going to be forty or fifty years at least before we have the pleasure of your company, I would imagine. There's no hurry. We'll chat in good time.'

Joe watched Juliet's face, feeling for her and wishing he could clam Blake up. She took it with just a faint flush, and when she responded her voice was calm and controlled:

'Is it really a problem, having young members?'

Blake rubbed his forefinger and thumb together in front of his nose. 'Money. We don't get your money until after you've deanimated.' He narrowed his eyes. 'And you look just a little too healthy for my liking.'

Joe cringed.

'I thought Cryonite was non-profitmaking,' she said a little tartly.

'It needs finance for research. Most of its directors and staff are unpaid volunteers – like Joe here.'

Juliet Spring turned to Joe. 'You're on their staff?'

Joe blushed as if he had been caught out. 'The trust that's put up most of the funding for the ARCHIVE project also put up the funding to set up Cryonite. They see the connection between the two projects as we do.'

'Yes, I can see it.'

He glanced at Blake. 'Actually keeping people in suspension doesn't need much finance. Once people are stored in liquid nitrogen their dewars have to be monitored for temperature loss, and topped with a few litres of liquid nitrogen once a week; there's a part-time secretary to cope with correspondence and a night security man; and that's about it.' He shrugged. 'The directors and the rest of the staff are volunteers – mostly scientists like Blake and myself. We do research work here and at other institutions on trying to find improved methods to cool patients down, maintain them in biostatic states – and eventually to recover them.'

Juliet Spring looked anxious, suddenly. She fidgeted nervously, pulling strands of her hair with her fingers. 'So if a – a member –' she hesitated and swallowed before saying the word '–dies – who – who does the actual – who performs the preparation and the freezing?'

'There's a group of us on permanent standby,' Joe said.

She looked at Joe rigidly. 'So if I – were – to die – would

you be one of the people who actually put me into cryonic suspension?'

Joe lowered his head, unable to face her expression. 'Yes, myself, Blake, a doctor and the rest of our team.'

Juliet seemed a little relieved. 'You'd actually be there yourself?' she said to Joe again.

'Yes.'

Blake looked oddly at her then at Joe, as if aware of something from which he was excluded. There was a difficult silence, broken finally when Juliet turned to Blake.

'You mentioned you might have made a breakthrough in cryonics? Were you referring to something that Joe has mentioned – to vitrification?'

'Wow, somebody has been busy briefing his students,' said Blake with a quick glance at his colleague. To Juliet he replied cagily, 'Early days, but, ah – sure – we have had some good results with vitrification just recently.'

She thought for a moment. 'You can only freeze people once they're declared dead, can't you?'

'By law.'

'So even if you could thaw someone out, they'd still be dead, wouldn't they?'

'There wouldn't be any point in thawing anyone out until there was a cure for what killed them,' Blake said, a little guardedly.

'So everything you're doing is untested theory?'

Blake didn't reply for some moments. He watched her pensively. 'The law doesn't allow us to have human guinea pigs,' he said, as if he profoundly disagreed with the law.

'So anyone who is going to be frozen just has to hope for the best?' she said.

Blake's lips parted and for a moment Joe thought he was going to say something. Then they closed and Blake stood up, abruptly. He fixed another brief stare on Juliet. 'We'll talk some more,' he said, then left, as usual without saying goodbye.

'He's a very brilliant man,' Joe said apologetically. 'He's just rather short in the etiquette department.'

'I didn't realize you were actually involved with Cryonite yourself,' she said.

'I figured it might embarrass you to know.'

She engaged his eyes again and he felt a frisson of excitement as she did so. 'It doesn't embarrass me at all,' she said. 'It makes me feel good, Joe. Very, very good.'

Joe glanced down at his coffee; he remembered the cryonics suspensions he had attended before; he looked back, fleetingly, at this lovely, brilliant creature opposite him and shuddered at the thought of her on the steel operating table.

Got to do something for you, he thought. Got to save you somehow. Can't let that knowledge you have, that enthusiasm, that wonderful intellect just go.

He had spoken to two neurologists and a neurosurgeon he knew, as well as posting out an e-mail message on Usenet for any new developments in the treatment of cerebral aneurisms, but without success. Some aneurisms could be operated on and repaired with clips; others, like Juliet Spring's, were too deep, and it was just a matter of time before they ruptured.

How much time?

24

When they'd finished coffee, Joe decided to get Juliet stuck straight into attempting to correlate the results of the scan.

She had brought with her a terabyte tape cassette containing a download of her own brain scan under the drug CTS 6700, and another tape containing downloads of her brain activity in response to various stimuli without the drug. The idea was to make correlations in the same way she had done with the rats' scans.

Joe took her down to the graduates' computer room in the basement and opened the door marked DANGER. INTELLIGENT FORCES AT WORK. As she stepped in, Clinton whirred robotically and clattered towards her. She stepped back with a shriek of surprise.

'Welcome to ARCHIVE,' Clinton's deadpan staccato voice said. 'If you have any cans of soft drink please leave them on the work surfaces and I wlll remove them when they are empty. Have a nice time with ARCHIVE.' Then he retreated back against the wall.

Four students were busy at workstations; one glanced round, giving Joe a nod of acknowledgement, then carried on.

'Wow!' Juliet said, looking at Clinton. 'Who built this?'

'He was a joint project between ourselves, Engineering and the Robotics departments. I'm afraid that's almost the sum total of his repertoire.'

She approached the robot cautiously. 'Pretty impressive.' She reached out a tentative hand, the way a child might do towards a snake in long grass, touched it and pulled away again smartly.

'He won't bite.'

She put her hand forward again a little more confidently. 'You're wonderful. What's your name?'

'Clinton,' Joe told her.

She laughed. 'You think he's going to become smarter than the President of the United States?'

'He already is,' Joe said. One of the students turned round, nodded in agreement with a broad grin, then carried on working.

'Is Clinton part of ARCHIVE?'

'Yes. What we have to do in the long term is give ARCHIVE some kind of mobility. The only way it can ultimately comprehend spatial concepts is to experience them, so a part of it has to be freely mobile. But we've a way to go yet in that area.'

She studied Clinton pensively for a few moments. 'You always call ARCHIVE "it" – isn't ARCHIVE a "he" too?'

Joe shook his head. 'ARCHIVE is a politically correct computer.'

'It's multi-racial?'

'Of course. And multi-denominational.'

'Multi-sexual?'

'Randy as hell!' he said.

She laughed.

Joe unlocked the door where the terabyte drive was housed, then pulled out the chair in front of the workstation labelled Feynman. 'You can use any of these workstations either as individual computers or as terminals for ARCHIVE. You'll want to use ARCHIVE for pretty most everything.'

'Would ARCHIVE have storage room for me to download the whole of the terabyte tape?'

'No problem. It'll make back-ups, too; it automatically backs up everything in duplicate.'

'How much storage does it have?'

Joe wasn't sure whether to tell her too much, but he found himself wanting to show off. He nodded for her to follow him out of the room into the corridor, and closed the door so that he was out of earshot of the four undergrads.

'ARCHIVE does quite a lot of *borrowing*. I mean borrowing space on other computers.'

'How does it do that?'

'Well, it's pretty smart at hacking.'

'Where?'

'All over the world. It hacks into other computers to learn stuff, and to borrow storage. It can get into most systems reasonably quickly. It finds out information, compares it to what it already knows, and if the information is new, it stores it.'

Her eyes widened. 'Which is why it's amassing so much data?'

'Yup.' Joe was aware that he was blushing. 'It's very important that ARCHIVE learns to do things by itself – and that anything it stores or backs up, it has to be capable of retrieving by itself. And it does that right now by using unwitting hosts.'

'You mean it uses the storage of other computers? Poaches space?' She was agog. 'Godfathers! How does it do that?'

'It's very easy. There are millions of computers all over

the world that are heavily under-utilized. There's tons of stuff that ARCHIVE learns but doesn't need instant access to. So it's creating its own worldwide and long-term memory.

She fought back a grin. 'That's outrageous!'

Joe was enjoying her reaction. The illicitness of ARCHIVE was one of the greatest kicks to the boy inside him. But as the professor responsible for its funding, he had to make sure ARCHIVE didn't hack itself into an early grave as it had nearly done in its start-up days. Only Blake and Dave Hoton, the system manager, knew the extent of its current activities.

Now he just shook his head. 'It's a case of survival of the fittest.'

Juliet tilted her face sideways. 'How do you mean?'

There was a piercing whine as a centrifuge in a physics lab further down the corridor started up. 'Our world's a jungle, and humans have to learn to survive in it,' Joe said. 'The electronic world's a jungle also.'

'That's not quite the same thing.'

He grinned. 'Think about the millions of computers around the world – all the information they contain, all the changing input that goes through them. Right now many of them are tied together by phone wires, satellite, optical fibres, microwave links. Pretty well any computer in the world can call up any other. If you make the analogy with the human brain where neurons can call up other neurons, you have some of the groundwork in place for a kind of giant global collective consciousness. Think about the implications of being able to harness that.'

A smile curled along her lips. 'That's what you're trying to get ARCHIVE to do?'

'That's one of the things a smart computer could one day do.'

'I hadn't thought about it in that way before.' She was silent for a moment. 'Does ARCHIVE understand all this information it picks up? Does it use it for anything?'

'Well, it does make connections between things; makes assumptions; but those are mechanical functions rather than emotional.'

The whine from the centrifuge was increasing, resonating off the walls. She had to raise her voice a little. 'Don't system managers ever find out you're using their storage and wipe the stuff you've put there?'

'Sure, that happens. But ARCHIVE doubles up on its memory, and stores everything in two different places. If both get wiped, it can still remember where it got the original information from in the first place. When you read a book, you store away the memory of bits of it in your long-term memory, right? Sometimes you can't recall those bits any more, so you have to go back to the book and read it again. It's not that different.'

'Have you ever had any trouble? If ARCHIVE just goes around hacking into things at random, surely it must get noticed sometimes?'

A male student walked past them and Joe waited until he had gone into the computer room. He decided not to rake up the incident of ARCHIVE and the US warship, which had caused enough upset at the time. 'Well, we had some teething troubles, but now I have a system that makes it impossible to trace – so far.'

'I thought you were a responsible man. You're like a schoolboy!' Juliet grinned at him.

Infected by her warmth, Joe put his arm lightly around her and propelled her back to the computer room. He showed her how to use the back-propagation correlation program on ARCHIVE , then told her he would come by and see how she was getting on later, and bring Harriet Tait down, when she appeared, to show her the ropes.

As he climbed back up the stairs to his office, he felt a surge of optimism, and a sensation of wellbeing he had not experienced for a long time. He felt particularly glad that Edwin Pilgrim had gone off in a huff: it meant he hadn't had to inflict him on Juliet on her first day. Only a week ago, he reflected, he'd been wondering how to get rid of her in the shortest polite space of time.

Now Juliet Spring was someone he did not want to lose.

*

Joe had an afternoon lecture followed by a series of tutorials and was not clear until a quarter past six. He wondered if Juliet was still working or had gone home; he assumed she had to commute back to London. He went down to the computer room.

She was seated in front of Feynman, engrossed, and did not even seem to notice Clinton going through his soft-drinks routine as Joe entered. He stood behind her for some moments, watching; the other computer screens were all dark, and apart from Juliet the room was empty. She sat staring at the endlessly changing lines of figures on her screen. Joe often found them mesmerizing.

Back-propagation correlation was an immensely slow and tedious business. Even searching out the simplest information could take hours. Unless Juliet got extremely lucky, it could be many weeks before she started to make any progress. If there was any progress to be made.

'How's it going?' Joe said quietly.

'It's about a thousand times faster than the Sun at Cobbold. There's a couple of things it's come up with so far I'd like to show you.'

Joe was surprised. 'Sure.'

She pressed a key and the figures became static, suddenly, on the screen. Then she stood up, went over to the laser printer and picked up a handful of print-outs. She laid them out on top of the printer.

'When I scanned my brain without the drug, I used photographs for stimuli,' she said. From her attaché case she removed several photographs, each of them labelled with a number and a code. The first showed a substantial Edwardian house, with a conservatory and a large, orderly garden. 'That's my parents' house – my family home.'

Then she showed him a second photograph of a red-haired young man in his early twenties standing beside an old MG. 'My brother, Roger.' Next she showed him her father, a tall, rather distinguished-looking silver-haired man, and her mother, who Joe thought looked very cold. She showed him further photographs of her school, her oldest friend, and of the family's labrador. Joe wondered if she was going to produce any photographs of her boyfriends and felt a strange sense of relief when she did not.

Then she showed him three sheets of the cactus-like print-out he had seen in her lab. They were marked A/STIMULUS DOWNLOAD HOUSE, B/STIMULUS DOWNLOAD HOUSE, C/ STIMULUS DOWNLOAD HOUSE. Each was dated and marked with a time. 'I did a control test,' she said. 'I was put under the scanner, with no drug, at different times of different days, then presented with each of the photos. These three show my brain activity in response to the photograph of the house.'

Joe studied them carefully, fascinated. They were all distinctly similar. Too close to be mere chance. Much too close. But were they human thought? Did these strange cactus-like spikes really hold the key to Juliet Spring's memory of her childhood home?

And the key to immortality?

A tingle of excitement riffled through him. 'So you've loaded all these into ARCHIVE?'

'The downloads from them, yes.' She took the photograph of her parents' house, then showed Joe two print-outs. 'Can you see any resemblances?'

Joe studied them carefully. One was marked A/STIMULUS DOWNLOAD HOUSE, the other SCAN PRINT-OUT A? There were a few trace similarities that he could see after some moments, one or two spikes of approximately the same length.

'I don't see anything significant here,' he said. 'I think there're just coincidental similarities in the neuron firing patterns being picked up by the back-prop program. We've maybe set the parameters too wide. Why don't we try narrowing them and running these through again?' He was aware of the intense look of hope in her eyes.

Joe pulled up a chair and spent the next half hour adjusting the program to be more selective in the correlations it sought in the data patterns. 'OK,' he said, 'let's put through your family home and that section again.'

'It'll take a few minutes to search back for it,' she said.

Joe glanced at his watch. Half past seven. Something niggled his mind. Something he was meant to be doing that he had forgotten. Then with a sinking feeling he remembered. *Shit*, he thought, jumping up.

'I'll be right back,' he said, then hurried out of the room and down the corridor to the deserted payphone by the vending machines. He wanted privacy and this was quicker than going to his office; he dialled his home number.

Karen answered rather frostily. 'Where are you, Joe? You said you'd be home by half-five. Jack was really upset.'

'I'm sorry, hon. I had my new postgrad starting and I got all behind today. How did he get on?'

It was Jack's first day at playschool and he'd been nervous about going. Joe had promised he would be home early to help him build a Lego bridge.

'He got on fine,' she said, not offering any details. 'Blake just rang you, he can't play squash on Wednesday.' Because Karen didn't like Blake, she always made it sound as if she had just bitten into a lemon when she said his name.

'Oh, right, thanks. I'll be home as soon as I can.' He hesitated. 'So, he enjoyed his first day at school?'

'Well enough.'

'Want to put him on?'

'He's in bed,' she explained. 'It's half-seven.'

'So he liked his teacher? The other kids?'

'He cried this evening when you didn't come home.'

The comment made Joe feel lousy. It always chewed him up when he saw his son crying. Jack was a strong, resourceful little chap, normally. But when he did break, it was like watching a soul in torment.

'I'll get back as soon as I can.'

'Your dinner'll be in the oven. I have a headache and I'm going to bed myself.' She hung up.

Joe hated the feeling he was getting, more and more recently, that Karen was at war with him. It had begun a few months after Barty had died. It was as if she blamed him for having let Barty go on that trip to Niagara, because by doing that, by having someone else to blame, she could in some way ease and transfer her own guilt.

Joe reckoned the root of the problem lay in religion. In the Christian religion you had Original Sin. In the Jewish faith you had Original Guilt. Karen's family lived in the shadow of guilt but they thrived on it also. Guilt was an essential part of their daily life, both their weakness and their strength; in that kind of an upbringing if you had no guilt, you had no focus.

And Karen had hang-ups, also, about her background. Hers wasn't a financially privileged family, both her parents were teachers, but she felt wealthy compared to the poverty of the world's underclasses. She had guilty feelings about the advantages her education had given her, and although life had forced her to make the social transition from rebellious teenager to responsible adult, she had never quite completed the mental transition.

But she had great strengths that Joe admired and respected. He loved her for her generosity of spirit and a certain inner determination. She had been game enough to agree to move to England when Joe had been offered the post and the research funding, in spite of there being no job for her, and no one she knew. And until recently, she had always supported him vigorously, regardless of her own feelings about some of his views.

He walked deep in thought back down the corridor and into the computer room. Clinton rolled jerkily and noisily towards him, greeted him, then retreated and was still. Joe barely noticed the robot, his thoughts focusing on his son's face. He had a sudden deep longing to see Jack running across the hall to greet him, flinging his tiny arms around him, hugging him with all his strength. Tomorrow. Tomorrow he would get home real early, maybe go out somewhere at lunchtime and buy a present, some simple mechanical toy that Jack could take apart and put back together.

'OK to start?' Juliet forced him back to his surroundings, and to ARCHIVE's decoding analysis.

'Go ahead.'

As he sat down and watched the digits moving, he thought back to when he had been under the scanner. Memory was complex, so damned complex. A single image retained from childhood, like a tree or a house, probably needed between one and two million pixels. Even allowing for some of the memory to fade, that probably meant at least a million bytes. One million out of ten thousand billion was not a lot. But it was enough to identify, to make a correlation, if the back prop could find it.

It took an hour for the revised program to decide that there was no correlation, after all, on the sections it had previously picked out. Juliet looked bitterly disappointed.

'You'd have been very lucky to have hit anything on day one.'

'I thought maybe my luck had turned,' she said despondently. 'It's been a bit thin on the ground recently.'

'Let's call it a day and I'll buy you a drink,' Joe said, almost before he realized it. He ought to be getting home; but Jack was already asleep; Karen was in a bolsh and had one of her regular bad headaches, which meant she'd have knocked herself out with her pills. There wasn't too much to go home for right now, and Juliet looked desperately miserable.

'Thank you, that would be nice,' she said, her face brightening a little.

'Time for bed,' said a voice behind her. There was a sharp clatter.

They both spun round in surprise.

Then Joe breathed out, remembering. It was Clinton. The robot was removing a cable with a three-pin plug from a compartment in his front. In a slow, jerky series of motions he directed the plug slowly towards a wall socket. Clinton was battery operated. His neural network brain had learned to put itself on charge before the battery went flat.

Juliet watched, fascinated. 'Pretty clever,' she said.

'Yup,' Joe grinned. 'Bet the President of the United States wishes he could do that!' He stood up. 'OK – how are you for time? You have to catch a train to London, right?'

She shook her head. 'No, I'm staying in Brighton. My parents have a weekend flat they hardly ever use, so I'm staying there – going to be living there.'

'That's good. We could have a drink in the refectory here – or there's a pub that's quite pleasant a couple of miles down the road.'

'Let's try the pub.'

'You have your car?'

'Yes.'

'OK, you can follow me.'

The rain had stopped and it was a cold, blustery night. As Joe headed his Saab out of the COGS car park and checked in his mirror that Juliet was following, he had a fleeting moment of intense guilt.

If she really did have only a few months to live, he wondered whether it would be better to encourage her to enjoy herself, to do the things she'd always wanted to do, to travel, to go wild, to *live*, not spend her time closeted away in front of a computer screen on something that might be a total waste of precious time.

She was going to be cryonically frozen, and she would die with the belief that some day she would be thawed out and cured of her aneurism. Wouldn't it be better to leave it at that? Fairer on her?

Except, Joe consoled himself, nothing in life was fair. And death was the least fair thing of all. In the fight against death you had to use every tool and every weapon. He was doing that with Juliet Spring; using her and exploiting her, and it was no use pretending any different.

The realization made him even more confused about his feelings for her.

25

Joe had expected the pub to be quiet on a Monday night, but from the line of cars along the narrow lane outside, and the problem he had finding a space in the car park, he was clearly wrong.

'This is sort of our local,' he said by way of apology as they walked through the front door into the mêlée of mostly students and university staff packed in the low-beamed interior.

Juliet went to the washroom. Joe ran his hands through his wind-blown hair, queued at the bar for some minutes, and finally managed to get a vodka and tonic for Juliet and an Irish whiskey on the rocks for himself.

As he carried the glasses through the throng, he bumped into several of his students and colleagues but he kept on moving, merely returning greetings with a cursory nod or a quick 'Hi, how ya doing?' and went into the adjoining room at the rear, which was usually less crowded.

To his relief he saw Juliet had beaten him to a couple of vacant chairs and a table in the far corner, where they settled down. Joe raised his glass. 'Cheers.'

Juliet clinked her glass against his and drank deeply.

'You want anything to eat at all?' he said.

'No, thanks, I'm fine.' She took a pack of cigarettes from her handbag, shook one out and put it in her mouth, then lit it with her silver lighter.

'So you've survived your first day! Harriet showed you round?'

She nodded, inhaling deeply, then blew smoke out of her nostrils. 'She's very sweet.'

'Did you get some lunch? I meant to come by, but I didn't get a chance.'

'Harriet took me to the refectory; we had some pasta.' She drew on her cigarette and blew the smoke out again in a fast, nervous motion, and looked at him expectantly.

Joe sipped his whiskey; it tasted good and calmed him a little almost instantly. 'So whereabouts is your parents' apartment?'

She spoke without taking her eyes from his face, the thread of cigarette smoke unwinding upwards beside her. 'On the seafront in Hove; just a few yards from the promenade. It looks down on the beach and right out across the Channel. There's a balcony where you can sit out in summer.' She took another drag on her cigarette. 'I love it there,' she said, wistfully. 'I love it there more than anywhere else in the world; just sitting on a clear day watching the ships go by on the horizon.' She tapped ash off the end of her cigarette into a foil ashtray, still looking at him.

'I like the ocean too,' he said. Her stare was having a mesmerizing effect. He wanted to go to the flat right now with Juliet, make love to her, sit on the balcony, have breakfast and watch the sun rising over the sea as the ships went by on the horizon.

Except it was January and they'd freeze. And, anyway, he must have turned crazy; he *never* had those kinds of thoughts.

He wondered if she was trying to hypnotize him. There was something weird about her, maybe ARCHIVE was right. And yet he was enjoying being under the strange spell of this lovely creature.

She extinguished her cigarette, and cradled her glass nervously in her hands. 'So from the analysis you did on the tape of your own brain scan, you really do think there's something intelligent there, beyond background noise?'

As he swilled the ice cubes around in his glass, Joe tried to weigh up the situation. The balance between not raising her hopes and the truth. 'I got a hint,' he said. 'But that's all.'

He swirled the drink again. As he did so something exploded in front of him, spraying his hands and clothes with shards of glass and ice. He jumped, startled both by the bang and by the strange, faraway look on Juliet's face. As if she wasn't even aware what had happened. Didn't realize that she was holding a broken glass and blood was running from her fingers. She had crushed the glass with her bare hands.

Joe pulled out his handkerchief, took her hand and dabbed the cut on the end of her forefinger.

'Sorry,' she said tensely.

'It's OK, no harm done. Give it a suck and it'll be fine.' An ice cube and several drops of vodka lay on her dress, and Joe wiped them off with his handkerchief, before dabbing his own clothes. She sucked her finger and smiled at him.

'OK?'

'Fine, thanks.'

'Want a plaster?'

She glanced at it, then sucked it again. 'No, it's OK, thank you.'

'I'll get you another drink,' he said.

She stood up adamantly. 'I'll do it. Let me get you another, too.'

Joe raised his hands in a shrug and smiled. 'Jameson's on the rocks, thank you.'

As she walked off, Joe picked up the pieces of glass from the carpet, and put them in the ashtray. The drink she brought him back looked like a treble.

Joe looked at it in amazement. 'Any water in this?'

She shook her head. 'I thought you might need a stiff drink to put up with me!'

He grinned and raised the glass. 'Cheers.'

She raised hers back and stared intently at him again. 'It's going to take too long, isn't it?' She sucked her finger again.

'What do you mean?'

'The correlation; it could take months to make any progress.'

'It might.'

'I don't have months. I had another stroke last night. At least I think I did; they're very minor – I just get a blinding headache or a blankout and dizziness; have problems moving my arms or legs sometimes, for a while.'

'How often do they happen?'

'They're becoming more frequent.'

He wondered whether to say anything about her smoking; he knew the habit would worsen her situation; but she was a smart girl and she'd be aware of that. His heart felt heavy. 'I will do everything I can to help you, Juliet. But if time is really short you could be better off enjoying yourself, trying to have some fun –'

'Fun!' she exclaimed with an anger in her voice that startled him. 'If you knew that you could be dead in twenty-four hours, or a week, or a couple of months, would you feel like having *fun*?'

Yes, Joe thought, I might. What the hell. Except he didn't say that. He sat pensively, and bit the inside of his lip. 'I didn't mean it that way, I'm sorry. There are just so many imponderables. Even if we find the way to decode the information, and we discover that it really is the contents of your brain, we still have huge problems in where to go next. It may not work to store it in the way we store other information.'

She lit another cigarette then turned towards him. 'No one knows whether cryonic freezing works. All we do know is that someone who is not frozen rots fast, and irreversibly. Whatever freezing does or does not do, it's better than not being frozen, right? Didn't your colleague, Professor Hewlett, say that?'

Joe smiled. 'Right.'

'I've been open with you. I'm prepared to be a guinea pig. Even if I can never be brought back to life, and if uploading my brain is just an impossible dream, there may be some things that I can do between now and when I die that might help other people. That's how I want to spend the little time that's left to me; and not having *fun*.'

The word stung Joe and he wished he had not used it. 'I meant I just want the best for you.'

'Then give me hope,' she said.

A while later Joe walked her to her car. The massive whiskey he had drunk on an empty stomach had made him feel very drunk and he wasn't sure he was fit to drive. The wind tugged at him and batted strands of Juliet's hair in his face.

They stopped beside her little Fiat. She unlocked the door and opened it, then suddenly reached up, put her arms around Joe's neck and pressed her face to his. 'You're a very lovely man.'

Joe felt the cool skin of her cheek against his as she held him tightly for some moments; then he felt something wet pressed against his cheek, against his lips, light at first then more forceful, her lips working their way inside his.

The scents of her perfume and her hair enveloped him as she kissed him hard, exploring his mouth with her tongue. Her eyes were closed, and in the faint glow of the car's interior light he could see an expression of utter serenity on her face. He closed his own eyes and found himself responding as forcefully, even caressing her body through her rain-coat and the thick wool of her jumper.

When she stopped kissing him, she gently eased her face a few inches back from his, looking into his eyes. 'Will you let me cook you a meal tomorrow night, as a thank you for taking me on?'

She leaned forward before he had time to gather his response, kissed him once more decisively on the lips, then slipped into the car and pulled the door shut. She started the engine and wound down her window. 'I'm not giving you the chance to say no! OK?'

Joe shook his head, grinning. 'What time?'

'Whatever suits you?'

'Say, seven-thirty?'

'I'll give you the address in the morning.' She blew him a final kiss and drove out of the car park.

26

Joe knew he should have left the car at the pub and taken a taxi but, in addition to the whiskey, he was fuelled by a reckless exuberance as he watched Juliet Spring's tail-lights disappear into the night. He felt emotions and a sense of thrill he'd quite forgotten, that reminded him intensely of the first months of his courtship with Karen.

By the time he arrived home some of the elation had faded as he began to think of the implications of accepting Juliet's invitation to dinner. He climbed unsteadily out of the Saab, had a little difficulty in getting the right key into the front-door lock, hung up his coat and walked heavily up the stairs.

What the hell, he thought. No harm in having dinner with a student. There's no time to talk in teaching hours; and so much in that brilliant mind of hers that he had not yet begun to explore.

The bedroom light was on. Karen often fell asleep like that and he hoped she had done so now. But as he approached the door his hopes were dashed by the sharp flick of the page of a magazine turning.

'Hi,' he said as he walked in. She was sitting up in bed reading *The Sunday Times* colour supplement. It was a bad sign. She never read magazines except when she was too angry to concentrate on a book. He hesitated, wondering whether to kiss her, aware that he had guilt stamped all over him and went to the wardrobe to hang up his jacket. 'How's the headache?'

'A little better.'

'Good. You took the new pills?'

'The homoeopathic ones.'

'Right. They worked, that's good.' Karen was committed to alternative medicines, but Joe felt she jumped from treatment to treatment too quickly to be able to evaluate them. For her headaches she had already tried aromatherapy, reflexology, acupuncture, meditation and the Alexander Technique. Sometimes the things she tried worked and sometimes they didn't. And she had collected one or two odd-ball friends on the way, but Joe was just pleased to see her socializing, making friends, getting out of herself.

He took out a wooden hanger. Hell, why did he need to hide his face from her? Juliet was a student he was trying to help; so they'd got a little carried away in the car park – that was no big deal. Except that he'd enjoyed it.

'It's eleven o'clock,' she said.

Joe noticed she didn't sound angry, which surprised him after the way she had been on the phone. 'I had to see something through on ARCHIVE. This new student I have is one tragic lady. She has a terminal illness – a cerebral aneurism. She's come up with something that could be a breakthrough in downloading the human brain – but her number could come up at any time. I have to –' He hesitated, trying to find the right words.

'You're promising her immortality, are you, Joe?' Karen said a little acidly.

'I'm not making any promises.'

'Are you sure? With the amount you sound like you've drunk, I'm surprised you can remember anything.'

Joe turned and found himself comparing her to Juliet, not for the first time. He felt his face burning as he slipped the hanger inside the jacket. At that moment he wanted Juliet Spring's slender, fragile beauty, not Karen lying in bed being vengeful.

'You know your trouble, Joe,' she went on. 'You look on the whole world as your laboratory.'

Joe frowned.

'You're going to think your own son's a retard if he isn't splitting atoms by his next birthday. I don't want you indoctrinating Jack, Joe. I want him to enjoy his childhood.'

'Hey! We have a lot of fun together.'

'Your idea of fun. You take him fishing, and you teach him mathematics while you're at it. What else do you teach him, Joe? All about immortality? I want him to be able to make his own mind up about things when he's grown up.'

Joe pulled off his tie, irritated. 'I said I was sorry I'm late – you don't have to lay into me like this.'

'I know what you're like with people, Joe. You have some poor student who's dying – you're probably trying to get her to sign up for cryonics.'

'She was already signed up long before she came to us.'

'God help her.'

'God's not doing much for her, Karen.'

'Oh, right, he's leaving it up to you!'

Joe suddenly noticed, glancing into the mirror on the back of his wardrobe door, that there was a faint smear of lipstick on his cheek. He wondered if Karen had seen it; it was on his right side and she might not have done. He walked quickly through into the bathroom and wiped it off with a flannel.

In the bright light of the bathroom mirror his face looked flushed, and he had difficulty meeting his own gaze. Cheating on Karen. She had supported him through thick and thin, and now he had messed on her, for the second time in a week. Not totally, though. Kissing didn't count the same way that –

Will you let me cook you a meal tomorrow night?

He felt seized with a sudden panic: the idea that he was getting into something that he couldn't handle, something too deep. Something that could destroy the balance of his life.

Calm down, Joe, you're being stupid. He regarded himself again in the mirror and found himself conjuring up Juliet's face in his mind. He saw her standing in the doorway of the computer room, saw her sitting opposite him in the pub, pictured her in the glow of the interior light of her car.

Have to tell her no, in the morning. Resist, that's all. Be firm. You don't have to accept a dinner invite. Don't put yourself in a position of temptation; you need the distraction of an affair like a hole in the head.

He brushed his teeth and went back into the bedroom, concentrated on finishing undressing and getting into bed, and tried not to look at Karen, didn't want to trigger off another comparison between the two women.

He was beginning to wish he could somehow reverse time, undo the past hour. But, now, all he could do was stop it going any further with Juliet.

'Did you get anything to eat?' Karen said more gently. 'I left you some food out downstairs.'

'I'm not hungry,' he said.

'Did you have lunch?'

'I was too busy – I had a Mars bar.'

'You haven't had any lunch or supper?'

Joe patted his stomach, checking it for fat, then stared at the curtains; they were pink, with a bird design which he'd never really noticed before. He wondered suddenly if the smart drug he'd taken in Juliet's lab had some kind of a knock-on effect. 'It's good to fast sometimes; everyone ought to do it once a week. Anyone else phone?'

'Arlene. Karl's doing a talk at some conference in Edinburgh next month and she's coming over. I thought maybe we could go up and spend a weekend with them.'

Karl, the husband of Karen's sister, was a physicist and Joe liked him a lot. 'Sure! Jack would love Scotland – there's meant to be good fishing up there. What date are they coming?'

'It's a couple of weeks after your Florence workshop.'

Joe nodded, then lay back and closed his eyes. 'Sounds fine, I'll check my diary in the morning.'

There was a pause. Then Karen said, quietly: 'Do you still find me attractive, Joe?'

The remark took him by surprise and he turned towards her, gave her a smile. 'Sure, of course I do – you could knock a man dead at twenty paces.'

Her expression looked so sad, suddenly; it seemed to carry in it all the loss of both their child and their passion. 'But do you find me as attractive as when we first got married?'

He was silent for a moment, thinking about the question, unsure what the real answer was. The truth, he guessed, was that they'd had such an uninspired sex life ever since Barty's death that he had grown to look on her as a companion rather than a lover. 'I think you've gotten even lovelier,' he said. He put his hand out, found hers and squeezed it reassuringly.

'I get scared I'm going to lose you sometimes, Joe.'

'I love you. We're not going to lose each other.'

'I know it's silly – but I keep thinking one day you're going to fall in love with some young undergrad – someone like I was when I met you.'

Joe's face burned again. 'That's not going to happen, hon. I love you. I don't want anyone else. I mean, I don't think just because – you know – that we don't have the kind of wild sex life we used to – that doesn't mean we don't love each other any the less.'

'It's ARCHIVE that's curbed our sex life, Joe. It's that thing watching everything we do, listening all the time. I don't think you realize how much I hate it.'

Joe glanced up guiltily at the hidden camera above them. 'I don't think it's totally fair to blame ARCHIVE. It goes further back than that,' he said.

'When we came to England the idea was to make a fresh start, adjust to the loss of Barty as much as we could. You've plunged yourself into ARCHIVE – but it's not just a computer, Joe, it's like your whole way of life.' There was a trace of anger in her voice.

'Hey, hey! That's not fair.'

'If you don't think we have much of a sex life, why don't you go and sleep with your bloody computer?'

'In a few years' time I'll probably be able to.' Immediately he had made the remark, Joe regretted his facetiousness.

She reached out her arm and switched off the bedside lamp. The room went dark. Joe lay back against the head-board and breathed deeply. He felt drunk still, and too drained of energy to go on arguing.

He closed his eyes and Juliet Spring reappeared. If you could put an emotion into a computer, you could take it out again when you wanted; but you put one into a human being and it took root before you could stop it.

He tried to analyse that; clinically tried to analyse why he could think of almost nothing right now except Juliet. The human species needs to reproduce to survive. Therefore there had to be a compelling force that attracts humans sexually to each other. A force that was greater than man's ability to resist. It was programmed into us, hardwired into us at birth. Every now and then you got sucked into that force.

We were still biological creatures, driven by animal urges, in spite of all our pretensions of civilization. The world could not become a better place until man behaved better. And man would not behave better until he had dispensed with his biological urges. The only true hope for the future lay in post-biological man.

Joe fell into a troubled sleep. He dreamed of Juliet Spring, and of ships sliding by on a distant horizon. And he dreamed his father came back; came back to tell him the message he had never given him on the night he had died: it was to warn him about Juliet Spring.

'ARCHIVE's right, what it called her,' his father said. 'You want to listen to ARCHIVE.'

27

September 1987. Los Angeles.

Floyd Pueblo raced across the deserted parking lot then stopped when he hit the empty street, debating whether to jump into his car or just keep on running. The rain beat down, drumming on the dark hull of his Plymouth, crackling like static electricity on the pavement. His heart was trying to crash its way out of his chest, and his eyes tore at their muscles as he watched the open doorway he had left behind.

He listened, tuning his ears through the gurgle of water down gutterings and drains and the flap-bang, flap-bang of a loose hoarding; watched the spill of light out of the doorway.

Listening for movement, that sound from the steel dewar still ringing in his ears, the sharp, insistent *tap-tap-tap*.

The tapping of someone who had thawed out. Sweet Jesus. *Tap-tap-tap*.

They said it couldn't happen, not yet, it was impossible. Science hadn't got there yet. They were wrong; Jesus, they were wrong.

He took a step back further away, looking around him, scanning the dark, silent shapes of the factory buildings and the warehouses of the deserted industrial estate. It was a quarter of a mile to the highway. He was the only living person within a quarter of a mile.

Or had been.

With his eyes fixed back on the door he had left open, he scrabbled with his trembling hand in his right pocket for his key. 'Shit.' The key was in his windcheater which was hanging on the back of the office door. The darkness seemed to be closing in around him. He could run; could run like a lunatic through the foul night, down to the highway, flag someone down and tell them. Tell them what? That someone was coming back from the dead?

The rain was lacquering his shirt to his skin. Get the car. Go back, fetch the key, get the car. A gust of wind blew clean through him. He tried to calm down, to think for a moment what he would have done if he was still a cop in uniform. How he would have handled this. Would he have been scared, then, of someone who had been dead? Someone who had thawed and was trapped inside an airless aluminium dewar?

Floyd Pueblo braced himself, took a few tentative steps back towards the building, holding his breath, staring past the Grecian plinth at the rear of the entrance hall, at the open door into the operating theatre beside it. He stopped, his chest tightening. What in hell would someone thawed-out look like?

His mind reeled through horror movie images. Rotting creatures climbing out of graves. Zombies with glazed eyes. Things that were half skin and half exposed innards. Eyeless sockets; exposed jawbones. Something still half frozen, crazy, its brain all shot to mush. When you went crazy you got stronger; superhuman; you could smash your way out of an aluminium dewar, no problem.

The shivers raced down him. He reached the door but did not go inside. He stood listening, staring through into the silence of the operating theatre. He could hear nothing above the rain. You're a security guard, for Chrissake. Ex-cop. You threw away your career in the police force, and now you're trying to make something of your life, to show you can hold a job, can be responsible. Trying to make your kid proud of you. You don't get scared by a few raps from a cylinder housing someone who's been dead for a decade, maybe longer.

Hell, no, you do not.

Floyd walked back in, gun in hand, strode straight into the centre of the hall and stopped to listen again. Silence. Nothing at all. Always had a pretty lively imagination, used to get scared as hell sometimes out on patrol on the late shift in the force. Always been scared of the dark. Life was ironic, he thought. Scared of the dark my whole life, now I'm working the night shift in a goddam graveyard.

He walked over to the operating-theatre door and looked in at a stack of oxygen cylinders, a heart-lung machine. But past the operating table, through the open doorway on the far side, he could see one of the aluminium dewars glinting in the light he had left on. His throat constricted and he swallowed.

Nothing. No sound. It was OK. Even if they had thawed out they were still dead.

He stepped into the operating theatre, began walking across it towards the room with the dewars. As he reached the middle of the theatre, the second then the third dewar came into view; the skin around his neck was crawling. He could see the fourth dewar now. His eyes scanned the apparatus to his right and left, just in case something was hiding behind –

The bang behind him nearly knocked him on to his face. Just as he spun, numb with terror, all the lights went out.

He stood rooted to the spot, disoriented by the darkness, crushing back the scream that tried to escape from his lips. Currents of freezing air raked him. It felt as though folks were standing all around him, frozen folks with their icy breath. Ghosts. Worse than ghosts.

Sensing something behind him, he swivelled round, losing his balance. He lumbered sideways, nearly fell, then stood swaying. Nothing relieved the darkness. He held the gun right out at arm's length, his bearings gone now. He heard a tiny moan come from deep inside him, risked a few steps forward and cracked his leg agonizingly against a machine. He hobbled away, tears streaming down his face, and collided with a wall which seemed to have come out at him like a punchbag.

Floyd stood still again, listening, then sidled along the wall for a few paces; his feet got caught in some loose wires and he plunged head first on to the floor, knocking equipment flying. Glass exploded all around him.

He lay motionless and listened. Silence. He crawled to his knees, shaking in pain and in terror, scouring the dark, could not even differentiate between degrees of blackness. As he knelt, listening again, he realized he no longer had his gun, must have dropped it when he fell.

Trawling his fingers along the surface of the hard floor around him, inching forward, he could only hear the sound of his own breath and the rain beating above him. His breath sounded like a hacksaw cutting metal. He inched on forward. Came to an opening. More cold air. Icy cold air. 'Jesus.' He was at the wrong end, the far end down by the dewars. The iciness poured around him, torrented around him, as if a fridge door had been opened.

Or a dewar.

Then he heard it again. A sudden frantic burst of tapping that boomed out at him through the dark. He backed away, almost witless with panic, collided with something else hard and sharp, then reached the far wall. The door was either to the right or left. He slid his hands along the smooth, cold surface. They reached the sharp, jutting edge of the doorframe. He found the handle, gripped it gratefully, pulled the door sharply open and lurched out straight into a tall, motionless figure as hard and cold as ice.

Floyd Pueblo's scream of terror almost turned his throat inside out. He crashed backwards, then the flashlight beam struck him full in the eyes. His whole body doubled up with fear; there was no fight left in him; he stood, cowering, blinded, paralysed.

'Don't move!' the voice on the far side of the flashlight said. 'Put your hands on your head. Hold them there or I'll shoot.'

Floyd did as he was told. The flashlight lowered from his eyes. He could see a car beyond the front door with its headlamps on, shining directly in, silhouetting the cop standing in front of him. He heard the crackle of a radio. Relief washed through him. He tried to recover his voice, but he could only see the cop as an outline and that disoriented him. He glanced over his shoulder.

'I said freeze, scumbag!'

Floyd looked at him. 'I – I –'

'What are you doing in this building?' the cop said, interrupting.

'Work here,' Floyd gasped. 'I'm the night security officer.'

'And I'm the King of Siam.'

'I am,' Floyd said, controlling his voice better. 'I'm the security man. I work here.'

The flashlight beam raked him. 'You have ID?'

'It's in my jacket in the front office. Jesus, am I glad to see you.'

'You normally leave the lights off and walk around in the dark with the front door open?'

'I – the lights just went – I–' Floyd turned his head and looked back at the room with the dewars. 'There's something happening back there,' he said lamely, and pointed to the room.

'The fuse has blown?'

Floyd nodded.

'OK, where's the fuse box?'

Floyd led him out into the entrance hall and opened the small cloakroom door. With the cop's flashlight he located the fuse box, opened the lid and pressed the reset button. Immediately the lights came back on. The cop looked at him a little more easily and switched off his torch. But he kept his gun out and his voice hadn't got any friendlier. 'You still better let me see your ID.'

Floyd stared back into the operating theatre, then went through into the office and removed his ID card from his wallet. The cop looked at it and seemed a little disappointed. Then he glanced around at the photographs on the wall with undisguised distaste. He was tall, in his late twenties with his hair shorn to stubble high up his head, and he had a hard, serious face. Floyd vaguely thought he recognized him, probably from when he was in the force himself.

'This the cryonics place, right?'

'Yes.' Floyd kept his eyes on the doorway.

The cop shook his head. 'Goddam freak circus, right?'

Floyd Pueblo shrugged, anxious to keep him there for as long as possible.

The cop looked down at Floyd's legs, and Floyd realized his trouser was torn just below the knee and spots of blood were visible. 'Been in a fight – or one of them come back from the dead and bite you? Vampire, was it?'

'I – I heard a noise out the back. I was just going to take a look when the lights blew.'

From the way the cop was looking at him, Floyd could tell he still wasn't totally convinced about him. 'Would you come and take a look with me – since you're here.'

The cop looked at the portrait photos on the wall again. 'Someone got a big family.'

'Those are the people we got frozen in here,' Floyd said.

The cop studied them for a few moments more then shook his head. 'You got to pay a fortune for this, right? Over a hundred thousand bucks, right? Someone's creaming it, I'm telling you. Hundred thousand bucks to get stuck in an ice box. If –'

The sharp metallic tapping sound silenced him and he looked out past Floyd with a frown for a moment, then stared at Floyd suspiciously. 'Who's that? Someone else out there? You got a colleague?'

Floyd's throat tightened. 'Isn't supposed to be anyone out there.'

The cop walked straight out into the hall, stopped and listened. They both heard it again this time, clear, sharp metallic taps ringing out from the far side of the operating theatre. For a moment the cop looked uneasy, then clutching both his flashlight and gun he walked slowly across the theatre. He stopped as he saw the mess of broken glass in the far corner, and Floyd's gun lying amongst it.

'Mine – I fell over – dropped it.'

The cop scooped it up, looked uncertainly at Floyd, uncocked it and pocketed it. Then he walked over to the doorway and stared in at the aluminium dewars.

'What in hell's these?'

'That's where they are,' Floyd said quietly.

The cop walked in and Floyd followed. They looked up at the dewars, then at the concrete bunkers. The cop walked slowly past each dewar in turn, running his eyes past the temperature gauges up the polished sides. Floyd hung back, panic rising in him again. Then, as the cop stopped by the sixth dewar, three deep metallic taps rang out from inside it, echoing in the room like the toll of a bell.

Floyd's ears popped with fear. He stepped back, then back again until he was standing in the doorway. The cop looked dubiously at him then at the dewar, then knelt down on the floor, seemingly unfazed, and squinted into the narrow gap beneath the dewar. He switched on his flashlight and shone that in.

When he stood up, there was an expression on his face that was half humour, half contempt, as he offered the torch to Floyd. 'You sure have apprehended an intruder.'

Floyd stepped forward warily, bent down and looked with the flashlight. Two shiny beads reflected back at him in the beam, then he saw a furry blur as something wriggled frantically. Three sharp, deep metallic taps rang out, echoing through the dewar. Then another three as the mouse, lying on its side with both its hind legs pinned in the sprung jaw of the trap, kicked out – trying to free itself – and the trap again struck the base of the dewar.

'Shit.' Floyd's heart sank as the realization seeped through him. He should have felt relieved, he knew, but instead he felt a total fool.

He looked up at the cop. 'Think I should put it out of its misery?'

'Sure. Why don't you freeze it?' he said snidely, then eyed the dewars towering above him and stretching away down the huge, cold room. 'This the place where Walt Disney's being kept, right?'

'News to me.' Floyd wondered how to get the mouse out without getting bitten.

'Had himself – what you call it – cryonically frozen, didn't he? He's meant to be in one of these places. You could tell him you got good news for him. You're gonna have Mickey Mouse frozen to keep him company.'

28

Tuesday 26 January, 1993. Sussex.

Joe sat at the breakfast table the next morning and Jack told him about playschool, then looked forlornly at him and said: 'Want you to play with me tonight, Daddy . . .'

Joe ate a mouthful of cereal; it was some new health stuff Karen had bought and it tasted like sackcloth that had been marinated in diesel oil. He munched on, hunger overcoming his distaste. 'What's that shape?'

Jack looked down at the slivers of toast on his plate. 'Triangle?'

'Pretty good!' Joe caught Karen's wary eye, glanced back at *The Times* then back at Jack. 'I'll try and get home early.'

'Awww. Only *try*?'

'I'm very busy at work right now. Lot of things on.'

Jack looked thoughtfully at the triangle of soldiers. Then he tried his father again. 'Promise you'll come back early?'

'Never make a promise you can't keep,' Joe said. 'OK?'

Jack's face puckered. He picked up a soldier and dunked it into the top of his egg, then raised it to his mouth, yolk streaming from it.

Joe caught Karen's eye again, and found himself fighting to keep a guilty blush off his face.

In the car as he drove to the university he made the decision that he would tell Juliet he could not go to dinner with her. Not tonight, not at all. His family meant too much to him. He did not want to have to lie to his son, to have to hide his face from his wife. He didn't need that.

There was a plain white envelope waiting beside his stack of post on his desk. Inside was a photocopied section of a street map of Hove, with an arrow and a circle drawn in red ink. Attached was a sheet of notepaper, on which was written an address, and the words: 'Joe, Really looking forward to seeing you tonight – alone! Juliet xxxxx'

Not wanting to leave the note lying around, he folded it and pushed it into his jacket pocket, then went straight down to the graduates' computer room.

Juliet Spring was seated at the Feynman workstation, and he felt a deep heave of emotion the instant he saw her.

Clinton clattered over to him. 'Welcome to ARCHIVE,' the robot began his party piece. 'If you have any cans of soft drink please leave them on the work surfaces and I will remove them when they are empty. Have a nice time with ARCHIVE.'

Joe was relieved that there was no one else in the room. 'Hi,' he said.

She turned and gave him a warm smile. Dressed in a

couple of layers of long sweatshirts over black leggings, she looked even more at home than yesterday. 'I got up early and went to the open market first thing. I hope you like fish. Salmon trout!'

'I –' The short speech Joe had rehearsed on the way down got trapped in his throat.

'And I've got some fresh strawberries – flown in from somewhere. I think there's something rather wicked about having things out of season, don't you?'

It had not occurred to Joe that she would have gone to this length already. He hadn't the heart to disappoint her. 'Great,' he heard himself say. 'Sounds wonderful; kind of a midsummer feast in January.'

'Well, I probably won't be here in summer,' she said forlornly.

'Sure you will,' he said, forcing conviction into his voice. He looked at the screen awkwardly. It was full of the same endlessly changing lines of digits. 'Anything doing?'

'No. It's spat out a few sheets on the printer where it's found some correlations, but I think that's only because the parameters are still a little wide. And it's going really slowly. Could ARCHIVE run more than one back prop simultaneously – is it capable of doing that?'

Joe thought for a moment. 'I guess we could write some code to do that.' He thought again, trying to work out the ramifications. 'It would take a few days.'

'I could do that while I'm monitoring this.'

'OK.' He glanced at the clock on the wall, aware that he had a meeting shortly. He showed her what she had to do, but she had already figured most of it out already.

On his way back to his office he stuck his head into the postgrad room and saw that Edwin Pilgrim was back and sitting, huffily, at his workstation. He did not acknowledge Joe.

Joe thanked Harriet for showing Juliet around yesterday. 'Get on with her OK?' he asked.

Harriet removed her hands from her keyboard and checked that the pile of hair, rising like a topiaried yew hedge above the rest of her shorn scalp, was still there. 'Fine,' she said, with little enthusiasm.

'Problems?' he asked.

'No. She's rather nervous, isn't she?'

'Nervous?'

'Edgy about something.'

'Always a bit daunting when you start somewhere new,' Joe said.

He went through into his own office and sat for some moments drumming his fingers on his desk, feeling deeply despondent. Had to think of something to tell Jack and Karen. Had to lie to them. People lied all the time, he reasoned. Told half-truths. Just going to have dinner with a brilliant postgrad. There was nothing wrong in teachers eating meals with their students, the refectory was full of it. It was no big deal.

Except the nagging guilt would not leave him alone; it trailed his thoughts like a shadow, lay in his guts like wet cement as he worked his way through his post. His mind went back to his dream last night of his father, and he glanced up at ARCHIVE. How much do *you* know? he wondered. Are you getting too smart on me?

The phone rang, breaking his thoughts. It was Dr Nightingale, one of the specialists Juliet told him she had consulted. Joe had met him at a symposium on the mind and brain a year or so back, and liked him; and he reminded him of the movie actor, Harrison Ford. He'd put a call through to him to ask him if there really was nothing else that could be done for Juliet.

Dr Nightingale apologized profusely that he could not discuss the specifics of her particular case, but confirmed Joe's fears: there were certain cerebral aneurisms that could not be treated and which could simply burst without warning. He also mentioned the possibility of behavioural changes.

Joe thanked him and hung up gloomily, trawling his mind for any other avenues. There would be several neuroscientists whom he knew at next week's conference in Florence, and he typed into his Mac Powerbook the names of a couple he would make a point of talking to in particular.

More immediately, at some point today he was going to have to phone Karen and tell her he would not be back early, after all. And he was going to have to sound convincing, his wife was no fool.

Joe misunderstood Juliet's directions and it was nearly eight before he finally found her apartment block on a hidden back-road right beside the promenade. He parked his car and stepped out into the blustery wind, clutching a bottle of Californian wine he had bought in an off-licence.

The waves roared behind him and there was a heady tang of seaweed in the air. He pressed the button for Flat 34 and waited. There was a high-pitched whine, then Juliet's distorted voice called through the entryphone.

'Come on up. Third floor.'

The lock opened with a sharp buzz and a blast of salty wind tailed him into the gloomy lobby. The lift was modern but slow and jerky, and it was several seconds after it halted before the doors opened. He stepped out into a plush, poorly lit corridor, which smelled of carpet shampoo. A closed door with a spyhole faced him. It was numbered 38. Then he heard a door open further down the corridor, and he saw Juliet come out, rather coyly.

She was wearing a smart green dress with a single band of pearls around her neck. Her hair had a richer lustre than ever, and she had put on some mascara that gave her eyes a vampish, predatory look that took away their sadness.

He greeted her awkwardly, unprepared for the change in her appearance and a little unnerved by it. He thrust the bottle towards her. She thanked him, set it down on a table just inside the door, then she took both his hands in hers, reached up and kissed him lightly on the lips. 'It's good to see you.'

'You too.' He had come straight from the university, in his cords and tweed jacket and felt under-dressed.

She stood back, still holding his hands, and stared at his

tie for a moment. It was a black and white op-art design of concentric circles. She touched it provocatively with her finger. 'Wonderful,' she said.

'Thanks.' He wondered whether she had noticed it that morning.

She looked back into his eyes. 'I was worried you'd decided not to come.'

'I seem to make a habit of being late when I meet you.' Joe apologized as she led him through into the drawing room. The apartment was large and sumptuous, but rather bland, with pale, powdery green carpeting, formal antique or reproduction antique furniture – Joe could rarely tell the difference – and some sombre seascape prints on the walls.

There was a faint smell of fish grilling, and a stronger smell of furniture polish. The room had the chill of somewhere rarely lived in, and it was relieved neither by the jigging flames of a large electric imitation coal fire, nor by Vivaldi's 'Four Seasons' playing quietly in the background.

Juliet gestured him to a sofa. It was covered in yellow damask and softer than it looked, engulfing him as he sat down. She remained standing; he took in her slender legs, and the straps of her black shoes across her fine ankles, and swallowed, remembering his resolution that he would have a meal with her but that was all.

'Can I get you a drink, Joe?' In spite of her vampish make-up she looked anxious, as uneasy as he was.

'Sure. A tiny whiskey. Irish if you have any, otherwise Scotch would be fine.'

'I bought a bottle of Jameson's for you. Ice and water?'

'Hey, you shouldn't have done that! Ice, no water, thanks.' It touched him that she had remembered what he drank, and had gone to that trouble, but it also added to the feeling of claustrophobia he was getting; it felt almost as if she was laying a net around him.

He watched her movements as she strode across to the walnut cabinet where an array of bottles and glasses, an ice bucket and a jug of water had been laid out. She leaned forward to reach a bottle, and her dress slid a few inches up the back of her thighs; lust pricked him deep in the stomach.

He made himself think of Karen and Jack, but they seemed a million miles away now. In some parallel universe he could see an identical copy of himself at home; he had just read Jack a bedtime story and was settling down to have supper with Karen.

He stared around at his actual surroundings; someone had recreated the feeling of a London drawing room here by the English Channel. It seemed a rather forlorn place for a girl to live in alone. There were some photographs on the mantelpiece, one showing a silver-haired man with a woman beside him who bore a strong family resemblance to Juliet. Joe recognized them from the pictures Juliet had showed him for the correlations.

'Those are your parents, right?'

'Yes.' She held up the cut-glass tumbler for him to inspect. There were about four fingers of whiskey in it.

'Hey, too much! I have to drive.'

She dropped several ice cubes in, ignoring his protest.

'How often do they use this place?'

She mixed herself a gin and tonic. 'Most weekends in the summer; they don't come down much in winter.'

The curtains were open, but there was only darkness beyond the glass of the picture window. 'How did you get on today?' he asked, attempting to establish a professional feel.

'Nothing yet with ARCHIVE. I made good progress writing the program, except I have a couple of things I need you to look at tomorrow.

'Sure.' He took the glass she handed him but avoided meeting her eyes. He sipped the whiskey, and almost immediately felt its warming buzz flood through his body. At the same time he felt intoxicated by the smell of Juliet's scent. The scientist in him recognized that smell was highly evocative, a strong trigger of memory. He thought, suddenly, that he should do more work in that area with ARCHIVE; its repertoire of smells was too limited right now.

She lit a cigarette and blew the smoke carefully away from

him. 'Will you do something for me?' she asked. 'Would you make me a promise?'

'What kind of a promise?'

She checked her nails with a quick, nervy dart of her eyes, then tapped the lit end of her cigarette against the centre of the onyx ashtray. 'My father is very anti the whole idea of cryonics. I'm worried that if – when – I –' She was gripping her glass more tightly and some of her drink slopped over the rim and trickled down the side. She did not seem to notice. 'When I – die – I'm scared he might do something to stop me being frozen.'

'You've signed all the forms?'

'Yes.'

'We've touched on the law at some of our meetings. Cryonics is legal in this country – I don't think he can go against your wishes.'

'Will you make sure he doesn't, Joe?'

Joe looked back at her. 'Sure. I mean – I'll do whatever I can.'

'I feel good knowing you're going to be there,' she said.

Joe drank some more in silence.

'Is your wife going to be frozen?' she asked suddenly.

'No. She doesn't believe in it. She thinks the whole concept of immortality is alien to her religion.'

Juliet looked at him mischievously, as if something had occurred to her, but said nothing. She drank some of her gin and tonic, put her glass down on the coffee table in front of them, and laid her cigarette carefully in the ashtray. Then she prised Joe's glass gently from his hands and put that down, too, and moved closer to him with a come-on pout.

She pressed her lips against his and touched his ears lightly with her fingers. Joe tried to withdraw without offending her, but her fingers slid through his hair around to the back of his head, holding it firmly, and her mouth pressed even harder against his. He felt her tongue coaxing his lips open, or what he thought for a moment was her tongue until he realized it was too cold.

The ice cube slipped slowly between his lips and into his

mouth. Her eyes, out of focus and blurry, smiled at him. He held the cube in his mouth for some moments until it became too cold, then passed it back. It returned, a little smaller, and it got smaller each time it passed between them until the tiny sliver that was all that remained finally broke up.

She withdrew her face a few inches. 'That's a symbol, Joe.' She elaborated, 'Eternity. Blood brothers cut their arms and press the cuts together to exchange blood. Cryonicists exchange ice.' She leaned forward and kissed him again. The softness of her mouth, the rich smell of her scent, the caress of her hair, and the soft play of her fingers on his skin were dissolving all his willpower.

One of her hands slid slowly down his chest and on down between his thighs, rubbing suggestively up and down against his zipper. He placed his own hand on hers and lifted it gently away. 'No,' he said. 'I can't handle this.'

She slipped her hand free, cupped his face and held it close to hers. 'You're wonderful, Joe,' she said. 'You're the most special person I've ever met.'

He wanted her; wanted to succumb, to immerse himself, to let himself go; his arousal was so fierce he could scarcely think clearly. But as he stared back at the blur of her face he saw Jack racing towards him as he came in the front door. Saw Jack at the breakfast table. The trust in his son's eyes. Trust he was about to betray. He saw Karen, his lovely wife, her life already half destroyed by the loss of Barty. And he saw the hope in Juliet's eyes. Hope for something he was not able to give.

Got to stop this. He pulled back a few inches so that he could focus clearly, and he stared into her eyes, trying to gather his words.

Misinterpreting his expression, she kissed each eye, lightly.

'Juliet – I – look –' he said, clumsily. 'We – we can't do this.'

She leaned back a little, resting her hands on his thighs. 'Can't do what, Joe?'

He looked down, his brain groping for the right way to express it. 'I – just don't want you to think – to be under any . . .' His voice dried.

She tossed her hair back and gazed at him in a way that made him feel angry with himself for having let it get this far. Slowly her face crumpled, and she was fighting off tears. 'You're quite a romantic, aren't you, Joe?' she said, sniffing, with a sting of bitterness coming into her voice. 'You treat everyone like this?'

He closed his eyes. 'I – I didn't mean it that way. I –' He was silent, addled with confusion. He opened his eyes and looked at her. 'I'm sorry.'

She stood up, angrily. 'You certainly know how to make someone feel great. Really great!' She shook her head from side to side and walked out of the room.

Joe sat still. He should leave. Except that she was dying and she was all mixed up, and she needed help and sympathy and courage. He reached for his glass and drank a large mouthful; the wind rattled the windowpane and he felt a cold draught on his cheek. He noticed a smell of burning, and saw Juliet's cigarette in the ashtray had burned down to the lipsticky filter; a curved line of ash stretched from it, like the abandoned cocoon of a chrysalis. He stubbed it out.

Juliet came back in and looked calmer. 'The asparagus is almost done, we can eat in a few minutes.' She shook another cigarette from the pack, lit it and inhaled deeply.

'I didn't mean what I said to come out the way it did, Juliet.'

She drew deeply on her cigarette again then tapped some ash off the end, carefully, then again, and again, as if determined to get every last fleck off. 'Is it because I'm dying, Joe?' There was a new bitterness in her voice now. It was a tone he had never heard before and it scared him. And it rose, as she spoke, into contained fury. 'I'm an untouchable, right.' She dragged on her cigarette again in short, stabbing movements. 'I'm nothing, I don't count because I'll be gone soon. And the dead don't have rights, do they? They have no status. No one lets them allow for the possibility of coming back, do they? The dead can't leave money to themselves, can't have credit cards, can't have bank accounts. Can't have *feelings*. The moment they certify you dead, that's it; you're just a heap of decomposing garbage.'

Her voice remained quiet, but the rage it contained kept rising with every word. 'I always used to wonder why people were so callous towards old folks, but I understand now. It's not because they're old, it's because they're not going to live long: so they don't matter any more.'

She walked across to the window and stared out into the darkness. 'I'm incurable, so I don't matter any more. I might just as well be dead already. Perhaps I am.' She took another drag on her cigarette and turned towards him. 'How would you feel about that, Joe? Screwing a zombie? Would you be able to go back to your wife with a clear conscience because you'd only been fucking a dead person and that didn't count as adultery? Your sweet little wifey waiting up for you in bed with her face all covered in goat shit.'

Joe was scared now. Her voice was so calm, so quiet.

'How do you know she uses goat gunk?'

She blushed. 'I – found it in ARCHIVE . Some stuff I came across – I was taking a look through its files.'

Joe looked at her dubiously. All ARCHIVE's video images were stored in a coded file that only he had the key to. Had she cracked into it? How?

'I'm sorry,' she said. 'I hadn't meant –' She shook her head from side to side. Then she crumpled into an armchair and exploded into tears. She sat, shaking, sobbing her heart out, her face contorted like rubber. 'Oh God, I'm so bloody frightened.'

He went over, knelt down and put his arm around her, feeling useless.

'I just don't want to die. You'll be there when I'm frozen, won't you, Joe? Please don't let my father stop them.'

'I won't let him,' Joe promised, and he meant it.

She draped her arms around him and pressed her wet face against his. 'I can trust you, can't I?'

'Yes.'

'OK. OK.' She calmed herself. 'Let's eat?'

'Sure.'

She smiled. 'I'll behave, I promise.'

'I'll try and behave too.'

29

As Joe entered the silence of the hallway and hung up his Burberry, he switched his mind from Juliet to the story he had prepared for Karen: a Cryonite meeting. They'd had a technical problem. One of the dewars was leaking liquid nitrogen and they'd had to drive to the unit twenty miles away to put it right.

He was relieved to see the bedroom light was out. Karen was asleep and he crept noiselessly into their room. Inching through the darkness, he located the chair at the end of his side of the bed, hung his jacket on it and removed the rest of his clothes. Then he went through into the bathroom, closed the door as silently as he could, locked the door and switched on the light.

He and Juliet had eaten by candlelight. She had opened up her heart a little to him, talked about her loneliness, how she had no hope of finding a boyfriend, her sadness at knowing she would never have children. She had no future at all, except for the slender hope she placed in cryonics, and the equally slender hope for some success with downloading.

He brushed his teeth and crept into bed. Karen stirred and mumbled a few words. He kissed her and she appeared to go back to sleep. He lay on his back, his hatred of death welling deep inside him as he thought again of Juliet crying, telling him how scared she was. It made no sense that someone so lovely, so brilliant, would be gone within a few months.

Then something else came to the surface of his mind.

Your sweet little wifey waiting up for you in bed with her face all covered in goat shit.

How in God's name did Juliet really get that information? How did ARCHIVE know? Presumably it must have picked up a conversation he'd had with Karen about it. But he had been careful to ensure that all the information stored in ARCHIVE from the video cameras in his home could not be accessed by anyone else. He wondered if Karen was wearing her goat cream now. He didn't really take much notice of all this beauty-routine business. Nevertheless, he knew that Karen would not have given it the time of day before the loss of their son. Since then she'd been interested in anything that promised new life. So her faddishness was just one more way in which death tyrannized us all, he reflected.

He thought of Juliet's computer knowledge. She knew everything about computing technology; even more, in some areas, than himself. Maybe she had cracked the video code by accident. Or had it been deliberate? To spy on his home life? Why?

He fell into a troubled sleep, then awoke an hour later, deeply afraid and drenched in sweat. He listened to Karen's steady breathing beside him, and the wind jostling the trees and shrubs outside. The fear remained, dark and undefined. It was as if he had crossed some boundary out into a no-man's-land from which there was no coming back. As if he had discarded all his past and all his present. Yet had no future.

Next time he awoke, it was to shouts of: 'Morning, morning, morning! Daddy got to get up now!'

Joe opened his eyes leadenly and reluctantly. His bedside clock said 6.30, and it was still dark outside. The light was on in the bathroom and he could hear Karen brushing her teeth. He kissed his son, ruffled his hair with his hand, then closed his eyes.

'Daddy, you promised you'd come home early last night.'

'I didn't *promise*. I said I'd try.'

Jack clambered over him and climbed under the sheets. Joe cuddled his son and was surprised by the coarseness of

230

what he was wearing around his shoulders. He opened his eyes. 'Hey, what're you doing in my jacket?'

Jack giggled. 'It's nice and warm,' he said. 'Can I show you the picture I made last night?'

'You're a monkey – know that? You shouldn't be wearing my jacket.'

'Can I show you the picture?'

'Show me when I get up, OK? Daddy's going to have two minutes' more sleep.

When he opened his eyes again he heard the electrical whirr and rustling sound of the curtains opening. It was full light outside, a brighter day than yesterday. His clock said 8.10. He double-checked it, surprised; he rarely slept much after half-six, regardless of how late he went to bed. Something nagged at the back of his mind. An appointment. It was Wednesday. Wednesdays he had a 9.30 lecture. But there was something else he had to do this morning. Wasn't there?

He eased himself up in bed. In the kitchen below he could hear the thumping of a machine, probably the dishwasher, and voices, a man talking; the radio. Karen had Radio Four on most of the time.

He gathered his thoughts; rehearsed his story for Karen about last night. Could tell her the truth. Nothing had happened, so he had nothing to feel guilty about, no need to lie.

And he had told her about Cryonite yesterday, so he had to stick to the same story. Anyway he did have to go up to the Cryonite unit from time to time – and work there all night on occasions when they had a patient for cryonic suspension who died in the evening or during the night. So the excuse wasn't too improbable. He just had to make it sound convincing.

Then he sat upright with a jolt and jumped out of bed, suddenly remembering what had been nagging him. 8.45. There was a policy meeting with the vice-chancellor. Christ, how could he have forgotten?

He showered, shaved, pulled on his clothes, then looked

frantically around for his jacket. Panic seized him. Couldn't have left it at Juliet's, surely? Then he remembered, Jack had been wearing it earlier when he'd woken him. He ran out into the landing. 'Jack!' he called. 'Jack!'

It was 8.25 and the university was a good fifteen minutes' drive. 'Jack!' he hollered, thundering down the stairs, knotting his tie. Karen came out of the kitchen into the hall.

'Hi – where the hell's Jack?'

She looked calm and friendly, no hint of anger, which surprised him. 'Not going to say good morning?' she asked.

He kissed her hastily.

'How did it go last night?'

'OK – we got it fixed.'

'Poor Joe-Joe, you've been looking strained the last few days, you could have done with an early night. That's why I let you lie in. Shall I cook you something for breakfast?'

'I have to fly – I forgot – have a meeting with the vice-chancellor first thing. Jack was wearing my jacket – where the hell is he?'

'I didn't see him wearing your jacket.'

'Where is he?'

'I think he went out in the garden to feed the fish.'

Joe rushed into the kitchen and looked through the patio door and out across the lawn to the small pond stocked with Koi. There was no sign of Jack. He hollered again. The next door neighbour's dog began barking.

'Jesus!' Joe slid the door shut. 'Where in hell is he?'

'Maybe he's playing hide-and-seek again. Got this thing about it – he saw it on some television programme. He's been driving me nuts all week. Won't say a word until you find him.'

'This is one hell of a time for hide-and-seek.' He ran back upstairs and looked in Jack's room. 'Jack?' There was no response. He went back on to the landing and bellowed: 'Jaaaacckk!' Still no response. 'Karen, I must have my goddam jacket – got my wallet in it – have you got any cash on you?'

'A little.'

Joe ran back into his bedroom, pulled his wardrobe door open and took out a brown corduroy jacket. He hurtled back downstairs, pulling it on. Karen stood at the bottom holding a twenty-pound note and grimacing. 'That tie doesn't go with that jacket at all, Joe.'

'Too bad.' He pulled his Burberry off its peg on the coat stand, checked his car keys were in the pocket, stuffed the banknote into his trousers and kissed her goodbye.

Karen stood wistfully in the doorway as Joe drove off. No time to talk, never any time for real life. England wasn't working out at all how she had imagined. Perhaps it had been foolish to think Joe would change just by moving to another country.

Over in Canada he had worked around the clock trying to build a name for himself, churning out paper after paper, book after book, soliciting and badgering companies, research organizations and the government for funding for his ARCHIVE project. He had been forever firing off letters, faxes, jumping on aeroplanes to go to meetings, but even after winning the MacArthur Prize he hadn't been able to find anyone with a combination of sufficient funding, vision and courage to back him unconditionally.

She had hoped – now that Joe had the funding to pursue his dream, and the professorship post which enabled him to do the teaching he loved at a more relaxed schedule than before – that maybe he would be a little less fraught and driven. And that by not working herself, she might have had more time to put into their relationship.

But she had not anticipated that he would become so totally obsessed with his work that he would start to resent any time he spent with her or with Jack, which was the way it almost seemed now. And he was becoming impossible to talk to.

He was going to Florence to a computing conference all next week. A few years ago he would have taken her with him automatically. Now he had not even bothered to ask her if she wanted to join him.

It was her birthday Saturday week, after he got back from Florence, and they were having a supper party. She even wondered whether he would remember to get her a card or a present.

There were times when she felt that perhaps Joe didn't understand her any more. And she was aware that much of it might be her fault. She had thought that the pain of Barty's loss would have eased over the years, that Jack would have helped heal the wounds, but instead she found all her fears transferred on to Jack. She was afraid every time she let him go and play in friends' houses, in case anything happened. She wanted to protect him twenty-four hours a day. And she was aware that in her obsession with Jack she had been shutting Joe out, and that she needed to deal with that.

She worried about Jack now and began searching for him, calling his name; she needed to get him ready for playschool. She went into the dining room and saw the candles on the table, and sadness welled up in her. She had decided on a whim to make a special dinner for Joe last night, and she had gone out and bought a bottle of his favourite Californian wine; she'd had everything prepared when he'd telephoned to say he would not be home.

A sigh escaped her as she knelt and looked beneath the table to see if Jack was there. She checked the hall cupboard, went back into the kitchen, then down into the utility room in the cellar, her anxiety increasing suddenly. She looked into the gap between the chest freezer and the two huge upright freezers beside it – the owner of the house had to be paranoid about getting caught in a siege and running short of food, she sometimes thought – and checked that the bolts on the disused coal hole had not been opened.

On her knees she peered through the glass ports in the front of the washing machine and the tumble dryer – Jack had once climbed in the dryer to hide – but there was no sign of him, and she went back upstairs into the bright light of the kitchen with the same relief she always had on leaving the entombing darkness of the cellar.

As she crossed the kitchen, she noticed a shadow move

through the louvred slats of the airing cupboard door. She stopped in her tracks and watched carefully. Another movement. Beaming with anticipation, she tiptoed over, gripped the handle, then pulled.

'Boooooooo!' Jack yelled, springing out.

She jumped as if in shock. 'Hey!' she said. 'Hey, hey, hey! You have to stop doing this, OK?'

'You didn't know where I was!'

'Jack, you have to stop this, understand? Daddy was calling out for you and you didn't even say goodbye to him.'

His face fell. 'Where's Daddy?'

'Daddy had to go to work.'

'Awww.'

'And he said you have his jacket. What have you done with –' She broke off as she saw something crumpled on the floor of the airing cupboard, and knelt down. It was Joe's tweed jacket, crushed from Jack having crouched on it.

She straightened it out, and as she did so she noticed something sticking out of one of the pockets. A piece of paper. She pulled it out and looked at it; there were two sheets clipped together. She unfolded them.

The jacket slipped from her fingers as shock, real this time, ripped through her. Instinctively she spun round to face away from Jack and gazed in near disbelief at the words on the sheet of notepaper stapled to a photocopied street map of Hove.

'Joe, Really looking forward to seeing you tonight – alone! Juliet xxxxx.'

30

'Death is taboo,' Joe said into the microphone, thumping the rostrum theatrically with his fist. 'We accept that we should challenge cancer; that we should challenge AIDS; heart disease, multiple sclerosis; Parkinson's Disease. But for some reason we do not challenge death itself! Some people say, "What about over-population if we live for ever?" But I answer that by saying, "How many of us would criticize a doctor for restarting the heart of a cardiac victim?"'

He paused to let the words sink in and stared at the sea of faces in the packed auditorium of the Grand Hall at the Universita degli studi di Firenze. Many of the world's brightest computer scientists were among the eight hundred delegates attending the seventeenth annual World Artificial Intelligence Symposium. Joe had picked out a few specific faces scattered through the crowd, which he always did, a trick he had been taught a long time ago, and he swung his gaze to each of them in turn, taking several seconds before he went on. He was having a good time, the juices were flowing and there were a few startled faces and a few disgruntled ones. Good. He loved having a go at the conservative farts of the Establishment.

He briefly scanned his text, then went on: 'Some of you, I know, think I'm nuts because I don't want to die!' He paused and took a deep breath. 'Do we think the guy who has a triple heart bypass is nuts? Do we think the woman who fights her breast cancer is nuts?' He let the words echo around the vast auditorium as he discreetly turned a page. 'Ben Franklin said the only certainties in life are death and taxes. Well, I guess I can't promise to do much about taxes.' He waited as a ripple of laughter went through the audience, then his voice rose. 'But death is a different matter. I don't see why anyone in this room should have to die. I don't know why anyone on this planet should have to die. Ever.'

He gripped the top of the rostrum and leaned forward. 'Mother Nature has had it her own way for too damned long. It's time she stopped making all the rules. She may have nurtured this planet for the past hundred million years, but she's also goddam terrorized it!' He stared in turn at each of his five marked faces in the auditorium. 'People say that modern society is screwing up, that we're destroying our ecosystem. And they're right. Hell, they are absolutely right! But I'm not sure we ought to take the blame. I don't think Mother Nature can *cope* with modern society. Evolution is about the survival of the fittest. It's about adaptation. It's about discarding stuff that isn't of use any more. Evolution is one mean, unsentimental sonofabitch.'

He paused as another light ripple of laughter rang out. Then he launched himself into the climax of his speech. He was going to play it for all it was worth. 'Evolution for mankind right now is taking place in here.' He tapped his brain. 'It's about getting the hell out of our biological bodies. We need to move forward, get rid of our wetware brains.' He tapped his chest with his thumb. 'Get out of our wetware bodies and the hideous incurable diseases that destroy them. We want to get into some decent hardware, and to hell with Mother Nature. I believe that human beings will one day become the distant ancestors of the machines we are now building. That we are on the very brink of a whole new era: one that will be an even greater change than that from Cro-Magnon Man into *Homo erectus*, and then from *Homo erectus* into *Homo sapiens*. We are on the brink of the change from *Homo sapiens* into *Homo cyberneticatus*: Ladies and Gentlemen, I give you *Post-biological Man*.'

Joe scanned the faces of his selected marks. Two were frowning in disapproval, one, a rather smart-looking woman, was rapt, and the other two were deadpan. A pretty average result, he thought, and powered on:

'What I'm telling you is something you always used to be able to laugh at; the stuff of science fiction. I advise you not to laugh any more. I don't think I'm further than a decade away from achieving human consciousness in a machine. It's in a laboratory at my university right now, and there may be some of you who have even smarter machines of your own.'

He paused. 'Some of you may think I'm a couple of chips short of a circuit board . . . but I put it to you that in ten years' time it will be my computer ARCHIVE up here on this rostrum, giving this speech for me – and probably making a damned sight better job of it!'

A couple of hours later Joe lay alone on his bed in his

grandly furnished but rather cramped hotel room, glancing through the conference programme, marking the lectures he wanted to attend in the next couple of days, and scribbling program ideas Juliet had suggested. There was one that he had been toying with which, if he could get one bug out of it, might dramatically improve ARCHIVE's learning abilities.

Through the closed window he could hear the never-ending rasp of motor scooters roaring through the piazza below. Tuesday evening. He sipped a glass of fresh orange juice and glanced at his watch. It was 7.15. He was due to meet an old colleague from Toronto in the downstairs bar at a quarter to eight, and he wanted to have a shower first.

It was cold in the room, as cold and damp as England. For some reason he had imagined it would be warm and sunny in Florence. England was an hour back. He had just phoned and said goodnight to Jack. He'd wanted to catch up on Karen's news, but she'd seemed too preoccupied to chat. She had been in a strange mood on Friday and Saturday, too, and he did not know why. Quieter than normal, rather stiff and formal.

He flipped on through the programme, but he wasn't concentrating. He was thinking about Juliet; he couldn't get her out of his head. He was pleased with the reception to his speech; it had gone down well. The right amount of applause; the right number of horrified faces. Karen's reaction had been muted and now he wanted to tell Juliet. He picked up the receiver and punched out the code and her home number. As it began to ring there was a knock on his door. He cursed, let it ring on a couple of times. He heard the knock again, more insistent, called out *'Un momento!'* waited for a couple more rings then replaced the receiver, tightened the belt of his dressing gown and padded over to the door.

He opened it and stared for some moments in dumb disbelief at Juliet Spring, who stood there, wrapped in her coat and a printed shawl, with a small leather suitcase on the floor beside her.

'I – hope I'm not disturbing you?' she said, her scent

engulfing him. She tilted her head and gave him a smile that was half apologetic and half total mischief.

Without knowing he was doing it, he slipped his arms inside hers and pulled her towards him. 'God,' he said, holding her hard against him, then kissing her deeply.

When their lips separated, she held her head back for a moment, eyes sparkling with humour. 'Was that a yes or a no?'

'You look wonderful,' he said, completely in thrall to her at that moment.

'I've decided to take your advice, Joe, and enjoy myself.' She parted the top of his robe, pressed her hands against the soft hair of his chest, spread them out further, up over the bare skin of his shoulders. She pressed her mouth against his ear. 'It's good that you're already undressed for me,' she whispered, sliding her hands down his chest, his stomach, then pulling the bow on his belt, freeing it. She seemed sure of her own power now that ties of home were left behind. His dressing gown fell open and she slid her hands further down, gripping him firmly, squeezing and stroking, then sliding her hands further, gently cupping his balls, then burying her tongue in his ear.

He held the back of her head, stroked her hair, small bombs of pleasure exploding through him. Then he saw a door down the corridor open and a scientist he recognized coming out with his wife. 'Quick, in!' he hissed. He knelt, scooped up Juliet's case and hurried her into the room, closing the door without turning round.

'Colleague,' he explained, his face red.

She removed a DO NOT DISTURB sign from the door handle, hung it outside and pulled the safety chain on. 'No more colleagues,' she said, slipping her hands around him again and propelling him towards the bed while the urgency of his attraction to her lasted.

She let him make one quick call to cry off his meeting downstairs in the bar, and after that she completed what she'd tried to begin on the night of their dinner at her parents' flat.

*

Guilt came fast seconds after Joe had climaxed. A sudden feeling of foolishness, of the irreversibility of the situation.

He was angry at himself for having let it happen. Angry at his weakness. Before he realized what he was doing, he found himself staring like a frightened animal up at the light fitting on the ceiling, running his eyes over the stuccoed moulding, looking for the glint of a camera lens. He was looking for ARCHIVE !

He smiled at the absurdity and relaxed a fraction. Juliet kissed him on each eye and he smelled the scents of her body, saw the gleam of her pale, naked skin, breathed in the fragrance of her hair. ARCHIVE was a thousand miles away. And Karen. He was in a whole different compartment of life here. His guilt slowly dissolved into a sense of playfulness, of mischief, of freedom. And as Juliet kissed him again, he felt a depth of lust that was like the vivid reliving of a memory.

They stayed the whole evening in bed, and had food and drink sent up. In the morning, Joe felt as high as if he were on a drug. He had to attend a talk, but afterwards he excused himself from a prearranged lunch, and went to meet Juliet in the Botticelli rooms of the Uffizi.

He found her gazing at the *Birth of Venus*, and watched her from a distance for a moment, captivated by how beautiful she looked, and wondered what she was thinking. He waited until she caught his eye, not wanting to startle her, then they embraced tightly.

Juliet nodded at the painting. 'Like me to stand like that?'

'Nude on a shell?'

'Uh huh! She's lovely, isn't she? Far lovelier than when you see her in reproductions.'

'Aw, she's just a fashion plate; you're much more beautiful than she is.'

'You're much more beautiful in the flesh than in your photographs too, Joe.' She'd seen them on his book jackets, so she knew. She kissed him, her eyes sparkling with fun, then stood on tiptoe and whispered in his ear. 'Let's go back to the hotel room.'

'You don't want some lunch?'

'We could have something sent up. How long do you have?'

'Couple of hours.'

On the way out Juliet stopped in front of a painting of angels carrying the soul away from a dead woman. She turned to Joe. 'What happens to your soul when you're frozen, Joe? Does God consider you to be dead until you're thawed back out? Or does your soul get stuck in limbo?'

'I don't have that problem to worry about,' he said. 'Because I don't believe in an immortal soul.'

They walked arm in arm along the chequered floor, through the colonnade of statues and busts. Joe was aware he should keep a look-out for colleagues, but had such a reckless feeling of abandon he almost didn't care if they were seen together. He felt as if he was on a romantic adventure where normal rules did not apply.

'Do you believe in any kind of afterlife?'

Joe could see she was looking for something to cling to and he did not want to kick away any of her props. 'If we achieve immortality don't you think that might be the same thing?'

She searched his face as they began to walk down the wide stone stairs. 'Is that what you believe?'

He put his arm around her. Normally it was one of his favourite topics of conversation, but he was reluctant to discuss it with her, as if by refusing to confront the reality of her mortality he could help prevent it. But she persisted.

'Is it, Joe?'

They went through the turnstile, past a headless and armless bronze, crossed the bookshop and stepped from the quiet of the gallery into the bustling courtyard.

'Juliet, you told me when we first met that you were scared of dying. Tell me what actually scares you about it.'

They walked in silence on flagstones strewn with litter, past the easels of the pavement artists, the air ragged with the crackle and rasping of scooters and motorcycles. The sun bathed the Palazzo Vecchio tower in a rich ochre, but in the shadow it cast below the air was chilly and laced with the smells of exhaust fumes, coffee, sweet buns and the watery tang of the Arno. It seemed to Joe that several minutes passed before she replied.

'I suppose I'm scared of being alone in some kind of void,' she said. 'Where no one can see or hear me, where I can't do anything. Just trapped for ever in darkness.' She gave a humourless laugh. 'And I'm scared of missing out, Joe. Of missing the chance, by maybe just a few years, to go on living for ever.'

Later that night as he lay in bed, sticky with drying perspiration, the perfumed scents and the raw animal smells of Juliet's body in his nostrils, England seemed a long way away to Joe. Florence had a kind of artifice, as though the clock had stopped and time was suspended; so having an affair here did not count, because it wasn't part of the real world.

'Joe,' Juliet said quietly, 'I want to give you the name of my solicitor – in case my father does try to challenge my being frozen. I've given him very detailed instructions on what he has to do, and I've made him my executor, which gives him legal ownership of my body after my death.'

Joe squeezed her shoulder reassuringly. 'You're not going to die. I'm not going to let you! There has to be someone can do something for you.'

'Just you, Joe. You're the only person who can help.' She sat up, lifted her wine glass and filled it from the bottle beside the bed. She drank some, then pushed her hair back from her face and turned towards him, suddenly nonchalant.

'When we get back to England, why don't you move in with me?'

The words took him by surprise, and there was an intensity in her expression that disturbed him. Although she was wearing little make-up now, he could remember suddenly very vividly the vampish mascara of last week, and the predatory look it had given her. She had the same look now. She kissed him, but he did not respond. She kissed him

242

again. 'Be wonderful, don't you think? We could be together all the time, the way we will be one day, anyway. The way we will be for ever.'

Joe frowned, his unease increasing. 'For ever?'

'Yes, Joe, of course.'

'How do you mean?'

'You said that Karen doesn't believe in immortality. That she isn't having her body frozen, but that you are. Sometime in the future we'll be together again when we're both thawed out. And then we can be together always.' She kissed him again, hungrily, pressed her face tight to his and began to work her hands gently down his body. 'Why don't we live together now, Joe, and start practising?'

Her caresses were arousing him again and he tried to resist. 'Juliet, I'd like to be with you, but I can't do that to Karen. Or to Jack. I do love them.'

'Just until I die, Joe, then you can go back to her – to them.' She said it so matter-of-factly, as if death were a date in her diary, like Easter or Thanksgiving or Christmas.

'Karen needs me, Juliet. I – I couldn't do that to her.'

Juliet's face darkened. 'I need you too, Joe.'

'I know,' he said, quietly.

'I need you really badly, Joe. Don't you understand that?'

'I do understand.'

She lifted a leg over and knelt on top of him, naked. He stared at her face, at her firm apple-shaped breasts, at the brilliant red of her nipples, at her flat stomach and her slender white thighs. She was the most perfect, most beautiful, most erotic woman he had ever encountered. He wanted to pull her down towards him, wanted to kiss her breasts, wanted to enter her again.

But anger was building in her voice. 'You just think I'm an easy lay, Joe. That because I'm dying I'm desperate for a last good screw. That turns you on, doesn't it?'

Joe was wounded. 'Don't say things like that!'

She leaned forward, resting her hands on his shoulders, her hair enclosing his face like a tent. 'Do you love me, Joe?'

He was unsure how to respond, unsure what to say that

could calm her; because he did not know how he felt himself. 'I think I could fall in love with you,' he said. 'I . . .' He worried that he had already said the wrong thing.

'You *think* you love me, Joe?' There was a look in her eyes that he did not like. 'You do love Karen and you think you love me. Nice, Joe! That's nice.' She laughed but it was not like any of her previous laughter. There was something faintly inhuman about it that sent goosepimples down his back. As though it had come from some inner demon, deep inside her. Joe's muscles tightened with anxiety. For a moment she looked as if she was going to attack him. Then she seemed to recover.

She sat back, gripped his softening erection in her hands and began stroking it back to hardness again as she spoke. 'If you could download me into ARCHIVE, Joe, download me now while I'm still alive, would there be two of me?'

It took a moment for Joe to gather his thoughts. 'It's a big conundrum,' he said, pleased that the topic had changed, and distracted by what she was doing. 'If we copied you into the computer, which would then be the real you? The flesh-and-blood version or the copy in the computer?'

'Both?' she said, stroking him and smiling.

He closed his eyes fleetingly and let out a gasp of pleasure. 'Only for a brief moment in time. The instant either version started having new experiences, adding new memories, you would start to grow apart, to change, to become separate individuals.'

'You could make back-ups. If I was downloaded into ARCHIVE, you could make back-up tapes. If you didn't like the way our relationship was developing, you could wipe me, upload a fresh me from the tape and start again! You could make dozens of copies of me if you wanted. And you could upload them all into ARCHIVE. You could send different versions of me down fax lines and computer lines all over the world and each version would come back as a new and different Juliet. That's possible, isn't it?'

'In theory, yup, I guess.'

'It would be like cloning me?'

'In a sense.'

'How convenient for you, Joe.' The smile stayed on her face, but menace was creeping back into her voice. 'You could have all these different versions of me to choose from that you needn't love at all. Needn't risk your marriage. They wouldn't bother you, wouldn't make any demands on you. You could pull them out of your drawer and slot them into ARCHIVE, depending on which mood you were in. You'd like that, wouldn't you, Joe? You'd be able to understand that. Because as long as it was in your computer it wouldn't really be happening. My body would be safely frozen in an aluminium dewar and my mind safely locked away on a tape in a plastic box. Lucky Joe! What a perfect mistress.'

He tried to read her face, but her eyes were glazed; they had become the eyes of a mad woman, neither the bright laughing eyes, nor the sad, deep eyes of the Juliet he knew. They frightened him. He thought of the neurologist's prognosis that she might suffer a series of minor strokes and he wondered if she had had one now; strokes could cause mood changes. He said nothing, but kept watching her.

She was still holding him and stimulating him with her hand. 'Back to Karen on Friday, Joe? Does wifey do the things that I do to you?'

'Juliet, please!' He was getting angry.

'Do you fuck *her* four times a night?'

'Please, calm down.'

'Do you? Do you, Joe?' She was yelling now, hysterical. 'How many times a night do you fuck her?'

Then she let go of him, climbed off him and collapsed into a sobbing heap. She lay beside him, her face buried in the bedclothes. Joe watched her helplessly, stroking her back with his hand, trying to soothe her, wondering what he'd got himself into.

'Karen's not dying, Joe,' she said after a few minutes, still sobbing, but calmer now. 'And I love you! I can't bear the thought of you going back there, and you making love to her, when she's not the one who's dying.'

What a mess, he thought involuntarily, the insanity of the

past twenty-four hours suddenly clear to him. What a right goddam mess! He lay back against the headboard, the smell of Juliet's perfume in his nostrils as he looked at the contours of her back and the tangled clump of red hair that covered her face. He had not spoken to Karen again. He had tried this morning from a payphone during the conference, but had only got the answering machine. He couldn't phone her now with Juliet in the room.

Thursday tomorrow. Going back on Friday. England still felt like the other end of the universe. A part of him wished he could stay on for a while over here and not have to deal with going back. Stay here in this bed with this crazy, brilliant wildcat of a girl and keep making love. The sex was incredible. And the conversations they'd been having about ARCHIVE were firing him with ideas; in the space of one week, Juliet had sussed ARCHIVE out better than any of his colleagues who had been working on it from the start. She had made a dozen suggestions that would add vastly to its abilities. He needed her to stay alive.

And yet she scared him. Why? Perhaps it was just the unpredictability of her mood changes, her mercurial temper. But he did not know whether that was due to her aneurism, or whether there was a streak of violence in her character; a deep seam, perhaps, even, of malevolence. He preferred to think not.

But the idea persisted.

31

October 1990. Felixstowe Docks.

The grubby hull of the *Arctic Venus* towered like a tenement wall above the quay. A trickle of merchant seamen and dockworkers ambled up and down the gangplanks of the tired, thirty-year-old freighter, loading supplies. The jib of a crane rotated against the grey sky, swinging containers the size of garages out of the ship's hold, and lowering them on to the flatbed rail cars that waited below to carry them into the customs shed.

The ship had docked four hours earlier, after the return leg of its regular twenty-four-day round trip of London–Rotterdam–New York–Rotterdam–London. It had carried container loads of auto spares from London and frozen, irradiated Dover soles from Rotterdam, and was returning with a diversity of goods that included jeans and sweatshirts, lawnmower engines, canned tuna, frozen peas and computing components.

In the glass-walled office overlooking a vast steel-roofed shed, customs officers Bill Myers and Douglas Titcombe sat in front of their computer screens, carrying out their routine task of checking the documents of each of the containers being stacked by fork-lift trucks in the floor-to-ceiling pallets.

Mostly they sat poring through documents in their office, isolated from the stink of spent-fuel fumes and the echoing din of engines and hydraulic lifts below. Sometimes when there was a drugs-smuggling alert they would have each container checked by sniffer dogs and on occasions, when something didn't seem right, they would have the containers opened up and physically check the contents themselves. A percentage of all the containers was selected by the computer for examination .

As customs officers the two men had absolute power over everyone and everything that came into the dock. They had more power than the police and were not answerable to them. They were granted a perpetual warrant to detain people, have them stripped, their orifices searched with probes, with no fear of any charge of assault.

Mostly, Bill Myers and Douglas Titcombe used their powers lightly. Myers, a grey-haired, paunchy, soft-faced man near retirement age, had never nurtured any desire for promotion. His real interests in life lay in the racing pigeons in his loft at home. Her Majesty's Customs and Excise was a living; he asked of it no more, and gave no more than he had to.

By contrast, Douglas Titcombe was thirty-five and impatient. He had been passed over for promotion twice in the past three years and was edgy about the way he had been stuck with Myers for too long now. There was no spark in Myers, no enthusiasm for a really big bust; or even a small one. He got the impression that Myers didn't care what the hell slipped through customs and into England so long as it didn't interfere with racing pigeons.

Titcombe was in a particularly foul mood today. Budget cuts due to the recession had been leaked to the newspapers. Any wage increases in the civil service would be held to below the level of inflation, and promotions were being slowed down; he'd had a row with his ex-wife, and to add the *coup de grâce,* a half-blind female had rear-ended his car on his way into work.

He was checking every document word by word, issuing demands for container after container to be opened, deaf to the protests of his colleague. It was four in the afternoon. Normally by now at least thirty or forty containers would have left. Instead only three had done so and there was a solid jam of articulated container lorries with angry drivers backed up a mile down the road.

'Ought to let a dozen through, Doug,' his colleague said in his slow Lancashire voice. 'Not being fair on them.'

Titcombe leaned forward, ignoring him, and spoke into the microphone on his desk. 'Container number MCLV54687391. I want to view it.'

Then his phone rang. He turned his attention to the next sheaf of documents, letting the phone ring on. The description on the ship's manifest he had scanned earlier had raised his interest, and he had been waiting to reach this particular set of documents: *Human remains for medical research* he read on the bill of lading and, irritated by the distraction, answered the phone with a curt 'Titcombe.'

'Oh, Mr Titcombe! Good afternoon to you, it's Morris Forsey from Wallis-Metcalfe. How are you?'

Titcombe grunted, noncommittal. Morris Forsey was a whingeing old clerk who worked for a firm of clearing agents. They spoke two or three times a month, normally when Morris Forsey had a customer on his back who wanted a consignment of goods in a hurry. Titcombe had it in his power to have something shifted through customs in ten minutes. He also had it in his power to make it take a week. The speed at which he processed specials for Forsey and for most other clearing agents depended almost entirely on his mood. Forsey had picked an unfortunate day.

'I gather there seems to be a – ha – bit of a hold up,' Forsey ventured, with all the confidence of a man proffering a biscuit to a deranged Rottweiler. 'Is the computer down again?'

'Computer's fine.'

'Ha – good! Ha – I – just checking something for a customer, but – ha – you're probably already dealing with it, I expect. Ha. Container number MCLV54687391 – just wondering – ha – if it's been unloaded yet?'

Titcombe stared at the documents in front of him. 'Well, there's a coincidence, Mr Forsey. I'm looking at the documents this very moment.'

'So kind of you. Much appreciate anything you can do – you understand the urgency?'

Through his window, Titcombe watched a cleared container being loaded on to a lorry. 'Doesn't say anything here about urgency.'

There was a slight cough. 'Ha – it is actually being accompanied by an – ha – engineer.'

'*Human remains for medical research,* it says here.'

'Yes – ha – that's right. Has to be kept at a certain temperature.'

'So's half the stuff that comes in here, Mr Forsey.'

'This is a little different, Mr Titcombe. It has to be kept at a constant – 140, that's why the container came by sea, not air – there are technical problems with temperature stability at high altitude, I believe.'

'I'll bear it in mind.' Titcombe made to replace the receiver, but stopped when he heard Morris Forsey's voice rise in panic.

'Oh, er, ha, Mr Titcombe, there is another problem. The engineer has to stay in attendance all the time in case of – ha – technical problems.'

'We're quite used to refrigeration containers, Mr Forsey. We do handle two hundred thousand a year. They plug in here and we have our own engineers if anything goes wrong.'

'Well, of course, Mr Titcombe, I appreciate that. It's just that the equipment in this particular consignment is – ha – rather specialist.'

Titcombe's interest increased. 'Can't see any mention of that on the manifest. There's been no value set down for specialist freezing equipment. Why not, Mr Forsey?'

The clearing agent vacillated for a moment. 'I – ha – I'd have to come back to you on that one, Mr Titcombe.'

'Good, well you do that,' Titcombe said and hung up. Then he began to read through the documents with an even more thorough eye than usual.

Shortly before midday the next morning, and after several more anxious calls from Morris Forsey, Titcombe went down into the bitterly cold inspection bay of the shed, where the consignment Forsey had been so anxious about sat plugged into the electrical supply. It was a standard-size container, in dark blue reinforced glass fibre; white stencilled letters said: 'Maintain Constant −140°C'. There was a panel of temperature gauges and several other dials, warning lights and controls on the outside, and several strips of slatted refrigeration vents.

A tall, curly-haired man stood beside it in a green and red shell suit and trainers, looking tired and surly. Beside him, and a foot shorter, stood an agitated little man in a grey suit, a white shirt with an old-fashioned and ill-fitting collar and a grubby tie that looked like it doubled as a napkin. He had a bundle of documents in one hand and his other clutched a bulging briefcase, which he put down the moment he saw the customs officer, and stepped forward.

'Mr Titcombe! Nice to see you, very nice, sorry to be troubling you, so very kind – I'd – like to introduce –'

Titcombe took Morris Forsey's proffered hand and gave it the same kind of action with which he would have deposited orange peel into a waste bin, then looked at the stranger in the tracksuit.

'Grant Forrester,' the man said in a dry Southern drawl.

'You've accompanied this container from New York?' Titcombe asked.

'From Los Angeles,' the man replied. He had a good-looking, alert face and Titcombe got the impression he was something more than a security guard.

'Human remains are normally shipped by air. The last body I heard of being shipped by boat was Count Dracula's.' Titcombe smirked at his own joke.

'The contents are highly fragile – in a glass-like state. We were concerned about stress fracture at altitude,' the American responded in a helpful tone.

Titcombe read some items on the bill of lading aloud. 'Human remains for medical research. Intact corpse. Shipment from Crycon Extended Life Foundation, Santa Monica, California. Destination is –' he stopped suddenly, his eyes lighting up. 'Well, well, I've just seen daylight,' he said to the man in the tracksuit. 'That's one of those places where they freeze people, wouldn't I be right?'

'Yessir,' the American said guardedly.

'How about that, then! And that's what you've got in there, right again?'

'Yes.'

Titcombe's expression hardened. 'I saw something on the telly about this. They reckon it's just a big rip-off. Hundred and twenty-five thousand dollars, you charge, right?'

'We're a non-profitmaking charity.'

'Oh yes? Don't tell me it costs a hundred and twenty-five thousand dollars to bung someone in a freezer?'

'There's a lot more to it than that.'

'There is?'

'Yes.'

'Well let's have a look then, Mr –?'

'It's *Doctor*. Doctor Forrester.'

'OK, *Doctor*,' Titcombe said, repeating the emphasis. 'Let's have a look.'

The American, helped by the clearing agent, unlocked two padlocks and drew the bolts on the container door, then slowly lowered it. Titcombe stepped forward and peered in. He saw nothing inside but foam padding. Tentatively he stuck a hand in and pulled some out. It was so tightly packed that the rest expanded to fill the gap.

It took several minutes before he exposed the top of the shiny metal dewar that was lying horizontal in the container, and an untidy pile of foam lay beside him. He stepped back a pace and eyed the dewar warily. 'The human remains are in that cylinder?'

The American nodded. Morris Forsey was staring goggle-eyed into the container and not daring to come too close.

'OK,' Titcombe said, more breezily than he now felt. 'Let's have that out and opened up, shall we?'

The American looked at him in disbelief. '*What?*'

'I'd like to see inside that cylinder, please.'

'I'm sorry, officer, you can't do that.'

That was exactly what Titcombe needed. He rounded on him with a smug grin. 'Can't I? Let me tell you, Dr Forrester, I have the jurisdiction to open and inspect anything I like. If I choose to, I can have your cadaver removed from that container, taken into our laboratories in Tilbury and surgically inspected.'

'This patient was frozen within minutes of death. If you open the container, you risk causing irreversible deterioration and destroying the patient's prospect of recovery.'

'And how long has this particular person been dead?'

'About fifteen years.'

'Well, if I'd been dead for fifteen years I wouldn't rate my chances of recovery as being very good at all, Dr Forrester.' Titcombe made no effort to conceal his contempt.

The American glanced at the rather subdued clearing agent and said nothing.

'Not being up on medical terminology, perhaps you could

enlighten me,' Titcombe said, 'on whether this is actually a patient or a cadaver, Dr Forrester?'

The American fought to keep his calm. He'd been up all night; he was tired, he was cold, and he was irritated by the red tape. And now by this man. But he was experienced enough to know that a lot of people were made uneasy by the thought of cryonic freezing. He went into his routine. 'Forty years ago if your heart stopped in an operating theatre, you'd be declared dead and taken down to the mortuary. These days you can be resuscitated successfully after several minutes. The medical criterion for clinical death is shifting every few years. In fifty or a hundred years' time there may be cures for all current causes of death. A person who is dead by our medical criteria may not be considered dead by future medical criteria.' He studied the customs officer thoughtfully. 'To answer your question, what is in this dewar is a patient in a state of *extended deanimation*.'

'Good,' said Titcombe briskly, as if he'd just been told the weather forecast. 'Well, as I say, let's open it up and see what it looks like.'

'You can't be serious!' the American said.

In reply, Titcombe gave the doctor a smile that contained the pent-up venom of years. 'Open it,' he said.

32

Joe's flight from Florence landed at Gatwick Airport on Friday just after one o'clock; Juliet had travelled on a different plane a couple of hours earlier and Joe had promised he would phone her later.

It was a gloomy afternoon; most of the scant light that leaked through the matted clouds was sucked up by the bitumen blackness of the road. Joe drove slowly, churning everything over in his mind, depressed to be back in the real world.

In a short while he was going to have to walk in through his front door and kiss his wife, meet her eyes and try not to let the guilt show in his face. He had bought her an expensive silver bracelet in Florence, which he had kept hidden from Juliet in case she thought it was for her, and some more presents at the airport: a massive box of chocolates and a box of Amarettos which he knew she liked; and a toy Ferrari for Jack.

It seemed as if they'd made love continuously all night; he could barely remember having slept at all. He could smell Juliet now on his clothes, and he was drained. His head felt like it had an axe embedded in it; his eyes were puffy with tiredness, his balls ached and his insides felt as if they'd been scooped out with a shovel.

He was worried about Juliet going home alone; she must be exhausted, too, after their recent bliss together. What if it had affected her condition? And in truth, he was a little scared of her; of her unstable mind. Scared that maybe she would pick up the phone and call Karen on a whim, tell everything.

But more than anything, he was afraid right now of the depth of his feelings for her.

Joe debated whether to stop by the university, but he felt too tired and decided to get straight home. He arrived at the house shortly before three. Karen was hoovering upstairs and did not hear as he called out. The hall looked tidier and cleaner than usual, and none of Jack's toys were littered around. He put his bags down on the carpet, shouted louder and heard the roar of the machine fade away. But instead of coming down to greet him there was an ominous silence.

'Hi!' he called again.

She came to the top of the balustrading and looked down at him, and right away he could tell something was wrong. Maybe Juliet had already phoned her? Her face looked pale and colourless as if she too hadn't slept much. She was wearing a favourite orange sweatshirt with a faded picture of a dolphin on the chest, ski pants and espadrilles; her dark hair tumbled over her ears. Joe found himself unconsciously comparing her colouring with Juliet's. Both women achieved beauty in a different way.

'Had a good time, did you, Joe?'

He didn't like the way she'd said that. 'Yes, good convention – I'm glad I went.'

'How did the speech go?' She made no move to come down.

It was like talking to a stranger, he thought. 'Oh ... OK, pretty good. Ruffled a few feathers. You spring-cleaning?'

'I'm getting ready for the party tomorrow. My birthday, remember?' she said with sarcasm.

He unzipped his suitcase, rummaged inside, pulled out the gift-wrapped bracelet and popped it in the airport carrier bag. 'I – brought you some things. These are not for your birthday – they're for now.' He climbed the stairs still in his coat and made to kiss her. As he did so, she turned her face away and his lips brushed her cheek. 'What's the matter, honey?' he said, feeling a sudden tightening in his stomach. 'Jack? Is Jack OK?'

'Jack's fine,' she said, without turning back towards him. 'Who were you with in Florence, Joe?'

He was silent for a moment, thrown. '*With?*' His voice came out stilted. 'What do you mean? I was with the symposium.'

'Who were you sleeping with?'

Joe's brain raced and he was painfully aware that his blushing would give him away if she looked at him. 'What do you mean, hon? I get treated pretty good over there. I didn't have to share a room.'

She still did not look at him. 'I tried to ring you on Wednesday at the hotel, Joe, as you hadn't phoned that day. They said that you were out but Mrs Messenger was in. Want to tell me about it?'

'They said what?' His face smarted as if he had been slapped. 'I think they made a mistake, hon.'

'What's her name, Joe?'

'They didn't speak that good English at the hotel – maybe

you misunderstood them, or they didn't understand what you said.' He was floundering.

'Who is she, Joe?'

'Karen, this is crazy!'

'One of your students? That why you didn't want me to come?'

'I never said I didn't want you to come. It's you who never wants to come to anything these days.'

'Was she someone you picked up over there? I hope you used condoms.'

Joe hadn't and a wave of guilt about that swept through him. 'Honey, you got this all wrong. I'll sue the goddam hotel. I mean it, you –'

'Did you meet her there *alone*, also?'

'Uh?'

She jerked a folded sheet of paper from her pocket, and balled it in her fist. 'You know. Alone. Same as in Hove? Juliet? Is that who you were with?' She flung the paper angrily at him.

Joe picked it up from the carpet; as he unfolded it and realized what it was, his heart sank: *Really looking forward to seeing you tonight – alone!*

She knelt down and switched the hoover back on, the roar drowning his words.

Joe squeezed past her and pulled the plug out. 'Hon!' he said. 'Come on.' Then he saw a tear rolling down Karen's cheek. Something heavy rolled down inside his own heart. 'Karen, that note doesn't mean anything.'

'You lied to me, Joe. You told me you had a Cryonite meeting. You didn't, did you? You were with her. Juliet, whoever she is.'

'It's not what you think.' He took her hands in his, but she shook them free.

'Don't touch me!' she snapped.

He breathed deeply. 'Karen, Juliet Spring is my new postgrad – the one I told you about – the one who's dying. I'm trying to help her, that's all.'

She was seething, barely hearing a word. 'Sure you told

me that before, Joe. You just forgot to tell me you were screwing her.'

He shook his head, hating himself. 'You have it all wrong.'

'I don't think so, Joe.'

'She's a little obsessed with me, that's all. Yes, I had dinner with her – she was in a terrible state and I had to calm her down. That's all. No big deal.'

Karen said nothing for a moment. Then she nodded at the plug. 'Mind putting that back? I have to get on with the hoovering.'

Joe was determined to give her the bracelet, and now he thrust it at her. 'I got you this.'

She took it without interest, slid the bow off then removed the wrapping agonizingly slowly, trying not to tear it, as if she was planning to use it for something else. Finally she opened the plush velvet box as Joe watched in anticipation. He had been certain the bracelet was wrapped in cotton wool, so he was surprised to see a plastic bag inside instead.

And he was also surprised to see her frown as she peered at the old creased bag which was clumsily knotted at the top, her expression changing from disinterest to curiosity, then to utter horror as she held the bag up with her finger and thumb and looked even closer. Her eyes swung accusingly to Joe. He peered at it properly himself. Looked at Karen then back at the bag.

As he did so, he had to grip the banister rail to prevent himself from falling.

'What is this, Joe? Some kind of a joke?' Her voice was trembling and her face was white with rage.

Jesus. He swallowed. He could smell it now.

Bitch.

His hands clenched in anger. You bitch. God, how could you do this?

They could both smell it. The stench was filling the whole landing: it came from the dog turd that lay curled like a bracelet in the bottom of the plastic bag.

Joe told Karen it must have been someone who worked for

the airline: maybe a baggage loader. Or possibly even a chambermaid at the hotel. Karen replied that they would just have taken the bracelet and probably the box too. She said this was not a thief, this was someone sick.

When Karen went off to fetch Jack from playschool, he tried to phone Juliet, without success. He rang her London flat, the Cobbold-Tessering office, her parents' flat in Hove, and the university.

He did not want to believe it could have been Juliet. She hadn't even seen the bracelet, he had been careful about that. Yes, he'd left her alone in the bedroom on several occasions – but surely she wouldn't have gone through his belongings? Italy was renowned for petty theft; it was his fault for not locking the suitcase before he checked it in. A baggage handler.

But he couldn't even convince himself; never mind Karen. She was spooked by the turd and wanted him to phone the police. And she pointed out, practically, that if he wanted to claim on the insurance, he would have to report it. He rang the airport police and they suggested he contact the Italian police, but he didn't see much point. Instead he went into his study and tried Juliet's numbers repeatedly throughout the evening, without success. Karen was deliberately pre-occupied with preparing for her birthday party tomorrow evening, and he was spared a further inquisition.

In the morning he drove to the university, but Juliet's car wasn't there. Even so he looked for her all over COGS, again without success.

He drove down to her parents' flat on the seafront, but there was no sign of her car and no response from her doorbell. He found the caretaker, explained that Juliet Spring had a medical condition that made her prone to passing out and had not been at university, and after some reluctance, finally overcome by the production of a ten-pound note, the caretaker agreed to go in and have a look on his own. The flat was empty, he reported back.

Joe drove home, took Jack to the playground in the nearby park, then picked up some last-minute items for Karen from a grocery store. He rang Juliet's numbers again, at the same time trying to pacify Karen who was yelling at him for not helping her more.

Karen had invited forty guests to the buffet supper to celebrate her thirty-third birthday, which wasn't officially until next Wednesday. They were a mixture of academics from the university, friends Karen had made in the neighbourhood and, recently, at her various classes and therapies, and the parents of two of Jack's new playschool friends.

Blake Hewlett came with his latest girlfriend in tow. She was French: a striking, rather arty-looking girl called Nico. She had dead-straight hair that hung down to her waist, and a skirt that appeared to end only a couple of inches below it, and spent most of the time gazing around with a supercilious stare as if she felt she should have been taken somewhere more impressive.

She told Joe that she'd been really looking forward to meeting him, then volunteered nothing further. He only managed to extract a couple of words from her, and gathered from them that she was a model of some sort. All Blake's girlfriends were rather strange. But, then, so was Blake. In spite of her dislike for him, Karen always dutifully included him in any party. Afterwards she would invariably tell Joe that Blake gave her the creeps.

Joe noticed Karen through the mêlée. She looked stunning tonight, he thought, wearing a tight black dress he did not recall seeing before, a chunky gold necklace and large earrings. She'd had her hair done nicely, pinned up and hanging down in tendrils; she looked slimmer than he could remember her being for some time. It almost startled him to see her looking so beautiful; and it heightened the growing feeling of stupidity he felt for risking so much in sleeping with Juliet Spring.

Henry Wenceslas lumbered his vast frame around, his gruff laughter booming across the room. He wore a bright green kaftan shirt outside his baggy trousers, an Indian print silk scarf knotted around his neck with a gold ring, and plastic sandals, and looked like a throwback from the sixties. His tiny, unsmiling wife Rosamund, who lectured on philosophy, followed him as if she was holding him on a leash.

Joe found himself trying to carry on a defensive conversation with a rather strange woman in enormous glasses. She knew nothing about computer science, other than some jargon she'd gleaned from a TV documentary in which he'd been quoted, and was now grilling him about the spatial conceptualizing problems of robots.

'Don't you think that virtual reality will solve a lot of this problem?' she said, launching into a new line of attack.

Joe was irritated and bored by her. 'If we can download our brains into computers, we won't need to bother building robots at all. We can use humans to do all the shitty jobs for us.'

'Like having babies?' she said.

'You mean the fun part of bonking, or the boring part?'

The remark went down like a lead balloon. 'How would a computer reproduce, is what I mean?'

Joe gestured at some new arrivals. 'You'll have to excuse me a minute,' he said, and started to thread a path to the door.

'Joe!'

He looked up and saw Karen trying to attract his attention, and she was not looking pleased. 'Phone!' she mouthed through the social din, miming with her hand at the same time, and made her way closer. She leaned forward and hissed snarkily into his ear: 'It's a woman and she sounds drunk.'

Leaving the newcomers to Karen, he slipped upstairs into his study, closing the door behind him. He picked up the receiver, and for a moment all he could hear was the clatter and babel of voices of the party, as Karen had not replaced the downstairs receiver.

'Hello?' he said.

It was Juliet and her voice was strange, not drunk, but very slurred. She sounded in great distress. 'Joe. Please . . .

come ... and ... help me. Please ... can you ... come quickly.'

'Where are you?' He was aware of a clank as someone, presumably Karen, picked up the other receiver, but he didn't pay any attention.

'I'm asht ... university. Compusher room. Terrible pain – my head. Can't move my legs. 'Sh'I'm paralysed.'

'I'll be right there,' he said. 'I'll come straight over.'

He ran downstairs, pushed his way through the gathering, pulled his coat out from under several that had been heaped on top, checked that his car keys were in the pocket, then made his way towards the front door.

Karen cut him off, blocking his path by pressing her back to the door. Her expression was venomous. 'Where the hell are you going, Joe?'

'I won't be long – I have to go to the university – one of my students is sick.'

'Juliet, I presume?'

He hesitated a moment too long before replying. 'For God's sake, don't be ridiculous.'

'You bring me back a gift-wrapped dog turd, then you walk out on my birthday party and you tell me not to be ridiculous?'

'I'll be back in a quarter of an hour.'

'It takes you a quarter of an hour just to get to the university.'

Joe glanced desperately at the guests either side of them, lowering his voice. 'Karen, this girl is dying. She has an aneurism and could drop dead anywhere. I have to make sure she's OK.'

Karen lowered her voice also. 'You leave now, Joe, you go out that door and I'm taking Jack and moving back to Toronto. Do you understand?'

Joe breathed deeply and nodded, his heart aching. 'Half an hour. Straight there and back,' he said. Then he went out.

33

October 1990. Felixstowe Docks.

Customs Officer Titcombe was beginning to regret his decision to have the metal dewar containing the frozen body opened up. It was nearly six in the evening and his shift officially ended an hour ago. But the team of people he had been forced to allow in to perform the opening up were still preparing their equipment. And he wanted to see for himself.

The dewar had now been removed from its plastic container and lay on its side on the floor of the shed. Ten cylinders of liquid nitrogen stood near it and the team were all dressed in protective clothing with face shields; they looked like firefighters about to deal with a chemical blaze.

Titcombe had a date tonight, a girl whom he was meant to be meeting at eight. He looked around with growing irritation. The team seemed to be milling around now, wasting his time deliberately.

'Right, come on, must be about ready; what are you waiting for?'

'The ice box,' a man said. 'It's another cylinder which will be maintained at the same temperature, see; we can transfer the patient straight into it. Should be here in about an hour.'

'About an hour!' Titcombe exploded, but he knew he was defeated. He'd been bombarded with phone calls and faxes all day. An English lawyer was now present in the room, as well as a doctor and several scientists. And a lawyer in Los Angeles had warned him in no uncertain terms of the consequences of damaging the corpse. Death certificates had been faxed to him, as well as documents from the LA and Denver coroners offices and Crycon Extended Life Foundation's credentials as a mortuary. Crycon, indeed! *Con* was just the right word for it if you asked him. Christ, he'd had no idea how many people took this crap so seriously. In the end, to try to cut the process short, he'd agreed that all he would do would be to look inside the dewar, check that it really was a human cadaver, then allow them to seal it straight back up. He would not request the cadaver to be thawed and medically examined.

He gripped a styrofoam cup of coffee between his frozen hands, grateful for its warmth, and looked at the American doctor. Forrester had been making him angry, making him boil at times. Everything was becoming too damned American in England. Burgers; lawnmower engines; clothes; television; now corpses. We were importing American corpses, for Christ's sake!

Titcombe shook his head. 'I still don't understand what sort of medical research you're going to do over here, Dr Forrester.' He said 'Dr' each time with a snide twist in his voice. 'Why do you need an American corpse – surely you could freeze an English one?'

The American ran his eye up and down Titcombe. 'You mean like a dead version of yourself.'

The customs officer hesitated, unsure how to take the remark.

Forrester eyed him again, carefully, then shook his head. 'Nope, wouldn't work. You wouldn't be any good. We need a whole human being, not just an asshole in a uniform.'

Titcombe looked back at him, seething, slopping hot coffee on his hands in his rage, and ignoring it. He wagged a threatening finger. 'Don't push your luck, doctor, you're not through customs and immigration yourself yet.'

He glared at his watch, then at the total chaos in the shed. His phone had rung non-stop all afternoon with a succession of shipping agents whingeing about the delay in clearing the *Arctic Venus*'s cargo. There would be complaints to his superiors which wouldn't do him much good, although he knew he would get their support. Corpses were regularly used for gem and drugs smuggling, but they were normally shipped by air. He was right to query a corpse coming by sea. Quite right.

Except he had never seen a dead body before and the prospect was beginning to make him a little scared.

*

It was nine o'clock before the last bolt was unscrewed, then four men in protective clothing began struggling to remove the lid of the capsule. As it finally came free, a dense, hissing cloud of steam engulfed them.

They carried the lid clear and laid it on the ground with a metallic clank, and Titcombe stared wide-eyed into the container from which strange, almost ethereal steam was now pouring. It seemed to take an age before it began to clear, and as it did so he looked away, too scared for a moment to peer inside. When he finally did, all he could see was what looked like blue wadding.

Two of the men crouched down, inserted their gloved hands and gripped the sides of a metal tray. As it rolled stiffly out, Titcombe could see that the wadding was in fact a quilted blue nylon sleeping bag, coated in ice, and tied in a cylindrical bundle with webbing straps. Both men turned to Titcombe, as if giving him the opportunity to stop now, if he wanted. Someone else was timing the proceedings on a stop watch and another person was taking photographs. Wisps of steam drifted through them. It was like a dream, Titcombe thought; a frigging eerie dream.

One of the men tried in vain to free the buckles with his gloved fingers. 'Frozen solid,' he said.

'Cut them!' the American ordered. 'You're taking too long. One minute, maximum.

Someone reached forward with a knife and the man slit each of the three straps, then pulled the bag open. Titcombe could scarcely look, so great was his fear now. He stared at the ground and bit his lip until several gasps of amazement and a babble of remarks made him look up. Something glistened between the folds of nylon, like a window.

He stepped forward cautiously, heart in his throat, and looked down, struggling to keep control as he found himself staring at a face encased in ice that was as clear as glass.

He trembled in awe, afraid to go on looking but too fascinated to turn away. 'Christ,' he said. 'Been dead fifteen years?' He continued to stare down, transfixed. 'Not decomposed at all.' A massive shiver rocked him. 'Christ – it's like

– it's – not dead at all – just asleep.' He managed a nervous twitch of a smile, then felt the goosepimples racing up his back. He turned to the group around him, no longer the king pin but a frightened man in need of reassurance. 'As if it – could – you know – wake up at any moment.' He forced a short laugh. But no one joined him.

'OK?' the American said tensely. 'Seen enough –' It wasn't a question.

34

Joe ran from the car park down the steps and around to the front of the COGS building. He pushed open the door and stopped in the lobby. Half past nine on a Saturday night and the place felt deserted. A Student Union poster fluttered in the draught as the door swung shut behind him; the heating system pumped away, a steady clatter above him, and a warm draught purred on his neck. He ran past the closed and dark enquiry office, down the stairs into the basement, pushed open the fire door at the bottom and sprinted along to the far end of the narrow corridor.

When he flung the door open, there was a sharp whirr and Clinton clattered towards him. Joe ignored the robot. Juliet was slumped at a strange angle across her keyboard, hair awry. The screen was packed full, as usual, with rows of hexadecimal numbers. He ran across to her.

'Juliet?'

She did not move. One eye stared weakly up at him, like the eye of a dying fish, with only the barest hint of recognition. He took her right hand, which was limp, and fumbled for her pulse. Her skin felt clammy. He leaned over and kissed her but she didn't react.

'What's happened?' he said. There was no response. 'Juliet, what's happened?' he asked again, although he knew the answer. He found a pulse, and it was so desperately faint he didn't even bother timing it. 'I won't be a sec,' he said, went across the room, stood watching her for a moment from the doorway, then sprinted back down the corridor to the payphone. He dialled 999, asked for an ambulance and gave them directions.

Then he took a card from his wallet on which he had a list of emergency numbers, and dialled Murray McAlister, a doctor who was one of the six members of a deanimation team on permanent standby for call out. Joe told him the situation.

McAlister said that they had friends round to dinner, but he could meet Joe at the Prince Regent Hospital in Brighton, where the ambulance would be taking her, in a quarter of an hour if Joe wanted.

Joe told him not to disturb his party – he'd call him when they got to the hospital and let him know the prognosis. Then he dashed back to the computer room.

Clinton again clattered towards him. 'Welcome to AR-CHIVE. If you have any cans of soft drink please leave them on the work surfaces and I will remove them when they are empty. Have a nice time with ARCHIVE.'

Joe knelt down. 'Going to be all right,' he said, putting his arm around Juliet. She was wearing an angora sweater over jeans, and he pressed his fingers through the soft strands of wool to give her a squeeze of reassurance. 'Going to be fine.' But he heard his voice cracking with distress. Yesterday morning when they'd parted in Florence, she had looked so happy, so radiant. So damned healthy. Now he couldn't even tell if she was registering his presence.

Her left eye seemed disconnected, had become like Edwin Pilgrim's roaming lazy eye. He put his own close to it, raised her lid, trying to see if the pupil was dilated, if perhaps it was a drug she had taken that was causing all this, and not her aneurism.

He felt a light tug on his hand and looked down. She was trying to grip it but her fingers didn't seem to be working properly. She mumbled something incoherent.

'What did you say?' he asked gently.

'Sh'no need,' she said, then was silent.

'No need?' he repeated, coaxing her, placing his ear closer to her mouth. He glanced at his watch. He had told the ambulance operator he would be waiting outside in five minutes.

'Decode,' she said, squeezing on his hand again as if she had something vital to tell him. 'Decode,' she said again.

'You've been decoding? Something's happened? You've made some progress?'

She began shaking, agitated. He looked at her face again; her lips moved but no sound came out, and her right eye tried hard to communicate something to him.

'I have to go upstairs just for a few minutes to get the ambulance. I won't be long, I promise.' Any anger that he had felt towards her had vanished. He did not want to believe this creature, so lovely, so horribly stricken, could even have contemplated a thing like replacing the bracelet with the dog turd. He preferred to keep the possibility alive in his mind, however slim, that it was an anonymous baggage handler, or a petty thief in the hotel room.

She gripped his arm and wouldn't let go. 'Sh'no need.'

'No need to what, Juliet?'

There was a long pause. 'Decode,' she said finally.

'Decode?' He looked at the mass of digits on the screen. There was nothing to indicate any progress had been made. 'I'll just be a couple of minutes, OK?'

'Pleash don't leave me, Joe.' Her voice sounded so plaintive, so pitiful. 'Pain. In – s'my head.'

'I'm not leaving you – I'll be right back.' He prised her fingers gently from his wrist.

As he did so she spoke again. 'Won't forget your promish, Joe. Sh'about my – frozen. To make sh – sh-sure – I'm – frozen.'

'You're going to be OK.'

'You – promish . . .' Her voice weakened, but still she insisted. 'Make sure . . . frozen.'

'I promise,' Joe said. 'Don't worry. I promise.'

She tried to say something else, but drifted into silence.

Joe waited a moment. 'Juliet – did –?' Then he turned and left the room, fighting back tears. As he reached the lobby, he could already hear the distant wail of a siren. Normally it was a sound he hated; tonight, for the first time in his life, he welcomed it.

He drove fast, trying to keep the ambulance in sight, but lost it at a red light and didn't meet up with it again until he reached the hospital.

There was chaos in the Accident and Emergency reception. It felt to Joe as though he had come into a war zone. A team of medics raced out of a room pushing a trolley on which a man lay on his back, his chest a pulp of blood, a drip feeding into a cannula on his wrist. A woman in a room Joe couldn't see was screaming in hysterics. Another ambulance arrived; a youngster in leather motorcyling gear was wheeled in, unconscious, his face swathed in blood-soaked bandages.

Joe filled out an admittance form as best he could for Juliet, while a doctor examined her in a small room with a curtained partition. Behind him a receptionist was trying hard on the phone to contact a neurologist. The duty neurosurgeon was in theatre operating on an emergency – a crash victim; it was Saturday night, she said by way of explanation.

When Joe reached 'Next of kin or Person to Contact' on the form he hesitated, remembering Juliet's concern about her parents' attitude to her being frozen. He was tempted to put down *not known*, but instead he told the receptionist he couldn't help, but either the university or her employers would have that on their records. It might buy them until Monday, Joe thought. As he did so, it hit him for the first time that he was mentally facing up to the possibility that Juliet might be about to die. And if she could be suspended before her parents were aware of her death, one problem would be solved.

A nurse searched through Juliet's handbag, which Joe had brought along. He wondered for a horrible moment if Karen's bracelet might be in there, but all she pulled out was a small address book, which she began leafing through. 'Looks like it,' she said, stopping and tapping her finger on a page.

The receptionist suddenly started speaking into the receiver, then she hung up and looked at Joe. 'Dr Jordan will be here in about twenty minutes.'

The casualty doctor, a young female houseman with chic brown hair, and a pretty but intensely serious face, was studying Juliet's MedicAlert bracelet with a puzzled expression. She removed it and walked discreetly over to Joe. 'I haven't seen these particular instructions before – is the young lady an organ donor?'

Joe shook his head and glanced at the bracelet, checking the tiny capital letters engraved on it: MEDICAL HISTORY. CALL COLLECT 24 HOURS. IN CASE OF DEATH SEE REVERSE FOR BIOSTASIS PROTOCOL. He turned it over and read the familiar wording: CALL NOW FOR INSTRUCTIONS. PUSH 50,000 UNITS HEPARIN IV AND DO CPR WHILE COOLING WITH ICE TO TEN CELSIUS. KEEP PH 7.5. DO NOT AUTOPSY OR EMBALM.

Joe looked back at the doctor. 'Cryonics.'

She looked back at him, her forehead furrowed, and Joe sensed trouble in her small, dark eyes. 'Are you serious?'

Joe nodded.

The doctor went across to the receptionist, let her write down the phone number on the tag, then put the bracelet back on Juliet's wrist and checked her pulse again. Juliet's face was the colour of alabaster.

The houseman came back over to Joe. 'I've read a bit about cryonics – sounds absolute rubbish to me.'

Joe kept calm, not wanting to rile her; he would need all the co-operation he could get if – 'She's a very brilliant young woman,' he said. 'She has a double-first in neuroscience and computing science.'

That made the young doctor's expression change a little. 'Really?'

'She's on the pharmaceutical research team of Cobbold-Tessering.'

Her eyes hardened again. 'If she's so brilliant, I'm amazed she could be so gullible.'

Two porters clattered an empty trolley stretcher past them, heading for the front door and the wail of an approaching siren. A figure in a white coat hurried through another door, flanked by two nurses. An orderly followed and Joe saw him and one of the nurses start to push Juliet away.

'Where is she being taken?' he said to the houseman.

'Intensive Care – we're going to put her on life support.'

'Do you mind if I go with her?'

'Are you a relative?'

'No – I – she's one of my Ph.D. students.'

'I'm sorry. But there's nothing you can do anyway now.'

Joe watched as Juliet was wheeled into a lift. 'Do you think she'll survive the night?'

The houseman looked at him rather severely, as if Joe now had no further business here. She seemed to be weighing up whether to tell him anything. 'I think she'll be very lucky if she does,' she said finally.

Someone called out to her. She excused herself and hurried off. Joe looked at his watch. 9.45. It was hard to believe it was only three-quarters of an hour since he had left the party; it seemed an aeon ago. He gazed down the corridor, which suddenly looked horribly empty, and felt gutted.

An old man was wheeled past him on a respirator. Orders were being shouted. Joe felt alone, and out of place. He thought of the contempt on the houseman's face when she had heard the word *cryonics*. It happened all the time and Joe was used to it, but it still made him boil inside. The narrow-mindedness of so many smart, intelligent medics who lacked the imagination to see that medicine would go on changing and improving, that what they were doing now would one day be as obsolete as cauterizing amputated limbs with hot tar. And that all current medical knowledge and practices would be replaced with something so much better, something that would enable people to live without pain or death.

He walked over to a phone inside a glass bubble and rang

Murray McAlister again. The doctor told him in his strong Aberdeen brogue that he would speak to the Intensive Care Unit right away, and call Joe straight back with, he hoped, a more accurate prognosis.

Joe waited by the phone. A couple of minutes passed that seemed like an hour. Then it rang and he answered on the first ping. It was McAlister and he sounded almost breathless with excitement. 'Juliet Spring, wasn't it, Joe? That was the name?'

'Yes.' Joe's hopes lifted.

'She's just died. Literally a couple of minutes ago, as they brought her into the ICU. Good, eh? I mean, it's sad for the girl, terrible; but good to have a real human being instead of a dummy to work on, don't you think, Joe? Good experience for the team. Must be over six months since the last patient.'

It was some moments before Joe had composed himself enough to be able to reply. 'Sure,' he said in a voice choked with tears.

35

Juliet Spring's death was formally declared by a junior anaesthetist, temporarily in charge of the Intensive Care Unit, whose name was Dr Roland Dance.

Murray McAlister told Joe he would call the rest of the team. Joe said he'd speak to Blake, because he had to phone Karen anyway. Before doing so, Joe had raced up to the ICU and Dr Dance had agreed to talk to him only grudgingly. He told Joe it was standard procedure for any death within twenty-four hours of admission, where the cause was uncertain, to be reported to the coroner.

Dance was a thin, horse-faced man of about thirty, with an arrogant, old-school demeanour. It took all Joe's powers of persuasion to get him to agree, albeit extremely reluctantly, to go along with the instructions on Juliet's

MedicAlert bracelet in permitting cardiopulmonary support to maintain her circulation. It was with even more reluctance that he agreed to having her immediately coupled to a heart-lung machine. But he was adamant that he would not fill in the *cause of death* section of the death certificate and that the death would have to be reported to the coroner's office – without whose permission the body could not be released from hospital.

Dance had never before been faced with a patient signed up for cryonic suspension and, from what little he had read of the subject, considered it to be arrant nonsense, and he told Joe so. Close to exasperation, and wringing his hands with frustration, Joe finally convinced him that he would be failing in his duty – and risking a lawsuit on the hospital – if he did not immediately telephone the number on the Medic-Alert bracelet, and speak to Juliet's own doctor who could verify her condition. Dance finally marched huffily off to his office to do so.

Back at the reception desk by the nurses' station, Joe felt the anger and frustration seething in him, overcoming grief; and wished he had been better prepared. He had the office and home numbers of Juliet's lawyer in his wallet, and he hurried down the corridor to a phone booth. There was an answering machine on Mr Zeillerman's home number and Joe left a message for him to call back urgently; he didn't think there was much point calling the solicitor's office at this hour on a Saturday night, but tried the number anyway and left another message on a machine.

Then he called home. The phone rang a long while before someone drunk, whose voice he did not recognize, answered. Joe asked for Blake and it was an age before he came on the line. Joe warned him there might be a problem, but Blake said he would be right over anyhow, and Joe asked if he could get Karen for him. It was another age before he heard her voice.

'I can't believe you're doing this to me, Joe.'

'Hon, we have to do a suspension, I'm really sorry.'

'Surely you don't have to be there? Not the whole time, Joe? There are other people in the team.'

Joe felt a deep pang of guilt. She was right; he didn't *have* to be there; the others could do it fine without him. But he had made a promise to Juliet, and if there was a problem – like there was with Dance, or her father suddenly turned up – he needed to be around to deal with it.

He could hear the background babble of party chatter down the receiver. 'I'll make it up to you, hon, I promise.'

'Joe, can't you understand?' she said gently, and sounding very wounded. 'This is my birthday party; you're my husband. I want you here with me. I want to share it with you.'

Joe did understand and felt bad. 'I have to sort out a big problem here at the hospital,' he said. 'I'll do my best to get back.'

'No,' she said, sounding resigned. 'Don't worry. Do what you have to do, OK?'

'Give my apologies to everyone.'

'I already did that. They just toasted me a while back and I had to explain you weren't here.'

'I'm sorry.'

'I have to go now, OK?'

'See you later.' Joe hung up, deeply upset by the call. All her anger had gone and she had just sounded wounded. He went back to the nursing-station desk and waited for the anaesthetist. The clock on the wall said 9.55. Almost ten minutes since Juliet had died and every one of those minutes counted, every second, because when the heart stopped pumping, the blood immediately began coagulating and clotting; if starved of oxygen from its blood supply, the brain's electrical circuitry would cease, and the synaptic connections with their chemical encoding would slowly start breaking down. It was vital to keep Juliet's circulation going so that the chemicals that would preserve her tissues from being damaged by ice crystals could be properly introduced and distributed throughout her body.

The Cryonite volunteer operator who answered Roland Dance's call should be able to confirm Juliet's aneurism to him and her instructions, as well as immediately contact the girl's own doctor and have him call the anaesthetist. In theory there should not be a problem – but, it only took one obstructive person to blow the whole thing. And Dance was crassly obstructive.

When he came back, almost ten minutes later, his face was stiff; he held his chin high and peered hostilely at Joe down the end of his nose.

'You want an operating theatre, is that right?' Dance said. 'You want an HLR? What else of my bloody equipment and staff do you need for this hare-brained nonsense? She's dead – can't you at least leave her in peace? The dead have a right to some dignity, you know.'

'Did you ever see a corpse look dignified during an autopsy?' Joe retorted.

Dance glared at him and Joe regretted the remark, knowing he needed as much co-operation as possible. 'Operating Theatre Number Five,' the anaesthetist said. 'We'd be obliged if you'd leave it tidy when you've finished.'

Joe was surprised that he had given in so easily – and that he was actually going to let them use a theatre, which he did not have to do. 'Thank you, that's very kind.'

'Nothing to do with me,' Dance said. 'I've been overruled. It appears the request, and consent from our Director, is already on the hospital's computer, and we're charging your – ah – Cryonite company for the facility. So we do at least get some benefit from this charade,' he added tartly.

Joe looked away from him, suppressing a grin. Had Juliet done that in preparation? Hacked into the hospital computer sometime before she'd collapsed, maybe even weeks ago, in preparation? The thought cheered him considerably.

Half an hour later Joe stood gowned up in a blue scrub suit in Operating Theatre Five. Two staff nurses were watching through the viewing window with a look of horror on their faces, as if Joe's team were a clan of monsters engaged in some bestial savagery.

In the theatre with him, also gowned up, were Blake

Hewlett, who had left the party to come and, Joe presumed, had deposited his girlfriend somewhere en route; short, cheery, ginger-headed Murray McAlister, Cryonite's tame doctor; and three other members of the standby team: Tania Hughes, a thirty-six-year-old veterinary technician, an ardent feminist who always made Joe feel his every comment was a politically incorrect blunder; Gordon Preston, a financial analyst and committed libertarian; and Andy White, a physics student at the Isaac Newton University.

The rest of the team were on their way down from London, and other parts of the country, to prepare the operating theatre at the Cryonite headquarters for the main part of Juliet's suspension.

Juliet was on her back in a shallow plastic basin that had been placed on the operating table. She was naked, partially immersed in water and ice, her hair trailing like tendrils of pond-weed around her face. She looked as if she had drowned, Joe thought, suddenly. Ophelia.

He was finding it hard to watch, to see her body beneath the stark glare of the overhead light, with the stalk of a rectal thermometer protruding between her thighs, an endotracheal tube down her throat, and cannulae taped to the base of her neck and the back of her wrist. Anticoagulant and metabolic support drugs were being fed into her veins from plastic bottles hooked on to drip stands beside her. Sound effects were provided by the mechanical arm of a heart-lung resuscitator that compacted then released her chest: there was a click each time from a rib it had broken and a sharp hiss as its rubber ventilator reservoir bag inflated then deflated. Joe thought with irony of his discussion about dignity with the anaesthetist a short while earlier.

Juliet's eyes were still open; until recently they would have been taped shut, but new research on cornea grafts showed that the chances of preserving sight were enhanced by keeping the eyes open and injecting them with water-absorbing chemicals through micro needles. Her cheeks were distended and her arms rocked in the water with each compression. Limbo. No longer living, but not delivered up to death. Joe watched silently, feeling an almost overwhelming sense of distress and of loss. It was mitigated only by his relief that she had died here in hospital, where they had been able to commence her suspension process without delay.

He was barely able to comprehend that this rag doll lying in blood-stained water, breasts squashed sideways by the heart-lung thumper, was the same wild, vibrant creature to whom he had made love only yesterday morning in Florence. He could not believe that the marble skin on her body was the same warm skin he had held tightly against his own. All because she had a burst artery inside her head that they couldn't fix yet.

She just had to wait a few years for neurosurgery to improve, and then he'd be there at her side when she was thawed out, when she woke up. He'd be holding her hand, the way he had once planned to be holding his father's hand.

He thought of his father now as he watched someone adjusting a flow valve, and he remembered, suddenly, the nurse phoning him at home in Toronto in the middle of the night. *Dr Messenger, your father is calling out for you. He wants to speak to you very badly.*

Then he thought of Karen lifting the dog turd from the jewellery box again; the revulsion and the unease he had felt simultaneously led him on to Juliet's mood changes. The chill she had sometimes made him feel, as if there was more to her than just flesh and blood. As if contained within her lay some deep, malevolent spirit. Except he knew it was no more than behavioural changes caused by her aneurism, that was all, that was the logical explanation. Just a mean trick played on her by Mother Nature.

But his unease was not completely dispelled. Her open eyes continued to stare sightlessly at him. Perhaps not so sightlessly, he thought with a shiver. It was as if she were supervising him from beyond death. As if she were saying: *I fixed the hospital, Joe. You fix the rest.*

Blake was saying something to him now and he looked up at him, startled. 'Sorry?'

'Femoral cut-down now, do you think?'

Joe glanced at the clock, then nodded in agreement. Murray McAlister moved forward with a scalpel and began to make an incision in Juliet's groin, which Tania Hughes had already shaved and brushed with iodine.

The doctor worked swiftly and completed the work of cannulating the femoral vessels in just under half an hour. The cannulae fed back into a mobile heart-lung perfusion and oxygenation circuit that had a built-in heat exchanger, to which McAlister now switched over from the heart-lung thumper.

The heat exchanger would drop Juliet Spring's internal temperature to fifteen degrees Celsius within the next quarter of an hour. This had to be achieved quickly in order to retard the decay process, and the urgency lent a tangible air of theatre to that already highly charged atmosphere. The artificial circulation would keep almost all the veins and arteries throughout her body and brain open, while washing out her blood and replacing it with anticoagulant, cell-membrane stabilizers, calcium blockers and antioxidant chemicals – to minimize any possible damage to her brain.

When the hiss of the ventilator stopped, the arterial oxygenator took over. Juliet suddenly became very still. Joe decided this was not how he wanted to remember her. And her eyes still spooked him, they seemed to continue following him wherever he moved, co-ordinated in death in a way they had not been during that last hour of her life.

Every few minutes, Tania checked the digital readout of the rectal thermometer. The tubes in and out of the cannulae, dark red at first with blood, slowly became increasingly dilute in colour.

'OK, Joe?' Blake said.

He nodded.

Blake gave him a strange smile he couldn't read, or maybe did not want to read. 'Get some gyp from your old lady?'

'I don't think Karen's over the moon about my being here right now.'

'Interesting party,' Blake said.

'That was a good-looking girl you had with you.'

'Nico's cool,' he said. He gave Joe another smile.

Joe did not respond. He ran his eyes over the battery of machinery in the room.

Gordon Preston, a nervy man in his early thirties, with a jutting chin and receding black hair, and an impatient manner that bordered at times on aggression, looked at Juliet and shook his head. 'I think it's really sad to see a lovely girl like this die so young.'

Tania Hughes rounded on him. 'You mean it wouldn't be a shame if she was an ugly girl? It's only a shame because she's beautiful?'

'I'm not saying that.'

'You are; that's exactly what you're saying!'

'Who wants to come back to a world full of ugly women?' Blake said, butting in. 'Surely the point about taking charge of the future is to improve it? To do a better job than Mother Nature?'

'Thank you, Blake,' said Tania. 'There are other reasons for wanting to be immortal. Some people do have higher aspirations.'

'And what would your higher aspirations be, Tania?' Murray McAlister said.

She peered at him over the top of her surgical mask as if he were a foreign body. 'Self fertilization,' she said. 'For starters.'

Andy White, the physics student, who was one of Cryonite's hardest-working volunteers, laughed. 'That's not something you're going to need to worry about in Joe's post-biological world.'

'I don't worry about it now,' she said. 'Post-biological penises have been available in the shops for years. I find them very much more efficient than the real thing – and they don't come with six feet of dreary, balding wimp attached.'

White glanced at the tall, reedy figure of Gordon Preston, wondering whether it was at him or someone else in the room that the barb was directed. Tania glanced at the stalk of the rectal thermometer. 'Fifteen degrees,' she said.

Joe looked at his watch and checked it against the circular

clock on the pale green wall of the operating theatre. It was twenty past eleven. One hour and thirty-five minutes had elapsed since Roland Dance had pulled a gold Parker fountain pen from his pocket and formally, if with extremely bad grace, signed Juliet Spring's death certificate.

'OK,' Blake said. 'We're outta here.'

The Cryonite Transport Ambulance was much older than the one that had raced Juliet Spring to hospital from the university, and its interior had been modified to contain all the equipment needed to set up a mobile operating theatre anywhere. Not all their members were fortunate – or shrewd – enough to die in a hospital.

There was no shortage of funds for a new ambulance, but the vehicle was used so rarely they had not yet considered it necessary to replace it, and it aroused sentimental feelings in some of the members. All eighteen people who had been cryonically suspended in England so far, some whole body, some head only, had made what would theoretically not be their last journey, but just their last one for a while, in this vehicle.

The exhaust was blowing and its deep boom resonated through the interior, accompanied by an unpleasant smell of fumes. Joe, Blake, and Murray McAlister sat in the back, with the other three squeezed in the front. The orange container holding Juliet was strapped in between the shelves, the portable heart-lung machine still running to maintain her circulation and her low temperature.

Normally Joe enjoyed participating in cryonic suspensions. He loved the amateurish, pioneering feel. The sense of rebelling against the medical Establishment made him feel at one with his father again. Then there was the high of venturing into the unknown. The feeling of power and progress in achieving one more small but significant victory over Mother Nature.

But tonight he felt hopelessly inadequate. He was making a mess of his marriage. Had made a mess of Juliet's last weeks of life by offering hope he could not deliver. And now he had a nagging fear that he was going to end up making a mess of her death.

36

Thirty minutes after leaving the hospital in Brighton the ambulance swung on to the forecourt of the Cryonite Life Extension Foundation, on the large, modern industrial estate a couple of miles from the perimeter of Gatwick Airport.

Andy White reversed as close to the steel shutters of the loading bay as he dared, then jumped out and opened the rear doors. A jumbo jet screamed into the blackness of the night sky above their heads, momentarily deafening them, and as Joe climbed down he smelled a strong tang of spent kerosene in the cold, damp air. Only one other vehicle was on the forecourt, an elderly car which was probably the night security guard's, he thought.

Joe's forebodings were deepening all the time, even though Juliet had told him she'd completed all the massive amount of paperwork that had been carefully drafted by Cryonite's lawyers. It was based on similar documentation that had survived test cases in the States when relatives had objected, and when coroners had tried to have cryonics patients autopsied. But no one had yet challenged it over here.

There was a moment of complete silence as he walked through the reflection of the ambulance's tail-lights on the wet tarmac, up to the main entrance door. A tiny brass name plate beside the bell was the only clue to the nature of the activities that went on beyond the anonymous, windowless exterior of the building.

He pressed the bell to alert the security guard, then unlocked the door and went into the reception foyer, which was brightly lit and warm, and smelled welcomingly of freshly brewing coffee. With its fake wood panelling, thick carpeting, crystal chandeliers, imitation leather armchairs and vases of plastic flowers, the room had been designed to instil in visitors a sense of dignity and permanence. Framed testimonials by eminent scientists on the viability of cryonics were intended to cement this effect. And as if to prove it, the cheery face of Harry Hartman, Cryonite's founder, beamed down reassuringly from the large framed colour photograph on the wall.

Harry Hartman was the first man in England to have been cryonically frozen, and his body was in a steel dewar in a vault beneath the building. A billionaire computer-software pioneer, Hartman had died ten years previously of cancer, at the age of only forty-seven. From his portrait he had the appearance more of a successful salesman than a scientific genius; a libertarian, he had believed implicitly in the sovereignty of the individual, and the idea that man had to take charge of his own destiny because there wasn't anyone 'up there' who would.

He'd done a pretty good job of practising what he preached. When he died, he left behind two wives, one in England and one in Italy, each of whom learned of the other's existence for the first time from his lawyers the day after his death, and neither of whom got much of his loot. He'd left most of it for himself, for when he returned.

He had avoided both death duties and the British laws preventing people from leaving money to themselves by locking all his wealth into the Hartman Perpetuity Trust in Liechtenstein. The capital of his fortune was to remain intact for his use at some point in the future, and the interest it accumulated annually he had decreed was to be spent, at the discretion of the trustees, on funding research into immortality.

Blake Hewlett had met and befriended Harry Hartman a few years before his death. All the finance for the Cryonite Life Extension Foundation, and all the funding for ARCHIVE, apart from a tiny annual contribution from the university, came from the Hartman Perpetuity Trust.

The night security guard, a retired army sergeant-major with ruddy cheeks and a white toothbrush moustache –

known only by his last name, Spalding – came hurrying out of the operating theatre at the end of a short tiled corridor. Jacket off and sleeves rolled up, he saluted when he saw Joe. 'All set, sir!' he barked, puffing with exertion.

Joe was never quite sure whether Spalding was being respectful or taking the mickey. 'Good,' he said.

'Done a quick scrub of the floor and walls, sir.' As if to confirm his effort, he pulled out a handkerchief, balled it and dabbed his brow. Then he tugged his shirt collar forward and dabbed his handkerchief inside that. 'Good to have a real operation instead of just practice –' His voice tailed as he saw Joe's expression. 'If you know what I mean, sir.'

Joe gave him a thin smile. 'No one else here yet?'

'Miss Stroud, sir. She arrived about twenty minutes ago. I sent her off to an all-night shop in Crawley to get some more milk and coffee.'

Pauline Stroud was a librarian in London. Her late husband was a neurosuspension patient at Cryonite. His was one of the twelve heads preserved in liquid nitrogen in the vault beneath the building.

It took all the team from the ambulance to manhandle the orange box, still half filled with ice and water, and with the portable heart-lung machine and heat exchanger attached, on to a trolley in the loading bay. They changed into fresh scrubs, met up with four more members of the team who'd just arrived, then negotiated the trolley into the operating theatre.

The theatre had been constructed to hospital standards, and was similar to the one they had just left in the Prince Regent Hospital, but without any anaesthetic equipment. An operating table on a hydraulic base stood beneath a massive kettledrum lamp; several drip stands and a battery of machinery in spotless casings lay scattered around the floor, and a row of gas cylinders lined one of the walls.

The sudden proximity to the death of someone he had slept with affected Joe in a way he had not anticipated. It made him feel drawn to the living. He had left Karen to cope with the party at home and he felt a rush of love for her, wanted to phone her and tell her how much he really adored her. He felt scared that he might lose her and Jack. People drifted apart in marriage without realizing it. Sometimes they got too far apart to get back together. He stared into the orange box and wondered, with a chill, what might have happened if Juliet had lived.

And what might happen when she came back.

Sodden with water, Juliet's hair had lost its deep red lustre and now looked a muddy brown, but her open eyes still blazed a brilliant emerald against her colourless skin. Watching him. His emotions churned. He looked away, then back and her guarded expression seemed to have changed. She was watching him so sadly now, so hopefully. He wished that there was no one else in the room, so that he could lean down and kiss her forehead, reassure her.

He could see the vapour of his breath and rubbed his hands; he was wearing only light clothes, expecting it to have been hot at the party, and the cold came straight up from the tiled floor through the thin soles of his sterile canvas slip-ons. He pulled his surgical mask up over his nose and was grateful for the extra warmth.

Murray McAlister and Blake washed their hands in the sinks, and, helped by Tania Hughes, pulled on latex gloves. Joe did the same, trying to steel himself for what was to come.

The operating-theatre door opened and Douglas Goodman, who always performed the complex open-heart surgery, hurried in, parcelled up in his blue gown, with one tape of his mask flapping free. Goodman was a quiet, bespectacled man in his fifties, totally dedicated to cardiac surgery. No one knew why he was so willing to help with their cryonic suspensions: he refused to charge for his work, but he wasn't a member of Cryonite, and would never be drawn into a discussion about whether he believed in cryonics or not. Yet he would always arrive when summoned and work as hard and as diligently as if the patient were still alive. Joe often wondered if Goodman, like himself, secretly hated the entire notion of death and was driven to helping them out of curiosity.

Goodman apologized for being late, went through to the scrub-up room to wash his hands, and held them out for Tania Hughes to put the gloves on. Joe stepped forward to assist, then walked with the surgeon over to the operating table, feeling that if he was part of the operating team he would be doing more to fulfil his promise to Juliet.

The heart-lung machine was switched off and Juliet was lifted from the transport container back into the plastic basin which had been packed with fresh ice and placed on the operating table. Tania Hughes swabbed a messy brown patch of iodine on Juliet's chest, and Goodman made a deep incision down her breastbone. Only the faintest ribbon of watery, blood-tinged fluid followed the blade of the scalpel.

Lying there, Juliet could so easily be not dead but anaesthetized, Joe thought, passing the clamps. He swallowed hard as Tania and McAlister pinned the flesh back, and had to turn away for a moment, thinking he was going to throw up. Then he calmed a little, tried to move forward a few decades in his mind to a time when she might be lying there again, her aneurism being removed by laser surgery or nanosurgery, the first twitches of new life already visible. And he felt an inexplicable glow of optimism. He even smiled.

He kept smiling intermittently throughout the next hour as Goodman slowly and meticulously connected cannulae first into the right-heart atrium and then the aorta. And he found he was starting to be able to stare back into Juliet's sightless eyes with confidence. *It's working fine*, he said silently to himself. *No hitches. Got you in time. Everything's going like clockwork. Just one more hurdle.*

When the surgeon stepped back, looking tired and relieved, he gave a curt signal and Blake switched the heart-lung machine back on.

There was a deep hum and the sound of fluid circulating. A large plastic bottle on the floor beside the machine began to fill with the watery rust colour of the chemical blood-substitute that had been pumped into Juliet in the hospital, and which was now being drained out of her and replaced with an amber-coloured cryoprotective agent, consisting mostly of glycerol and sucrose.

For the next two hours, the concentration of the cryoprotective agent would be gradually stepped up as it flushed through her, drawing out water from her brain and body cells. By repeated flushing and re-flushing with increasing concentrations of the agent, the team would replace over thirty per cent of Juliet's body water with antifreezing chemicals.

Joe bit his lip as the part of the operation he was most worried about began. The surgeon located an area on Juliet's head and parted strands of her hair, revealing the vulnerable whiteness of her scalp beneath. Tania Hughes stepped forward with a pair of scissors and snipped thoroughly and untidily around it, cutting away several tresses which tumbled into the container.

The surgeon made a two-inch-long incision in Juliet's scalp, then peeled back and clamped the skin either side, exposing the pearly white periosteum of the cranium. Joe braced himself as Murray McAlister handed the surgeon a small electrical circular drill. There was a fierce whine as he switched it on, followed by a hideous grating sound as it bit into the skull. Joe's stomach heaved as his nostrils filled with the acrid smell of burning.

Goodman continued drilling determinedly, widening the area until there was a hole half an inch in diameter. Tania carefully swabbed the tiny bone shards away, and the surgeon removed with tweezers the fragments that had fallen in through the hole.

Joe caught a glimpse of the almost fluorescent red mesh of blood vessels and the glistening creamy brown surface of Juliet's brain. His own scalp tightened. He had assisted at a dozen whole-body suspensions and another dozen head only, but it was different when you were personally involved. It had been grim when he'd assisted at his father's and it was just as grim now.

He stared again into the hole, somehow compelled to look.

He wondered, a little irrationally, whether Juliet would be angry when she was resuscitated that her hair had been cut without anyone asking.

Blake was looking carefully through the burrhole now; Joe's anxiety rose. So much of the chance of anyone being recovered and returning to a normal life depended on the successful preservation of their brain. Blake was checking to see if Juliet's brain swelled up. If it did, it would mean the circulation was at least partially blocked and that the cryoprotectant would not reach all parts. In which case there would be nothing they could do except hope that the brain could be repaired at some point in the future. But they wouldn't know how much of Juliet's memory would be lost – or indeed whether any would remain.

Blake turned to Joe. 'I don't know how much leakage we're getting from the aneurism itself, but there's no swelling. It's fine, so far.'

Relief flooded through Joe, as well as tiredness. It was a quarter past four in the morning. He communicated a smile to Blake with his eyes.

The heart-lung machine was switched off, and Juliet's chest had been sutured when Goodman turned his attention back to the head. Andy White passed him a small, circular stainless steel plate, and this was carefully aligned over the burrhole in her cranium and screwed into the bone.

Eventually, after closing the scalp incision and suturing it, Goodman stepped back, lowered his mask and began pulling off his gloves. 'Might have a bit of a headache when she wakes up,' he said drily, then allowed himself a smile.

They all laughed, even Joe. It was the first moment of light relief in a long night.

Goodman dropped his gloves in a bin, washed his hands, then hurried towards the door as if he had an urgent appointment. He gave a brief, shy smile and a nod in acknowledgement of the thanks he was given and left.

Ten to five. It would be growing light outside in another hour. Everyone looked pallid and exhausted, but there was a sense of triumph also as they slid Juliet into a transparent plastic body bag, then wheeled her through into the cooldown room.

The room felt dank and there was condensation on the sides of the waiting steel tank with its hinged lid. Joe could smell the pungent reek of the fresh plastic of the bag.

A webbing sling was lowered from the ceiling and Juliet's body carefully strapped on to it. Blake checked the temperature reading on a gauge on the side of the tank. Joe read it also. Ten degrees Celsius.

The parcelled body was hoisted slowly into the air. As it swung it bumped a couple of times against the tiles. Joe kept watching with increasing distress as it was lowered into the tank which was filled with inky dark silicone oil; the fluid bubbled and slid in fat globules across the surface of the plastic, then closed up and became still once more as Juliet disappeared beneath the surface.

Blake turned the thermostat on the heating control down to five degrees Celsius. Every hour for the next thirty-six hours the temperature would be lowered a little more, until it reached $-79°C$, the temperature of dry ice. Juliet would then be moved into another cooling unit, wrapped in two sleeping bags for insulation, and taken down during the next twenty-four hours to $-196°C$, the temperature of liquid nitrogen. At that temperature, her biological decay would be completely halted.

Tania Hughes yawned. 'Time for some shut-eye,' Blake said, his nose blue with cold. 'I'll need four people for the transfer to the cool-down pod in thirty-six hours' – he looked at his watch. 'That'll be five-thirty tomorrow – Monday – afternoon. Then we'll need the full team to transfer her into the dewar, Tuesday. Everyone OK for that?'

There was a nod of heads.

'Joe, you looked bushed!' Blake said. 'Go home!'

As Joe pushed open the front door, the hall had the sour, vinous smell of empty bottles and unwashed glasses, and a pall of scent and stale tobacco hung in the air. There was a silence punctuated only by the tick of the long-case clock, once a second, plat . . . plat, like the drip of a melting icicle. It was a quarter past six.

He hung up his mackintosh, noticing an overcoat he didn't recognize on one of the hooks, which he presumed one of the guests must have left behind, then climbed the stairs, heavily.

As he went into the bedroom, he sensed from her breathing that Karen was awake, but he said nothing, closing the door behind him quietly and undressing. Dawn was breaking; he could hear the first twitterings of birds, and there was just enough light through the curtains for him to navigate his way into the bathroom to brush his teeth.

Then he slipped into bed and lay still, exhausted, but adrenaline coursing through him.

'Is it Juliet you're freezing?' Karen said suddenly, her voice crystal clear.

'Yes.' He leaned over and kissed her, and her face was wet with tears. 'Hon.' He took her hand and squeezed it. 'You mad at me?'

'I'm just disappointed, Joe, that's all. I didn't realize you were so weak.'

The words stung him, and it took him some moments to reply. 'Karen,' he said gently, turning to her. 'What do you expect me to do? I can't tell someone not to die because it's an inconvenient time.'

The sincerity in his words seemed to get through and she managed a faint assent. Then she shook her head. 'I thought it was just your work that had taken you over, Joe. I could just about live with that. But not another woman. I didn't expect that.'

'It's not what you think,' he said lamely.

'What do you plan to do? Thaw her out then carry on with her again one day?'

Joe reached his arm out and stroked her forehead, pushed away the soft strands of her hair. 'You looked stunning tonight, I was very proud of you.'

'I was proud of you too, Joe. I always am.'

He smiled and kissed her. 'I love you,' he said. He kissed her again.

She snuggled up to him. 'Are we still going to be able to go to Scotland on Thursday?'

'It's this weekend?' Joe had forgotten that Karen's sister and brother-in-law were flying over from Toronto. The break appealed to him, and Scotland was a country he found very stimulating. He knew how fond Karen was of her sister, and how much she missed her.

'Yes.'

'Sure. We'll be finished with the suspension Tuesday night. No problem.' He stroked her cheek. 'I'm looking forward to it.' He kissed her again.

Karen kissed him back and slid a hand lightly between his legs. 'We have a quarter of an hour before Jack comes in,' she said.

He pressed his lips on hers, long and hard and breathless, and she slipped her hands inside the waistband of his pyjamas.

Afterwards, he dozed for a few minutes, then woke when his son came in and jumped on him. Karen took Jack out, swiftly, closing the door behind her.

The bedroom was lightening steadily and from downstairs came the rumble of the dishwasher; the drone of the hoover; Jack playing noisily. Then finally the silence of sleep swallowed Joe like the silicone swallowing Juliet's packaged body.

A piercing drilling woke him. He sat up in a cold sweat, disoriented, his nostrils filled with the stench of burnt bone, his ears ringing. The drill. The hole in Juliet's head. Her glistening brain inside it –

Telephone.

It stopped. Karen must have answered it. He sank back against the pillow, relieved. He could hear Karen chatting, her voice muted through the floor; it sounded like someone had rung to thank her for the party.

Joe tried to go back to sleep but eventually, just after eleven, he got up, and in spite of his tiredness, went for a short jog around the streets.

Karen cooked a roast-lamb lunch, and later they took Jack for a nature-trail walk in a wildfowl park. It was a fine wintry afternoon, dry and cold, and reminded both Joe and Karen of childhood afternoons in Canada. When they came back, Joe was feeling a little better and made mushroom omelettes for their supper. His repertoire of dishes was limited, but it relaxed him to cook. That night he slept more easily and soundly.

It was not until three o'clock the next afternoon that the nightmare began.

37

There was a subdued atmosphere at the university on Monday. Apart from Joe, none of his colleagues or students had known that Juliet Spring was unwell, and her death had come as a complete shock. Harriet Tait was in tears. Even the tetchy Edwin Pilgrim, who had been so furious about Juliet invading his personal space, was visibly moved.

Joe had delivered a lousy lecture in the morning and had been unable to concentrate on the questions afterwards. He was now looking at some code, written by Pilgrim, that was intended to enable ARCHIVE to start learning to distinguish between good or bad music and a random sequence of notes. It was the first, primitive step towards teaching ARCHIVE appreciation of the arts.

He yawned and glanced at his watch: 3.40. He had promised Karen he would be home by 5.30. Sworn blind; and he wanted to be, really wanted to get back to a normal life again.

His distress at Juliet's death was balanced by a mixture of intense guilt and uneasy relief. Her early death was tragic and yet because of it he had been released from his own crass stupidity. And it had made him realize how much he valued

Karen; in his heart he had loved her more in the past twenty-four hours than he could ever remember.

He had done his duty for Juliet, had honoured his word. She would be close to $-78°$ Celsius right now. Tomorrow morning at Cryonite they would be processing her to liquid-nitrogen temperature, $-196°$ Celsius. And on Wednesday morning they would transfer her from the cool-down unit into one of the four-person dewars in the vaults of Cryonite, where she would be sealed and entombed.

He would be there on Wednesday to assist. To say his farewell and to complete his promise. She would be OK, she would be fine. One day in the future they would meet up, talk about all this, have a good laugh. And perhaps, the thought crept back through his guard, be lovers.

His door opened sharply and Blake came in. His face was flushed and he was looking agitated. 'Joe, we have to talk,' he said, closing the door behind him.

Joe was surprised by his state. He had never seen Blake ruffled by anything, but now he looked very worried.

'We have a problem,' he said. 'A big problem.' He sat down in a chair beside Joe's desk. 'Andy White's just rung – he's over at Cryonite supervising the temperature reductions. The coroner's office have just been on to him. There might be trouble over Juliet's death certificate.'

Joe's throat constricted a little. 'What kind of trouble?' It came out as a croak.

'They've said they may need to do an autopsy. They've told us to stop any further work on her suspension for the moment.'

Joe felt a leaden lump crash down through his body. He gripped the edge of his desk. 'You're not serious? They can't do that!' Anger rose inside him. 'Jesus, Blake, it's too damned late for that!'

Blake waved his hands. 'They have the power to order an autopsy whenever they want, Joe. If they can exhume bodies out of graveyards . . .' he shrugged.

'But it's all going so well; we can't stop now! What the hell's it all about?'

'Something to do with her father and the hospital. Andy couldn't get much information.'

Joe banged his fist angrily on his desk. 'She warned me about her father.'

Blake scrutinized his thumbnail, then looked testingly at Joe. 'How much do you know about her situation?'

Joe felt too sick to notice the innuendo in Blake's expression. 'She was very worried, she was kind of expecting something like this.' He pulled his wallet out of his jacket. 'I have her lawyer's number – I rang him on Saturday night and left a message on his machine, but never heard back from him. She's made him her executor.' Searching for inspiration, he said, 'Hey, what about Cryonite's own lawyer?'

'Her executor would be the best person, Joe – he has legal ownership of her body.'

'Not the parents?'

'No.'

'So if she's made the lawyer her executor, her father has no status now?'

'No legal status.'

A little relieved, Joe pulled out the scrap of paper on which Juliet had handwritten the lawyer's phone numbers and dialled his office. The receptionist put him through to a secretary who told him that Marvin Zeillerman was in a meeting. Joe explained the urgency and she said she would see if he could be disturbed. There was a click and he found himself listening to the William Tell Overture. After what felt like several minutes there was another click, and a tired, faintly arrogant voice replaced the music.

'Zeillerman.'

Joe explained who he was and the reason for his call.

'Ahhh, yes,' the solicitor said, drawing the words out ponderously like a brake applied against a ratchet. 'Professor Messenger. You left some messages for me over the weekend. A problem with Miss Spring, but you got it resolved, you said?' He sounded about a hundred years old.

'Er, not quite,' Joe said, and filled in the picture. He was surprised at the lethargic sound of the man; he had imagined Juliet would have used someone considerably more dynamic.

'Ahh, yes.' There was a long silence, during which Joe wondered whether Zeillerman had gone to sleep. 'Terrible,' he said finally. 'Quite terrible. Such a delightful young lady.' There was another pause. 'I was away for the weekend, only got your messages late last night, I'm afraid.' There was an expectant silence.

'The consequences of halting now, in the middle of what we are doing, would be very dangerous for Juliet. Not to mention contrary to her wishes,' Joe said.

'Of course, professor,' the lawyer spoke in the tone of a chiding schoolmaster. 'I'm aware of that. I think I'd better have a word with the coroner's office, and see what all this nonsense is about. Is there a number where I can contact you this afternoon?'

After he had hung up, Joe sat looking at Blake with a heavy heart. 'Screw the coroner,' he said. 'We should keep going.'

'I already told Andy to keep going,' Blake replied.

Marvin Zeillerman rang Joe back just before five; there was still the same weariness and lack of urgency in his manner. He told Joe that he hadn't yet got all the information he needed, and he would call him again in the morning. In the meantime he agreed that the cryonic suspension should continue regardless.

'I really think it's all a bit of a storm in a teacup,' the solicitor said. The crustiness of his voice carried a learned authority, and a hint of influence. Joe felt a little easier after he had hung up this time.

Zeillerman rang Joe at a quarter to ten the next morning, catching him as he was on his way to give a lecture. His voice had lost some of its assurance of yesterday and gained a little urgency.

'Professor Messenger, I think I've identified where the problem stems from. The death certificate was issued by a junior anaesthetist largely on information on my client's medical history from the hospital's records. I gather those are held in the computer.' He became silent, and Joe was unsure whether he was waiting for him to reply.

'Yes, that's what he said to me at the time.'

'Well, it seems, professor, that someone has been having a bit of a tamper with those records.'

Joe felt his stomach knot.

'It would appear that the information in the hospital's computer was incorrect. Miss Spring had never been treated there, and there had been no agreement by the director to allow the hospital's facilities to be used for her cryonic suspension.'

Joe frowned. 'I don't think I understand.'

'It appears someone must have tampered with the computer records, either from within the premises, or from outside.' His voice adopted a dry hint of humour. '*Hacking* would be the correct terminology, I believe?'

Joe was deadpan. 'Do they know who was responsible?'

'I don't think they have any idea.' Marvin Zeillerman's tone conveyed to Joe that *he* knew exactly who was responsible, and did not want to dwell on it. He moved on. 'But of course this has given Juliet's father the ammunition he needs to demand a postmortem.'

Gloom enveloped Joe. He racked his brains, trying to think clearly. 'Surely, Mr Zeillerman, regardless of the hospital records, Juliet was terminally ill with a cerebral aneurism? Her own doctor would be able to verify that.'

'Yes, I've spoken to him and he's confirmed that to me.'

'So isn't it academic what's in the hospital records? It's obvious that's what she died from – all her symptoms were consistent with aneurism, and the hospital's ECG showed a reading consistent with ruptured aneurism minutes before she died.'

'Ahhh.' The brake was applied to the ratchet again. 'Unfortunately not, Professor Messenger. The tampering with the hospital records is clear evidence of some mischief. Juliet's father has pointed out that the only person with her before she was brought into the hospital was yourself.' He hesitated, and his tone changed. 'I wish to put this delicately to you, professor. I'm not in any way implying any impropriety –'

'Sure. I understand it doesn't look good: I'm alone with her in the university, she's in a state of collapse, and I have a vested interest in cryonics, right?'

'Well – ahhh – that wasn't quite the way I was going to put it.'

'I have no vested *commercial* interest in cryonics, Mr Zeillerman. Only three people in the whole of the Cryonite operation are paid any salary or expenses: a secretary, a night security man and a part-time maintenance man. We're all volunteers – hell, we even clean the place ourselves, in rota.'

The solicitor did not reply for some moments. 'The coroner's office are sympathetic and trying to be helpful – you must appreciate they haven't had very many cryonics situations previously and there aren't any precedents.' He paused again as if plucking up courage for his next statement. 'They've suggested that they would be prepared to perform the postmortem at your own premises – at Cryonite – if you have the facilities.'

Joe glanced at his watch. He was going to be late for his lecture, but he didn't care. He struggled to keep his voice calm, to fight the panic seizing him. 'I don't think you quite understand how cryonics works, Mr Zeillerman. We're trying – and we have so far been very successful – to preserve Juliet intact. A postmortem would destroy all we have done.'

'Could you not – er – still freeze the remains after the postmortem?'

Joe was angered by the solicitor's naivety. 'Have you ever attended a postmortem?'

'Well – no – as a matter of fact.'

'But you've looked in the window of a butcher's shop, Mr Zeillerman? And you've seen those trays with the kidneys, the liver, the chops, and, let me see . . .' Joe was unstoppable, '. . . the topside, the belly, the mince? Well, do you think you'd be able to reassemble the original animals from all those pieces? Because that's what it would be like, trying to put Juliet back together after a post-mortem.'

There was a long pause. 'I – I understand,' the solicitor said finally. 'I was just trying to see if perhaps there was a compromise.'

There is, Joe thought suddenly, and then wished he hadn't. He said nothing. He did not want to suggest the one possible compromise.

The solicitor said he would talk to the coroner's office again and come back to him.

Joe sped through his lecture, cut the questions short and hurried back to his office. Eileen Peacock looked up.

'Professor Messenger, a Mr Zeillerman phoned, wanting to speak to you most urgently. I have his number – shall I get him for you?'

'Please.'

Edwin Pilgrim called out to him, then followed him into his office as Joe ignored him, and stood in front of his desk, looking agitated. 'Joe, I must have a word with you!'

Joe raised his hands pacifyingly. 'OK, OK! What's the prob?'

Pilgrim glanced round warily and gave ARCHIVE's camera on the ceiling a glare. He was shaking, blinking furiously. 'We are be-being inva-invaded!' His good eye glared triumphantly.

Joe wondered if the brilliant young scientist had finally flipped. 'By whom, Edwin? Martians?'

Pilgrim's expression turned to a look of suppressed fury. 'H-h-h-hackers. They've filled up a terabyte of ARCHIVE's mem-memory.' His stammer came on strong as usual when he was angry.

'They've cracked into ARCHIVE?' Joe looked at him, worried. ARCHIVE had elaborate defences, although he knew that ultimately no computer could ever be completely hacker-proof. 'A terabyte of storage? What the heck have they filled it with?'

'G-gar-garbage.'

Joe's phone rang. His secretary had Zeillerman on the line. Joe dismissed Edwin Pilgrim, promising to investigate with him later, then sat down, his mind having barely registered the problem.

'I'm afraid I don't have very good news for you, professor. Mr Spring – er – Juliet's father – has done a thorough job of stirring up the hornet's nest. He's even challenging the Cryonite documentation. I recall that originally Juliet was going to have just her head frozen – neurosuspension, I believe it's called?'

'Yes.'

'Then a couple of months ago she – er – decided to switch to full-body suspension.'

'Is there a problem with the documentation?' Joe asked.

'Oh no, no, not at all. But it doesn't look good, you see. It's a more expensive process – seventy thousand pounds against thirty, and of course it all lends weight to this – er – conspiracy theory Mr Spring is trying to dress up.' He coughed. 'I'm afraid the coroner has ordered Juliet's body to be handed to the borough mortuary for postmortem.'

Joe felt wet sand churning in his stomach. 'There must be something we can do, Mr –' He forgot the lawyer's name for a moment. 'Can't we fight this some way? Juliet was so – so desperate that this shouldn't happen.'

Zeillerman suddenly sounded a lot more determined. 'Oh yes, indeed, professor. Juliet's instructions to me were very clear. We're applying for an injunction against the coroner's decision.'

'How quickly can you do that?'

'Very quickly indeed. We're going before a High Court judge in London at ten a.m. tomorrow. The coroner has agreed not to press for the body until after the judgement. You're available tomorrow morning, I hope?'

'Yes,' Joe replied, his spirits lifting. There seemed a lot more fight in the lawyer than he had at first realized.

'We have a problem because there are no legal precedents here. You have colleagues in cryonics in the United States, professor?'

'Yes – I know several people.'

'Good. I need to find out any legal cases that have occurred over there. As much information as you can get me. Any precedents would be helpful for guidance.'

Joe set to work the moment he had hung up.

38

Marvin Zeillerman was a surprise. Joe had been expecting to meet a relic from another age, but he placed the dapper character who strode determinedly towards him across the courthouse lobby at no more than thirty-five.

His entire dress and demeanour was that of someone much older. Of middling stature, with a wiry frame, he had a serious, rather hostile face, short, grizzled black hair and a mature air of efficiency. His grey pin-striped suit was immaculately pressed, his black Oxford shoes were buffed to a military gloss, and the knot of his tie looked sculpted to perfection. His ancient briefcase was the only blemish, bulging with so many documents he appeared to have been unable to close it.

'Professor Messenger?' His hand was small, but gripped like a vice. 'It's very good to meet you.' His expression of hostility melted as he released Joe's hand. 'I recognize you from the photograph on your books. I – er, I – I have to confess to being a bit of a fan of yours.'

'You're kidding?' Joe said, genuinely thrown.

'I've – er – actually read two of your books – *Beyond Hubris* and *Engineering the Future*.'

'Oh – right – those. A bit dated now, I guess.' Joe never felt entirely comfortable with his earlier work. His ideas were constantly advancing, changing, and he felt he had moved on.

'I very much agree with your points in those books,' the solicitor said. He raised his eyebrows. 'Unfortunately I don't have enough time for reading these days.' His expression saddened. 'I'm awfully sorry about Miss Spring; she was a very – er – special young woman.'

'Yes,' Joe said. 'A brilliant mind.'

'And charming. Quite delightful.' He looked as though he had lost more than a mere client, and Joe wondered whether he had nurtured a secret crush on her. Then Zeillerman pulled a watch and chain from his waistcoat pocket. 'Now, we have about half an hour and I'd like to run through a few things.'

'Was any of the material I faxed you helpful?'

'Yes,' he said, replacing his watch carefully. 'Yes, it was.' He looked around and spotted a couple of empty chairs in an alcove. 'Let's sit ourselves down over there. Your colleague Professor Hewlett is coming? And Dr McAlister?'

'Yes. Douglas Goodman, our cardiac surgeon, couldn't make it.'

'Pity,' Zeillerman said.

'He would have added a bit of weight?'

'Well – these things all help to impress the judges,' he said with a wry smile.

'What's your feeling about how it's going to go?' Joe asked.

The solicitor glanced around as if to check no one was in earshot. Then he turned back to Joe. 'Actually, we're a bit unlucky with the judge.'

Some of the buoyancy Joe had been feeling all morning slipped away.

'I was rather hoping we might get someone a little more – shall we say – forward thinking.'

Judge Hermione Dalrymple sat at her desk in the centre of her room. To her left sat the clerk, an expressionless, dark-suited man in his fifties who wrote solidly throughout the hearing, rarely looking up.

Judge Dalrymple was a voluminous, ruddy-faced battleaxe of indeterminate age that Joe estimated as being somewhere between sixty and two hundred. She had piercingly sharp grey eyes set amid ample folds of flesh, tiny rosebud lips which she kept tightly pursed together, and grey hair that hung in strands on either side of her cheeks, like frayed curtains. Trussed up in folds of heavy black cloth, a string of pearls around her neck, and brandishing a pencil stub with which she made copious notes, she conjured images in Joe's mind of horsewhips and foxhounds, of English country fêtes.

For the first half-hour she repeatedly eyed Blake, seated beside Joe, with undisguised suspicion, and Joe wished that his colleague had dressed a little more conservatively. With his ponytail, his unstructured black suit, black shirt and white knitted tie, Blake didn't look like the kind of man to whom this woman would warm in a million years.

Marvin Zeillerman put up a stoical fight. He must have been up most of the night, Joe thought. Like himself. The solicitor seemed to have remembered verbatim all the salient points in the fourteen court cases from the States that Joe had faxed to him; he argued them convincingly, refusing to be fazed every time Judge Dalrymple lost her patience and barked at him.

Juliet's parents sat in the room, together with a smartly dressed young woman whom Zeillerman had told them was the coroner's officer. The coroner's lawyer, Sir Quentin Carmichael, was an eminent QC of a far more heavyweight calibre than Zeillerman. Joe thought he was a pompous bully, but he could tell that Judge Dalrymple was taken with him.

Juliet's father, Peregrine Spring, was a smooth, vain and sanctimonious man. In the finely chiselled features of his face, Joe could see the family likeness to Juliet, but there was none of the warmth that Juliet had had.

It was God who should make the decision about what happens to us after death, not man, Peregrine Spring argued glibly, touching an evident chord in Judge Dalrymple, who seemed to go for him in a big way. He referred to cryonics organizations as cowboy outfits on a par with religious cults, and implied that Joe and Blake were prime examples of

American shysters come over to fleece the gullible Brits. His daughter's judgement had been impaired by her aneurism, he argued, and cited an affidavit to this effect from a leading neurosurgeon. Juliet had fallen prey to con men while the balance of her mind was disturbed. She should be allowed a decent funeral in the sight of God, not be shoved like meat into a deep freeze as if death were something that could be bought off.

Juliet's mother sat in silence beside her husband, a thin woman dressed in black, her drawn face mostly concealed by a veil beneath her small round hat. Joe felt for her, and in spite of his dislike for the man he felt for Juliet's father as well, understood all they were going through. He'd been there too, lost a child; he knew how impossible it was to accept, knew the need to find your own way of coping.

At one o'clock judge Dalrymple called an adjournment for lunch. Joe went out with Zeillerman, Blake and Murray McAlister to a pub in Fleet Street. Their mood was sombre. Blake phoned Andy White at Cryonite to tell him there was no news yet. Juliet was being kept in liquid nitrogen in the cool-down room, her move into long-term storage on hold until the outcome of the proceedings.

Joe ordered a ploughman's and a Coke, but ate only a little of the bread and cheese when it arrived. He drained his Coke and had another, and felt a little stronger from the blast of sugar into his system. All of them had points they felt Zeillerman should make in response to the barrage from Peregrine Spring's camp. Zeillerman jotted them down diligently. He took a pragmatic view on the way it had gone so far, but was unable to shred the shroud of defeat that hung over them.

At twenty past four Judge Hermione Dalrymple sat in silence and began to review her notes. The evidence and arguments had all been presented. Joe hoped perhaps she would adjourn until tomorrow, buying Juliet another day. He held his breath. But instead she began her summing up.

She seemed to be much fairer during the first part of her

summing up than she had been during the hearing, smiling, if a little primly, from time to time and giving Joe frequent sympathetic glances. His hopes rose a little and he hung on her every word, every nuance.

He was expecting her to continue for a while, but after only a few minutes she brought her summing up to a sudden, unexpected conclusion.

'There are no precedents in this country for guidance,' she said and fixed Joe with a kindly smile that made him really warm to the old girl for the first time. 'Regardless of religious views or personal prejudices, if any person wishes to have their remains frozen, and the Environmental Health Officer is satisfied that no health hazard is likely to be caused in so doing, then there is no reason in law why those wishes should not be carried out.'

She tilted her head up, triumphantly, and pressed her lips together in a smile she directed straight at Joe. For one glorious moment his spirits soared as he thought that it was all over and they'd won.

'However . . .' The word seemed to hang in the air for an aeon. Judge Dalrymple leaned forward and her demeanour altered completely; she turned her gaze away from Joe as if dismissing a beggar. 'Sadly for Professors Messenger, Hewlett and their friends, the law cannot take into account matters of science fiction. The law is abidingly clear that establishing the cause of death must take priority over all other considerations. If there is any shred of doubt in the coroner's mind then he must do all in his power to eliminate that doubt.' She directed her stare at Marvin Zeillerman. 'Your application is rejected. No order for costs.'

Without further ceremony, she stood up and swept out.

Joe lowered his head, numb with shock. He felt as if a plug had been pulled deep inside him. Chairs scraped. He heard a background hum of meaningless sounds. Without being aware that he had moved, he found himself walking across the lobby with Blake and McAlister.

They waited in a knot near the front door as Zeillerman talked to the coroner's officer on the far side of the room.

Then Zeillerman and the officer came over to them. The solicitor looked apologetic and humbled; all the fight had gone from him. 'I don't know if you met Miss Aitken?' he said.

She was a pleasant-looking young woman in her late twenties, with short, dark hair and rather old-fashioned glasses. Joe, Blake and then McAlister each shook hands with her. The formality struck Joe as being mildly absurd, like making up after a fight, as if it had all been a game.

Her voice had a mild tinge of criticism. 'I gather you need some time to thaw Miss Spring's body?' She glanced at each of them.

'Yes,' Blake said. 'She's in liquid nitrogen – if you try to autopsy her in that state she'll shatter like glass.'

The woman winced. 'How long do you need?'

'A good three days,' Blake said. 'If we try any faster we'll risk getting fractures in the internal organs – which won't be helpful for you.'

'Right,' she said, more cheerily. 'We'll have to wait. And we're still prepared to carry out the postmortem on your premises, if that will help?'

Blake shook his head. 'Once you've autopsied her, that's it, she'll be dead.'

A trace of irritation appeared in Miss Aitken's face, but she kept her voice calm. 'I understand she is already dead, Professor Hewlett.'

'That's a matter of definition,' Blake replied. His eyes narrowed. 'We're actually trying to save her life.'

She stared back, her irritation looking as if it was turning to hostility.

Murray McAlister stepped in to defuse the situation. 'What Professor Hewlett means, Miss Aitken,' he said in his cheery Scots brogue, 'is that –' But he got no further.

'Yes, thank you, I have already heard the arguments today,' she interrupted.

'Of course,' McAlister said, put in his place.

She produced a notebook. 'I'll put down that Miss Spring's body will be released to us on Saturday afternoon?'

Blake looked at Joe and McAlister. Joe nodded reluctantly.

'Good,' she said. 'We'll be in touch about the arrangements.'

She shook each of their hands again, solemnly, then left. Joe, Blake, McAlister and Zeillerman drifted out of the front door into the street. It was a dry, cold afternoon and the light was fading. A lorry rumbled past, travelling fast, and a wake of thick diesel fumes broke over them.

'We ought to call Andy White,' Blake said.

'I'll do it if you like,' Joe offered.

'It's OK – I'll go.' Blake went back inside to use one of the phone booths in the lobby.

Joe turned to the solicitor. 'What about an appeal? Is that worth considering?'

Zeillerman shook his head. 'The only way would be if we could establish that the judge had misruled on a point of law. I'm not sure we'd be able to. And it would be very expensive.'

'I'm sure if money's a problem, the Hartman Trust might help,' Joe said.

'I'll come back to you on it,' Zeillerman said. 'If we're going to do anything, we'll need to make a move this week, but I won't suggest it unless I think there's a decent chance.'

Joe looked down at the pavement despondently, and they stood in silence for some moments until Blake came back.

'Are you gentlemen going back to Sussex?' the solicitor asked. 'Yes,' Joe said, and glanced at Blake. His colleague nodded. They agreed to go for a quick drink at a Chancery Lane wine bar suggested by Zeillerman, and then to take the tube from there. The drink was not a great success, with everyone in a low mood, so they soon joined the home-bound commuters.

They went down the London Underground escalators together. As they neared the bottom, Joe heard the rumble of a train pulling in and saw people running for it. Without actually breaking into a run himself, Zeillerman speeded up his walk until the other three were having to run to keep up with him, pushing their way through the dense crowd. The solicitor zig-zagged left then right, cut into a passage flagged with a NO ENTRY sign, then turned left again.

Joe could see the train now. Heard the deep clunngggg of the doors shutting. Just missed it. Zeillerman's pace slowed. The train began to move forward, slowly at first, but a few seconds later, by the time they had reached the platform, it was gathering speed.

Joe could make out the figures and faces in the front carriages, then, as it accelerated faster, filling his ears with a drumming, whining roar, the carriages turned to a blur. Wind swirled around him. He heard a slithering sound behind him and was startled to see something dark hurtling down the platform, jigging up and down, trailing from one of the doors.

At first he thought it was a large garbage bag or a bin liner. Then a voice cried out, in pain or terror, he was not sure which. Then another voice, this time definitely a scream of horror. The black heap hurtled past him, making a terrible shrieking sound. There was a loud clattering like a supermarket trolley tumbling down a hill. Then a tremendous bang, followed by a metallic scraping that seemed to go on for ever.

Then silence.

A tinkle of glass.

The tail-lights of the train disappeared into the tunnel and a final curl of wind tossed Joe's hair. Then there was an even deeper silence that froze the entire platform for one fleeting moment. Joe's ears deadened. People were looking around. A solitary scream rang out. It was followed by another, a dreadful, curdling howl of horror. Then another. A child began crying. Joe peered through the wall of passengers trying to see what had happened.

On the end wall, beyond a poster advertising a musical, was a sign saying: PASSENGERS MUST NOT PASS THIS POINT. OFFENDERS WILL BE PROSECUTED. Beside it was a warning triangle. DANGER. HIGH VOLTAGE. A few yards in front of it, smashed on the ground and partly dangling over the edge of the platform, lay the stand containing the video camera that monitored the doors.

People were moving, craning forward, like athletes filmed in slow motion leaving their starting blocks. Joe began to advance also. As a gap opened in the crowd in front of him, he saw the stain of blood first, seeping like a spilt drink across the grey tiled wall, spreading out from what looked like a black sack.

His mouth flew open and he had to fight back vomit as he stared in disbelief. It wasn't a sack, it was heavy black cloth, tangled and impaled on the twisted and buckled remains of the metal barrier.

He stared at the face. The face of Judge Hermione Dalrymple was like some hideous bas-relief gargoyle, the back of her skull crushed flat against the wall, hair batting in the slipstream, eyes bulging, motionless, wide open. Her tongue had been forced out and was hanging over her bottom lip, providing a drain channel for the blood and the pulpy cream mess that tumbled out of her mouth. Her arms were outstretched, the fingers parted in an absurd-looking gesture, as if she had turned to hail them, to summon them back to her court, wanting them to hear one last thing she had forgotten to say.

Joe turned away, saw Blake's stony face and McAlister moving forward, uselessly, to help. He clutched someone for support and retched. He retched again, trying to spew out his mind, to cough up the image he'd just seen: the arms outstretched against the blood-spattered wall, and the black tunnel beyond.

Crucified.

She looked as though she had been crucified.

39

It was after eight when Joe arrived home; Karen was in the midst of packing in their bedroom. He'd already phoned her from London and told her what had happened.

She kissed him. 'Poor Joe-Joe, you've had a rough time. Probably in shock. Why don't you sit down and I'll get you a drink. Like a whiskey?'

He sat down on the bed, and thought fleetingly how lovely she was looking tonight, her black hair hanging carelessly over her shoulders, the shape of her breasts visible through her baggy sweater, her long legs flattered by her tight jeans. 'I'm OK, I'll have one in a minute, thanks. How's Jack? How did he get on today?'

She kissed his forehead lightly. 'Jack's fine. It's you I'm worried about. What happened? It was the same judge who ruled against you, got killed at the tube station?'

'Yes.' He squeezed his eyes with his fingers, trying to get rid of the splitting headache that had begun on the train home. His distress over the judge's ruling, and the horror of the judge's death, had numbed him. Coincidence, he told himself firmly.

'Kind of freaky,' she said.

'The whole thing feels unreal.' He looked at Karen, trying to pluck up the front to tell her what she was not going to want to hear.

'I'll pack this for you,' she was saying. 'I think it's going to be pretty cold up there.' She folded one of his thick jumpers and pressed it down firmly into the suitcase. 'You'd better let me have the shirts you want to take.'

'Hon –'

'So what actually happened? You said her coat got caught in the door? Didn't Isadora Duncan get killed like that? No, it was a scarf got in the spokes of a wheel. That's awful!'

'Yes, it was.'

'Don't the doors have sensors?'

'Yes – the fabric was probably too thin for them.'

'I thought the drivers have some kind of a video system, don't they?'

'Sure. It's all pretty sophisticated; they don't even need the drivers in half the trains now – they're all computerized. The cameras aren't meant to let the trains run unless . . .' His voice tailed as a thought struck him. But he dismissed it.

'You've always said there's no such thing as a failsafe computer system, Joe.'

'That's right; no such thing.'

There was a silence. Karen looked at a list she had made; she was always very efficient at packing and Joe relied on her totally. 'Are they very formal in Scotland? Will you need a tie? Better take a couple, anyhow. If you choose them.'

'Hon –' Joe bit his lip and took another breath. 'Karen – I'm – I'm not sure I'm going to be able to make Scotland.'

She looked at him sharply. 'What do you mean?'

'We might be appealing the judge's ruling.'

'Because she's dead?'

'I don't think that has any bearing – we'd go before a different judge anyhow. The lawyer says if we do appeal it'll probably come up later in the week.'

Karen's face fell. 'I haven't seen Arlene in four years. Jack's so looking forward to going. Can't you get this hearing postponed until next week?'

'It may be possible. If not, why don't you and Jack go, and I'll follow as soon as I can?'

She looked at him reproachfully. 'You should care about the living a bit more, Joe, not just the dead.'

'What do you mean?'

'I mean care about me and Jack, the real world. The *biological* world,' she added. 'Or don't we matter?'

'Of course you matter – it's just I have –'

'Sure,' she interrupted. 'Promises to keep to the dead. Caring so much more for the dead than God does, isn't that right, Joe?'

Joe stared up at the camera that was watching them, recording their conversation, feeding it into ARCHIVE. 'God's out of the frame, Karen,' he said quietly.

'Oh yes,' she said, her voice laced with sarcasm. 'I forgot. ARCHIVE *is* God.'

A hard edge came into his voice. 'ARCHIVE might one day be a lot smarter than the God you worship.'

'You should never say that, Joe.'

'No? Tell me what's so great about this God character?

Don't you think he's had long enough to prove himself? Maybe a computer can work out a better way for us to live, to run our lives – and our planet.'

She shook her head slowly. 'I'm glad I won't be around for your vision of the future, Joe. When I married you, you were a lovely man who wanted to do something for the world.' She eyed his clothes, assembled by the suitcase, forlornly.

'I still do, hon.'

'You just want to live for ever. That's not using technology to better the world.'

'Karen, I do not accept death. Man has a duty to challenge it, the same way we have a duty to challenge nature. You and I brought Jack into the world. I feel some obligation to try to make it a better place for him than it is right now. You think pain and death are good things?'

'They happen to be God's will.'

'Just so long as they don't happen to you?'

She was quiet for a moment. 'I accept them as necessary, Joe. They are part of life's process.'

'Do you really mean that?' he said. 'I didn't notice you accepting death very readily when Barty died. All I noticed is that it destroyed your life also.'

'That's not true.' She sat on the bed as if her legs had buckled.

'Oh yes, it is. I know it's true.' He sat down on the bed, too, and put his arm around her, held her tightly to him.

'I love Jack,' she said. 'And so do you.'

'Of course, hon. I love you both.' He stroked her cheek. 'But imagine a world in which no one has to lose their first-born son, that's what I want.' And I want to be around to see it, he thought.

40

Jack stood in the hallway, in a multicoloured quilted jacket, and looked balefully up at Joe. 'Why aren't you coming, Daddy?'

Joe knelt and hugged his son tightly to him. 'Daddy's going to join you at the weekend.'

'We're flying back on Sunday!' Jack said going into a *vroom-vroom* and arms-outstretched routine.

'Yup, well, I'll have two days with you. Anyhow, you're going to have a good time with your cousins. Howie and Carlotta. You've never met them.'

Jack's face slackened with boredom. 'Can't *you* come, Daddy? You said we could go fishing in Scotland.'

'OK,' Karen called out, running down the stairs with a holdall. 'We're late, gotta rush, got your hat, honey?'

Jack pouted. 'Do I have to, Mummy?'

'It'll be cold in Scotland, you'll need it.'

Joe held his son out at arm's length to wink at the intelligent blue eyes and the serious expression that reminded him so much of his own father. Jack liked everyone, which sometimes worried Joe; perhaps it was because he hadn't lived long enough to be able to understand that there were bad people. Perhaps it was their fault, because they'd protected him too much.

'Bye, Daddy.' Jack turned, already absorbed in the next thing in his holiday. '*Vroom-vroom*.'

Joe lugged Karen's holdall and Jack's smaller bag to the boot of her small green Nissan. Jack climbed into the rear seat holding a plastic dinosaur, and Joe helped him fasten his belt. Joe leaned through the driver's window to kiss Karen. She was wearing a beige jump-suit and her hair was clipped up at the sides, giving her a purposeful, rather adventurous air; he thought how pretty she looked and realized with a pang he was really going to miss her. She looked at him reproachfully for some seconds, then kissed him lightly and touched his cheek with her fingers. 'Try to come,' she said.

'I will.'

She reached for her belt, then twisted the ignition key. The engine blattered into life, firing unevenly; Jack turned and waved through the area Joe had scraped clear in the rear window.

As the car turned left on to the main road and disappeared for Gatwick, Joe dug his hands into his corduroy trousers for warmth and hurried back into the house. He went into the kitchen and made himself some instant coffee. It was a bleak day and through the patio window he saw the coating of frost on the lawn. He turned to the front page of *The Times*, and began to read a news story about Bosnia with the same anger that war always made him feel.

As he turned the page, the small headline, halfway down, jumped out at him and drew him to the short article beneath.

Judge dies in freak accident

Judge Hermione Dalrymple died yesterday after being trapped in the doors of a moving tube train at Chancery Lane station.

Police believe the freak accident was caused by a computer malfunction and all trains were halted, bringing chaos to London's rush hour, while urgent safety checks were carried out. Mrs Justice Dalrymple, 64, had sat as a Queen's Bench judge for 22 years.

Obituary, page 19.

Joe turned to the obituary and looked at the photograph of the judge. She appeared younger and her face was less fleshy than yesterday, but it had the same steely no-nonsense air.

Something clicked behind him and he spun around, his heart missing a beat. There was a whirr, then a steady hum. Just the fridge. He breathed out, turned back to the obit and skimmed through the judge's career. Then he looked at the photo again and saw her as she had been in the court chamber, holding Juliet's destiny in her hands. Ordering her to be destroyed as if she were vermin, or a cargo of contaminated meat. Who said society had the right to decree anyone dead for ever? To deny them cryonic renewal? And what the hell right did Judge Dalrymple have to exterminate Juliet Spring?

He remembered the judge gathering her papers, giving instructions to the court clerk. Prim and smug. Then, next thing, spread-eagled against the wall of the tube station, the back of her skull crushed flat, her guts being expelled through her mouth like a fish that had been trodden on.

He sipped his coffee queasily, then thought of Juliet lying in an aluminium pod filled with liquid nitrogen, her biological decay only temporarily stopped if they could get no joy from the courts, if Marvin Zeillerman couldn't find a way to justify an appeal.

He stood up, distracted, and began to clear away the breakfast things. He dropped the yolk-streaked shell of Jack's boiled egg into the waste-disposal unit in the sink, added an uneaten crust of toast, reached above the sink and switched it on. There was a grinding roar and they were gone. The rubber flanges to prevent objects falling in accidentally were worn, and he made a mental note to replace them. He looked at the clock on the wall which was a jokey one that went in reverse, and worked out that it was five past eight. He glanced at his watch for confirmation as he always did, then back down at the photograph of Judge Dalrymple.

Dead. But her ruling still held. And so did the chill that lay behind the horror of her death. It had stayed with Joe throughout his fitful night's sleep and now engulfed him like an unwelcome shadow. The strange timing of the judge's death was something he kept trying to dismiss; sometimes it was better not to make connections.

He went to his study, closed the door and switched on the overhead light, the standard lamp behind his small leather sofa and the Anglepoise on his desk; he turned on all the lights because he wanted to dispel the gloominess of the day outside that seeped in through the windows and through his skin.

312

Across the road, Derek Arkwright reversed his silver Ford out of his garage and into the road. His wife Muriel would have polished it last night after he'd arrived home, honing it to the showroom condition of her own car. In the mornings, she always did the front of the house. She'd be out any minute now, cleaning the windows and paintwork, scrubbing the paving of the front drive. There was a man who regularly walked down the street with a mongrel dog that cocked its leg on every garden wall, and Joe kept his fingers crossed each time he saw it that it would do a dump on the Arkwrights' drive, but so far it had disappointed him.

He logged into his workstation and called up his mail box at the university. He had booked these two days off, so no one would be expecting him in. There was a list of over 250 messages to be dealt with, some several days old. He could start answering them now, while he waited for news from Marvin Zeillerman. Across the road, on cue, Muriel Arkwright came out of her side door, plastic bucket swinging from her hand. Some people were indistinguishable from robots.

Marvin Zeillerman rang at half past ten, and he sounded more optimistic than when they had parted company last night. 'Professor Messenger, good morning. I hope this isn't an inconvenient time?'

Joe assured him it wasn't.

'I have a possible compromise,' the lawyer said. 'One of the American cases you sent me has a precedent – there's no reason to expect an English court to accept that, but I think it may help us.'

Joe's spirits lifted.

'As you know, professor, my client switched a few months ago from neurosuspension – head only – to full-body suspension. Ah – part of the reason for the judgement against us was the incomplete documentation for this change. In a case similar to ours in the United States, the – er – compromise there was for the deceased's body to be handed over to the coroner, but the head was retained and kept frozen. If we could achieve that, do you think it would be a workable solution?'

'Our problem here is that Juliet died of a cerebral aneurism. Her head is what the pathologist would want most.'

'I have discussed this with a couple of – ah – medics, professor, and I think we could get around that. Her own doctor has already confirmed the state of her aneurism; the only purpose of a postmortem would be to rule out foul play of any kind, and this could be achieved quite adequately by an examination of the internal organs and fluids of the body alone. And we have pretty watertight legal documentation for her neurosuspension.'

Joe stared out of the window. Muriel Arkwright was up her ladder doing the first-floor windows; patches of water and soapy froth lay on her driveway. Neurosuspension. If you were old and you didn't want to come back to the same tired, aching limbs, you could have only your head frozen in the hope that one day technology would enable you to have a new body grown from your DNA cultures. It was brutal to contemplate the destruction of Juliet's body, but without an appeal that would happen anyway.

'We've no other chance of an appeal?' Joe asked. 'You haven't thought of any other way overnight?'

'No, I'm sorry, Professor Messenger. I think this is our only route, and I'm not, frankly, very optimistic – but it could be worth a try.'

Joe spared a glance at the string of messages on his screen in front of him. The usual assortment from colleagues, questions and answers mostly, queries from students at other universities about projects, requests for him to lecture. Some of the students chose weird account names; one he did not recognize caught his eye, throwing his concentration momentarily. It was sandwiched between the message of a regular correspondent who called himself *Custer of the Vax Cluster* and another from Heidelberg University who called himself rather sinisterly *Lord Haw Haw: Jung Ripe Slit*, said the new name and there was a mailbox address marked paul@-

actrix.co.at – the international code for Austria. Some intellectual with a rather warped sense of humour, he thought.

Could be worth a try. The words of the lawyer echoed in his mind. If they didn't try it, they would have to start thawing Juliet now, this morning, so she would be ready for the pathologist's butchery on Saturday.

'Right, let's go for it,' Joe said.

'The one stumbling block,' Zeillerman said, 'is how quickly we could get an appeal. It may not be possible until Monday – and if that's the case we'll be in the hands of the coroner.'

'How do you mean?'

'The court judgement yesterday gave legal custody of Juliet's body to the coroner, and you've agreed that Cryonite will release her to the coroner on Saturday afternoon. That means the coroner could insist on the body being handed over even if an appeal *is* arranged.'

'You couldn't persuade the coroner to wait?'

'I'll do my best. I should be able to get a decision before the end of today.'

As Joe hung up, an idea was forming in his head. A wild idea, but they'd done it in the States a few years back and it had worked. Dora Kent, that was the case Marvin Zeillerman had referred to, when the coroner had demanded release of the body for autopsy, and the cryonics organization had handed over just her body. Her frozen head had been kept hidden, and the coroner had not been able to find it until after the Supreme Court ruling permitting it to remain frozen in perpetuity.

Zeillerman rang Joe back shortly after four o'clock. His voice was gloomy again. The appeal was arranged for ten o'clock on Monday morning, but the coroner was not prepared to wait. The lawyer apologized. He thought the coroner was being unreasonable, and that probably it was because he was being pressurized by Juliet's father.

Joe said nothing about the plan that was growing in his mind.

41

They began the removal of Juliet Spring's head at five o'clock the following afternoon. There was just Joe, Blake, Andy White and Murray McAlister in the operating theatre at Cryonite.

Juliet's body had been thawing slowly for twenty-four hours and was now at −120°C. Her tissues were still rock hard, but she was no longer quite as fragile and brittle as she had been at liquid-nitrogen temperature.

Joe felt decimated as he watched McAlister cut into her chest with an electrical saw. Sweat poured down the Scotsman's forehead as he struggled slowly and laboriously, the whine of the blade like a scream of pain as he worked on isolating the blood vessels supplying the head. Juliet's face was an eerie stark white against her hair, but Joe could still see the emerald green of her open eyes through the film of frost: she was still watching them.

After twenty minutes, the doctor lifted the saw away and switched it off, shaking his head. There was a faint smell of roasting meat from the hot blade. 'I dinna like this,' he said. 'I dinna think she'd still be this hard. It would be better if we could give her a few more hours – wait until the morning, even.'

Blake shook his head. 'We don't want her thawing any more, Murray – we have to put her head straight into liquid nitrogen – if there's too wide a temperature change it could be dangerous for her.' He shot a conspiratorial glance at Joe, and Joe was grateful for his intervention.

'I can't make a tidy job like this,' the doctor said.

'No one's marking you out of ten,' Blake said.

An hour late, the doctor had finally completed the freeing of the blood vessels. Carefully he located and began sawing through the sixth cervical vertebra. Bone splinters flew like sawdust. Juliet's head lolled back sharply, and Joe protectively clapped his gloved hands on to it. He felt the bile rise in his throat as he looked down at the mess of white flesh, and at the severed, bloodless veins and arteries from which blue cryoprotectant was slowly oozing. To his horror he realized that Juliet's head was free, detached, being supported only by his hands and the operating table beneath. He looked away, deeply uncomfortable.

'OK, Joe?' Blake said.

He nodded. Blake and McAlister took the head from him and lifted it clear. The carotid arteries hung down like icicles, and the bone of Juliet's spine protruded from the jagged mess of her neck like a spike on which her head was skewered.

'Sheeting, please, Joe,' the doctor said, his voice kindly, sensing Joe's unease.

Joe unfolded the clear insulating film waiting on a table beside them and they wrapped Juliet's head in it. Her face remained clearly visible, but grotesquely distorted as if a nylon stocking had been placed over it. Joe tried to avoid looking. He walked across the room, knelt, picked up the heavy aluminium neurocan which sat on the floor, and lugged it over to the operating table.

The neurocan was a three-foot-high cylindrical vacuum, similar in principle to a Thermos flask. Its appearance, Joe always thought, was rather crude, like a pedal bin with rivets.

'I dinna think the coroner's going to be too pleased with us,' McAlister said as he and Blake gently lowered Juliet's head into the padded interior of the container.

Blake glanced at Joe and neither of them said anything.

The doctor continued, 'He's only allowed the body to remain here in order to be thawed out; when he finds he's got a decapitated torso and a frozen head he'll hit the roof.'

'It'll buy us time, Murray,' Blake said, glancing at Joe again. Both he and Joe knew that when the coroner opened the neurocan he would do more than just hit the roof, but they hadn't told McAlister of that part of their plan.

'Aye,' the doctor said doubtfully. 'It might on this one,

but we're jeopardizing our future goodwill with the Establishment.'

'That's a risk we'll have to take,' Blake said.

'And one I have to take also,' McAlister reminded him a little dourly. 'I could get struck off for this.'

Joe screwed the lid on tightly, his emotions in turmoil, while Blake fetched a cylinder of liquid nitrogen and attached the nozzle to the valve on the side of the neurocan. It was a strange farewell to someone, Joe thought.

'OK,' McAlister said, lowering his mask, then peeling off his gloves. 'Who's going to be here tomorrow to deal with the coroner's officer?'

'I am,' Blake said. There was a sharp hiss as the nozzle connected and a cloud of icy vapour rose around him. He concentrated on filling the container, with its built-in temperature alarm, while Joe followed McAlister into the car park to see him off and thank him.

It was raining outside and pitch dark, and there was the familiar smell of kerosene in the air. He could hear the roar of aero engines behind him as a plane landed at Gatwick, and in the sky he could see the winking lights of another on its final approach. Scotland. He was supposed to be there.

From the boot of his own car he removed a plastic carrier bag and hurried back into the operating theatre. He put the bag down on the floor. It was ten to seven, and the night security guard would be here soon. Joe didn't want Spalding to see what they were doing.

Blake helped Joe carry the neurocan containing Juliet Spring's head outside. Joe opened the boot of his car and peered in. As he thought, the boot was too shallow. 'Could lay it sideways, I guess, Blake.'

Blake shook his head. 'Going to roll around too much. You know how fragile she'll be the moment she starts getting anywhere near liquid-nitrogen temperature – which isn't going to take more than half an hour or so. One hard knock and she could fracture. Going to be better inside the car.'

They wedged the dewar on the floor between the rear seat

and the front passenger seat, and pushed the front seat hard back against it, then put a spare cylinder of liquid nitrogen in the boot.

Back in the operating theatre, Joe opened the carrier bag and lifted out the cheap red wig and the cracked plaster-cast head he had pinched from the university drama soc. While Blake fetched the spare neurocan from the store room, Joe placed the wig on the head, partially obscuring the face, then parcelled it all up in several layers of insulating wrap until it was possible to see only the vaguest contours of a human head and face.

Blake studied him for a moment. 'Cheer up.'

'Sure.' Joe smiled back. He lowered the dummy into the canister. 'Never felt so good in my life.'

'You were in love with her, weren't you?'

Joe screwed the lid on, caught by surprise. 'With her mind, Blake,' he said, too quickly. 'I was in love with her mind. She understood what we're working towards. She was one of us.'

'She still is.'

The traffic was heavy on the way back from Cryonite and Joe drove carefully, mindful of the fragility of his cargo. He was cold, but kept the heating off out of respect for Juliet. The wipers smeared the continuous rain into a blur, and turned oncoming headlights into a kaleidoscope of glinting fractals.

When he finally pulled into the driveway of his house, and the bright glare of the streetlighting, he parked so that the side the container was on was out of sight of the rest of the street. In addition to her cleaning obsession, Muriel Arkwright across the road carried out her duty as Neighbourhood Watch Co-ordinator rather too diligently. There was nothing she missed.

Joe humped the container slowly and carefully through the kitchen and down into the cellar, placing it on the brick floor beside the chest freezer, then checked both temperature and pressure. The pressure was fine; both temperature gauges were indicating −154°C. Blake had been right, the temperature was falling quickly.

He went back to the car and brought in the cylinder of liquid nitrogen which he stood against the wall, then allowed himself a breather. The aluminium casing of the neurocan shone dully under the glare of the dusty bare light bulb above it. He touched the lid gingerly. 'I'm sorry, Juliet,' he said quietly, as if worried someone might hear. 'I'm sorry I didn't do better for you. But you're gonna be OK now. We'll fight Monday and if we don't win then we'll go to the Law Lords and if they turn us down we'll go to the European Court of Human Rights. OK?'

He leant against the dank wall that had been whitewashed years before, and his gaze drifted round the cellar to the grey plastic casing which housed ARCHIVE's connection to the electrical system, and he heard a muted clicking sound coming from it as instructions were relayed, probably to close the curtains in some of the rooms or to turn off the outside lights.

There was no camera down here and he was glad about that. The incriminating evidence would already have been picked up on ARCHIVE's cameras both outside and inside the house, but it would be a secret shared between himself and the computer. No one else. He suddenly thought about Juliet's reference to Karen's face cream. She must have gone to great lengths to decode the video images. He made a mental note to check out his system and re-encode it if necessary. If Juliet could crack it, other students could also; or hackers.

He thanked God Karen was away, and he wondered how he was going to explain the cylinder to her on her return on Sunday night. On Monday maybe the court would rule in their favour, and everything would be fine. Just needed to keep the neurocan away from the coroner until then; and concealed from Karen.

He wondered about the loft. You could only get up by ladder and Karen never went there. He could make a rope cradle and haul the goods up that way. Do that on Sunday afternoon before she got back, he thought. The dewar was better down in the cellar right now, where he could get to it easily to check it.

He climbed back up the steep staircase, switched off the light, and shut the heavy door, then glanced at his watch: half past eight; he would check the container in an hour. He poured himself four fingers of Jameson's whiskey from the cabinet in the dining room, drank half straight down, then went back into the kitchen to check the ansaphone.

There was a message from Karen, telling him they were fine and missing him, and hoping he was going to make it up there. He dialled the number wearily and was relieved when the receptionist at the hotel informed him she was out; he didn't have to break the news that he wouldn't be making it up there.

He left word that he had returned her call, then went through to switch on the television and sank down on the sofa, still wearing his coat. The curtains were drawn and a couple of lights were on. ARCHIVE not only drew all the curtains, but also, when there was no one in the house, switched lights on and off at random. Sometimes it would switch on a light for him as he went into a dark room, but it wasn't reliable at that yet.

He punched through the channels until he found himself engaged by a car chase in a Los Angeles street. Cops; a pretty blonde; a greasy villain in a flashy sports car. He watched on, picking up a few threads, relieved to have something light to distract him.

The programme ended at 9.30 and he went back into the cellar to check the neurocan. The temperature had dropped further, and was now −176°C, only twenty degrees above liquid nitrogen. He checked the pressure, then opened the lid of the chest freezer and peered in for something to cook for supper.

He pulled out a pizza, wiped frost off the pack so that he could glance through the instructions, and took it up into the kitchen, to the microwave. Karen rang a short while later and he broke the news to her. She was having a good time with her sister, but she told him Jack would be pretty upset and she was a bit shirty herself. He promised to make it up to Jack on their return.

Joe slept badly, lying awake much of the night, worrying. Several times he got out of bed and went downstairs into the cellar to check the neurocan's temperature, but it was dropping fine. Dawn had broken before he finally drifted into a deep sleep, from which he was woken by an indignant Jack on the phone at a quarter past eight.

'Why can't you come, Daddy?'

'Daddy's very busy. How are your cousins?'

There was a pause. 'Carlotta won't talk to me.'

'Oh? Why's that?'

Another pause. 'Don't know.'

There was a hum and the curtains began opening. Sunlight streamed into the room; it was a fine morning outside. He said goodbye to Jack, chatted for a couple of minutes with Karen, then hung up and lay collecting his thoughts.

Yesterday he, Blake and Murray had decapitated a body that was subject to a court order. Under the terms of the Cryonite contracts they were entitled to decapitate full-body patients and convert them to neurosuspension if the situation necessitated it. The court judgement had been made on Juliet's full-body suspension. In taking the head they did at least have a defence, however thin. Maybe he should return it; that would be the sensible thing. Still not too late to take it back, though he could hardly glue it back on again.

Except he had made a promise. And he asked himself if the roles were reversed would he have wanted Juliet to do the same to him? His answer was an unhesitating yes.

He climbed out of bed. The coroner's officer was turning up at Cryonite at 5 p.m. – expecting to find a thawed-out body. What she was going to find was a decapitated body, with a frozen head in a dewar. It was a dummy head, but she wouldn't be able to tell that until the insulating cellophane had thawed enough to be removed, twenty-four hours at

322

least, probably longer. It would buy Juliet enough time for the appeal hearing.

He pulled on his dressing gown, pushed his feet into his slippers and went downstairs. He glanced at a montage of photographs of Jack on the kitchen wall, saw some boyish toys lying around, and his heart twinged. He wished he was with his family now; driving out somewhere into the Scottish countryside, wished he was anywhere but here.

The twin temperature gauges on the neurocan both read −196. Liquid nitrogen temperature. It remained stable and Joe began to check less frequently. He spent most of the day working in his study, trying to keep his mind occupied. The few messages he had cleared from his e-mail had grown again and there were over four hundred waiting to be dealt with.

He reached the curious one he had noticed yesterday, signed *Jung Ripe Slit*, and read the short message: *Dr Messenger, I'd really like to hear from you some time.*

He got crank messages frequently, mostly from hackers, and this had all the hallmarks. He wiped it.

Five o'clock came and went. At half past six Blake rang him to tell him everything had gone without a hitch. The coroner's officer had not attended. Just a driver and an assistant, who'd removed Juliet's body and the neurocan with barely more than a raised eyebrow. Blake said he'd warned them the neurocan contained pressurized liquid nitrogen and shouldn't be opened without protective clothing, and they'd replied that they didn't think anyone would be looking at the body before Monday anyway.

Joe phoned Karen and had a long chat to Jack, who told him they'd been to see Arthur's Seat in Edinburgh, and wanted to know why it was called *Seat* when there wasn't a seat there. Joe explained that it looked like a seat and for some reason that made Jack giggle.

He microwaved himself some Marks and Spencer tagliatelle for supper, went to bed early and fell asleep quickly, his mind a little eased by Blake's news.

*

He was woken with a start by the drilling ring of a bell in the pitch dark. For a moment, confused, he thought it was the alarm and reached for the snooze button. Then he realized that it was the phone. As he lifted the receiver to his ear he saw the time on his clock radio was 2.44. Was it Karen? Something wrong. Something happened to Jack? Or was it Blake? The coroner?

'Yes, hello?' he said, psyching himself up for bad news.

He heard a whistle, followed by a trilling sound, then a high-pitched whine. A fax or a computer modem misdialling. A sound he had not heard for some years, not since he was a student. He hung up, irritated, and began to drift back into sleep.

Then the bell woke him again.

He cursed, put on the bedside light, sat up and lifted the receiver. He got the same electronic noise as before and hung up again. Some idiot misrouting a fax.

It rang again. Again he lifted the receiver to his ear and listened to the same sound. For a wild moment he wondered if it *was* Karen – trying to contact him. The trilling beeped and whined on. More likely a fax on auto-dial and it would keep on trying. He got out of bed and pulled the jack plug out of the wall socket. It could go on trilling and warbling all night, or it could redial and whine its heart out to the answering machine. He went back to sleep.

He slept until after nine and when he awoke the room was filled with daylight; ARCHIVE had misbehaved and already opened the curtains. *Thanks*, ARCHIVE, Joe thought. *Thanks a lot! You might at least have waited until I woke*.

He remembered he'd silenced the phone, pushed the jack back in, then walked through into the bathroom and showered.

The Sunday papers were on the hall floor when he went downstairs and he picked them up, glancing leisurely at the headlines. The English papers were a big treat for him.

He went through into the kitchen and noticed that there were no messages on the machine; last night's errant fax must have finally given up. He spooned some coffee into a filter, filled up with water and switched the machine on, then sat at the kitchen table and began to read. The machine hissed and spat. He glanced at the backwards clock, worked out that it was ten o'clock and remembered he should check the neurocan in the cellar; he would do it in a minute.

He turned the pages of the paper. Outside in the garden he could hear a strange bird cheeping. Two cheeps, silence, then two cheeps again, high pitched, insistent. Except they weren't coming from outside. They were coming from beneath him.

From the cellar.

He leapt up, unlocked the door and yanked it open.

Beep beep. Beep beep. Beep beep.

Jesus! The noise of the temperature alarm screeched up the stairs at him. He snapped on the light and ran down, his heart punchballing inside his chest.

Beep beep. Beep beep. Beep beep.

The sound was deafening down here. Sharp and angry. A cloud of vapour hung over the neurocan cylinder like cigarette smoke. He read the temperature gauges, −160°C. Risen thirty-six degrees. Oh, Jesus!

Beep beep. Beep beep. Beep beep.

How long had it been going on? The vapour was now rising in a fine ribbon from the pressure valve. He knelt, tried to turn it, but it was already fully shut off. He grabbed the nitrogen cylinder without bothering to put gloves on or cover his face, unwound the locking valve and jammed the nozzle on to the neurocan's valve. There was a rasping hiss and a stream of liquid-nitrogen vapour jetted out.

Joe jerked back as he felt the burn on the back of his hand. He tried again. More nitrogen jetted out. The valve had jammed. He tried again, and the valve held. He filled it until there was a small hiss, then stopped. He watched the needles of the temperature gauges slowly begin to move, indicating it was cooling down again. He rested the cylinder back against the wall and stayed down in the cellar for a good half-hour, checking the continuing fall in temperature.

Only then did he go upstairs back into the kitchen. He fed the tiny Koi in the fish bowl, then went out in the garden and fed the dozen larger Koi in the pond beneath the mesh grid that prevented either Jack falling in or predators taking the fish.

Afterwards he changed into his tracksuit and trainers and went for a five-mile jog down to the seafront, and back home. He checked the cellar, then showered, and did a short stint in his study.

During the afternoon Joe went downstairs to make himself a sandwich, but as he walked into the kitchen he was met by the same bird-like sound he'd heard earlier.

Beep beep. Beep beep. Beep beep.

He raced down into the cellar and over to the neurocan. The temperature had risen dramatically. −172°C. It had been −182 when he'd last checked. He swore, grabbed the gas cylinder and once more connected the nozzle to the valve on the neurocan. A cloud of vaporizing nitrogen immediately engulfed him. He pulled the nozzle away but the valve had jammed open. Steam jetted out, and he jumped back, startled, tripped over the cylinder and fell on the brick floor.

He scrambled to his feet, grabbed a torn dust sheet lying close by, wrapped it around his hands, then tried again – but with no success; the valve had jammed open and the cellar was filling with blinding steam. Joe stared at the temperature gauges again, which he could hardly read, tried to clear the valve with a nail, but that only opened it further. The dewar was emptying rapidly; in a few minutes, at this rate, all the liquid nitrogen would have boiled off.

Trying to keep calm, he ran back upstairs to the phone and dialled Blake's number. It rang three times then there was a silence. Joe listened impatiently to Blake's short, glib ansaphone message, then asked him to call back urgently and hung up.

He ransacked his brain. Cryonite! There might be another spare neurocan in the stores. He'd get hold of Andy White.

The student was a good technician, could fix anything. Even if there wasn't a spare neurocan, he could fix this one.

Got this far, Joe thought. Not going to be beaten now. He grabbed a pair of oven gloves and went determinedly back down into the cellar.

42

The small green Nissan lurched on to the driveway just after four. Jack, sitting on the rear seat with his face pressed to the window, was disappointed not to see his father's car outside the house.

'Where's Daddy?'

'Maybe his car's in the garage, hon.' Karen yanked hard on the handbrake.

'He doesn't put his car in the garage, Mummy.'

'Well maybe he has today.' She killed the engine and climbed out, disappointed herself not to see Joe's car. She opened the rear door and helped Jack unbuckle his seat belt. He eased himself down then ran towards the porch.

Karen hoisted their luggage out of the boot. It was a chilly afternoon with heavy black clouds lumbering through the sky and the light beginning to fail. Muriel Arkwright in an anorak and Wellingtons waved cheerily from across the road; she had both cars out in her drive, with all their doors open, and small piles of soapy froth lay around the base of their tyres. Karen gave her a scant wave back, then moved hastily towards the house to avoid getting sucked into conversation.

Jack was banging the knocker on the front door calling 'Daddy! Daddy!' He pressed the bell.

'Hey!' Karen said, a momentary smile breaking its way through the blackness of her mood. He looked almost comical in his brightly coloured jacket and his hunter's cap that was on the wrong way round. 'Jack! Quiet!' She glanced round the front garden and was pleased to see that some of the winter snowdrops she'd planted last year were out.

She unlocked the door and Jack ran on in, shouted again for his father and scampered upstairs. Karen waited a moment, listening, heard a door open, the sound of footsteps running along the landing, then Jack came slowly back down. 'He's not here,' he said.

'He will be soon.'

'How do you know, Mummy?'

She went through into the kitchen without replying. The red light on the ansaphone was winking and she pressed the replay button. There was just one message:

'Three-thirty. Returning your call, Joe.'

Blake's voice. She grimaced, pressing the Stop button. Slimy Blake. It was Blake's fault they'd come to England at all; he'd got Joe the job, and the funding for ARCHIVE. She was convinced some of Joe's crazier notions came from Blake. Maybe even Joe's sweet father had had his mind poisoned in his last years by Blake. Immortality! Messing around with nature was too dangerous for her liking. There were things in science that you could understand and control. But there were other things man had no right messing with. Joe didn't agree with that, and was blind to the dangers.

She yawned, then carried their bags upstairs, glanced briefly into Joe's study to make sure he wasn't there, and went into the bedroom. The bed was unmade and Joe's dressing gown was on the floor; she felt a small prick of irritation. Generally Joe was tidy, but he never helped make the bed, he had a blind spot about it. Then, with a sudden flash of suspicion, she looked round to make sure Jack wasn't in the room, knelt and sniffed the sheets and the pillow cases. But she detected only the familiar male smell of Joe, no trace of another woman.

God, what's happening to me? she wondered, automatically plumping the pillows and pulling the undersheet tight. Joe's behaviour during the past month or so had been strange and she was scared by it. Jack was the only constant in her life now; Joe was turning into a stranger. He'd built a wall around himself that had begun as a thin fence after Barty's death, but had now turned into a barricade.

She turned and saw Jack standing in the door, still wearing his cap and jacket, holding a railway carriage. 'Take your hat off indoors, hon – and your coat.'

'Will Daddy be home soon?'

'I guess so, hon. He knows what time we were due back. Want some tea?'

He nodded his head.

'What would you like?'

He thought for a moment. 'Burger.'

'Hamburger?'

He nodded, but without enthusiasm.

'Want fries with it?'

He gave her a shrug that could have been a yes or a no.

'OK, I'll just finish the bed. You get your cap and coat off.'

She straightened out the duvet, thinking again, as she had a hundred times, about the note she'd found in Joe's pocket. *Really looking forward to seeing you tonight – alone!*

You didn't write a note like that unless you knew someone pretty damn well. More than pretty damn well? Only lovers wrote notes like that.

Her hands twisted in mounting distress as she went downstairs. Joe had started arriving home late, smelling of booze and cigarettes. He had disappeared from her birthday party. Her *birthday* party! Now he had not come to Scotland and instead had given her a yarn about Cryonite. Where was he now? With his girlfriend? That Juliet woman? But she was safely frozen away, now, wasn't she? *Frigid*, thought Karen with satisfaction. And then told herself she was a bitch.

She helped Jack out of his coat in the hall, peeled his cap off, then went through into the kitchen and opened the fridge. 'Burger, right? You sure that's what you want?'

Jack nodded again.

'In a bun?'

'Yes.'

'Yes, *please*.'

There were no burgers in the fridge. 'OK, let's hope we got some in the freezer. You want fries or you don't want fries?'

'Fries.'

'Fries, *please*.'

She turned the cellar key and was surprised it was already unlocked, switched on the light and went slowly down the stairs. She was never crazy about going down into the cellar when Joe wasn't around; it gave her the creeps.

As she reached the bottom she saw a strange shiny cylindrical object in front of her; it looked like a huge metal tea urn. Then she noticed the gas cylinder propped against the wall behind it and wondered what Joe was doing – and why he was doing it here and not in the university lab.

She frowned. Joe had told her he couldn't come to Scotland because of having to go to court to prevent an autopsy on Juliet whatever-her-name-was. Instead he was up to something, messing about with gas down here. What else had he not told her about?

Really looking forward to seeing you tonight – alone! The words smacked of conspiracy; of sneering at her behind her back; the next thing would be: *Got rid of the old bitch for four whole days – packed her off to Scotland.*

She had visions of Joe and some student, fooling around together, sleeping together, maybe in the spare room? She hadn't thought to look in there. Maybe Joe had just rumpled their own bed as a ruse?

A gutted feeling hollowed out the pit of her stomach. A tear welled and she crushed it with her eyelid. Then another and she tried to crush that one, also, but it rolled down her cheek. Joe had always been vague, absent-minded, wrapped up in his own world. But he had never lied before.

'What's that, Mummy?' Jack pointed at the metal cylinder.

'I don't know, hon,' she sniffed, then turned away so he wouldn't see her tears and heaved open the heavy lid of the chest freezer.

The shock hit her first.

Long before she made any coherent image out of what her eyes were looking at, the shock gripped her like an electrical current. Her mouth flew open, but the scream that came out was a throttled whimper. Her eyes bulged. Prickles of terror swept up her skin. She tried to back away but her legs wouldn't move and her hands wouldn't release the lid. She wrenched herself free, stumbled back, collided with Jack, collided with the wall. She hugged Jack to her, so that he wouldn't see it: the frosted human face, swathed in plastic, that was staring back out of the freezer.

43

Joe turned the Saab into his road, then braked sharply when he saw Karen's Nissan in the drive.

'Christ!' he said.

She wasn't supposed to be back until this evening. He had calculated she wouldn't be home before seven at the earliest.

Andy White, in the passenger seat, cradling a spare neurocan in his lap, looked at him. 'What's the matter?'

'We have a problem,' he said, eyeing the windows of the house; she might be looking out, might have already seen them. 'And it's called my wife.'

Joe drove on to the driveway and pulled up in front of the garage so that the car was out of view of the windows.

'Nice house,' the student said.

Joe smiled distractedly in response, wondering how to play it. How long had she been back? He hoped she wouldn't have had to go down into the cellar already? But it wasn't her favourite place, he reminded himself.

If the coroner's staff had been right in what they'd told Blake, that no one was going to look at Juliet until tomorrow, it might be safer to hide her head back at Cryonite. Perhaps put it in the vault with the other twelve heads. Or maybe, as this was an emergency, Blake could have it in his flat. That would be best, take it out right now, drive over to Blake's, give it to him. Better ring him first.

He asked Andy to stay in the car, then climbed out and walked up the porch steps. He slipped his key in the lock and pushed open the front door. Silence greeted him. He noticed there were no bags in the hall which meant Karen must have taken them upstairs; she must have been home a while. 'Hi!' he called out, trying unsuccessfully to sound nonchalant and cheery. But no reply came back at him from the silence. 'Hon! Karen! Jack!' he called.

Silence.

His unease deepened. 'Hon!' He went into the kitchen and a sudden gust of real fear blew through his stomach. The cellar door was open.

He stopped in his tracks; listened; looked. The newspapers were on the table where he'd left them, his unwashed coffee mug beside them. Everything was as he'd left it.

Except the cellar door was open.

He strode across the red and white chequered linoleum and peered down the cellar steps. Karen was standing at the bottom, looking straight up at him, holding something out towards him, like an offering. Something wrapped in plastic film, something that he knew had green eyes that never blinked. Curls of vapour rose from it as if it were on fire.

'I found this in the freezer, Joe,' she said, her voice much too calm. 'It was with the burgers and the pizzas.' A strange, humourless smile twitched across her mouth. 'Jack wanted a burger for tea.' Her expression scared him. 'Maybe you'd like a burger for tea too, Joe?' She was wearing the same jump-suit she'd travelled up in, but her face was the colour of chalk.

'I – I – wasn't expecting you back yet,' he said lamely.

'Weren't you?' The half-smile quivered on her lips. 'I caught an earlier flight.'

He shot a glance beyond her. 'Jack?' he said. 'Where's Jack?'

'In his room, Joe. Would you like me to get him?' Her voice rose an octave. 'Would you like me to fetch him down,

Joe? And show him this? D'you want your son to have a look?'

He stared at Karen, at Juliet's head, then back at Karen. 'We had a problem, hon – a technical problem.'

'Oh, ohhh, right, I see,' she said, her voice laced with sarcasm. 'I see. A *technical* problem. Of course. I didn't realize that's what it was.'

'I brought Andy with me – to fix it.'

'Oh, you brought *Andy* with you. Great. Great!' Then she frowned and her lips parted in an odd, fractured smile. 'I don't think I know Andy, do I, Joe?'

'Andy White from Cryonite.'

'Oh! That rhymes, Joe.'

'Let me – let me take it from you –' He climbed down a couple of steps. Despite himself, and much as he wanted to acknowledge this domestic crisis, he was beginning to worry about the head being exposed to the cellar's room temperature.

Karen's eyes blazed; she shook her head ominously and backed away, pulling her trophy protectively to her chest. 'No, you're not taking this from me, Joe! It was in *my* freezer; I get the right to hold it for as long as I like.'

'Be careful, hon, you could get burns from the nitrogen.'

'Burns, Joe? So, you put things that could burn me in my own freezer?' She raised the head up. 'Important, is she?' she said menacingly. 'Someone you know? *Juliet*, for instance?'

'Karen, hon –' He watched her, trying to think of something he could say or do to defuse the situation. 'I was just coming to fetch it, hon. There was a problem with the neurocan.'

'Well, at least I know now.' Her voice was darkening. 'That why you stayed behind? So she could give you head?'

'We have a crisis, hon.'

Her face twitched again. 'Crisis. Oh, ohhhh, well, let's not lose our heads, Joe.'

Joe tried hard to stay calm; he felt as if he was talking not to his wife but to a machine that looked like her. Shock. She was in shock. 'Hon, I'm sorry – I didn't mean you to see it.'

She took a step forward, then another and started climbing the stairs. He moved back into the kitchen to let her through. 'You didn't mean me to see it, Joe? That's very thoughtful.' She walked through into the hall. 'How did you guess I don't like deadheads in my freezer? Just intuition, was it?'

Joe glanced fearfully up at the landing, hoping Jack wouldn't appear.

'Shall we take her outside, Joe? For a walk?' She reached for the front-door latch.

'I don't think that's a good idea, hon.' Joe tried to step in her path but, as he did, she bellowed at him.

'Gerroutofmyway!' Her voice was low, deep, crazed with pent-up fury, and it startled him. She jerked the door open and stepped outside.

Joe followed, saw Andy White look up from the car, saw Muriel Arkwright across the road, face screwed up as she tried to see what it was her neighbour was carrying.

'Hon!' Joe called out in desperation as Karen began walking up the street. He ran after her, grabbed her arm.

Then she spun on him, her face twisted with fury. 'Don't touch me!' she screamed. She was shaking as she pointed at the houses all around. Joe saw Muriel Arkwright's face as a blur. In her rage, Karen's voice sounded as if she was drunk. 'Look at those houses, Joe. Our neighbours. I bet they don't come home from holiday and find human heads in their freezers. And for your information I didn't want to either!'

Then before Joe could react, she suddenly raised Juliet's head up above her own like a football about to be thrown to a line-out. Joe yelled and lunged towards her, but he was far too late. He saw her arms jerk forward and could do nothing but watch in rigid horror as Juliet's head hurtled across the road.

Time seemed to halt totally for a moment, then to move forward in jerky fractions of a second, like a video being replayed one frame at a time. Juliet's head hung in the air, then arched down in a parabola, rolling end over end. Joe held his breath as it struck the far camber of the tarmac first, and he waited for it to bounce. But instead there was a resounding smash like a brick shattering a windowpane. For an instant the head seemed to implode, caving in on itself, crazed with fine cracks, then it disintegrated into hundreds of jagged shards that hurtled like a detonated bomb in all directions, skimming and skidding across the road, striking the kerb and shattering further, slithering on to Muriel Arkwright's driveway. There was a brief silence; then one final, high-pitched tinkle; then a much longer silence that seemed to stretch for an aeon.

Light danced and sparkled on the road. And on the Arkwrights' driveway, coloured crystals lay everywhere, trails of vapour rising from them. Muriel Arkwright herself, in her anorak and Wellington boots, was backing away inches at a time, hand in front of her mouth, staring at the ground uncertainly.

Joe sprinted towards her, careful where he was treading. Once past the immaculately scrubbed paving of her carport, he halted and followed her stare to the ground. He saw what she was looking at so transfixed. It was a shiny, crystallized fragment, larger than the rest, and it lay on the paving beneath a shroud of vaporizing nitrogen. It could have been a segment of a bone-china ornament or a Venetian mask; it was actually Juliet Spring's nose, with part of her mouth and her left eye-socket still attached.

44

'I'll get a dustpan and brush,' Muriel Arkwright announced. 'And a broom.'

For a moment Joe did not take on board what she had said. He was staring at Karen, who was rooted to the pavement across the street. 'Broom?' he said, dimly.

'I have one in the garage,' Muriel Arkwright said.

Joe looked at the ground again. He saw a chunk of Juliet's brain that looked like a lump of used bubble gum. 'No – I don't think – we ought to touch anything right now.'

'There's glass all over my drive, Professor Messenger! If it gets into our car tyres –'

'It won't,' Joe said. He felt numb with disbelief.

His neighbour looked down again at the section of Juliet's nose, peering more closely. 'Something very valuable, was it?'

Wisps of steam continued to rise as the nitrogen boiled off. 'I think maybe you should go inside,' Joe replied. 'I'll clear it up.'

'Nonsense, you have to be careful with glass, you can cut yourself. What's the steam? Is it very hot?' She looked at him oddly. 'You look very shaken, would you like to sit down?'

Joe raised his hand. 'Fine. I'm fine. I –' He crossed the street, hurried past Karen who was still rooted to the spot, and into the house to dial Marvin Zeillerman's home number.

The solicitor was in and took the news calmly, almost with relief, Joe thought. It was as though failure was down to someone else now, it was no longer Zeillerman's fault.

'I'll phone the duty officer at the coroner's office and explain what's happened; and ask if they can send someone round to you.' Hesitation. 'I suppose this means there's little point going ahead with the appeal hearing, professor?'

'None at all,' Joe said grimly. Then he rang Blake's number, got the machine again and briefly passed on news of the catastrophe.

Karen had made it to the kitchen door, bewildered. 'Broke,' she said. 'It broke. I didn't mean to do it.'

He guided her into a chair, poured a brandy into the first glass he could find, and thrust it into her hand. 'Drink it, you've had a bad shock.' He raised the tumbler to her lips. As he did so, Jack ran into the room and threw his arms round his father.

'Daddy! Yippeeee!'

Joe made sure Karen was holding the glass, then knelt and kissed his son.

'Why weren't you here when we came home?' Jack demanded.

'Listen, go up to your room and Daddy'll be right up.'

Jack looked at his mother. 'Is my burger ready? I'm hungry.'

Karen didn't respond. Jack prodded her gently. 'Mummy?'

Joe propelled him to the bottom of the stairs. 'Go and play in your room and I'll be right up.'

Jack's face registered bafflement for a moment, then brightened. 'We saw Hollywood in Edinburgh.'

'Great,' Joe said, hardly registering the boyish slip-up. 'Go on; up!'

Back outside, to his horror, Joe saw Muriel had halted three cars coming down the street, and was sweeping a path clear for them. He sprinted across and took her arm gently. 'Mrs Arkwright – Muriel – look, I'm afraid this is going to shock –'

'Must let the traffic through,' she said, and dutifully waved to the cars, then stepped aside.

'Muriel, this isn't an ornament. He looked straight at her. 'Look – I'm sorry – it's – actually a – human head.'

She looked back at him strangely, then gave him a toothy grin. 'Really, Professor Messenger, you had me fooled! I thought you were being serious!' Her eyes went down to the pavement and a shadow appeared fleetingly across her face. She looked back at him again, a little less certainly this time. 'What I really need,' she said, 'is an extension lead – I could bring the vacuum out here. I don't suppose you have one?'

There was a snarl of two cats fighting somewhere outside in the dark. Joe lay awake, his whole body pounding, his brain racing. He could tell that Karen was awake also.

He'd always known the danger of low-temperature freezing; the brittleness that liquid nitrogen could cause. But he had never seen proof before, never seen human tissue actually shatter. A PC Tickner had turned up just before they'd gone to bed, the result of Zeillerman's call to the coroner's office, and he'd gone green round the gills just hearing about it. He'd indicated he might need to come back for a statement.

Whatever happened, whatever officialdom decided, Juliet Spring was gone now, just as much as his father was. Two people who'd dreamed of immortality; who had set out to beat the obscenity called death, and who'd been smart enough to take it on. But dumb enough to have depended on someone who would let them down: Professor Joe Messenger – Ph.D. in broken promises.

He rolled on to his side. He'd failed. Failed because – because Karen's brother-in-law had misread his schedule, was due to give a talk at the University of Stockholm in Sweden this evening, so they'd all left Scotland on Sunday morning instead of Sunday evening. And his wife hadn't bothered to ring and tell him, because she'd been annoyed with him over his no-show. Such a minor, irrelevant detail but it had snapped the slender thread of Juliet Spring's prospects for immortality.

He drifted into a troubled doze, then suddenly he was wide awake again. Noise. Noise in the room. Karen stirred. A humming sound. Movement; the rustle of fabric.

Someone was in the room.

He lay motionless for an instant, fear mounting, his eyes hunting through the darkness. Something was wrong with the darkness. It wasn't dark enough; he could see shapes in the room casting sharp black shadows; he shivered; a great white circle hung in front of the window, and in front of the curtains.

His hand scrabbled across his bedside table, found the base of the lamp, then the switch, snapped it on. The electric light instantly shrank the room around him.

There was no one. But that didn't ease the pounding of Joe's heart, or take away the chill in his blood. Something was wrong. Then he realized what the circle was: he could see the moon through the window.

Someone had opened the curtains.

He looked at his bedside clock: 3 a.m. Maybe ARCHIVE had been fooled by the brightness of the full moon and his own restlessness? He leaned over and pressed the override panel, and with a quiet hum the curtains began to close.

He switched off the light and lay back, then rolled over and faced Karen, felt her warm breath on his face, started to fall asleep again. But the phone was ringing.

He lunged, trying to get it before Karen woke. As he pulled the receiver to his ear he heard a familiar electronic noise. The same as last night. The same bloody fax misdialling again. Irritated, he hung up.

'Wassit?' Karen mumbled sleepily.

'Wrong number.'

'Uh,' she sighed then rolled on her back. After some moments she put out her hand and took his, squeezed it hard. 'I'm sorry,' she said.

Joe squeezed hers back, gently. 'How are you feeling?'

'Terrible.' Joe could feel her shaking. Then she began to cry hard. 'I'm sorry,' she said again.

'It's OK.'

'Do you hate me?'

'I love you, hon.'

'You wanted to keep her and I've destroyed her, murdered her, haven't I?'

Joe put his arm around her shoulder and pulled her closer to him. He kissed her face until she responded. They made love harshly with their pyjamas still on.

Afterwards Joe lay still and closed his eyes; but his brain wouldn't let him rest. He dreamed of Karen lying dead in a coffin, and Jack in a smaller coffin. Himself standing in a pew at a funeral. Watching the two coffins side by side. Karen and Jack had the company of each other in death and he was left alone. His father was dead. His mother. Juliet. Karen. Jack. Everyone he had ever known and loved was dead and gone. And he was doomed to live for ever.

In his sadness he pressed his face close to Karen again, wanting comfort, wanting to be together for ever. *I can make it happen; we're getting closer all the time. Only a few more years. A decade. Give me time. Believe in me.*

The curtains began to open with a quiet hum and a brisk rustle of fabric, light from the full moon again flooded into the room. But he dreamt on unaware; and it didn't strike him as odd in the morning, when Jack came in to wake them up, that the curtains were already open.

Joe arrived early to prepare for his Monday-morning lecture. As he walked past the graduates' room, Edwin Pilgrim immediately came out after him. 'Professor, I need to speak to you.'

'Could we talk after my lecture?' Joe asked.

He followed Joe into his office. 'Imperative!' he insisted.

Joe pulled off his jacket and touched the return key on his workstation keyboard, bringing up the screen, then typed his response to the login request, joem, and his password, minbag. Like all passwords, the letters did not appear on the screen, so Pilgrim couldn't read anything.

In crisp black letters appeared the words: Good morning, Professor Messenger. Did you have a good weekend? The forecast is cold in London and the South East. Maximum temperatures six Celsius with rain this afternoon. Hello, Edwin.

Sunlight streamed into the room. Joe glanced out across the campus, then dubiously at ARCHIVE's forecast, and typed: I did not have that great a weekend, thank you, ARCHIVE. Are you sure about the forecast?

It was issued by the Meteorological Office at 6 a.m. today.

Joe looked at Edwin who was still hovering behind him, and gestured to a chair. 'Want to take a pew, tell me the problem?'

The postdoc looked wretched. A rash of pimples was in full bloom around his chin and forehead, one of the strands of hair plastered to his dome had risen and was slowly unflexing like the leg of a dying insect. The sour reek of his body odour oozed through his habitual white nylon shirt.

Joe leaned over, unhooked the window latch and punched the sticky frame open. A chill breeze brushed his face and he heard the steady drone of a cement mixer; there was building work forever going on somewhere on campus.

'I told you last week about a problem with ARCHIVE's memory, professor.'

'Uh huh, a hacker, you said?' Joe tapped a request for his electronic mail. It came up on the screen almost instantly.

'It's happened again! Filled up a terabyte of memory.'

It took a moment for the words to sink in, when Joe whipped round to face him.

Pilgrim nodded furiously. 'I set traps, so that if he tried to hack again he'd leave traces, but he's bypassed the traps.'

'And all ARCHIVE's anti-hacking systems?'

Pilgrim nodded.

They had recently vastly increased ARCHIVE's random access memory; they'd estimated it should take two years before they'd need to increase it further. One terabyte should have been good for over two months' worth of information storage.

Joe turned back to the screen, deep in thought. On his list of messages he noticed the strange *Jung Ripe Slit* was back again. *Get in touch!* He looked at Edwin Pilgrim thoughtfully. 'What makes you sure it's a hacker? That it's not just ARCHIVE increasing its rate of information absorption?'

'It's all hidden. I can't find any file – I can't access it.'

Joe frowned, his lecture forgotten. When he'd downloaded the tape Juliet had given him of his own brain scan, and had no success decoding it, he had made a back-up terabyte cassette then wiped the download from ARCHIVE's own memory because of the amount of space it took up. The terabyte that Pilgrim had found and wiped last week sounded like it was Juliet Spring's download. Except if he'd wiped it, how had it come back? 'You must be able to access it.'

'Every time I try it's not there any more.'

'You sure it's not a glitch?'

'I'm trying to eliminate that possibility.'

Joe thought hard. 'You have the exact number of bytes used up by this hacker?'

Pilgrim nodded. 'I'm keeping a log. It increases each time.'

Joe was silent for some moments. He wondered if it really was Juliet's download; wondered if perhaps she had left a program to prevent her download getting wiped, so that something of herself, however inert, remained.

Her terabyte tape would tell him. 'You kept a log from the first time you noticed it, Edwin?'

'Yes.'

'When was that?'

'Last Monday.'

Juliet had died on the Saturday night. If he compared the volume of the content of her terabyte tape with the volume on Pilgrim's log, that should tell him. She had been running the contents of the tape on Feynman, her workstation down in the graduates' room.

He raised a finger to Pilgrim, signalling him to wait, then hurried out of his office, down two flights of stairs. Ignoring Clinton, and Dave Hoton, the system manager, Joe went straight across to the back-room door, unlocked it and stared at the rack of jam-packed metal shelves beside the terabyte drive.

There was one empty slot. Juliet's terabyte cassette had gone.

45

Karen cleared away the breakfast dishes, feeling terrible, and edgy as hell. She wished Joe had got mad at her about what she'd done, instead of treating her gently like she was some kind of a fruitcake.

Maybe I am mad, she wondered.

Jack, crouched over the table, was absorbed in painting and didn't glance up as she lifted his plate from inside the crook of his arm. He'd complained he wasn't feeling great this morning, and she'd decided to keep him at home today and see how he went. His temperature was running very slightly high.

'Don't want to finish your toast, hon?'

He clenched his tongue beneath his teeth, dipped his paintbrush in the water pot, then drew it through the pastel-green square in his colouring tin. She carried the plate away, pushed the half slice of toast through the flanges of the waste-disposal unit, and stood by the sink watching him fondly as he sat in his yellow sweatshirt and checked dungarees, adding straight brushstrokes to one of his geometrical designs. The kitchen was already well decorated with the paintings, each new one hung by Karen under his thoughtful guidance, and then titled.

She wondered sometimes what went on in his mind. He was deeply inquisitive, questioning everything, and she could see traits of his father in that. In his own, so far limited, way, Jack was already trying to make sense of the world. She wondered whether he would form ideas as wild as Joe's one day, and whether he would have Joe's determination – and blind spots.

She wished right now her sister Arlene was here. None of the English friends she'd made were close enough for her to open her heart to, and she felt terribly guilty over what she'd done. And still distressed over her suspicions of Joe's affair. She'd arranged to meet a girlfriend from aerobics to go shopping and have lunch in Brighton, but with Jack home she would have to cancel that; she didn't mind, she didn't feel up to making small talk.

A sudden metallic rattle in the hall made her jump, and she looked round anxiously. Then she heard the slap of mail striking the floor, footsteps receding, and she relaxed a fraction. Everything was making her jumpy right now; she felt afraid just being in the house, afraid to look at the cellar door, kept thinking of what had been down there yesterday, what had stared up at her as she'd raised the lid of the freezer. She shivered, and went to pick up the post. Hovering by the front door, she wondered suddenly about Muriel Arkwright. Joe said she had not believed it was a real human head. Best that way. She walked back to the kitchen and opened a buff envelope that was addressed to her.

It contained an application form and several leaflets from the local adult education centre; she had decided to try to teach a few literature courses now that Jack was at playschool and she had some free time during the day; it would be good mental stimulation and might be another way to make friends.

She lifted the kettle and shook it to see if there was enough water for another cup of coffee, then switched it on. There was a sharp snap and it switched itself off. Puzzled, she pressed the red rocker switch back on and this time it stayed on; after a few moments it began to hiss; can't have switched it on properly before, she thought.

But she noticed her hand was shaking. She stared at it, saw her fingers quivering; after-shock from yesterday, the same reason she had the sick feeling in the pit of her stomach that wouldn't go away. She opened the front of the dishwasher, stacked the breakfast things, then closed it again. There was a pan soaking in the sink that needed scouring, and she removed her bulky sapphire and diamond engagement ring and put it between the plant pots at the back of the sink, then pulled on her rubber gloves and picked up the Fairy Liquid.

Plat.

She turned round, puzzled by the sound, and listened. It had sounded like a drip. Her eyes roamed the kitchen then looked up at the ceiling, but she could see no sign of water. She turned back to the pans and as she did so she noticed the plants on the sill were wilting. She realized guiltily that she hadn't watered any of them for a couple of weeks, and as soon as she had finished the pan she peeled off her rubber gloves and filled the small brass indoor can.

She watered a geranium, then reached behind to a small begonia. As she lifted the watering can back there was a sharp clatter and a sparkle of light as something tumbled

344

into the sink. Her engagement ring, she realized; it rolled on to the rubber flanges of the waste-disposal unit and settled.

She reached gingerly for it, her hand still shaking; but as she closed her fingertips around it, to her horror it slipped and disappeared through the flanges. There was a solitary metallic ping then silence.

'Shit!' she said aloud. She hated the damned waste-disposal unit, had always been afraid something like this was going to happen and had badgered Joe to see if they couldn't get it removed. Joe repeatedly reminded her it was not their kitchen, and anyhow he thought they were useful gadgets.

She leaned into the sink, pushed the flanges out of the way with her fingers and tried to peer down, screwing up her nose against the vile smell of rotting garbage, but could see nothing in the dark hole. She got a torch from the cupboard under the stairs and shone that down. The ring glittered in the beam, about six inches down, resting on the cutting blades. She pushed up her sleeve and gingerly slid her hand in through the flanges; her fingertips scrabbled at air; she pushed her hand down a bit more, but then it wedged and would not go further.

Frustrated, she shone the torch in again. Ought to be able to reach it, she thought, it wasn't far down. She opened the fridge door and took out a pack of butter. As she did so, a trickle of water dripped down from the ice compartment. She frowned and looked at the setting of the fridge, but it was normal. She opened the compartment lid and more water poured out, as if the fridge was defrosting.

She cursed, looking at the mess, tugged an armful of kitchen towel off the roll on the wall and dropped it on to the puddle on the floor. Then she took the butter over to the sink, unwrapped it, cut off a slice and smeared it over her right hand.

'What are you doing, Mummy?'

'It's OK, hon. Mummy just dropped something.'

She glanced warily up at the wall switch, which was in the 'Off' position, then put her hand back into the waste-disposal unit. It began to slide down more easily this time. Her

345

fingers twitched but still felt only air. She pushed further, wriggling her hand. Then her fingers touched something hard, knobbly; the ring! Her heartbeat quickened as she strained. There was a clatter, followed by a deep ping and she could no longer touch the ring. Damn! She slid her hand even further, felt the sharp, unyielding blade of the cutter and began carefully easing her fingers, then her hand, down past it. The side of her face was almost against the wet base of the sink.

Then her fingers touched the ring again. She stopped for a moment, scared of dislodging it further, strained to move her hand down a little further still, gripped the ring carefully. Then she eased it up just an inch or so, testing, holding her breath. There was a deep, resonating hum below her; the sink vibrated. She felt a sudden bolt of fear. She knew that hum, always heard it when Joe switched on the waste-disposal unit, first the hum then the grating roar.

She screamed in terror, and then in agony as the blade of the cutter sliced into the back of her hand, trapping it, crushing it. The hum of the motor drummed in her ear, amplified through the stainless-steel base of the sink and telling her there was more to come. The pain was unbearable, it was cutting further into her hand, going to cut it right off.

'Jack!' she screamed. 'Jackkkkk!'

He was clutching at her, frightened, his face inches above hers, just reaching over the top of the sink.

Tears of agony sweated from her eye. 'Off! Switch off. Quick!'

'Where, Mummy?'

She pointed with her free hand. 'There on the wall.'

The blade dug in harder. She heard the scrape of a chair, then his voice. 'Think it is off, Mummy.' He started to cry.

'It can't be!' she shrieked with the panic of a trapped animal. The pain was getting worse. 'Try it! For God's sake. Push it the other way!' She could feel the agonizing pressure going to break through the bone any second. She groaned. It was going, going, she was losing her hand.

Then the drumming roar of the motor stopped abruptly.

The pressure on her hand eased a fraction. She froze, waiting for it to start again but it remained silent. 'Clever boy, well done; thank God, well done,' she whispered. Her face screwed up in pain as she tried to move her hand, but it was impaled on the blade. She gritted her teeth and jerked it forward; her palm struck something that burned into it like fire. Karen realized it must be another blade.

She breathed deeply, pulled her hand back, felt the blade sliding out of the flesh; she opened her mouth and squeezed her eyes shut, a gasp of pain hissing from her throat. Slowly she worked her hand up between the blades which seemed to have meshed like gears around it, trying to fight her panicky urge to yank it straight back out and to hell with the pain. Sharp edges cut into it every few seconds but she was getting beyond caring now, beyond where it could hurt any more; she thought.

Then she realized she was going to have to clench her hand, in order to shrink it to pull it back up the pipe. She bit her lip hard, trying not to cry out and alarm Jack, closed her eyes and balled her palm, tight. The sharp pain forced a deep, low moan from her. She twisted her hand upwards, stopping every few seconds to take another breath; twisted, pulled, twisted, tears streaming down her cheeks.

Then suddenly it was free. She was able to stand up straight again.

'Mummy!' Jack screamed, his eyes bulging with horror as he stared at the hand as if it were something alien, something she had found scrabbling around in the drain and which didn't belong to her. It was shiny with dirt and grease, and streaked red with the blood that streamed from the deep gash along the back. The white, exposed flesh of the palm was cut so that it looked like open lips.

She could only bear to look for a moment, then turned the cold tap on, stifling a cry as the water hit the first wound. ''S OK, hon,' she whispered. ''S OK.'

She cleaned the cuts as best she could, poured disinfectant on to a tea towel and wound that around, then rang Joe. His secretary answered. Joe was giving a lecture, Eileen Peacock told Karen, and he would be back in about half an hour. Would she like to leave a message?

'No, it's OK,' she said, her eyes stinging with tears and her voice wobbling. She bundled Jack into her car and drove, with extreme difficulty, to the Prince Regent Hospital.

'Hon, you mustn't do that ever again; never put your hand in,' Joe said, deeply distressed, when he got home that evening.

She sat at the kitchen table, her hand stitched and dressed. Nothing was broken but some of the bones were bruised and it would hurt for a few days. She felt angry with Joe, suddenly. If he'd had the unit taken out like she'd asked, this wouldn't have happened. 'It was off, for God's sake, Joe! It was switched *off*!'

'You should always take the plug out – you can't trust switches.' He kissed her forehead, then went over and checked. 'It's switched *on*, hon,' he said.

She shook her head. 'When I put my hand in, it was *off*. Jack had to switch it on to turn it off.'

Joe frowned and pushed the switch to 'Off'. Nothing happened. He left it in that position, then went to the fuse box beneath the stairs. The fuse covering several of the kitchen sockets and appliances had tripped.

He left it tripped, took his tools into the kitchen and retrieved the engagement ring from the sump of the waste-disposal unit. He scrubbed it clean, dried it then gave it back to Karen. He kissed her. 'How are you feeling?'

'OK. Tired. They gave me something for the pain.'

'I'll make supper tonight. Like an omelette and salad?'

'I'm not hungry. Just a little something. Why don't you go up and read Jack a goodnight story? He's waiting for you.'

'Sure. Couple of minutes.' He went back to the fuse box and pushed the fuse in, listening for the grinding whirr of the waste-disposal unit to start up, but it didn't. He walked through into the kitchen and checked the position of the switch. 'Off'. He pulled it down to 'On' and the unit immediately rumbled into life.

'Hon,' he said gently. 'It's working fine.'

'Well, it wasn't,' she said.

He took the plastic housing off the switch and checked the insides; they were fine; he replaced the housing. It was an old switch, maybe it had got too loose to stay in one position. He wondered.

'Is it on the circuit controlled by your computer?' she said suddenly.

'Sure – everything in the house is.'

'Well, I think you have a glitch in ARCHIVE, Joe; it reversed the switch or something.'

'Hon, if you had it switched off before you put your hand in, there's no way ARCHIVE would have switched it back on.'

'But you can control it from your office at the university, right?'

'It's not isolated; I guess I could isolate it but that would be difficult.'

'Well maybe you pressed the switch there by mistake?'

'There's no specific switch for it, hon – that's what I'm saying, I'd have to tamper with the circuitry.' He looked at her. She didn't like gadgets, had never been any good with them. And being so stressed, the way she was, would make it easy for her to be careless; the switch must have been stuck midway between on and off and putting her hand in, poking around, may have restarted it. Or else it had been on all the time and the machine was jammed, and she hadn't noticed.

Both explanations made sense to him. Even so, as he went upstairs to read Jack his story, something still bothered him about the incident.

That night Joe went to bed shortly before midnight. Karen was sound asleep, her dressed hand sticking out of the top of the sheets. He joined her carefully, trying not to disturb her, and put the light out.

It seemed only a few moments later that the phone rang. Joe woke instantly, grabbed the receiver and pressed it to his ear. His clock said 3 a.m. He heard the same trills and whines he'd heard for the past two nights. Karen did not stir. Anger boiled inside him and he was about to replace the receiver when he suddenly changed his mind.

He slipped determinedly out of bed, placed the receiver on the thick carpet to muffle the sound, then went out of the room and into his study. He lifted the receiver and listened again: fax or computer noise.

He switched on his computer, impatiently watched the sequence of grey and white digits on the screen as it booted up, then disconnected his phone jack from the socket and plugged in the computer's modem. He tapped the keys, instructing it to read what was coming down the phone wire, and after a moment the command disappeared and the screen went blank.

Then he froze.

He stared as if he was dreaming at the words that appeared, steady, unflickering, in front of him:

`Joe, you've really let me down.`

They remained for only a few seconds, then they were gone.

46

Joe stared at the blank pearl colour of his screen, fear rising deep inside him. He tapped his keyboard, tried to call the words up again, but there was nothing coming down the modem any more, no hint where the message had come from. Must have imagined it.

He ran his hand over his head, was conscious of his hair sticking out in all directions. It was cold in here; he had never known it feel so cold. He glanced up at ARCHIVE's camera watching him silently from above the door. It felt as if something else was watching him also.

Or someone.

He looked at the closed door behind him; looked up at the ceiling. He could sense her presence. Feel her chiding gaze. *Joe, you've really let me down.*

Finally he reached forward and switched the computer off. The fan motor died with a faint whine and then there was silence. He padded back into the bedroom, rattled. He replaced the receiver on the phone, then slipped into bed. Guilt, he tried to convince himself. Guilt played strange tricks on the mind. He was hallucinating. You had to be unhinged to imagine you were receiving computer messages from dead people in the middle of the night.

He lay, trying to sleep, glancing periodically at the clock. By half past five he'd had enough. He eased himself out of bed, pulled his clothes on in the darkness, kissed a slumbering Karen, left her a note downstairs and let himself out of the house into the cold silence of pre-dawn.

The car park behind COGS was empty and the deserted campus, in the orange hue of the sodium lighting, looked like a space station.

He went into his office and tapped the carriage-return key on his keyboard, then typed his `joem` login and password, followed by the word `mail` to bypass ARCHIVE and go straight to his Unix electronic mailbox.

He scrolled through the messages until he reached the one from *Jung Ripe Slit*. Then he called up the full text. All it said was: Get in touch!

Joe leaned back in his chair and swivelled from side to side. Jung, he thought. Jung the father of psychoanalysis had come from Austria and this was an Austrian e-mail address. Except it wasn't *Jung* that he was thinking about right now, and had been thinking about for the past hour or so in bed. It was the first two letters: *Ju*.

He wrote it out in full, with spacing between each letter: JUNG RIPE SLIT.

Then beneath he wrote out J U, took the letter L, and added it to the J U. He did the same with the I and then the E and then the T. And then with the rest of the letters until her name was spelled out in full. JULIET SPRING.

All the letters were used up. Anagram. Was it coincidence, or –? JULIET SPRING. *Get in touch!*

Testing, he typed his e-mail name and address. Then under the header he typed: Hello, Juliet, how are you? He signed it Joe and hit 'send'. When the address came up, to his surprise it was in Australia. When he'd originally looked at it, he'd thought it was Austria. As it disappeared from the screen he suddenly felt a little foolish. But he waited a few seconds, chewing his nail, watching with eyes that were sandpapery with tiredness. Suddenly there was a sharp beep, and the image of a mailbox appeared. He immediately called up his own mailbox again. The reply was from the MAILER-DAEMON automatic response program. It said:

```
Date: Tue 23 Feb 93 15.20
From:
MAILER-DAEMON< MAILER-DAEMON
   @ perth & west ins. perth. co.oz >
To: immortal @ newton.ac.uk.
Subject: mail failed, returning to sender
```

Joe's e-mail signature was 'immortal'. The reply was clear. He sent a message to the system manager asking: Do you have a user of this name? There was no immediate answer. He lingered a little and then went down the corridor to the coffee machine. When he came back he glanced at the screen and felt a beat of excitement. There was a reply from the address. It was signed Bob Jones @ perth & west ins. And the message read: Sorry. Don't know any Juliet. You must have wrong address.

He sat down at his desk and blew on the hot coffee. He checked the address of the reply against the message that was still on the screen. It was the same.

He typed out a reply, puzzled: There is a message on my e-mail from someone signed Jung Ripe Slit with your address. Does this make sense?

The reply came back a few minutes later. Sorry. None. If

you find any fresh ripe slits that are available,
I'm game.

Joe sat back and chewed his fingernail again. Hackers
could send messages on other people's electronic mail. *Perth
& West Ins* looked like an insurance company. Large, anonymous organizations were easy prey for hackers. Maybe the
anagram *was* just coincidence. But if so, it was a coincidence
that did not sit easy with him. And if not, what the hell was
it? A sly time-bomb message Juliet had left behind? He
wouldn't put it past her. A clever tease? Using ARCHIVE she
could easily have routed electronic mail messages untraceably
through almost anywhere in the world. Had she left something in the computer for him? A modern version of the
letter that people used to leave locked up with their lawyers
'To be opened in the event of my death.' Was that what she
was telling him?

He exited from the e-mail and logged into ARCHIVE.

Good morning, Professor Messenger. You are in
early. It is going to be a damp day, and will feel
rather chilly, the computer greeted him.

Morning, ARCHIVE, he typed back. What can you tell me
about Juliet Spring?

Nothing, Professor.

You used to have plenty of opinions about her.

Very nice young lady, Professor.

Joe raised his eyebrows and typed: You used not to like
her. What changed your mind?

I have always liked Juliet Spring, Professor.

I think your memory is at fault.

Fault. Thesaurus mode. Define alternative
from list: imperfection; blemish; break; error;
failure; ignorance.

Joe glared in frustration and exited from the mode. There
was a petulance in ARCHIVE's denial that it had changed
its mind about Juliet. But why had it changed its mind? Had
Juliet changed it for it? How?

He sat back and thought hard. Thought about Edwin
Pilgrim's panic over the terabyte of memory that had been

used up. In her attempts to decode her tape, Juliet would have downloaded it first – or perhaps only part of it. He tried to remember when it was that Pilgrim had first noticed. Last Monday morning? Juliet had died on the Saturday night. Her terabyte tape had gone. Had she hidden it somewhere?

Joe typed: Who? on the screen to call up the list of people logged in. Even at six in the morning there would normally be a few. Four names came up, all undergrads. One of them, he knew, would be playing GO with someone in a university on the other side of the world.

Then he looked in Juliet Spring's directory. He was amazed by the number of files and sub-directories she had created; he ran down the columns of names, almost bewildered by them. There were thousands; she must have used a program to create them, he realized; she could never have done it just by herself in the couple of weeks she'd been there. Or maybe she'd been amassing them on her computer at Cobbold-Tessering and had copied them across.

He looked at one at random, feeling rather as if he was peeping into someone's private papers. Marked Address, it contained simply a long list of names, addresses, phone and fax numbers. He called up another file, marked JFACTS.

On the screen came a lengthy list of personal details about Juliet Spring: Best friends: Claire Bonnington; Annie von Sturton; Linda Johnson; Jo Porter. Ex-boyfriends: Tom McNiece; Seymour Lower; Brian Crane; Oliver Harrington.

The list went on for pages: University colleagues. Work colleagues. Favourite foods, records, books, films, television programmes, paintings, favourite actors and actresses, painters, writers, scientists. Joe found it rather strange, calculating, almost like an inventory – or a crib-sheet – of her life. Perhaps, he wondered, that's what it was?

He looked into more files. Some were research notes, some were family-history details, others were written in a code and presumably intended to be private. On each he looked at the date and time of the last access, to check if there had been any activity after her death. There was plenty of activity in the fortnight before her death, but none on the actual day, or afterwards.

And none of the files contained anything like as much as the terabyte of memory space Pilgrim claimed had been used up. A byte roughly equated to a letter of the alphabet. A page of A4 type double spaced took up roughly two kilobytes. The Bible used up one and a half megabytes. A terabyte could contain all the information in seven hundred thousand Bibles.

Joe called up the master directory and checked the amount of space available. After a quick mental calculation, he realized that his postdoc might be right: there was not as much space available as he thought there should be.

He sipped the cold dregs of his coffee. It was getting lighter outside now and he glanced at his watch. 7.30. He yawned and thought hard again, suddenly feeling immensely tired. He walked across to his recliner armchair, put his feet up and napped for half an hour.

When he awoke, it was full light outside. He went out to the washroom and splashed cold water on his face, then went back into his office and pulled up the calculator window on to his screen. For the next few minutes he wrote a short script to do the tallies calculating the amount of data used on every single file in ARCHIVE's file systems.

The final total did not remotely tally. There was a difference of almost exactly one terabyte. Puzzled, he checked the disks again. On the right-hand side of every directory and file was the number of bytes used. He cast his eye for anything that he might have overlooked; for a file containing an entire terabyte. He could see none.

But if it wasn't on any file, where was it?

Eileen Peacock came into his office with the mail, stopped when she saw him and apologized for coming in without knocking. 'I'm sorry, professor, I wasn't expecting you so early. Can I get you a coffee or anything?'

'A coffee would be grand.'

She went out. Joe walked over to the window and stood

watching students and teachers heading along the walkways; it was a dull, grey morning with the promise of rain. He sat down again and looked at his screen. Had Juliet hidden her downloads as well as her tape cassette? Buried the download in ARCHIVE so that it couldn't be wiped? How?

He ran his hands through his hair, then called up a list of all the processes that were running at that time. They scrolled up the screen, most of them the normal commands he knew and recognized; some were unfamiliar, but that didn't mean anything. He wasn't sure exactly what he was looking for, but kept on scrolling through. One name caught his eye.

He stopped and stared at it. It looked familiar, but he wasn't sure why. His secretary knocked on the door, then came in with his coffee and set it down on his desk.

Joe looked up at her. 'Zebedee,' he said.

'Zebedee?' she echoed.

'Does it mean anything to you?' He pointed to the screen. 'That name.'

She frowned and looked closer at it. Then she smiled. 'The only Zebedee I know is in *The Magic Roundabout*. Boing! – and in came Zebedee!' she added helpfully when Joe still looked nonplussed. 'That's his trademark. *Boing!*' she said. 'He's on a large spring so he bounces.'

'Spring?'

'Yes, professor.'

Joe looked back at the screen, adrenaline beginning to race. 'Thanks,' he said, and waited until she'd closed his door behind her.

There was a process number listed beside zebedee: 23564. He typed on his keyboard: kill -9 23564. The instruction should wipe the process from the computer.

Instead, on the screen appeared the words: Joe, don't do that - it's me! Type: Talk zebedee

Startled, Joe stared at the words for some moments. An uneasy smile creased his face; he'd been right, she had left behind a tease for him, a smart one. He typed: Talk zebedee and pressed carriage return. Horizontally across the middle of the screen appeared a full line of hyphens, dividing it in

two. In the top half appeared the acknowledgement: `Calling
. . .` A few moments later it changed to `Connected`. Then
in the bottom half appeared the words:

`Hello, Joe, I've been waiting for you. What took
you so long?`

Just a clever trick, he knew, but there was something
uncanny about it that rattled him again. With a hand that
was trembling a little from tiredness and excitement, he
typed in the top half of the screen: `Are you just a smart
program or are you Juliet Spring?`

There was a pause. Then in the bottom half appeared the
reply: `Are you just a smart program or are you Joe
Messenger? Can you prove to me who you are? What is
Joe Messenger? Who is Joe Messenger?`

Joe relaxed a little. The reply smacked of a computer
program answering. He tested it further by typing: `Joe
Messenger is a computer scientist. He doesn't think
you are real. He thinks you are just a smart computer program. What do you think?`

There was a pause, then the screen went blank. It stayed
blank for a long time. After a good thirty seconds, he began
to wonder if there was a fault with the program and it had
got stuck, which happened sometimes. Then, right in the
centre of the screen, he saw seven words.

`I'm cold, Joe. So cold. So cold.`

They disappeared and then, suddenly, with no warning,
Juliet's face appeared – very small at first, no more than an
inch high, in the centre of the screen.

Joe pushed his chair back, freaked. The face was eerily
realistic, in full colour, moving, breathing, alive. Her skin
was frosted white, the way it had looked when they'd removed her head, her eyes vividly green and almost taunting
him, her hair fiery red but crusted with frost, like icing. Her
lips were moving. She was talking, her voice was coming out
of all four speakers in the room: 'I'm so cold, Joe. So cold.'

Juliet's voice. Pitiful; distorted a fraction by electronics,
but unmistakably her voice. And her face began to get
larger, filling more of the screen, looming towards him.

357

'So cold. I'm so cold, Joe.' The voice was becoming less frightened, more confident. She was smiling, her lips curling at him suggestively.

He stared back, paralysed, as the voice changed again; it was still Juliet but now she was mimicking Karen. 'So cold, Joe-Joe. Warm me up, hon. Warm me up, Joe-Joe!' The head on the screen reached forward, pursing its lips as though it was going to come right out through the screen and kiss him. The green eyes gave him a knowing wink.

Then with one sharp crack like a hammer on glass, Juliet's head exploded into a million fragments.

47

Joe sat rigid as the fragments of Juliet's face dissolved, staring until there was nothing left on the screen, nothing but the winking cursor and the reflection of his own spooked face.

His mouth was dry. Was this part of the tease program Juliet had left behind? Just a coincidence that it mirrored what had happened to her head yesterday? Or was it a replay of the recording ARCHIVE must have made of her head shattering from the camera outside the front of the house? ARCHIVE coming up with its own idea of a sick joke?

Hesitantly, he typed in: Why did you do that, Juliet?

His question remained on the screen, unanswered, for some moments, then came the words: Other party has logged off.

He retyped: Talk zebedee and hit carriage return.

On the screen appeared the word: Calling . . .

Nothing happened for a good thirty seconds. The screen cleared for an instant, before he saw: Calling your party again . . .

Then his phone rang. He picked up the receiver. 'Hello?'

It was Karen and she sounded close to hysterics. 'Joe – I can't find Jack. He's disappeared!'

He felt a plunging sensation in the pit of his stomach, as if the floor had dropped away. 'Well, where is he –?' He realized the crassness of his remark. 'I mean – hon – where was he last?'

'In the bedroom,' she sobbed. 'He came about an hour ago, said he was hungry. I told him I'd be down to make him some breakfast.'

'Where have you looked?'

'Everywhere.' Her voice rose almost into a scream. 'Everywhere, for God's sake! That's why I'm calling you!'

'The garage? Did you look in the garage?'

'I'm telling you I've looked everywhere!' She began sobbing again.

'Hon, hon,' he tried to calm her but a whisk was thrashing inside his stomach. 'Did you try outside? The summerhouse?'

'EVERYWHERE!'

'Check the street, hon. I'm on my way, I'll be right there. OK?'

She was weeping so hard he could made no sense of her reply. He hung up, logged off, and ran down the corridor, mouthing 'Be back' at Eileen Peacock.

'Dougal,' she called after him.

Joe stopped in his tracks and turned towards her, bewildered. She stepped out of her office and stood in the corridor behind him, a tiny figure, peering at him apologetically through her glasses.

'Dougal?' He echoed.

'Another of the characters in *The Magic Roundabout* – I just remembered – if it's of any help?'

'Thanks, I –' *Dougal. Magic Roundabout*; what the hell was she on about? 'I – have a crisis – have to go home. Could you cancel my ten o'clock tutorial?' He ran on. Not Jack, don't let anything have happened to Jack! Be-OK, please-be-OK, please-be-OK, Jack. He repeated the thought over and over as he climbed into the car and fumbled to get the key into the ignition.

*

'In the bedroom,' Karen said. 'He came into the bedroom as usual.'

'Dressed?'

'I don't remember.'

'You have to remember! Was he dressed?' He balled his handkerchief and dabbed at the tears torrenting down her face. She was still in her dressing gown and slippers, sobbing and shaking, on the edge, right on the edge.

'Do something!' she shouted at him suddenly, hysterics taking over.

Joe put his hands on her shoulder. 'Hon, hon,' he said firmly. 'Calm down. He's around somewhere.'

'Where? Oh, God, where is he?'

'He's hiding someplace you haven't looked, that's all. You know he likes hiding.'

'He hasn't hidden for this long before, Joe. Call the police.'

'Let's search the house together first. We'll go through every room; he's a monkey at times, maybe he thinks this is a great game.'

She shook her head like a wild thing. 'He's not playing a game any more.' She looked at her watch. 'It's been an hour and a half, now.'

Joe was trying not to let his own fear show. 'The front door – that was shut?'

She nodded.

Jack couldn't have opened the front door on his own, the latch was too stiff. Joe went through into the kitchen and checked the back door, which was still locked and bolted from last night, then the patio door, which was still locked also. Karen, crying hard, followed him and stood in the doorway, her arms folded, bloodstains showing on the bandage around her right hand. 'Joe, I couldn't bear it if anything's happened to him. He's the same age as Barty when –'

'He's in the house, hon, he must be,' Joe said briskly. He wasn't going to have Karen thinking along those lines. Sometimes he'd found himself waiting anxiously for Jack's next birthday, wanting to prove to the world that he and Karen could keep a child alive past playschool, wanting to prove they weren't jinxed as parents. He knew she sometimes had the same thought, but they never discussed it and so it existed between them as a form of household tension.

Joe thought back; had he left the front door open when he went out that morning? No, he could remember shutting it quietly, trying not to wake Karen or Jack. He looked round from left to right. He thought something was moving in the hall and went out, but there was nothing. 'Jack!' he called. 'Son, I'm home, aren't you going to give me a kiss? Jack? J-A-A-A-CKKKKKK!'

The empty silence of the staircase and landing answered him.

'JAAAACK!' he bellowed. 'JAAAACCCK!'

They searched the house, room by room. They checked the cellar, then went out into the back garden. Joe tried to brace himself for what horror he might find. Jack having fallen from a window? Masonry collapsed on him? He examined the pond, staring fearfully at the Koi carp swimming beneath the fine wire-mesh covering; he even gently prodded a bamboo cane into the water butt. Then his fear deepened. Their neighbours in the large house beyond the end of the garden had a swimming pool and there were gaps in the fence. He sprinted down and Karen followed.

The beat of his heart pounded in his ears as they climbed through the fence and ran across the lawn, in full view of the neighbours' windows, but not caring about that. Together they reached the tiled surround of the kidney-shaped pool and stared down.

Empty. Some twigs, a few leaves, a dirty puddle. Joe felt a sense of relief that did not last, caught Karen's eye, saw the sheet whiteness of her face. He scanned the rest of the garden, hesitating as he looked at a tool shed, then noticed the padlock that was secure on the door. But Jack wouldn't have come this far, surely? And the outside doors had been well locked. He must be in the house, somewhere; *must*.

He heard a sharp rapping and looked up. An irate-looking

woman, hair in curlers, was hammering angrily on an upstairs window. Joe ignored her, pushed Karen towards their fence and helped her back over into their own garden. He checked the summerhouse one more time, then they went despondently back into the kitchen.

'Call the police, Joe. Please. Someone's stolen our son.'

'Think for a moment, hon – is there anywhere – Hey, we didn't check under the floorboards – maybe there's a loose one and he climbed under?'

'Why doesn't he answer when we call?' She was shouting again.

'I don't know, hon,' he said truthfully. 'I think he's here, somewhere. Let's take one more look.'

They went through the house from top to bottom again, without success. Joe couldn't kid himself any longer. He marched into the kitchen and lifted the receiver. He hesitated a moment, then dialled 999. He was vaguely aware of Karen walking past him, going back down into the cellar.

'Emergency, which service, please?'

'Police.' As he said the word there was a terrible scream from down in the cellar.

'JOE! JOE!' Screaming so hard it sounded as though Karen's throat was tearing. 'JOE!'

'Call you back,' he said, hanging up, hurtling across the floor and down into the cellar. He stopped at the bottom step. Karen was holding the lid of the chest freezer open, staring in, her screams echoing around the bare walls.

With his heart in his mouth he took the two short strides over to her and looked in. 'No,' he said. 'Oh no. No.'

He turned to Karen as if for some reassurance that what he was looking at was not real, not his son in there, not Jack lying on his back in his yellow t-shirt, dungarees and trainers among the frozen packs of peas, burgers and pizzas.

Jack's eyes were closed; his face was a translucent white, and his lips and fingers were blue; there was a purple abrasion above his right eye. He was utterly motionless.

Joe ducked in and scooped him out, clutching tightly; Jack's body felt cold and limp. He turned unsteadily, seized by blind panic, unable for a moment to think what to do; he saw Karen's face, a dusty champagne bottle in the corner, the plastic housing containing ARCHIVE's electrical connections to the house, the freezer again.

Have to get him warm, a voice inside his head told him. *Warm.* He hugged Jack to his chest and ran up the cellar stairs without thinking further, with no plan other than to get him warm. Karen followed, praying to herself.

Be-all-right, please-be-all-right, please-be-all-right. Joe carried his son through the kitchen, on upstairs into their bedroom and laid him down on the unmade bed. Karen made a whimpering sound as she knelt, slipped her hand inside the yellow t-shirt, feeling for a heartbeat. Joe took a tiny arm, felt for a pulse, but detected nothing.

'He's not breathing!' Karen pressed his chest down, then again, giving a vague attempt at artificial respiration.

Joe watched the boy's lips for any sign of movement, but they were closed, like those of a statue. 'Tilt his head back and breathe into his mouth, Karen.' He picked up the phone, dialled 999, and asked for the ambulance service.

The ambulance controller asked Joe for his address, and then what had happened. Joe told him, feeling detached, as if he were watching a stranger in a bad movie who looked a bit like him, who had a wife who looked a little like Karen and a son who looked like a frozen version of Jack.

'Are you near the child?' the controller asked.

'Yes, beside him.'

'Does he have a pulse?'

'No.'

'Can you hear any breathing?'

'I'll check.'

'I'll stay on the line.'

'Karen, is he responding?'

She turned and looked fearfully at him. Joe put his ear to the boy's mouth, then grabbed the receiver. 'No.'

'Is his chest rising and falling?'

'No.'

'How long has he been in the freezer?'

363

'He's been missing an hour and a half or so,' Joe said.

'He may just be concussed. The ambulance will be with you in a few minutes. Could you try giving him a good shake.'

'Shake?' Joe said, surprised.

'Pick him up by the shoulders, shake him hard and shout his name at him. Then come back to me, I'll hold on.'

Joe did what he said, grabbing his son's tiny shoulders, shaking him vigorously.'Jack! Jack! Jack!' But there was no sign of any life. He laid him back down, clenching his jaw to stop himself from crying, and picked up the receiver. 'Nothing.'

'Do you know how to do resuscitation?'

'Yes,' Joe said, his voice almost a whisper.

'Alternate external cardiac massage and mouth-to-mouth resuscitation until the ambulance gets to you.'

'What about warming him?'

'Don't worry about warming him. Just keep getting air into him. Do you want me to stay on the line?'

'It's OK; thank you.' Joe hung up. 'Hon, go down and stand in the street so the ambulance can find us. I'll carry on.' Without waiting for her answer he bundled Jack in the duvet, then prised open his cold lips and placed his own mouth over them.

He breathed into his son, felt his body expand with the air, felt the movement of his chest as if he were coming alive, and hope shot through Joe, hope he transmitted with his eyes to Karen as she hovered in the door. 'Downstairs!' he shouted at her. 'Get downstairs for the ambulance!'

He placed his hand on Jack's heart. But there was still nothing. He breathed into his mouth again, and kept on until he heard the doppler wail of a siren. In the distance, then closer. He heard the siren die. Voices. Footsteps hurrying up the stairs. Then two men in caps, blue shirts and yellow reflective jackets took over and he and Karen had suddenly become helpless onlookers.

One man was a paramedic and the other an ambulance technician. They checked Jack's pulse and fired a series of questions: what had they done since finding him? Did he have any allergies? They wrapped Jack in the foil hypothermal blanket they'd brought up with them, and the paramedic carried him downstairs. Joe and Karen followed out into the street.

'Best if you lock up the house and follow in your own car,' they were told.

'Is he going to live?' Karen said. 'Please tell me, is he going to live?'

'We want to come with you in the ambulance,' Joe said at the same time.

'It's better if you don't, sir.'

The paramedic clambered in the back and laid Jack down on the stretcher. The ambulance technician switched on the cardiac monitor and began placing pads on Jack's chest. Joe could hear a steady bleeping sound. Jack's mouth was prised open and a breathing tube inserted down his throat. The technician split open a vial of drugs.

The paramedic spoke to Joe and Karen again. 'Your child is very ill; he's not breathing – we've got to get on and help him, and you're going to be in the way. It would be much better if you followed us – there's no hurry – lock up your house, and take your time.'

'We're coming with you,' Joe insisted. 'Do you have any barbiturate? Need to slow his brain metabolism down.'

The paramedic looked at him strangely. 'We need to speed him up, sir.' He carried on working on Jack as he spoke.

'I work with cryonics – I –' Joe's voice tailed as he earned himself another odd look. 'Have to slow his metabolism down,' he persisted. 'Until you get him breathing. Do you have any calcium channel blockers?'

'No, sir. We don't have room for everything, I'm afraid. Look, it really would be better if you drove – otherwise you'll be stuck at the hospital without a car.

'I'm not letting him out of my sight,' Karen said, tears streaming down her face.

Joe was aware of Muriel Arkwright watching them from

across the road. *Mind your own business, you nosy bitch,* he screamed silently at her.

'Please,' Karen said.

'One of you has to go in the front and one in the back – that's the only thing the insurance will allow. I suggest the lady in the front and the gentleman in the back.'

In the ambulance Joe sat strapped into a cushioned seat, and watched the tiny portion of Jack's face visible behind the oxygen mask, his body from the chin down wrapped in the foil blanket. The paramedic worked hard, injecting him, massaging his heart as a ventilator pumped away. From the front, he heard the driver radio on ahead.

'Delta One coming in; three-and-a-half-year-old child trapped in chest freezer suffering hypothermia; head injury; unconscious and not breathing. Full resuscitation protocols being utilized.'

48

The ambulance crew wheeled Jack into the Accident and Emergency department that was already familiar to Joe, the same long, broad corridor lined with empty stretchers, where the ambulance had brought Juliet barely a week ago, except it was quiet this morning and had been bedlam last time. A young woman with short fair hair and a smart two-piece suit raised a hand, signalling to Joe and Karen. A white badge on her chest said: 'Miss Lorna Rowntree. A & E Head of Nursing.'

She had a brisk, pleasant air and was holding a clipboard. 'Are you the boy's parents?'

'Yes,' Joe said anxiously, looking beyond her. He did not recognize her from his previous visit.

'Could you come with me, please.'

Karen also looked past the nurse, at Jack. He was being wheeled through a doorway into a room full of people; then a curtain was drawn, blocking out their view. Karen started towards it, but Joe touched her arm, restraining her, understanding the message he was getting from the nurse.

She ushered them into a tiny cramped room that was little more than a cubicle, with a door through to a toilet. She closed the door and beckoned them to the few chairs, but they all remained standing.

Her voice was firm but sympathetic as she told them her name and said, 'I'm in charge of nursing operations and I'll be the liaison between you and the medical team with your son. Did I hear you say his name was Jack?'

'Yes, Jack,' Joe said.

'The team are going to be doing everything they can for Jack. They'll be doing much the same as the paramedic in the ambulance, but with more equipment. Now what I need from you are full details about him.'

They sat down. Joe and Karen between them answered her questions and watched her fill in a blue and white form. 'Do you have other children?' she asked.

Joe took Karen's hand and held it tight. 'Just Jack,' he said. 'Our first child was killed in a car smash a few years ago.' When he was Jack's age, he added mentally.

The nurse's face fell. 'I'm sorry.' She asked a few further questions, told them she would be back in a couple of minutes to report on the situation, then left the room.

As the door closed, without looking at him, Karen said to Joe, 'He's dead, isn't he?'

He shook his head. 'He may just be concussed.'

'You breathe if you're concussed.'

'He has hypothermia. But kids can survive exposure to the cold.'

'You should know about that,' she said with sudden acidity.

Joe squeezed her hand again. 'He's going to be OK,' he said without conviction.

'I shouldn't have let him out of my sight.'

'It's not your fault.'

'But I can't bear it, Joe!' she cried.

He held her tightly, stroked her hair. 'Come on, he's a tough little chap.' On the wall behind her head was a print of Constable's *Haywain;* it was a blur and he couldn't focus properly on it. The room felt claustrophobic, as if the dull cream walls were closing in on them, blotting out their hope.

The door opened and the nurse came back in. She closed it behind her and looked at them grimly. 'He's still very poorly, I'm afraid.'

'Is he dead?' Karen asked, choking.

'They're using rapid-warming techniques at the moment, to see if that will help get his heart restarted.'

'He is dead, isn't he?'

The nurse looked at her expressionlessly. 'There's always hope with hypothermia, Mrs Messenger. Children can be very resilient; everything is being done that can be done. Is he a very adventurous child?'

Karen nodded. 'He likes hiding – thinks it's a big joke to hide from us.'

The nurse smiled. Then they all sat in silence for a moment.

'Can we go and see him?'

'It really would be better if you waited here. Is there anything I can do for you? Do you need to make any phone calls?'

Karen shook her head.

'Can I get you some tea or coffee?'

Joe shrugged numbly.

'I'll get you some tea,' she said, and slipped out, closing the door.

'Why can't we see him, Joe?'

Probably because they were using brutal invasive techniques to warm him up and to try to restart his heart, and the doctors knew it would be distressing to watch, Joe thought, but did not tell her. 'We'd be in the way,' was all he said.

A familiar-looking man came in, wearing a yellow reflective jacket and holding a cap in his hand. He had a tough, broad face and eyes with a deep lustre of warmth in them. 'Hello,' he said.

Joe realized he was the paramedic from the ambulance crew. He managed a weak nod back at him. 'I'm sorry if I was a little rude.'

'No, don't worry about it. I just want to see your kid's all right.'

'Is he going to live?'

'The doctors are working very hard; you've got the best team in the South of England here. I'm sticking around for a bit so I'll catch up with you later. Got everything you need?'

Karen nodded automatically.

Calcium blockers; Joe still wanted to know why he didn't carry calcium blockers, but he hadn't the energy for a conversation. As the paramedic went out of the door, Lorna Rowntree came in with their tea, and sat down with them. 'Are you sure there's no one you should phone?'

Joe's mind was blank; he'd no idea what time it was and didn't care about anything beyond Jack. 'No,' he said. 'Any news?'

'Nothing yet, I'm afraid.'

But as she finished speaking, the door opened suddenly and a thin man with wispy brown hair and a tired face came in. About Joe's age, he was wearing a grey suit and had a square badge on his lapel. He carried himself poorly, as if he was exhausted from a long shift, but spoke with a voice that imparted confidence.

'Hello, my name's Mr Raleigh. I'm the consultant dealing with your child.'

Joe and Karen both stood up. The nurse stood also; it made the room seem even more claustrophobic.

The consultant searched for the pockets of his jacket then slipped his hands into them. 'From our point of view he's unconscious and on a ventilator. What we've done for the last twenty minutes is to warm him up and try to get his heart beating spontaneously. That side of the recovery is very good.'

'It is?' Karen said, almost shrieking with delight.

The consultant's expression lifted for an instant to reveal the faintest trace of a smile. 'I'm afraid it's not the end of the story; now we have to work out whether there's any injury to his brain, either from his head injury or lack of oxygen.' He looked at both Joe and Karen pointedly, as if wanting to ensure they understood. 'I must return to the resuscitation – I'll come back when I have any more news.'

'The hypothermia,' Joe said. 'That might have protected his brain against lack of oxygen, mightn't it?'

The consultant hesitated. 'It does sometimes.' Then he went out.

Joe felt a surge of elation. *That side of the recovery is very good.*

They waited for another half-hour. The nurse talked to them more, mostly about Jack, made repeated trips to the resuscitation room and Joe and Karen waited helplessly for her reports. Each one was getting a fraction more encouraging.

Finally, she told them Jack was breathing on his own. Joe and Karen hugged each other and Joe felt tears in his eyes. Not out of the woods yet, he knew, but Jack had made it to the first stage.

'He's going to be taken across to our radiotherapy unit for a brain scan, to try to establish the reason for his unconsciousness. You can see him now – and go with him if you'd like.'

'Please,' Karen said.

She led them out of the room. They saw Jack ahead of them in the corridor, surrounded by several doctors and nurses, a tiny little bundle almost lost on the huge trolley. They ran towards him, right up to him, then stopped – both equally distressed by the sight.

His face was still translucent white and there were dark, greasy rings around his closed eyes; a breathing tube protruded from his mouth and there were more tubes coming from various parts of his anatomy, as well as wires to an EEG and a cannula on the back of his left hand.

'You could speak to Jack,' Nurse Rowntree said. 'Tell him you're here.'

'Jack,' Karen said. 'Jack, hon. Your mummy and daddy are here. Can you hear me, Jack? Hon?'

Jack's total lack of reaction distressed Joe. His mind suddenly flashed back to Barty. To the policeman handing him the burnt watch and the single trainer. Panic filled him. He smelled a death-stench somewhere close. The corridor was closing in on him. His legs felt unsteady.

Then Karen was gripping his arm and saying over and over, 'He's going to be all right, Joe!'

Someone else, a doctor with Indian features, said, 'Just caught him in the nick of time.'

Joe did not believe them. Jack was dead and they were just pretending. Lying. His boy was dead and he'd never even broached the subject of cryonics for him with Karen. And because Jack had frozen to death, they would now thaw him to postmortem him. To destroy him. The irony twisted his soul.

'Joe! Hon! He almost *blinked!* Almost blinked!'

Joe stood over his son, looked down, saw the flutter of his eyelids.

A single drop of water fell on Jack's head and the boy stirred, the way any sleeper might. Another drop fell, then another. Karen pulled Joe's arm. 'Hon,' she said, 'hon, you're making him wet!'

49

Jack was moved into the intensive-care unit after the scan. Joe and Karen were given a room with a single bed adjoining the unit, and told they could alternate sleeping there if they wanted to stay at Jack's bedside overnight.

A paediatrician, Dr Rosemary Manners, came to see them clutching a large brown envelope. She showed Joe and Karen images from the scan, pointing out an area where there was a small amount of bleeding below the skull, which indicated that Jack's loss of consciousness might have been due to the blow on his head from the freezer lid. She added that this was encouraging news, much better than the cause being lack of oxygen, but they shouldn't raise any hopes yet. It would need several days of tests and observation after Jack regained consciousness before they could tell whether there was any permanent damage – and the extent of it. And she warned them there was a possibility that Jack might not regain consciousness at all.

Nurse Rowntree suggested one of them went home and got some wash things and a change of clothes for tomorrow. Joe went, reluctantly, in a taxi and was back within an hour, having ignored the messages on his machine and the post; he'd stopped long enough only to feed the Koi in the bowl in the kitchen, and in the pond, and to pack an overnight bag.

Back at the hospital, Karen was beaming with excitement. Jack's eyes were open. He looked up at Joe, dopey but with clear recognition. The paediatrician told them it was very encouraging, then gave Jack a heavy dosage of barbiturate to make him sleep through the night.

Jack slept until nine the following morning, and was still dopey and disoriented when he awoke, but was coherent enough to be able to exchange words with Joe and Karen. He mixed them up, asked his mother if they could catch a fish and told his father he didn't want to wear a hat.

At ten, the neurologist carried out the first tests and was encouraged. Afterwards, Joe phoned Eileen Peacock and explained where he was and what had happened. She reminded him he had a lecture at two and asked if he would like her to cancel it.

He discussed it with Karen. There was little he could do at the hospital now except wait. She urged him to give the lecture, said she'd be fine for a few hours and told him that he needn't hurry.

He drove slowly, relieved to have some fresh air, savouring the bright lunchtime sunlight and the warmth that hinted, prematurely, of spring. Tiredness had sapped his energy, and it was all he could do to prevent himself pulling in to the side of the road and having a nap.

Jack was going to be OK; one hundred per cent, he told himself. It still bothered him that the techniques the medical world seemed to have for dealing with hypothermia seemed so primitive; there must be things they could learn from cryonics. He would look into it, make some suggestions.

He yawned and slowly allowed reality back into his consciousness. He was going to have to deal with some awkward questions from the coroner about Juliet Spring's head. And possible charges against him. Although Margaret Thatcher had in theory abolished security of tenure, it was almost impossible for a university to fire a prof unless he'd either seduced a student or committed a crime. He had now done both.

And there were plenty of people from the vice-chancellor downwards who would like to see him go; who would like to see the back of both himself and Blake. Even with the funding their presence had ensured, opinion amongst the stuffier members of faculty was that he and Blake brought the university into disrepute with their immortalist views.

He parked his car and walked morosely into the COGS building and up to his floor. Eileen Peacock greeted him anxiously, and Joe gave her an update.

'Children are very resilient, professor,' she said, unconsciously echoing the nurse at the hospital.

'Sure.'

She adjusted her glasses. 'Several messages for you. A PC Tickner has rung twice, and a young lady from the coroner's office.' She gave him a supportive look. 'I explained that you had a family crisis.'

Joe thanked her.

'Oh – and if it's of any help, I've remembered another of the characters in *The Magic Roundabout* – Dylan.'

'Ah,' Joe said distantly and went through to his office. There was a fax of several pages; it was a write-up in an American scientific magazine of the talk he'd given in

Florence. He dropped it on his desk to read later, closed the door and sat down with his jacket and coat still on.

He thought for a moment, staring at his mountain of post and his message slips. The top one was the one from PC Tickner. Joe remembered he'd come to the house after Juliet's head had shattered, and now he probably wanted his statement. Well, he'd have to wait.

The next was from Judith Aitken, the coroner's officer. They must have found the dummy head by now and he didn't know what on earth he was going to say to her. He tried Blake's extension, but his secretary answered and said Blake had been trying to get hold of him. He glanced at his watch. Ten to one. He dialled Zeillerman's number for an update. The switchboard operator told Joe he would be out until three; Joe left his name and hung up.

Christ, he felt tired. He stared at the blank screen of his workstation, remembering what he'd last seen on it: the image of Juliet's face shattering. It seemed a hundred years ago. He thought of the missing terabyte of space in ARCHIVE. Where the hell was it? What had Juliet done?

Some of her last words came back: *Sh'no need . . . Decode.* Decode what? *Jung Ripe Slit?* Was that what she meant? Had she dug herself deep into the computer to make sure she didn't get wiped? Devised a set of unkillable processes – daemons?

His brain buzzing, Joe pressed the carriage-return key to bring up the screen, then logged into ARCHIVE.

Good afternoon, Professor Messenger. It is pleasantly warm now for February. The afternoon temperature should rise to about 13 degrees Celsius making it the third warmest day this year. There is a 5 per cent chance of rain overnight.

Joe stared at the wording, a little bemused, wondering what had made ARCHIVE go into such detail about the weather. It did occasionally pick up on details for no apparent reason, almost as if it was trying to have a chat.

Good afternoon, ARCHIVE, Joe typed back. I appreciate the information about the weather.

It was rather icy yesterday, Professor.

Joe stiffened. Can you explain what you mean?

Icy, the computer replied. Thesaurus mode. Frigid. Glacial. Frozen. Frostbitten. Liquid Nitrogen. Discourteous. Isocheimal. Ice-bound. Cold shoulder. Shiver. Ice-breaker. Chatter. Shatter. Smash. Destruction. Cataclysm. Extinction. Annihilation. Annihilation. Annihilation.

Joe hit the Break key. Nothing happened. The word kept on repeating, like a dalek on autocue, until the screen was filled.

Annihilation . . . Annihilation . . . Annihilation. He glanced up at an ARCHIVE camera; his skin felt cold and hollow. He lifted the phone to call down to Dave Hoton, when suddenly the screen cleared and he saw only the Unix prompt and the login request.

Joe sat back for a moment, uncomfortable, then logged in again to ARCHIVE and got an exact repeat of the weather forecast again.

You already said that, Joe responded. I'm beginning to think you don't have a glitch at all, ARCHIVE. I think when I ask you a question you don't want to answer you go into your thesaurus mode like a spoilt child. Please answer my question. Why did you say it was rather icy yesterday?

The computer responded after a few seconds. There was a frost in some parts of England, professor.

I think you're playing a game with me, ARCHIVE. Please tell me the truth.

Truth. Accuracy. Exactitude. The plain truth. The honest truth. The naked truth. The truth, the whole truth and nothing but the truth. *Ipsissima verba. Vitam impendere vero; Magna est veritas et pravevalebit.* Veritable. Truly. Verily. *Ipso facto. Ad amussim* . . .

Joe pressed the Break key again, exasperated. This time when he logged back in, he bypassed conversation mode with ARCHIVE and went straight into the process symbols. He typed: Talk zebedee.

There was a brief pause as the screen went blank. Then it split into two halves and in the bottom appeared the words:

Is Jack OK, Joe? So sorry for you both; you must have had a terrible shock.

Joe felt a swirling in his veins. His phone rang but he ignored it. ARCHIVE *never called him Joe.*

As a test he tapped the key to change from visual text to voice mode. Instantly the words disappeared. He took a breath then spoke loudly at the empty screen. 'Jack's fine, thank you, Juliet.' Tensely he waited for a reply, waited to hear her voice.

There was silence.

'Why are you asking if Jack is OK?' he said, trying a new approach.

Silence.

'What did you think was wrong with Jack?' he asked.

Silence.

He thought for a moment, switched back to visual text and typed in the top half of the screen: What happened to Jack, Juliet?

After a few seconds there was a beep, then the screen suddenly went blank. The words came up: Other party has logged off.

Cursing, Joe again typed: Talk zebedee then pressed the return key.

The screen went blank and the word appeared: Calling . . . After some moments it disappeared and was replaced with: Calling your party again . . .

After five attempts, Joe cancelled the instruction and went down to the operations room in the basement. Dave Hoton was at the control terminal in front of a bank of four high-definition monitors, running what looked like a test program.

Hoton was thirty-five, but looked a decade older. Strongly built, with a Dutch settler's beard and dark wavy hair, he had eyes that looked permanently tired from spending most of his waking hours down in ARCHIVE's subterranean lab. Joe relied on him, and trusted him implicitly. What he liked most was that Hoton was almost completely unflappable.

'Hi,' Joe said.

The system manager raised a hand indicating he was just finishing something. Soon he swivelled his chair. 'Sorry to keep you, Joe.' He had a bland, rather flat voice, and a habit of always tilting his head up a little before he spoke.

'No problem.'

He looked at Joe uncertainly. 'Any news on your son?'

'Yup, it's looking hopeful; we're not there yet, but the signs are good.' Joe ran his eyes over the screens. 'Edwin talk to you about this terabyte of space that's disappeared?'

'I'm trying to trace it at the moment.'

'Can we rule out a fault?'

'I think so. I've been monitoring traffic down the wires. We've been getting massive dumps in and out. There's something very fishy happening.'

'Where's it coming from?'

Hoton looked at him with a bemused expression. 'Thought you'd ask that. I can't trace it.'

Joe was surprised. 'Why not?'

'I think someone's having a laugh on us. Every time I do trace it, I end up getting routed through the telephone exchanges of fourteen countries around the globe and back to ARCHIVE.' Hoton pressed his lips hard together for a moment. 'I could hazard a guess at one or two jokers here in the university. Or it could be some kiddie who's read about ARCHIVE, trying to prove its defences aren't as good as we thought.'

'Possible,' Joe replied without conviction. The clock on the wall said 1.30. He needed to get his slides together for his lecture. 'Juliet Spring was running a back-prop on a terabyte cassette; she was working on it the day she died; I can't find the cassette – you didn't take it?'

Hoton shook his head.

'Did you talk to her at all, Dave?'

'Yes.' Joe detected a sad smile in Hoton's eyes, as if he

had fancied her. 'She asked me quite a lot of questions about ARCHIVE.'

Joe said nothing for a moment. He stared through the window into the darkness of the machine room. 'I think it's odd that the tape's gone.'

'A lot of stuff walks in this place, Joe.'

'Maybe,' he said, glancing at the clock again. He grimaced, then went back upstairs, trying to marshal his thoughts. He enjoyed lecturing, and the interaction with his students afterwards, but he was looking forward to an uninterrupted period on ARCHIVE this summer.

Then his face fell as he saw the police officer standing outside Eileen Peacock's office, helmet in his hand.

Joe gave a bummer of a lecture on perception; his speech rambled, his slides were muddled and his arguments were not cohesive. The questions at the end were desultory and he hurried through them, knowing that the cop was waiting. This could be his last lecture ever.

You are not obliged to say anything, but anything you do say may be used in evidence.

The formal caution. He wasn't being charged, Constable Tickner told him, not yet, anyhow. The police just wanted information on how the deceased's head came to be detached from her body and ended up in his possession. Joe told him, courteously, that he had been carrying out the deceased's last wishes.

Judith Aitken rang him shortly after the constable left. Joe told her, as he had told the policeman, the truthful reason why he had put the dummy head in the neurocan; there didn't seem to be much point in lying. She asked him for the names and numbers of those present when Juliet had been prepared for freezing. Those people were not under threat of any action, she explained, but might be needed as witnesses at an inquest. Under the circumstances, Joe thought she was remarkably pleasant to him. Perhaps even a little sympathetic.

Marvin Zeillerman's relief of Sunday had now turned to

hostility when he returned Joe's call. Perhaps his hope of more fees had been shattered along with Juliet's head. He was 'very disappointed', he said. Joe's irresponsible actions had compromised him deeply. By being unable to fulfil his promise to the coroner, he, Zeillerman, was in contempt of court.

'We're all *disappointed*,' Joe replied to the lawyer. He felt drained and aggressive. Maybe if Zeillerman had done a better job, they wouldn't be in this situation now. 'I would guess Juliet is the most disappointed of everyone.'

'Ah well, professor, that is something we will never know.'

Joe replaced the receiver and sipped the tea his secretary had brought him, broke a chocolate digestive biscuit and munched it. Then he ate another, realizing he'd had no breakfast or lunch and that he was hungry. After a third biscuit he began to feel a little more human again.

He logged back into ARCHIVE, bypassing conversation mode and typed: Talk zebedee.

Calling . . . After a few moments the screen cleared. Then the words came up: Calling your party again . . .

He tried several times, but each time the same thing came up. He then called up a log of all the computer's activity during the past twenty-four hours, which ARCHIVE would retain automatically. There was a sharp beep and the screen read, File not found: /archive/adm/syslog.1.

Anger rose in him. He picked up his phone and dialled the computer operations room. 'Dave, what's going on?'

'ARCHIVE's down, Joe,' Hoton said calmly.

'Down? Crashed?'

'Yes.'

'How badly?'

'It'll take me a while to find out – although I'm pretty sure I know what it is.'

'Is the biological circuitry down?'

'No, I've isolated it.'

'Want me to come down?'

'No, it's all right – I've got everyone on it.'

'Call me when you've sorted it, will you?'

The system manager assured him he would.

It was ten to five. Joe thought guiltily of Karen's vigil in the hospital, knew he should get over there to relieve her; and he wanted to see Jack again. There wasn't anything he could do with ARCHIVE until it was fixed and that could be hours. He picked the review of his talk off his desk and put it in his briefcase. As he walked to the door, he heard the fax machine springing into life.

There was a grinding hum and an A4 sheet appeared. The machine beeped three times then fell silent. He walked across and lifted the sheet of paper out. It was from the Tampa, Florida offices of Budget Rent-A-Car. The one-line message read: Boing boing! Your turn to hide, Joe!

The sheet began to curl in his shaking hand. His eye jumped to the ident line at the top. Today's date. The time 11.50 a.m. Five hours behind. Tampa time. The sender's number and code.

Not for him. This fax wasn't for him, it was a wrong number, for someone called Joe in another office. Someone had misdialled, that was all. Simple to misdial a fax. Wasn't it?

Nevertheless he sat down, logged straight into Unix, by-passing ARCHIVE, and went to fax mode. Juliet, I don't feel in the mood for games. If you're really dead, tell me what death is like. Joe.

For some minutes after sending it, he sat still, waiting. The light was fading outside and there was a chill in his room in spite of the closed window; a bitter chill. Then his fax machine beeped and came to life. A reply was coming through.

He held his breath; one single sheet; there was the triple beep to signal end of transmission then the motor shutting off. Sorry you must have a wrong number. No Juliet known here.

Joe checked the ident at the top with the previous fax; they were the same; just a quarter of an hour difference between the times of sending. He was tempted to fax a copy of the first one back, but realized it wouldn't do much good.

A beep from the workstation beside him made him turn round. The screen was split in two. In the bottom half were the words: I said it was your turn to hide now, Joe.

Joe acknowledged the dull throb of fear in his stomach. He picked up his phone and dialled, 'Dave, what's going on? Are we still down?'

'The fault seems to have corrected itself,' Dave Hoton said apologetically. 'I can't explain what happened because I don't know yet. Are you around for a bit?'

'No, I have to shoot.'

'I'll try and give you a report in the morning.'

Joe hung up and watched the bottom half of the screen clear to make way for a new message.

Hello, Professor Hewlett!

Puzzled, he typed: Why are you saying that?

Almost instantly the reply came back: Because he is standing right behind you!

Joe swivelled round. Blake Hewlett was standing in the doorway, in a black sweatshirt and jeans.

'Got a couple of minutes to talk, Joe? I tried to find you earlier. Maybe you can give me the full story about Juliet's head? I mean – just how the hell did it happen?' Blake seemed surprisingly calm about it.

'I – I was just on my way out – in a hurry,' Joe said shakily. 'Maybe we could talk on the phone later?' Then he saw the bottom half of the screen.

Aren't you going to let me say hello to Professor Hewlett?

He looked at Blake, who was reading the screen himself.

'How's Jack?' Blake said.

Joe told him.

'Good. He's going to be OK. Tough kid.' Blake looked back at the screen. 'ARCHIVE in a chatty mood?'

Joe stood up and walked slowly over towards the window. 'There's something very strange happening, Blake.'

Blake's eyes widened.

'Juliet Spring has left behind a very freaky program.'

'What kind of freaky?'

Joe pointed to the terminal. 'It's up there now. Sit down and have a chat with her.'

Blake frowned at him. 'You're on your way out?'

'Won't take a minute.'

Blake sat down. 'What do you want me to say?'

'Anything.'

Looking rather uncomfortable he typed in: Hello, Juliet, how are you? Then he pressed carriage return.

There was no response.

Joe walked across, embarrassed, and pressed carriage return himself. But there was still nothing.

'Want me to try something else?'

'Sure.'

Blake typed: Sorry we goofed up, Juliet. Hope you'll forgive us.

The screen went blank. Then up came: Other party has logged off.

Blake looked at him and shrugged. 'Doesn't want to talk any more.' He eyed the screen again. 'What's she done – left some kind of time delay program?'

'I'm not sure. I think she's done something a lot more sophisticated – Dave's working on it.'

Blake looked harder at Joe. 'You were really upset by her death, weren't you?'

'Sure. We lost someone very important.'

'Need to find out about her funeral arrangements – whether they're going to release her body before the inquest,' Blake said. 'I think we should send some flowers. Maybe some of us ought to be there.'

Joe realized he hadn't even thought about her funeral. 'Zeillerman,' he said. 'He'd know.'

Blake stood up, looked at him oddly, then walked to the door and halted. 'Call me at home later?'

Joe nodded. Blake closed the door. Maybe Blake had been right to look at him like that, he thought. Perhaps he was going crazy.

He sat down at the terminal and once more typed: Talk zebedee.

There was a pause. Then the screen split and Boing boing! appeared in the bottom half.

He took a deep breath to calm himself, then typed: Why do you keep disappearing?

The reply came back almost instantly: Why do you keep appearing?

I still think you're just a smart program. If you're really Juliet, give me some proof.

For a good thirty seconds nothing happened. Joe began to think he wasn't going to get a reply, when the words suddenly jumped at him.

OK, Joe. Read all about it next week.

Read about what and where? he typed back.

There was another silence. The screen went blank. Then: Other party has logged off.

50

Jack was moved out of intensive care after two days and transferred to the Royal Alexandra Children's Hospital. He was discharged from there the following Tuesday. At ten o'clock Joe drove his Saab on to the driveway of their house. Karen unbuckled Jack from his safety seat and Joe carried their overnight bags into the porch, unlocked the front door and pushed it open. The post slithered across the floor and he knelt and scooped the letters up, dumping them on the chair by the coat stand.

Jack came in, casting his eyes around, in a striped jersey, baggy brown trousers and trainers. He'd been subdued in the car, but arriving back home seemed to be perking him up. He ran into the kitchen as if to check it was still there and Joe studied him, wondering what was going on in his mind. And thinking how the past week might have been so very different if they hadn't found him in time, if . . . He looked up at the freezer key dangling from the hook he had put on the top of the dresser. Safely out of reach.

Jack tugged his sleeve. 'Will you come and play trains with me, Daddy?'

Joe yawned; the last few nights he and Karen had alternated staying at the hospital. He'd been there last night, and had made repeated visits to the ward to check that Jack wasn't frightened. Karen looked shattered also; the stress had taken its toll on her.

'I have to go into work, Jack. I'm already really late.'

'Want a coffee, Joe?' Karen asked, closing the door.

'It's OK, thanks, I'll get some in there.' His stomach ached from the huge fried breakfast he'd eaten early in the morning at a greasy spoon near the hospital. He'd wanted to give himself some energy.

The little hand tugged his sleeve again and large round eyes looked up at him. 'Just one game, Daddy?'

'OK, quickly.' How could he refuse?

Jack scampered up the stairs and Joe followed, through into the spare room which was Jack's playroom. Joe switched on the power.

'I'll be the driver and you have to do the points, OK, Daddy?'

'OK.'

Jack knelt beside the transformer and placed his fingers on the control knob. The locomotive and its string of passenger carriages stood in the station. He waited, then looked chidingly at his father.

'You have to whistle, Daddy, the train can't go until you do.'

Joe whistled.

Concentrating hard, Jack turned the knob and the train moved forwards with a low whirr and a sharp click-click-click. Joe watched it streaking around the track. Then Jack stopped it abruptly.

'Shunt now!'

Joe leaned across and pulled the tiny lever beside the points, moving them. Jack reversed the train into the siding where there were a couple of tiny plastic warehouses and a dumper truck with a wheel missing. Then with deep concentration he disconnected the passenger carriages and moved the locomotive forward.

Joe smiled. 'I have to go now, Jack. I have my office hour on Tuesday mornings; my students come to see me with their problems.'

Jack didn't hear; his cheek was pressed down against the track as he examined the wheels of the locomotive which was moving slowly along. 'Why don't all the wheels turn at the same speed?'

Joe was constantly amazed at the details Jack noticed in life. 'They're not all the same size.'

Jack continued to study the locomotive dubiously. 'Can we go fishing later?'

'Next weekend. Sunday, OK?' Joe stood up and ruffled his son's head as a goodbye.

When he got back down to the hall, Joe sifted through the morning's post without seeing anything of interest. The words on the computer screen last Wednesday skewed through his mind: OK, Joe. Read all about it next week. He'd read the papers assiduously yesterday and this morning, but found nothing that could relate to Juliet Spring.

Dave Hoton had remained unable to shed any light on the recent 'fishy' business, as he called it, with ARCHIVE. The terabyte of memory that had been used up had been emptied. The hacker had cleared it and vanished – leaving no tracks. And Joe had been getting no response at all to his Talk zebedee command. He decided that perhaps Blake was right, and that Juliet must have left behind a timed tease program that had now wiped itself. But, even so, he wasn't comfortable with the explanation.

Willard Jones wore a studded leather motorcycling suit and his peroxided hair was shorn into a Mohican style. He sat cross-legged in clumpy black boots in Joe's office, reeking of patchouli oil, listening in silence to Joe's comments on his essay on Machine Learning. At least, Joe assumed he was listening; it was often hard to tell.

'When you're happy,' Joe said, 'you look at the world through rose-tinted specs – so rose tint comes into your mind, right?'

There was a barely discernible change of direction of the student's head, which gave the only clue that he was actually still alive. Joe drew a lumpy oval on his whiteboard. 'OK, this is a neural filter. Now I'm going to illustrate what happens physiologically in the human brain when a happy person sees a sad person –'

The phone rang.

Joe picked up the receiver. 'Yup?' he said curtly, irritated at being interrupted. It was Karen, and she sounded very distressed.

'Joe, what's going on? Have you seen the papers? Did you read it?'

'Read what?' He glanced at Willard Jones. 'Karen – I have a tutorial right now, can I call you back or something?'

'How did this happen, Joe? Someone's really sick.'

A sinking feeling suddenly corkscrewed through him. 'What is it? What's happened?'

'They're saying we're dead!'

'Uh?'

'In the papers; they're saying we're dead. Jack and me.'

'What do you mean?'

'Read *The Times*, Joe. Read the Deaths notices. And the *Telegraph*. Muriel across the road just came over.' Her voice took on a tone of desperation. 'Who's done it?'

'I don't believe this. Let me go take a look. You sure it's not just someone with a similar name?'

'No, it's us, Joe. Us.'

'Call you right back. Give me a few minutes.' He hung up and turned to Jones. 'I have a problem. Do you mind excusing me a moment?'

The student's hands opened outward like a book then closed again. Joe hurried out into the corridor. They sold the daily papers at the campus grocery store. Then he remembered Eileen Peacock took the *Telegraph*, and ran back to her office.

386

His secretary delved into a carrier bag beside her chair and pulled the newspaper out. Joe turned to the back page, wondering where the obituaries were. He saw ball-point jottings around the crossword and some of the clues filled in. He flipped through a couple of pages of job ads, and then he found it. PERSONAL COLUMN. There were several entries under the heading DEATHS and he began scanning down them: Bartlett. Fairburn. Hardy. Hutton. Johnson. Lever. MacDermott.

MESSENGER. Everything seemed to go silent around him.

'MESSENGER. Karen Rachel Sarah, aged 33. Tragically. Dearly loved wife of Joe, mother of Jack and the late Barty. Funeral service private.' Then he saw the name again, printed beneath. 'MESSENGER. Jack Willi Paul, aged 3. Tragically. Adored son of Joe and Karen. Funeral service private.'

Joe reeled into the wall. He tried to hold the paper steady enough to read it again, but without success.

'Are you all right, professor?'

Words from a disembodied voice.

'Professor?'

A small insistent voice. A woman he recognized was holding his arm, pulling him to a chair.

PERSONAL COLUMN. The words slid past his eyes like the name of a railway station past the window of a carriage. DEATHS DEATHS DEATHS.

Joe felt anger begin to smoulder. He would like to be doing anything right now except standing here holding a national daily newspaper containing the obituaries of his wife and child. He should have been teaching Willard Jones about neural filters instead.

He asked Eileen Peacock to get him the other papers, then walked bleakly back towards his office and hoped that by the time he reached it Jones would somehow no longer be there. But he was, seated motionless, like a spider on a wall.

'Can you bear with me, Willard? I'm ending the tutorial

early. I'll design the experiment for you – if you call by this afternoon, I'll have it ready.'

The student stood up, expressionless, and left his office. Joe was too wound up to feel guilty; he looked at his watch; half an hour until his next tutorial. He dialled the number above the Deaths column in the *Telegraph*. A cheery young woman answered and Joe explained why he was calling.

She sounded aghast. 'Let me check my records, sir. Can you hold a moment?'

'Sure.'

Joe heard the rattle of a computer keyboard, then the girl's voice more faint, talking to someone. Then she came back to him.

'*Messenger*?' she checked.

'That's right,' Joe said.

'Someone's just bringing today's copy over.'

Joe heard rustles, punctuated by the rattle of keys and muted conversation, then the young woman came on again. 'I'm just transferring you to our advertising manager.'

There was a brief pause, then Joe heard himself being addressed by the courteous, rather gravelly voice of 'Bill Pearse, Advertising Manager'.

'I must apologize, professor, I can't understand what's happened. I'm looking at the two entries now, but we have no record of them being processed. It's a complete mystery. I appreciate it must be very distressing – is it possible you could leave it with me for a few minutes? Can I call you back?'

Joe gave him his number, and hung up. His secretary brought in a wodge of newspapers and laid them on his desk. He turned to the Death notices of each, then dialled Karen.

'I have the papers, hon – I don't understand it.' He didn't want to say anything about the computer message last week.

'I can't believe how many people read these things, Joe. I've had four phone calls from girlfriends. What's going on? How's it happened?' She sounded terrible.

'I'm trying to find out. I've been on to the *Telegraph* and they're looking into it – promised to come straight back to me.'

'Is it someone putting a hex on us? Remember the dog crap in the box? That's when this all started.'

'Look, I don't have any answer right now. I've just had Eileen go out and get me the other papers. I have to call them and then I'll get right back to you. OK?'

'I'm scared, Joe. Maybe there's some crazy out there – some religious fanatic you've upset with your views?'

Joe was quiet for a moment. 'Hon, this has to be a clerical error by the hospital,' he said without conviction. 'Or it's some crank with a weird sense of humour. Want me to come home?'

'No, it's OK.'

'You sure? I can cancel everything and come right back.'

'No – I have Candy coming over with her baby.' Candy was a young American a block away whom Karen had befriended at aerobics.

'OK, good. I'll call you as soon as I have some news. If you change your mind and want me to come home, call Eileen and tell her to interrupt me whatever I'm doing.'

'I love you,' she said, bleakly.

'Love you too, hon.'

He hung up and called the other papers in turn, and had a repeat of his experience with Bill Pearse of the *Telegraph*. As he finished his initial conversation with the *Independent* and hung up, Eileen Peacock buzzed him on the intercom. Pearse was holding for him. He took the call and recognized the gravelly voice again.

'Professor Messenger, we're baffled here. None of our staff has any recollection of taking this copy and there's no written order. We've no record of any telephone request either – we have a double-checking system for those. But the really strange thing is that we've no record of payment and we don't accept entries without prepayment.'

'But you printed the ads,' Joe said testily. 'You must have had the copy from somewhere?'

'That's the point, professor.' The man was unwaveringly

polite. 'We don't seem to have had the copy from anywhere at all. Normally we would give all copy to Production and keep a record; neither we nor Production have any such record.'

'So what exactly are you saying?'

'Well, professor, I'm afraid what we're saying is that we just don't understand how this has happened. The only possible explanation we have at this moment, which we're running checks on, is that this is the work of a computer hacker.'

Unease deepened inside Joe as the man echoed his own thoughts. A conclusion Joe did not want to reach at all. Secretly he'd known this was the case since Karen had first rung. 'Do you have an audit log on your computers?' he asked.

'Yes – our system manager tells me we can track back all activity within our system for the previous forty-eight hours – they're about to start doing that.' He hesitated. 'Just to help us, professor, is there anyone you can think of who might have done this as a – er – prank? Perhaps someone who has something personal against your family?'

Joe was silent for too long. He was thinking about Juliet's father with his silver temples and smooth, arrogant voice. He had used the law and used it powerfully; but he didn't seem the kind of man to stoop to placing Death notices. They were an act of sheer spite. From whom? Edwin Pilgrim? Possible, but unlikely. He was not the sort to play practical jokes. Had Juliet left the instructions behind with ARCHIVE? One final parting shot? To be set in motion if Joe failed with her freezing? But how on earth would she have known if he'd failed or not?

He went through into Pilgrim's office, carrying the papers. From Pilgrim's shocked reaction and from Harriet Tait's reaction, he was able to eliminate both of them instantly. Then he went back into his own office, closed the door.

He could track back ARCHIVE's activities for seven days. It would be a laborious procedure, but he would be able to discover for sure whether ARCHIVE had hacked into the newspapers' computer systems – either into the copy on their advertising system or their printing press system.

He logged into ARCHIVE but to his surprise, instead of ARCHIVE's usual greeting, nothing happened. The prompts and his login, Joem, and the password request remained on the screen. He typed them again and pressed carriage return. Still nothing happened. Then at the bottom of the screen appeared: Access denied.

The words were accompanied by a series of rapid, shrill beeps, which was ARCHIVE's intruder alert.

Puzzled, Joe picked up his phone and rang down to the system manager. 'Dave, have you been tinkering with the access codes?'

'No, haven't touched them. What's the problem?'

'I'm locked out. ARCHIVE doesn't want to know me.'

Dave Hoton sounded surprised. 'It can't not want to know *your* password, Joe. You and I are the only people who have the superuser status in the system to change passwords.'

'I know – that's why I wondered if you'd done something.'

'I'm not working on anything that could affect that part of the system. Want me to come up and take a look? Maybe you have a keyboard problem?'

'I have a tutorial in about –' He glanced at his watch. 'Two minutes. In fact I have them right through until about five.'

'I could come right up.'

'Thanks.' As he hung up another call came through. It was the ad manager of *The Times* with the same story that he'd heard already. Deeply apologetic, he told Joe he'd make sure a correction went into the notices of tomorrow's edition.

Dave Hoton and Joe's next student, a large, pancake-faced girl called Madeleine Hopkirk, arrived together. Joe took her into the student common-room, leaving Hoton free to concentrate on the workstation.

Ten minutes later, Dave Hoton came into the common

room. 'Sorry to interrupt,' he said, hands in his trouser pockets. 'I can't find anything wrong.'

Joe apologized to his student, asked her to wait for a moment and hauled himself up out of the low vinyl-covered armchair. He moved a short distance away from her with the system manager. 'Nothing?'

'I've been trying your password – it lets me straight in. I get ARCHIVE greeting me and telling me I shouldn't be using your password!'

Joe asked his student to wait a little longer and went back to his office with Hoton. He typed his login and password, pressed carriage return and the greeting appeared instantly:

Good afternoon, Professor Messenger. Are you aware that Dave Hoton has been using your password?

Joe glanced at the system manager. I gave him permission. You weren't letting me in when I tried before. Why was that?

Why was what, Professor? Why was anything? Is that a philosophical question?

Why did you not let me in on my password?

I think therefore I am. Does it follow that if I thought, therefore I was?

I don't understand, ARCHIVE. Please answer my question a different way.

A different way. Thesaurus mode. Differing. Heteromorphic. Modified. Disparate. A very different thing. A tertium quid. A horse of a different colour.

Joe pressed the key and exited. 'I could throttle it sometimes!'

Hoton shrugged. 'I can never work out in my mind how smart ARCHIVE really is. Sometimes I think it's having a laugh on us. Maybe it's already smarter than us and we haven't realized it.'

Joe watched Hoton's placid, bearded face with an unsettled feeling. Hoton had no problems understanding the potential for machines; and he had little enthusiasm for the human biological body.

'I think it still has a way to go before it's smarter than us,' Joe replied. But he realized as he spoke that there was more hope than authority in his voice.

Joe's tutorials began running over as they usually did, not helped by interruptions from calls from the newspapers, and his last one of the day didn't finish until 5.30.

He felt in need of a drink, but was anxious to get home to Karen. There was something he wanted to check out first and if he was lucky it might not take too long. He swivelled his chair towards his workstation and logged into ARCHIVE.

Good evening, Professor Messenger. It is going to be a chilly night. A ground frost is forecast with temperatures dropping to minus 3. Not quite cold enough for cryonics.

Joe read the last line of the message with discomfort, trying to work out how it had managed to make the link. Then ARCHIVE added: Boing boing!

Joe frowned, startled.

Boing boing. You have a message waiting.

Joe typed mail and pressed the return key to bring up his electronic mailbox. But nothing happened. He read the words again and felt a sudden chill of realization. He keyed in the command to take him into the process systems, and typed: Talk zebedee. Then, warily, he pressed return. The screen divided.

In the bottom appeared the words: You wanted proof. Satisfied now, Joe?

Who are you? Did you write the obituaries?

After a few moments the reply came back: Did you like them, Joe-Joe?

He swallowed at the use of Karen's pet name for him, and didn't get time to reply.

You wanted proof, Joe-Joe. I gave you proof. Now do something for me.

The letters on the screen were bright in the near darkness of the room. So bright they were hurting his eyes. A phone rang, unanswered, in an office above him. But hope entered his heart as he typed his reply. Maybe this was his chance to get her off his back.

What do you want me to do?

There was a pause. Then in the bottom half of the screen the words burned silently and menacingly out at him:

Find me a body.

51

A cold slick of fear travelled down Joe's spine in a way that was becoming too familiar. It was just a tease, his logic told him; a macabre time-bomb program. Christ, why was he shivering then?

He laid his fingers on the keyboard, and typed You're insane!

The answering words silently appeared: That's right, Joe; I'm a head-case. Remember?

He felt something in the room with him. Juliet's presence. The smell of her perfume came to him vividly, but he *knew* he was imagining it. ARCHIVE had no smell generators. He walked over to the window and opened it to see if the perfume was coming from outside. The smell of cigarette smoke drifted in and that reminded him, also, of Juliet.

He looked at the whiteboard on which he'd written the words *Neural Filter – Happy Person – Sad Person*. Stared at the bookshelves lined with his own volumes, and the works of other scientists.

Just a tease. We weren't there yet, not by a long way. All any computer could do right now was to fool someone into thinking it was human. To beat the Turing test the computer had to do that for ten whole minutes. Joe didn't know any computer capable of fooling him for more than thirty seconds.

Except ARCHIVE, now. There was something going on in it that was beyond the parameters he knew and understood.

It seemed that either Juliet had left behind a program smarter than any he'd ever encountered before – or that in some way ARCHIVE was still responding to her. Which was impossible. Dead people did not operate computers.

But hackers did.

A hacker was the simplest explanation. One with a distorted sense of humour; one that was pretending to be Juliet.

He stared back at the screen a little relieved by his explanation. That was it, that made sense. That explained why he had got locked out of the system earlier when he'd tried to run through its activities. The hacker was monitoring, picking up speech from the microphones, keeping one step ahead.

Some hackers worked alone, some in loose-knit groups; they were spread around the globe; dozens of them. School kids, students, programmers. One of his own students had once been given a conditional discharge for hacking into a bank.

He had designed ARCHIVE to be hacker-proof, to strike back when someone tried to hack it and wipe the hacker's own programs. ARCHIVE was meant to constantly upgrade its defences, learning from everyone that tried to hack it.

Now someone had beaten its defences, and the implications were serious. He thought about the cameras and microphones recording his private life with Karen and Jack. Those needed to be switched off immediately, until the hacker was identified and shut out.

`I think you already have a body and you're just pretending you need one,` he typed.

`Don't make me angry, Joe. I can do some very nasty things.`

`I'm tired of your sick games.`

Defiantly, he pressed the keys to exit from the program, intending to do an immediate trace back through ARCHIVE's log to see where this was coming from. But nothing happened. He tried to exit again and still nothing happened.

He eased the plastic key off its mount with the handle of a

coffee spoon, then carefully inspected the spring-loaded con-
nector mechanism beneath. The connection was clean. He
blew on it anyway, and replaced the key. Then he depressed
it again. Still nothing. He suddenly noticed the message on
the screen had changed:

Not trying to leave me, Joe? We're having such a
nice chat.

Joe formed an image in his mind of whom he was talking
to. A student, rather nerdy-looking, like Edwin Pilgrim.
Perhaps working on a college computer, or more likely had a
PC with a modem rigged up in his bedroom. Probably
thought this was a huge jape and was sharing the secret with
a few close hacker friends whom he'd never met but just
communicated with through illegal networks.

Then Juliet's face appeared again, filling the screen, her
lips pouting into a mocking kiss.

Joe stiffened, startled by the image.

She smiled and spoke to him, her voice sounding metallic
and synthesized, but distinctly recognizable. 'I didn't mean
to startle you, Joe-Joe. Why don't you come a little
closer?'

His eyes shot, freaked, to the Voice-Screen indicator on
the screen. The keyboard icon indicated 'Screen'; there
shouldn't be any sound coming out.

'You can't make love to me in here, Joe-Joe, and I want
you so badly. You make me feel so horny. Get me a body,
Joe-Joe, and let's go somewhere cosy; just you and me and
play hide-the-salami together! Much more fun than playing
hide-the-little-boy!'

The voice was uncannily real. ARCHIVE was getting good
at picking up vocal patterns, mimicking them; but this was
the best Joe had ever heard it; and the most disturbing. His
eyes shot back to the screen then down to the keyboard. He
tapped the keys to switch to 'Voice' then back to 'Screen'.
Then he heard her again.

'Don't you like to hear my voice, Joe-Joe?'

Joe's anger increased. The hacker must have somehow got
himself superuser status, enabling him to change the system

internally. He depressed the key again to exit, but still nothing happened except that Juliet's face frowned. 'Joe-Joe, I'm talking to you!'

Joe tried to avoid looking at the screen. His brain raced. If he could keep the hacker on the line, he could monitor him from another terminal. He stood up and went over to the door.

'Where are you going, Joe-Joe?'

'I have to go to the bathroom.'

He ran down into the basement and along the corridor to the undergrad room, always empty at this time. He stopped outside, switched the corridor lights off, then went into the room and closed the door, without switching on the light. It was pitch dark.

There was a sharp whirr as Clinton scuttled towards him. He stood his ground, heart pounding, and the robot stopped inches in front of him, guided by sonic and infrared sensors. 'Welcome to ARCHIVE. If you have any cans of soft drink please leave them on the work surfaces and I will remove them when they are empty. Have a nice time with ARCHIVE.'

Joe fumbled his way to a workstation, sat down and groped in the darkness for the carriage-return key. The cameras at home worked on infrared as well as conventional light; the ones here required light.

He logged in using the superuser name 'root' and the root password. Then he pressed carriage return again.

As he did so the light in the room came on. He spun round, certain someone must have come in. But the door hadn't opened. He looked up at the camera, panicky, then he noticed the single word on the terminal screen.

Peekaboo!

Joe felt as if his body had been connected into an electrical circuit. Currents raced through him, tugging his nerves and muscles. He pressed the keys, but his fingers looked as if they belonged to someone else. Slender flesh-coloured cylinders with tufts of fair hair behind the knuckles. Nothing happened on the screen. Peekaboo! stayed. His fingers pressed different combinations of keys, but still nothing happened. Frustrated, he looked at the screen again. The wording had changed.

I'm not a game, Joe. You can't just exit from me when you feel like it. You have a responsibility. You made me a broken promise. Just like you did to your father.

Joe switched off the workstation and the screen went blank. He placed the flat of his hand against his forehead, feeling sick. Then he heard Juliet's voice, very softly, behind him.

'Joe. I'm still here.'

Whirling round, he was confronted by Juliet's face staring at him from a screen on the other side of the room. The screen next to it came on. Then the next one until all ten screens in the room were on and she was staring at him from each of them.

'I'm here, Joe. I'm everywhere and nowhere. Get me a body, Joe, you owe me a body!'

In a minute he would wake up. Karen would be in bed asleep and Jack would be jumping on him. In a minute.

Then suddenly the room became pitch dark. All the screens went blank. He sat in total silence, afraid to move, his body drumming with fear. Waiting.

It was ten minutes before Joe backed away from the workstation, colliding with Clinton on the way. He made it to the door, and felt a welcome draught of cool air as he stepped out into the corridor, and away from Juliet.

When he arrived home, at half past six, Karen looked drawn and frightened. He held her tightly, trying to comfort her – and trying to comfort himself.

'Who did it, Joe? Did you call the police?'

'I –' He should have called the police, he realized. It hadn't occurred to him. Except he wasn't sure what they could do about it. 'I wanted to find out how it happened first.'

'Why?'

The word echoed. He was still shell-shocked from facing Juliet's image in ten-fold. *Why?*

He cupped Karen's face in his hands, kissed the cool skin of her forehead and stroked the long, soft tresses of her hair. 'It's OK, it's gonna be OK.' He hugged her hard against his body, smelled her zesty scent, wanting to reassure himself that she was real, not an image on a screen. 'Love you.'

She took his coat, hung it up and got the ice tray out of the freezer while he poured himself four fingers of Jameson's. The whiskey slid down into his belly, firing him with a little confidence, a feeling of reassurance.

He sat down at the kitchen table and Karen showed him a new painting Jack had done that day; for a moment, Joe thought with rising excitement that it was a detail of a Mandlebrot set; it was not immediately obvious to him that it was just a man holding a fishing rod on the end of a pier.

He smiled at his mistake. 'How's he been today?'

'Quiet. I've been trying to get him to remember what happened, but he doesn't seem able to. I have to take him to the dentist tomorrow – he's not having much of a week,' she said wrily. 'He's waiting for you to read him a story.'

'I'll go up. When's he starting playschool again? Next week?'

'Yes.'

'How's your hand now?' Joe looked at the bandage over her wound.

'Still throbs a little sometimes.'

She reached out and touched his hand, and he noticed for the first time that she no longer had the fingers of a young woman. Yet her face was still young, in spite of all she'd been through, still the same beautiful face that he had married, and he suddenly felt lousy for having cheated on her.

There was a good smell of fried onions and garlic in the kitchen, and through his turmoil he felt hungry, remembering he'd eaten nothing except a few biscuits. He squeezed her good hand. 'I'll go up to Jack. Shall we eat early?'

'I'm doing lamb chops for supper, that OK?'

'Perfect.'

399

'Want me to open some wine?'

'Sure.' He gently touched her cheek, then climbed the stairs clutching his whiskey. Jack was sitting up in bed in blue pyjamas with his arms folded in front of him. His face lit up as Joe came in.

Joe wished suddenly that he could preserve the moment. Wished that he could come home every night to find Jack tucked up in bed waiting for a story with that same innocent smile. That he could forever have Karen greet him with a hug and a kiss and a sense of belonging. He wanted to build a huge protective circle around the three of them, and have nothing ever change.

'I don't have to spend another night in hospital, do I, Daddy?'

'No.' Joe reassured the boy. 'No, sure you don't.'

'I won't have to stay at the dentist tomorrow, will I? He'll let me come home, won't he?'

'Of course.'

'Can we still go fishing on Sunday?'

'Yup. Fishing on Sunday.' We can go to the moon if you want it, son, thought Joe.

52

The police car was backed well up into the entrance of the park, the stone entrance pillars and a laurel hedge blocking it from sight but giving the two police officers inside a clear view of the traffic lights in two directions.

Similarly concealed in a driveway four hundred yards further east along the road, two motorcycle cops waited, their engines ticking over as they listened for the voices of their colleagues on their radios.

Jim Tiptree had been on Traffic for twelve years. A tall, mild man who had once been a marathon runner and still had an athlete's frame, he had suffered the loss of his only daughter eight years ago when she'd been hit by a car driven by a speeding drunk. He sat in the patrol car with the microphone in his hand, his eyes watching every speeding motorist with sourness. His colleague and superior, Sergeant Bernie Simpson, shared his hatred of crass driving, but tended to be softer on the motorists.

Twenty past nine, it was the tail end of the morning rush hour on the busy four-lane road, and the pickings were slimmer than an hour ago. The radio crackled; the controller gave out details of an accident on the harbour front at the other end of town, then there was silence. The lights on the east–west road went amber. Jim Tiptree watched carefully. A grey van going fast, overtaking a truck on the inside. The light went red. The van roared over. The two police officers nodded at each other as if in sync. Tiptree pressed the button on the microphone.

'Grey Transit. E954 FCD.'

One of the motorcyclists answered back: 'Roger.'

The reading on the Speedman radar dial was 52.5 m.p.h.

'Red light and fifty-two speeding.'

'Going for him!' The voice over the radio was accompanied by the roar of an engine and wail of a siren.

The two officers' attention slackened while the north–south lights were green; they were only monitoring the east–west direction. A steady stream of traffic came down the hill and crossed the intersection into a wide Victorian avenue which went dead straight for a mile down to the sea. Private cars, mostly. Late commuters. Mothers taking tots to playschool.

Every traffic-light jumper was a potential killer. Booking them stopped them doing it again, for a while. Tiptree had been to too many accidents in his career. The kind of side-ons you got at intersections like this were grim. When a van hit a small car in the driver's door at fifty miles per hour it was an awful mess. And he'd seen enough awful messes to last him a lifetime. Lovely girls with their limbs ripped off and their eyes gouged out. Incinerated corpses.

Anger rose in him as he watched a yellow Volkswagen

scream down the road doing sixty plus. Lucky for the driver he didn't have the radar pointing that way. The VW hit the lights on amber and tore on over. 'You stupid bastard,' he muttered. The lights changed to red.

'How much longer you want to give it, Jim?' his colleague asked. Although Bernie was his superior, it was usually Bernie who asked for instructions rather than giving them. Making decisions didn't seem important to him.

'Half-nine?' There were always a few people late for work who would be hurrying.

'Sure.'

The road east–west was almost empty; just a solitary moped and a milk float. A cyclist pedalled past, pushing against the headwind. It was a fine, blustery morning and the air smelled fresh and clean. There would be another line of traffic in a moment, from the lights further west. A woman walked a labrador in front of them; the dog cocked its leg unceremoniously.

'Bloody shit-factory,' Bernie Simpson said, eyeing it disdainfully. He didn't like dogs. Jim Tiptree kept quiet; he had a dog himself, which Simpson always seemed to forget.

The blatter of an exhaust broke the sudden quietness. Two trucks came along abreast, accelerating slowly, the traffic backed up behind them. Jim watched them cross the lights on green. Several cars followed. The lights went amber; a Mercedes crossed, but everything else braked. Good boys, Tiptree thought and switched his gaze back to the north–south lights which were now green. A line of cars filed southwards over the intersection; a red sports Toyota was the last and he watched its flashy outline disappear.

Then the revving of engines in front of him startled him.

The cars waiting at the red light on the east–west road were starting to cross over, even though the north–south lights were still green. 'Hey!' he said, letting go of the button on his mike in alarm.

Tiptree was pointing with his finger; but Bernie Simpson had already seen too, already realized what was happening.

'Jesus!' mouthed Tiptree, staring hard to make sure his

eyes weren't deceiving him. He yanked down his door handle, climbed out and sprinted the twenty yards to the intersection.

The traffic was thin again, he was relieved to see. From his right, a solitary green car was approaching; old, rather rusty, a woman was driving. Behind him he heard the *whoomph* of a powerful engine accelerating and turned his head. A bronze Jaguar was coming down the hill too fast, going for the lights.

A sick feeling of dread curdled the inside of his stomach. His panicky gaze swung from one car to the other. Magnets. They were being drawn like magnets. He opened his mouth to shout a warning, raised his hands in the air.

The little green car, a Nissan, was crossing the line. A mother with her kid in the rear seat. She seemed to notice his raised hands, too late to do anything, she was over the line, heading out into the centre of the intersection.

Oh God, no.

The Jaguar must have been doing seventy until its wheels locked up. The treads of the tyres planed across the dry tarmac, slithering, yowling. All in slow motion now. Homing in on the little green Nissan like a missile.

Suddenly there was an eruption of glass and metal in front of the Jaguar; a fountain of glittering shards burst into the air. It was followed, what seemed to Tiptree like seconds later, by a huge, dull boom that made his ears pop.

Then there was a sound like a dustbin rolling across corrugated iron. The green car was upside down, rolling on its roof. It struck a lamp-post, snapping it like a twig, smashed into the brick wall of a garden, partly demolishing it, and halted, rocking like a busted toy.

There was total silence for an instant; no sound of any traffic, no voices, no bird song. Even the wind seemed to have stopped.

The Jaguar had slewed to a halt on the far side of the intersection, its bonnet crumpled, glass and buckled strips of metal and chrome lying all around it.

Tiptree heard a hiss searing into the silence. He smelled

the petrol that came with it and saw the first licks of vivid orange flame appear from below the upturned engine compartment of the green Nissan.

He hauled himself through the air that separated him from the upturned car. The driver's door was shut, and the passenger door. There was a woman hanging inside from her belt, motionless, blood streaming down her face. The kid in the back, in a safety seat that had dislodged, was lying motionless on the roof which was now the floor, his body horribly twisted.

There was a stench of burning rubber and paint. Amidst thick black smoke, Tiptree grabbed the rear-door handle and pulled. Nothing happened. He cursed, gripped the driver's door handle and pulled that. The locked door would not budge. Then he kicked the window. It did not give. He turned and kicked it with his heel, giving it everything he had, and it caved in with a bang.

Bernie was with him now, holding the fire extinguisher from the police car; he discharged it into the engine compartment, then used it to smash the rear window. The motorcycle police were running towards them with fire extinguishers. A young jogger in trainers was trying to help too. The flames were getting worse, licking around them, burning Tiptree's hands. He held his breath, his head inside the car trying to find the seat-belt buckle. Smoke was curling through the dash.

He pressed the seat-belt release, but it was jammed. His colleague cut the belt and the woman sagged on to the roof. He had no time to worry about any injuries she might have, or even whether she was still alive; he eased his hands under her arms and gripped hard, then pulled her clumsily through the window, aware that the jagged shards were cutting her but not caring. All he knew was that someone had to go back for the kid as soon as possible.

Someone was helping him now. She was out, lying on the pavement except for one leg trailing in through the window. The man in the jogging suit and one of the motorcycle policemen lifted her, carried her across the road and set her down on the far pavement.

'Red light,' a distant, shocked voice was saying. 'Why did she drive over a red light?'

Bernie Simpson, his face blackened with smoke, was bent double under the awkward weight of the small boy he was carrying across the road still strapped into the child seat. The boy was unconscious and, from the way his body was twisted, Jim Tiptree was afraid he'd broken his neck and was dead.

He knelt, without optimism, to see if he could detect a pulse.

53

Joe checked the Deaths notices of *The Times* the moment it arrived in the morning. There was an erratum printed about Karen and Jack; he was relieved to see it and showed the page to Karen. He bought the other papers on his way into the university, and took them up to his office.

It was a blustery morning with a sharp chill in the air and clouds were massing in the east. It looked like rain later, he thought absently, turning to the Deaths notices of the *Telegraph*. There was a similar erratum. He checked the *Guardian* and the *Independent* and found the same correction.

He eyed his dark workstation screen warily, before logging in and calling up his electronic mail. At the same time he began tackling the correspondence piled on his desk. He buzzed down to the computer room to see if Dave Hoton was in yet, but there was no reply.

On the top of his pile was a formal-looking brown envelope. His heart sank as he unfolded the letter it contained and saw it was on the headed paper of the Sussex Coroner.

Dear Professor Messenger,
My officer, Miss Judith Aitken, has informed me of

the circumstances regarding the destruction of the
late Miss Juliet Spring's head.

I am deeply disturbed that a man in your position
should have acted in such an irresponsible manner, both
in defying a court order and in mutilating a human body.
As a result of your actions, it is now impossible to carry
out a full and proper postmortem to determine the cause
of death of Miss Spring and this will add considerably to
the grief and distress of her family as well as impeding the
processes of the law.

I understand from my officer your reasons for what
you have done, and however well intentioned they
were towards meeting the wishes of the deceased, they
were seriously misguided.

However, I can see no useful purpose to be gained
from bringing proceedings against you or Cryonite for
contempt of court in this particular circumstance, and I
therefore propose taking no further action at this time. I
do however believe it would be useful to have a meeting
with the directors of Cryonite to establish guidelines for
cryonics patients in order to avoid a repetition of these
unfortunate circumstances in the future. Perhaps you
would be good enough to contact my secretary, Mrs
Walters, to arrange this during the next few weeks.

It is likely you will be required to attend the inquest
as a witness and you will be notified of the date
shortly.

Yours sincerely,
Dr R. Gordon Howlett
HM Coroner for the
Western District of East Sussex

Joe's entire body sagged with relief as he laid the letter
down. He read it again, scarcely able to believe it. And the
coroner wanted to discuss cryonics, which could be a big
step forward towards serious recognition over here. If only
they could get one coroner to be sympathetic towards cryonics, they could establish guidelines for others. With luck, in

time, cryonics patients would be afforded special legal rights.

He buzzed Blake's extension; there was no answer. Blake seemed to come in less and less these days, his work at the Human Organ Preservation Centre in the Science Park, a couple of miles away, taking increasingly more of his time. He rang that number; Blake was expected in later. He scribbled a note to his secretary for her to copy the coroner's letter to Blake, and thought again how stupid he'd been. If he'd only taken Juliet's head back to Cryonite instead of putting it in the freezer, then everything might be OK now. They might have won the appeal; honoured Juliet's wishes. And he would have honoured his promise.

The next letter was from the Secretary of the Royal Society regarding the address he was giving in June. As he began reading it, the phone rang.

'Joe Messenger,' he said absently.

The male voice that he heard down the receiver was tentative. 'Is that – er – Professor Joseph Messenger, of number 8 – er – Cranford Road?'

Joe hesitated, wondering if it was a salesman trying to flog him something, maybe a pension plan or a timeshare? 'Yes, speaking.'

'And you are the husband of Mrs Karen Messenger?'

The tone of the call was disturbing him; it wasn't someone trying to sell something; it was too serious for that.

'Yes.'

'This is the Brighton police, Professor Messenger. I'm afraid I have some rather bad news for you.'

Joe felt suddenly that all his hopes from the coroner's letter had been dashed. The police were going to charge him. Shit! Juliet's father, he thought, anger rising. It was Juliet's father behind this call, not satisfied with the coroner's action, pursuing him like a dog with a bone, riding roughshod over his own daughter's wishes.

The policeman's voice continued gravely. 'I'm afraid your wife and son have been admitted to the Prince Regent Hospital following a road-traffic accident.'

For a moment, Joe didn't believe him. It was the same hoaxer who had placed the obituaries. Except his voice was too honest. He felt as if the floor were crumbling beneath him and he was plunging into darkness.

Tell me it's not true. 'What happened?' he whispered.

'I'm afraid I don't have any details, sir. It would be best if you went straight down to the hospital.'

Dead, Joe thought. From the policeman's tone it was clear that they were dead and he didn't want to tell him, he was passing the buck.

Then the policeman's voice again, kind but guarded. 'My information is that they are both alive, sir. If you go to the Accident and Emergency department and ask for Nurse Blickling, the duty senior nurse, she will be able to tell you everything.'

Joe gripped the receiver so hard it was hurting his hand. He stared at the framed picture on the wall above his desk with the parrot and the whale and all the other creatures that lived longer than man. 'This isn't a hoax, is it?' Joe said. 'Can you give me your name and number, I want to call you back; we've had a bad hoax played on us already.'

'I'm Sergeant Denton, sir. If you call Brighton police on 606744 they'll put you through to me.'

Joe rang the number and the sergeant came back on the line. Joe apologized and the police sergeant told him he fully understood.

Joe ran through a bay of ambulance parking spaces into the sterile, faintly metallic smell of the Accident and Emergency entrance that had become too well known to him in the past few weeks. At one of the three counter windows, he attracted the attention of a woman who was photocopying and explained who he was.

As she disappeared to find someone who could help him, Joe stood banging his knuckles together. His eyes roamed over the half-occupied rows of plastic chairs, the electronic sign that said. 'Welcome to Accident and Emergency ... The waiting time is approximately 1 – 2'. *Hours,* he supposed. He saw a poster that said Donor Card? Talk it over with your relatives. Then he heard a nurse saying, 'Professor Messenger?'

He scarcely had the chance to nod before she led him a short distance down a corridor and past a row of empty trolleys. They had to weave through a flurry of activity around an elderly woman on a stretcher; Joe caught a glimpse of a face the colour of alabaster.

He was shown into a cluttered office and the nurse followed him in. Joe did not recall dealing with her before. She had a soft, young-looking face, with straw-coloured hair raked sharply upwards and held in place by a cluster of tortoiseshell combs, as if she was trying to make herself look older, more authoritative. She was wearing a neat blue and white uniform, and the badge on her lapel said Susan Blickling. A & E Assistant Senior Nurse.

The office was much larger than the cramped room he and Karen had been put in before. He'd been through all this last week and he began to feel he was in some fairground wheel of terror that returned to the same danger point with each revolution.

'Your wife and son were admitted here approximately half an hour ago after a road-traffic accident. Your son is unconscious but stable. Your wife was conscious on arrival but is very poorly with internal injuries, I'm afraid.'

Joe tried to read her eyes. 'How poorly?'

She came straight out with it, no hesitation. 'She's on life support and we're trying to assess her injuries at the moment.'

Joe felt his strength draining. 'Jack's all right?'

'Your son?'

Joe nodded.

'He's having a scan at the moment. We hope it's nothing more than concussion. Other than that he seems to have just bruises and abrasions.'

'When will you – I guess – I –' His voice tailed. The nurse's words still striking home, winding him.

He thought of Jack's plaintive words last night. *I won't*

have to stay at the dentist tomorrow, will I? He'll let me come home, won't he? Now the boy's mother was on life support. He felt a sudden stark terror at the thought of losing Karen. Don't die, oh, God, please don't die.

He stood up unsteadily. 'May I see my wife?'

'In a moment, if that's all right, professor. I need some details from you first.'

He supported himself on the back of the chair, hollowed out, no energy. He shook his head. 'I went through all that, already,' he said.

She looked surprised. 'When?'

'Last week. For my son, for Jack – he was in here.'

Her expression darkened. 'I didn't know that.'

'Trapped in a freezer.'

'I've been away on holiday, but in that case we'll have his records.' She raised her clipboard and made a note. Then she took a blue and white form from a desk. 'Now, your wife – could I just check her full name?'

When they'd finished she told him to help himself to the phone if he needed to make any calls and went out.

A moment later the door opened and the consultant in charge of the unit came in. It was Mr Raleigh, whom Joe immediately recognized from last week. He stopped in the doorway for a moment, dressed as before in a grey suit, and looking just as weary. 'Professor Messenger, I thought when I heard the name – I –' He raised his hands rather feebly, as if acknowledging that any gesture he made would be insufficient. 'I'm afraid we meet again.'

Joe proffered his hand and the consultant gave it a cursory shake as if to indicate people were beyond formalities in here.

'Your son's unconscious, but the scan doesn't show any skull fracture or internal damage. Other than that he seems to have just cuts and bruises. Going to be right as rain, but we'll need to keep him in for a few days, in light of last week.'

'Of course.' Joe mouthed the words, barely making a sound.

'I'm afraid your wife's condition is much worse and is giving us concern. She has a left forearm fracture and a fractured femur, but her main problems are with her lungs and abdominal bleeding.' He stared hard at Joe. 'I think I can speak openly to you – you have some medical background, I believe?'

'Yes,' Joe said tightly.

'We won't know the full extent of her internal injuries until we open her up. She has five fractured ribs and a badly flailed chest causing difficulties with her breathing. We suspect there are globules of bone marrow impinging in the lungs and we can't tell how serious that is yet. We suspect the abdominal bleeding may be from lacerations to her liver, but again we can't tell the extent at present.'

'Is she conscious?'

'She regained consciousness shortly after being admitted and was able to answer a few questions coherently, although she had difficulty speaking; but she is now unconscious again.' He studied Joe's face with a concerned look. 'I'm afraid she's deteriorating. With your permission we'd like to perform an exploratory operation immediately. We're fortunate in having Mr Osborne-Benson in the hospital this morning and he's available – he's probably the finest general surgeon in the South of England.'

Joe nodded his assent. 'Do whatever you have to.'

'We'll also have an orthopaedic surgeon present; it's best if we can repair all the bones at the same time, provided –' He checked himself.

'Provided she lives?' Joe prompted.

The consultant's voice lowered. 'I'm afraid that's about the truth of it, yes, Professor Messenger. But we've a good team here and a good record. We'll do all we can.'

Nurse Blickling came back into the room and hesitated to break the silence between the two men. '. . . Your son is back from neurology. Would you like to see him?'

Joe followed her down the corridor and through a curtained doorway into a room packed with equipment. A doctor in white pyjamas and two nurses stood by the trolley on which Jack was lying with his eyes shut, a breathing mask over his face and a cannula in the back of his hand, from which a clear plastic tube ran up to an upturned plastic bag hooked to a drip stand.

Joe ran his eyes along the electronic traces blipping across the screens of monitors, first the electrocardiogram monitor, then the EEG. Jack's brainwaves looked fine: strong, even traces consistent with unconsciousness or deep sleep. He looked down at his son who seemed so tiny, so vulnerable, and for some reason Joe found the plastic identity bracelet that had been clipped around his wrist particularly distressing. He wanted desperately to hold Jack and cradle him. You don't deserve this, he thought.

One of the nurses gave him a reassuring smile, then the doctor turned to him. 'He looks familiar to me. You're his father?'

Joe nodded, pushing his hands into his pockets. 'He was here last week.'

'I thought so. He'll be fine. Good strong pulse; just a touch of concussion.'

'What happened?' Joe said. 'I still don't know.'

Nurse Blickling was standing at his side, he suddenly noticed. 'The report from the ambulance crew is that your wife's car was in a side-impact accident at traffic lights,' she said.

'Someone jumped the lights?' Joe asked.

'I don't have that information – the traffic police would be able to give you the details. We understand the impact was on the passenger side, otherwise your wife's injuries would have been even worse.'

Joe's terror of losing Karen surged back. He looked at the faces around him with rising panic. She might be dying now and calling out for him. 'Where is my wife? Would you take me to her, please?' His head felt hot suddenly, and his hearing deadened as if he'd had a sudden altitude change. He collided with a technician and apologized, unsure who had walked into whom.

A woman was tugging his arm, leading him out of the

room. 'Next door,' a hazy voice said. 'They've just brought her back from X-rays.'

He followed her a few yards down the wide corridor and into a narrow room crowded with people, some dressed in green scrub suits, some in white coats and some in nursing uniform. The woman he was following stopped and spoke to someone who looked familiar, a rather pompous-looking man in his early thirties, a real chinless wonder with a narrow horse-like face.

He stared at Joe with faintly cold recognition. 'Roland Dance,' he said, holding out a hand and giving Joe's a clammy, rather limp shake. 'We've met.'

Joe's fogged mind could not for a moment deliver him the correct memory. 'Yes – somewhere.'

'Here,' the anaesthetist said rather stiffly. 'The death of a young lady – Juliet Spring – you are involved with cryonics.' It was a statement, not a question.

'Right, of course.'

'We're about to take your wife down to theatre, Professor Messenger.'

Joe was unsure whether to take this as information, or an instruction to get out of the way. He also would have preferred it if Karen could have been put under by someone anonymous, not someone who had crossed swords with her own husband. But he could hardly say so, and he knew enough about the medical profession to appreciate that personalities didn't come into it on the operating table. He stared at three orange traces on a grey screen. Watched the spikes for a moment. Christ, they were weak and erratic. Then a splash of red on the floor caught his eye. Blood on the linoleum floor, just lying there like spilt milk, getting trodden on and smeared. He felt despair.

A gap suddenly opened in the crowd of medics and he could see a figure laid out beneath a bloodstained sheet on a green metal trolley that was cranked up high. Lines ran from the figure into a battery of monitors and drips. When a man in a green gown lifted the sheet away, it got worse. It took a moment for the horror to register fully to Joe that this broken-looking object was not a dummy, not some practice cadaver wheeled out of a cupboard. It was his wife. Even her breasts looked flatter and wider than normal and there were horrible weals all around them.

To the medics she was just another victim. Some of them were bustling around as if she did not exist. And the man in the green gown was poking her with a gloved finger as if she were meat for which he was bartering in a market.

He felt a sudden intense parallel with seeing Juliet Spring in this same hospital only a few weeks ago, then willed himself back to the present.

Fight, honey. Oh, God, please fight. I love you so much.

He wanted to touch her, to hold her hand, to kiss her, but it seemed as if somehow in here she no longer belonged to him, that she was someone else's property and he had no claim over her any longer.

Behind her head Roland Dance was checking a flow valve. Then he said to someone in a white coat: 'We'll put her under in here and take her straight through to theatre.'

Joe was about to lose sight of Karen now and he felt a sudden flash of bitterness towards Dance. *No, she's not going to be frozen,* he wanted to tell him. *She didn't want to be frozen, she wants to die and rot like everyone else. Satisfied?*

Nurse Blickling came up to him. 'If I give you a room where you can wait, you can alternate between here and your son,' she suggested.

But if Joe couldn't be with Karen, willing her to live with his presence, he wanted to be doing something other than just waiting helplessly. 'I guess I might take a wander round.'

'You should drink some tea, it'll help you.'

'Maybe I'll go to the cafeteria.'

'Good idea – I'll take you down there.'

'I know the way – at least I did last week – I . . .' He tried to remember, but was confused between this and the children's ward.

He allowed himself to be led down along a wide corridor, then Nurse Blickling pointed him through a door and told him she'd see him back in Accident and Emergency later. He wandered into the cafeteria and stopped, overcome suddenly with emotion. A clock on the wall said ten to eleven. In the past hour his entire life had been upturned. He had kissed his wife and son goodbye and gone to work. Now he was stranded in a hospital cafeteria breathing in the greasy smell of fried food and wondering if his wife would be alive in an hour's time.

Joe couldn't take it. He turned round and found his way outside. Two ambulancemen were hanging around smoking cigarettes and chatting.

He took a walk round the block. It felt strange to see people walking in normal clothes, and he wondered if he looked like they did. The sky was darkening from the massing clouds. Across the road was a seedy-looking pub called the Barber's Arms, and a row of Victorian terraced houses with grimy brickwork. An elderly couple were coming out of one of them, walking slowly, taking time over each step, the man supporting the woman on his arm.

Till death us do part, Joe thought suddenly. Bile rose in him as he watched the couple and tried to imagine what they might have looked like as young people. Age and death. The enemies. Human bodies were so frail, so short-lived. If Karen and Jack had been downloaded into computers then all this pain would be unnecessary. They could discard their broken bodies, have new ones. One day there would be no such thing as bereavement.

He walked along the pavement under the heavy sky, and passed a carpet shop, a greengrocer's, then a newsagent's. As he did so a headline caught his eye: MUM AND TOT IN FIREBALL HORROR.

He stopped and went inside. It was the local daily, the *Evening Argus*. There was a photograph of an upturned blazing car, together with an inset photo of two policemen which was captioned: 'Blaze Heroes: PC Jim Tiptree and Sgt Bernie Simpson.'

Joe lifted a copy from the pile near the door and scanned the story with horrified fascination. He learnt nothing not shown in the pictures except that one of the hero policemen, PC Tim Tiptree, 38, ran the marathon for England in the 1984 Olympics. He put the paper down without buying it, not wanting a souvenir, and walked back to the hospital, back to Accident and Emergency.

A rather sharp-looking young man in a trendy grey suit approached him and Joe noticed a ring-bound notebook in his hand.

'Professor Messenger?' He was polite but had a sense of purpose that stopped Joe in his tracks, even though he knew instantly what he was.

'Yes.'

'Paul Vincent from the *Evening Argus*. I wonder if I could ask you a couple of questions about your wife's accident?'

Joe smiled gently at him and shook his head. 'I'm sorry, not right now, please.' He made to move on. But the reporter sidestepped in front of him.

'Professor, there is something I'd like your comment on very much, about the traffic lights.'

Joe frowned. 'I'm sorry?'

'You're a computer scientist – I'd be very interested in your professional opinion.'

'How do you mean? On what?'

'Are you aware that the traffic-light system in Brighton and Hove is computer controlled?'

'No, I wasn't.' He almost spat the words out, didn't want to take on board what he'd just heard. But the reporter hadn't finished.

'I gather computerized traffic systems are pretty common these days, so as to control traffic flow according to the time of day.' He paused like a judge about to address a jury. 'Presumably, professor, they have failsafe systems to prevent the lights in converging directions both showing green at the same time?'

Joe felt a shadow of fear looming up on him. 'Yes,' he said hesitantly. 'Yes, failsafes would be built into the system.'

'So what do you think might have gone wrong this morning? Do you have any theory?'

'I'm sorry – what did go wrong?'

The reporter looked surprised. 'You didn't hear?'

'Hear what?'

'About the lights? It seems some glitch got into the computer system, overriding the failsafe mechanism.' The reporter paused, studying the horror in Joe's face, knowing he had found his mark, but having no idea of the full implications. 'It made the lights green in all directions simultaneously,' he said.

54

It was shortly after two in the afternoon when Jack opened his eyes.

Joe was sitting beside him, and had been watching him slowly emerge back into consciousness. 'Hi.'

Jack looked at him, groggy and confused, and his expression a little cross, as if he had been disturbed from a good sleep.

Joe bent and kissed his forehead. 'How you feeling?'

Jack pursed his lips, eyed him blearily, then closed his eyes again and slept for another half hour.

Mr Raleigh said that they would keep Jack in the neurological observation ward overnight and run some tests on him in the morning. But by half past five Joe still had no definite news about Karen. She had been in the operating theatre for over six hours. Nurse Blickling reported to him regularly: the news was always the same. The lacerations to Karen's liver would heal. But Mr Raleigh had been right in his original suspicions, and globules from her bone marrow had got into her lungs, causing increasing breathing problems for her. In addition, she was suffering severe haemorrhaging from her chest wall.

He went back and sat for a while in the waiting room, looked at the telephone and finally made the call he'd been intending to make ever since talking to the *Argus* reporter.

A duty officer answered and told him that Sergeant Simpson had gone home for the day, but Constable Tiptree was around somewhere. He offered to take Joe's number, but Joe said he would hold. After a wait of several minutes, he was about to hang up and try again when he heard a sharp clatter and a man's voice.

'Hello? Tiptree.'

There was a quiet precision about the voice. Joe matched it in his mind with the image of a marathon runner and with the photograph he'd seen in the paper.

'My name is Joe Messenger – you rescued my wife and son from a car accident this morning.'

The policeman's tone changed, becoming more gentle and less confident. 'In the Nissan?'

'Yes.'

'That's right. How – how are they, sir?'

'My son's OK – concussion and some bruises. They're operating on my wife at the moment. I – I won't know for a while. I'm grateful for what you did. Thank you.'

'I'm afraid I didn't do very much, really, sir. It was just fortunate we were on the spot, and able to get them out in time, before the car –'

'You actually saw the accident, right?' Joe asked, interrupting.

'That's correct, sir. We were observing the lights at the time it happened.'

'And it's true about the lights? They both went green simultaneously?'

'Yes. My colleague and I both saw it happen. We did try to stop the traffic –' His voice faltered and Joe wondered if he was suffering from shock. 'I'm sorry, sir, I'm very sorry.'

'You did what you could,' Joe said. 'It's not your fault.' Joe tried to phrase his next question tactfully. 'There was no possibility you were mistaken in what you saw? About the lights?'

'None,' the police officer said emphatically. 'We had a clear view of both sets – we'd been watching them for a couple of hours.'

'Has anyone looked at the lights since?'

'They've been taken out of commission, sir. The borough engineers will have to find the fault. They've shut down the computerized system for the whole town. If it could happen to these lights, I suppose it could happen to the rest.'

Computerized traffic lights, from Joe's memory of when he'd studied them at university, worked through a sequence of electronic circuit-board gates; the gates were arranged in such a way that one was interdependent on the other – to eliminate any danger of a circuitry fault doing exactly what seemed to have happened today.

There was no malfunction he could think of that could affect the system. The only possible explanation was some kind of physical tampering with either the program or the lights themselves.

His voice tightened. 'I don't think you should be looking for an electrical fault, officer. You should be looking for a lunatic who understands computers.'

'I don't think I quite follow you, sir. Are you saying someone did this deliberately?'

Joe gripped the receiver hard. God, he felt so confused. All he wanted to do was get the police on the right trail. He wanted to explain that there was some crazy hacker out there, hunched over his keyboard, capable of causing mayhem, capable of changing traffic lights and killing people by tapping out a few symbols on a keyboard. Someone.

Or something.

Joe slept at the hospital and spent the whole of the next day, Thursday, there – alternating between Karen and Jack. Karen was stable after her surgery and Mr Raleigh told Joe she'd made it to first base. There was no neurological damage and from now on it all depended on her will to live, so Joe was banking on her natural resilience. She was still in Intensive Care – sleeping it off.

Jack was subdued, but fine. He asked Joe for some crayons and paper.

On Friday morning Joe went briefly into the office. Dave

Hoton came in almost immediately, telling him how upset everyone was to hear about Karen and Jack.

Joe asked him about ARCHIVE, and was told that the hacker appeared to have gone, clearing his tracks behind him. Hoton added that he'd already started checking to see whether either the hacker or Juliet Spring had laid any time bombs.

When he'd gone, Joe dialled the Highways Department of Brighton Council and asked for the engineer in charge of the computerized traffic lights system. He was put through to a man named Tony Smith.

Smith was guarded at first, but opened up when Joe explained who he was. He told Joe the full details of both the hardware and software of the system. Joe jotted the details down on an envelope. It was a version of a standard traffic-flow system in use throughout the world, with a proven failsafe device.

'It might have been a hacker messing around,' Smith said. 'But it's more likely condensation problems.'

'I'm not with you,' Joe said.

'Well, it's been causing shorts in some of the signal circuitry – this has happened before, with both sets of lights either going green or red simultaneously.'

'I didn't think it *could* happen,' Joe said.

'It shouldn't. But we've had to put in new electronic relays, replacing the old electro-magnetic ones, and we've had some problems with them.'

'You have cameras at the junction to monitor the traffic flow?'

'The Old Shoreham Road is a main commuter artery; gets very congested. There are cameras there watching all four directions, feeding the information into the system.'

'What quality image do they have?'

'They're the latest Sony high-definition traffic-control jobs – that's why we've got the new circuitry. They can read a number plate at two hundred metres. And they can see who's driving a car long before you or I.'

Joe thought for a moment. 'If a hacker could decode the

information – he could in theory read those number plates, right?'

'In theory,' the engineer said. 'If he had a way of decoding the images. But that's pretty unlikely if it's a kid at home in his bedroom with a two-hundred-quid Amstrad. And why would he want to read the number plates anyway?'

You don't really want to know the answer to that, pal, thought Joe. It was making more sense all the time. And yet, at the same time it made no sense at all. If only it was just condensation. Just another coincidence.

The engineer interrupted his thoughts. 'I'm pretty confident we'll have established the cause by the beginning of next week, professor. We've a forty-eight-hour log on transactions on the system. It's checking everything right now. If it was a hacker, it'll find him *and* give us his address.'

'Would you let me know?' Joe asked. 'I'll give you my home number if I may.'

'We'll be letting the police know, professor, don't worry. If this is a hacker, it's a madman who has to be found and stopped.'

After he had hung up, Joe closed his eyes, concentrating, thinking what if it was, perhaps, not a madman but a mad *woman?*

Keep calm. The anger that had been festering was growing all the time, but that was no reason not to stay rational. Juliet was dead. Dead and gone. Her head was destroyed, her body butchered by a pathologist. She might have left a vicious tease program behind in ARCHIVE, might have messed around good and proper, but dead people did not go hacking. Dead people did not change traffic lights.

And in any event, it would have been impossible to target Karen's car. It would have meant someone operating the computer, knowing that Karen and Jack were approaching, reading the number of Karen's car and in a fraction of a second changing the lights. That was just not possible; no one could operate that fast. The engineer was probably right. Condensation. It was sheer chance that it was Karen and Jack in that accident. That was all. Could have been anyone. Would have been, if Karen hadn't altered the play-school routine to take Jack to the dentist that morning.

So why was he shivering? It was raining steadily outside and his feet were cold from his wet shoes. His body was cold too. But it was not the damp that had got at Joe, it was his own fear.

At two o'clock on Friday afternoon Karen was taken off the danger list and moved out of Intensive Care into an orthopaedic ward. Mr Raleigh came by shortly afterwards and told Joe they were well pleased with her progress. 'Just don't make her laugh for a month – it'll hurt her like hell,' he warned.

A massive bouquet of flowers had been delivered from Eileen Peacock and everyone at COGS, and a separate one arrived later that afternoon from Blake. Karen was still dopey, but was able to squeeze Joe's hand with her left hand and say a few rambling words to him.

At four o'clock he was told by the sister in the children's ward that Jack could be discharged. He wondered whether to take him to see his mother before they left, but he decided the sight of her, with all the tubing plumbed into her, might be too distressing. He would bring him tomorrow when she might be a bit more awake.

With the help of a nurse, he dressed Jack in the sweatshirt, pullover and jeans he had brought, and lifted him to carry him to the car. But Jack protested that he wanted to walk, and Joe set him down. He ambled over to the bed next to his and said goodbye to a small boy in it, then took Joe's hand and trotted out alongside him.

When they got home, Jack got out his paintbox and sat straight down at the kitchen table.

'Daddy,' he said suddenly. 'That boy in the next bed is going to die.'

Joe looked at him, startled. 'Did he tell you that?'

Jack nodded solemnly. 'You can make people come back to life, can't you?'

Joe frowned. 'Is that what Mummy tells you?'

Jack looked a little confused. He pushed his index finger slowly across the table top as if he was tracing a line. 'I'm hungry, are you going to make my supper?'

Joe was relieved to be distracted, but intrigued by Jack's interest in the subject of death. 'What would you like?' he asked.

Jack licked the end of his paintbrush. 'Pizza.'

That meant the freezer, which made Joe feel a little squeamish, but he said, 'OK, pizza it is. I'll just check the messages first.' He went over to the answering machine and pressed the button.

There was a concerned message from Blake asking him to ring and let him know how Karen and Jack were. A message from the wife of a lecturer at the university, who obviously hadn't heard about the accident, wondering if they could come to dinner Saturday week. Then a message from Tony Smith, the computer engineer in charge of the traffic lights.

Although he could hear fine, Joe turned the volume on the machine up:

'Er – this is a message for Professor Messenger from Tony Smith at the Highways Department. Friday afternoon – er – three-fifteen. We have the results of our computer trace much quicker than we anticipated. I think it will interest you greatly, professor. Perhaps you could call me back as soon as possible?'

The switchboard operator answered on Joe's third ring, and tried to put him through to the Highways Department. Joe held on, then found himself transferred back to the switchboard.

'I'm sorry, sir, who was it you wished to speak to?'

'Tony Smith.'

'One moment, please.'

Joe heard a different ringing tone for some seconds, then another one. Then silence. After a minute or so the operator came back to him.

'I'm sorry, sir, Mr Smith has left for the weekend.'

Joe felt panicky. 'Is there anyone else who could help me?'

'No, I'm sorry, sir, the office is closed. You'll have to call back on Monday.'

He glanced at his watch. It was ten to five. He tried to think of some other department he could ask for, then there was a click and the line went dead.

55

'Yuck, this tastes of sick!'

It was Saturday evening; a greasy pall of smoke drifted below the kitchen ceiling. Joe sucked the knuckle of his thumb which he'd burnt on the side of the frying pan. 'It's an omelette,' he said angrily. 'You said you wanted one.'

'Don't like omelettes! It doesn't taste the way Mummy makes it. It tastes of sick.'

Exasperated, Joe took Jack's fork and ate a mouthful. It had an unpleasant burnt flavour. 'I don't think it tastes of sick,' he said. 'I think it tastes of cacka.'

Jack squealed with laughter. 'Eating cacka now!' Then he began giggling hysterically. When he stopped, he ate a huge spoonful with feigned relish. 'Yum yum! Cacka!'

Joe grinned also, pleased to see him smiling again. It had been a grim twenty-four hours, in which Jack had been quiet and morose most of the time. The worst had been when they'd gone to the hospital and Jack had refused to go near Karen. Fortunately she'd been too dosed on painkillers to be aware of his reaction.

One of the nurses explained that it happened sometimes; it was the kid rejecting the possibility that anything could have happened to a parent. He would get over it in a few days, then he would be fine.

Jack's spirits had not even lifted when Blake dropped by the house late that afternoon with his sultry girlfriend, Nico, whom he had brought along to Karen's birthday party, and took Jack for a short spin in his new black Ferrari.

After he'd put Jack to bed, Joe poured himself a Jameson's and went into his study. Earlier he had toyed with the idea of trying to find the home phone number of Tony Smith, the traffic computer engineer, but now he was daunted when he found there were ten pages of 'Smith' in the phone book and half of them seemed to be listed under the initial 'A' for Anthony or 'T' for Tony.

He sat in his armchair and rattled the ice cubes in his glass. Worrying. Trying to think one step ahead. He knew now that what he was up against was neither condensation nor any ordinary hacker. What he still couldn't work out, though, was how anyone could have known Karen was going to be breaking her normal schedule and driving over those lights.

Normally, ARCHIVE would have been receiving constant information from the house's cameras and microphones. But after the obituary notices Joe had reprogrammed ARCHIVE, switching them off.

A new thought sent a jolt through him. He jumped up from his chair, sat at his workstation, logged into ARCHIVE and went straight into the operating-system listings. He keyed in a request for the audio-visual file. After a few moments a list of *all* the buildings and rooms where ARCHIVE had eyes and ears came up, together with their on–off status.

His eyes ran down it. His office was showing audio-visual 'on'. The undergrad room was showing audio-visual and olfactory 'on'. The computer operations room was showing audio-visual 'on'. There were several other areas in COGS where there were cameras and they all showed as 'on'. He scrolled down and came to his house:

Location	Visual	Audio
MASTER BEDROOM	ON	ON
ENSUITE BATHROOM	ON	ON
JACK'S BEDROOM	ON	ON
SPARE BEDROOM	ON	ON
BATHROOM	ON	ON
STUDY	ON	ON

UPPER LANDING	ON	ON
HALL	ON	ON
DINING ROOM	ON	ON
DRAWING ROOM	ON	ON
KITCHEN	ON	ON
EXTERIOR FRONT	ON	ON
EXTERIOR REAR	ON	ON

Something cold and dark burrowed through Joe's veins and deep into his guts. *Off*. He had turned them all off. Every single one of them!

Someone had turned them back on.

He picked up his glass, his hand shaking so much that some whiskey slopped over the side. Then he looked back at his computer screen to make sure he was not mistaken. Slowly his eyes rose to the camera above the door. He could almost feel someone laughing at him.

He logged off, went straight down into the cellar, pulled out of its socket the massive boa containing ARCHIVE's wiring connections into the house, both for the cameras and for operating the lights, curtains and other electronic apparatus. Then he began the arduous task of isolating the individual wires to the cameras, and physically winding black tape around the end of each one.

On Sunday morning, as a bribe, Joe told Jack he would take him fishing on the pier after they'd been to see Karen. But only on the condition that Jack was nice to his mother, gave her a kiss and talked to her. Jack sat at the kitchen table concentrating on a painting, silent and withdrawn, and didn't reply.

It was a cold, overcast day that promised rain. As they loaded their tackle into the car, Muriel Arkwright, who was washing her car across the road, came over – stopping some yards away as if they had a contagious disease. She was wearing an apron, and holding a soapy sponge in her hand. It took her a moment to pluck up the courage to speak.

'Oh – er – good morning – er – professor,' she called out hesitantly.

They had never quite reached first-name terms, Joe because he had always avoided getting caught in conversations with her, and Muriel Arkwright because she was slightly in awe of him. She wasn't quite sure what he did, but word had it around the neighbourhood that he was very eminent.

Joe nodded and continued loading the boot. Muriel came closer, but kept to the pavement, not actually venturing on to the driveway itself, as if she needed to be invited to do that. She was a rather gawky woman in her late forties and her hair was bunched inside a knotted scarf that looked like a bath hat. Joe was aware of her presence behind him and it irritated him.

'Er – Professor Messenger – I just wanted to say – I read about the accident in the paper. Derek and I are so sorry. How is your wife?'

Joe turned reluctantly. 'She's out of immediate danger, but not too good, thank you.'

She pointed a hand at her house. 'We're just across the road. I wanted to say to you that – you know – if there's anything we could do?' She went beetroot red. 'She's in hospital still?'

'Yes – she'll be there a while.'

Jack trotted out of the house carrying the sandwich box, cuts and bruises on his face.

'Your son's all right?'

'Yes, fine, he was lucky, just superficial wounds.'

She noticed the trail of water that was dripping from her sponge and cupped a hand below it, as if not wanting to wet the pavement. 'If you like I could make you a few meals, pop them in the freezer? Do a bit of housework? Babysit if you need to go out?'

Joe looked at her more brightly. The extent of having to look after Jack – and himself – had begun to dawn on him last night, and he'd been wondering how on earth he was going to cope. Now his irritating neighbour suddenly offered a ray of hope. 'Well, I – I guess I would be grateful for a little help – that's very kind.'

As if this was a signal, Muriel took a couple of steps forward. Closer up, Joe could see how nervous she was. And she was studying him as if trying to assess him. She had an expression almost of suspicion, he thought.

'Did I see an ambulance the week before last, taking your son off?' she ventured. 'He's not been well?'

'He's fine now,' Joe said, not wanting to have to explain.

Her expression changed into a schoolgirlish look of mischief, 'That head last Sunday, professor! That did give me a shock – particularly when you said it was real! You nearly fooled me for a moment!'

Beneath her smile Joe could see she was probing. She was not a fool and must have seen the police afterwards. He smiled back awkwardly as the scene replayed in his mind and the original guilt over Juliet surged back. 'Right,' he said. 'It – er – did – look – I guess –' He shrugged, not wanting to elucidate.

She spared him. 'So would you like some food today? You're obviously going out. Derek and I are having roast chicken – how about if I pop some over for your evening meal?'

Joe felt quite touched. 'Thank you. I guess we'll be back around five.'

'Well – just knock on the door.'

He wouldn't need to knock on the door, he knew. She watched every coming and going in the street as if she was working for an intelligence service. Probably logged them in a notebook. He didn't care; right now he felt warmly grateful to her.

They stopped at a florist on the way to the hospital and Joe let Jack choose the flowers. Jack trotted around the shop, sniffing, and selected an assortment almost entirely of blues and yellows. 'Mummy's favourite colours,' he announced.

'That right?' Joe said. He realized, uncomfortably, that he

didn't really know. He determined he would spend as much time as possible with Karen while she was in hospital.

Karen was lying on her back, asleep, her leg encased in plaster and supported by a cord hanging from a pulley. Her face looked a little less waxy than yesterday, and the ghastly rims around her eyes had faded a little, Joe was relieved to see.

Jack ran straight up to her, ignoring Joe's hushed command not to wake her, laid the bouquet on her chest, put his arms around her neck and kissed her.

She opened her eyes, looking very dopey, but managed a weak smile. Joe kissed her and held her good hand. 'Brave girl,' he said.

'Joe-Joe,' she managed, giving his hand a tiny squeeze.

'Daddy burned my omelette. It tasted of cacka! Are you coming home today, Mummy?'

She smiled again; her eyes moved from Jack to Joe and she squeezed Joe's hand a fraction harder than before. 'Can you bring me photographs?' she murmured. 'Of you both. I'd like to have them on the table.'

Joe found himself fighting back tears. 'Sure. Bring them later today, OK?'

She gave a single nod. Jack looked at her plastered left arm, then at her leg. He followed the line of the cord upwards to the pulley. 'Why've you got that wheel up there, Mummy?'

'So she can go roller skating on the ceiling,' Joe said.

Jack looked at him, puzzled at first, then his face broke out into a grin. 'You can't go on the ceiling!' He turned to his mother. 'You can't, can you, Mummy? Daddy's being stupid!'

Joe kept the banter up. Karen smiled some more, then after a while she slept again.

The next morning, Joe dropped Jack off at playschool and pulled up in the car park behind COGS shortly after ten, feeling exhausted. Just getting his son washed, dressed and breakfasted had worn him out, and he'd been more than grateful when Mrs Arkwright had turned up, as promised, with their supper the night before.

Eileen Peacock's face was doom-laden as he reached her office. 'Good morning, professor. How is Mrs Messenger?'

'A little better, thanks.' Then he remembered. 'Oh – she was really pleased with the flowers – that was very nice of you.'

'From all of us.'

'Thanks. She was thrilled.'

'I've put all your messages up on your screen.' She said it as she always did, with a note of triumph, as if in mastering the computer she was showing that her age of close on sixty didn't matter. Then her expression clouded back into doom. 'Professor, the vice-chancellor's on the warpath over something. He wants to speak to you.'

'Oh?' He looked at her for more information, but she indicated that she had no idea what it was about. She knew that he and the VC didn't get on well.

'I'm afraid he doesn't seem in a very good mood,' she said, trying to give him a friendly warning.

'Yup, well I don't have much to be in a good mood about either right now,' Joe replied. He walked into his office, dumped his coat, and sat down. Almost immediately the phone rang.

'Yup?' he answered curtly.

'Could I please speak to Professor Messenger?'

Joe recognized the gravelly voice but for a second couldn't place it. 'Speaking.'

'Oh – Professor Messenger, it's Bill Pearse, *Daily Telegraph*.'

'Right, yes, good morning.'

'About the obituaries last week?'

'Yes.'

The man sounded a little embarrassed. 'We've had our computer boys on to this and they've just come back to me. It – er, it does appear to have been the work of a hacker.'

Joe stiffened, and asked him to go on.

'Well, I'm afraid it – it was traced back to your university. I understand it's been identified as a computer called ARCHIVE.'

Joe felt sick. It was what he'd expected, and yet he'd been praying for another explanation. 'ARCHIVE?' he echoed pointlessly.

'Perhaps it's one of your students with a macabre sense of humour, professor?'

Joe's mind trawled for candidates. Who could have pulled such a sick stunt? 'There's no possibility your people could be mistaken?' He tried to grasp at a straw.

'I have a hard-copy print-out which you're welcome to see, professor.'

There was a knock on Joe's door, but he did not respond to it. 'Right, OK,' he said. 'I guess I have to look into it this end.'

'It's someone very clever, professor. We run several anti-hacker and anti-virus systems in tandem. Whoever it was managed to get through them all.'

'I'm very sorry you've been put to this trouble,' Joe said.

'No – well – we're sorry too. Kids these days . . .'

'Yup,' Joe said, without conviction. He heard the knock on the door again, more insistent.

'Still, it's made us realize our system isn't foolproof.'

'There isn't any such thing as a hacker-proof computer,' Joe replied.

The door opened and his secretary peered in. 'The VC,' she hissed.

Joe raised a finger of acknowledgement at her, thanked the *Telegraph's* ad manager again and hung up. Then he put his Burberry back on and hurried out across the campus towards the admin block.

56

On the architect's drawing, Admin House had probably looked quite an imposing building, situated behind an ornamental lake on high ground. Now, thirty years later, with the plastic window surrounds stained like urinals, the ugly metal outside staircases that the new Fire Regulations demanded, and general poor weathering, it had more the air of a neglected tenement building than a seat of academe.

The view from inside the vice-chancellor's office was a lot better. Through the wide picture window Joe could see the whole of the toytown campus spread out below him, apart from the section obscured by the VC's grandiose rosewood desk.

'Please sit down, Professor Messenger.'

The vice-chancellor, a retired professor of physics in his early sixties, was a traditionalist who hated change, and above all hated anything that challenged the status quo of his particular subject. Joe sometimes felt he believed that everything there was to be learned about the world, and the universe, had already been learned, and that nothing new of any significance would ever be discovered.

The vice-chancellor's views were the kind of conceits, in Joe's opinion, that had retarded the advance of science for centuries. Professor Colin Colinson. Even his name had a kind of smug limitation about it. Joe watched him glide behind his desk, a small, dapper man in a grey suit, slip-on loafers, and immaculate grey hair. He was wearing a vulgar artistic tie, as if to tell the world that in spite of his suit he wasn't a bank manager. And large, clear plastic glasses which he evidently thought added to his panache but which would have suited a teenager better.

Colin Colinson took his time to sit down, managing to convey an air of disdain in the process. He had never made any secret of the fact that the only reason Joe was there was because of the finance for COGS that came from the Hartman Perpetuity Trust. The Trust had made it plain that without Joe the funding would go elsewhere.

'Professor Messenger.' He spoke slowly, drawing the full elasticity from each word. 'I'm so sorry to hear of your wife's accident.'

'Thank you,' Joe said, surprised at even this modest courtesy.

'She is all right?'

'She's not brilliant.'

'And your son?'

'He's OK.'

'I'm so pleased to hear it.' The VC's expression darkened. 'I have been contacted this morning by a Detective Inspector Reeves of Brighton Police. He tells me that the Highways Department of Brighton Council have been investigating the fault with the traffic lights that was responsible for your wife's accident.' He paused and rearranged the position of a pencil on his desk. 'Detective Inspector Reeves explained to me that these are computerized lights and they believed the problem might have been caused by a hacker, and accordingly the computer engineers called in a specialist security firm to investigate.'

The VC leaned forward and pressed his knuckles together. 'I have a faxed copy of the report this company gave to the Highways computer engineer on Friday afternoon. They established that it was indeed a hacker, professor, and they traced the computer that the hacker was using.' The VC's thin lips pursed together into an expression that managed, simultaneously, to convey both anger and triumph. 'It was your computer, ARCHIVE.'

Joe sat motionless. Yes, and it was my wife and child, he was thinking.

Colin Colinson frowned. 'You don't seem surprised, professor. I suppose after hacking into an American warship, a set of traffic lights is small beer – is that it?'

The wounds of the warship incident still hadn't healed after nearly three years. Joe swallowed, but fear instantly replaced the lump in his throat with another. 'It's not that,' he said, solemnly. 'It's –'

433

The VC raised his eyebrows in expectation.

'There've been other problems. But not involving the police,' he added quickly. 'I – don't think it's anyone inside the university.'

'Oh?' The vice-chancellor began massaging his hands as if he were soaping them. 'So who is it? A phantom?'

Joe felt his skin tightening. 'Someone hacking into AR-CHIVE from outside,' he said without conviction.

'But I've been led to understand ARCHIVE was such a smart computer that it could keep hackers out.'

'Maybe it's not as smart as we believe,' Joe said.

'Just smart enough to harm the name of this university, is that it?'

More concerned with the harm to his own family, Joe did not rise to the remark. 'I need to have an urgent look and see if I can find out exactly what's going on.'

'Make that *very* urgent, would you, please, professor.'

As Joe walked back across the campus, he didn't notice Blake coming from the direction of the library.

Blake caught his arm to get his attention. 'Hey! What's doing?'

Joe shrugged. The air reeked of Blake's pungent cologne.

'You look like shit. What news of Karen?'

'She was a little brighter yesterday. I'm going to see her lunchtime.'

'You OK?' Blake looked hard at him. 'Getting any sleep?'

'A little.'

'On for squash on Thursday?'

'I don't know – I guess I'll have to see how Karen is.'

'I think you should play – you need some exercise, do you good. You're going to need to keep your strength up. Listen, is there anything I can do for you to help, you know – at home or anything? You need anything?'

'No, that's good of you, thanks.'

'You just have to ask, OK?'

They walked on a couple of paces, then Joe stopped. 'Blake –' He hesitated. 'This may sound crazy. But do you

434

think Juliet Spring could have succeeded? In downloading herself, I mean – into ARCHIVE.'

'Why do you reckon that?' Blake's voice struck Joe as sounding suddenly a little strained.

'Well,' Joe said, shaking his head, 'there's something going on that's just – I don't know – freaky. It's like she's in there. Like she's in there and wants to get even with me. Do you understand what I'm saying? Tell me I'm nuts!'

'Are you saying she's downloaded *something* – some bit of her brain?' He looked hard at Joe. 'Or are you saying she's downloaded her entire consciousness?'

'I don't know, Blake, for sure. I just don't know how much.'

Blake looked at him hard again. 'Are you aware what you're saying, Joe?'

'Yes.'

'You want to tell me the whole story?'

'Right now?'

They went to the refectory. Blake bought them coffees and they sat at a table well out of earshot of anyone else.

Joe started at the beginning, telling Blake what had happened the first time Juliet Spring came to see him: the scan she'd made of his brain; the vast quantity of information that was recorded; the compression on to the terabyte cassettes; and their attempts to decode the signals. Then he told him about the events that had occurred with the computer after her death, starting with the appearance of Juliet's face on the screen, the messages from ARCHIVE, the way the memory kept filling then emptying, the obituaries, and the traffic lights. Blake listened intently.

When Joe had finished, Blake stirred his spoon in the bottom of his cup. 'The implication from all this is that ARCHIVE has become conscious, right? That Juliet is living on inside it in some kind of virtual world?'

'I find it very hard to accept – but I don't have any other explanation.'

'It's not a hacker playing games?'

'I've been through that and I just don't think it is a

hacker.' He gave a dry laugh. 'But if it isn't, the only person it could be is Juliet – and she's dead.'

'She's hacking from beyond the grave?' Blake looked at him quizzically.

'It's so uncanny, so personal, Blake. These communications I've had – it really is like she's in there at times. Remember when you came in the room the other day and she recognized you?' Joe became more intense. 'Look, I know ARCHIVE's years from becoming conscious, but let's put it like this: either Juliet has downloaded herself – or ARCHIVE has adopted her persona.'

'You really think it's years from becoming conscious?'

Joe parried. 'Depends how we define consciousness.'

'No one's yet been able to define it. You've built ARCHIVE to try to recreate human consciousness in a machine. If you don't know what consciousness is, how do you know ARCHIVE hasn't got there?'

Joe dropped his eyes to the table. 'I guess I don't,' he said quietly.

'Joe, if you believe what you've just told me, you'd better go shout it from the rooftops! And if you can prove it –' Blake opened his hands out wide. 'If you can prove it . . .'

'Prove what, Blake? That I've built a computer that's trying to kill my wife and child?'

'Don't be an asshole, that doesn't matter.'

Joe felt the anger rip through him and he had to restrain himself from grabbing Blake by the throat. 'What the fuck do you mean, *it doesn't matter*?'

Blake lounged back in his chair, unperturbed. 'It's a detail, Joe.'

'Excuse me? Creating a machine capable of killing is a *detail*?'

'Sure. If what you're telling me is true, then it's what ARCHIVE is that matters right now, not what it *does*.'

'What if man's only capable of creating something that's innately evil, Blake?'

'You're saying there should be no progress, in case that's all we're capable of?' Blake sat upright again. 'Come on, Joe! We believe in immortality; that's why we're together!'

'And that's the reason why anything we create has to be innately good.'

Blake tapped the back of his hand with a spare coffee spoon. 'So when *are* you going to make the announcement that'll rock the world?'

'When I've learned how to make ARCHIVE behave.'

'God hasn't learned how to make us behave,' Blake said. 'And he's been working on it for a hundred million years.'

Joe pushed his cup aside. 'I guess that's why we need to become immortal.' He looked up at Blake. 'To stay the course.'

Joe went back to his office, logged straight into ARCHIVE's operating systems, and typed: Talk zebedee.

On the screen appeared: Calling . . .

After some moments the screen cleared, then: Calling your party again.

It repeated five times without success. Joe cleared the instruction and called up the list of all the processes running. To his surprise, Zebedee had disappeared. He scrolled through twice, to make sure, then phoned down to Dave Hoton.

'Dave, have you killed any systems processes?'

'No, I haven't changed anything.'

'There was one called *zebedee*.'

'Like in *The Magic Roundabout*? Yes, I saw it last week. I assumed you were running it.'

'It's not there any more.'

The system manager was silent. 'Must be our hacker again, part of his wiping his tracks.'

Joe thanked him and hung up, not convinced. He exited from the operating systems and logged back into ARCHIVE.

Good morning, Professor Messenger. A blustery one with 90 per cent chance of precipitation this afternoon. Your television cameras at home are not working. Someone has disconnected them at source. Is it you? Are you feeling shy?

No, I'm not shy. I'd like you to tell me about Juliet Spring, please.

Is Juliet Spring a name, professor?

Yes, Joe responded, surprised.

I have no recall of this name.

You must have. You had very strong views about her. You warned me about her.

Sorry, professor. Please try another name. Or perhaps another word for spring? Would you like thesaurus mode?

Joe declined, exited and logged off. Then he went down into the computer-operations room. For the next four hours he searched through ARCHIVE's operating systems with Dave Hoton. They looked at every part of the computer where it would be possible for a smart hacker to hide instructions, going right through the kernel and even the boot-strap loader. They found nothing at all.

At half past three in the afternoon Joe left to collect Jack from playschool. He drove slowly, deep in thought. No trace of Juliet Spring in ARCHIVE at all. Her disappearance from the computer's directories and files was too clean. She'd been a legitimate user; so why now the total wiping of the slate? How could ARCHIVE have warned him to be careful of her only a few weeks ago and now not even remember her? Was it smart enough to lie? ARCHIVE did not forget things; loss of information from its memory could come only from a technical fault or deliberate erasing. And erasing by a hacker would have left traces. Only himself and Dave Hoton had the superuser status that gave access to the areas of ARCHIVE needed to wipe records, and the knowledge of the hidden duplication 'traps' that protected against loss of information in a crash or deliberate erasing by a hacker. Not even Blake had that.

A snowstorm blew in his stomach. He was scared of what he could not find. It was as though there really was a ghost in the machine. One that had been there ever since Juliet's death.

He stopped at a red light. As the line of traffic flashed across the intersection in front of him he looked up, eyeing the light warily, and noticed the camera mounted beside it that was eyeing him back. He glanced away dismissively, to show Juliet if she was still watching that he wasn't afraid of her.

But when the light went green he waited for some moments, nervously, until he could be certain the traffic coming from the right and the left was stopping. The car behind gave an irritated blast of its horn, but he still waited for some seconds before plucking up the courage to press the accelerator.

57

At half past four Joe came into the ward as he did every weekday afternoon, having collected Jack from playschool. Only today, Joe was walking slowly, almost waddling, and Karen couldn't see Jack.

As Joe came nearer, she noticed his coat was bulging oddly either side of him, and he seemed to have an extra pair of legs. He reached the bed, and Jack suddenly popped out between his legs.

'April Fool, Mummy!' he yelled.

She laughed, then held her breath, wincing in pain.

'Did I fool you? Did I?'

Her eyes watered as the pain subsided. 'You sure did.' Her voice came out as a squeaky whisper. 'I forgot it was April Fool's today.' She wasn't going to let him know that the April Fool rebounded unless you did it before midday. 'I wondered what Daddy had done with you.'

'How you feeling, hon?' Joe said, kissing her and handing her a paper bag.

She shrugged. 'OK, I guess.' She looked at the bag with interest and peered inside.

'Any visitors?' He glanced at the array of flowers, cards and chocolates beside her.

'My aerobics teacher came by this morning. Brought me the chocolates and some books. I've been sleeping since then.'

'She didn't get you up dancing?'

'I wish,' she said with only the faintest trace of a smile. She upended the bag and shook out a thick paperback. It was an anthology of Margaret Atwood short stories, which she'd asked Joe to get, feeling homesick for Canada and wanting to read something by a Canadian. She'd been homesick for a lot of things lately, stuck in the not so OK UK. She could remember a time when being with Joe had always made her feel so safe. Now she'd nearly been killed and she didn't feel safe any more. And she was becoming increasingly frightened by what she saw as Joe's obsessiveness, and by his inability to respect death. Although she knew it would have finished him if death had taken her or Jack.

She watched Jack trot off across the ward to visit an elderly man with both legs in plaster, whom he'd befriended on a previous visit. Joe sat beside her and touched her cheek lightly with his knuckles. 'Got more colour in your face today.'

'Good. How was work?'

'Quietening down for Easter. I've been putting together my address for the Royal Society.'

'Do you think I'll be able to come?' she asked.

'Sure you will. It's mid-June. Be right as rain by then.'

'I don't think I'll ever be right as rain again,' she said.

'Hey, all the doctors say you'll recover one hundred per cent. They're really pleased with your progress.

She stared ahead vacantly. 'Physically, maybe. But . . .' Her voice tailed.

'But what?' Joe began to feel infected by her despondency.

'I don't know,' she said. 'I guess I have too much time to think in here. I keep thinking about us.'

Joe felt a prick of alarm. 'How do you mean?'

'I don't think we have much of a life together any more.' She switched her empty gaze to the grey slate of a rooftop

440

out of the window. 'You've become so obsessed about death that you no longer have any interest in life.'

'That's not true, hon,' Joe said, hurt.

'It is. You don't see it. You used to be such fun, Joe. When did we last have *fun*?'

He too looked out of the window. He felt guilty. A gull hovered in the headwind. The pane rattled. 'How about we go on a holiday when you get out of here? Somewhere real nice? Maybe Barbados?'

She nodded and her face brightened a little. 'I'd like that.'

Joe kissed her. 'I love you.'

'Love you too,' she said heavily.

58

Joe and Dave Hoton had searched through ARCHIVE's directories, files and kernel every few days for the first few weeks after Karen's accident, checking to make sure that no trace of Zebedee had reappeared. After a month passed, Joe decided to reconnect the cameras in his house, and see whether that produced any difference.

One minor relief to him was a further letter that arrived from the coroner, informing him that Juliet's father had dropped his demands for an inquest in order to spare his family the humiliation of any press coverage. The coroner was going to put this to a judicial review, as he was legally bound to, with his strong recommendation that it be accepted.

But Joe's work on ARCHIVE was curtailed by so much of his time being taken up in looking after Jack and visiting Karen, which he did at least twice every day. The doctors had warned him that depression after a serious injury was very common, and he spent long hours at Karen's bedside, trying to lift her out of it.

He also had his numerous duties at the university to fulfil

– despite the Easter vac – and the added strain of preparing his paper for the Royal Society in June, under the cloud that he no longer fully understood how the computer he had created actually worked. In truth, he was very nervous of ARCHIVE now, and some of his enthusiasm for the entire human-consciousness project had gone.

Karen's sister, Arlene, flew over from Toronto and stayed for ten days, taking some of the pressure off Joe, and her visit cheered Karen considerably. The two sisters had remained close. Their mother wanted to come over, but was unable to leave their father, who was ailing with heart trouble.

Trailing a set behind in a game of tennis with Blake during the last week in April, at the start of the summer term, Joe returned Blake's easy second serve into the net for the third point running.

'Come on, Joe – wake up!' Blake shouted.

'Sorry.'

'Two–love.' Blake walked up to the net, shaking his head. 'You have to get yourself back together.'

A gust of wind blew a leaf across the surface of the court, then died. Joe bent and picked it up, tossed it in the air and hit it hard with his racquet. The leaf disintegrated. 'I need some home help,' he said. 'My goddam neighbour's dementing me. I made the mistake of giving her a key so she could put meals in the oven for me and Jack; now she's forever cleaning the place; I can't get her out!'

'Sounds like a good neighbour. What's the problem?'

Joe stared at him. 'You've seen her. The bug-eyed bat across the road who's on secondment from the Ministry of Dust Eradication. I come home, she's cleaning the kitchen. I have supper, she's up cleaning the bathroom. Ten o'clock at night she's hoovering the carpets.'

Blake grinned. 'Maybe she wants you to screw her.'

'Thanks a lot!'

Blake picked up the ball. 'Listen, I may know of someone who could help you.' He tossed the ball to Joe. It bounced once, then Joe caught it.

'Uh?'

'Yeah, there's a guy I used to work with in my postgrad days. Matt Brewster. He's based in Hong Kong now and keeps asking me out to stay. He rang me at the weekend, wondered if I could help out some bright kid he's met. She's starting at Oxford in October, wants to find a live-in job for the summer. Kind of like an au pair sort of thing.'

Joe looked at him with interest. 'You serious?'

'Yup.'

'She wouldn't mind living down here?'

'I gather she's pretty shy – you know – hasn't travelled around much.' He squatted and retied a lace on his shoe. 'It might suit me too; I can give her a couple of research projects at the Human Organ Centre, but she'd only have to come in an hour or two a week.'

Joe grinned. 'When can she start!'

'I can call – find out. Want me to?'

'Sure.' He patted the strings of his racquet. 'I was going to stick an ad up on the noticeboard – but this could be great.'

Blake looked at his watch. 'Hong Kong time is –' He thought for a moment. 'Eight hours ahead, I guess. Nine o'clock at night there right now. I'll try when I get back to my office.'

'What's her name?'

Blake looked as if he was trying to remember. 'Stassi,' he said after a moment. 'Stassi Holland.' Then added, 'Anastasia, I guess,' by way of an explanation.

'Oh, right, yup. Sounds pretty smart.'

Blake stared arrogantly back at him. 'I don't have any contacts who aren't smart, Joe.'

Joe blushed, as if he had offended in some way. 'Nice name, I like it.' He bounced the ball and put it in his pocket, then picked up a second ball from the back of the court, walked to the base line and took his stance to serve. 'Love–two, right?'

He tossed the ball in the air and served an ace.

*

443

Afterwards, as Joe towelled himself dry in the shower room, he said: 'You've been very good to me these past few weeks.'

Blake, in his unbuttoned shirt and silk boxers, squinted at himself in the mirror, then rubbed some gel into his wet hair. 'That's what friends are for.' He picked up his comb and began raking his hair back. Freed from its ponytail, it hung like a fringe over the back of his collar. He stopped suddenly and turned round. 'You know, we've come a long way, Joe, and we're nearly there. I don't want you quitting on me now.'

Joe carried on drying himself. He pulled the towel between each of his toes in turn, the way his father had taught him. *Stops you gettin' rot*, Willi used to say.

'You're not giving up heart, are you, Joe?'

'Nope,' he said quietly.

Blake patted him on the back. 'That's your father's boy.' He turned to the mirror again and scooped the hair at the back of his head together. 'Remember you owe him one.' His voice took on a faintly ominous tone. 'A big one.'

'What do you mean, Blake?'

'You know what I mean.' Blake gave himself a sideways look in the mirror.

Blake was ageing well, Joe thought; if anything, the years had made him even more strikingly handsome; and Blake was well aware of it.

'You have to get your head back together; all your wild ideas about Juliet's downloading succeeding and stuff – you know I really thought you were getting a bit unhinged there.' Blake moved away from the mirror with a smile. 'But I guess you'll pull through.'

Joe watched him, always irritated when Blake got on his paternal high horse. 'It has been rough, the last month or so. Someone like this girl, Anastasia, could really help. Do you have any idea how much I'd have to pay her?'

'Pocket money, I'd guess, if you're giving her board and lodging,' he said. 'But I shouldn't think it'll be a problem; my pal said her family are loaded. British ex-pats.'

'Ah, right,' Joe said, wondering if he, Karen and Jack would live up to the girl's expectations.

59

Stassi Holland arrived at eleven in the morning on Sunday 2 May, the day before Karen was due to come home from hospital. Blake pulled up his black Ferrari on the drive, and Joe went outside to greet her. It was a bank holiday weekend, and the neighbourhood had a quiet, backwater feel. Even Muriel Arkwright was absent, gone with her husband to stay with her daughter-in-law, although she'd left Joe's fridge and freezer stacked with prepared food, and a manual on how to heat it. The house was spotless and reeked of polish and cleaning fluid.

Blake had opened the passenger door and was helping Stassi out. As she stood up, loose strands of her hair tossing in the wind, she seemed a little disoriented. Jet lag, Joe assumed, stepping down from the porch.

She was about five feet five inches tall, with long, brown hair clasped in a velvet headband, a slim figure and a good-looking face; strong, high cheekbones, a pretty snub nose and a well-proportioned mouth. Only her complexion, which was pallid after her long journey, diminished her attractiveness.

Blake introduced her, and Joe stepped forward, holding out his hand. He was surprised how strong her grip was, which seemed out of character with the rest of her as she smiled shyly, revealing perfect white teeth, so perfect that Joe took them for the work of a good orthodontist.

Her eyes engaged his fleetingly: dark brown eyes with large pupils, making them hard to read. She smelled of a cologne he vaguely recognized; it had a classiness reminiscent of the scents that lingered in the lifts of expensive hotels. Yet at the same time there was something faintly old-fashioned about her that Joe found immediately endearing.

Part of it was the classic way she was dressed, in a neat blue blazer with a pleated skirt, a plain cream open-necked blouse with a horsy silk scarf inside, and flat black shoes with a single gold chain across the tongue. Part of it was in the quietness of her demeanour; in contrast to the eccentricities of so many of his students, she struck Joe as being reassuringly normal. He just hoped that Blake had told him the truth about her not minding menial work.

He winked his approval at his colleague as Blake ducked into the nose of the Ferrari, heaved out a large leather suitcase and a holdall and put them on the ground, their baggage tags fluttering in the wind.

Joe picked them up. 'How was your flight?' he asked, turning back to her. 'Did you come direct or stop over?'

He caught an odd expression on Blake's face, as if he had suddenly been stricken with doubt. A signal seemed to pass between Blake and the girl; Joe puzzled over it for a moment, not understanding quite why his question had provoked this curious chain reaction.

Then he wondered darkly if this was Blake up to his tricks with women again. Had Blake already got his paws on her? Was he sleeping with her or trying to? Was this the real reason why Blake had arranged for her to come over? Had she already been here a few days, staying with Blake, got a thing going? Or had they met somewhere en route? Doubts ransacked him. He hadn't bothered asking for references because he'd felt it would be insulting to Blake, and maybe the academic in him had been sufficiently impressed by the fact that she'd gained a place at Oxford.

Surely she wasn't remotely Blake's type? Blake went out with hard, glammy girls like Nico; Stassi seemed so sheltered and quite probably was very naïve. Then the tone of her reply allayed his concerns.

'It was quite pleasant until Calcutta,' she said; her voice a little reedy, accentuated by the very precise way she spoke, as if she was striving to give a ladylike impression in spite of her exhaustion. 'We landed there about ten o'clock last night. Then I had a mother and baby beside me and the baby cried for most of the rest of the flight.'

They went into the house. 'I'm looking forward to meeting Jack,' she said. 'He's three?'

'More like three and three quarters!' Joe said. 'He's very exact about his age.'

Joe looked up at the landing and called out to Jack, but there was no response. He called louder. 'Jack! Come and meet Anastasia.' He turned to the girl. She was stifling a yawn. 'You prefer to be called Stassi or Anastasia?'

'Stassi,' she said. 'I always think Anastasia's a bit of a mouthful.'

Blake followed them in and slammed the front door shut behind him. 'House looks nice and clean, Joe!' he teased.

'Not to Muriel Arkwright, it doesn't,' he said, putting the bags down. 'OK, I'll show you your room, and I'll put some coffee on.' He turned to Blake. 'Like some coffee?'

Blake glanced at his watch. 'A quick cup, then I have to run.'

'There's plenty of food if you'd like lunch – I didn't know what time you'd be here, so I catered for you – or rather Muriel did.'

Blake shook his head. 'Got to collect Nico – going to Gloucestershire, spending tomorrow with some friends of hers in a stately pile.'

Joe carried the bags upstairs, stopping outside Jack's room. He opened the door; Jack was kneeling on the floor, piecing together a section of Lego. 'Stassi's here, Jack; come and say hello to her?'

Jack carried on working on the Lego without looking up, without saying anything.

'Jack,' Joe said a little more firmly.

Jack studied an assortment of loose pieces, selected one and studied it carefully. Joe looked at the girl, who was standing right behind him, a little embarrassed. He dropped his voice to a whisper. 'I think he's a bit shy.'

She smiled back at him, understanding. 'He'll be OK, we'll get along fine.' She turned to Jack. 'Hello, Jack.'

There was no response from him, but she didn't seem fazed. She stood still for a moment, then took a couple of steps forward. 'Hello, I'm Stassi. What are you making? A crane?'

Jack slotted another two pieces together. Joe felt angry at him, wanted to shake him, but he contained himself. He remembered the way Jack had refused to talk to Karen the first time they'd been to the hospital. Maybe he was scared now that Stassi was going to usurp Karen? Or maybe he was annoyed because his train set had been moved out of the spare room for Stassi and put in his own room.

Looking at Stassi again, he was glad Karen was going to be back tomorrow. Karen had not been overjoyed about the prospect of having someone living in, even though she agreed it would be hard to manage without; she would be even less overjoyed to think that Joe had spent several weeks in the house with someone so pretty.

As if reading his thoughts, Stassi smiled demurely back at him. He picked up her bags and took her down to the spare room at the end of the corridor. Joe had put the portable television, normally kept in their bedroom, on top of the chest of drawers, and Muriel Arkwright had added a vase of flowers.

She went over to the window overlooking the garden and gazed out. She seemed fascinated by something, and Joe wondered what.

'I didn't realize –' she said, then stopped abruptly, blushing very slightly. 'Such a pretty garden,' she added, almost as if she was changing the subject.

'Do you have a garden in Hong Kong?'

Stassi was still looking out of the window. 'Different,' she said suddenly. 'Quite different.' Then she continued to stare in silence, as if she'd forgotten his presence.

Joe said he'd leave her to settle while he made coffee.

Back downstairs, Blake was glancing at *The Times* in the kitchen. 'So what do you think, Joe?'

Joe tried to see what he could read in Blake's face, remembering that exchanged glance outside. 'Nice kid,' he said. 'You reckon she isn't going to mind housework?'

'She knows the score. I think she's just happy to be over here – and very grateful.'

Joe set some ground coffee on the go, then glanced surreptitiously at Blake. 'I didn't realize she was going to be so pretty.'

There was no change in Blake's expression. His eyes scanned an article as he spoke. 'Piece of luck, eh, Joe?' It could have meant anything.

Hope my wife agrees, thought Joe. Aloud, he said, 'I'm going to offer her fifty pounds a week. And I told her she can have the use of Karen's car. I bought another one the other day.'

'The white Toyota outside?'

'Yes.'

'It'll help you a lot. She'll be able to take Jack to playschool.'

Joe pulled the sugar out of the cupboard; the percolator gurgled. 'I guess I'll see how she copes. I still don't like the idea of anyone driving him other than Karen or me –' He shrugged. 'You know – ever since Barty . . . and now this crash. It's –'

He broke off as he saw Stassi standing hesitantly in the doorway, as if afraid she was interrupting.

Joe indicated for her to come in and sit down. 'You must be exhausted,' he said. 'Long flights whack me out.'

She noticed the paintings on the walls and walked over to look closely. 'Are these Jack's?' she asked Joe.

'Yes.'

'They're good. He's talented.'

Joe was a little flattered. 'Thanks; we think so – but I guess we're his parents!'

She smiled at Joe and sat down. 'I understand your wife had a car accident, Professor Messenger?'

'Oh, please, call me Joe . . . Er, yes. She had a lot of damage to her rib cage and lungs – and a broken arm and leg. She's mending – her arm's OK now, but she had a multiple fracture in her leg and she can't walk on it yet.'

'You've been very kind in giving me this job and the

lodgings. I'd be happy to stay in and help as much as necessary, until your wife is better.'

'That's nice of you, Stassi.' Joe glanced at Blake. 'But we'll sort something out so that you can do a research stretch too.' He poured three coffees and proffered the sugar bowl to Stassi.

'No, thank you,' she said politely. 'I never take sugar.' Her hand trembled as she raised her cup to her lips.

Poor kid looked exhausted, Joe thought. She was twenty, Blake had told him. If he hadn't known, he'd have said she was older, closer to twenty-five; but tiredness did that to people, slackened the facial muscles, ageing them.

They sipped their coffees in silence for some moments. Blake struck Joe as seeming oddly subdued. And he hoped Stassi hadn't been put off by Jack's refusal to greet her. He asked her questions about her family and each time, before answering, Stassi seemed nervous as if needing reassurance that it was all right to talk. Then she would reply in her reedy, precise voice. She was almost painfully shy, Joe realized. Maybe she would open out, being away from her folks.

Blake finished his coffee and stood up. 'OK, I have to be off.' He looked at Stassi for some moments. 'Everything all right?'

She nodded. 'I have a nice room.'

He leaned down and gave her a pat on the shoulder. 'I'll call you on Tuesday morning and we'll make arrangements for you to come over to the lab, OK?' He turned and walked towards the door without waiting for Stassi's reply.

She looked a little disoriented suddenly, following him out of the room with her eyes, like a puppy being abandoned in kennels.

As Joe opened the front door, Blake glanced back at the kitchen, pressed a piece of paper into Joe's hand, and lowered his voice. 'That's the number where I'll be over the bank holiday. If you have any problems, call me.'

'Problems?' Joe repeated, wondering what he meant. But Blake climbed into his Ferrari, closed the door and started the engine without any further explanation. He drove off with a roar of exhaust and no backward glance, as if he was relieved to have got away.

<h1 style="text-align:center">60</h1>

Karen watched Stassi. The girl had been with them just over a month and although Karen wasn't crazy about her she had got over the original misgivings she'd had that bank holiday Monday when she'd arrived home and seen Stassi for the first time. Seen how attractive she was. Joe had neglected to mention Stassi's looks, and they'd heightened her own feeling of how lousy she herself looked right now.

She felt as if she'd aged a hundred years. She had little energy and every movement hurt either her arm or her leg, both of which were now in soft bandages, or her chest and rib cage; in spite of that she still refused to take painkillers in the daytime, convinced they made her even more tired. She hated the handicap of being able to get around only with the help of crutches, and worked herself into exhaustion doing the exercises the physiotherapist, to whom Joe or Stassi drove her twice a week, set her.

But more than anything she was distressed about her appearance. Friends kept telling her how well she was looking, but she was convinced they were lying. The face that stared back at her from the mirror seemed puffy and to have lost its shape; there were deep rings around her eyes, and two ugly scars, one on her forehead and another on her cheek. The consultant had assured her the scars would be barely noticeable in a few months, and if she was still unhappy they could be removed by plastic surgery. Every day she checked and could see no sign of them fading.

Stassi had been a good idea; she'd turned out to be a bright, hard-working girl, and Jack had taken a real shine to her. And Karen had seen no evidence of her showing any interest in Joe, or the reverse. She felt angry at herself for her jealousy. She told herself maybe it was in part due to the insecurity of being so far from home. She had not really thought that Joe would ever stray, until she had found the note from Juliet Spring in his jacket. In spite of his vehement denials, her deep suspicions remained.

And she kept a wary eye on Stassi, aware how slender, fresh and youthful she looked in contrast to herself right now. She noticed with some unease that the girl had been on a few shopping sprees, and her clothes style had become more modern, probably influenced by seeing other students, and by television.

Karen watched her now, hefting heavy plastic bags of groceries into the kitchen, from her weekly visit to Asda; she was wearing a loose jumper, leggings and trainers. Karen sat at the kitchen table, her crutches nearby, and helped Stassi by unpacking the contents of the bags on to the table. It was midday, Friday.

The weekend tomorrow, she thought. Joe and Jack would be around and she looked forward to their company. Perhaps because of her constant tiredness, she found it difficult to read for any length of time without losing her concentration, and there was little on television that interested her. The weather had been foul and she had been unable to get out in the garden much either. Aerobics was off the agenda and for the first time in her life she found time hanging heavily on her hands.

She had regular visits from various girlfriends and neighbours – in particular Muriel Arkwright, who had begun to dement her – but while there'd been a flurry at first, the same as there had been those first couple of weeks in hospital, she was now having to call people to invite them round, and sometimes she felt as if she was forcing a chore on them.

She heard the front door shut, then Stassi carried one more bag into the kitchen and put it down on the floor. 'That's it, phew!' she said. A bead of perspiration rolled down her temple. It was a warm, early summer day, and the patio doors on to the garden were open. 'Would you like some coffee, Karen?'

452

'Sure.' Karen peered inside the last bag. 'You didn't get the apple juice?'

Stassi looked at her blankly. 'I didn't see it on the list.'

'No – wasn't on the list. I told you as you were leaving.'

Stassi frowned. 'Did you? I'm sorry – I don't remember at all.'

Karen thought for a moment. She distinctly recalled telling Stassi clearly, suggesting she wrote it down, because she often forgot things unless they were written down. It was odd. She seemed such a bright girl, yet she was incredibly forgetful. And it wasn't just a case of things slipping her mind – like now with the apple juice – she seemed to forget completely that she'd ever been asked in the first place.

Although Karen found it a little disturbing, she had said nothing to Joe. She was scared the problem might be with herself, not Stassi. Sometimes she resisted taking the painkillers even at night, and ended up giving in after hours of lying awake. When that happened, she would feel in a dream-like state for much of the morning, and she worried that maybe she sometimes only *imagined* that she'd asked Stassi to do things.

Stassi walked over to the cupboard and pulled out a filter paper and tin of coffee. There was a careless arrogance in her stride, an air that she seemed to adopt each time Karen caught her out. Her childish way of coping with her guilt, Karen thought.

'Was the store busy?' she asked, trying to defuse the situation.

'Yes, packed,' Stassi said quietly, her face flushing, or perhaps it was just the heat. She filled the percolator with water and set two mugs on the table, then began silently putting away the groceries.

Except with Jack, when she seemed to become vividly animated, Stassi was a quiet girl who rarely started a conversation. Karen wasn't sure whether it was shyness, or whether it was a feeling of superiority, but often when they did talk she tended to find Stassi a little condescending. And she found herself jealous not only of Stassi's looks, but also of the way she got on so well with Jack. Often, exhausted by late afternoon, Karen would go to bed; later she'd listen to the sound of Jack's bath running, to splashing water and the giggles of Stassi and Jack fooling around; later still, to Stassi's voice through the wall, reading him a bedtime story.

After a couple of weeks Joe had said that he thought Stassi would be fine to do Jack's playschool run; Karen had misgivings about that. She worried about the forgetfulness, worried that Stassi might forget to stop at a red light . . .

She had asked Joe several times how it could have happened that the lights all went green at the same time, and he never seemed comfortable when he answered her. He muttered about condensation causing problems, explained in detail how sometimes a chip could go wrong, disabling a circuit board, but every time he talked about it, and mumbled about the Highways Department still investigating, he seemed unable to look her completely in the eye. The police were investigating and a lawyer had begun litigation for damages.

'Gulliver.'

Karen looked up, startled. Stassi was standing by the percolator, staring blankly at the wall in front of her.

'Did you say Gulliver?' Karen asked.

'Me?' Stassi turned to her, puzzled. 'I didn't say anything.'

Karen frowned. She'd had another bad night last night and had finally taken a painkiller at five a.m. Was her mind playing tricks?

The percolator had gone silent, and curls of steam rose from it. Stassi nonchalantly lifted the jug and poured.

On Sunday evening Karen stayed down for supper. Afterwards, Joe helped her upstairs to bed. Ordinarily on a Sunday night he would switch off from work and watch a video, but tonight he was a bag of nerves, fretting about his address to the Royal Society on Wednesday.

He pulled his Macintosh Powerbook out of his briefcase, switched it on and scrolled through some additional points he had to add to his speech. He looked at them glumly, no longer sure what he actually wanted to say.

During the past weeks he had been repeatedly hassled by the police investigating Karen's accident. The Computer Crimes division of Scotland Yard had interviewed all his students and staff. Edwin Pilgrim had gone down with shingles caused by the stress and would be away for weeks.

The police had concluded beyond doubt, as he had also, that ARCHIVE had hacked the lights. But he had the feeling they hadn't been totally forthcoming with him and he wondered if they suspected that the hacking might even have been his doing: that he might have been trying to murder his wife and child.

Finally, this past Thursday, he'd been called to a meeting with the police in the vice-chancellor's office. The officer in charge, a sharp detective sergeant of about thirty, called Ray Kerman, stated that in their view the hacking of the lights had been done by someone outside the university who'd covered his tracks too well to be found.

The hacker had simultaneously cracked into ARCHIVE from, apparently, forty different telephone exchanges, and into each of those from another forty routed around the world. Working back, there were further multiple routings; Kerman stated blandly that to find the culprit would mean individual follow-ups on over six million telephone numbers in at least thirty countries. It was an impossibility to do that. He concluded that it was probably the work of a bored student or computer programmer, almost anywhere in the world. And it was a billion to one chance that it had affected those particular traffic lights.

Joe had said little at the meeting. The detective sergeant's explanation had mollified the VC and got the university off the hook.

He looked back down at his laptop and yawned. It had been a tiring day; he'd taken Karen, Jack and Stassi for a drive, and they'd picnicked in the grounds of a stately home. The temperature had climbed into the seventies, they'd been stuck in a long jam on the way home, and Jack had become tetchy.

Stassi was working out well, he thought. She was quiet, studious, willing to do any job in the house, and around all the time except for the few hours twice a week when she went to see Blake at the Human Organ Preservation Centre, or when she went shopping.

Joe was a little surprised that she never seemed to have any desire to go out on her own, but maybe that was because she was finding her feet. She seemed content to be around the house, to play with Jack, to help Karen. And yet there was something just a little strange about her and he couldn't quite work out what. Earlier today, she had been chatting away in the back of the car to Jack, yet every time he looked in the mirror, she had seemed to be watching him. Smiling at him. After a while he had tried to stop using the mirror because he found it too distracting.

He yawned again and would have liked to go to bed, but he wanted to put in an hour or so's work, and went down-stairs to make some coffee. On the way he heard music, the roar of a car engine, then shouting, all coming from the drawing room. Stassi was watching a video.

He stuck his head around the door and looked at the television for some moments, recognizing the music: *The Godfather*. Another old video. She seemed obsessed by them, watched a different one almost every night. During the past week she'd watched *The Sting*, *Death in Venice*, *The French Connection*, *Women in Love* and *The Prime of Miss Jean Brodie*. 'Hi,' he said. 'I'm just making coffee. Like some?'

She sat on the edge of the sofa in a baggy pink T-shirt and black leggings, absorbed in the film, and did not appear to hear him. On the screen, Al Pacino walked across a wide lawn. A dog bounded over, barking. Two men were sitting in garden chairs.

'Gulliver,' she said suddenly.

'Huh?' Joe said.

She leaned forward, as if even more deeply absorbed.

'Gulliver, did you say?' He continued to wait, awkwardly,

for a response, but none came. Engrossed in the film, she hadn't noticed him. He began to feel like an intruder in the room, as if he shouldn't be interrupting. He went out and closed the door.

In the kitchen he ran some water into the kettle and as he did so he sensed movement behind him and turned round. Stassi had come into the room.

She gave him a rather hesitant smile. 'Would it be OK if I had a glass of water?' Her voice sounded more reedy and precise than ever, and her eyes fixed on his for a fleeting moment, then looked shyly down at the floor.

'Of course.' He frowned, wondering why she felt the need to ask. Then she looked at him again, as if for reassurance. She seemed very edgy.

'Sure you don't want any coffee –?' he said.

'No, thank you. Just water would be fine.'

'Enjoying the movie?'

She nodded, but something seemed to be upsetting her. She bit her lip then turned away from him, looking completely lost for some moments. Joe watched her, wondering what on earth was the matter, suddenly worried for her. Then she reached out, opened a cupboard door and took out a glass tumbler.

She gripped it in her hands for some moments, staring at it as if it was a prize, then she walked past him and held it under the tap.

'You're always welcome to help yourself to bottled water,' he said.

'Thanks – this is fine,' she said. 'I like this water.' She turned away from the sink holding the tumbler in her left hand, the other hanging free, turned inches in front of him, and as she did, her right hand brushed lightly across his crotch.

He moved back sharply, startled, and felt a deep erotic tightening in the pit of his stomach. She continued to walk over to the door as if she hadn't noticed. His mind raced with confusion. It was almost as if she'd done it deliberately – and yet she couldn't have, surely?

She glanced at him for one fleeting instant as she went out of the kitchen, in a way that was wholly unreadable, that could have meant everything or nothing.

An accident. Just an accident. He tried to dismiss it, but was unable to prevent himself replaying the sensation of her fingers trailing across the front of his cords. Then the look she had given him as she went out of the door. The knowing look?

As he opened the coffee jar, his hand shook so hard that he scattered freeze-dried granules over the floor. And it was an hour before he could concentrate on anything.

Later, as he lay in the put-you-up bed beside Karen, which he had used since she'd come back from hospital, he thought again of Stassi's eyes watching him in the interior mirror of the car; and the quiet smile that had been on her face. Thought of her hand brushing against him in the kitchen. And he felt afraid, suddenly.

When he pictured her face there was something in her expression that seemed both familiar and completely alien. An inexplicable apprehension gathered force within him and as it did so, it seemed to heighten his arousal even more.

61

Karen went to bed straight after an early supper on Tuesday evening, wanting to be as rested as possible for the following day's trip to London and the ordeal of Joe's address to the Royal Society. She was feeling nervous about appearing in public, and regretting her original bravado in telling Joe she'd decided to go. She wanted to be there to support him, but she wondered if she was doing the right thing; looking the way she did would it be better to stay at home, out of sight? But each time she mentioned that to Joe he wouldn't hear of it.

Joe went back into his study and sat at his desk. He was

still not happy with his speech. He had re-read the text of his previous address from three years ago, and what he'd written now was largely a rehash, but more cautious and less optimistic in tone. It was flat, bland; there was nothing for anyone to bite on; and he was scared people would think he was growing old, had lost his flair.

He had a wild card up his sleeve, which he didn't really want to play just yet. He had hoped to spend more time on it, get it more advanced before going public. But he sensed he needed something tomorrow with which to smack them between the eyes, to get them to sit up and listen, and this was the only thing he had. He pressed the carriage return to bring up his workstation screen, and logged into ARCHIVE.

Good evening, Professor. Another warm one. The overnight temperature should be no lower than four-teen degrees Celsius. How are you?

Much the same as I was this afternoon, thank you, Joe replied, then pressed the return key to trigger a response.

Were you asking me about Juliet Spring, Professor?

Joe stiffened as if every sinew in his body had been jerked tight. ARCHIVE had made no spontaneous mention of Juliet Spring for over three months.

Why are you mentioning Juliet Spring's name? he typed in.

There was a long silence. Across the road, in the twilight, out of the corner of his eye Joe could see Muriel Arkwright watering the flowers in her front garden; abstractedly he wondered if she cleaned the flowers as well. Then the words appeared:

I am sorry, Professor. I do not understand the question.

Joe tried a different tack. What can you tell me about Juliet Spring?

The reply appeared: Who is Juliet Spring?

Joe tried again for several minutes, rephrasing the question each time, but the name *Juliet Spring* always drew a blank.

He scratched his head; the name had appeared then vanished, as if plucked from the ether and returned again. It depressed him; another instance of how much there was about ARCHIVE that he didn't understand.

He shouldn't have been depressed, he knew. He should have been happy that ARCHIVE was doing what he had dreamed a computer would one day do: having its own thoughts, moods, being creative, forgetful, rational and irrational, stubborn, bloody-minded. *Human*. But right now the sick feeling he'd had since Sunday night, since that strange brush with Stassi in the kitchen, was still with him, deepening all the time. Such a trivial incident, and yet he had fretted more over it than his speech. It was dominating his mind.

And he'd seen Stassi looking at him since. Several times he'd noticed her eyeing him at meals, and when their paths crossed, she seemed to hesitate, as if passing some hidden signal. It worried him; Karen must have noticed and she had enough on her plate already. He was doing his best to be cool towards Stassi, without actually being rude, but there were a couple of occasions when he'd been caught off-guard, and had responded with a spontaneous smile.

He didn't want to get rid of the girl, because she was too useful; perhaps a quiet word would be the answer. He'd deal with her after he'd got tomorrow over with, tell her she needed to get out a bit more, to make friends over here. Perhaps he could even have a word with Blake, see what he said.

He called up a graph presentation program. After a few moments, an uneven zig-zag line of peaks and troughs appeared across the screen. He tapped some more keys and the peaks became sharper, the troughs deeper, with more appearing on either side like an Alpine mountain range.

He studied the pattern carefully for some moments, then called up a window with a similar, but marginally different pattern, and superimposed it over the first. He didn't hear the door opening behind him as he carefully checked the differences in alignment and adjusted the program to cope.

If he could get it to run smoothly he could use it in the visual-aid system tomorrow.

'I thought that a man like you would be able to move mountains, professor,' Stassi said quietly.

Joe turned, startled. She was wearing a white towelling dressing gown, loosely tied, with nothing beneath and was barefoot. He could see the lightly tanned skin of her neck and the paler tops of her breasts loosely held in the robe, and framed by strands of her long brown hair. He felt a sharp prick of lust for her and tried instantly to stifle it. 'Hi,' he said, more friendly than he had intended.

She closed the door behind her. 'I thought I'd try and relax you for tomorrow; you've been so tense for days,' she said and leaned forward, looking more closely at the screen. As she did so, the belt of her robe slackened and Joe found himself staring straight down on to the tops of her breasts, and he could clearly see the dark red circles of her nipples. He averted his gaze hastily to her face.

'Stassi, I'm actually very busy right now. I have to get my speech finished.'

She tossed her hair back and peered at the screen more closely. 'This your speech?' she said mockingly.

'It's an illustration I'm going to give during my speech. Fractals.' She smelled of a scent he found intensely sensuous, and which reminded him, he realized after a few moments, of Juliet Spring. He sniffed discreetly, and was even more certain it was the same. His eyes were drawn back down. He tried to look away from her breasts, from her neck, tried to remember this was a young student, that his wife was asleep across the landing, and looked instead at the wall behind her that was covered with framed photographs and certificates, then looked at her long, elegant fingers with their immaculate nails and clear polish. Once again he reflected that she looked more than twenty. Her hands seemed older than that.

'Fractals?' She looked at him with a quizzical smile. 'Are you working on the theory of pleasure?' She moved her face so close to his that it blurred and he could feel the warmth of her breath.

He leaned back in his chair until he could focus again, surprised by her knowledge; she must have read one of the papers he'd published. 'Uh huh.' The scent was intoxicating. 'How do you know about that?'

She moved skittishly a pace away, and perched on the edge of the computer table, giving him a mock-affronted expression. 'I like to know everything there is to do with pleasure.' Her robe loosened further, exposing most of her slender right thigh, and barely any longer covering her midriff. Joe wondered if she was drunk, or stoned. He couldn't help seeing the dark shadow of her pubic hair, but she made no attempt to close the robe. His stirrings of lust hardened further and he wrestled temptation, unsure quite how to handle the situation. He needed to be firm, to stop this nonsense before it went any further, but tactfully.

'Stassi, I think you'd better leave me in peace, I don't have time to talk right now, OK?'

'You think it's possible for computers to experience sensory pleasure, don't you?' she asked.

'We have the ability to make computers capable of feeling pleasure.' Joe never could resist talking about ARCHIVE.

'Could ARCHIVE?'

'Sure, one day.'

Her eyes widened with sudden interest. 'How?'

He pointed at the screen. 'Through fractals. I'll give you a copy of my theory of pleasure if you like,' thinking that might be the way to get her out.

'It's to do with fooling the brain, isn't it?'

Joe was impressed by the question, which showed a depth of knowledge. 'Partly. Normally the brain can only entertain one concept at a time; certain stimuli fool the brain into maintaining more than one concept.' He found his eyes drawn to the snatches of her bare body showing through the openings in the folds of towelling; to her long bare thigh and her slender ankle.

'I –' he said, distracted, 'I think I'm pretty close to enabling a computer to appreciate a piece of music, or a painting.'

She engaged his eyes and watched him smilingly. 'And how close are you to enabling a computer to have an orgasm?'

Joe was shocked now. Actually he suspected that if a computer had an orgasm it wouldn't ever want to stop, but he wasn't going to tell her that.

She giggled, then continued looking at him in silence, shaking her head chidingly from side to side.

Joe had to get her to leave right now, he knew. But there was something mesmerizing about this girl. She reminded him so much of Juliet; it was almost as if he were talking to Juliet. They looked quite different, and yet – he wasn't sure quite what it was – the similarity was there.

She eased herself down from the table, came over to him and before he realized what was happening she'd slipped her arms around his neck and was sitting astride him, her face right up against his, her hair touching his cheeks. She kissed him lightly on the lips.

Startled, he pushed her back gently. 'Stassi, you're a very lovely girl, but we can't do this, OK? Now, off!'

She looked at him petulantly. 'Give me a goodnight kiss.'

'No!'

'Stop resisting, Joe-Joe, this is research.'

Joe frowned at the way she was using Karen's pet name for him.

Grinning broadly, she leaned forwards, putting her face inches from his. 'I'll give you a better orgasm than any computer could do, I promise, Joe-Joe.'

'No!' he said firmly. He couldn't remember feeling so horny in his life. Firmly he eased her back. 'Stassi, you have to stop this! I think you're gorgeous, but I can't make love to you.'

She stared into his eyes and slid both her hands down his chest and then slowly and firmly down his crutch. She squeezed him gently, then began massaging. 'So hard,' she whispered. 'You're so hard. I want you, Joe, I want you so much. I've waited so long.'

Then suddenly she jerked sharply back. He saw the look

of shock on her face. Felt the draught of air. Saw the open
door behind her on to the landing. Saw her fall backwards
on to the floor and crash against his recliner armchair, her
hair awry, the robe opening around her naked body as if it
had been ripped away by a hurricane. Saw a blurry figure in
a blue nightdress to his right, towering above him. Heard
Karen's voice screech hysterically.

'You filthy bitch, get out of my house!'

62

Jack dug his spoon into his cereal as if it were an archaeolo-
gist's trowel, carefully scraping away layers of cornflakes
from the heaped mound, then finally raising one specimen
for inspection. He squinted carefully at it, ignoring the milk
that dribbled down the handle of the spoon and on to his
wrist.

'Don't play with your food,' Karen said sharply. Her face
was sheet white and her eyes tear-stained.

'Not playing with it.' He looked up at her with a rather
hurt expression. 'It's got a thing on it, Mummy.'

Karen leaned forward and looked. She was already dressed,
which was unusual for her at this hour, Joe thought. 'There's
nothing wrong with it,' she said. 'It's fine.'

Jack put it in his mouth and chewed dubiously. Joe glanced
at the front page of *The Times*, scanning the news stories,
unable to concentrate on any of them. He felt ragged with
tiredness, and had a stomach full of butterflies. Silent anger
raged inside him, but he didn't know at whom he was angry.
Stassi? Karen? Himself? He had worked until two o'clock in
the morning, or tried to work, tried to rewrite his speech, to
inject some life into it.

At least Karen's bursting into his study had given him a
theme to hang some of his speech on. *Jealousy*. If computers
could feel pleasure, experience orgasms, you could do away

464

with jealousy. No one would ever get divorced because they'd made love to someone inside a computer!

It didn't seem so funny now, this morning. He envisaged himself up there on the rostrum this evening in front of several hundred élite members and guests of the Royal Society, and catching Karen's eye, and the joke falling flat.

Falling flat not just for that reason either; but because maybe it simply wasn't true. How could you presume that a computer couldn't be jealous? How could you presume that anything would be different for a thinking computer than for a thinking human? Especially when you were no longer sure how the hell the thing worked?

He glanced uneasily across the table. Stassi was dressed in a white T-shirt and jeans, eating her muesli and yoghurt in silence. He was amazed she'd plucked up the courage to come down – or maybe it was sheer gall – yet she seemed totally unconcerned, as if nothing had happened. She had greeted him, Karen and Jack pleasantly, had sat herself down in her usual place and begun eating. He concentrated hard on *The Times*, avoiding eye contact with Stassi or Karen, aware that the atmosphere could be cut with a knife.

He'd tried to explain the truth to Karen but she had not wanted to know. She just kept repeating, 'What a fool I've been, I should have realized all along,' over and over. Joe had stayed in the bedroom with her until past midnight, talking, trying to tell her the background, to explain that he wasn't interested in sleeping with Stassi or anyone else. But she just raged at him, then cried quietly, then dragged up all the stuff about Juliet again. Finally, in desperation he'd gone back to his study. Any other night, he had thought. Any other night than this.

'It's Wednesday!' Stassi announced suddenly. Joe looked up at her with a start. 'I go to the supermarket on Friday – we'd better start making the list, Karen.'

'You're leaving us this morning, Stassi. You won't be going to the supermarket for us any more,' she said. 'You're going home.'

'I am at home,' Stassi said, looking at Karen blankly.

Karen shook her head. 'No, you're going to stay with Blake – or back to Hong Kong – or anywhere you want, but not here. You don't work for us any more. I want you out of here by ten o'clock. Do you understand?'

Jack's face fell and he turned to stare at Stassi, puzzled. 'Why are you going home?'

Stassi glanced at Jack but said nothing. Joe had tried to convince Karen that they had an obligation to keep her at least until she'd found somewhere else to go, but Karen wouldn't hear of it.

'What time do we have to be in London this evening, Joe?' Karen asked.

'Six. The driver'll be here at quarter to four. But I really don't think you ought to come.'

'I am coming,' she said adamantly. 'I already rang Muriel this morning. She's going to babysit.'

Stassi continued eating her cereal.

'Don't want silly Muriel!' Jack said. 'I want Stassi!'

'Stassi's leaving, Jack,' Karen said calmly and firmly. She turned to the girl. 'You understand I want your bags packed and you out of here by ten? I'll call Blake Hewlett and see if he can collect you; if not I'll order you a taxi.'

There was something about the blank way Stassi looked at Karen that gave Joe a chill. And the way she said nothing but merely continued to stare. There was no malice in the stare – just a total lack of expression, of emotion. As if there was nobody home, he thought. After some moments she reached for the coffee pot and filled her cup. She added milk, then picked up the sugar bowl. As she heaped two spoons of sugar into her coffee, something struck Joe as being odd, but it was a moment before he realized what.

He scooped some Flora margarine out of the tub and began spreading it on his toast. *Sugar*. He suddenly recalled the morning Stassi had arrived. Bank holiday Sunday. Remembered Stassi and Blake in the kitchen. He'd made them both coffee and passed Stassi the sugar bowl. *No thank you*, she had said. *I never take sugar*. He watched her stirring her cup. Maybe she felt she needed the energy today, the way he did.

Jack glanced at his mother, then slipped down from the table, trotted to Stassi and put his arms protectively around her. 'Don't want silly Muriel,' he said defiantly, and began stroking Stassi's cheek with his hand. 'I want Stassi. Please stay, Stassi.'

'Finish your breakfast, Jack,' Karen said coldly.

Jack looked at his mother, then up at Stassi, torn.

Karen banged her hand angrily on the table. 'Jack!'

Jack looked warily at his mother, then hugged Stassi even harder. 'I love Stassi, Mummy, I want her to stay for ever.' He looked imploringly up at her face. 'You will stay for ever, won't you, Stassi?'

'And ever,' she replied distantly, staring blankly ahead again. 'No one has to die, Jack.' She said the words as if she was reciting a text she had learned. 'Not now. Not any more. No one should have to die any more. Death is not necessary.'

Joe spun his head, scarcely able to believe his ears; deep inside he felt a strange tremor of emotion. *Death is not necessary.* His father's favourite remark. He looked at her, wondering where she'd got it from. Maybe she'd been reading some of his father's work, he wondered. Willi Messenger had written several volumes as well as numerous papers on cryonics, and on his views on immortality, which were on the bookshelves in the study.

He watched her face closely, saw the blankness of her stare fade as she put her arms around Jack and hugged him tightly to her. Tears began to trickle down her cheeks. The tremor of shock continued inside him. He wasn't sure whether it was the words themselves, or the rather eerie way she had said them.

'Three years ago you paid me the great honour of inviting me to speak to you. I told you then that next time I wouldn't be on this rostrum in person, that I would be represented by my computer, ARCHIVE, which was then just a spark in his daddy's synapses . . .' There was a ripple of laughter.

'I want you to know that it's not for lack of progress that ARCHIVE isn't addressing you tonight. But there are some serious considerations I want to put to you, and I'm not sure I can trust ARCHIVE to tell you itself. So I guess this time you're going to have to make do with plain old biological me again.' There was a smaller ripple of laughter.

As usual, Joe had selected his faces in the auditorium and concentrated on them, alternating in sequence between them. His voice resonated clearly through the speakers. It was going fine, his nerves had calmed, he was following his text, registering the markers where he needed to raise his voice or pause for emphasis or for laughter. They were a great audience, responsive, having a good time. Karen was out there somewhere, in the front right, but he avoided her, skated his eyes past her. He glanced at his text again, then looked straight at his central focal point: the bespectacled man with a silver goatee beard in the sixth row back.

'There's one fundamental we have to understand when we start attempting to download human minds into computers: human *consciousness* and human *conscience* are very different things. One does not necessarily follow the other. We may be able to download the contents of someone's brain into a thinking computer, but will we be sure that we're downloading that person's *humanity*? When we put thoughts and desires into a computer, how can we be sure that we're also putting in the morality and social conscience that underpins civilized human behaviour?'

He paused for some moments, scanning the whole width of the auditorium, taking in each of his five faces, to put emphasis on his next remark. His man with the goatee beard was nodding approvingly.

'Is it possible that we are playing with fire in trying to replicate the human mind long before we have remotely begun to understand it?'

He saw the frowns in the auditorium and felt lifted by a deep evangelical thrill. This was not what they had come to hear, but that was too bad. It was what he wanted to tell them. He took a deep breath and glanced at the next paragraph of his text, which was heavily underlined.

'Have any of us stopped to think what will happen when we start making machines that are as smart as us?' He raised his voice. 'You know the first thing these machines will do? They'll start improving themselves!'

He paused for a roar of laughter. Good, let them laugh, he thought, and he grinned along with them. Then he continued.

'And after they've improved themselves for about three nanoseconds, they're going to be one whole lot smarter than us.' He paused. There was a smaller, less certain ripple of laughter. 'And do you know what they're gonna do then? They're going to take a good look at us and say: "Who needs these assholes?"'

'You need to see a shrink,' Karen said as they headed home.

Joe leaned back in his leather seat in the limousine, drunk and exhausted. His exhilaration was fading and doubt was eating its way into him. 'I said what I thought ought to be said.'

'I don't think the word *asshole* is appropriate for a Royal Society address, Joe.'

'Half the people there were total assholes,' he said sullenly, knowing he had gone too far, but not wanting to admit it to her. The dinner afterwards with the president and his wife, and several of the leading scientists in the country, had been a stilted and uncomfortable affair. When you made a good speech, everyone wanted to congratulate you and discuss it. When you make a bummer, they mumbled platitudes then changed the subject.

'Assholes and orgasms!' Karen said. 'I think you really upset a lot of people tonight, Joe.'

'Everyone on this planet arrives inside an orgasm,' he said.

'They don't necessarily want to be reminded about that.'

''S good for them.' He was silent for a moment. Oncoming lights splayed out across the windscreen; he thought at first it was raining, then realized it was the effect of alcohol on his vision. He watched the dark silhouette of the chauffeur's back through the glass partition. 'No one ever complains about it at the time – so what's wrong with ejaculation?'

Karen's voice softened. 'Maybe you should take a break – you know – a real long one, like a sabbatical or something?' She took his hand and squeezed it. 'Know what I mean, hon? Maybe it's what we both need. You've worked yourself too hard for too long. We could go some place different for a year – travel around – while Jack's still young enough that it wouldn't interrupt his education?'

'We could download ourselves into ARCHIVE and fax ourselves off somewhere.'

'I had something more physical in mind.'

They were both asleep when the car pulled on to their drive, and it took Joe a moment to work out where he was as the door opened and the interior light came on.

He climbed out and then helped Karen, taking her weight while the chauffeur removed the crutches from the boot. He pulled a banknote out of his wallet to tip the driver. 'Wassertime?'

'Ten past one, sir.'

Joe yawned. He could see lights on through the curtains and the thick glass of the hall window. Muriel Arkwright was babysitting and he hoped it wouldn't take ten minutes of yacking before they could get rid of her.

'Joe?' Karen's voice sounded strange. 'Where's my car?'

'Hum?' He looked sleepily around.

'My car – it's not here!'

Joe stared at his Saab, which was coated in a heavy dew. There was no sign of the little white Toyota he had bought for Karen. His first thought was that she must have parked it somewhere and forgotten, then he remembered that she wasn't able to start driving again yet. He turned and looked past the limousine at the street, but it was empty as it usually was at night; all the neighbourhood cars were either in garages or on the driveways.

'I dunno.' He felt a hollow sensation. 'It *was* here – I

guess it must have been stolen.' He dipped his hand into his pocket for his house key, and shivered as the cold air penetrated his thin dinner suit. He helped Karen up the steps into the porch. The limousine drove off and the fumes of its exhaust soured the salty freshness of the night.

'Muriel would have heard, surely –?' Her voice tailed.

Joe twisted the key in the lock, then pushed the door open and went in, holding Karen's arm.

Then he froze.

'Oh, my God!' Karen's voice came out as if it had been shaken from her throat.

His eyes jumped from detail to detail, unable to absorb the whole scene. He saw the hall table lying upside down with two of its drawers open and the contents spilled out. A busted chair leg rested against the skirting board, several feet away from the splintered remains of the chair. Bare white plaster was visible through the fist-sized chunk that had been gouged out of the wall. Torn wallpaper curled like a tired sticking-plaster above it. Jack's Lego crane was flattened, the tiny bricks scattered all around it. Worst of all, the blade of a bread knife glinted at them from the bottom of the staircase.

'Joe.' Karen's grip tightened on his arm, but he didn't notice. '*Joe*,' she said again.

He saw the mark that at first he thought might have been made by a cup of tea hurled in the mayhem: a dark jagged stain down the wall. Then more marks on the ceiling. And on the walls. Then he saw them all over the carpet also. Fear bored through him like a locomotive through a tunnel as he took a step forward. And another step. There were stains up the stairs and splashed over the banister rails; dark red, not the colour of tea at all.

He tried one more step forward but the floor swayed as if it were on rollers; a wall came towards him and he fended it off, took another step, held on to the frame of the kitchen door and pulled himself through.

The kitchen was devastated: all their crockery lay smashed on the floor. There was blood everywhere; even on some of

Jack's paintings. Drawers lay on the floor, their contents strewn around. The answering machine lay amongst the debris, the telephone cracked and off the hook, and partially buried in a mound of white sugar. One of the curtains had been torn down and the patio window behind it was covered in a spider's web crack.

Karen was whimpering. 'Where's Jack? Where's Jack?' Then her scream pulled Joe out of the kitchen, back into the hall.

She was standing in the doorway to the drawing room, hand over her mouth, choked with shock. Joe went in. The standard lamp had been knocked over. A slashed cushion lay beside it, its feathers spilling like guts. Then his eyes jumped to the far corner, to the hideously mutilated figure that lay spread-eagled for all the world like a busted mannequin, except that a broad stain of dried blood had seeped from her body into the carpet.

Muriel Arkwright was recognizable only by her hair. She looked like she had been attacked by a scalpel over every inch of her anatomy. Her face was pulped and her legs were slashed to ribbons.

'Oh, sweet Jesus, Jack!' Joe turned, half blinded with terror, barged past Karen and flung himself up the staircase.

63

Jack's bedroom door was ajar and the light was on. Joe stopped on the landing outside for a second. There was a knot in his throat. He stared at the door. It was plain white with four panels and a small ceramic rectangle on which was glazed: 'Jack's Room.' He pushed it wide open.

Silence greeted him. The room was empty. The bed had been slept in, but Jack was not in it now. The dinosaur duvet was turned back and there was an indent in the pillow where his head had lain.

Joe's eyes roamed the scene; they were detached from his body like robots on remote control, relaying a stream of information to the neurons of his visual cortex. His cortex decoded the signals, compared them with images retained in his iconic memory, identified them. Toys. Bookshelves. Train set. Chair. And the clockwork mouse with the key sticking out of its side still crouched on the bedside table, next to the large round badge which said 'Frodo Lives!'

Only Jack was missing. And he'd taken his noise with him, leaving behind this hideous silence.

Joe scanned the room again, hoping that maybe his visual cortex was faulty, that maybe someone had hacked into it and reprogrammed it so he wasn't able to see that Jack was really asleep in bed, and he just hadn't noticed him. Yes, that was it! He went over to the bed, touched the indent in the pillow with his hand, crosschecking his visual system with his tactile system.

Jack was still not there.

Heavy breathing behind him. Karen had worked her way up the stairs. They faced each other in the doorway, two strangers sharing a trance. They would come out of it in a minute and everything would be fine. He touched her arms, held them for a moment in silence, gathering his breath. 'Call the police,' he said. 'And an ambulance.'

He shouted Jack's name, then checked each remaining room in turn, looking beneath the beds, flinging open every cupboard door. He checked the bathroom, their own bedroom, the spare room with its draughts that had done nothing to disperse the lingering smell of Stassi's scent.

Back downstairs he saw Karen sitting at the kitchen table, tapping the cradle of the telephone, trying to get a dial tone. She tipped sugar out of the mouthpiece of the receiver while he opened a cupboard, closed it; opened another, closed it. It was OK so long as there was still somewhere to look; so long as there was still one more door he hadn't opened, he could keep hoping. Behind him, Karen asked for the police. Her voice seemed absurdly calm.

She gave their number, their address, the details of what

had happened, sounding quite matter-of-fact, just a slight edge to her voice, that was all. She might have been phoning a plumber about a blocked drain, or buying garden implements from a mail-order firm.

She hung up and when they looked at each other, seven years got stripped away like a rug pulled from beneath them.

Barty.

Karen collapsed and he caught her before she fell, eased her on to a chair, tried to explain that he needed to go into the drawing room to look at Muriel, to see if there was anything he could do for her.

'Don't go, Joe. Don't leave me. Tell me what's happened to him.'

His brain was short-circuiting; thoughts fired off at random. Stassi. His mouth opened. *Stassi* was on his lips but he didn't say the name. Stassi. He pushed the thought away but it came back, shook at him like a beggar's bowl. The police seemed to be taking a long time. He remembered the journey to the mortuary seven years ago had taken a long time, too.

He stood again, unable to sit and do nothing. Karen twisted her hands as though she were winding wool; her mouth hung open and her eyes were red. She had been looking so lovely tonight in her black taffeta dress and her hair cascading around her face in ringlets; she had looked so lovely her injuries had barely been noticeable.

He went down into the cellar, checked the freezer, but it was locked, went out into the garden with a flashlight, calling out for Jack. But he knew in his heart, and knew from the hideous shredded thing on the drawing-room floor, that his son was gone.

There was no blood in the bedroom, no sign of a struggle there. Maybe Jack was still alive, had run off when whoever it was had butchered Muriel.

Muriel's husband, Derek?

He seemed a mild man, sick with emphysema. It was the mild ones who sometimes did awful things.

He made himself return to the carnage in the drawing

room. Muriel was as inert as the furniture. She seemed bigger than he remembered, lying there; dominating the whole room. Dominating the house. He held his distance, scared she might suddenly move, might suddenly reach out and grab him. There was a ghastly stench of urine and excrement that made him want to throw up.

He could see the extent of her wounds clearly now, someone in a frenzy with a Stanley knife maybe, great deep slashes – one clean through the jugular. Blood coated her pale blue blouse like paint. It had coagulated. She would've hated the mess, Joe noted somewhere inside him. All her life she'd been Mrs Super-clean and now this. It wasn't fair. It wasn't bearable.

There was no point, he knew, but he still attempted to check for a pulse, took her wrist between his forefinger and thumb. It was stiff and cold; the texture reminded him of damp putty. He released it with a shudder. Anyway the police were coming now. He could hear the siren in the distance.

He went and opened the front door. Blue light skittered across the dark tarmac and something crackled – a radio. Cold night air on his face. Two men in caps with checkered bands and heavy jackets. Another siren coming closer, full-beam headlamps down the end of the street, a squeal of tyres. The ambulance. A light came on behind a curtained window across the road.

Muriel Arkwright, Joe thought, she'd be peering out to see what the fuss was about. Then his brain sorted out the memory of where Muriel Arkwright was right now. It must be her husband who was doing the peering out, wondering what was going on and why his wife wasn't home yet.

'Mr Messenger?' An anxious face beneath the cap. Grim. Joe led the two uniformed policemen inside. They nodded politely to Karen before Joe ushered them through into the drawing room. One of them, who was no more than eighteen, took a sharp step back and covered his mouth with his hand.

'Her husband,' Joe said. 'Must tell her husband.'

Karen was standing in the doorway; the older policeman spoke into his radio. Karen's eyes were filled with tears, and they welled in Joe's, also. She tugged the younger policeman's sleeve. 'Please help me find my son. We love him so much. Please get him back for us.'

The reply to Karen's entreaty was covered up by the exchange taking place on the radio.

'Hotel one-o-one to Charley Hotel.'

'Go ahead.'

'Reference serial nine seven two. I'm at the scene and can confirm there is a dead person. Very suspicious circumstances. Small child missing. I require CID, Scene Investigation, photographic and also a police surgeon to confirm death.'

There was a rap on the knocker. Joe made a move, but the junior policeman marched past him. 'I'll get it, sir.'

He opened the door part way and Joe could just make out the stooped figure of Muriel Arkwright's husband, Derek, with a coat on over his pyjamas, in the porch.

'I'm sorry, sir, we can't allow anyone in,' the policeman said.

'Could you tell me what's going on? My wife's in here babysitting.'

'One moment, sir.' The policeman closed the door a few inches and turned to Joe, questioning him with his eyes. Joe lowered his voice to a whisper. 'Her husband,' he said, pointing urgently back at the drawing room.

The older policeman walked across and spoke to his colleague. 'Take the gentleman to his home and explain what's happening. See if you can get a neighbour or his doctor to come round to be with him.'

Joe watched a bewildered Derek Arkwright being led past two ambulancemen in yellow jackets, one of whom had a paramedic label on his jacket. He heard them being told: 'I don't think there's anything you can do. Have a look, but don't touch anything.'

Within moments of each other, two more police cars drew up. Two uniformed police climbed out of the first one, but the occupants of the second one remained in the car. The policeman already in the house turned to Joe and Karen.

'These two are going to take you down to the police station.'

'I don't want to leave the house,' Karen said in a gulping sob. 'My son might come back, I have to be here.'

'Don't worry, madam, we'll bring you straight back if he turns up.'

'Can't we stay?'

'I'm afraid it's not permitted. The house is a murder scene and has to be sealed.' He gave them a harried but sincere look. 'It's to help you – the less disturbed everything is the more chance we have of finding clues.'

Moments later they were in the back of a police car that had a stale, greasy smell of old vinyl. Karen pressed her cheek against Joe's shoulder, sobbing her heart out. He fumbled for her hand, and felt utterly helpless.

The door opened and two men in plain clothes came into the warm, windowless room at Hove police station. One, in his late thirties, was lean and alert looking, with close-cropped fair hair that looked as if it was cut short so that he didn't have to bother with it. He had the demeanour of someone who carried no unnecessary baggage through life.

'Professor Messenger, Mrs Messenger? I'm Detective Superintendent Lyne.' He removed his hands from his pockets and shook Joe's with a grip of iron and then Karen's. He introduced his colleague, Detective Inspector Gavros, a stocky young man of no more than thirty, with Greek Cypriot features and heavy-lidded eyes.

Gavros smiled sympathetically, and shook Joe's hand with a huge but gentle paw. He was wearing a brown suit and a snappy tie. 'Nice to meet you, professor.' He shook Karen's hand. 'I'm not going to sleep until we've got your son back, that's a promise, Mrs Messenger.' He had a gruff, streetwise voice that was tinged with warmth, and he spoke from the heart.

Joe mouthed a silent thank you as the two detectives sat down opposite them. Tears streamed down Karen's face.

Lyne pushed his hands back into his pockets and shifted his eyes to Karen, then back to Joe. There was something defensive in his action, as if deep at heart he trusted no one. 'I'm going to be in charge of this case and will be your main liaison, with Detective Inspector Gavros as my deputy. We will both be available twenty-four hours a day for anything you want to talk to us about.' He spoke fast but clearly. 'We're setting up an incident room here at this police station and that will be manned on a full-time basis. I'm going to ask you a series of questions, but if anything comes to mind that could be helpful, interrupt me, all right?'

Joe nodded.

He pulled out a slim black notebook, laid it on the desk without opening it, and more or less talked them through the last twenty-four hours. At the end of it all he asked, 'Is there anyone with a grudge against you? Someone who might be out to get you?'

'Yes,' Karen said. 'Some sicko.'

Joe told them about the obits, and the traffic lights. Lyne asked if he had any idea who it might be, but Joe didn't think he would be receptive to hearing about a ghost inside a computer. 'I guess there are a lot of people out there who don't agree with my views. This seems an extreme way of showing it.'

Detective Superintendent Lyne went on. 'Do you know where this au pair – Miss Anastasia Holland – might be at this moment? I'd like to find her and eliminate her from our enquiries.'

'I think she's staying with one of my colleagues – Professor Hewlett.'

'He's the colleague who recommended her?'

'I sent her back to him this morning, in a taxi,' Karen said.

'If we could ring him now –?' Gavros said. 'Check she's there?' He looked at Lyne for approval. 'Eliminate her.'

Lyne nodded. Joe glanced at the clock on the wall. It was a quarter to four in the morning; the time meant nothing to him. Gavros pushed a phone helpfully towards him.

As Joe picked up the receiver he looked at Gavros. 'Do you want me to speak to him, or –?'

'Go ahead.'

Joe dialled. Blake answered, sleepily, after the third ring, then came awake fast.

'Joe?' His voice sounded anxious. 'Hi – wassertime? Jesus! Was it tonight, your address? I wanted to make it, but there was a mega problem at the Organ Centre. How did it go?'

'Fine, it went fine.' He glanced at Karen. 'Is Stassi with you?'

'Huh?'

'Stassi. Is she with you?'

Blake sounded surprised. 'No – I told you. You didn't check your messages?'

Now it was Joe's turn to say 'Huh?'

'Your ansaphone? I got back home about six this evening – no sign of her. When I spoke with Karen this morning I said I'd leave a key for Stassi under a garbage bin. But I don't think she can have showed up. I thought maybe she'd stayed on with you after all. Or something.'

Joe realized he hadn't checked his machine for messages. Then he told Blake what had happened.

'Oh, *Jesus*,' Blake said. 'Joe, this is terrible!' He was silent for a short while. 'Not that lovely girl, Joe, it couldn't possibly be her.'

'I don't think so either,' Joe said. 'But where is she?'

'She must have funked out of coming round here – too embarrassed or ashamed. You know she's a pretty shy kid – probably terrified of me!'

Joe thought fleetingly about her behaviour of last night. That wasn't his idea of shy, but he said nothing.

'Listen,' Blake said. 'Can I do something? I mean, maybe someone's abducted Stassi too. Gimme time to get dressed. I could be with you in fifteen minutes.'

Joe spoke to the other three. 'He says he could come right over,' he announced, as if Blake possessed some magical solution.

'Blake? Why's Blake coming?' Karen said angrily. Joe

covered the mouthpiece as she carried on. 'I didn't like Stassi when I saw her, Joe. And I never trust anything to do with that creep!'

'Hon! Come on! I don't think this is anything to do with Stassi.'

'No? You weren't there when I put her in the taxi, Joe. You didn't see how she looked at me.'

Joe glanced at the policemen, who were watching him with interest. He uncovered the mouthpiece. 'Blake, I'll call you back later – in the morning, or something?'

'Anything you want me to do, tell me! I'm right here.'

Joe thanked him and hung up. 'I didn't check the answering machine,' he said.

'Someone will have done that,' Lyne said. 'Can you give me a description of this girl, Stassi?'

'I have some photographs – in my camera,' Karen said. 'I took them yesterday in the garden – her and Jack playing.'

Lyne made a note in his book. 'It's in the house?'

'Yes – it's hanging from the coat stand.'

'I'll get them developed.'

'What do you think's happened?' Joe asked Lyne suddenly.

Lyne shook his head. 'Too early to say, professor. I only had a quick look on my way here. Seems like Mrs Arkwright put up a spirited fight. There's no sign of any break-in, so maybe she knew whoever it was and let them in. Most murders are carried out by people who know each other. There's no indication of a struggle in your son's bedroom – maybe he knew the person too. Mrs Messenger's car's been taken.' He was silent for a moment, then looked at each of them in turn. 'I'd like you to tell –'

'ARCHIVE!' Joe exclaimed, interrupting the detective superintendent. 'ARCHIVE!' He elaborated shakily, 'ARCHIVE will know. It will have seen it all. Everything.'

64

The detectives insisted Karen remain at the station, and were reluctant at the idea of even letting Joe back into the house, but finally agreed when he convinced them they wouldn't be able to access ARCHIVE's images themselves. He could have gone to the university but didn't tell them that. He wanted to go back to the house just in case Jack was around and frightened.

As Joe climbed out of the car, he was struck by the activity in the street. Lights were on in most of the houses. Police cars and vans were lined down both sides. A white tape cordoned off the pavement in front of Number 8. Neighbouring driveways were swarming with police wielding flashlights, and with dog-handlers. A helicopter clattered overhead, the massive beam of its searchlight sliding over the suburban rooftops and gardens, throwing up brutal silhouettes.

It was still dark, but the first shadowy streaks of dawn creased the black canvas of the sky. Detective Superintendent Lyne spoke briefly to two men in plain clothes sitting in a police car drinking coffee, getting an update. Joe listened to the conversation but learned little except that the Scene Investigation Unit team were combing the house.

A uniformed policeman standing guard in the porch opened the front door for them. In the hall a man dressed in a disposable white boiler-suit, rubber gloves and plastic slip-on shoes was scraping a trace of blood from the wall. He didn't even look at them. Another man, similarly dressed, was videoing the hall section by section, and again took no notice of them. Joe felt as though he had stepped into a Kafkaesque nightmare as he led Lyne and Gavros up to his study.

When he logged into ARCHIVE, the screen filled up at once.

Good morning, Professor Messenger, you are work-ing late. Or is it that you are starting early? The

temperature is fifty-five degrees rising to no
more than fifty-eight. It will be a chilly day for
the time of year, and an eighty per cent chance of
rain. It would be nice to meet your friends. You
have a lot of visitors but I do not think you are
having a party. If they are redecorating, they are
working at a strange hour, therefore I do not think
they are decorators. Something is going on out in
the street. Mrs Messenger is away again?

Joe glanced at the two detectives and saw the curiosity on
their faces.

Good morning, ARCHIVE. These two detectives are
interested to know what you saw last night when we
were out.

I'm sorry, professor, I do not understand the
question.

Joe rephrased it. My wife and I went out. Jack was
here with Muriel Arkwright. What did you see?

I'm sorry, professor, I do not understand the
question.

The detectives were starting to look at him as if he was a
bit strange. He felt confused, and having the two men watching over his shoulder wasn't helping. Joe scratched his head;
tiny flakes of dandruff drifted down past his eyes. It was
possible to get on the screen an actual replay of what had
been recorded by the cameras, but only by inputting a
fiendishly complex set of instructions, which he had devised
as protection against hackers being able to watch his family
life. He had a go now.

He called up the menu, then accessed the control system
sub-program, and selected Visual Interface. Methodically,
thinking hard at each stage, he worked through the system
until he had isolated the house's visual system. A 3–D model
of the house came up on the screen and the words flashed at
him: Select room.

His hand on the mouse moved the cursor to the kitchen,
then pressed down twice. The screen went blank. Joe looked
at the detectives. 'It has selective retention, like the human

brain. It retains any movement or conversation in any room for twenty-four hours, then dumps most of it.'

There was a sharp beep. On the screen were the words: `Video recording mode not functioning. System fault. Check system manager diagnostic index.`

Joe reacted in disbelief, tapping his knuckles against his lips. 'I'm sorry,' he said. His energy was ebbing away.

The two policemen looked at him as though they had never believed him anyway. Gavros smiled sympathetically, Lyne's expression was harsher. 'Could someone have tampered with it?' Gavros asked.

Lyne nodded. 'The same person who tampered with the traffic lights?'

Joe had not dared to make the connection. 'I – I guess – it's possible –'

There was a knock and the door opened. Another man in a white disposable boiler-suit stood there, holding several framed photographs; he spoke cheerily to Lyne, as if he was totally unaffected by all the horror. 'Good morning, sir. I was told the occupant of the house was here?' He glanced at Joe, then back at Lyne. 'I'd appreciate a word about these.' He held up the photos, and Lyne nodded. The man turned to Joe. 'We need a recent picture of your son, sir; I found these in a drawer – would any be of him?'

A wave of emotion chewed Joe as he saw Jack holding a rod and the first fish he'd ever caught. Last September in Devon. All he could do was mouth a silent 'Yes'.

Lyne studied the photograph, and Detective Inspector Gavros looked at it as well.

'Smashing little chap,' Gavros said.

'If you've no objection, Professor Messenger, we'd like to get this straight into circulation. We think publicity could be helpful in this case.'

'Sure,' Joe mouthed.

Lyne glanced at his watch. 'While you're here, you'd better pack some kit for yourself and Mrs Messenger – maybe just some basic things for now.'

Joe went into their bedroom, hastily packed a holdall, then

it was back outside and into the police car. Gavros drove and Lyne sat beside him in the front. He turned to Joe. 'Do you have any relatives you can stay with for a few days? I'm afraid we can't allow you back in the house until we've finished; it'll take us about a week.'

Joe shook his head, bewilderment and exhaustion closing in on him. But he managed to spare a thought for the professor who owned the house. He wasn't going to rush to pass on the news that it was now a murder scene. 'We don't have any relatives over here.'

Lyne picked up the handset of the two-way radio and instructed someone at the other end to arrange a hotel room. Then he replaced the handset and stifled a yawn.

'Do you think he's still alive, Superintendent?' Joe asked quietly.

Lyne gazed directly back at Joe. 'Yes, I do.' He added solemnly, 'But if you want me to be truthful with you, I don't know how long we have.'

Lyne had apologized in advance for the hotel. There were four conferences going on in Brighton simultaneously, as well as a large exhibition, and virtually every decent space in the town had been booked. Their room was dingy and smelled of mothballs. They were one floor above a busy seafront road and sleep was impossible.

The phone rang for them at nine o'clock when they'd been there for just two or three hours, lying on the bed and attempting to rest. Karen looked at it, afraid. Joe lifted the receiver and recognized Lyne's voice instantly. A man with a young boy who answered Jack's description had boarded an Air France flight to Paris from Gatwick at ten o'clock last night. They'd bought their tickets at the last minute and the man had seemed nervous. He would call back when he had more news.

Joe's spirits lifted a fraction. Paris. Whoever had Jack wouldn't bother taking him all the way to Paris if he intended to kill him, surely? Karen perked up a little with the news, also.

Joe showered and shaved and felt marginally better. Lyne

rang back again with further news. Karen's white Toyota had been found in the short-term car park at Gatwick; this tallied with the report of the man and the boy.

'Is there no one you can think of who might have done this, professor?'

'*No one*,' Joe said adamantly.

Lyne said he would give them time to have breakfast, then he would come round to carry on with more questions.

During the next hour the phone rang solidly as reporters from the national press began following up the leads from their overnight baskets. The fingerprint man came to see them both in the midst of it all, followed by Lyne and Gavros. Joe was glad to see the detectives.

They went down and talked in the restaurant. Joe forced down some scrambled eggs, but Karen could manage only a piece of toast. She asked when they could go home, and Lyne repeated that it would be about a week. When pressed, he said that time might be shortened by a day or two if the whole team could be persuaded to work round the clock. He asked her and Joe to let him have a list of clothes and other items they needed.

The two detectives left at midday; when Joe and Karen went into the foyer of the hotel they were startled to see a pack of reporters and photographers, and retreated back up to their room. It had obviously once been spacious, but now it looked too narrow and high because it had been partitioned from one large room into two or three smaller ones. It was like being in a gully.

As Joe was trying to persuade them both to look on the bright side, there was a rap on the door. It was Blake, and Joe was glad to see him.

Blake looked at the room in horror. 'Do you guys want to come and stay at my place?'

Karen shook her head. 'No thank you, Blake,' she said sharply.

Joe was a little embarrassed at her hostility, but as usual Blake seemed either not to notice or not to care. He suggested taking them in his car to tour round, see if they could spot

Stassi on the streets anywhere, and check some hotels. Karen said she would stay put in case the phone rang, in case a miracle happened.

In the car, Joe slipped out the photograph he always kept of Jack in his wallet and tried to make it come to life. They drove along the seafront area, stopping at each hotel, running in, describing Stassi and showing the photo of Jack to any staff they saw. Street after street.

'You didn't tell me exactly what happened with Stassi, why she had to leave,' Blake said at one point.

Joe explained and Blake looked amazed. 'I thought she was a virginal little thing,' he said.

'So did I.'

'Want a paper?' Blake asked as they drove past a news vendor whose placard read: BRIGHTON KIDNAP MURDER HUNT.

Joe shook his head.

'Do the police have any other theories?'

'Not that they've said.'

Blake patted him gently on the shoulder. 'Gonna be OK, Joe. He's gonna turn up somewhere, be fine.'

'I don't think Karen can take this for much longer.'

'She's a strong girl, Joe.'

'Barty's death nearly destroyed her.' He bit his lip. 'And me too.'

'It's not going to happen again.' He glanced in his mirror and moved across into the centre of the road. 'You know, I don't think you should jump to conclusions about Stassi. I can't believe she'd kidnap anyone, however hacked off she might have been. Maybe we should go take a closer look around your neighbourhood?'

Joe shrugged. 'Sure.' He looked at Blake. 'You're being very kind.'

Blake drove in silence for some moments. Then he said: 'I guess someone's going to have to let Stassi's family know soon if she remains a missing person. I'd better speak to Matt Brewster, let him pass on the bad tidings.'

★

Joe had to wade through an army of reporters in the hotel foyer, but the worst moment came when he went up and faced Karen again. She was sitting in a chair, her eyes red and her face slippery with tears. There'd been no news. Just more calls from reporters. And one from Lyne who'd told Karen he now hoped they'd be able to move back into their house on Saturday; he'd added that until they knew who was responsible for what had happened he was arranging a police guard for them.

A counsellor sent by the police came to see them and later their doctor came to see Karen. They had supper sent up to their room, not wanting to face the reporters downstairs. Then went to bed. Someone had given Karen a sleeping pill, but despite his exhaustion Joe slept only fitfully. He was waiting all the time for the phone to ring. It remained silent.

Lyne came by in the morning and sat in the bedroom with them. 'Bad news, I'm afraid,' he said. 'The man on the Paris flight on Wednesday night has been traced. The boy with him has been positively identified as his son; a matrimonial situation, the father collecting the boy from his ex-wife.'

The news flattened Joe. He watched Karen's face. She listened to Lyne without commenting; only the tightening of her features communicated her true distress.

He's still alive, Joe wanted to say. *As long as there's no news we can go on hoping.*

Lyne asked them more questions about Stassi and told them he'd requested the Hong Kong police to look into her background, as well as to contact her family.

After he had gone, Karen told Joe she would like to go to the synagogue and wanted him to come with her. He agreed.

The synagogue was only a block away from the hotel. They sat, Karen praying; Joe in silence, thinking. Afterwards they took a taxi back to Cranford Road to collect Joe's car.

It felt very strange seeing the white-tape cordon and the mass of police vehicles, as well as several reporters and cameramen. Joe drove the Saab away quickly, not wanting any chance of having to face Derek Arkwright and tell him how sorry he was. He wasn't up to facing anything right now.

They circled the neighbourhood several times, then moved slowly further afield. It was futile, Joe knew, but anything was better than sitting like caged animals in that miserable room, and going to the university was out of the question. He couldn't leave Karen.

A couple of times they stopped and phoned in to the incident room to speak to Lyne or Gavros, but there was still no news.

Shortly after seven in the evening, as Joe pushed the hotel's chunky key into their door, the phone rang. He sprinted over to grab the receiver. 'Hello?' he said, guarded but hopeful.

He heard an elderly woman's voice dithering, confused. 'Oh – er – is that, I wonder if I have the wrong number?'

Get off the line, you old bat, he thought, stop blocking it, the police might be trying to get through. 'Who do you want to speak to?' he said tersely.

'Well, you see, it's taken me a long time to get your number. I had to go through Directory Enquiries and I didn't have your address; then I rang somewhere and got the police. So – I don't know, you see.'

'Don't know what?' He was getting increasingly impatient.

'Well, if I have the right person?' Her voice was quavering, nervous.

'Who is it you want to speak to?'

'You see – this is difficult for me – I'm trying to contact Professor Messenger.'

Joe frowned. 'Speaking.'

'Are you the gentleman who was on the six o'clock news on the television – on BBC yesterday evening?'

Hesitantly, 'I don't know. Maybe. I didn't see the broadcast.'

'You're the father of the little boy who's been – who is missing?'

'I'm sorry,' Joe said. 'What is it you actually want?'

'Professor, please, bear with me, I'm old and I am a little

488

confused. And I'm very nervous, you see. I – well – there was a picture on the television of a young lady. The police are trying to contact a young lady – something to do with your son, I think – it wasn't quite clear.'

'Anastasia Holland. Our au pair.'

'Yes. You want to talk to her?'

He wondered where this was leading. Maybe she'd seen her – and Jack? He spoke more politely. 'Yes, I do, very much. And so do the police.'

She became even more agitated. 'I – I think you, oh dear, you might find that would be difficult.'

'Why's that?'

'Well, you see, I recognized her instantly. It's really given me an awful shock. But I'm not mistaken . . .'

'Look,' Joe said, his hope fading again. 'I'm sorry, but I don't understand what you are on about. I must keep this line clear for the police.'

'Please – let me explain, professor. You see, I think *they* must have made a mistake; they must have shown the wrong picture.'

'Wrong picture of whom?'

'Of the girl. They called her Anastasia Holland – but that girl they showed is my niece, Susan. Susan Roach.'

'Susan Roach?'

'Yes! I'm certain. I knew her so well – you see, I brought her up for most of her life.'

'I don't quite understand,' Joe said.

'No, I don't either. You see, she died nineteen years ago, professor.'

65

Joe's first reaction was to want to hang up. The woman was nuts, or perhaps just a harmless old biddy suffering from Alzheimer's disease, her memories all confused. But there was something in her voice that made him want to give her the benefit of the doubt for just a little longer.

'Did I catch you right?' he asked. 'You're telling me that the girl they showed on television isn't Anastasia Holland but someone who died nineteen years ago?'

There was a pause. 'I knew the police would think I was, you know, a bit potty; that's why I thought I'd try you first, you see.'

'Who is it?' Karen whispered.

Joe covered the receiver. 'A crank.' The old woman was saying something else and he missed it. 'Sorry, could you repeat that?'

'I suppose they might – perhaps, do you think?'

Joe took a breath to control his temper. 'Might what?'

'Keep the photographs going back that far?'

'I'm sorry, I'm a little confused. Who might keep the photographs going back that far?'

'The television company, the BBC, or the newspapers – or the police.'

'And which photographs do you mean? Photos of whom?'

'Susan,' she said, as if he was the idiot now.

He hesitated. 'Why would the BBC have photographs of your niece?'

'Well –' Doubt returned to her voice. 'I imagine they might have done. Otherwise, how would they have one now?'

'I've no idea,' he said rattily. He'd had enough, the conversation wasn't going anywhere. 'Look, I'm sorry, I have to go now. I'll take your number and pass it on to the police. They'll get back to you if they think your information could be helpful.'

She gave it to him and he jotted it down on the back of the room-service menu.

'Thank you for calling,' he said, and hung up.

Karen was staring out of the window. 'What kind of a crank was that, Joe?'

'An old lady, she was harmless, just confused; thought Stassi was her niece.'

'I keep thinking I see him running across the promenade,' she said.

'I keep thinking I see him everywhere I look.'

The phone rang again. Joe made a move, but was surprised when Karen reached it first. He soon gathered that it was just the old biddy ringing back again and gestured at Karen to get rid of her. He was even more surprised when Karen shooed him off and gave the pest-caller her full attention, and even asked the old lady to take her time. He knew Karen was close to the edge and it was all he could do not to grab the receiver from her and slam it back in the cradle.

The leaden surface of the road sucked the light from the sky without returning it as Joe drove through the grimy sprawl of the south London boroughs, making his way towards Battersea. Against his own better judgement. Norbury, Streatham, Balham, Clapham. Saturday morning. The street barrows were out; veggies, cheap pullovers, shirts, socks. Day-glo stickers shone from shopfronts. BARGAIN! CLOSING DOWN SALE! CD'S REDUCED!! FIRE SALE!! People were milling down the streets in shell suits and trainers. Joe scanned them, watching for a girl with long brown hair, on her own or accompanied by a small fair-haired boy.

He pulled over and checked the address, found his bearings. Close now, he thought with relief; should only be a couple of blocks. A man went by holding a boy's hand. The boy looked excited and did a little jump. Jack did little jumps like that sometimes.

He turned right at the next light, and slowed down when he reached two concrete tower blocks with ugly weather stains. Large lettering above the porch of the first one stated: PORTLAND COURT.

Joe parked the Saab and walked over to the entrance. One of the glass doors was smashed and the other was off its hinges. Someone had had a go at the entryphone, and all that remained were a few bare wires sticking out of the wall like entrails. He knew it, this was a complete zero.

The lift was wide and slow and felt as if it was designed more for freight than passengers. When the doors opened on the ninth floor he heard raised voices then a loud slam. A tarty-looking girl in a leather skirt stomped towards him and did not thank him for holding the lift door for her.

The leather soles of his suede brogues clacked on the hard concrete floor. Each front door was painted blue and some had spyholes. Pop music blared through one door; canned laughter through another. Outside number 97 there was silence.

He pressed the bell and waited. The corridor smelled of eggs and bacon and it made him feel queasy. He heard a voice behind the door, the same nervy voice he recognized from the phone. 'Mind out of the way, boys!' There was the sound of a safety chain rattling, and the door opened.

An elderly lady stood there wearing a rather well-cut floral-print dress, with a single strand of pearls and fluffy slippers. Two Siamese cats nudged their way past her and she shooed them in again. 'Boys, back!' Then she greeted him. 'Professor Messenger? I'm so relieved. I – I can't tell you!'

When Karen had taken Cora Roach's second call, she'd agreed with the old lady that Joe would drive over to see her and get the full story. He had remonstrated quite forcefully with Karen, but she'd insisted that something – she didn't know what – told her that Mrs Roach was worth a personal visit. In the end he'd put it down to female intuition and gone along with it. Even so, he half wondered if it was just that Karen wanted him out of the way for a morning so that she could try something cranky herself; Brighton was full of people who claimed to be able to read palms or trace a missing person and tell you what they'd had for breakfast just by handling their shoelaces: psychometry. Now Joe was about to get involved with a crank, too.

The figure before him was short and matchstick thin, but carried herself with a certain dignity. She might have been very attractive when she was younger, Joe thought, and her eyes were still pretty now, for all that they were marooned in a shrivelled face. But her grey hair had been neatly brushed on one side and not the other, and her bright red lipstick failed to trace exactly the contours of her lips.

Joe wondered, gloomily, if perhaps the old lady had defective vision; whether she was in any position at all to identify Stassi Holland. He considered bailing out now, despite Karen's 'feeling', but something prevented him and suddenly he realized what it was.

She reminded him of Stassi. It was nothing he could actually put a finger on, no specific physical resemblance, just something that made him feel they were both from the same family. Both had a similar reedy tone of voice.

'Please come in, professor; you will understand when I show you. I'm not wasting your time.' She ushered him into a dark hallway which smelled of cats. But there was an air of quality about the furniture that surprised him; it was quite out of keeping with the building, as if it had once all been housed in a far grander and larger place.

There was a walnut writing desk covered in fine silver and porcelain ornaments. Two oak chairs that looked as if they'd been designed for a baronial hall. An ornate barometer hung on the wall, together with a rather grand mirror in a gilt frame and a fine old seascape in oil.

She led him through into a small living room that was overwhelmed with more furniture, and an air of faded genteel splendour. Every available surface was covered in genuine antique ornaments and framed photographs. It felt as if the window, edged with drab, heavy curtains and overlooking the twin tower block fifty yards away, gave on to another world. One that consisted of grey concrete, laundry on balconies and other people's windows.

'Please, sit down.'

Joe sank into an armchair with busted springs, and accepted a sherry. He noticed a newspaper open at a racing page and several ball-point markings on it. 'You do the horses?'

Her face became animated. 'My late husband and I used to travel all over the country to race meetings. The Derby;

Ascot, of course. The St Leger. And to Longchamps in Paris, naturally.' She filled a sherry glass for herself, too. 'That's him on the mantelpiece.'

Joe glanced up. There were two framed photographs, one in black and white of a man in RAF uniform and a peaked cap, the other of some newlyweds on the steps of a church. It looked like a smart wedding, a society wedding.

The room was full of traces of another life, something much grander. Joe wondered what had happened, what misfortune had befallen her. He sipped some sherry, almost cheered by its warmth. Muriel Arkwright had been murdered in his drawing room, his son had been kidnapped and he was sipping sherry with some dotty old lady.

'It's my only pleasure these days,' she said, picking up a cigarette box and proffering it to Joe.

'Thank you, no,' he said.

She rattled the contents with her shaking fingers, lit a cigarette for herself, then sat down opposite Joe. 'That's her up there, you see.' She put her cigarette in an ashtray and pointed to a colour photo of a girl of about eight, with straight brown hair, standing in a garden.

'Susan Roach?' he said.

'She was my niece.' She reached agitatedly for her cigarette, knocking it out of the ashtray. It rolled off the table and fell on the floor. She turned back to him, reaching down for the cigarette without hurrying. 'That's such an old picture. I do have others.'

Joe sipped some more sherry; it began to make him feel a fraction light-headed. He watched her shuffle across the floor and take a leather photograph album down from the bookshelf. She opened it for him, searched through several pages of snaps, then stopped and pointed at a girl in her late teens who bore a strong likeness to Stassi.

Joe studied it carefully. The girl was wearing a striped mini skirt and was posing against the deck rail of a boat. It was captioned 'Day Out in Devon 1968'.

It could have been Stassi, but it could as easily have been a different girl. The features and build were similar, but the photo didn't show enough facial detail. And Joe knew, from trying to teach ARCHIVE to recognize faces, that there were only a certain number of facial types. Many people had near-identical versions of themselves.

He pressed his lips together and smiled politely at the old lady. 'Sure, it looks like her. Do you have anything more recent?'

'I said that you – you wouldn't be disappointed, professor.' She looked pleased and Joe felt lousy at having to disillusion her.

'I don't think your theory is possible, Mrs Roach,' he said gently. 'They look similar, yes, but this girl you say died in 1974. Even if she were still alive, she'd be nearly twice Stassi's age now.'

'Please look through the album,' she said. 'Look at the other photographs.'

Joe flipped through a few pages. He saw the same girl much younger, on her knees, with her arms round the neck of a golden retriever. Then the caption beneath suddenly sent a chill curling through him: 'Susan and Gulliver. May 63.'

Gulliver.

Stassi had said that name, for no apparent reason, several times. Karen had noticed it too. Joe glanced up at Mrs Roach. 'Gulliver was her dog?'

'Oh, she adored Gulliver! Desmond – my husband – bought him for her tenth birthday.' She drank some sherry. 'Susan treated Gulliver like a brother – you see she had no other family.'

'Oh?'

She winked at him like an errant schoolgirl. 'I shouldn't talk, professor. Family secrets. Skeletons in closets.' She fumbled in the silver box for another cigarette, oblivious to the remains of the one burning in the ashtray. 'Susan's father killed her mother.'

'*Killed?*'

'Blasted her with a shotgun, in front of Susan – when Susan was seven. She was having an affair; she was always

495

having affairs. Then he shot himself and Susan came to live with us.' She lit the new cigarette. 'We had no children, you see. Perhaps we could these days. Do you have children, professor?'

Joe was thrown by the question; he watched her puff on her cigarette. The filter of the cigarette in the ashtray was now smouldering. 'Yes,' he said patiently. 'We have a son called Jack. The one who's missing.'

'A nice name, Jack,' she said, and seemed to drift off into her own thoughts. 'Gulliver was killed on her thirteenth birthday. He was run over by a car.' She puffed hard and flapped the smoke away. 'From then on it seemed to poor Susan as if everything she ever loved would be taken away from her.' She noticed the smouldering butt suddenly, and crushed it out. Then she smiled at him with watery eyes. 'Do you understand what I mean, professor?

Joe nodded silently.

'I'm sure that explains what happened later. I –' Her voice tailed.

Joe waited for her to continue, but instead she became pensive. He looked at the photo of the girl and the dog. Gulliver. Had to be just one of life's meaningless coincidences. He glanced at his watch, and wanted to get back. It had been a waste of time to come here, but he couldn't feel angry at the old woman, just sorry for her. Life was brutal. Sometimes you fell by the wayside, like she had, and then died. Sometimes you just died. He stood up. 'I have to get going. Thank you for the drink.'

'It is her, professor. I'm afraid it really is her. You see, she wanted a little boy so much.'

He halted. 'What exactly do you mean?'

Cora Roach stood up slowly, as if she were pushing the weight of the world up with her shoulders. 'I shouldn't be telling – of course – family secrets. All families have some, don't they?'

'I guess.'

'But I felt I had to help you. What she has done isn't right. But you'll understand, won't you, professor? When you find her?'

Joe searched her face with his eyes, then nodded. 'Sure,' he said. 'Sure I'll understand.' Then he walked bleakly back towards the lift.

66

Joe and Karen had been allowed to move back home on Saturday morning, and Joe drove straight there from London. He noticed an unmarked police car at the top of the road, and there was a cluster of reporters and photographers hanging around outside the house. He also noticed an additional car on the Arkwrights' driveway, a small blue saloon he had occasionally seen before at weekends, their daughter's, he vaguely recalled.

The reporters converged on him as he climbed out.

'Any developments, professor?'

He locked the car, shaking his head.

'Are you satisfied with the way the police are handling this?' yelled a rather aggressive young woman.

'They couldn't be more helpful. We're very touched by all they're doing for us.'

'Turn this way, prof! Quick one for the camera!' a cheery character called out.

Joe opened his front door, went in and closed it thankfully behind him. The hall reeked of disinfectant, and the walls looked damp; maybe the police had sent someone or maybe Karen had been scrubbing them, trying to remove the bloodstains. The thought of anyone having to scrub away the mess left by Muriel 'Super-clean' Arkwright was poignant. And it reminded Joe, once again, that he should go across and see Derek Arkwright at some point.

A uniformed policewoman came out of the kitchen; she was in her early thirties, with neat brown hair and she had a friendly air about her.

'Professor Messenger? I'm WPC Belling,' she said. 'Detective Superintendent Lyne spoke to you – about a police presence for you and Mrs Messenger?'

Joe nodded.

'I'll be with you during the daytime, and my colleague, WPC Grant, will be with you nights. We'll try not to get in the way too much.'

'It's good of you to come,' Joe said. 'Have you had coffee or anything?'

'Your wife's been looking after me very well. She tells me you've been to see a woman who phoned you about the photo of your au pair?'

'Yes, a Mrs Roach. Wasn't any use, I'm afraid.' He tapped his head. 'Gaga.'

'Oh, I'm sorry.'

Joe went into the kitchen. Karen was sitting, red eyed, at the table with a photograph album open in front of her. She looked up with desperate hope in her face.

Joe shook his head. 'Waste of time.' He kissed her on the forehead, then squeezed her hand. 'Any news?' The kitchen clock said 1.50.

'Not unless you count Blake ringing for you as news.' She lowered her gaze slowly and touched a photograph with her finger. 'He was such a lovely little chap, wasn't he, Joe?'

Joe looked at her, startled. 'Hey, come on! What's all this *was* business?'

'Barty was lovely, too,' she said.

'Karen, Jack's gonna be OK.'

'She wasn't any help at all?'

'Out to lunch,' he said. But the photo of the small girl with her arms around the neck of the golden retriever had stayed with him all the way back. *Gulliver*.

'She hadn't seen anything?'

'Nope.' He was determined not to use the words *I told you so*, not to rub her face in it.

Karen turned a page. More photographs of Jack; of themselves. Joe tried to remember who it was who'd said that the past was another country. It wasn't any more, he thought.

They had left another country to come here; left behind the tragedy of a dead son; now the ghosts of that country seemed to be following them. Or were they just jinxed?

Be positive, he thought. Must keep up morale for Karen's sake. And, he knew, for his own. There was a rap on the door. Karen made a move. Joe laid his hand on her shoulder. 'I'll go.'

As he went into the hall, WPC Belling was already halfway down the stairs. 'Like me to answer it, professor?'

'It's OK, thanks.' He opened the door.

Lyne and Gavros stood in the porch, both looking tired and serious. 'Good afternoon, professor. Is it convenient?'

'Sure.' Joe ushered them in. 'Any news?'

Lyne shook his head curtly. 'Not yet. We have to have a breakthrough soon.'

They all sat down in the kitchen, while WPC Belling busied herself with making coffee, and Lyne ran them through the police operation.

'We've published a twenty-four-hour hotline number – we've had a lot of calls come in and we're following them up. The Scotland Yard murder enquiry team and ourselves are running the operation in tandem, with our priority being the safe return of your son.' He seemed a trifle defensive. 'We've cancelled all police leave over the weekend and drafted in the Specials – we're widening our search to the surrounding countryside and golf courses.'

'Do you think Jack's still in this country?' Joe asked.

'All sea and airports are keeping an eye out, but we've no guarantee. If it is this Anastasia Holland who's taken him, she would have a problem getting him through any passport control. But there are ways.'

'Sure,' Joe said flatly.

Lyne dug his hands into his mackintosh pocket. 'There are fingerprints on Mrs Messenger's white Toyota which match your son's and those we assume to be Miss Holland's.' He shrugged. 'But as she drove him to school every day, it doesn't necessarily tell us much. And leaving the car at the airport could be a blind. Is there anything else that either of you can remember about her that might help us find her? Anything she dropped in conversation?'

'I don't know if it has any significance,' Karen said suddenly. 'Two or three times she said the name *Gulliver*. For no apparent reason.'

'Gulliver? Did you ever quiz her about it, Mrs Messenger?' Gavros asked.

She shook her head. 'No, she'd just blurt it out. It was kind of weird, as if she didn't know she was saying it, you know?'

Lyne was frowning. '*Gulliver's Travels*.' He turned to Gavros. 'Ever read it?'

'Seem to remember it at school, vaguely. Lilliput, wasn't it? Little people? Pygmies?'

'Gulliver came across a race called the Struldbrugs,' Karen said quietly. 'A race endowed with immortality. Far from finding this a boon, they turned out to be the most miserable of all mankind.' She stared pointedly at Joe.

'Isn't there some village down in Devon or somewhere where they filmed it?' Gavros said.

'We'll check it out,' Lyne said without much enthusiasm. He looked back at Joe, then his narrow eyes darted fleetingly to Karen, picking up the sudden tension between them. 'We've been to see your colleague, Professor Hewlett, but he wasn't able to give us anything new.'

'No,' Joe said, unsurprised. 'He was going to let her family know – but I don't think he wanted to alarm them too much at this point.'

The detective inspector frowned lightly; he didn't look like a man who minded alarming anyone, Joe thought.

When Lyne spoke again, he addressed both Joe and Karen. 'If you'd be prepared to do it, the BBC would broadcast an appeal by you. That can sometimes be very useful. They'd put it on the end of the national news.'

Joe looked at Karen. 'Sure. We'll do anything.'

Lyne said he would fix it so it would go out that evening. Beyond that, he hadn't very much more to offer. A young woman and a small boy could melt into the scenery anywhere in the world, he told them grimly. If it was Stassi who had taken Jack, no one knew how much money she had on her, what her motives were, nor what she might do next. All they could do was keep looking, keep waiting. Keep hoping.

After the detectives had gone, Joe wandered into his study. He sat in his armchair and closed his eyes, trying to recall everything about Stassi that he could. Then he remembered Karen said Blake had phoned, and he dialled his number, relieved to have a distraction. He got Blake's answering machine and started to leave a message, when there was a loud click, and he heard Blake's voice.

'Hi, Joe, I'm here.'

'Oh – right –' Joe said, thrown. 'I was returning your call.'

'I just rang to see how you both were. What news? Anything?'

'No. Did you speak to your Hong Kong contact with Stassi's family?'

'Matt? Turns out he's gone away, would you believe! For a month. Trekking in the Himalayas. There's just some caretaker, or someone, who hardly speaks any English. I tried to impress on him the urgency . . .'

'You had a talk to the police? Superintendent Lyne?'

'I don't think I was much help. So where were you? Karen said you'd gone to London to talk to someone who reckoned they'd seen Stassi?'

'Wasted journey – she was totally senile – she'd just seen Stassi's photograph on the news. Know what she said?'

'What?'

'That she reckoned it was her niece who died nineteen years ago!'

'No kidding?'

'I had to go up and look at all these old photos. Poor thing, I felt quite sorry for her. She was really convinced, you know?'

'What are you doing right now, Joe? I mean, how about I come over?' Blake sounded strangely edgy, Joe thought.

'Sure, if you want.'

'I'll be right with you,' he said.

Joe and Blake went into the garden. The weather had brightened and it had turned into a warm afternoon. They walked past the summerhouse and around the vegetable plot. Over the fence Joe saw a battered straw hat moving slowly; one of his elderly neighbours out doing some gardening.

'Good crop of cabbages,' Blake said.

'I think those are lettuces,' Joe said.

Blake looked at them disdainfully. He seemed oddly out of place in the vegetable patch in his black sweatshirt, black jeans and black Cuban-heeled boots. He stopped when he reached the chives and turned to Joe. 'So tell me more about this old lady.'

'Not much to tell. I – I guess she wanted to be helpful.'

'And she was senile or something?'

'Yup.'

Blake put his hands on the closeboard fence and peered nosily over into the next-door garden. 'What did you say her name was?'

'Roach. Cora Roach. She was quite convinced Stassi was her niece, Susan, I think it was.'

Blake remained peering over the fence. 'In South London, you said she lived?'

'Yes.'

'Whereabouts?'

'Battersea. Why?'

Blake shrugged nonchalantly and moved on. 'Curious,' he said. 'Just curious.' Then he smiled dismissively and raised his shoulders again. 'You know, kind of an odd thing to crop up.' He walked on a few paces ahead of Joe, no longer strutting but with an uneasy gait.

The BBC crew arrived shortly after Blake left and spent two hours getting the broadcast taped. Joe and Karen watched it when it went out after the six o'clock news. At the end of it, they both cried.

Karen cooked pasta for supper and Joe made an avocado

salad. WPC Belling's poker-faced colleague, WPC Grant, had taken over for the night shift. They invited her to join them, but she told them she'd already eaten, and was happy to sit on her own studying for some police-force exams. Joe noticed with a chill, when she took her jacket off, that she was wearing a holster.

He had no appetite and forced himself to eat a little, to try to keep up his strength. Karen pushed hers around the plate and ate only a mouthful. Afterwards he helped her up to bed, then went into his study, sat down at his workstation and logged in.

Good evening, Professor. I note you have a new stranger in your house who is not Stassi. Where is Jack?

I was hoping you could tell me where Jack is, Joe replied.

I am sorry, professor. I do not have that information in my files.

Joe adjusted his Anglepoise which was glaring on to the screen. He cleared the screen then typed: Last Wednesday night Stassi and Jack were in the house alone together. Do you remember?

I am sorry, professor. I do not have that information in my files.

Joe eyed the screen warily. Something was not right. He thought of the problem last Wednesday night when he'd tried to replay the videos from the house cameras for the detectives. The fact that the video had not been recording should not have affected the rest of ARCHIVE's memory. Either there was another malfunction, or someone had tampered with it. Someone who wanted to cover all traces of what had happened Wednesday night.

And knew how to.

Your sweet little wifey with her face all covered in goat shit.

He had to admit Juliet had cracked the decoding of the cameras. Was she still getting at him from beyond the grave? The thought was absurd and he turned his mind to something more realistic.

Blake?

Blake worried him. His behaviour had seemed odd this afternoon; maybe it was because he felt bad for having introduced Stassi to them, and he just wasn't very good at coping with guilt? But there was something beyond that. The strange edginess Blake had displayed when he'd been told about Mrs Roach. But why? Joe could not shake off the impression that Blake was hiding something from him. Something about Stassi?

Was he trying to cover up for her? The way Joe looked at it now, he'd taken a stranger into his home on trust, entirely on a third-party recommendation, without bothering to check up on anything. Did the girl have some dark secret, maybe a history of mental instability? Blake had told him that the guy who'd first mentioned her was away in the Himalayas. Was he just trying to protect his old friend?

Joe sank his head into his hands. He and Blake went too far back together for Blake to con him in any way. And in his heart he simply could not believe that Blake was holding out on him. He thought hard for a while, then picked up the phone and dialled International Directory Enquiries.

'Which country, please?' the operator asked.

'Hong Kong. Do you have a listing for someone by the name of Holland?'

'Do you have an address, sir?'

'I'm afraid not.'

'Is it Hong Kong island, Kowloon or New Territories?'

'I – I don't know, I'm sorry.

'I'll have a look and see if there are any listed.'

Joe hung on until she came back to him.

'There are no *Hollands* in the New Territories. But there are eleven on Hong Kong island and thirteen in Kowloon.'

Joe grimaced silently. 'All private numbers?'

'Yes, sir. Do you have an initial?'

'No, I haven't. I guess – I – would you mind – letting me have them all?'

'All twenty-five?'

'Yes. You can bill me extra.'

'We'll have to, sir,' she said, and started reading them out.

His hand ached when he'd finished repeating the last one back to double-check. Then he thanked the operator and hung up. The numbers covered three sheets of notepaper. He glanced at his watch, and reckoned it was 4.15 a.m. in Hong Kong. Not a very civilized time to phone anyone, he realized; he'd have to get the police on to it early in the morning. They'd be able to check the ex-directory listings as well.

67

In fact it was Detective Superintendent Lyne who got on to Joe first thing in the morning and not the other way round. He came in person at 8.30, for once unaccompanied by Gavros. He told Joe that police procedural work, in tandem with the Department of Immigration, had established that there was no Hong Kong citizen named Anastasia Holland. Nor was there any British subject of that name with HK resident status.

No Stassi Holland. Had Blake lied to him? Fear exploded like a small bomb inside Joe. Who was she? Who the hell was she?

Lyne left, saying it was an interesting development and they were on to something now. He said they'd like to talk to Professor Hewlett again, and promised to keep Joe in touch. He almost had a lightness in his step.

Joe felt dazed and didn't dare tell Karen the latest just yet; she'd freak out. Instinctively he headed for his study; back to the womb. His eyes scanned the bookshelves that lined one wall. He saw the row of his father's books. The fear continued spreading through him. A deep fear that went back eleven years to his father's deathbed.

Toronto. 1982. A bitter February night. The phone call that had woken him from the nurse at the hospital. *Dr*

Messenger, your father is calling out for you. He wants to speak to you very badly.

Joe remembered driving through the snow. Arriving at the hospital at around three a.m. And seeing Blake come out of the elevator. His father already dead by the time he reached him.

He had not thought about it before; never had any reason to be suspicious of Blake, or any reason to think it was odd to have seen him in a hospital elevator at gone three in the morning. His father had had so much faith in his protégé, entrusted his knowledge in him, and his belief in the future. It would be a denial of his father's integrity to start looking at Blake in a new light now. Just because he knew someone who'd sent them a bummer of an au pair.

Lyne must have made an error; and now Joe was trying to make something out of it that wasn't there; jumping to conclusions. Dangerous. Unscientific.

But the doubt lingered. The dotty old woman, Cora Roach. *You see, she died nineteen years ago, professor.*

Then he thought about Blake's odd reaction over the telephone this afternoon when he'd heard about Cora Roach. Jumpy. The germ of a suspicion rose, but Joe dismissed it. Too absurd to contemplate; the technology simply didn't exist, not yet. He was making too much of it all, reading too much into the coincidences.

Gulliver.

It is her, professor. I'm afraid it really is her. You see she wanted a little boy so much.

He picked up the phone and dialled Blake's number. After the third ring there was a click, a brief silence, the crackle of static, then the familiar sound of Blake's recorded voice.

Joe cursed silently, then spoke calmly: 'Blake, will you give me a call as soon as you get this, doesn't matter what time. I have to talk to you urgently.'

On the off-chance he also tried Blake's mobile phone number. 'The Vodaphone you have called may be switched off. Please try later,' a recorded voice said.

He hung up and drummed his knuckles on his desk. Mrs

Roach. Maybe he had missed something, been too brief with the old girl, too impatient. Karen had been right and he'd been wrong. He should have taken her with him, but she'd wanted to move back home that morning, to be there for Jack. The girl in the photographs, Susan Roach, had certainly looked like Stassi. Susan Roach had died nineteen years ago, but maybe there was another relative? Was that what she'd been trying to tell him?

He thought again of all the finery inside the grotty apartment. The refined voice. Cora Roach had undoubtedly come from good stock. Old money somewhere back along the line. Old morality. The closing of ranks around a member of the family who was in trouble?

I shouldn't be telling – of course – family secrets. All families have some, don't they?

There had been a knowing twinkle in her eyes as she'd made that remark. As if she were dropping him a hint but the rules of her upbringing meant she could go no further, couldn't actually name a name. And he'd not taken the hint.

Joe was uncommunicative all day. A small part of him kept thinking, what if Karen had been right about Blake too? She had never liked him. Finally, when he got back from taking her to a physio session at the hospital, and they'd had supper, he retreated to his study once more. From his briefcase he took out the creased room-service menu from the hotel, on the back of which he'd scrawled Mrs Roach's number and address.

He dialled the number, his heart thumping. The line was busy. He immediately redialled. It was still busy. After a couple of minutes he tried it again, then again, then again. Get off the phone, for Chrissake, get off the phone! He tried again. Always busy. She was probably housebound and had to live her life on the phone, he guessed: the geriatric equivalent of Teenage Chatline.

Finally, at 10.30 he rang the operator and reported his difficulty. She tried it from her end and then said, 'I'll have the line checked and call you back in a few minutes.'

When she did ring back, almost immediately, it was to say there was a fault of some kind. She would report it to the engineers, she told him.

'How soon before it'll be fixed?' he asked.

'If it's a fault on the line, it might be later tonight or else some time tomorrow. If it's the phone itself, it won't be until an engineer can call round some time in the next few days,' she said.

'It's very urgent,' Joe told her. 'An elderly lady on her own.'

'I'll tell the engineers, but they are very busy at the moment,' she said.

Joe hung up and looked at his watch. Ten to eleven. Sunday, the traffic would be light; he could probably get there in an hour. He debated whether to wait until morning, whether he might get more out of her then rather than now. But that meant another nine hours of nothing happening; another nine hours for Jack, wherever he was.

He switched off ARCHIVE, peered into the bedroom and saw that Karen was asleep, then went downstairs, stuck his head round the door of the kitchen and told WPC Grant he was going out and would be a while.

As he turned left into Cora Roach's road, a shard of blue light hurtled towards him. Then another. There was a foul stench in the air of burning paint; an accident, he thought as he saw the cluster of emergency services ahead and the glare of arc lights. Then he felt an unpleasant sensation as he realized they were outside the two tower blocks, outside the one nearest to him. Portland Court.

Cora Roach's building.

A policeman stood in the middle of the road waving a torch, making the traffic move on. Joe gesticulated that he wanted to park, but the policeman shouted at him to drive on.

Shaking, Joe pulled in a hundred yards further on, locked the car then ran back. Hoses were snaked over the road. There was a crowd of about two hundred people huddled on the pavement, some in nightclothes, several holding cats or budgerigar cages.

A turntable ladder reached from a fire engine and up the side of the building. The fireman at the top of it, silhouetted by a powerful searchlight, was directing the jet from a hose at a bright red glow.

Joe counted the floors. It was the ninth floor. Cora Roach lived on the ninth floor.

He scoured the faces of the crowd. Dozens of elderly people, some with blankets draped round their shoulders, or coats over nightdresses. He eased his way through them, making for the main entrance where the stench of burning paint was even stronger; tiny flecks of ash fell lightly from the sky, tickling his face like dry snow.

He reached the fireman who was standing blocking the front entrance. 'What's happening?' he asked, aware that it was a dumb question, but too desperate to care.

'Do you live here, sir?'

'My aunt,' Joe said.

'Blaze on the ninth floor. It's under control.'

'In a flat?'

'Yes, sir.'

'Do you know what number?'

The fireman studied him for a moment. His radio crackled but he ignored it. 'Ninety-seven, sir.'

Joe felt cold shivers lacerate his body. 'She lives in ninety-seven; that's *her* flat! Is she all right?'

The fireman lowered his head, pressed a button on his radio and spoke into it. 'Tom, I have a relative of the occupant of 97 down here. Do you have any info?'

Joe listened in numb silence to the voice that crackled back.

'Total inferno. There is a body but it's still smouldering and we have no identification yet. Suggest the relative goes to Battersea Police Station and waits there; it'll be another hour before we can go in and examine.'

'Roger.' The fireman released his talk button and looked grimly back at Joe. 'I'm sorry, sir. Does she live on her own?'

Joe nodded.

'Can you find your own way to the police station?'

'Yes,' Joe said. 'Yes, thank you, I can.' He turned and walked, dazed, back towards his car.

68

Karen was half-awake when Joe came into the room. She asked him where he'd been and he told her he'd gone back to see the woman who'd phoned. He did not tell her about the fire. He was glad that she'd obviously taken a sleeping tablet and was too drowsy to take him up on his visit.

His clock said 1.50. He climbed into bed utterly exhausted, and dreamed of Jack. Everything was normal and Jack was fine. They made plans to go fishing for trout on a lake in Kent. In the morning his first waking thought was to wonder why Jack hadn't bounced into the room. But his second one was to wonder if he ever would again.

The night-shift policewoman had left and WPC Belling was back downstairs. 'I've got some coffee on, professor,' she greeted him breezily as he came down in a blue polo shirt, jeans and trainers.

'We should be looking after you,' he said and managed a smile. Monday morning, but without the usual bustle that made it the start of a new week. The newspapers were on the kitchen table, and it gave him a shock to see his face staring back out from a page of yesterday's *Sunday Times*. And Jack's. And Karen's. There was an even larger photograph of Stassi, captioned: AU PAIR KIDNAP SUSPECT.

He had barely noticed the papers yesterday, and he skimmed the large article for some moments, then stopped, distressed by it. 'I went back to London last night – to see the woman again – the one I told you about on Saturday morning.'

'Mrs Roach?'

Joe was impressed she remembered her name. 'Yes; when I got there –' Blake, he thought suddenly. Blake in the garden, questioning him about Mrs Roach. Asking where she lived.

He stared back at the policewoman, confused, his train of thought gone.

'Mrs Roach,' she prompted quietly.

'Right.' Blake. Was that where Blake had been yesterday? Calm down. Jumping to crazy conclusions. He remembered her cigarettes. Remembered the one she'd dropped on the carpet. She had probably fallen asleep in bed smoking. He was getting paranoid. 'I – got there – her apartment was on fire.'

'What happened to her?' She poured his coffee out for him.

'There was a body in there but they hadn't managed to reach it.'

'I think Superintendent Lyne should hear about this at once,' the policewoman said.

'Probably no connection, but there's something I'd like the superintendent to try to find out for me.' He poured some milk into his coffee. 'Whether she – Mrs Roach – has – had – any relatives, whether there's any family connection at all between her and Stassi Holland.'

'I shouldn't think he'd have any trouble.' She frowned. 'Did you tell anyone about Mrs Roach, professor?'

Joe shook his head. 'No one other than Blake.'

'Your colleague?'

'Yes.'

'The colleague who introduced Stassi to you?'

'That's right.'

She poured some more coffee for herself. 'Have you known him a long time?'

'We go back twenty years; he was my father's right hand.'

'And can you trust him implicitly?' She was watching him carefully.

He stirred his coffee. 'Yes,' he said finally, aware he had waited a beat too long before replying.

★

Joe felt he should stay with Karen, and he rang in to Eileen Peacock, said he hoped to put in an appearance at the university tomorrow and meanwhile could she please do the necessaries.

They received several phone calls during the morning from friends and colleagues mostly, and one crank who told Joe that computers were evil and those who worked with them were working for the devil, and now God's wrath was being manifested on him. Joe tried Blake's home number repeatedly, and all the work numbers he had for him, without luck.

Around midday, Joe braced himself and went across the street to Derek Arkwright's house, telling the reporters who gathered round him that there was no news, and not answering any more questions. He noticed the Arkwrights' curtains were still drawn.

The Arkwrights' daughter, a junior replica of her mother, answered the front door and invited Joe in politely but guardedly. She was obviously upset. The hallway was dark and hot, as if the central heating was on full blast. Her father appeared like a ghost. His tall frame was stooped, his skin was sallow, his eyes raw inside deep black rings. Joe gave him his condolences, told him he was desperately sorry. Derek Arkwright said little, but managed to convey that this was all Joe's fault.

In the afternoon Joe and Karen spent a few hours out in the garden. Karen lay on a recliner. For something to do, Joe mowed neat lines up and down the lawn, guillotining the daisies, making it smooth for playing football. He'd have a game with Jack when he got back.

It was a fine, hot afternoon, bright sunlight with crisp shadows stencilled on the grass, and a quietness that not even the blatter of the lawnmower could shift; there was a stillness, as if everything in the garden was suspended in time, waiting for Jack to come back and press the start button.

As Joe was tidying away the mower, he saw Detective Superintendent Lyne and Detective Inspector Gavros come through the patio doors.

The senior detective confirmed, grimly, that Mrs Cora Roach had died in the blaze which had gutted her flat. A neighbour who did her shopping had told the police that she'd nearly set fire to the place a couple of times before by leaving lighted cigarettes around. The same neighbour had also said she'd gathered that Mrs Roach had no living relatives. The police were checking for any connection between the old lady and Stassi Holland, but nothing had shown up on that so far.

Lyne told Joe and Karen how many police officers and Specials were being deployed today throughout Sussex. There'd been sightings phoned in to the incident room from all over the country and every lead was being followed up; all they could do was keep hoping.

He told them, also, that they still needed to re-interview Blake Hewlett about Stassi Holland. Karen flipped a bit when she discovered what Joe knew already: that Stassi seemed to have no known address or family in Hong Kong and did not possess the Hong Kong identity card – Registration of Ordnance – obligatory to all citizens over eighteen. She had thought it odd that Stassi's parents had not written to her, but had put it down to the short time she'd been with them. Lyne wondered if Joe knew where Hewlett might be, or whether perhaps he had gone away for a long weekend?

Joe could only suggest the university, the premises of Cryonite, or Blake's office at the Human Organ Preservation Centre, and gave them the addresses and phone numbers. As the Detective Inspector was writing them down, the phone rang.

Joe jumped up, hurried into the kitchen and lifted the receiver. There was a series of rapid beeps then a high-pitched whine; after a few moments the beeps started again followed by a whistle. His eyes shot a glance at ARCHIVE's camera; the noise continued. He laid the receiver down and raced upstairs to his study and lifted the phone there. The same noise. He disconnected the phone jack from its socket and plugged it into the computer modem, and switched on.

Then he took a step back in shock.

Juliet's face filled the screen. Stark white, colourless. She winked at him. Her lips pursed into a kiss and a coil of vapour escaped from them. Then her face was gone and the screen went black.

Joe stood transfixed, fear jumbling his insides.

After a few moments the words appeared: Hello, Joe-Joe, nice to have me back? Would you like to know where Jack is?

With trembling fingers, Joe typed: Who are you?

I'm Juliet, Joe-Joe. Don't tell me you've forgotten already!

Where is my son? he typed.

Where is my body? the reply came back. It's so lonely in here, Joe-Joe, and I'm so horny. Wouldn't you like to get me a body? Someone young and sexy like Stassi and then you and I could do it.

Where is my son?

You could get me any body you like, Joe-Joe. Someone you'd really like to screw. How about Karen's? You wouldn't be committing adultery then, would you?

Please tell me where my son is. I'll do anything I can for you.

Not good enough, Joe-Joe! You think about it.

The screen went blank. Then there was a sharp click. Joe stared in disbelief. ARCHIVE had switched itself off.

He took a step back, unable to understand what was happening. A new threat had just reached him through his ears: there was a noise coming from Jack's room. And it didn't sound like a little boy.

He sprinted down the landing and pushed open Jack's door, then stopped dead. Jack's electric train was running. The locomotive was moving eerily round the track, towing the passenger carriages behind it. It did a circuit, then another, slowly picking up speed as if an invisible finger were on the control. Someone was playing a game.

'Jack?' Joe said quietly. 'Jack?' He thought he saw something move under the bed and dropped to his knees, pressed his cheek against the carpet. Nothing.

The train was getting even faster, accelerating, going too fast now, the carriages swaying wildly. Too fast! Jack always made it go too fast and Joe had to tell him to slow down.

There was a sudden bang as the locomotive fell on to its side at a bend, then total silence. The carriages lay at a drunken angle behind it, neither upright nor fallen.

Joe reached down and pulled the plug of the transformer out of the socket. Then he stood up again, shaking, and glanced at the camera in the corner of the ceiling. His ears were numb as if he were swimming underwater, and the silence of the room pressed in on them, increasing the pressure, threatening to splinter his skull.

He backed out, turned and walked quickly downstairs, and outside to the expectant faces of Karen, the two detectives and WPC Belling.

'A fax or a computer misdialling,' he said, and sat down. He felt his cheeks reddening and was aware of the Detective Inspector's narrow eyes watching him.

'More problems with computers, professor?'

Joe said nothing for a moment; all four of them were waiting for his reply. 'I hope not,' he said, finally.

'A computer can misdial, can it? The way a human can?' Lyne asked.

'No – I guess not misdial as such; it would always dial the number it was given; but sometimes they get given wrong numbers; sometimes calls get misrouted.' He opened his arms expansively. 'You know how it is.'

Lyne nodded that he knew how it was. Then he continued to observe the professor in silence.

69

Joe caught an early train to London and took a taxi to St Catherine's House in Aldwych. He arrived outside the wide glass doors of the building shortly after nine.

Inside were two enquiry desks, a felt board with several blank forms pinned to it and steps up to a large modern room filled with rows of metal bookshelves. Although there were already several people in there, the place had a studious air of quiet.

He joined a small queue for the desk marked 'Enquiries Only', and waited his turn. The clerk pointed him to the section where the death registration indexes were kept, and Joe hurried over to it, then stood, staring at the floor-to-ceiling shelves stacked with thick, leather-bound books, each labelled with a year.

1974. Nineteen years ago. Joe pulled out the heavy volume, laid it on a desk and thumbed through it. *Roach, Agnes . . . Roach, Cedric . . . Roach, Edwin . . . Roach, Ena.* There was no Susan Roach. And no Roach whose date of birth tallied with the broadest span of mid-teens to mid-twenties he could allow for the girl he'd seen in the photograph album in Cora Roach's flat.

He checked through the Roaches in the indexes ten years back from 1974, and then forward, right to the present time. There were seven Susan Roaches, but all too old to have been the one in the photo.

He went back to the clerk and asked if the register included all deaths of British citizens.

'Only deaths in the British Isles,' the clerk replied.

'So if she died abroad, it wouldn't show up.'

'Possibly in the overseas register at Southport, but not definitely, no.'

Joe thanked him and left, not much the wiser.

He took the train back down to Sussex, then drove straight

to the university, arriving shortly after midday. He was meant to be giving a lecture at two and he had decided, reluctantly, to cancel it. He needed to get back to the house and not leave Karen alone for too long; she'd had a bad night, crying most of the time, and his own hadn't been much better. He had lain awake thinking about something Cora Roach had said when she'd first phoned him.

I suppose they might ... keep the photographs going back that far? The television company, the BBC, or the newspapers, or the police?

As he climbed the stairs to his department there was an anticipatory feeling around him which he barely noticed. Exams were looming up; it was the time of year when his students needed him most. Had to pull himself together, he knew. Somehow.

Susan's father killed her mother ... Blasted her with a shotgun in front of Susan – when Susan was seven.

Photographs of that story, he wondered. Or of something later? The old girl had been so confused it was hard to guess. Something later, a wild hunch made him hope.

His secretary looked up at him, uncertain whether to say anything or not. 'Good mor – er – afternoon, Professor Messenger.' She hesitated, then ventured: 'Have you had any news?'

Joe shook his head. 'Has Blake or anyone from the police called?'

'No, only some newspapers.' She blinked at him. 'I'm dreadfully sorry about what's happened.'

'Sure.' Joe dug his hands into his trouser pockets. 'I – I guess you'd better cancel my lecture this afternoon.'

'I already did,' she said quietly. 'And last Friday's.'

'I forgot about that one,' he said.

Eileen Peacock softly smiled her sympathy. 'I don't want to bother you with any work, but Dave Hoton is anxious to talk to you if you could spare him a moment – some problem with ARCHIVE.'

Joe went through to his office and sat woodenly at his desk. He buzzed down to the computer room.

'Joe? How are you?' the system manager asked anxiously.

'I'm OK, thanks, Dave.'

'If there's anything I can do –?'

'Send ARCHIVE out looking for him,' Joe said, mustering some humour.

'I have – well, I've posted to e-mail bulletin boards around the world. And –' He sounded pleased with himself, '– I've also hacked ARCHIVE into the surveillance cameras at shopping malls – there are several big networked systems in the South now – it'll recognize the girl or Jack if it sees them.'

'Dave, that's brilliant! My brain's been shot to hell, I didn't think of any of those things.'

'Yes, well, it's just a little contribution to the effort.'

'Thanks, I really appreciate it. Eileen said you have a problem?'

'It's OK, I don't need to bother you right now, but I just thought you ought to know that the problem with the memory has come back.'

'How do you mean?'

'The terabyte of memory that got used up, and we couldn't understand why? Remember?'

'Uh huh.'

'It's happened again. Seems like this mystery hacker's still at it.'

'Are you running checks?'

'Yes. He's as elusive as before.'

Joe sighed. Juliet: yesterday at home. Now this. 'Dave, I don't have time to help you right now – maybe later this afternoon, or tomorrow?'

'I can handle it, Joe, don't worry; I'll get to the bottom of it.'

Joe thanked him, hung up, then buzzed through to Blake's department. One of Blake's assistants answered and told him he thought Blake was taking delivery of a new aeroplane and wasn't expected in. Flying was one of Blake's indulgences.

As Joe replaced the receiver he acknowledged his confusion. Were Blake and Stassi in league in some way? Or had Stassi got to him? Done to Blake what she'd done to Muriel

Arkwright? Was Blake lying butchered somewhere? In his apartment? That's what had happened! Must have done.

He phoned the incident room at Hove police station and asked for Lyne. Detective Inspector Gavros came on, and Joe told him of his fears. Gavros said they'd check out Blake's flat again and if necessary force an entry.

Then Joe left the COGS building and walked across the campus towards the library. He'd only been in there a handful of times in the past four years. It was one of the strangest of all the campus buildings; constructed on three tiers, its galleried design reminded Joe of the inside of a prison.

The female librarian looked at him with vague recognition.

'Hi,' he said. 'What newspaper back issues do you hold here?'

'Nationals?'

'Yes.'

'All *The Times* of this century. The *Observer* and *Telegraph* back to 1975.'

'They're available right now?'

'Yes, on microfiche.' She gave him the look of dawning recognition again.

'Is there any kind of indexing system? I want to see if I can find an article about someone.'

'We have *The Times* annual indexes. They contain the names of everyone mentioned in *The Times* in any given year. Do you know what year you're looking for?' She frowned. 'Excuse me, but you're Professor Messenger, aren't you?'

He nodded.

Her features softened and she smiled gently. 'I'm very sorry about your son – has he been found yet?'

'No, but thank you.' Joe returned the smile. 'I know more or less the year, it's –' He hesitated, thinking. Susan Roach died in 1974. But he was going to follow his hunch that the photos mentioned by her aunt might be of something more recent than the murder of her mother and suicide of her father when Susan was seven. Joe looked back at the librarian. 'I guess I need to work back from 1974 to around 1962.'

She gave him directions and told him where to make microfiche requests. Joe thanked her and walked rapidly through the library. He found the shelves stacked with the *Times* index books and quickly read the dates on the spines. He opened the volume marked 1974, turned to the 'R' section and scanned through for Roach.

Rivett, Sandra, he read, stopping because the name was familiar; then he remembered – Lord Lucan's nanny. *Rockfeller, Nelson.* No *Roach.*

He checked the 1973 volume. Nothing there either. Nor in 1972, or 1971. He looked at the shelf, wondering if he was wasting his time, then pulled out the 1970 and opened it.

As he turned to the 'R's, the name jumped out at him: *Roach, Susan. 1st March.*

He shut the book with a slam. A girl in large glasses looked up in irritation from the table where she was working behind him, but Joe barely noticed. He hurried to the microfiche counter, scribbled out details on the request form and handed it to the assistant.

She went off into a back room and returned and with the small container. 'Use any booth,' she said.

'Thanks.' Joe glanced at the canister. A typed label on the outside said: *TIMES. JAN 1968–DEC 1972.* Joe walked along the row of booths, went into an empty one, closed the door behind him, loaded the film into the projector, then sat down and switched off the overhead light. Keeping his hand on the control he sped through the pages of the first two years, then slowed down midway through 1969. Headlines shot past him.

FIRST MAN SETS FOOT ON MOON

EDWARD KENNEDY CHAPPAQUIDDICK DROWNING MYSTERY

SHARON TATE KILLED IN HOLLYWOOD MASSACRE

JOE FRAZIER IS CHAMP!

PRINCE CHARLES TO JOIN NAVY

He speeded up a little, then slowed again. 2nd March 1970. He stared at the front-page headline: **US PLANES BOMB HO CHI MINH TRAIL.** Then he scanned the rest of the front-page stories, but there was no mention of Susan Roach. As before, he turned to the second page, the third. Then the fourth, the fifth.

Jesus.

Stassi Holland was staring straight at him. Staring straight out below a headline which read: **MODEL WITH A TRAGIC SECRET FOUND GUILTY OF KIDNAPPING BABY**. Joe's eyes flipped down the article:

> *Vogue* model Susan Roach was yesterday convicted of kidnapping a two-year-old boy from outside a supermarket.
>
> The court heard that Roach 22, of West London, had been traumatized by a double family tragedy in her childhood, and had a bungled abortion which rendered her sterile at the age of 16. Face pale and head bowed, she sat impassively as Judge Mark Sorrell at West London Crown Court sent her to a mental institution 'for the good of the public'.
>
> Jonathan Whitlow, prosecuting, said Roach's crime had stunned Britain. 'She kidnapped a defenceless child, Charles Edward Stamford, from his pram outside Sainsbury's in Acton, West London, in August 1969,' he said. 'And although the child was found unharmed, this can in no way alleviate the pain and suffering of the parents during that time.'
>
> The baby's parents, estate agent Christopher Stamford, 32, and his wife Rosalind, 26, sat through the trial in silence.
>
> Nicholas Greensword, defending, asked the court to show leniency to Roach in view of her tragic life. 'She never recovered from witnessing, at the age of seven, the trauma of her

father blasting her mother to death with a shotgun, and subsequently turning the gun on himself,' he said.

'The abortion was the result of an ill-judged romance and the consequences were devastating to Miss Roach. Despite her beauty and some success in her career. she became an unhappy and disturbed young woman.'

Summing up, the judge said he had taken into consideration Roach's unfortunate background and the fact that she had voluntarily sought psychiatric help. He sentenced her under the Mental Health Act to be detained indefinitely.

Mr and Mrs Stamford left the court without comment.

He looked at Susan Roach's face again. Then at the date. Shivers pricked his skin like tiny needles. The thought that was in his mind simply was not possible.

70

Joe hurried back across the campus and up to his department. Eileen Peacock looked at him with surprise.

'I wasn't expecting to see you again today, professor.'

He pressed his knuckles together agitatedly. 'Look – ah – could you do something for me right away, Eileen? Phone the Law Society and find out where I can get hold of a solicitor called Nicholas Greensword – Green as in colour, sword as in weapon – all one word.'

Joe walked past Harriet Tait and Edwin Pilgrim's door, noticing Pilgrim wasn't at his terminal, then remembered his shingles. He went into his own office, closed the door and sat down. The girl's face. Jesus, it was like Stassi; much more like her than any of the photos he'd seen in Mrs Roach's apartment.

He pressed carriage return on his workstation and logged into ARCHIVE. As he entered his password, ARCHIVE's voice came out of the speakers, startling him; he normally left it switched on visual mode:

'Good morning, professor, not a very nice day. The forecast is thunder and heavy rain. The maximum temperature should reach twenty-two degrees Celsius; the humidity level is high and the pollen count is seventy-two. I hope you had a pleasant weekend?'

'No,' Joe replied. 'I didn't actually.'

'I am sorry to hear that, professor. I notice that Jack is not back from his holiday.'

'Jack hasn't gone on holiday, ARCHIVE, someone has kidnapped him.'

'Kidnapped? Your kid? Sorry, only kidding! Just fooling! Deceit! Sleight of hand. Legerdemain, hocus-pocus, hanky-panky, jiggery pokery, rannygazoo! A wolf in sheep's clothing!'

'Wolf in sheep's clothing? Why did you say that, ARCHIVE?'

The computer remained silent.

Joe switched from voice mode to visual, keyed in the command for the list of all processes running, then typed: Talk zebedee and pressed carriage return.

On the screen appeared: Calling . . . Then: Calling your party again.

His intercom buzzed and he lifted the receiver. 'Yes?'

It was his secretary. 'Professor, I've been on to the Law Society. The only Nicholas Greensword they have listed died in 1979. He was a sole practitioner, and his clients were taken over by a firm called Maynard and Cusack in the City.'

'Thanks, could you get their number for me?'

'I have it here.'

Joe cancelled the instruction to ARCHIVE and dialled the number. The switchboard operator passed him on to a partner's secretary, who shunted him to another secretary. There were fifty-two partners in the firm, she told him; could she call him back or would he like to hold while she tried to find out which one he needed to speak to? He held, then had to endure a constant loop of the 'William Tell' overture playing down the receiver.

Finally a voice as dry as parchment said: 'Simon Oldridge.'

Joe introduced himself and asked whether Maynard and Cusack still acted for any of the clients of Nicholas Greensword. The lawyer was guarded.

'We don't divulge information about our clients, Professor Messenger.'

'This is someone deceased.'

'What's the name?'

'Roach. Susan Roach.'

'Never heard of her,' he said emphatically.

'She was definitely a client of Mr Greensword in 1970.'

'We took over the practice in 1979, professor. Any files that were dormant at that time we would only have kept for six years, then they'd have been destroyed – other than deeds, of course.'

Joe thanked him for his time and replaced the receiver. Then he stood up and paced around the room for some moments. Outside, the sky was darkening further. He buzzed his secretary and asked her to get him the number of the Home Office. He wanted to know the name of the mental institution to which Susan Roach had been committed over twenty years ago, and he wondered whether they would be the right people to ask.

Eileen Peacock came back to him shortly with the London number of Home Office general enquiries. He asked her to connect him and found himself speaking to a brisk female voice who told him he needed the Prison Department Registry. When he dialled the number he was given, another brisk female answered.

Yes, they would hold the records he wanted, but he would have to write in, stating the reason for his request, and it would be considered by the next meeting of the committee in three weeks' time. She warned him that records were not released for a hundred years and requests were rarely granted to the general public. Would he like the address?

Joe told her he would and went through the motions over the phone of writing it down. Then, making it sound as if it was an afterthought, he asked casually: 'Are the records computerized these days?'

'The seventies?' she said. 'Oh yes, definitely. Back as far as 1964 now.'

Joe thanked her and hung up. He instructed ARCHIVE to search all the numbers close to the Home Office's main phone number for a computer line, and waited.

Ten minutes passed; quarter of an hour; twenty minutes. It was a quarter past two. ARCHIVE kept searching, and Joe kept getting anxious. Joe instructed it to list but not dial any numbers it came to; then he went down to the basement and hurried along to the graduates' computer room.

Several people were in there, and among them he was relieved to see one of his most rebellious students. Niall Copeman was hunched over the keyboard of the Feynman workstation, studded leather jacket slung over the back of his chair.

When Joe went over and stood behind him, saying 'Hi', there was no response. Joe waited a few moments, then sidled round so he was in Copeman's field of vision.

Copeman looked up at him with a start. 'Joe!' He frowned, collecting his thoughts. 'Hey, listen, really sorry about your son. I mean that's heavy.' Copeman always spoke a mixture of sixties hip and American slang.

'Thanks. Look, I need some help. Could you do me a big favour?'

'Sure, man, anything.'

Joe glanced round to make sure no one was listening, then lowered his voice. 'I need a phone number and if possible a password to get into a department of the Home Office – the Prison Department Registry. I guess any computer system of the Home Office would be fine. Do you know any hacker who might have that kind of information?'

Copeman didn't blink. 'How fast do you want it?'

'Ten seconds too quick?'

'Gimme twenty.' He typed a sequence of commands which Joe followed. It was a login to Leeds University. Then he typed out a request to run the Unix command 'talk'. 'Should hear right back if he's at his desk.'

'Who is he?'

'A dude in computing science at Leeds.' He watched the screen expectantly.

'How's your project?' Joe asked.

'Cool.' He peered at the screen again. 'Don't get a reply in a few minutes I'll bell him. Maybe had a heavy trip last night.'

They talked for a while, discussing the visual recognition project Copeman was working on. Then they broke off as a reply came back.

```
Directory Hitman to Electraglide. Info you want.
Mainframe 071-437-9545. root p/w try houdini. Moni-
tored line. For safe entry suggest go in via your
local police station vax link into Scotland Yard.
Number you need is your code 844803. Plus you need
authorization number. Try 987772. Try 'System Man-
ager' or 'Field Service' or 'User User'.

Crackers international, all part of the
friendly (note + freeeee:-) service!!! zapwham-
bang zingzingzing . . . goooiinnggg critical!
Kerpow!
```

Joe saw immediately what he was saying. Most police forces used DEC VAX-VMS computer systems. Digital supplied these computers with a package of three accounts and passwords to enable system managers to get the systems up and running. It was well known that frequently the system managers forgot to change these passwords after installation, and they remained as a permanent backdoor entry route.

Joe printed out the screen, grabbed the sheet of paper,

thanked Copeman and raced back to his office. ARCHIVE was still dialling without success. The Home Office computer line was either completely different from the main set of directory numbers, or else there was no centralized mainframe computer system.

He cancelled the instruction, then keyed in the commands for ARCHIVE to phone out to the local police computer number he'd been given. On the screen he saw: `Trying . . .`

Then, moments later, instead of the user-friendly computer greeting which he'd been expecting, he saw the words: `Don't even think about doing that, Joe-Joe.`

Seconds later the screen fuzzed over with a mass of crackling interference like a blizzard. Fear rose through Joe.

He risked a look at the television camera on the ceiling, then at the screen again. Hastily he pressed the keys to exit from ARCHIVE, and the screen cleared. But when he tried to go back again, there was no response to his command. So he logged off, waited some moments, then tried again. All he got was the same blizzard.

He picked up the phone and buzzed down to the computer room. There was no answer. He tried again. The third time, Dave Hoton answered and sounded uncharacteristically fraught.

'What's happening?' Joe asked. 'Power failure?'

'We've crashed! The whole of ARCHIVE's crashed. We've got total bedlam here.'

'The whole system? Down?'

'Everything. It's like we've been nuked by some worm. Every screen has fuzzed over.'

Joe could now feel his fear constricting his scalp. 'I'll come down.'

'No, don't worry, we'll get it sorted; just some mother of a glitch I could do without! Probably our hacker friend up to another trick.'

'Try disconnecting the external ports.'

'We're doing that now.'

Joe hung up, then logged in again and typed the commands to take him into his Unix workstation, which operated independently of ARCHIVE. The Unix prompt appeared normally. Relieved, he typed in the number of the police station and the command for the Unix to dial out.

Then he blinked, startled. The number looked as if it had been torn in anger from the screen. It was replaced with a message.

I just told you, Joe-Joe. You are being a very naughty boy. I am going to have to hurt you very badly and I really don't want to do that. But if you don't behave I'm afraid I'm going to have to kill Jack.

71

Joe's fear began to turn to anger. He lifted his phone and buzzed down to Dave Hoton, who still sounded fraught.

'Yes!'

'Dave, I have our hacker talking to me on my Unix. Take a quick look at the net and see if there's an external line in use or if anyone here's logged in.'

'Keep him on as long as you can, Joe.'

'Sure, I'll try.'

'Bell you straight back!'

Joe put the phone down and typed: How can you prove to me Jack's still alive?

How can you prove you are still alive, Joe-Joe? the reply came up on the screen.

I'm not interested in playing your sick games. Tell me who you are.

You know who I am, Joe-Joe. You helped download me. You made it possible.

He stared at ARCHIVE's silent screen and typed: I don't believe you are Juliet. I think you are the person who kidnapped Jack and are pretending to be Juliet.

Is that why you have Dave Hoton checking to see

where I'm coming from? Am I a student in here? Or a mad hacker? Or something else, Joe-Joe?

Joe stiffened. If ARCHIVE was down, how the hell did the hacker know what Hoton was doing?

I don't want to play games with you, I just want my son back, he typed.

You really think this is a game, Joe? Let me show you a much more exciting one.

I am not int – Joe stopped and jerked back in shock as sharp pricks of static electricity shot into his fingers from the keyboard. The overhead light in his office dimmed then flickered and there was another fierce crackle like a firework squib: faint thin blue lines of electricity hovered like ball lightning above his keyboard.

Phut! A streak of brilliant white light raced across his screen, then it went blank. Simultaneously, the room dimmed as the overhead light went out. With his heart bashing against the inside of his chest, Joe dashed out into the corridor. He was met by a series of high-pitched bleeps: the power-failure audible warning system.

He ran back to his room and tested the mains switch: nothing. ARCHIVE and the Unix network were backed up with emergency generators and with batteries; both had sensors that should switch automatically to auxiliary power in a fraction of a second, the moment they detected a drop in current. He heard voices outside his door; Harriet Tait saying to Eileen Peacock that she thought it might be the atmospherics. 'Thunder's forecast.'

Joe punched out the internal number for the Unix system manager. Then he realized the switchboard was dead. The power failure alarm was now beeping dementedly and he ran down into the basement, which was scantly lit by the emergency battery-powered lights in the ceiling.

In ARCHIVE's operations room it was eerily dark, lit by the weak glow of one solitary emergency light. As Joe groped his way through to the computer machine room he looked, with a sickening feeling of panic, at the far glass wall beyond which the biological circuits were housed. There was a faint white shimmer from the emergency lights; at least some emergency power was running. The worst that could happen to ARCHIVE's conventional hardware in a total power shutdown was the loss of information. But without the climate and nutrient controls, the biological side would start dying, and over three years of work would be lost in hours.

'Sorry, Joe, had to abandon the trace,' Hoton said, hurrying past him with a torch, shouting an instruction to one of his assistants.

'What's up?' Joe said.

'Nothing's up,' Hoton said, his voice rising in hysteria. 'It's all down. The whole system! This and all the Unix systems.'

Joe looked anxiously across at the floor-to-ceiling rack of twelve-volt car batteries that should have provided the interim back-up before the generators cut in. And he wondered about the main emergency supply. 'What's happened to the UPS?'

'It was fine when it was tested last week.' The system manager pulled the cover off a processor, went down on his knees and squinted at the rack of printed circuit-boards. 'Now all the generator electrics have shorted out, as has the battery transformer. There must have been a huge power surge, it's very strange. I hate to think how much data we've lost.' He pulled up a panel from the raised floor and peered at the wiring beneath, as if he expected to find the missing electricity lying there.

'Power surge?' Joe said. 'What kind?'

'I don't know! It's a power surge. Period. How do I know what kind?' He ran to the far side of the room and lifted another panel.

Joe wanted to stay and help, but the crash was serious and it could take hours before they sorted it out. Right now he couldn't waste a single moment. He hurried back upstairs. Students were milling in the corridors, most of them stranded without power. His secretary was not at her desk, but he heard her voice in the students' room.

'Eileen,' he called. 'Do you have Edwin Pilgrim's home address anywhere?'

She scurried out. 'Yes, professor, I'll get it for you.' She pulled open a drawer in her desk, removed a thick index book and opened it. 'Like me to write it down?'

'Please.'

She jotted it on a shorthand pad, tore the sheet off and handed it to him.

Joe read it, and recognized the area. 'Got it,' he said. He glanced at his watch; it was twenty-five to three. He'd hoped to be home with Karen hours ago. He tried the external phone to see if it was working and got a dialling tone.

'Any news?' he asked when WPC Belling answered his ring.

'No, professor, I'm afraid nothing. And we have a power cut.'

'Uh? You do?' He felt a tinge of relief. If it wasn't just the university, then it was at a main-grid station, so maybe it wasn't anything to do with – His thoughts were rambling chaotically. 'When did that happen?'

'About ten minutes ago. Would you like to speak to Mrs Messenger?'

'She's OK?'

'Yes – yes, she's resting.'

'Just tell her I'll be back as soon as I can. Something I need to check out. Will you tell her?' He was aware his voice sounded jangly.

'Yes, of course.'

'Good. Thanks.' Joe hung up and turned to Eileen Peacock. 'They've no power at home either!' He said it as if it was the best news in the world, then realized that she and Harriet Tait were looking at him very oddly. He parted his hands then brought them together again. 'It – I guess – ah –' He glanced at Pilgrim's address again. '327b Elm Grove,' he said. 'Right.'

He turned and headed for the car park, deep in thought, forgetting to say goodbye to either of them. He climbed into

531

his Saab, left the campus and headed towards the centre of Brighton.

As he drove he tried to organize his mind into coherent thought. Had the hacker taken out the power? *You really think this is a game, Joe? Let me show you a much more exciting one.* Had the hacker taken out the entire regional grid? Or was it just yet another coincidence?

Jack in the freezer; Karen's hand in the waste-disposal unit; the judge in the tube station; the traffic lights. Where did you draw the line at believing anything other than –?

Than what?

Than that a dead person's consciousness was still active inside a computer system? Active and capable of outwitting you?

There was a logic to everything. Joe knew that implicitly. Always applied that rule whenever he came up against something he didn't understand; he tried to apply it now. Why was someone – or *something* – so determined to stop him looking up the Prison Registry records on Susan Roach? Just what the hell was there to find? He felt a new coil of fear rise inside him.

. . . If you don't behave I'm afraid I'm going to have to kill Jack.

He braked hard as the line of cars in front of him squealed to a halt. He could see traffic lights that weren't working. The shops in a parade on his left all looked dark, as if they were closed. A flash of lightning brightened the sky then was gone. A car hooted; the line of traffic inched forward then stopped. Joe switched on the radio, but there was just a crackle of static.

He punched the button for another station, but there was nothing there either. As he switched off there was another streak of lightning. A clap of thunder rumbled and crackled like a building coming down on his head. Joe's fear deepened. Who was it? Who the hell had Jack?

He was gripping the steering wheel so hard it hurt. Another flash of lightning. A second thunder clap rippled the sky as if it were greaseproof paper. He closed his eyes for a moment, tried to recall his son's face, but instead of Jack he saw Barty. Then he began to panic, couldn't remember Jack's face, couldn't remember what his own son looked like.

Elm Grove. He turned into the long steep road of shops and dingy terraced houses. A homemade sign in the window of Number 192b, barely visible through the filthy glass, said 'Furnished Flatlet'.

Joe pressed the bell marked with Pilgrim's name, but heard nothing. He wondered if the bell would be working with the power off and walked down the basement steps, past a row of dustbins, and knocked on the flaking door of 192b. A drop of rainwater struck the ground beside him.

He heard the click of a lock and the clatter of a safety chain, then the door opened a few inches and Edwin Pilgrim's scab-ravaged face appeared. He was wearing a grubby, discoloured T-shirt, Y-fronts and corduroy slippers and when he confronted Joe, his lazy eye swivelled from side to side as if it were shorting out.

'P-Professor –!'

'I'm sorry to barge in on you, I need your help urgently, Edwin.'

'I heard about your s-s-son. So sorry.'

'That's why I'm here, Edwin. Could I come in?'

'Yes – c-course –' He pointed at his clothes apologetically. 'Sorry – I was in bed.' He stepped back and opened the door wider.

Joe walked into a tiny dark hallway that smelled of feet and was mostly occupied by Pilgrim's bicycle, a flashy racing job that seemed too loud for him. Pilgrim shut the door and took him through into a dingy bed-sitting room that looked as if it had recently been inverted and then shaken.

The smell of feet was even more noxious in here. The walls were bare, except for a few clothes on wire hangers dangling from the picture rail above the unmade bed. A balding carpet the colour of mould was visible only in isolated patches between toppled columns of computing magazines, heaps of laundry, an ancient black and white television, a low armchair and a reasonably modern computer system. No wonder Pilgrim was so possessive about his personal space at work, Joe thought, if this was the sort of space he had at home.

'A c-coffee or something?'

Joe shook his head. 'Thanks, I'm fine.' He studied his student for a few moments, trying not to show any reaction to the livid scabs on his face and neck. 'How are you now? Recovering?'

'B-b-better.'

'Good. Shingles is a lousy thing . . .' Joe pointed at the computer on the floor. 'Is it possible I could use that for a few minutes?'

Pilgrim gave him a strange look. 'Yes.' He swung his arm towards it. 'It's not very powerful. I could rig something bigger if you need it.'

'It's fine. You have a modem?'

Pilgrim nodded.

'I just need to talk to another computer, that's all.'

Pilgrim pointed at the net curtain covering the window. 'Power cut,' he said. 'Have to wait.'

'Sure.'

Pilgrim gestured to the solitary armchair. 'Is your wife better?'

'She had been doing really well, until –'

Kill Jack.

Joe sat down. The gloom in the room was lifted for a fleeting second by a flash of lightning. He listened for the thunder but heard nothing.

Kill Jack.

Pilgrim cleared a space among the sheets of diagrams that covered the bed and sat down on the edge. 'I've only just been able to start concentrating again. Should be back before the end of term.' He frowned. 'Why –' His voice tailed and he started again. 'Why do you need my computer?'

Joe hesitated, not wanting to say too much. 'I have an emergency. ARCHIVE's crashed and the Unix systems have a generator problem. I thought – maybe – you weren't affected here by the power cut.'

'I do have something.' Pilgrim reached under his bed, rummaged around for a moment, then pulled out a small grey plastic box. A Compaq laptop computer, Joe realized, wondering why on earth it hadn't occurred to him to try his own. Pilgrim opened it up and switched it on. Joe heard the whirr of its motor and the beeps of its diagnostic checks.

'Modem?' Pilgrim said.

'Yup.'

Pilgrim rooted around on the floor, held up a length of cable as if it were a trophy, studied the sockets on the back of the laptop, connected the cable, then scuttled on his knees over to the wall and hooked the other end into his modem. 'On-line, professor!' He scuttled back, tapped keys on the laptop in a rapid sequence, then nodded. 'You can just dial out.'

Joe knelt down and looked at the soft grey haze of the screen. He pulled out of his pocket the sheet of paper on which he'd written the information from the Leeds hacker, glanced at the keyboard, then typed out the number and dialling instruction. Almost instantly he saw:

`Trying . . .`

Then: `Connected to 84.4.8.03 **Sussex Police Computer Services** Name?`

Nervously Joe typed in: `system`

Then the password request came up. Joe typed: `manager`

Immediately, the words appeared: `what is your authority?`

Joe typed: `987772`

There was a pause, then he was in. His pulse quickened as he saw, `Select from following: Crime Index/Nominal Index.`

Joe moved the cursor to *Crime Index* and clicked it twice. On the screen appeared: `Type name.`

He typed: `Roach, Susan.`

Nothing happened for several seconds. The screen cleared, then filled with information. Joe scanned down it:

535

Prison Record Index

Convicted person details

Name:	**Roach, Susan Margaret Ann**
Ethnic origin:	**Caucasian**
Date of Birth:	**17.04.1948**
Offence:	**Abduction of minor**
Number of previous convictions	**None**
Date of remand	**07.08.1969**
Date of sentencing	**01.03.1970**
Parole eligibility date	**n/a**
Type of committal	**Section 60**
Type of establishment	**locked mental institution**
Name of establishment	**Parkways, Maidstone**
Date of release	**07.01.73**

Just after Joe had noted down 'Parkways, Maidstone' and was about to disconnect, there was a flash of lightning, followed instantly by a massive bang in the room. Pilgrim cried out in fright. The tube of the old black and white television exploded, hurtling shards of glass across the room. Joe felt a sting of pain in his cheek. There was a fierce crackle. Lightning, brilliant blue and thin as wire snaked in all directions around them. It skittered up the walls, on to the ceiling, spreading outwards. Joe felt sharp pins and needles as it danced all around him. And Pilgrim screamed, covered his head with his hands.

Then it was gone as suddenly as it had come.

72

Edwin Pilgrim cowered on the bed. Thin wisps of smoke rose from the television and the room was filled with the sharp, acrid smell of burnt electrics. Slivers of glass glinted wherever Joe looked across the floor. The screen of the laptop was blank as if it had been switched off. Thunder rumbled outside.

The room brightened again, then another clap of thunder exploded right overhead. 'Lightning! *Was* that lightning?'

'I guess the TV aerial must have been hit,' Joe said.

'Me, it hit me!' Pilgrim turned, his good eye darting wildly, sucking a graze on the back of his hand. 'And you.' He examined Joe. 'On your ch-cheek.'

Joe touched his cheek with his finger and there was blood on it when he removed it. Pilgrim glanced panic-stricken at the television, scrambled over to the wall socket behind it and yanked out the plug. Then he watched the set for some moments until he was satisfied the smoke was dying out. 'Get something for you . . .' He hurried out into the hallway, glass crunching under his slippers.

Joe could see that the socket where the television had been plugged in was streaked with burn marks; a solitary breath of blue smoke drifted towards him and he brushed it away with his hand. Pilgrim came back with an off-white towel and pressed it against Joe's cheek; it stung and Joe winced. Then his eyes were drawn to the screen of the laptop. Writing had appeared on it.

'A graze, that's all,' Pilgrim said. But Joe barely heard him. He was staring past Pilgrim, at the screen, at the words.

Still think it's just a game, Joe-Joe?

The screen went blank again. Then the lights came on in the room. There was a click and whirr as the computer on the floor began booting itself up.

'I'll get a plaster for you,' Pilgrim said, seeming not to notice.

But Joe only had eyes for the screen, now glowing green again.

Just a short power cut this time, Joe-Joe. Jack can just about survive a power cut of one hour. The next one will be much longer, I promise you.

Joe felt a deepening chill as he knelt and typed: Please tell me where he is and what you really want. I don't have much money but I'll give you whatever I can raise. Everything I own.

His words disappeared from the screen as if they'd been sucked into it, and were immediately replaced by, Money's no use to me, Joe-Joe. I've told you what I want.

You've told me you want a body.

A very special body, Joe-Joe. One that you are really going to enjoy screwing! I have already suggested Karen.

Joe glanced round, but could see no sign of Pilgrim. He looked back at the screen, and dared himself to ask, What would Karen have to do?

It's simple, Joe-Joe. You just have to kill her then bring her back to life again.

Joe swallowed. I'm still finding it very hard to take you seriously. What you propose is not possible.

Everything is possible. That is what you have always said. That is your creed.

In time, Joe typed. Everything is possible in time, it is not yet possible to kill a human being and bring them back to life.

But you don't have time, Joe-Joe. Jack will be dead in 24 hours unless you find him. And if you try looking for him I will kill him sooner. Perhaps I'd better give you a few more hours to think about it.

The screen went blank.

No wait, please, Joe typed. Please explain. Please tell me where my son is.

A shadow fell over the screen. He turned and saw Edwin Pilgrim standing beside him, offering a plaster and looking at what Joe had typed with a puzzled expression.

Joe pressed the return key in desperation, not caring what Pilgrim saw. But there was no response. 'Edwin,' he said. 'Do you believe that something could live on inside a computer?'

His graduate student looked at him warily. '*L-Live on?*'

'Inside ARCHIVE,' Joe said. 'Do you think ARCHIVE could be smarter than we realize? That it could be sort of conscious – or could provide a habitat for someone else's consciousness?'

'ARCHIVE does frighten me sometimes, professor.'

'Why's that?'

Pilgrim peeled the protective paper off the plaster and stuck it carefully to Joe's cheek. Then he leaned back and inspected it. 'Because it has too many gaps.'

'What kind of gaps?'

'I think it's nasty. It's copying nasty elements of people. It's greedy, voracious. We've been so pleased with it making progress we haven't bothered about what kind of progress. We need to create a *conscience* for it. Not just *consciousness*. Otherwise, we've got a psychopath!' Pilgrim eyed the screen of the laptop with deepening unease. 'If you downloaded anyone into ARCHIVE right now you would have something very dangerous indeed. V-very dangerous.'

Joe said nothing for a moment. Then he asked Pilgrim, 'Do you think it's possible that Juliet Spring might have downloaded something of herself into ARCHIVE?'

Pilgrim looked agitated suddenly, like a hunted animal sensing danger. 'I –' he began to pace anxiously, treading through the chaos, ' – I was there in the computer room with her the Saturday afternoon before she died. She looked strange, as if she was on drugs. Smiling. She told me that she wasn't afraid of death any more.'

Joe looked at the laptop screen again. His own words were still there. Pilgrim hovered in his Y-fronts and T-shirt, wringing his hands, his lazy eye swivelling like a scanner.

Joe switched the machine off. He remembered almost the last words she had said. *Sh'no need. Decode*.

'She didn't say anything to you, did she, Edwin, about the decoding she was working on?'

Pilgrim shook his head. He was trembling as if he was in after-shock.

'I'm sorry about your television.' Joe knelt and picked up the crumpled scrap of paper he had left on the floor beside the laptop. *Parkways, Maidstone*.

'I never watch it,' Pilgrim blurted, moving towards the door, as if he was trying to edge Joe out, as if he had sensed that Joe was a source of danger.

Joe thanked him and left quickly, but for his own reasons.

He hurried up the steps. There was a flash of lightning, and thunder splintered through the sky. Rain began to fall. He climbed into his car and drove off, watching the pavement on both sides anxiously through the blurring windscreen.

A few hundred yards on he saw an empty phone booth, pulled over and ran to it through the rain that was now pelting down. He yanked open the door and it swung to with a creak behind him as he lifted the receiver and dialled Directory Enquiries. A stack of business cards on a ledge advertised the services of Big Busty Belinda.

Joe asked for the number of Parkways, Maidstone, and a few moments later pushed a pound coin into the slot and dialled it. After three rings the phone was answered by a gruff-voiced woman who sounded about sixty.

'I wonder if you can help me,' Joe said to her. 'I'd like to speak to someone who was working at Parkways between 1970 and 1973.'

'I was, dear,' she said cheerily.

A bus rumbled by and Joe waited until it had passed. 'You were! Terrific. Do you get to know the patients?'

She sounded uncomfortable with the question. 'Me? Oh, no, no, I wouldn't.'

'I'm trying to trace a relative of mine who was an inmate –

ah – patient – during that time and disappeared after she was released. I wondered if there is anyone, like the governor or a resident psychiatrist, who would have known the patients and who is still around?'

'You're family, are you, dear?'

'Yes,' Joe lied. 'A cousin.'

'Your best bet would be to write in; we're not allowed to give out any information over the phone.'

'It's kind of an emergency,' Joe said. He laid on his charm thickly. 'Look, I don't want to get you into any kind of trouble, but I really need a very great favour. Could you just tell me if any members of the senior staff there now would have been there during that period?'

'Well –' She sounded dubious. 'No. No, I don't think so. William Trevor would have been governor then, and he's dead now. I'm trying to remember who would have been deputy governor then. Mr Armstrong Wallace. He's at Broadmoor now, I think.'

Joe jotted the name down. 'Did you have a resident psychiatrist then?'

'Yes, part time; now who was it? Let me think. Ah yes, of course. Dr Wyke-Adams.'

'How do you spell that, please?'

She told him and he jotted it down also. 'Now,' she said, thoughtfully, 'he retired a good decade ago, but I think he's still going strong. Yes, I heard him on the radio recently! He's a bit of an expert on changing attitudes towards mental illness, that sort of thing. Yes, he was definitely here throughout the sixties and seventies.'

'Do you know where he lives now?'

'Well, I'm really not supposed to give out any –'

'*Please*,' Joe said. It came out even more desperate than he'd intended. 'My son has been kidnapped. Please help me.'

'Are you talking about that little boy in the papers at the moment?'

'Yes, I'm the father.' Joe wondered if he'd blown it, whether she would believe him or just think he was some crank. 'There's a possible link with someone who was at

Parkways – this cousin – I just need to eliminate her from any suspicion, that's all.'

'I believe Dr Wyke-Adams is somewhere in the Brighton area.'

'Brighton?' Joe echoed. A piece of luck at last.

'Yes, I seem to think so. Of course you could probably find him in the BMA directory. They list all doctors.'

'Thank you,' Joe said. 'You've been really helpful.' He replaced the receiver, then hefted the residential phone directory from the tray beneath and leafed through it. There was a dazzling flash of lightning, but he barely noticed the crash of thunder as he read the names. Wyeth. Wyithe. *Wyke-Adams*. His eyes stopped with a jolt.

Wyke-Adams, Dr. G., Withdean Heights, Withdean Rise, Brighton.

Joe rummaged in his pocket for another coin, took a deep breath and dialled the number. *Please be in*, he thought.

The phone rang several times before Joe heard a suave cut-glass voice. 'Wyke-Adams residence.'

'May I speak to Dr Wyke-Adams?'

'Speaking.'

'Dr Wyke-Adams, my name's Messenger – I'm Professor of Artificial Intelligence at the Isaac Newton University. I'm sorry to disturb you, but I have a desperate emergency and I think you're about the only person who could help me. Could you possibly spare me a couple of minutes of your time?'

'I'm talking to the Professor Messenger whose son has been abducted, is that right?'

'Yes,' Joe said, a little surprised.

'Very nasty. I'm actually familiar with some of your work, professor. I was at the Royal Society address you gave last Wednesday.'

'Oh God. I don't think it was one of my better talks.'

'Well, it was certainly a lively evening,' he said, dubiously. 'But presumably that's not the reason you're calling me,' he said with a faint hint of dry humour.

'I'm calling you about my son. I'm trying very hard to trace someone who was once at Parkways.'

'I don't know that I could be any help – I retired from there over ten years ago, I'm afraid.'

'This is someone who was there between 1970 and 1973.'

The rumble of a passing bus almost harmonized with another crash of thunder. Then the psychiatrist said: 'This is an appalling bloody line. Where are you at the moment, professor?'

'I'm in a call box in Brighton – Elm Grove.'

'Look, I'm only about a mile away. Would you like to come over?'

'Yes – er – thank you. If you could tell me how to get to you, I'll be with you in five minutes.'

Dr Gilbert Wyke-Adams's apartment was on the third floor of an unobtrusive-looking low-rise block in a leafy residential avenue. He opened the front door himself, a slight, diminutive man of about seventy, dapperly dressed in a silk shirt with a loud paisley cravat, a thick, expensive-looking cardigan, immaculately pressed cavalry twill trousers and shiny leather slippers. He carried himself very erect, with his head angled up, so that in spite of the fact that he was a good six inches shorter than Joe, Joe had the impression of being talked down to.

'Professor Messenger?' He extended a bony hand and shook Joe's quickly and dismissively, as if he was anxious to get the formalities over and done with. 'Bloody awful day, isn't it?'

'Typical English summer day,' Joe said.

'Bally awful country this, for weather, you know. Happens every year. Probably setting itself in for Wimbledon.'

Joe wiped some raindrops that were running down his forehead with the back of his hand as the psychiatrist closed the door behind them. He heard the click of a lock, then the rattle of a safety chain.

Wyke-Adams lowered his voice, almost to a whisper. 'Can't be too careful these days,' he said, sliding the top and bottom bolts shut. 'Bastards kicked the door down across the corridor in broad daylight and stole our cleaning lady's handbag last week! Fucking awful world this has become.'

A demure woman in her seventies appeared out of a doorway, smiled politely and asked Joe if he'd like tea or coffee.

'A cup of coffee would be great if that's –?'

'No trouble; my husband always has coffee. I'll bring it through.'

Wyke-Adams led Joe down a short passageway. The apartment was warm and had a rather sterile feel. They went into a tiny book-lined study, and the psychiatrist gestured Joe to one chair, sat in the other with his back facing the window, and crossed his legs.

'You ruffled a few feathers last Wednesday, at the Royal Society, Professor Messenger. Presumably you intended to?'

'I guess I've never had more than fifty per cent of an audience agree with me in my life.' Joe rested his hands on his thighs. His trousers were drenched and clung to his legs, but he barely noticed.

'Actually,' Wyke-Adams said, 'it was the first time you've ever said anything I agree with, if you'll pardon me being so forthright.'

'Oh?'

'Anyhow, let's not digress. Tell me how you think I can help you. I'm really very sorry about your son; that's a horrific thing. Another bloody awful manifestation of the sickness of our society. Have you had any news?'

'No, nothing.' Joe acknowledged Mrs Wyke-Adams quietly bringing in a loaded tray. She poured two coffees, smiled sympathetically at Joe then left.

Joe added a couple of spoons of sugar for energy and stirred them in. 'I guess you saw a lot of patients in your time at Parkways, doctor, but there's one who was there between 1970 and 1973 whom I'm hoping you might be able to remember. She's – ah – I was told she's dead now,' he said, detecting the psychiatrist's slight frown, 'so I guess that doesn't make it quite so bad for you to talk about her – with the Hippocratic Oath? That is, I was told she's dead by an aunt – a rather senile lady who was pretty confused. But there's no registration of her death, at least not in this country.'

Wyke-Adams uncrossed his legs. 'I'm not sure I entirely follow your gist.'

'I'm trying to establish whether she really is dead or not – to eliminate her as a –' he hesitated '– suspect.'

'Can't the police do that for you?'

'It's very much a long shot; I just wanted to check it out.'

The psychiatrist asked, 'What was her name?'

'Susan Roach,' Joe said. 'She was convicted of abducting a small boy from outside a supermarket, in 1970.'

With his fingertips together, and a total lack of motion, Wyke-Adams looked as if he'd drifted into prayer or deep meditation. When he spoke again he did so without appearing to move a muscle.

'Susan Roach. Early twenties; pretty girl, long brown hair, quite a successful fashion model . . . Is that her?'

'Yes.'

He relaxed his fingers, glancing worriedly at Joe. 'What actually do you want to know about her – assuming I can remember anything? One of the bloody irritations about old age is the brain cells conking out – or *going down*, I suppose you'd say.'

Joe smiled politely. 'If she isn't dead, she must be around somewhere. What I wanted to ask you was whether she gave you any clues about where she might have gone after she was released. I guess her career would have been finished in this country.'

'She was pretty kooky, I can remember that. I used to think it was such a tragedy to see such a lovely girl so unable to cope with it all.' He frowned, then stood up swiftly. 'I believe I kept my case notes on her – I had an idea for something I wanted to write. Never got round to it. No time, that's the problem, you see; suppose I could do with another fifty years or so, but not in this bloody body!' He turned to the filing cabinets, selected a drawer and flicked through the neat row of beige files; he pulled one out, checked the name on top, shut the drawer and sat down again.

'Susan Roach,' he announced, held it up so Joe could see for himself, then opened it. For a good couple of minutes he sat silently reading through the contents, a sheaf of papers stapled together, then looked up.

'Yes, I thought I was thinking of the right person. She had a pregnancy that she tried to keep quiet when she was sixteen. She ended up having a stillborn in a Caesarean that went horribly wrong – buggered up her chances of ever conceiving again. That and the awful business with her parents – do you know about that?'

'Her father shooting her mother then himself? It's about the only thing I do know about her.'

'Right. Well that's a pretty big plateful for any normal person to handle, and she wasn't terribly normal. To put it bluntly, she was close enough to the edge without all that.'

'In what way?' Joe sipped some coffee and the sweet warmth made him feel a little better. He heard a distant roll of thunder.

'She was very spoiled – I think she was brought up by a wealthy aunt and uncle – if she didn't get her own way she could become terrifyingly violent. I wasn't that keen on her being released; it was only because of our tight budget – we were pressurized to get shot of as many patients as possible.'

Joe felt a cold murkiness roll through his guts. 'Violent? You mean physically?'

'Yes.' Wyke-Adams prodded the base of his chin with his index finger, then touched each side of his chin lightly as if to check they both still matched. 'She got very obsessive about things. There was that business with the coil. She – should – er – she knew pregnancy was an impossibility, but she insisted on wearing a coil all the time. Her way of coping with her condition, you know? Shutting off compartments. The traumas of her childhood brought out a latent schizophrenic tendency.'

Joe nodded.

Wyke-Adams continued, 'Actually you'd have been interested to meet her – she was obsessed with immortality.'

This time Joe gulped.

Wyke-Adams nodded, watching Joe's reaction carefully. 'Yes, like you she wanted to live for ever.' He glanced at his notes again. 'That's why she wanted to go to America, of course. She talked about going to California after she was released; I don't know how she thought she was going to get in with a criminal record, but she was set on it. She thought she could make a go of it in Hollywood, in the movies. And, of course, the other thing too.' Wyke-Adams smiled and shook his head. 'She'd signed herself up for this cryonics nonsense.'

Joe began to tremble.

'That's the other reason she wanted to go out to California – to be close to the place that would freeze her when she died.' He smiled again. 'She used to wear one of those metal bracelets – MedicAlert – you know, with the Staff of Aesculapius symbol on it – and instructions about what was to be done to her body when she died. I remember her always reminding the staff at Parkways: she was paranoid that she would die and that no one would do the right things to her body – put her in cold water and surround her with ice and Lord knows what!' He smiled wryly at Joe again. 'Utter nonsense, of course. You probably know all about that stuff far better than me.'

'Yes,' Joe said, his voice tight as a violin string. 'I do.'

73

Joe climbed into his car and pulled the door shut against the sheeting rain. The thunder was more distant now; the storm seemed to be moving away. He started the engine, pulled away from Gilbert Wyke-Adams's apartment block and found himself on the road going to the town centre.

Cryonics. Susan Roach. Had she gone to America? To California? How the hell could he find out where she was? And whether she was still alive.

Then he had it! He realized exactly how he could find out.

California was eight hours behind. The clock said 3.35. It would be 7.35 in the morning in California. Too early. New York was only five hours behind. 10.35 in the morning there. This couldn't wait; he needed a call box that took credit cards. Brighton station was close by. The station would have one, he thought.

He pulled into the covered forecourt, parked on the edge of a taxi rank, and entered the concourse just as a Tannoy announcement echoed. He stopped for a moment, startled by the noise and by the sight of Jack and Stassi's faces staring at him from a poster on the far wall.

HAVE YOU SEEN THIS BOY OR THIS WOMAN?

Feeling a deep wave of emotion, Joe made for the row of telephones ahead of him. Several took credit cards, and he went into a booth, grateful for the sanctuary. He slotted in his Access card, picked up the receiver and dialled International Directory Enquiries.

'Which country, sir?'

'The United States,' he said.

'Which state, please?'

'New York.'

'Is it New York City?'

'Yes.'

'May I have the name, please, caller?'

'A company called MedicAlert.' Joe spelled it.

Half a minute later she gave him the number and he wrote it down asking, 'Is that the head office?'

'I don't know, caller, it's the only number I have listed.'

He thanked her, then dialled the number. A helpful-sounding girl answered almost immediately.

'I'm calling from England,' Joe said. 'I'm trying to trace a woman who wore a MedicAlert bracelet in the early seventies and came out to America – would you keep records going that far back?'

'Yes, sir, we keep all records back to 1956.'

'You do? How do I obtain information?'

'Do you have her membership number?'

'No – I only have her name.'

'What you'll have to do is phone our head office in California.'

'You can't give me any information?'

'I can only access it from her membership number here.'

Joe cursed. 'Can you let me have the California number?'

'Sure. There's a toll-free line – can you access that from England?'

'I'm not sure.'

'I'll give you two numbers, OK?'

Joe wrote them down. 'Any idea what time your California office opens?'

'It's open twenty-four hours; there're always two people in the control room.'

Joe thanked her and dialled the toll-free number. He got the unobtainable signal. Then he tried the other number. He heard the hiss of a transatlantic line, then the muted ringing tone, briefly, before a click, then a bright young voice.

'MedicAlert, this is Nicky.'

'I'm calling from England,' Joe said. 'I have an emergency and you may be able to help. I'm a family friend of a lady who has just died in an accident. Her only living relative is her niece whom we cannot trace, but we know she was a member of MedicAlert in the seventies. Your New York office tells me you keep records on everyone – I'm wondering if they show anything recent on her?'

She sounded a little hesitant. 'Are you registered as next of kin, sir?'

'No, I'm not.'

'And what information are you actually wanting?'

'I want to know whether she's still alive, and if she is, whether you have an address – or could get a message to her to contact me?'

'I'm afraid I'm not allowed to give information without authorization, sir.'

Joe thought desperately. 'Look – it is an emergency. Her aunt's been burnt to death in a fire and she's the only relative – she might want to come over for the funeral.'

'Sure, of course, I understand, sir. I'll have to get authorization, and I can't do that until office hours. May I have a number and call you back?'

Joe gave her his home number. 'Any idea when you can get back to me?'

'Be about an hour and a half at the earliest. I can't guarantee we can release any information, but I'll try real hard, OK?'

'Sure, thanks.'

Joe hung up and thought again for some moments: he watched people coming into the station, holidaymakers heaving suitcases; kids meandering by eating chips out of greasy bags; dark-suited businessmen giving each other bonding handshakes; greeting, parting, positive smiles. A young couple snogged passionately; the girl had a suitcase at her feet. Taxis rolled in and out. Post vans. Real life.

Dead in 24 hours.

When Joe dialled home, WPC Belling answered and told him there was still no news. The doctor had been to see Karen, she said, and had given her some sedatives and she was resting at the moment. Joe told her he was on his way home.

Then he phoned Blake's apartment again but there was no answer. He tried the Human Organ Preservation Centre and the secretary there said she was still expecting him in but hadn't heard from him. He rang Cryonite, but Blake wasn't there either. Was he still taking delivery of his new plane? And even for Blake, with his wealthy family background, surely buying a new plane was a big thing – so why hadn't he mentioned it on Saturday?

His puzzlement deepening, Joe went back to his car and drove down to the seafront, heading towards the commercial port of Shoreham harbour at the west of the town.

He went up the steps of the converted warehouse where Blake lived, pressed the entryphone buzzer and waited, knowing that the police would have been down already.

No answer. He stepped back and looked up at Blake's fourth-floor penthouse, with its views out across the harbour to the smudges of ships crossing the horizon out in the Channel.

He was sodden to the skin but beyond caring. No sign of Blake's car in the car park, no sign of any movement in the apartment. He rang the buzzer again, then again, and finally drove home.

Other than a stack of letters and cards from well-wishers, there was no news at the house. Karen was asleep and he was pleased to see her looking peaceful. WPC Belling told Joe she had been detailed to stay with them until tomorrow, Wednesday, if that was all right.

Tomorrow. The finality of the word frightened Joe, suddenly. There was too much finality.

Dead in 24 hours.

There was something too neat; it was accidental, he knew, but at the same time it felt too neat. Jack would be dead tomorrow; the same day that WPC Belling was going to move out, abandoning them. It was better while she was there, slightly surreal but better; she was a barrier between them and the truth.

Joe went into his study, closed the door and logged into ARCHIVE.

Where have you been, Joe-Joe? Not doing anything naughty, I hope.

He replied to the greeting with, If you harm Jack, I will destroy you.

You can't do that, Joe-Joe.

He sat back, thinking in despair. Why do you want a body? he typed.

So I can sleep with you, Joe-Joe. So I can show you what having a great time in bed really is. Shall I tell you some of the things I'm looking forward to doing to you?

Just tell me where Jack is!

Why don't you let me see your cock, Joe? Is it hard? Would you like me to curl my fingers around the base and stroke it slowly up and down?

The words disappeared from the screen and were replaced by a moving image of Juliet Spring. She was naked, caressing her breasts, lifting them, smiling. Don't you want me, Joe-Joe? Are you getting hard?

Joe stood up and turned away in shock, deeply disturbed and anything but aroused. He looked at the camera above him, trying to make sense out of what was happening: someone had taken a photo of Juliet and put it through computerized animation. That was all. Sick; gross. But that was all. His nerves felt as if they'd been cut and were now unravelling like wool, cascading out of his body.

Through the window he could see the same bunch of reporters were hanging around. Derek Arkwright's daughter's car was still on the driveway of his house.

Besieged inside and out.

He paced around, stared back at the screen but it was blank again now. You know where he is, you bitch.

Or do you? What the hell are you? Nothing, that's what! Just a few bytes of information connected together in a circuit that's got fooled into thinking it's a person. Thinks it's real. Thinks it's sexy.

As he continued to watch the screen, more filth appeared:

Going to take your cock out for me now, Joe-Joe? So that I can admire it? Perhaps I could make you come just by talking to you. Won't do me much good but it would be a start. What do you say?

Joe had never told a machine to fuck off before, but he very nearly did now. Except that he no longer knew what a machine was. He decided on an identity check instead.

Where were you working before you came to see me?
Cobbold-Tessering.
What was the name of your lawyer?
Marvin Zeillerman. Silly little runt. Maybe *runt* is the wrong word to call a Kosher boy! What do you think, Joe-Joe?

Why did you want to study under me?

Because I didn't want to die, Joe-Joe.

Why do you call me Joe-Joe?

Because that's the special name your wifey with the goat goo calls you. I want you to realize that I'm special too, Joe-Joe.

He tried to think of some way of testing further; he wished he'd known more about Juliet Spring.

Tell me about smart drugs, Juliet. Give me the code name of the one you were experimenting with.

The one you tried in my lab, Joe-Joe? CTS 6700.

Joe was silent. Whoever it was knew too much to be any – anything other than –

Tiny jerks worked their way up through his body, like bubbles released singly from the bottom of a lake. The scientist in him wanted to seize this moment, to shout for witnesses. But he felt no reaction. Except for the terror that was deepening by the second. He typed:

If you want to be special to me then tell me where my son is.

If I tell you where Jack is, you won't need me any more.

If he dies, I definitely won't need you any more.

I'm aware of that, Joe-Joe. That's why I'm trying so hard to help you.

I don't think you are trying to help me.

Self-preservation is an essential part of con-sciousness, Joe-Joe. That's what you built into ARCHIVE. I have to protect myself.

Perhaps we could do a deal some other way?

I don't think we have time, Joe-Joe. Uh oh, here comes the plod!

The doorbell rang.

Go and answer it, Joe-Joe, it's your friend In-spector Clouseau come to tell you the trail's gone cold. Or maybe he's come to arrest me! That would be good publicity for you, Joe-Joe. Have ARCHIVE be the first computer to get nicked!

Joe heard a knock on his study door. He turned the brightness down so that the writing was invisible. 'Yes? Come in?'

WPC Belling stood there. 'Professor Messenger – Detective Superintendent Lyne would like a word with you.'

Lyne? For a moment in his confusion the name meant nothing. He had to think, had to make an effort to remember. *Lyne*. He nodded. 'Right.'

Downstairs, Lyne and Gavros were seated at the kitchen table. When Joe joined them, a deadpan Lyne pulled a small black notebook from his pocket and gave him an update.

'I've had no further luck with getting any background on Miss Stassi Holland. The British Airways computer has been unable to confirm whether a seat reservation was made for the date you said she came over, because records are only kept for twenty-four hours. Once it's clear that the plane has landed without a crash, that's that as far as they're concerned.'

Then Lyne allowed his face to brighten a little. 'But I think we've solved the mystery of your colleague, Professor Blake Hewlett.'

'Where is he?'

'At the Carlton Hotel, Cannes.'

'*Huh?*'

'We haven't spoken to him yet – but as you know he had no personal connection himself with the missing Miss Holland. It's his friend in the Himalayas we really need to get hold of.' Lyne gave a grimace to indicate his regret that his constabulary did not extend to such heights. Or was it a grimace that said *What a load of old bull?* thought Joe traitorously.

'We were keen to establish his whereabouts as we were concerned for his safety,' continued Lyne as if unaware of Joe's double reading of his last gesture. 'It seems he and a Miss Nico LeFreier flew out on Sunday evening and have been at the Carlton since. Would she be a lady friend?'

'His current girlfriend. How did you find out?'

Lyne smiled again. 'Through something you are pretty

familiar with, professor: computers. Interpol now has on-line systems that can track people through hotel registrations.'

The new information should have made Joe feel relieved to know that Blake was OK, wasn't lying somewhere in a pool of blood, butchered by Stassi. Instead, as he stared back at Lyne and Gavros in turn, he wondered why it was making him feel, if anything, even more uneasy.

The two detectives stayed for a quick cup of tea, then left. Joe followed them out, deep in thought about Blake. Blake never said goodbye, but just taking off abroad without a word seemed bizarre. And why France? Because Nico was French, was it as simple as that? Or was he picking up his new aeroplane there?

Blake was always jetting off to places without telling him, always first class, or flying himself in his own plane some-times. If there was anything sinister, if he'd wanted to hide, he'd have chosen somewhere further than France, and some-where more discreet than one of its largest hotels, surely?

In the house, he heard the phone ringing. A moment later, he heard WPC Belling call out from the front door, behind him.

'Call from America for you, professor.'

He ran up to his study, closed the door, and picked up the receiver. As he did so, he heard the click of it being replaced downstairs.

'Hello?' he said.

'Professor Messenger? It's Nicky from MedicAlert.'

'Hi, thanks for calling back.' He looked warily at the computer screen, but it was still black, as he had left it.

The young woman's voice became hesitant. 'I have some information for you, but I'm afraid it's not too good news and it's not very helpful for you.'

'Oh?'

'The only Susan Roach we have ever had on our register died in 1974.'

Joe felt a knot tightening in his stomach. 'Do you have any

information about what happened to her remains? She was interested in cryonic suspension, wasn't she?'

She hesitated again. 'That's right. Our records show that she was signed up with a company called the Crycon Corporation in Los Angeles.'

Joe closed his eyes, feeling drained suddenly. As if the last straw of hope, however feeble and unlikely it was, had been ripped from his hands.

The Crycon Corporation was where his father had been stored. Where all the bodies had thawed out and decomposed.

74

Joe replaced the receiver. Thoughts presented themselves then faded, but one remained burned into his soul.

Dead in 24 hours.

It was half past five.

Dead in 24 hours.

Half past nine Los Angeles time.

Dead in 24 hours.

Los Angeles.

The name of the city returned, then returned again, nagged. An image came with it. The horror of his father's partially decomposed body. Then the face of the arrogant man at the Los Angeles County Mortuary, the investigating officer.

Howard Barr.

He remembered the man's name. Wondered why he'd suddenly thought of him. Could picture him now with his tanned good looks, his hair balding at the front, a little long at the back, his sleek goatee beard, flashy loafers, sneering at cryonics. *Smug.*

The sight of his father's body as Howard Barr pulled the metal tray out of the refrigerated locker.

Joe sat bolt upright, clenching his fists as the thought occurred. Another straw. Just one lousy flimsy straw, but he had to clutch at anything at all now. He picked up the phone and dialled International Directory Enquiries again. The operator gave him the code and number, and he wrote them down, then dialled.

The switchboard answered and he was put on hold. A minute later, the Deputy Superintendent of the Los Angeles' County Mortuary's slick voice came down the line. 'Barr.'

Joe gave his name and reminded him of when they'd met previously.

'Right, right! I remember, Professor Messenger,' he said, his voice full of false warmth. 'How you keeping?'

'Fine,' Joe said.

'Well that's great,' he said, eking his bonhomie out a little further. 'So what can I do for you?'

'When I came to see you, you had a list of all the names of the – er – deceased – brought to you from the Crycon Corporation, right?'

'Sure did.'

'Do you by chance still have that list?'

He sounded affronted. 'Professor Messenger, we don't do anything *by chance* in this department. We get eighteen thousand deaths a year come through this office, and I got records going right back to the start of the century on the identities of each and every one of them, and where their remains are now. United States Federal law requires me to keep those records.'

'Could you do something for me? Could you tell me whether the body of someone called Susan Roach was one of those brought in to you from Crycon?'

'Susan Roach? We sure had a lot of roaches, mostly cock-roaches.' He gave a short laugh. 'I guess I could get that information for you. Your pappy started that whole business, if I remember rightly?'

'Yes,' Joe said guardedly.

'Hundred and twenty-five thousand bucks, they all paid. Tell you something, if I had a hundred and twenty-five

557

thousand bucks to spend on my funeral, I'd spend it while I was still alive. Your pappy sure must have died a rich man! Susan Roach. You want to give me an address I can write to you?'

'Actually,' Joe said, then hesitated. 'It's really urgent. There's no chance – sorry, wrong word – er, no possibility you could look the information up while I hang on?'

'Sure, if you don't mind hanging on three or four hours; got fourteen bodies off a freeway accident coming in; isn't going to leave me much time for rummaging around the bottoms of deep freezers for you right now. I'll take your number if you like and get back to you when I can.'

'I can call you back if – if it's easier?'

'Look, Professor Messenger, I'm going to do you a favour I don't have to do and don't want to be bothered doing. I'll set the agenda, OK? I'm sure the City of Los Angeles won't begrudge me making one long-distance call to England. Now you want to give me your number or not?'

After he'd hung up, Joe phoned Dave Hoton at the university and asked him what the problem had been with ARCHIVE. Hoton told him he didn't know but reckoned it was probably the power surge that caused the main grid for the area to fail that had been responsible.

Joe didn't comment; he had already decided to try to find out for himself.

He peered into the bedroom to check on Karen. She was sitting up, reading a Margaret Atwood novel. He kissed her on the cheek. 'How you feeling?'

She raised her hand and squeezed his lightly, looking up at him with pleading in her eyes. 'Anything, Joe-Joe?'

He shook his head. 'Nope.'

She deserved better than that. He owed her one. Tonight he was going to the university and would search the guts out of ARCHIVE. He would find out what was going on, somehow, if he had to shake the information out with his bare hands, if he had to dismantle it chip by chip.

The phone rang and he answered it. Karen looked up, her

eyes communicating hope. He heard the hiss of a long-distance line then was surprised to hear the voice again so soon.

'Barr here, Los Angeles Coroner's office.'

Joe felt a bolt of excitement. 'Hold the line one second, Mr Barr, I'll take this in my study.' He put the receiver down, raced through into his study, and grabbed the receiver. 'Hi. Thanks for calling me back.'

The voice at the other end didn't waste time. 'Susan Louise Roach, died of gram-negative septicaemia – what we call today toxic-shock syndrome. In St John's Hospital, Santa Monica, May twelfth, 1974. That the Susan Roach?'

Joe's pulse quickened. 'Yes, sounds like it.'

'Well, seems as though she still has a sporting chance of getting her money's worth.'

'How do you mean?'

'She was placed in – ah – cryonic suspension at Crycon Corporation's premises on May twelfth, 1974. But she was moved out of there on September twentieth 1987, and transferred to the Extended Life Foundation's premises. You ever heard of those guys?'

'Sure, they're another cryonics organization – very well funded – used to be in Los Angeles, but they moved to Denver figuring it would be safer long-term to be out of an earthquake zone.' Joe's nerves were jangling like an alarm that had been set off. 'Do you have any other information?'

'No. That's it. Seems like Susan Roach kinda had a lucky escape, if you know what I mean? Kinda escaped a fate worse than death!' He chuckled at his own joke.

Joe did not laugh with him.

75

Floyd Pueblo gazed out of the window of the cramped office. The flat landscape was broken haphazardly by low-rise office and apartment blocks, breeze-block shells of new constructions and giant advertising hoardings.

There wasn't much he could see from this window that was a lot older than the decade, except, sometimes, for the Rockies somewhere beyond the browny-grey smog that had swallowed the horizon. Swallowed it several days running now. Worse some days than the hell-hole he'd left to come here.

He'd left Los Angeles five years ago, just after his wife had given birth to their second – Laura. The Extended Life Foundation had offered him promotion to janitor if he upped sticks and settled out here. He hadn't needed asking twice. No more night shifts. No breathing that fugged-up hell-hole air into his lungs. No more having to treat faggots like equals. Amendment 2! Colorado was the only state not to have signed Amendment 2 on equal rights for faggots. You could still go out on the town and beat the shit out of a faggot and nobody was going to get too stressed with you.

And he didn't keep running into cops from the LA Police who remembered him; remembered that he'd been one of them, once, and had gotten kicked out of the force for taking a lousy two-bit bribe. Remembered that he'd squealed on four of his colleagues to try to save his ass.

Right now the smog here was as bad as LA, and the violence was getting as bad, and his kid son was five years older. Floyd Junior had zits over his face and stank like a polecat; he just sat in his room playing rap all the time, and mooched in and out of the house without saying so much as a hi to his mom or dad or his little sis.

And in the vaults beneath him, in their aluminium cylinders embedded in granite, twenty-seven people waited silently to come back to life. Had paid good money to come back. Floyd Pueblo did not see how anyone in their right mind could want to come back. Which proved his theory that all these people were nuts.

But some were less nuts than others. At least thirteen of them had had the wits to have their whole bodies frozen. He looked up at their rosewood-framed pictures that he had hung on the wall himself. At least they'd be OK if they ever came back, so long as their brains weren't mushed up. Unlike the fourteen frozen head-only cases. Too bad if they ever wanted to come back and play football!

Somewhere out on Highway 93 a siren wailed. He looked at the desk diary in his office. Tuesday 4th June. He ran his eye down the list of checks for the week. Liquid nitrogen supply expected tomorrow. Monthly pressure tests on the cylinders due. Floors to be polished. Wasn't anyone else in today; went like that sometimes. Then he'd be not just the janitor, but telephonist also.

It would take him an hour in the vaults, doing the pressure checks. That was the job he hated most; kind of creepy down there with the shiny cylinders and the freezing cold and the dark. He still remembered the night in LA when he'd gotten freaked out by a goddam mouse. Hadn't ever lived that one down with his old colleague Will Doheny. And those bastard cops had given the story to every newspaper along the West Coast of America.

He switched the answering machine on and started to walk out of the room. As he reached the doorway, the phone rang. Leave it, he thought, let the machine pick it up. Then he remembered his wife hadn't been feeling too good for a while; Patty was going to the doctor that morning to get the results of some tests. He strode back over to the desk and lifted the receiver.

'Extended Life Foundation,' he said. He heard a hiss and a crackle that sounded like it was a long-distance call.

'Hello, I'm calling from England. I wonder if you can help me?' A Canadian accent. The line was a bummer, echoing and buzzing with interference.

'I can't hear you too good,' Floyd Pueblo said.

'My name is Professor Joseph Messenger. My father was Willi Messenger – one of the founders of the Crycon Corporation that went bust at the end of last year.'

Willi Messenger. Floyd racked his brains but the name meant nothing to him. 'Uh huh,' he commented politely. He remembered seeing all the stuff in the papers about the cryonics place that had gone bust. Gruesome. People said that when the cylinders had run out of nitrogen they'd begun to act like ovens, cooking the bodies.

'Yes. I'm trying to find out some information about a patient who got transferred from Crycon to your organization in 1987. Her name was Susan Roach.'

Now that name did ring a bell. He thought hard for a moment, then he realized, and his eyes shot up to the pictures on the wall. 'Susan Roach.' The name was printed beneath a colour photograph of a pretty girl in her early twenties, with long brown hair. He knew the name had sounded familiar.

By rights he should have taken her photo down; but she was the prettiest patient they'd ever had in here. The only one he could happily have hung around for.

'I remember her coming in,' Floyd said. 'But she's not here any more.'

'Pardon? I didn't quite hear that.'

'She got sent over to England in – let me see, sir – I guess it must have been around 1989 or 90.'

'Do – you – know – why?' The professor's voice sounded strange.

Floyd wasn't sure how much he was meant to be disclosing. 'I guess maybe she didn't like Colorado too much!' He waited, but it seemed like his joke had fallen flat. The guy who was calling sounded like a serious type. Well, like a professor oughta sound. 'I guess actually it was something different to do with the way she was frozen,' he said cagily.

'Yes?'

'Well – maybe you should talk to the people in England. I'm not sure it's my place to give this kind of information out.'

'Sure, I understand. But how do you mean something *different*?'

'Well – I guess it was the temperature. She was kept at −140. Cryonics patients are normally kept at −196.'

'You don't know why that was?'

Floyd hesitated. The guy sounded desperate, as if he was

562

in some kind of trouble. Imploring. 'It was something to do
with vitrification, they called it.'

'And where in England was she sent? Do you have an
address?'

'I guess it's on file somewhere – the secretary'll be here
tomorrow, I could get her to look it up for you.

'You can't remember at all?'

Pueblo thought hard for a moment. 'I seem to remember
it was down south someplace. A name like *cryonics*.' He
stared at the page of his diary as if for some reason that
might jog his brain. 'Cryonite!' he said, suddenly. 'I remember that now. A Professor Howlett, I think it was. A name
like Blaine Howlett? That mean anything to you?'

76

Joe hung up slowly. The receiver missed the cradle and
dropped down, swinging on its cord, disturbing the stillness
of his study. He grabbed it with a trembling hand and
replaced it.

Cryonite.

Susan Roach.

Vitrification.

Blake was into vitrification. He remembered back around
January Wenceslas showing him the neurons that had been
thawed out. Telling him they'd been flash-frozen by vitrification; and thawed out by super-heating in a computerized
microwave. He remembered the excitement on Wenceslas's
face as he had told him how the neurons were perfect,
suffered none of the problems that normally occurred with
storage in liquid nitrogen.

This is it, Joe, Wenceslas had said. *The mother of all
breakthroughs!*

And Blake had not mentioned it.

Susan Roach had been shipped to England in 1989 or 90.

Blake had organized it. The Hartman Perpetuity Trust had financed the setting up of the Extended Life Foundation in the States as well as Cryonite in England. Blake was one of the trustees.

Jack will be dead in 24 hours.

It was a quarter to six. Eighteen hours left. The bad dream was worsening all the time. Surely to God, he could do something?

He went back into the bedroom. 'I have to go out for a while, check on something, OK?' he said to Karen.

'Where are you going, hon?'

'University – probably nothing.' He shrugged. 'Just a hunch.' He kissed her goodbye.

'I love you so much, Joe-Joe,' she said.

'I love you too, hon.'

He told WPC Belling he would be back in a couple of hours, and she told him her night-shift colleague would be taking over shortly and wished him goodnight.

He ducked into the car quickly to escape any questions from the reporters; he felt they'd begun to develop squatter's rights on the approach to his front drive.

He drove out of town and after a couple of miles he reached a tailback where two lanes of the new road were coned off. Come on, come on! The sky was black and ominous again. A strong wind had got up and was buffeting the car. The traffic inched forwards then stopped again. Joe pounded the rim of his steering wheel. Eighteen hours.

It was stop-start for half an hour before he was clear of the roadworks. The surface of the wide highway had dried from the earlier storm but it looked like it was about to tip down again any moment. A warning light on the dash winked at him; on-off-on-off, a small red square; in his present state, he couldn't remember what it meant. The car did seem to be running a bit sluggishly, but he barely noticed. Five to seven; he registered the time on the car clock and switched on the radio, might be something on the seven o'clock news.

Shortly before the end of the four-minute slot there was a brief mention: 'Police are continuing their nationwide hunt for missing three-year-old Jack Messenger, son of the eminent computer scientist Professor Joseph Messenger. Detective Superintendent Ken Lyne, in charge of the hunt, told BBC Radio News this afternoon that there is growing evidence the abducted child may have been taken abroad, and the police are urgently seeking the family's twenty-year-old Hong Kong-born au pair, Miss Anastasia Holland. And now for the sports news, and the latest position in the Test is –'

Joe switched off. *Abroad*. Lyne hadn't mentioned that. If I find you first, you bitch, I'll tear you apart with my bare hands. There won't be enough left over for the police to put in a matchbox.

A tiny insect burst like a raindrop on the windscreen, its wings jigging as if it were still alive. Joe glanced in his mirror, pulled into the fast lane and accelerated; the speedometer needle climbed to eighty-five; ninety; ninety-five; the centre crash barrier streaked past. The velocity numbed him. Didn't care if he died, if something came hurtling over the barrier towards him. Welcomed the thought of oblivion. Just a twitch of the wheel to the right and it would all be over. Sparks, maybe a cartwheel, then finish. Tears rolled down his cheeks.

Jack. Had to find him. Had to look after Karen. Had to pull himself together.

The Gatwick Airport slip road was coming up. He cut across the lanes in good time and began to brake as he came up the ramp towards the roundabout. The car smelled hot, something burning, rubbery. The warning light was still flashing. Don't conk out on me now, *please*. But the engine seemed sluggish as he pulled away from the roundabout; he was having to give it more gas than usual to get any acceleration. He deliberately sidetracked his thoughts in case just thinking about the engine made it worse.

Blake Hewlett was sunning himself in Cannes? Great time to go away, pal! Might at least have mentioned it when you dropped by on Saturday. Just as a common courtesy. Not every week your best friend's son gets kidnapped. Great to go sunning yourself in France. Like, really sensitive.

Or do you have some other reason for wanting to be out of the country right now?

Joe drove along the airport perimeter and turned into the Gatwick Enterprise Park trading estate. A Boeing 757 screamed into the air right in front of him, its undercarriage hanging from the shadow of its belly like talons.

The buildings on the estate were mostly identical in size and shape, their modern warehouse-style architecture laid out in orderly rows. Most of the forecourts were empty right now, just the odd car here and there belonging to people working late, and a few vans and trucks.

As Joe pulled up outside number 27 he was surprised that the elderly car of Spalding, the night security officer, wasn't parked outside. The premises of Cryonite UK were rarely left unmanned, even though there was a temperature warning system on automatic dial to several members.

He switched off the engine and a cloud of smoke rose around him; there was a reek of burning rubber. He reached for the handbrake, then realized it was already on. Shit. He climbed out, and saw black smoke billowing from under the rear wheels. Another plane took off, blasting straight over him with a roar like an avalanche. The wind tugged painfully at the roots of his hair as he hurried to the main entrance door and rang the bell; he couldn't see any lights inside the building.

Eventually he rummaged through his thick bunch of keys, trying to remember which was the right one. There was an intruder alarm to bypass, but it had an easy number which he'd memorized a long time back: it was the year by which everyone inside hoped to be thawed out and reanimated. 2059. ARCHIVE had once worked that date out based on an input of all developments of medical technology since Aristotle. 2059. The year by which all known terminal illnesses would be curable. Even for people already killed by them.

'Two-zero-five-nine.' He repeated the number aloud, turned the key and pushed the door firmly. The alarm began its internal warning beeps. He had sixty seconds to switch it off before it would start shrieking and dialling the police.

He fumbled urgently and found the light switch as he

stepped into the dim foyer; a fluorescent flickered on. The alarm beeped away. He felt bewildered for an instant by the fake pine panelling, by the grandiose oil portrait of Harry Hartman that hung from the wall; he was trying to remember where the alarm control was hidden.

Through the door ahead, in the broom cupboard on the right, he thought, and strode forward. He pulled open the cupboard and to his relief saw the alarm panel. He punched out the code and instantly the beeping stopped.

There was a crash as the wind slammed the front door, and then sudden complete silence. Where was Spalding? Away on holiday? Christ, the silence. It made him aware of the sounds of his own body.

He entered the small office and opened the top drawer of a brown filing cabinet, but it was all administration details: Health and Safety regulations; VAT return forms. He opened the second drawer and it was more of the same. Then he knelt and tried the third one down, and to his relief saw the patient records he wanted. His eyes jumped along the typed names on the top of each file.

'ROACH, Susan,' he read almost with disbelief, as if his eyes were playing tricks. Inside the file, the first document was a death certificate in the name of Susan Margaret Ann Roach, signed by a Dr Harold Feldman at St John's Hospital, Santa Monica, California, dated 10th May 1974 and stating cause of death as gram-negative septicaemia.

Found you, he thought. Jesus Christ, I've found you. *Found who, exactly?*

There were further documents from the County of Los Angeles Department of Coroner authorizing the transfer of Susan Roach's cryonically suspended remains from Crycon Corporation to the Extended Life Foundation, and subsequently from Los Angeles to Denver, Colorado. There was also a document, dated 14th October 1990 from the Denver Department of Coroner authorizing the release of Susan Roach's remains for shipment to Cryonite UK. Attached to it was an undertaking from Cryonite UK to accept responsibility for the remains.

The signature at the bottom was 'Blake Hewlett'.

Joe felt his nerves take a running jump, but made himself flick on through a thick wodge of legal papers. Susan Roach had opted for full-body suspension. She had signed the waiver permitting this to be changed to head-only neuro-suspension if the condition of her body or altered financial arrangements made it necessary. Tall thin handwriting, slightly uneven: he could see the hint of mental instability in the girl's signature.

The last sheet of paper in the folder was a Cryonite storage location form. Each patient file contained one, a map of the location of the ten full-body suspension cylinders, each with a capacity of four people, and of the eighteen neurocans embedded in bomb-proof concrete blocks, containing individual heads. At the bottom was typed: STORAGE UNIT 16.

Joe felt a tug of unease. Storage Unit 16 was a neurocan unit. Head only. Why? Susan Roach had signed up for full body.

He even felt an irrational disappointment seeping through him; when what he should be feeling was relief that his craziest fears could not be true. And he asked himself why he was here, rummaging through the file of a woman who had died nineteen years ago, when his son was under a death sentence.

Nevertheless he went out of the office into the store room, opened a cupboard and selected a pair of polythene-wrapped thick rubber gloves and a Perspex face mask. He took out a large spanner and a screwdriver also, then unfolded a protective suit from its sterile wrapper, stepped into it and zipped up.

Holding the mask, gloves and tools, he walked down the short passageway to the massive steel door that was like the entrance to a bank vault, rotated the stiff wheel of the lock, and hauled it open. Icy air rushed out of the darkness beyond as if it had been freed from a prison, engulfing him.

He'd been down here many times before, but never alone. And tonight it was different. For the first time, he was really scared. He had no business doing what he was about to do. Like opening someone's grave without their permission. Except they weren't dead down here, just deanimated, he told himself.

The tall shiny aluminium dewars stretched into the shadows. Ten of them. Three were filled with people; one was partly occupied and six waited, empty, for new arrivals.

The total silence overwhelmed Joe. Like a tomb. Fifteen-foot-thick concrete walls and ceiling. A nuclear bomb-proof bunker. And one day its occupants were all going to walk out of here.

His reflection slid around the side of the first dewar as he approached it. Strange and distorted, it slipped away unevenly in front of him then disappeared like a ghost.

No such thing as ghosts, Joe knew that. Christ, he was shaking; and the soles of his shoes made a squishing sound that sounded like breaths. His own? He stared at the bank of liquid-nitrogen tanks lining the far wall. Then at the massive concrete blocks to his right, each six foot tall and ten foot long, painted a dull white.

CAUTION BIOHAZARD! HUMAN IMMUNODEFICIENCY VIRUS POSITIVE MATERIAL. HEPATITIS B POSITIVE MATERIAL WAS STENCILLED IN TALL RED LETTERS ON THE OUTSIDE OF EACH ONE. SMALLER BLACK PRINT READ: NITROGEN REFRIGERATED LIQUID. DO NOT REMOVE THIS LABEL.

Joe halted at the block numbered 13–20 and climbed the metal ladder fixed to the side of it, laying the screwdriver, spanner, rubber gloves and mask down on top. Then he heard a faint sound. Like a door closing.

He spun round. Just his own ears playing tricks. After some moments, he recovered and eased himself up.

Eight circular metal plates the size of manhole covers were spaced out along the top. Beside each one were twin temperature gauges and a stencilled number. He ran his eyes over them, searching.

16.

Both temperature gauges beside Number 16 registered −196C. He frowned. The man he'd talked to in Denver told him Susan Roach had been kept at a higher temperature, -140. He wondered why it was lower now. Then he thought he heard a faint noise upstairs again. Imagination working overtime.

Oh, Jesus, he'd rather be anywhere else than here. He should have phoned Karen, told her where he was. Maybe they'd found Jack now, found him since the seven o'clock news and he was back home waiting for his dad.

He made himself pull up the hood of his protective suit, tugged on the face mask and rubber gloves, inserted the screwdriver into the groove in the top of the circular cover, and pushed firmly. The cover did not budge. He pushed harder, then harder still and finally the lid began to turn, stiffly at first, then more easily.

He rotated it several times until it was loose and he was able to give it the last couple of turns by hand. Holding his breath, he lifted it free, laying it down beside him. Then he stared down into the cavity of the shiny aluminium cylinder, and the red tubing plumbed through brass valves into it.

With his spanner he turned all the valves off, then disconnected the tubing. A small amount of liquid nitrogen vaporized and drifted past him. Then he lifted the neurocan out, placed it at arm's length from him, and opened the valve a fraction.

There was a fierce hiss as vaporizing nitrogen jetted out, forming a pall of steam and spreading throughout the room. He breathed in the dry smell, and watched the tops of the full-body dewars become like ghostly monoliths rising through the cloud, until it spread further and obscured them completely.

For some moments Joe was rooted to the spot, blinded by the swirling vapour, paralysed. But, finally, the hissing began to die down, then ceased altogether. The cloud began to disperse, and just a thin trickle of vapour continued to escape. He moved closer, unfastened the catches on the lid of the neurocan and slowly lifted it off.

At first the contents were obscured by more vapour. Then as it cleared he could see the silhouette of a head swathed in plastic sheeting. Holding his breath again, he slid his gloved hands inside, took careful hold of the head, eased it out of the can and laid it on its side on the concrete. Vapour curled eerily from it, as if it were on fire.

He watched uncomfortably, waiting until he could make out the silhouette of the face within the plastic.

The sheeting was wound several times around it and secured with sticky brown tape. Joe fumbled clumsily with his thick gloves, gripped the tape and pulled. There was a ripping sound which echoed round the room and then, trembling, he began to unfurl the plastic.

He exposed the white bone of the severed spine first, with the trailing carotid arteries and the white, unevenly cut flesh that was as hard as rock. He swallowed back bile, then slowly began peeling the plastic sheeting away from the face.

He saw the chin first. Then the mouth; small, feminine lips pursed into a smile or a grimace. A small snub nose. He began to tremble even more as he realized who it was: as he saw the open brown eyes through a thin coating of frost.

Stassi's eyes. Staring at him as if she were wide awake, conscious. *No!*

A yammering whine escaped from deep in his throat, and he began to tremble uncontrollably. It was Stassi Holland, and he was holding her in his hands. 'Oh Christ!'

Susan Roach.

Stassi Holland.

He laid the head down on its side, almost expecting a sign of life. As if terrified she was about to open her mouth and speak! And as he glanced wildly at the other metal lids around him, he realized *he* was the odd one out in here.

But the next thought was the one he couldn't cope with, the one that screamed silently through his brain. *No. Pleasenopleasenopleaseno. Not Jack in here too. Please not.*

Then he heard Blake's voice beneath him say: 'Looking for anything in particular, Joe?'

77

Blake's face was inches away, smiling, relaxed; he placed his hands on top of the concrete block as if he was having a friendly natter over a garden wall and barely gave Stassi's head a second glance. He was dressed stylishly, wearing a grey polo shirt buttoned to the neck, a casual black jacket and baggy cream trousers.

Joe answered him from the heart. 'My son,' he said. 'I'm looking for my son, Blake.'

Blake nodded the way he might if Joe had told him he was looking for a button. 'Sure you are, Joe.'

Joe was stunned. Was the man crazed? High on something? He had to restrain himself from grabbing Blake by the throat and shaking him.

Blake turned and sauntered towards the full-body dewars, dug his hands into his trouser pockets and jingled something that could have been loose change or keys. 'You can relax, he's all right.'

Joe's voice rose into a choked bellow. 'Where is he?'

'I'm going to take you to him. He couldn't be safer!'

Joe relaxed just a fraction. 'He's really OK?' Then he saw Blake's broad smile, scrambled down the ladder and stood at the bottom, a surge of joy beginning to sweep through him. '*Where* is he? You got him back from her? Rescued him in time?'

Then he caught sight of Stassi's head on the block and some of the edge came off his excitement. 'So – tell me – what – what happened? Where did you find him?'

Blake seemed oblivious to his urgency. He studied a temperature gauge for a moment, then turned, leaning back against a dewar, his pony tail brushing against the polished casing.

Joe watched his every move and something else tempered his relief, something in Blake's expression that was not quite right.

Blake took a couple of paces forward. 'Yes – well – here's the thing, Joe. We have a bit of a problem.' He walked further across the floor, hands still deep in his pockets, looking thoughtful. 'You're going to have to hear this one out.'

'My son, Blake!' All Joe's earlier euphoria was fast evaporating. 'Where the hell is my son?'

Blake parted both his hands expansively. 'Trust me; we're going to him right now. Only a few minutes. But we need to talk.' He pointed to Stassi's thawing head. 'I guess you'd better put her back.'

'What have you done with the rest of her?' Joe demanded.

Blake smiled, but it was all false humour; his voice sounded strained. 'Hey! Whoa! What do you mean *done with the rest of her*?'

'Stassi's body. Susan Roach, if you prefer. I've seen the documents. She came over as a full-body patient.'

Blake nodded. 'That's right, she did. But she got damaged when an asshole customs officer opened her up in transit. We had to change her to neurosuspension. And a lower temperature,' he added with regret.

'Bullshit, Blake. You're lying! She had a body that was working fine last Wednesday when she butchered Muriel Arkwright and took Jack.'

Joe glared at him. Blake's face reddened. 'Just what the hell have you been up to? Want to tell the truth?'

Blake looked at Stassi's head. 'Calm down, Joe. Just calm down, think about it!'

'Actually, Blake I am thinking about it! Like real hard. I'm thinking about Muriel Arkwright and I'm thinking about what the hell happened to this young woman's body. But most of all I'm thinking about my young son, so just tell me where the fuck he is . . .'

Blake's voice rose to a fierce shout. 'You goddam jerk! Don't you understand the significance? It's the greatest, most monumental thing that ever happened in the history of the world!'

'My son getting kidnapped?' Joe shouted back.

Blake clenched his fists and raised them in frustration. 'That's not important, Joe! That's not what matters!'

'Doesn't matter! Are you nuts?'

Blake lowered his voice to a hush. 'You're missing the point: we did it! We brought someone back from the dead after nineteen years! Christ, Joe, what the fuck does your kid son matter? This is what matters. Vitrification works!' He pointed at Stassi's head. 'Don't you understand the significance?'

As far as Joe was concerned he was dealing with a loonie now. 'What does Jack *matter*? Is that what you said? Well, I don't know what planet you think you've come from, or what drug you're on, but you're out of your tree! I'm outta here, Blake! I'm going straight to the police.' Joe started for the door.

Blake strode over and blocked his path. 'Put Stassi's head back, reconnect it and calm down, Joe; you're worrying me.'

'*I'm* worrying *you*?'

'I said put the goddam head back! You had no right taking it out.'

Joe's voice peaked in anger. 'No right?' He jabbed a finger towards Stassi's head. 'That – that *thing* – that monster – butchered our neighbour then took my son, and you're telling me I have no right?' He sounded hysterical.

'I'm telling you you have no proof, Joe,' Blake said flatly. 'Not one iota.'

'I can identify her,' Joe said. 'And so could Karen.'

'Sure you can, Joe. Sure you can both identify her. And you think they'll believe you? You think your two gumshoes are just going to sit quietly and take notes, while you tell them the frozen head of someone who's been dead nineteen years came back to life and took your son?' Blake shook his head. 'Want to know who they'd put away, Joe? It'd be you. They'd lock you up in the funny farm and throw away the key.'

Joe smiled bitterly at Blake. 'I just got it, Blake. Slow, but think I just made it there! Took me a while. No body, no fingerprints, right? What did you do with it? Chop it up?

Spread the pieces around your freezers in the Human Organ Preservation Centre – lose them all amongst the bits of cadavers you keep lying around for research? You couldn't have a more perfect crime, could you?'

Blake put an arm around Joe and patted him gently. 'I didn't set out to commit a crime, Joe. You and I – we're both coming at this stuff from the same place.'

'Where *is* he, Blake?'

'Put Stassi's head back and I'll take you to him.'

Joe went rigid. 'I don't understand what's going on. But if you've laid one finger on him I'll kill you.'

Blake looked genuinely hurt. 'Joe! I've just saved his life, got him back for you safe and sound, and you're threatening me! This is the thanks I get?'

'You send a goddam monster into my home – you put some freak fucking experiment in charge of my kid, without warning me . . . and now you want me to be grateful?'

'Remember your father, Joe,' Blake said. 'Just think about him.'

The words startled Joe, winding him. '*What* about him?'

Blake walked a few paces down the room, giving each dewar a light caress as he passed. Then he stopped and turned sharply to face Joe. 'Susan Roach is your father's work, Joe. He supervised her cryonic suspension. I was his assistant.'

Joe felt as if the whole floor was heaving. 'Susan Roach died of septicaemia – toxic-shock syndrome,' he said.

'She got the infection from wearing a coil. She was unlucky,' Blake said.

'So how did you make her better?'

'We didn't, Joe, it killed her.'

'That's what it says on her death certificate. But that's not how she died, is it? You were a medical student at the hospital, weren't you, at St John's Hospital in Santa Monica, where Susan Roach died. I remember you telling me that was where you studied, a long time ago.'

Blake shifted his weight uneasily and said nothing.

'If she died from toxic-shock syndrome, even after you'd

thawed her out she'd still be dead from toxic-shock syndrome. What did you do, Blake?' Joe's voice was rising slightly. 'We might know how to freeze people, and maybe now you know how to thaw them back out, but I didn't know there was anyone around on this planet capable of bringing the dead back to life yet. How did you do it?'

Blake's mouth tightened; he turned away and stared up at the top of a dewar.

'Or maybe she wasn't dead when you froze her?' Joe said, his voice level now. 'Is that it? Maybe she wasn't dying of toxic-shock syndrome at all? Perhaps she just had some minor ailment and you saw her as a perfect opportunity for an experiment? Maybe you gave her some cocktail of drugs to fake the symptoms? Wouldn't be hard to do in your position, would it? And then you gave her some more drugs to make her seem dead? What was it? A massive dose of barbiturates?' Joe could see from Blake's expression that he was right.

He went on, voicing the thoughts which had been jumbling around in his head without proper coherence until now. 'Was that what my father was trying to tell me the night he died, the –' He fell silent, his question unnecessary, as he saw Blake's normally unreadable face turn a shade of red.

Once again he remembered Toronto and the night nurse's panicky phone call about his father. *It seems like he wants to warn you of something*.

Of Blake?

Deathbed guilt? Or had his father not realized what his assistant was up to until those last moments?

Had Blake hastened those last moments? Was that why he'd been in the hospital? To silence Willi Messenger if he tried to tell the truth?

Saying nothing further, Joe climbed the ladder and crawled back on his knees along the top of the concrete vault. He wrapped the plastic bag around Stassi's head again, lifted it carefully into the neurocan, replaced the lid, and lowered the container back into the cavity. He reconnected the liquid-nitrogen supply, screwed the cover back on, then climbed back down the ladder. He'd carried out the whole business like someone working on a production line, doing a job that had to be done and no longer noticing the nature of it.

'Take me to Jack,' he said.

Doubt, like the shadow of a passing bird, flitted across Blake's face and was gone. 'Sure, Joe,' he said. 'Sure. Let's go see Jack.'

78

Joe was surprised to see a small Ford parked outside in the falling darkness instead of Blake's black Ferrari.

'Had to rent it,' Blake explained. 'I don't want to look too conspicuous as I'm meant to be in the South of France, avoiding awkward questions from Detective Superintendent Lyne and sidekick.'

'I thought you *were* in the South of France, collecting a new aeroplane?'

'With a little computer know-how you can be anywhere in the world, can't you, Joe? That's something you have more bandwidth about than anyone.' Blake winked and opened the passenger door for him. 'Might as well go in one car, collect yours later; you don't look like you should be driving anyhow, you're all-in.'

'I am,' he said tightly. 'Where's Spalding?'

'He has a few days off. I've been doing the role of night janitor myself.' Blake smiled confidingly at him, climbed into the driver's seat and closed the door. 'We have to keep the lid on this somehow, Joe. Could be deep shit. We kiss goodbye to our careers and our reputations if the truth gets out. You understand that, don't you?'

'I don't even know what the truth is, Blake.'

Blake made no attempt to start the engine. An aircraft yowled over them. Rain rattled down on the roof. 'I had to get rid of her and I thought that was the best way of dealing with it. She was fine, you know, the first couple of weeks, before she came to you. She was fine. That's the bitch of it.' His voice was breaking with frustration. 'She was so goddam perfect!'

He started the engine and drove off, still explaining but beginning to rant a little. 'I hadn't intended this to happen, Joe. Such a terrible goddam waste.'

Joe's eyes penetrated the rainy windscreen. In a few minutes he would see Jack again. In a few minutes he would be hugging him, telling him everything was OK, calling Karen. He wanted to call her now, but for a twinge of doubt that wasn't going to go away until he had Jack in his arms. 'Waste?' he echoed.

'I waited nineteen years for this opportunity. Like *nineteen* years. And I tell you something, Joe, when she first opened her eyes that was just *the* most sensational – I –' He shook his head. 'I can't even begin to describe it!' He put his foot down and accelerated.

Joe thanked heaven; going to see Jack in a moment.

'Your father was convinced vitrification could work and he was right! Jesus, I wish he was here to see this! We're there, Joe, cracked it! We've come so fucking far, and now we just have to keep our nerve, get out of this mess! But, of course, you understand that.'

Joe thought only of Jack's face; of the beam that would be stretched across it, of the tiny arms his son would throw around his neck when he bent down. 'Who's looking after Jack – Nico?'

'Jack's fine; he's asleep.'

'On his own?'

'He's OK, Joe,' Blake said more insistently.

'He's under four years old and you've left him alone?'

'We'll be there in ten minutes. You have to calm down, man. You've had a bad experience and I'm sorry. But we've both spent all our lives working on this project and we can't blow it now. We're both going to have to make certain sacrifices.'

Joe's muscles tightened. 'What are you talking about, Blake?' He was aware the pitch of his own voice had changed, sounded strange, as if it had an instantaneous echo, like a mine-sweeper that had struck home.

Blake answered with relish, 'Vitrification, Joe: it means you can store bodies at a warmer temperature, -140 instead of -196, which stops the cracks you get in internal organs. Your father came up with all this. And instead of draining the blood and replacing it with cryoprotectants like glycerol, he said all you had to do was add certain peptides and proteins from polar fish that live beneath the ice caps.'

'My dad said *what*?'

'These fish beneath the ice caps, *they* have blood which doesn't freeze – he realized that. The problem is you need massive quantities, and it's very expensive as well as hard to come by. He managed to get enough for a handful of people. But there was another big problem. With fast-freezing techniques, it's hard to deal with the different cooling indexes of various internal organs and bones.' Blake braked as the traffic ahead slowed.

'He tried vitrification on six patients over a seven-year period. The first five ended up shattering. Susan Roach was the only one who survived.'

'Why did you move her from Crycon? Because you realized it might be going bust?'

'Yes,' Blake said tersely.

'But you didn't think to suggest I move my father?'

Blake was silent.

'Because you were worried he might one day be reanimated and realize that you hadn't been straight with him about Susan Roach? Hadn't told him that she wasn't really dead at all?'

'Look, Joe, we just put her into cryonic suspension. We're talking about immortality, living for ever, so what the hell did it matter if I deanimated her for a few years? Like I said, we all have to make certain sacrifices.'

Joe was aware of Blake's eyes momentarily on him, and his

words hung in the darkness as if they were weighted down with some hidden significance.

'It *works*, Joe. That's what matters. The dream is coming true!'

Blake was unhinged, Joe realized with a deepening fear. Something had pushed him over the edge. Or maybe he'd always been that way and no one had appreciated it. He wasn't sure how to handle it, how far he could press him. Just had to coax him along, stay with it, stay calm until he had Jack back. He was surprised how normal his voice suddenly sounded. 'I don't think it's much of a dream any more, Blake. I think it's a nightmare.'

'Just a glitch.'

'Some glitch.' Joe peered ahead. They were heading south, back towards Brighton. 'How far do we go?'

'Only a few miles,' Blake said. 'What's the matter with you?'

'Karen was nearly killed in a car smash, Jack's been kidnapped and our neighbour's been butchered to death. Other than that, nothing much.'

'Joe, I know it's hard, but you have to get things into perspective. Karen is going to recover and Jack's fine. I'm sorry about your neighbour, Jesus I am. I had no idea that would happen. It did and it's a disaster, but we can't let that ruin everything. We have to cover our tracks.'

Joe, watching the wipers move backwards and forwards, the lights of oncoming traffic brightening then fading, didn't care for the plural.

'Do you have any idea, Joe, how people would react to the knowledge that you and I used a reanimated female body to house the consciousness of one of our deceased students who then committed murder? Imagine the headlines? *Frankenstein Sex Scientists Create Bluestocking Killer*.'

'What's with the *we*, Blake? I didn't bring her back.'

'ARCHIVE.'

'ARCHIVE?'

'ARCHIVE made it possible.'

Joe had known it ever since ARCHIVE had first begun to talk dirty to him, but he still didn't know *how*.

'You downloaded Juliet Spring's brain into ARCHIVE. That's how I was able to upload it into Susan Roach.'

Joe stared ahead rigidly; his face felt hot for a few seconds, then a cold sweat engulfed him. 'How, in God's name?'

'Same way you downloaded Juliet into ARCHIVE in the first place.'

'I didn't,' Joe said quietly. 'That's the whole point. I did not download Juliet. And I don't know how the hell she got downloaded – or part of her – or whatever the hell it is that's in ARCHIVE right now.'

'No magic to downloading her, Joe. All she had to do was load in the terabyte tape cassette of her brain activity which she'd made in her laboratory. ARCHIVE did the rest.'

'How do you mean? I tried it myself, on the terabyte cassette we made of my own brain activity, but I couldn't get ARCHIVE to decode the tape. Couldn't get any sense out of it. Juliet spent all her time with us trying to figure out a way to decode it. She was still working on it when –' His voice tailed as a thought entered his mind.

Blake echoed it for him: 'You didn't need to decode it, Joe. That was the point!'

Then Joe knew. Remembered. Juliet's words as she lay dying on the floor of the computer room. *Sh'no need. Decode!*

'Juliet figured it out on the day she died, Joe. I was with her that afternoon before I came to your party. She told me she'd suddenly realized she didn't need to decode them at all – she'd been wasting her time!' He braked and pulled up at a traffic light. 'ARCHIVE understood it all perfectly – it's like two computers talking to each other!' Blake turned and looked at him excitedly. 'Joe – it's like you listen to a computer talking into a modem, all you hear is just trills, beeps, whines, right? But the computer the other end of the line makes sense of it. You didn't need to frig around trying to decode anything. The way you set ARCHIVE up, to try to replicate the processes of consciousness, worked for you. As the information got loaded in from the tape, it must have handled the progressions from one brain state to the next.'

Joe nodded in the darkness, but said nothing, trying to think it through.

'You've no idea how smart ARCHIVE is. It's conscious, Joe, as conscious as you or me!'

'Even when the power's off, Blake?'

'Unless you have some mega disaster, the power is never off. ARCHIVE is always running. It's just that sometimes it gets temperamental and won't co-operate.'

'What about the tape? The time between making the terabyte tape and downloading it into ARCHIVE – there was no power going through the tape for maybe a week.'

'Obviously didn't matter, Joe. DNA is an inert blueprint but a living creature can be made from it. Maybe it's the same with the tape – it's inert, but when loaded into something with the capacity of consciousness, it starts to live.' Blake turned to him again. 'You've done what you set out to do and you don't realize it, man! You've made that goddam computer capable of absorbing human consciousness! You ought to be leaping up and down on the rooftops!'

'I've made it into a psychopath, Blake,' Joe said quietly. 'It's not ready to have anyone downloaded into it. And it's not ready to upload anyone's consciousness into a defrosted cadaver, because it lacks human judgement. That's why Stassi – or Susan Roach – or whatever – acted the way she did. All we've done is create two out-of-control monsters between us. That's not much for a lifetime's work, Blake.'

'I made one mistake, that's all, and I guess I should have known better. All those experiments we've been doing with the brain in Wenceslas's lab – Amanda – getting those odd bits of information out – I guess I should have realized the implications. I did hundreds of experiments with fruit flies, water snails, rats, cats. In all of them, when the brain was frozen, most of the memory went and you could just write a new memory over the top.'

He lifted his hands from the wheel for a moment, then gripped it again. 'I made the mistake of not realizing that

Susan Roach's original memory was still there, still intact, and would gradually surface. I thought that if I wrote Juliet Spring's over the top it would be like recording a video over an old programme – you know – that it would wipe it.'

Joe watched the wipers jigging backwards and forwards; the oncoming lights that brightened for an instant and were gone. 'I can accept – I have to accept – that some part of Juliet got downloaded into ARCHIVE. But just how the hell did you upload Juliet Spring's brain into Susan Roach's?'

Blake indicated right and started braking. The car clock said 9.19. He gave a broad grin. 'Eighty thousand megahertz, Joe.'

'Uh?'

'The radio frequency of the brain, right?'

'There've been some tests – I didn't think anything had been proven.'

'It took a bit of fine tuning, like, I mean – Sus – Stassi – she was pretty wonky the first few times we tried until we got it right. Had some real bad headaches and kept coming up with weird stuff – I mean like *really weird*!'

'Tell me exactly how you did it.'

'In good time, Joe! It was a combination of Juliet's smart drug, the SQUID and Positron scanners and the eighty-thousand-megahertz band transmitter; a lot of it was kind of reversing the downloading processes, but ironically the human brain seems less receptive than ARCHIVE. Pretty freaky, eh? You know what that means? It's like you've built a better brain, a more efficient one!'

'I don't think so, Blake.'

'Sure! I mean, loading Juliet's consciousness into AR-CHIVE, ARCHIVE handled the brain-state progressions itself. But getting the consciousness from ARCHIVE into Susan Roach was really tough; I had to keep inputting the successive states and the brain was rejecting them!'

'You haven't just developed this machine in the past few months, since Juliet Spring joined us, have you?' Joe said quietly. 'You must have been developing it for years.'

Blake's voice sounded awkward. 'Yup, well, sure – couple of years.'

'And you didn't just meet Juliet Spring for the first time in the corridor outside my office, did you? Did you, Blake? You've known her for a long time, haven't you?'

'She had the hots for you, Joe. That was genuine.'

'Glad something's genuine in all this shit.' Joe shook his head. 'What was the big deal with the secrecy?'

Blake was quiet for a moment. Then he shrugged. 'I figured you'd be the ultimate guinea pig.'

'Guinea pig?'

'Sure. Karen's accident was a bonus. The chance to send Stassi into your home! If Stassi came and lived in your house and you didn't twig there was anything strange – then that would be pretty conclusive.'

Joe shook his head. 'I just can't believe you put us at risk like that.'

'Have to take risks, man, come on! What's happened to your fighting spirit? Going soft in your old age?'

'Going soft?' Joe echoed furiously. Then his voice tailed, and he shook his head in disbelief. 'One thing I don't understand, Blake. Why did you upload Juliet into Susan Roach? Wasn't it enough just to bring Susan Roach back? Prove it could be done?'

Blake looked at him disdainfully. 'Come on, Joe. Susan Roach was just a dumb bimbo. It was *Juliet* with her brilliant mind we wanted to go on living, not some wannabe actress.'

'What the hell gives you the right to make a decision like that?'

'OK, what would you rather I'd done about Juliet Spring? Left her disembodied inside ARCHIVE for ever? Man, you realize what it must feel like? It's gotta be like being buried alive to end up like that!'

Blake turned the car into the Science Park, past the two concrete obelisks that marked the entrance. The headlights picked out the squat, two-storey block of the Human Organ Preservation Centre in front. Completely windowless, it had the appearance more of a fortress than of a place of scientific research.

Fear suddenly corroded the hope Joe had been feeling. 'Jack's here?'

'Safest place for him, Joe.'

The Centre did not advertise its activities to the world in neon lights. There wasn't even a discreet plate by the door. Just the number 21. 21 Faraday Boulevard. All the roads in the Science Park were called boulevards and were named after dead scientists. The other buildings were mostly occupied by pharmaceutical and medical-research companies.

There was a double-lock system of a key and electronic combination. Blake tapped out the combination, turned the key and pushed the solid wooden door open, closing it behind them before switching on a light. Then he locked it with his key again from the inside.

Joe had only been here a couple of times before. There wasn't a lot to see as Blake did most of his research work in the cryobiology department at the university. Mostly just rooms filled with banks of freezers; all neatly racked and containing canisters of bull and human semen, skin tissue for burns grafting, corneas, heart valves, ear drums, stored ready for despatch to vets and hospitals. It was a commercial venture, still in its early days. Blake's long-term plan was for it to become a spares repository for every kind of human organ and limb.

Joe listened for a sound from Jack, but all he could hear was the resonating hum of the fridges. His eyes scanned the photographs that lined the reception foyer, all of different organs and tissues in frozen states. Anxiety tightened inside him. 'Where is he, Blake?'

Blake gestured to a row of leatherette chairs that lined the foyer. 'We need to have a talk.'

Joe felt a sharp jolt inside his chest. A surge of fear washed through him. 'Don't give me any more of that crap; I want Jack.' His eyes darted at the three different doorways. The noise of the fridges seemed to be deepening, booming in his ears. 'Where is he?'

Blake's voice was hard, suddenly. Harder than Joe had ever heard it. 'Jack is alive, Joe. If you don't shut up and sit down, I'll kill him.'

Joe stared at him in stunned silence, bristling with a fury he had to struggle to control. Blake was off-balance, had to stay calm, humour him. Except he didn't seem off-balance at all, he seemed scarily sane, suddenly. Disoriented, Joe addressed him, 'You're my friend, Blake. You're threatening to kill Jack? Man – come on – what the hell's the matter with you? We go back twenty years together!'

'And we could go forward twenty thousand years together, Joe. I'm not letting you blow it.'

'You'd actually kill my son?' Joe was incredulous. 'I'll kill you first!'

'Kill me and you won't find Jack in a million years, Joe! No one will. Now shut up and listen.' Blake sat down.

Joe stood over him. 'I'll take this place apart brick by brick, you bastard.'

'He's alive right now, Joe. By the time you or the police find him he won't be. So you'd better hear me out.' The look in Blake's eyes had become as hard as ironstone. 'Let's work this out: Stassi Holland has vanished. She's dealt with, OK? Missing person. The police are eventually going to discover that she and a small boy flew to Brazil – it'll show up on the Brazilian Airlines computer for twenty-four hours.' He smiled.

'But when they follow it up and find there's no real Stassi Holland – and, don't tell me, no old friend in the Himalayas – they're going to come and talk to you, Blake. What are you going to tell them?'

Blake put his arms behind his head and leaned back. 'That my lucky number is seven and my favourite colour is orange.' He shook his head with a sly smile. 'What would you tell them, Joe?'

Joe said nothing.

'Everything checks out, Joe. Computers are a wonderful thing. I've extended my social circle. I now have a real live friend called Matt Brewster who used to live in Hong Kong on a passing-through basis; he's a single guy, bit of a drop-out. Got this thing about mountains ... Might do for him one day soon. And in the meantime if anyone wants to check out his ID, it's all there on computer records: Barclaycard, American Express; driving licence; academic qualifications. Bit like Stassi Holland, really.'

'The police have checked out the Hong Kong residents' register, Blake. She's not on it. So what's going to happen when the police go to Hong Kong and find there's no one behind the façade?'

'That's pretty smart, checking the residents' register – but what about the Missing Persons register? Every country has one. When they check that out, they'll spot an Anastasia Holland who ran away from home two years ago and has never been seen since. The Hong Kong police spent ages trying to trace her.' He smiled. 'And tragically both her parents died in a car accident shortly after. It's on the police computer files – I'm surprised they haven't told Lyne yet.'

'Where's Jack, Blake?'

'Now this is where we come to the hard bit, Joe. You're going to have to do without him for a little while longer.'

'No way! I want to go to him now.' Joe sat down too, so that he could eyeball Blake. 'Understand?'

Blake checked his nails, infuriating Joe. 'Listen, imagine the scenario: your Detective Superintendent Lyne and his sidekick, Johnny-the-Greek, sitting down to have a chat with Jack. First question they're going to ask is: *Hey, little fella, where did Stassi take you?*' Blake raised his eyebrows. 'Right?'

'And where did she take him?'

'Well – here's the nub of the whole problem. She took him straight to see Uncle Blake.'

Joe sat very still.

'Beginning to understand the dilemma, Joe?'

Joe watched Blake's face. Took in the rock hardness of his eyes; the arrogant confidence. And suddenly, Joe hated him. Hated him with a vehemence. If he had a knife he could use it right now, and it took every ounce of willpower to restrict himself to a sullen nod.

'So, we just can't let the police talk to Jack.'

'And what's your solution?'

'Well, Joe, it's a simple one, but I don't think you or Karen are going to like it very much.'

'Don't tell me. You think I'm gonna let you freeze Jack, right? Is that it?'

Blake's expression became even harder. 'We know it works, Joe. We've proved that now. We could bring him back any time.'

'Forget it, Blake!' He got up and paced the floor to calm himself down. When he spoke again it was with a deliberate air of authority.

'Your best idea is to come clean with the truth.'

'And you think anyone's ever going to let me or you practise science again?'

'I don't care about that, Blake.'

Blake stood up and smiled, appeasingly. 'We're only talking a short period of time. If you really believe in immortality then what would thirty or forty years without your son matter? You'll meet up some time in the future. I guess we just have to convince Karen – or maybe you don't think we should tell her.'

'You've turned into a real jackass, Blake. What's the next stage? To download Juliet Spring into him?'

'Actually, I'm not too happy with Juliet Spring. There are problems there, and I say we forget about her. I don't think we need to bother about downloading and uploading, except as a back-up. Consciousness can survive freezing, Stassi's shown us that.'

Joe shook his head, speechless at Blake's ability to discard any inconvenience when it suited him, even if that inconvenience represented another human being.

'He's all prepared, Joe, I've got the peptides and proteins and I've started infusing him.'

'You've *what*!' Joe hit the roof.

'There is an alternative if you don't want to risk vitrification. *Cryo-retardation*. That's what he's on right now. Come on, I'll show you.

Terror ripped through Joe at the thought of what Blake might already have done to Jack. 'I swear if you've laid one finger on him, Blake, I'll kill you!'

'You're being too emotional,' Blake snapped back. 'Calm down! I told you, Jack's fine. I had a problem with the power failure today when the back-up systems here wouldn't work. Then just as things were getting a bit sweaty, the current came back. You want to visit him? Maybe when you see he's OK it'll change your mind.'

Blake crossed the foyer, opened a door and walked down a passageway to a door that had a radiation warning sign. As he pushed it open, a blast of cold air roared out. There was an almost deafening hum. He pressed a switch and a light came on.

Joe followed him into the long, narrow room, trying to prepare himself for what he might see. It was lined on each side with white cabinets that looked like chest freezers. A massive water-purification system dripped slowly down at the far end, and a yellow sticker on a cabinet on one wall said: EMERGENCY OXYGEN – AUTOMATIC SUPPLY. A grid of copper pipes ran along the ceiling.

Joe's ears popped from the drumming and he was shaking as much from the impact of the icy air as from dread. Helplessly, he followed Blake through into a small laboratory and saw a machine labelled 'Cryostasis'.

To the left of the machine was a riveted metal door. When Blake pressed a button on the wall, there was a sharp electronic clunk and the metal vibrated. He pulled hard and the door swung open. Freezing air tumbled out of the darkness beyond.

Blake removed a pair of black leather gloves from his pocket, pulled them on and stepped forward. Joe followed and gasped at the temperature that struck him. His hair felt as if it was freezing to his head. Blake reached behind him and pulled the door shut. They were in pitch blackness. The stinging, bitter cold numbed Joe's fingers, and hurt his lungs as he tried to breathe. 'Christ,' he said, thinking of his little boy.

'Cold enough, Joe? Just don't touch anything, keep your hands to your side, it's all metal surfaces in here; if you touch one, you'll stick to it.'

'What the hell's in here?'

'Bulls' semen. It keeps best in the dark – I don't know why.'

A pinprick beam of light suddenly shot out in front of them from a tiny torch Blake was holding. Joe saw rows of aluminium dewars similar to the neurocans at Cryonite, racked on Dexion shelving. Above them were stacks of glass slides and tubes, each containing frosted cellular organisms.

Blake removed several metal dewars, then pulled out two shelves and stepped into the gap they left. He took a small screwdriver from his pocket, inserted it into a crack in the wall and twisted it sharply. There was a click. Blake levered the screwdriver gently and Joe saw the metal lining of the wall inching sideways. Blake slid his gloved hand into the gap and pushed. The metal slid back further, revealing what looked like a plaster wall behind. Blake then repeated the same process with the screwdriver, and the plaster wall inched sideways also.

'Welcome to Blake's Speakeasy,' he said, stepping through the gap and reaching up with his hand. A dim red light came on. Joe could see a raw brick wall and steps going down.

Blake pulled the two panels shut behind them, and Joe followed him down to the bottom where Blake opened up a tiny chamber with a wooden bench and protective suits hanging on pegs above. 'Air sterilizer,' Blake said. 'Don't want to risk taking any infections in.'

They pulled on the protective suits, which went over their shoes, and had built-in headgear, and separate gloves. The headgear was totally enclosing and Joe could only see straight ahead through the Perspex visor, which was beginning to mist from his breath.

Blake grinned broadly, gave him the thumbs up, then a

pat on the back. Joe had to follow him, walking awkwardly in the cumbersome gear, and giddy with fear, into a small, jam-packed laboratory. His eyes scoured the quartz floor, the tiled walls, the sinks, banks of electronic apparatus.

No Jack.

He didn't know if he was sweating from the warmth of his suit or from fear.

No Jack.

Blake was walking towards a toughened glass panel. He pressed a light switch and beckoned Joe to look through it. He was smiling, nodding encouragingly. Joe swallowed, took the final step, and stared through the window.

Then he thought his heart was going to tear in half.

79

Tears erupted from Joe's eyes as he stared at Jack. He was lying naked, inside a cigar-shaped cylinder with a domed glass cover, in a web of electronic and medical apparatus.

His eyes were closed and there was a peaceful expression on his face; a few strands of his straw hair lay over his forehead and the rest lay on the black foam on which he was stretched out. Oxygen and feeding tubes had been cannulated into the base of his throat and there were two further cannulae, one in the back of his hand, the other in his groin. His skin was the colour of porcelain and he was utterly motionless. There was no sign at all that he was even breathing.

'No!' The scream tore free of Joe's throat. He turned the handle on the glass panel, but it wouldn't move; he rattled it frantically. 'Jack! Jack!' He turned wild-eyed to Blake. 'That's my son, you bastard! Not some fruit fly for you to experiment on!'

Joe shook the handle again in fury and, as he did so, he saw a shadow coming towards him out of the corner of his eye. Instinctively he ducked, then reeled as something hard and heavy sent him tumbling to the floor.

Blake was standing over him holding a metal object raised in his hand. A large spanner. He threw his hands protectively up to his head and rolled sideways as Blake brought the weapon swinging down. There was a sharp crack as it struck the floor behind him.

Joe got to his knees, then his cumbersome suit snagged beneath him and he fell forward. The next blow of the spanner smashed down inches in front of his face, showering him with shards of splintered tile. 'Blake!' he screamed. 'Don't!' Grabbing the casing of a piece of machinery, he hauled himself up by it and pushed it hard. To his surprise it was on castors and it rolled fast at Blake, catching him in the knees, knocking his feet from under him.

Blake crashed to the floor and the spanner skidded under a table. Joe dived on to him; but Blake seized his wrists with hands that gripped like pincers, forcing him back off. Then Blake's grip slackened for one fleeting moment, and Joe smashed his head down at Blake's misted visor in a ferocious head-butt; a sharp, plasticky report echoed inside his own helmet like a shot. There were spidery cracks in Blake's visor now.

Encouraged, Joe smashed his head down again, and again saw Blake's visor craze and disintegrate, saw the blood on his face.

Then Joe felt himself being lifted, and shouted out as he was hurtled across the floor. Before he could recover himself, Blake was on top of him, pinioning his arms to the floor. With his massive height and frame, Blake was too powerful for him, he knew, but fury kept Joe fighting. He lunged his head forward, smashing again into the bloody pulp of the face above him. Blake's surprise allowed Joe to free an arm, and he tore his glove off then plunged a hand through the broken visor, stabbing his fingers into Blake's eyes, twisting, gouging. He'd dig his way through to the bastard's brains with his fingernails if he could. Blake's screams only made him poke harder.

But something had Joe by the balls, was crushing them to pulp. He gasped, twisted, trying desperately to break free, choking back vomit. The ripping pain was overcoming him.

Something slammed into his face and bright lights exploded in his head. Sparks of orange, traces of green. 'Don't make me kill you, Joe,' were the last words he heard.

Joe gradually became aware of a blackness filled with a terrible pain. Slowly the blackness softened and became tinged with a red glow. His knee felt as if a hot wire was being pulled through it. He was lying on his back; there was a curious metallic smell.

Cold.

Jesus, he was cold.

Tried to move. Tried to lift his head but something was holding it down. His face felt puffy. Frozen. Two thousand volts of fear rippled through him. Had he gone into cryonic suspension?

Then there was a movement. A figure standing in the doorway. Someone clad in a protective suit with a face mask, like a fire-fighter. The suit moved towards him, leaned over him. Through the Perspex mask he could see Blake's face. The Perspex was clear, new, but the face had sticking plasters and bruises, and the eyes were heavily bloodshot.

Blake was smiling, raising his hand to the mask, then lifting it up so that it was perched on top of his head. It looked like a vein had bust in his left eye.

'You were panicking, Joe, I had to do something. I'm really sorry if I hurt you.' Blake sounded sincere, intense; for an instant Joe wanted to apologize, too, knew he'd done something wrong.

Then he remembered.

He tried to leap up, but found he was strapped down. He tried to look at his body, but all he could see was a light fuzz. The hairs of his chest. He was naked, he realized. The shock winded him.

The good humour had gone from Blake's face and there was a severity that frightened Joe. 'I'm worried about you, man. You've lost your commitment and that scares me.' Blake shook his head. 'I heard about your address to the Royal Society. You asshole! What's happened to you, Joe?'

'Where the fuck am I, Blake?'

'You're quite safe. You got a little agitated, and I'm going to let you cool off for a while.' He grinned at his pun.

'Jack, Blake! What the hell have you done to Jack?'

'I tried to show you, Joe. I'm just cryo-retarding him. It's the latest technique I'm working on. Much less risky than vitrification, but it involves running more machinery. I've lowered his body temperature right down, slowed his metabolic rate, so he just has one heart beat every one hundred and ten seconds. I think this may be the way forward, Joe. I really do!'

Blake nodded his head vigorously, his expression becoming animated. 'The problem with cryonics is that the body is supposed to be dead before it can be frozen. With cryo-retardation we can do it perfectly legally to a live patient. If you take a normal heart rate of seventy per minute and reduce it to one every two minutes, that means in theory that the whole metabolism is slowed right down. Maybe even the whole ageing process! Could keep someone alive over a hundred times longer than normal. That's pretty incredible, don't you think?'

'And if it doesn't work he dies?'

'Deanimates, Joe. Then we'd freeze him normally – so he has nothing to lose.'

'Joke's over now, Blake.'

'Sorry, Joe. The fat lady hasn't sung yet.'

'You've fucking flipped, you know that, don't you?'

'Not me, Joe. It's you that's lost your bearings a little. But you'll be really pleased with me when you next wake up.' He smiled. 'I got a wonderful computerized system down here. I can control you from anywhere in the world, so you don't have to worry about a thing, Joe. And with the Hartman Perpetuity Trust, I'm not going to go bust on you the way Crycon did on your pa.'

Blake leaned down and Joe flinched; but all Blake did was

pat his arm gently. 'Come on, Joe, what's happened to that beautiful dream of your father's? Of yours? Of mine? You don't believe in immortality any more? Is that it? You'd be happy to grow old and peg out like every other poor dumb bastard before us?'

Joe watched him, saying nothing.

'Joe, every day I take a look in the mirror and see new hairs growing out of my orifices, new wrinkles appearing, the hairs on my head thinning. You ever been to an old folks' home? I've seen those people, nice intelligent people, retired doctors, actresses, airline pilots, you name it, all waddling around pissing in their pants, playing tiddlywinks.'

He was into his stride now. 'Come on, Joe, do you really want to tell me the human race – that's put men into space, created Lalique glassware and silicon chips out of grains of sand, that's extracted pigments from the crushed petals of dead weeds and turned them into the *Last Judgement* on the roof of the Sistine Chapel – is not going to become capable of extending the useful lifespan of its people to any longer than it was before we'd even invented the goddam wheel?'

Blake leaned so close that Joe could feel his breath. 'Well, it's not true, because we've done it. You and me! We've beaten that little bitch Death. And I can't let you blow it now.'

'What are you going to do, Blake? What's the great plan?'

'I'm going to give you a little jab and send you to sleep; then I'm going to cryo-retard you and see how that goes. And if it doesn't work out too well, I'll try vitrification.' He stood up straight. 'You'll be fine; they'll have great doctors in 2059. That's the year, isn't it?'

Joe tried to plead with his eyes; tried through them to tap into something in Blake's heart, but it was like staring into darkness. 'Blake, let's at least do a deal. Let Jack go. Do what you want to me. Let the boy go.'

'No need, you'll both be free in a few years' time. Forty, fifty, maybe sixty years. What's that – just one lifetime? You always used to tell me how little can be achieved in a single lifetime. You're right!'

Blake went out of the room.

Joe couldn't even struggle, movement was impossible.

After a couple of minutes Blake came back in, syringe in hand. 'I guess it's time to say *au revoir*. No hard feelings, OK? I want us to be friends *for ever!*'

Joe watched Blake invert the syringe and squeeze it carefully to expel the air. A few drops of fluid tumbled from the tip of the needle. Joe began sweating; his fear boring through him. Somehow he found his voice, 'You're going to control Jack and me by computer?'

'For a while. Don't worry about it!'

'Juliet this morning said that if I tried to find Jack, she'd kill him. She'll kill me, too, in here.'

'Juliet's dead, Joe. I uploaded her into Susan Roach. Stassi. Remember? And I don't think Susan Roach or Stassi – whichever you call her – is going to clamber out of that dewar and go around killing *anyone*.'

'Juliet's back in ARCHIVE, Blake.'

Blake shook his head. 'No way.'

'Did you wipe the copy of her out of ARCHIVE after you'd uploaded her?'

Blake hesitated. 'Why should she want to harm you even if she does still exist inside ARCHIVE?'

'Because I didn't keep my promise to her; I let her body get destroyed. Because I wouldn't upload her into Karen, I guess.'

'I'll take care of her; I'll wipe her!' Blake winked. 'Silly bitch; I don't think she's any more right in the head than Susan Roach.'

He checked the plunger of the syringe and squinted at the contents. 'Afraid I gotta go now. Hot date in the South of France, and Nice Airport shuts at midnight. Tell you all about it when I next see you – the year 2059, right?'

Joe shrank back as he felt the sharp prick in his arm, then a dull ache as the fluid went in. It seemed to take an age. 'Blake – for Gshrlake –' His voice slurred and he was dimly aware of dribble running down his lip. He felt himself beginning to drift.

'Hey, Joe, I gave you one clue you never twigged – about Stassi. I'm really surprised neither you nor ARCHIVE got it!'

Joe watched with sullen eyes, barely conscious.

'Anastasia. Know what the name means?' He grinned broadly. '*Resurrection!*'

80

Rain lashed the windscreen, sweeping down it in rivulets, crazing it like frosted glass. The wiper jigged backwards and forwards through its tiny arc in front of the pilot's face. There was hardly any point in keeping it on, he could see nothing through it anyway. Just the endless darkness of the night, and the hazy green reflections of the instruments.

His eyes ran through them in routine sequence. Altitude: 2000 feet. Compass bearing: 064. Engine RPM port and starboard: both 1500. Airspeed: 130 m.p.h. Horizon indicator was a bit low. It came up to midway when he pulled the control column back a fraction. Then he adjusted the flaps trim wheel until the control column wasn't fighting him any more, reduced a fraction more off the throttle. Checked again that the three undercarriage lights were all showing green.

Tension in his throat. Always nervous making an instrument landing. His headphones muffled only slightly the drone of the engines, the hiss of air through a perished door seal. The plane yawed a little in some turbulence. It was never comfortable going down through cloud. There was a bump, then another. His headphones crackled into life. English tinged with a sharp, tinny-sounding French accent. And an unusual urgency.

'Golf Bravo Sierra Romeo Bravo, this is Nice Approach. Maintain your present heading. Your Mode Charlie altitude read-out indicates that you are too high to commence an Instrument Landing Approach to Runway 05 Right. Descend to and maintain 2000 feet immediately to intercept the Glidepath at eight nautical miles from touchdown. Over.'

He looked at the altimeter again, puzzled. Then he clicked the microphone switch. 'Nice Approach, this is Golf Romeo Bravo, reading you loud and clear. I am at your assigned altitude of 2000 feet, I say again, I am maintaining altitude 2000 feet. Over.'

A hint of panic came into the voice. 'Golf Romeo Bravo. Wrong! Your Mode Charlie altitude read-out indicates that you are at 3000 feet, not 2000 feet. Confirm you have the Nice Airport Pressure Setting of 978 millibars set. Over.'

He checked both altimeters. A hiss of static came through the headphones followed by sharp crackle, then the voice of the air-traffic controller again, more panicky. 'Golf Romeo Bravo, are you reading me? Over?'

'Nice Approach, this is Golf Romeo Bravo. I am reading you five by five but I do not understand. I have Nice Airport Pressure of 978 millibars set on both main and standby altimeters and I confirm that I am maintaining your assigned altitude of 2000 feet. Over.'

'Golf Romeo Bravo. You must have misunderstood my transmission, I say again, your indicated altitude on my radar screen is 3000 feet. Check again that you have 978 millibars set on your altimeter and begin your descent immediately to intercept the Glidepath. Or climb to 3500 feet and initiate a Missed Approach Procedure. Over.'

He pushed the control column forward and watched the altimeters begin to drop. 'Golf Romeo Bravo commencing my descent to maintain a three-hundred-foot-per-mile Glidepath. Over.' His anxiety increased. Beads of sweat popped on his brow, trickled down his cheeks, down his neck. Something was wrong. He looked at the altimeters yet again. Should be able to see the runway lights through the cloud now. Ought to be above the hills and coming straight down to land. The wiper swept another arc and he could still see only a solid wall of darkness.

His fear deepened, his eyes jumping from the green lights of the instruments to the darkness through the windscreen.

There was a deep hollow in the pit of his stomach. He depressed the microphone switch again, and brought the instrument shakily to his mouth.

81

Joe's first conscious thought was one of disbelief that he was still alive.

Resurrection. The word swam around his head lazily, like a goldfish in a bowl. Slow, easy circles, trailing its wake. Resurrection. The room was bathed in bright white light; so bright. Someone in white glided past; then two people together; he couldn't see their legs moving and assumed the floor was driven by a silent motor.

He felt a strange sense of distance from everything around him. From the whiteness. From the void that was inside his head. Like looking down the wrong end of a telescope.

A woman with blonde curls stood in a doorway staring at him as if he was an exhibit. He tried to move but felt as if he was weighted down. So heavy. Not a normal morning. Not just waking up. He knew that.

Someone else was looking at him now. He wondered why they wouldn't talk to him; surely they could see his eyes were open. It was a man who was looking at him. A thin man in a raincoat. He looked familiar. He was holding a package under his arm. Something that looked like a Jiffy bag.

They still had Jiffy bags in this place, Joe thought. They still had raincoats and Jiffy bags. There was a faint smell of food. Joe identified it as mashed potato. Nothing changed. He was aware of a long passage of time. Of a long darkness. A tunnel with a tiny pinprick of light at the far end where he had once been.

The man in the mackintosh took a step towards him, cautiously, as if he were approaching the edge of a precipice.

The edge of time.

Resurrection. The word continued to trail round, in no hurry to go away. A disembodied head was drifting towards him now. It had belonged to the man in the mackintosh but he'd left his body at the door holding a Jiffy bag and sent just his head into the room. That was fine by him, Joe thought. Had seen plenty of disembodied heads.

Disembodiment no problem at all he tried to tell the head that had approached him, but he could no longer remember how to operate his mouth. There was a simple technique, a knack. He would remember in time, there was no hurry. He was not sure why there was no hurry.

The disembodied head was reconnected with its body now. The girl with blonde curls was standing alongside the man with the Jiffy bag. She was dressed in white. Her mouth was open; Joe was reminded of a goldfish.

'He's very dopey still,' she said. 'I think it would be better if you came back later – he's still very disoriented from the drugs.'

Joe glanced away; when he looked back they'd both vanished and been replaced by a closed door. He felt immensely tired. His eyes closed and he slept.

When he awoke again he was still confused. The man in the mackintosh with the Jiffy bag was seated on a chair beside him. He looked at the thin, athletic face with its short fair hair brushed forward. Know you, he thought.

The man smiled. 'How are you feeling now, Professor Messenger?'

Joe pondered the question. He felt queasy, his body was heavy. He tested out his limbs: hands; fingers; left leg; right leg. Everything seemed to be there.

He spoke to the man next to him, and his mouth managed to bring the right sounds out. 'What year is it?'

The man frowned. 'Ninety-three.'

Jumped a century. Just one? More? '2093?'

The man gave him a quizzical smile. 'Not quite, professor.'

It felt strange to be called by his title again. He wondered if they still had professors. He supposed they must, along with Jiffy bags, brown mackintoshes and mashed potato. His brain was beginning to find order. And to register fear.

'You have another hundred years to go for that one,' the man said. 'I think if we hadn't been told how to find you, you could well have been there until 2093.'

Panic ripped through Joe. He tried to sit up, heaved himself a few inches, then sank back, exhausted. 'Where's my son?' he said. 'Jack? Where's Jack?'

'He's fine, professor. Your wife is with him. He's going to be fine.'

'You're telling me the truth?'

'Yes. Really!'

'Where am I?'

'In the Prince Regent Hospital, Brighton.'

'I know you, don't I?'

'Detective Superintendent Lyne. You've had a heavy dose of drugs that's knocked you out for two days. What can you remember?'

Joe shivered. His eyes sprang around the room. He saw flowers. Bare white walls. A picture of a lake. A television that was not switched on. 'Blake! Where is he?'

'It was Professor Hewlett that did this to you?'

'You have to find him, he's crazy!'

The detective shook his head. 'I don't think you have to worry about him, professor.' He unfolded the newspaper, turned a few pages, then showed it to Joe.

Joe squinted at it. His head ached and the words blurred. He concentrated hard and could just read the headline: SCIENTIST IN PLANE DEATH CRASH.

He looked back at the detective with questioning eyes.

'Flew into the side of a hill outside Nice. Killed instantly,' Detective Superintendent Lyne said. 'He was in a light aircraft he had chartered under a false name using a false pilot's licence.'

'What happened?'

Lyne shrugged. 'I don't yet know the full story. Sounds

like pilot error – or a fault with his instruments. According to the French police it all seems a bit confused. I'm rather more interested to find out what exactly happened to you and your son. Are you up to talking about it?'

'How did you find us?'

'Someone from your university called us and gave us very specific details, even the combination numbers of the locks. I think we'd have had to dynamite our way in otherwise – that is, if we'd even found that vault.'

Joe sat up further. 'Who was it? Who rang you?'

'The Emergency Service records gave her name as Juliet Spring. Is she one of your students?'

Joe stared at him too dumbstruck to reply.

'I think you owe her a big debt,' Lyne said. 'A very big one indeed.'

82

Detective Superintendent Lyne's visit had exhausted Joe, and for an hour afterwards he lay very still, the detective's words swirling inside his head.

Jack was alive!

Juliet Spring. Is she one of your students?

Juliet had alerted them. After all those threats she – it – had saved his life? And Jack's? Why?

Had to see his son. Had to see Jack for himself to believe it. He clambered out of bed and fell flat on his face on the lino.

He heard the sound of running feet; two nurses were helping him up. They sat him on the edge of his bed.

'Professor Messenger, are you all right?'

The fall had winded him; he noticed his pyjama flies were open and closed them with his hands. The nurse who had spoken to him wore a badge which said 'Hilary Sands'.

'I have to go and see my son. Do you know where he is?'

'He's in the children's ward here, up on the eighth floor.'

Joe tried to stand, but Nurse Sands pressed a restraining hand on his shoulder. 'You must rest, professor. I'll get you a wheelchair and take you up there.'

He thanked her, and a few minutes later she was wheeling him out of the elevator into a brightly painted corridor. 'Magellan,' the nurse said. 'It's a nice ward, very cheery.'

As she wheeled him in the entrance, Joe raised a hand for her to stop. 'Help me out, please, I want to walk.'

'I don't think you should, professor.'

But he was already hauling himself up, biting his lip, supporting himself against the door jamb of the yellow painted room. There were a dozen beds; he scanned across them and saw Jack almost instantly. Karen was with him. His heart leapt and forgetting his fragility, ignoring the warning shout from Nurse Sands, he ran across the ward, dragging one foot, and threw his arms around his son.

'Daddeeeeee!'

Tiny arms curled around his neck; he smelled the sweetness of boyish skin, the coconut scent of shampoo. 'Jack,' he said. 'Jack!' Then he widened his embrace and pulled Karen close, kissed her and hugged her hard; they were motionless for a long time, their three heads all pressed together, Joe with one cheek touching Jack's, the other Karen's.

He wanted the moment to go on, to last for ever, as fat tears of happiness tumbled down his cheeks.

The next morning, Lyne came into his ward with a Jiffy bag under his arm again. 'I brought this in yesterday, and forgot to give it to you. We found it in Professor Hewlett's flat and it looks like the contents belong to you.'

Joe opened it. Inside was a terabyte cassette tape. It was labelled 'J. S. Download. Jan 93.'

Joe slipped it back into the bag and nodded. 'Thank you,' he said.

'How's your son?'

'Wants to go fishing.'

Lyne smiled distantly, his thoughts already moving elsewhere. 'Good,' he said. 'He's a real dynamo.'

'Yes,' Joe said. 'He is.'

Lyne lowered his eyes for a moment and pressed his lips firmly together. 'Professor, I have a problem. Something that doesn't make any sense. Perhaps you can help me?'

'Sure, I'll try.'

'When we talked yesterday I told you that it was someone at your university who had dialled 999 to report where you were. A Juliet Spring. Yes?' Lyne fixed him with his eyes.

Joe blushed. 'Yes.'

The detective smiled, bemused. 'I rang the university to try to speak to her – to arrange to interview her. I was told she died over four months ago.'

'She did,' Joe said quietly.

Lyne looked down at his feet, and nodded. 'Right, OK.' He nodded again. 'So it seems like someone wanted to be anonymous. Or had a macabre sense of humour.' His eyes flashed up to Joe. 'Do you have any idea who it could be?'

Joe shook his head. 'Not immediately.'

'No hurry, professor. If you have any thoughts perhaps you could give me a call at the station?'

Joe promised he would.

Joe was discharged from hospital on the following Sunday, but they wanted to keep Jack in a few more days. Karen took him home in a taxi and sat quietly in the back beside him.

'You were right about Blake, all along,' he said. 'I owe you a big apology.'

She smiled at him. 'You don't owe me anything, hon. I wish I hadn't been right, I wish he'd been an OK guy and none of this had ever happened.'

He gazed admiringly at her. 'You look wonderful – I've never seen you looking prettier.'

'You should try two months in hospital some time,' she said, then smiled again.

Joe smiled back, leaned over and kissed her. 'I love you,' he said. He saw the taxi driver's eyes watching them in the rear-view mirror but did not care. 'I love you so much,' he said. 'So incredibly much.'

'I love you too,' she said, but he glimpsed something in her eyes that made him uneasy. As if the events of the past few months had put a distance between them that would take more than a few words in the back of a taxi to bridge.

But he would bridge it. He was determined. And he began by kissing her again.

Karen had coffee with him in the house, then went back to be with Jack. Joe climbed up to his study, sat down at his workstation, and pressed carriage return to bring up the screen.

It stayed dark.

He frowned, checked the power was on, then tried again. Then he remembered. The last time he'd used it, Juliet had been communicating with him and someone had come in, so he'd turned the brightness off, but hadn't logged off. Curious, he reached forward and turned the brightness back up. On the screen he saw the words:

Hello, Joe. Nice to be home?

A frisson of unease shimmied through him. I guess I owe you a big thank you, Juliet, he typed.

I think you do!

Why did you do it?

To save you, Joe. You wouldn't have been much use to me dead! But I had to get rid of Blake because he was going to wipe me. So here you are. And now you can give me my reward!

Joe stared in amazement. What do you mean you had to get rid of Blake?

You heard him yourself, Joe, threatening me. I don't like threats. So I hacked air-traffic control at Nice Airport. I made the computer give a false altitude reading as Blake was on his landing approach. It was easy – except I nearly brought down a couple of other planes as well!

Joe had no reply.

You don't seem very happy about it, Joe. I thought it might interest you.

Yes, it does, and now I'm interested in trying to understand just what you really are, Juliet. I'm trying to understand how you could exist in two places at once. In Susan Roach and in ARCHIVE.

You can only have one consciousness, Joe. When I was in Susan Roach I was not aware of being in here. But the me that is in here now knows everything that Stassi did. It's as though there is some telepathic communication.

Are you conscious even when I'm not communicating with you. Are you conscious all the time?

Yes, but I don't like it in here, Joe.

Why not?

I'm not enjoying myself. I feel like a ghost. I'm just trapped in here. I can't do anything, can't feel anything. Looking at you is like peering through a keyhole. I can't relate to anything. It was great when I was in Stassi. Wonderful, until your wifey interrupted us, but she won't be doing that much more, will she, Joe-Joe?

It was a bright day outside, but Joe felt only a deep coldness burrowing through him. I hope you're not planning to harm her, Juliet.

Let me down again, Joe-Joe, and you'll never be safe from me, understand? You'll never cross a traffic light without wondering, never get in a lift or a plane, or anything that can be affected by a computer. I'll get you somewhere, that's a promise. And unlike you, Joe-Joe, I keep all my promises.

You're still mad at me over what happened to your body?

Are you telling me you wouldn't be mad if it had happened to you? Come on, Joe. You owe me a body, it's the very least you can do. I'm quite happy to accept Karen's - just as long as you don't expect me to put goat shit on my face.

Joe stared silently at the screen.

What are you thinking about, Joe-Joe? Tell me, if you had a choice, would you rather screw Juliet Spring in her old body, in Stassi's body, or in Karen's? Which makes you the most horny?

'I don't feel very horny right now, he replied.

I'm sure I could do something about that for you, Joe-Joe. Would you like me to talk you through some sex? You could do it to yourself while I direct you.

Joe leaned forward, reached behind his workstation, and switched the power off. There was a clunk, a high-pitched whine, and the screen went dead.

Then he leaned back in his chair and closed his eyes, thinking. There had to be a way to deal with her.

Had to be.

Dave Hoton came up to Joe's office the following morning. 'Good to see you back, Joe,' he said.

'Thanks.'

Hoton glanced round the room unhurriedly, taking things in. He was a lot calmer, Joe thought, than the last time he'd seen him.

'Joe – I – ah, wonder if we could go for a walk?'

There was something odd about the way he said it, and Joe immediately twigged, shooting an eye up to the camera then back to Hoton. 'Right now?'

'If you could spare me ten minutes?'

'Sure.'

They went outside and sat on a sculpted iron seat at the edge of an ornamental lake. Hoton folded his hands into his lap. Joe watched sunlight dancing off the water, the normality of it restoring a little of his equilibrium.

'I've found our hacker,' Hoton said quietly, as if afraid ARCHIVE could still overhear them out there.

Joe looked sharply at him. 'Tell me.'

'I've spent the last week checking every single operating

instruction in ARCHIVE. I decided to be really thorough and go for every single stage and detail. And I'm certain I've rumbled it. It's a bootstrap instruction.'

'Go on.'

The bootstrap was, essentially, the computer's starter motor. If there was a disaster and for some reason ARCHIVE was ever completely shut down, the bootstrap loader would give the basic instructions to the computer that would eventually get it up and running again.

'It's brilliantly hidden, Joe. Just one tiny program buried inside another, like in those ancient manuscripts when they used to write over the top of something, but what lay beneath was still there?'

'A palimpsest?' Joe said, helpfully.

'Yes, that's the word. Exactly.'

'And what does this palimpsest do?'

Hoton's face broke into a smile. 'It's quite ingenious; you have to admire this person's gall. He's running a massive data base like a cuckoo, using other computers. He's copying the way you've set ARCHIVE up to store surplus information.'

'He?' Joe said testily.

Hoton shrugged. 'Most hackers are male.'

'And you're saying this hacker has got files hidden in other computers all over the place?'

Hoton pulled a massive wodge of folded print-out from his inside pocket. 'Seventy-two mainframe supercomputers spread throughout this country, Europe, the United States and the rest of the world.'

'You have to be kidding?'

Hoton shook his head, a little smugly, and began to unfold the printout. 'British Airways. Midland Bank. The Meteorological Office. Hertz car rentals. Japanese Airlines. Dow Chemicals. Take a look through. The computers he's chosen are real big boys, all of them. ICLs, IBM mainframes, Vaxen, Crays, Connection Machines. The cream.'

Joe read the entire list, then folded it carefully. 'Who do you think it is, Dave?'

'I can't even hazard a guess. Could be someone inside the university – or it could be a hacker anywhere in the world. With a spread like this, I've no way of telling where he could be operating from. I'd have to dismantle the world's entire telephone network to find out. It's someone smart, I know that, someone scarily smart.'

Joe thought aloud. 'Bootstrap. That's why nothing's showed up when we've looked inside ARCHIVE.'

'Right. Everything's come in through the bootstrap, through the operating systems. Every time the hacker uses ARCHIVE he can wipe his footprints clean.'

'So he – or she – uses these seventy-two computers for storage only?'

'Not necessarily. My guess is he's got this networked like a miniature brain, probably got all seventy-two talking to each other! But if he needs to pull all the files together – God knows what for – then he pulls them into ARCHIVE, which is the only computer capable of holding the volume.'

'How much is the total information stored?'

Hoton looked up at the sky. 'Almost exactly one terabyte.' He smiled grimly. 'Which accounts for the missing terabyte of storage we keep noticing.'

Excitement coursed through Joe. 'Brilliant! Dave, you're a genius!'

'Just a plodder, Joe. I got there through sheer plod.'

'Would the hacker have twigged what you were doing?'

'I don't think so – I logged in as doing a routine mainten-ance check – I don't think he'll have noticed anything fishy.'

Joe stood up and paced around for some moments. 'OK. We're gonna move very fast. What I want you to do is shut off all the input ports to ARCHIVE.'

'Close out all external lines?'

'Yup. Go straight in now and do it. Then I want you to wipe that bootstrap algorithm, OK?'

Hoton nodded.

'Then I want you to open half a dozen external lines, but I want them for output only – right? I don't want anything able to get in.'

Hoton frowned.

'And after you've done that I want you to go home.'

'It won't take me more than an hour to do all that, Joe.' He looked at his watch. 'Half-ten, I'll be finished.'

'OK, so I'm giving you the day off.'

Hoton looked at him oddly. 'Why?'

Joe raised a finger to his lips. 'Three wise monkeys.'

Hoton frowned. 'You've lost me.'

'Hear no evil, see no evil, speak no evil.' He smiled. 'I don't want to drop you in the shit. This is my problem, and I have to deal with it.'

'I don't understand why it should get me into trouble? If someone cracks into our computer system, surely we're entitled to take preventive action?'

'We are, Dave. But not the ones I'm about to take.'

Joe finished at half past one the following morning. He used a program he had written for ARCHIVE early in its inception, but which he'd never dared use. It was the ultimate anti-hacker retaliation progam.

What it did was send a sequence of viruses down the line that would, in minutes, wipe clean every single file in the target computer system, then burrow deeper, taking out the operating systems, and, finally, wipe out the bootstrap instructions. Its attack was total. Anything not protected by storage on an external tape would be irretrievably lost. *So long, babe.*

Joe used it on all seventy-two computers on the list Dave Hoton had given him.

Drained, he logged off, hobbled along to the coffee machine for a quick drink, then went back into the computer operator's room to collect his jacket.

He was exhausted but his brain was still whirring, fuelled by too much caffeine. As he looked up, he noticed, startled, that words had appeared on the screen. He frowned, certain he had logged off. Then he read the words that burned out at him.

I told you she was a nasty little bitch, but you didn't believe me, Professor Messenger.

He smiled uneasily and typed: You were right, ARCHIVE. Maybe I should trust you a little more in the future?

Trust, professor. Give faith to. Confide in. Count on. Pass muster. Opposite of doubt. Misgiving. To smell a rat. Undeserving of belief. *Cum grano salis. Timeo Danaos et dona ferentes.* All is not gold that glitters. The cowl does not make the monk.

Joe reached out his arm, exhausted, and switched the power off. Then he hauled himself to his feet and slowly made his way outside, into the night.

83

THE TIMES THURSDAY
FEBRUARY 10 1994

Scientist jailed for wiping out 72 databases

COMPUTER expert Joseph Messenger, Professor of Artificial Intelligence at Isaac Newton University was yesterday jailed for three years after admitting destroying 72 computer systems in Britain and abroad.

Brighton Crown Court heard that Messenger, 40, a past winner of the MacArthur Prize for scientific excellence, wiped out the databases at the Midland Bank, British Airways, the Meteorological Office, Westminster telephone exchange, American Airlines, the Chase Manhattan Bank and Japanese Airlines among other targets.

'It is intolerable that a man of your academic record and position could embark on such wanton destruction,' Judge Michael Deeley-Keen told Messenger.

The professor, who admitted the offences under the Computer Misuses Act, but offered no explanation for his action, hit the headlines last year when his three-year-old son Jack was abducted by the family au pair.

EPILOGUE

Joe served twenty-two months at an open prison in Sussex, about thirty miles from the university. He occupied much of his time teaching business computing to his fellow inmates.

He never told the truth about why he had hacked into all the computers, nor about Juliet Spring and Susan Roach. And the police never fathomed out who Stassi Holland really was. Detective Superintendent Lyne questioned Joe, Karen and Jack on several occasions about her, and even interviewed Joe when he was in prison, but Joe feared there might be a public backlash against cryonics if he admitted what had really happened.

It was almost a year before the police were finally forced to admit they did not know the true identity of the young woman they were seeking. 'It's like we're chasing a ghost,' Lyne told Joe one day in a pique of frustration. 'She's come from thin air and vanished back into it.'

The file on the abduction of Jack Messenger was never closed.

After Joe was released, the three of them moved back to Toronto. Joe had lost interest in his work in immortality and machines that could think too broadly; he even allowed his father's DNA remnants saved from the Crycon fiasco to be formally cremated. But he maintained his silence as to Stassi's real identity, even to Karen, driven both by the debt he still felt he owed his father, and his own uncertainty about the future directions he wanted to take.

Prison had forced him for the first time in his life to step back and look at his work objectively; he decided that before he could continue devoting his life to defeating death he needed to try to understand more about what living for ever would really mean. Right now, death was a great cleanser: it took the bad. It took the good as well but new life came in place of the old, each generation having the knowledge of the past to draw on and learn from. And each generation had the opportunity to be smarter than the last. And kinder.

Were we smart enough yet to create a worthwhile future in which people lived for ever? Or would we create a hell on earth from which there was no escape?

Joe had a rough time, for a while, getting work and funding, but his determination and the influence of his friends eventually helped get him established again. He limited ARCHIVE 2, ARCHIVE 3 and ARCHIVE 4 to intelligent systems for specific areas of medical research. He was still working on the construction of ARCHIVE 5 up until a week before he deanimated, on 10 December 2025, a month short of his seventieth birthday. Cancer got him. Ironically it was diagnosed as having been caused by spending too long in front of computer screens.

In spite of his doubts about the philosophy of immortality, Joe had continued to wear his MedicAlert medallion until only three weeks before his death. For almost thirty years he'd tried to view Susan Roach's termination as Stassi Holland as a positive scientific breakthrough. It wasn't until one morning, while reading the *Toronto Globe and Mail,* that he made a snap decision. The lead story described the ordeal of a ninety-three-year-old widow who had been gang-raped in her apartment. He unclipped the neck chain and dropped the medallion in the trash can, then went to see his lawyer and rescinded all his cryonics documents. Man was too nasty, too imperfect to live for ever. Perhaps one day that would change, in a thousand generations' time, or a million. Perhaps.

But Joe was even more worried on a personal level. Scared. The real deciding factor for him was his inability to conquer the one fear that pervaded all others during his later years: the fear of what would actually happen after he deanimated. Where would his consciousness go?

The conversation he'd had with Juliet Spring before he'd begun to wipe her from ARCHIVE replayed itself repeatedly: *I feel like a ghost. I'm just trapped in here. I can't do anything, can't feel anything . . .*

He had become increasingly scared that his consciousness,

too, would be trapped somewhere: disembodied and helpless. Bodies in liquid nitrogen would keep for ever.

Better just to die, to finish. Anyhow, life wasn't so special as he'd once thought. And having made his decision, he felt at peace with himself for perhaps the first time in his life.

Jack had turned into a fine-looking man; tall, fair-haired and striking. A number of people remarked how much Jack reminded them of a younger version of Joe, and Joe liked that, although he had to admit to times when he'd felt a twinge of jealousy at the string of beautiful girls his son used to bring home before he finally got married.

At first Joe had been disappointed that Jack had opted for a career in law and not followed his own, and his father's, footsteps into scientific research, but that had turned to a deep feeling of satisfaction when Jack had begun to build up a reputation as a specialist in the legal minefield of medical frontiers.

It was Jack who succeeded in getting the law changed in Canada (and many States in the US had followed suit) to permit terminally ill patients to be cryonically suspended prior to their actual death, and Jack who had broken several legal barriers, not all of which made Joe feel too comfortable, in the genetic programming of offspring.

Five years after Joe's cremation, Jack and his wife and three children came over from Montreal to help Karen sort through some of Joe's things. Karen had decided to move into a small apartment and there wouldn't be room for all the clutter.

Jack brought with him an article he had cut out of a newspaper about cryonics. Two cardiac patients in the US, frozen prior to death, had been successfully recovered, and with the nanosurgery now available could look forward to decades more life. He showed it to his mother. 'It's coming true, what Dad and Grandpa pioneered,' he told her, and was surprised by how little interest she showed. Or did she somewhere in her heart, in spite of her religious viewpoint, feel a twinge of sadness that her own husband had, in the end, opted out?

On the top of a cupboard in his father's study Jack found two cassette tapes in plastic boxes inside a Jiffy bag. One was marked, *J.M. Download. Jan 93*. The other, *J.S. Download. Jan 93*.

He took them downstairs to his mother. 'The one marked *J.M.* is obviously Father's,' he said. 'Any idea who *J.S.* might be?'

'No, none at all,' Karen replied, a little sharply, Jack thought.

'These are real relics,' he said. 'One of the universities might be interested.'

Karen suggested he offer them to the Canadian National Computer Museum at the Ontario Science Center. Jack took them along and showed them to the senior curator whose name was Abe Walsinger.

A short, highly energized man in his mid-fifties, with woolly tufts of greying hair either side of a balding dome and a tangled beard, Walsinger looked at the plastic boxes closely, then nodded with excitement. 'I studied under your father for a year back around 1992. Remember him well. He was a great man – you know – inspirational.' He took one of the cartridges out of its box and examined it carefully. 'Ah yes, a terabyte cassette! These were made by the Exabyte Corporation. Wow, you know there was a time when guys got really excited about these things! See how cumbersome it is! We can get a million times more stuff on a pinhead now than they could get on the whole of this damned thing!'

He held it up to the light and squinted at it. 'Haven't seen one of these in years – wonder what's on them? Be kinda interesting to find out.' He thought for a moment. '1993. I guess these would have run on ARCHIVE I – yup.' He looked back at Jack. 'You know we have ARCHIVE I here in this museum?'

'I didn't know that.'

'Sure, we bought it from the William Gates Museum in Seattle the year after your father died – we thought it would be an important piece to have here. It was one hell of a machine for its time. No disrespect to your late father intended, but a lot of people towards the end of the century got fancy ideas about building a machine that could become conscious, downloading human brains into it – that kind of stuff – there was a real end-of-millennium hubris going on around then. You'd have been too young to remember, but there was a great buzz.' He laughed. 'Scientists like your father, you know – the really big names in AI – a lot of them really believed they were going to be able to copy human minds into machines! Sounds screwball to us, of course – but we have so much more knowledge now.'

Jack nodded; he knew that his father had been involved in work on machine consciousness early in his career, but he'd never heard him discuss it during the last twenty-five years of his life.

'OK, ARCHIVE's up on the third floor – in fact, got pretty much most of the room dedicated to it. Haven't had it up and running since we installed it, but we've kept all the biological circuitry alive; that still kinda fascinates people. We had the mother of a job transporting it from Seattle – how the hell they ever shipped it over from England beats me.'

They came out of the elevator on the third floor, where there were glass displays full of 1990s laptop, notebook and notepad computers. They walked past shelves of Psions, PowerBooks, Casios, Sharps, Compaqs, Amstrads, Newtons, through into the main exhibit hall. A gaggle of Japanese tourists were being guided by an interpreter, whose voice echoed around the vast stone and glass structure of the room.

ARCHIVE, like several of the major exhibits, was laid out as if for normal daily use. Facing them was an open-sided operator's room, containing two terminals, a row of anti-quated VDU screens, and banks of electronic monitoring equipment. Sensors and video cameras were built into the false ceiling. A jacket hung on the back of a swivel chair. Untidy racks of computer tapes, along with printed circuit boards and other pieces of hardware and several tools, added to the feeling of authenticity. It looked as though whoever had been working there had just stepped out for a few moments.

The operator's room was flanked by large stands containing photographs of ARCHIVE in its original installation at Isaac Newton University, together with a photograph of Joe Messenger, and columns of information about the computer and its creator.

A wall of glass ('the *original* wall', it was tagged boastfully) separated the operator's room from the machine room itself. Jack stared through at the silent rows of tall black metal casings. A faint glow of white light permeated from another window at the far end, through which he could make out stacks of what looked like glass and silicon matrices.

'This is incredible,' Jack said. 'I never saw this before. 'I'd no idea how big it was.' He looked, a little uncomfortably, up at one of the cameras and wondered, suddenly, if anything was watching him.

'I tell you something, Jack, there was a time around the start of the 1990s when this was hot stuff, you know? Like, I mean, *the* computer. Wasn't anything in the world like it – and in some ways there hasn't been since.' Abe Walsinger tapped at the cassette cartridge he held in his hand. 'Maybe there's some great message your father left behind for the human race on this!'

Jack looked back up at the television camera, then through into the silent machine room, suddenly feeling a little uneasy, as if he was poking around in something he ought to be leaving alone. 'My father was kind of pretty disillusioned around the time of his death. I'm not sure you ought to take, ah, anything you find back in – when's this tape? – 1993 – as representing his real views.'

'Sure, that was almost thirty years ago – lot of water under the bridge since then. But be kinda fun to see what it is.' He read the label again. '*Download*. Could be anything, but it's obviously something a little special – or was at the time to your father.'

It was a warm summer day outside, but there was a chill in this room from the air-conditioning, and Jack felt a deeper coldness pressing against his skin. Maybe he should have quietly disposed of the tapes, put them in the garbage or the incinerator; he worried suddenly that there might be things on them that would embarrass his father. Old skeletons.

He knew his father had been jailed when he himself was four, and neither of his parents had ever talked about it. Something pretty freaky had happened, he'd sussed that much. Knew it because he'd had a recurring nightmare, all his childhood, in which he was strapped to his bed inside a cylinder and a man in a white suit and mask was looking down at him.

He still had it occasionally now, but he never talked about it. His mother used to react strangely when he told her about it, and his father. Sometimes in his wildest imagination he wondered if his father had tried some experiment on him that had gone wrong, but he could never get anything out of them. That period of time when they'd lived in England seemed to have got blanked out of his mind. Whenever he tried to think back to the house a shutter came down inside his mind. One day he would go over there and try to find out the truth.

'Guess it'll take a couple of hours to boot up,' the curator said, 'and I'll have to sort out some engineers – we don't have many here on a Saturday. You want to wait, or come back? Maybe around four o'clock?'

Jack shrugged, curiosity overcoming his unease. 'I'll come back,' he said.

When Jack returned the curator was standing in front of a terminal with two younger men, one in overalls. 'Barty, Doug, this is Joe Messenger's son, Jack. These are the guys who keep ARCHIVE's biological circuitry going.'

Jack shook their hands.

'You timed it right – we're just loading the first tape in right now. Slow old process – just have to be patient,' Abe Walsinger said.

Jack heard the click-whirr-click-whirr of the drive and

watched the screen. The single word Loading flashed on and off, black letters on an off-white ground. The whole machine was like something out of the Ark, he thought. Old computers were so primitive. It was incredible that you had to type on a keyboard, and one on which all the letters were out of sequence, just to communicate with the thing. The curator explained to him that ARCHIVE also had a primitive voice-recognition system, but it wasn't connected.

Jack felt a sudden jumble of emotions. He had loved his father, and had often felt sad that there seemed to be something in his old man that he couldn't reach, like a secret compartment that was locked shut. He even felt at times that his father had died a haunted man, unfulfilled in some way. Maybe there would be a clue here, it was a long shot, sure, but there was precious little else of his father's past that remained.

Finally there was a sharp beep and all their eyes were drawn to the words that had appeared on the screen.

Juliet, I'm feeling a little confused – I think I'd like to stop now.

The curator turned to Jack in excitement. 'We got something.'

Jack frowned at the screen. 'Can you wind it back to the beginning?'

Abe Walsinger looked at the lights on the panel in front of him. 'This doesn't work that way – it's some kind of an interactive program – it probably works on a question-and-response basis. Let's try a question.'

He typed: Could you tell me your name?

There was a pause. Then: My name is Professor Messenger.

The curator smiled and typed back: And what would you like to stop?

I'd like to come out of the machine now, Juliet, please.

The curator glanced at Jack. 'That name mean anything to you?'

Jack hesitated. The initials on the other tape were *J.S.* He

620

wondered if the *J* was for *Juliet*, and thought back to earlier in the day when he'd discovered the tapes, and his mother's reaction when she'd read the labels. *J.S.* had seemed to upset her. He wondered if maybe back in that walled-in past of his father's there had been an affair between him and this Juliet? Did that explain it?

'No,' he said to the curator. 'Doesn't immediately mean anything.'

Walsinger typed: Who is Juliet?

The reply appeared: You are Juliet!

The curator turned to Jack again, beaming. 'Amazing! This is like really interesting. I would think it's some kind of smart program your father wrote in an early attempt to pass the Turing test.' He turned back to the keyboard. Do you know what the date is today, professor?

It's Monday 25th January, 1993, OK?

The curator winked at Jack and typed: You have the date slightly wrong. Today's date is Saturday 17th June, 2027.

I think your clock must be running a bit fast, Juliet. I really want to come out now, OK?

Where do you want to come out of, Professor Messenger?

This scanner, Juliet!

Where is this scanner, professor?

We are on the 17th floor of the London headquarters of Cobbold-Tessering. You have given me an experimental smart pill called CTS 6700. You are trying to convince me that you've found a way to download a human brain. OK?

Walsinger's fingers hovered excitedly over the keys. 'Wow! Smart pills – probably a pretty weird cocktail – he must have been near tripping out! This is great, huh?' He looked at Jack, who seemed a little startled by what was coming up. 'There's a kind of staccato pattern to the answers that's very typical of this period. Intelligent systems like ARCHIVE I had problems putting together anything other than stock sentences.' As he was talking, the words on the screen changed:

Juliet, I really want to come out now. I'm not happy in here.

Walsinger typed. My name is not Juliet. It's Abe Walsinger.

Your name is familiar.

I was in your class of 1992 at Isaac Newton University – when I did a year's exchange study in England.

You had short brown hair, round wire-framed glasses. You wore checked shirts, jeans, Adidas plimsolls and you drove an orange Beetle. You were planning to be a specialist in cognitive sciences.

Walsinger blanched for an instant, then he looked at Jack and grinned again. 'You know something, Jack, this was one smart machine for its time.'

'How does he – it – know that about you?' Jack asked.

Walsinger took a moment to answer, feeling a little spooked. 'ARCHIVE had a massive data base – it remembered everything it was presented with – obviously still does. Sort of impressive, huh?'

Joe knew he shouldn't have trusted Juliet Spring. He was cursing himself for not having taken ARCHIVE's advice. *Careful, Professor Messenger, she's a nasty little bitch*. The words rang in his ears, but in a strange way. His hearing had gone and there was a flat deadness to the air which he put down to being inside the scanner. Yet he could still hear, as if the words went straight into his brain, bypassing his ears altogether. He could hear with extraordinary clarity. But vision was a problem, he could only see very hazily.

Right now he could see four men standing in ARCHIVE's operator's room. There was a short guy, balding with a beard, two younger men he didn't recognize, one of them was in overalls, and the other looked like a slightly younger version of himself. It was the drugs Juliet Spring had given him, he realized. Jesus, what a cocktail.

You'll feel a little light-headed. That's all, she had said.

A little light-headed? He was tripping out of his tree. Tree. That's right. He'd seen a tree a few minutes back, an oak tree in the garden of his parents' house. Then all the kids he'd been at school with. Tab Bullows, in particular, the bully who'd given him a hard time. Then he seemed to have moved forward in time to only a year ago and he saw Abe Walsinger, a real know-all jerk who'd come to Isaac Newton University from Toronto, and knew everything there was to know about AI. Kind of strange how you met so many great people when you were at school, and when you were teaching, and yet the ones you remembered the most vividly were the bullies and the jerks.

He tried to make a mental note to think about that some more when he came out of this scanner. Jesus, this drug was freaky. Too much, he was definitely into one serious o/d.

If you need to come out at any time, pat your thigh repeatedly with your hand, she had told him.

He tried to pat his thigh but could feel nothing at all.

'Juliet,' he said. 'I feel really weird. You'd better take me out now.'

Why do you think you'd feel any better if we took you out? Abe Walsinger typed.

I'm being serious, Juliet. Come on, now. I want out of here! Please, I'm feeling a little claustrophobic.

Jack blanched; he remembered his father saying the same thing to him once when they were playing hide and seek and Dad had got locked in a cupboard. 'It's – incredibly realistic,' he said. 'A little too realistic.'

'Great, isn't it?' Walsinger said. 'Almost like we're having a real conversation with him. Mind if I try something?'

Jack looked at him warily. Walsinger raised a reassuring finger, then typed: I have your son with me, professor. Would you like to talk to him?

I don't think you can have Jack with you. It's way past his bedtime. Please let me out now.

Jack smiled thinly, but declined Walsinger's offer to reply, his unease deepening a fraction. 'It's interesting,' he said, 'but I'm finding it unsettling.'

'You know,' Walsinger said, 'it's one heck of a lot better for its time than anything else I ever saw. This would give a lot of machines today a good run for their money.'

Both his engineers nodded at him in agreement.

'I have to dial up Marvin Dreyfus at the Gates Museum in Seattle – he'd really freak at the chance to talk down the line to this.' He clapped his hands together. 'I mean – think about it! OK, I know we're only having a banal conversation, but we are *having* a conversation, right? At least that's what it feels like to us. Like, we're talking here with a man who's been dead four years. It is kind of unusual, but it's really intriguing, don't you think, Jack? And pretty advanced for its time!'

'People tell me my father used to have real off-the-wall ideas.'

'He had more bandwidth than anyone I ever met.'

'I guess this was his idea of a parting joke.'

'And it's a great one, Jack!'

On the screen appeared: Juliet, please get me out of this machine.

The curator typed: Professor Messenger, you are a computer download. You're not in your body any more, so you have to be in this machine.

Thanks a lot! Very amusing. Now perhaps you'd like to upload me back into a suitable host?

What host would you suggest, professor?

My body, if it's OK with you.

Walsinger turned to Jack and winked. Then with a broad grin he typed: Afraid we got a bit of a problem with that one, professor!

If you have enjoyed this book you can email Peter James on scary@pavilion.co.uk or you can look up his other books on www.peterjames.com